Death of Innocence

Written by

Richard Greene

Edited by Barbara Bowers

ISBN: 978-1-4349-9196-6

Library of Congress Control Number: 2008928974 Printed in the United States of America

Richard and his Lhasa Apso Jackson

About the Author

Richard Greene was born in Denver, Colorado, in 1939 and grew up in a small two-bedroom house in Englewood, a suburb of Denver. In 1954, his parents divorced, and his father moved to Houston, Texas. Soon after that, Richard dropped out of ninth grade, working at various jobs, including sacking groceries at a local supermarket and as an electrician's apprentice for a neighbor. He spent his summers with his dad, who owned 'The Texan' bar on the outskirts of Houston, Texas, where he got an education in life, unlike his friends back in Englewood, Colorado. In August 1956, at seventeen, Richard enlisted in the United States Navy. After boot camp and Yeoman School in March 1957, he was transferred to the USS Belle Grove LSD-2 (Landing Ship Dock), serving in the South Pacific, and took part in the atomic testing at Eniwetok and Bikini Atolls in 1958.

Honorably discharged in 1960, he worked at Samsonite Luggage for a short spell and then went to work for Burlington Truck Lines as a billing clerk. The trucking industry fascinated Richard, so he attended Denver Traffic School to learn the trucking industry's ins and outs. He worked as a dock supervisor for United Buckingham in Denver and a sales representative for Californian Motor Express in Fresno and Los Angeles, California. Moving back to Denver, he went to work as Claims Prevention Manager for Consolidated Freightways, which included investigating road accidents of CF trucks within 100 miles of Denver. After a year with Consolidated, he transferred from Denver to the

General Claims Department in Portland, Oregon. In 1973, Richard left the Claims Department to become a supervisor in the Collection Department for Consolidated, where he remained until his retirement in December 1995 as Manager of Collections.

Still residing in Portland, Oregon, Richard and his wife Cathy spend much of their time with their children and grandchildren. Richard's other interests are golf, long walks, reading, and oil painting.

You can email me at bellgrove3@aol.com and use YOUR BOOK in the subject line.

Please visit my web page, www.richardjgreene.net, or visit me on Facebook at https://www.facebook.com/richardgreene.7393 or on Twitter at https://twitter.com/@dickiejoe.
All of my books are available on Amazon as ebook or paperback.

Editorial Review by Manybooks of Death of Innocence by Richard Greene:
Posted on 8th of November, 2019 by Meg Stivison

This fictionalized account of the author's ancestors takes readers on a historical adventure through nineteenth-century America.

The author follows lightly fictionalized accounts of his ancestors' lives, moving through different cities and times. Of course, their emotional and private lives have been embellished, but their major life events are family history, and the wider historical events are accurate.

Readers are led through the lives of the men and women who eventually became the author's great-great-parents. Strong historical research deepens the narrative, and the author has paid careful attention to the details of everyday life in a different era.

The military sections are particularly well-researched. Themes of courage and determination recur repeatedly in the storylines, showing family traits in the military and daily life. Although the narrative moves between characters and between battles, there is a heavy sense of loss in most of the battles.

As the story progresses, tension builds because readers can't help rooting for the characters' success and worrying about their safety, even though we know how the battles will turn out.

There's a compelling sense of fate throughout this book because these ancestors must manage to be smart or occasionally lucky enough to survive the war in order to marry and have the children who ultimately led to the author's birth. This gives a heightened sense of destiny and importance to the relationships between soldiers and the women they'll later marry, especially in the first meetings or in seemingly minor decisions that ripple outwards.
Death of Innocence is an engaging family saga. The sense of destiny and family connection leading up to the present day gives extra intensity to everyday moments.

Contents

Prologue

While researching my family's history, I found my ancestors interesting, with each having a story of their own to tell. The problem was that most of the information was just "stuff" and a little boring without fiction to fill in the gaps between fact, family lore, and mystique. These individuals lived during one of the most important periods of our country's history, and to tell these stories, I have chosen to use all of the above, plus my imagination. For numerous reasons, I have taken author's liberties in many areas by making up some individuals, places, and events. In some cases, I found it necessary to change certain family members' names for this work of fiction. Besides those of historical correctness, other names in this story are purely fictional, and any resemblance to actual people, living or dead, is purely coincidental.

People of the South in 1860 would soon find themselves in the midst of a terrible civil war, whose architect, President Abraham Lincoln, would become known as the 'Widow Maker.' Never again would life in the South be as it had been before the great civil war.

Joseph Greene (my great-grandfather on my father's side) came to Florence, Alabama, searching for a better life than he had known while working his father's farm in southern Tennessee. His dreams of being a pilot of riverboats took him to the Tennessee River, where he met and fell in love with my great-grandmother, Mary W. McAlexander.

The McAlexander family consisted of Edward, his younger brother Alexander, and their sister Mary (my great-grandmother on my father's side). The McAlexander family was of some importance, living their innocent dream in northern Alabama, in a place called Florence, in the county of Lauderdale, located on the Tennessee River. Unknowingly, their lives were about to be caught up in a great struggle.

William Chrisman (my great, great grandfather on my father's side) lived in Kentucky, where he met and married Elizabeth Louisa Blackstone, a young Indian girl, against his family's wishes in 1837. Rather than accept William's wife, his family gave him money, and two young Negro slaves, suggesting that he take his bride and leave the county for the West. William and his young bride eventually settled on a farm near the town of New Site in Tallapoosa County, Alabama. There, they cut a life out of the wilderness and raised a family, never knowing that a great war would all but destroy them.

Andrew Jackson Patterson (my great, great grandfather on my mother's side) was a 43-year-old widower living on a farm in Anderson County, South Carolina, at the start of the Civil War. He was busy raising four children as best he could while secretly in love with a neighbor's daughter, who was twenty-five years younger than him. Even he would not be able to resist the fever of the Southern cause that tugged at him to defend his way of life. His decision to leave his farm and young children to join the war would take him to places of such violence he never dreamed possible.

While most of these families were not acquainted with one another, each was linked to the other by an invisible chain of events that would one day come together in another time and place, creating my family line.

Where does one start when telling the story of his own family? Out of so many people, how does one choose the correct place in time or with the correct person to begin such a story? After much struggling with this, I finally realized that all true stories end in death, and the end is often the best place to start. I hope you enjoy reading this mostly fictional story that is also fact-based on my family.

One

October 1873

Shreveport, Louisiana

The Yellow Fever Mound

In the early hours of a brisk October morning in 1873, three men stood in front of a large earthen mound in the Oakland Cemetery of Shreveport, Louisiana. The first was a big man with gray hair and beard known as Captain Benjamin Goodman, a river pilot of a sternwheeler. The second was Bob Colbert, a soft-spoken gentleman from Georgia who made his living as a gambler. The third was an ex-slave named Jonah, who had once been Captain Goodman's property until the Civil War freed him to be a slave of wage and industry. The three men had come to pay their last respects to someone buried beneath the large mound that now gave testimony to the fight the people of Shreveport had waged against a terrible death during the summer and fall of 1873.

Captain Goodman turned from the mound, where he watched the black and gray smoke rise from burned-out shacks along the Red River and a few expensive homes within the city. Knowing no other way to fight the fever and death that stalked them, the people of Shreveport had fought fear with fire by burning the homes and clothing of the dead. Fear prevented individual services, so mass graves were filled with the bodies of the fever victims. As Captain Goodman watched the scene in silence, images of burning cities along the Tennessee River during the Civil War marched through his memory. He relived the events of the past several days and the sadness they had carried into his life. Like the smoke he watched drift aimlessly into the sky, his mind drifted back across the years and miles to a time of innocence and splendor…a time before the Civil War.

August 1860

Joseph Samuel Greene

Lauderdale County, Alabama

Joseph Samuel Greene opened his eyes from a sound sleep and searched the darkness for what had awakened him. In the stillness of the dark room, he sat up on his elbows and looked out the open window into the night. Then Joseph groped in the dark for his pocket watch lying on the table beside the bed. Holding it in the light of the moon shining through the window across his bed, he saw it was only 3:40 a.m. With a soft sigh of frustration, he replaced the watch and turned onto his side, his head resting on the pillow, as he looked through the small open porthole into the black night. A slight breeze gently moved the limp curtains as it invaded the warm, stuffy room, carrying the smell of the Tennessee River. He closed his eyes, wanting sleep, but instead, his mind filled with useless things.

Irritated and sleepless, he got out of bed and walked to the open window. Moving the lace curtains aside with his hands, he leaned on the sill, looking into the early morning darkness and a sparse scattering of lights dotting the hillsides of Florence, Alabama. He looked up at the full moon and clusters of stars in a black sky that carried no evidence of rain to cool the unusually warm August night. The same slight breeze that played with the curtains danced across his moist body, his only relief from the warm night.

At twenty-seven, Joseph Greene was a handsome man of five feet ten inches, slender, boasting broad shoulders on a frame of 190 pounds. He was solid with little fat, resulting from hard work while growing up on his father's farm in Tennessee. A dark brown mustache adorned an otherwise clean-shaven face of friendly blue eyes, straight nose, thin lips, and dark brown hair, which he combed straight back without a part.

Returning to his bed, he sat on its edge and picked up the tin of small cigars from the table beside it. Opening the tin, he removed one of the thin, dark brown cylinders and put it between his lips. Striking a match across the underside of the nightstand, he touched the flame to the end of the cigar, giving it life. Then, with a puff of smoke, he blew out the match, returning the room to darkness. As he sat back against the headboard, his mind returned to the day of his mother's death while images of his father, two brothers, and sister he had not seen since he left home ten years ago passed through his memory. He filled his lungs with cigar smoke and exhaled while remembering his mother's pale face and ghost-like appearance as she lay in her bed, losing her battle with death.

He was the better part of ten the day he stood beside her bed, looking into the softness of her blue eyes as death took her. He remembered a light snow falling as the family gathered around the open grave that cold morning. He looked skyward into the black dots of snow falling from the gray sky, watching as they disappeared into the deep, dark pit that would soon hold his mother's pine coffin. Feeling as if the snowflakes were about to pull him into the darkness, he stepped back, took his father's hand, and looked up into his red, welling eyes. Then, leaning forward, he looked around his father at his two younger brothers and sister, all crying.

Then, glancing at the other mourners, he wondered why everyone was crying but him while a solemn man dressed in black read words from the Bible. Joseph only partly heard those words as he stared at the pine casket. The man stopped reading, closed the bible, and stopped back while four men lifted the coffin, and another pulled the wood braces from under it. Then, the four men lowered his mother's coffin, chased by the falling snow into the darkness. He gripped his father's hand tighter as two men threw shovels of heavy, wet dirt into the grave, sending back thunderous echoes that often visited his dreams. Now, his memory found the inscription on the wooden marker:

Anna Dorothy Greene
Beloved wife and Mother
b: Feb 1818 d: Jan 1845

Taking a drag from the thin cigar, he recalled how he and his father often quarreled after his mother's death, saying terrible things to one another. Blowing smoke into the darkness toward the open window, he recalled the day he had decided to run away.

June 1850

In the predawn morning of a day in early June 1850, a horse and its rider stood motionless atop a hill overlooking the Tennessee Valley and the Greene farm. The slender rider turned to look one last time at his father's farm, barely visible in the dim light. 'Suns coming up,' he whispered to himself. After he tugged at the small carpetbag tied to the saddle horn, making sure it was on tight, he took a last look and then turned the horse and disappeared over the hill toward the small river town of Gasten, Tennessee.

An angry young man of barely sixteen was running for freedom like a slave. He had watched his grandparents grow old and die working the land and then helplessly watched as it took his mother, the one person who truly understood him six years earlier. His father, Zachariah Greene, was a good God-fearing man who worked hard during the day, turning to the scriptures each night for guidance and enlightenment. However, Joseph had little use for such things, unlike his brothers and sister, who never seemed to mind the work and scriptures. Blaming the farm for taking his mother, he had come to hate the land and yearned to know what lay beyond the next hill.

Gasten, Tennessee, was one of many small towns along the Tennessee River, supported by both farming and commerce along the river. A dirty and often muddy main street made its way between restaurants, stores, hotels, a bank, and six saloons, among other businesses. Several whorehouses sat quietly yet conspicuously along the side streets closer to the docks. Away from the river on the other side of town, small, one- and two-room shacks dotted the hillside. Farther up the hill, larger homes sat in smugness, boasting of their occupants' wealth.

Joseph made his way to the livery, telling the proprietor that a man would soon arrive to claim the animal. He handed the man a note for his pa and money for oats, then gently patted his horse on the nose while looking into its big black eyes. Giving the animal a last hug, he whispered, "You're 'bout the only thing I'm gonna miss." Then he picked up his bag, hurried out the door of the livery, and made his way along the muddy street while glancing now and again over his shoulder, half expecting to see his father.

The journey from the livery stable took him past stores, saloons, and restaurants smelling of breakfast. At times, he paused to peek into a door or window before hurrying along his way, always fearfully glancing over his shoulder.

As he walked along the wooden boardwalks of Gasten, the bustling life fascinated him. It may have been a small town to some, but to Joseph Greene, it was quite large compared to the farm towns he was accustomed to. The sounds of boat whistles in the distance made his heart surge with excitement, and, quickly forgetting his hunger, he walked a little faster toward the sounds and smells of the river.

Rounding a corner, he stopped in awe as the river and its large ships filled the expanse before him. The scene was like something out of a painting. Various-sized ships rested along the piers, their smoke drifting lazily skyward from tall black stacks. Others were farther out in the river, coming into port, leaving, or sailing past the small town. Whites and slaves alike were busy on the docks at one labor or another. As he walked, he noticed a group of men and paused to watch as one tossed two small white cubes with black dots across the wooden planking that bounced off the side of a crate. As they came to rest, some men laughed and picked up their money while others cursed angrily.

Confused at the game's meaning, he walked along the pier only to stop at another group of men playing another strange game. Each man held pieces of stiff paper with colored images of red hearts, diamonds, black clovers, and a strange-looking black upside-down heart. After watching for a few moments, he decided it was a game requiring a little more thinking than the one with the cubes. As fascinated as he was with this game, he quickly glanced over his shoulder and continued along the pier where Negro slaves carried crates and boxes under the scrutiny of white men. Pausing to watch the Negro men, he felt empathy for the slaves whose desire for freedom seemed not so different from his own.

Continuing along the dock, he glanced at the line of ships, knowing he had to make a choice and sneak aboard one. But which one? Time was running out, and the fear of his pa catching up with him made his heart race. He glanced back along the dock, and his eyes settled on a freshly painted white sternwheeler getting ready to leave. He had no idea where she was bound as he ran toward her. Then, without any fear of getting caught or hurt, he tossed his bag on board and then jumped onto the stern, falling against a bale of cotton.

Sitting up, he glanced around in disbelief that no one had noticed him, but then he realized that everyone was facing either out across the river or toward the ship's bow. He turned and looked back toward the town in time to see the figure of his pa riding slowly along the pier with the horse he had left at the livery in tow. Joseph stepped back between some crates and watched from the safety of his hiding place until his pa disappeared behind a building.

The sound of the ship's whistle pierced his ears, startling him. Covering his ears with both hands, he turned and looked up at the tall, dark stacks spewing billows of black smoke into the cloudless blue sky. Then, he read the name SOUTHERN BELLE, painted in bold white letters on a black background beneath them. He looked back at the pier for his pa, and when he didn't see him, he found deep relief in his escape and a sudden sadness he hadn't anticipated. He lay down on the deck, his head on his carpetbag, and looked out across the river at the shacks and buildings that slowly passed as the ship began its way south and wondered what wondrous things lay ahead.

The destination had been Florence, Alabama, and now, ten years later and unable to sleep, he turned and looked toward the window. The warm night finally gave way to the morning sun that shone through the lace curtains, casting their pattern against the opposite wall. The clock on the far wall read 6:33 a.m. as he put his feet onto the cold floor, stood, and walked back to the window. The morning air was heavy, warning of another hot, humid day as he looked out across the city that was beginning to come to life. Turning from the window to the tall standing mirror in the corner of the room, he looked at his naked image covered in sunlight.

"You're gonna suffocate," he whispered while thinking of sitting in church dressed in his suit. He considered not going, but when he looked at the photograph of Mary McAlexander, he knew that would be a big disappointment to her, and he needed to keep up appearances for her family. After lighting the kerosene lamp, he walked to the closet, took out one of his two suits, and laid it across the bed's footboard.

Pouring cold water into a shaving mug, he mixed the water and soap with a small, stiff-bristled brush and stirred the mixture into a soapy lather. Methodically, he applied the lather to his face and shaved, careful of the handlebar mustache. After getting dressed in his black suit and white shirt, he retrieved a black tie from a hook on the back of the closet door. While looking at his image in the small mirror on top of the chest, he started to work on the tie, thinking of Mary patiently waiting for him on the church's steps. He smiled as he thought of how her face always brightened with a smile at seeing him. Joseph knew the problems he and Mary faced with her two brothers, Edward and Alex McAlexander. Their family was prominent in the county, and while both brothers were polite and friendly, he suspected they only tolerated him for their sister's sake. He and Mary had talked of marriage many times but wisely had never discussed the matter with her two older brothers.

His attention returned to his image in the mirror, and as his fingers fumbled with the tie, he remembered how his mother would tie it for him each Sunday morning as a child, and when finished, she playfully patted his head. He thought of the years spent behind the plow during the day and listening to the Bible verses his father read each night by the fireplace. The red-hot glowing embers always reminded him of the Hell his father talked of while reading the Bible. If the old man wasn't preaching from the Bible, he told hardship stories of when he was a young boy in Ireland. Joseph could repeat the stories word for word about his grandparents' struggle after leaving their hard lives searching for a better one in America. Remembering they died poor dirt farmers, he wondered if it had been any better.

Remembering his two brothers and sister, whom he had not seen in all these years, saddened him. There were times he even missed his father, but then he would remember how they had argued. Over the years, he thought about going back to see the old man, hoping they could sit down and talk, something they were never able to do after the death of his mother. But he knew now that going back was not an option, and he had no intention of returning to that poor, muddy way of life. He loved Mary and knew he had a future that could mean a river pilot's license and, perhaps, one day, a steamboat on the Tennessee River.

Finished with the tie, he buttoned his vest, put on his long black coat, stepped back into the light, and looked at his reflection in the tall oak-framed mirror. Satisfied with what he saw, he walked out of his room, closed the door behind him, and then descended the stairs and out the front door of the boarding house to the sound of riverboat whistles in the distance. Walking down the porch steps, he imagined the card games, glasses of whiskey, and loud music, the things he enjoyed most. There was money on the river, and he was determined to get his share so he could take Mary away from Florence to Louisiana or even Texas. As he walked toward the church, he remembered their first meeting.

April 1858

Guntersville, Alabama

Joseph was on the bridge of the Southern Belle, drinking a cup of coffee and watching the captain on the dock below checking the cargo against a manifest. Joseph chuckled softly as the captain took off his hat and scratched his head with one hand before saying something to the other man that Joseph knew was not in a friendly tone.

A black carriage pulled by two black horses and driven by a slender, well-dressed Negro, turned onto the pier. He skillfully guided the two horses along the pier and stopped next to the Southern Belle. The driver climbed down from his seat, opened the door, and helped a young woman step down from the carriage. Watching as she struggled to open a stubborn, white lace umbrella, Joseph smiled and wondered who she was.

The struggle won, she placed the open umbrella over her shoulder. Then, as she twirled it, she glanced up, and their eyes met for a moment. She then turned toward the carriage as a short, well-dressed, stocky man stepped down from the carriage, followed by another taller, well-dressed man. The latter spoke to the Negro driver, then turned to the lady and gestured toward the gangplank. As the three walked toward the boat, the woman looked up at Joseph just before the umbrella she twirled over her shoulder hid her face.

Captain Goodman called out as he hurried across the dock to greet them as they stepped onto the boat's gangplank. Joseph watched with curiosity as the captain politely tipped his hat to the woman, kissed her hand, and then shook the hands of the two men. 'Rather friendly,' Joseph thought, then he watched as all four laughed at something the captain had said while they walked up the gangplank. Wondering who they were while sipping the strong, bitter coffee, he briefly considered rushing down to manage an introduction but quickly decided against it. He took another sip and watched them stroll along the deck, talking and laughing like old friends. Hoping the young lady would look up at him again, disappointment filled him as they disappeared through a doorway.

The Southern Belle had been underway for several hours, slowly chasing the sun westward along the Tennessee River. Joseph was standing on the bow, quietly watching the last of the sun settle beyond the trees at the bend of the river up ahead. As the sound of the boat's hull cut through the murky water, a gentle, silent breeze carried with it the smells of the river.

A woman's soft voice interrupted his thoughts. "Beautiful, isn't it?"

Joseph turned, finding the young woman from the carriage standing a few feet away, enjoying the sunset's soft, warm colors. Barely able to control his delight in seeing her, he smiled. "Yes, it is."

"Sorry," she apologized shyly. "I didn't mean to be so forward, but it's just such a beautiful sight and better if shared with another, even a stranger."

Joseph couldn't take his eyes off her. "I agree."

The moment was interrupted by someone calling out. "Mary!"

Turning toward the voice, Joseph saw the taller of the two men he had seen earlier that day standing on the upper deck. "Alex is waiting."

She looked toward the man and then smiled at Joseph with raised eyebrows. "Alex is waiting."

Joseph smiled at her humor while considering the man waiting.

"My brother, Edward," she said, anticipating his thoughts. "Alex is my other brother."

Trying not to look too relieved, he turned from the brother, searching for something to say that wouldn't sound stupid.

The man who waited called to her again. "Mary, please, the others are waiting."

She glanced at her brother and then turned to Joseph. "He'll wait." Then she held out her hand. "My name is Mary McAlexander, Mister---"

He gently shook her hand and, with the other, took off his black riverboat hat. "Joseph Greene, Miss Mary, at your service."

"Are you traveling on business or pleasure, Mister Greene?"

"Neither," said Joseph, feeling a little embarrassed. "I'm the First Mate of the Southern Belle."

She smiled, looking interested. "Sounds very exciting."

The man on the stairs impatiently called to her a third time. "Mary, please."

She glanced at her brother, and when she turned, the smile had left her face. "I should go. My brothers get a little testy if they miss their evening meal."

Joseph chuckled as he put on his hat. "Most men do."

She smiled. "Good evening, Joseph Greene."

"Good evening, Miss Mary. Enjoy your meal."

She smiled warmly. "Perhaps I'll see you again before we reach our destination."

He watched as she turned and walked across the deck and up the stairs before disappearing through the doorway. Feeling slightly disappointed that she had not stopped to look back, he turned back to watch the last of the sunset, hoping they would meet again.

The next morning, Joseph was on the bridge with his coffee and thoughts of Mary McAlexander when the captain entered. "Good morning, Captain."

"Humph," grunted the captain, looking irritated as he picked up his cup and poured it full of coffee. Taking a sip of the hot, strong brew, he sat down in the captain's chair next to the window and put his cup on the sill of the bridge window. He took an empty pipe from his coat pocket, put it in his mouth, and looked up the river. "Saw you talking to Miss Mary McAlexander last evening."

Suddenly, Joseph felt uncomfortable.

Captain Goodman stared at the river up ahead. "Be careful, Laddie."

Joseph became puzzled. "Careful of what, Captain?"

"I've known that family for years," Goodman said as he turned from the river. "They're a highly respected family. They are a family of influence and have the money to back it."

Knowing the captain had rules about mingling with passengers, Joseph stammered, "It was an innocent meeting, Captain. I was---

"Didn't say it wasn't," interrupted the captain. "Who you talk to is your business as long as no harm comes from it. I'm sure it was innocent, just as you say." He stood to put one hand on Joseph's shoulder, then smiled wryly. "It's you, Laddie, I'm concerned about, not Miss Mary McAlexander." His expression was uneasy. "You and I come from different worlds, Laddie, and we travel in different circles than these folks do."

Joseph smiled, feeling like a young boy being talked to by a father or an uncle. "Who are they?"

Captain Goodman looked at his pocket watch. "Appears we have a little time." He turned to the helmsman and gestured with a nod of his head. "Mind the river. There's a few sand bars up ahead."

"Yes, sir," replied the helmsman as his eyes keenly searched the waters up ahead.

Captain Goodman gestured at the door. "Let's go down to my cabin, Laddie. I could use some Scotch in this coffee."

As they entered his quarters, the captain walked straight to the messy desk beside his unmade bunk. "Can I interest you in a drink, Laddie?"

"No thanks." Joseph watched as the captain plopped down in the chair at the desk and opened the lower left-hand drawer.

Retrieving a bottle of Scotch, Goodman pulled the cork out with his teeth, and while still holding it, he poured a small amount into his coffee, replaced the cork, and then put the bottle away. Then he leaned back in his chair, told Joseph to sit, and began to sip the Scotch and hot coffee.

Joseph took off his hat, set it on a small table, and sat in an uncomfortable chair beside it.

"To answer your question as to who they are," said the captain, "I'll tell you what I know." He paused for a sip of coffee, then stared out the open porthole of his cabin. "Their father was Alexander McAlexander, and their mother was a beauty by the name of Julia O'Neal." He smiled with affection at her memory. "A handsome lady of wealth and stature in her own right." He paused to take another sip of coffee. "It was their father, Alexander, who helped me get my first job on the river that started me on my illustrious career." The captain chuckled, shook his head, and took another sip before he continued. "Anyway, to make a long story short, they had three children I came to know over the years." He sat back, placed his feet on his desk, and rested the cup on his right leg. "Edward's the oldest, named after their uncle, Edward O'Neal. Alex is the second oldest named after their father, and I don't know Miss Mary's namesake."

He looked down at his cup while considering another drink but instead set the empty cup on the desk. "Shortly after Mary was born, Julia died. Alexander began drinking and doing all sorts of crazy things." Goodman looked sad as he gestured with one hand. "He was never the same after her death. That's when the trouble started. Julia had named her brother, the children's uncle, Edward O'Neal, executor of her will, which left a tidy sum of money and a few slaves to the children." Goodman paused. "Edward O'Neal was a powerful man around Marshall County back then, and I guess he still is. Irritated with Alexander for his drinking, he sought for and got custody of the children, becoming their benefactor, so to speak." The captain frowned as he shook his head. "Old man Alexander fought long and hard, but in the end, Edward O'Neal won."

Goodman put his feet back on the floor, looking sad as he leaned forward with his elbows on his desk. "Then the day came when their uncle realized he didn't want three additional children and split them up. He took young Edward to Florence with him, giving the boy the finest education at the best medical school. Today, Edward McAlexander is a fine, respected surgeon in Florence." He paused in thought. "Alex and Mary lived with their grandmother in the city of Madison. Alex was sent to law school and became an attorney while Mary attended the best boarding schools, and now the three jointly own a plantation east of Florence where Alex, his wife Ella, and their children live. "Alex is quite capable of handling both a law practice and the cotton farm, but I believe he loves his time on the farm more than his practice. Even though Alex physically works the farm, they all share the profits equally." Goodman shook his head once again with a sad expression. "Now comes the sad part; Edward married a beautiful young woman named Henrietta Koger a few years back and had a daughter they named Mary, after his sister. Henrietta died recently, so I believe they're on this boat."

Joseph looked on with interest, waiting for the explanation.

"Edward didn't say as much," said Goodman, gesturing with one hand. "But it appears he's taking his sister Mary back to be a nanny for his daughter." He looked at Joseph and smiled. "And there you have what I know about the McAlexander family. Wealthy, respected, good breeding, and damn nice people."

"What became of their father?" asked Joseph, looking curious.

Goodman shrugged. "Got sick and died several years back."

Joseph sat quietly, considering what the captain had told him, and then stood. "Well, thanks for the interesting story, Captain. I'll keep all that in mind if I have the opportunity to see her again."

Goodman smiled wryly. "I saw Miss Mary McAlexander after dinner last night, and she asked about you. Where you came from, what sort of man you are." Still grinning, Goodman continued, "Seemed to me she was more than a little interested, laddie, and that's why I told you to be careful."

Joseph smiled as his face flushed a little. "I best get up to the bridge."

The captain sat back in his chair and considered the young man's chances with Miss Mary McAlexander. After a quick moment, he decided that they were, at the very best, impossible. So, he smiled, opened the drawer to his desk, and retrieved the bottle of Scotch while Joseph picked up his hat and walked toward the door.

Joseph walked out of the cabin and down the dim passageway into the warm sunlight, finding Mary McAlexander standing alone at the railing, staring at the view of small shacks and farmlands along the river. Not wanting to startle her, he spoke softly from the doorway. "Good morning."

She turned and smiled shyly. "Good morning. Taking care of your morning duties?"

He smiled as he walked to the railing, leaning on it with both hands as he looked out across the river, thinking of Captain Goodman's story. "I suppose you could call it that." Then he smiled at her. "Sleep well last night?"

"Oh yes," she said with a smile. "There's something about the water and the gentle movement of the boat that puts me right to sleep."

"I know what you mean. I sleep better onboard than I do in my room in Florence."

"You have a place in Florence?" she asked with a surprised look.

"It isn't much," he shrugged. "But it's someplace to hang my hat and call home, as they say."

Mary smiled again. "I'm sure it's quite nice."

"Well, I don't know about that, but it serves its purpose."

Her face suddenly flushed with a small smile. "And what purpose would that be, Joseph?"

He shrugged. "Stability, I guess."

She laughed. "My brothers would be proud of you."

During the next several minutes, they talked about several subjects, none very important. Joseph felt completely at ease with her, as if he had known her all his life, because he usually felt a little uncomfortable around women. She admitted to turning twenty recently and told him she was moving in with her brother Edward in Florence.

Thinking the captain had been correct, he listened to her talk while taking in her oval-shaped face framed with dark brown hair under a light brown bonnet. Her lips were full, her eyes dark brown, and her long brown hair lay softly over the shawl covering her shoulder. Other than the red lip covering, she wore little makeup. She was slightly plump but not fat, and a tiny waist accentuated her full breasts.

Hearing a familiar voice speaking her name, Joseph turned, coming face to face with Edward, Mary's older brother. He was a good-looking man, standing some five feet nine inches tall with neatly cut, light brown hair and dark eyes that seemed to search for your soul as they looked into your eyes. His tanned face was clean-shaven, with a square jaw and thin lips. His tailored clothes showed off his broad shoulders and small waist. Joseph thought he looked more like a gambler than a physician.

Edward was a man filled with guilt over the loss of his wife, and it held him unmercifully in its grasp since he believed that, as a doctor, he should have been able to save the woman he loved. Although that was not true, he had never forgiven himself for her death.

Mary stepped away from the railing and took her brother's arm while gesturing toward Joseph with her free hand. "This nice young man was explaining the hazards of the river. Joseph Greene, this is my brother, Edward McAlexander."

Joseph stood a little taller as he offered his hand.

Edward politely shook his hand with a friendly, firm grip. "I'm honored, Joseph."

"The honor's mine, sir."

Edward placed his arm around his sister. "What position do you hold on board the Southern Belle?"

"First Mate."

Edward nodded approvingly and then looked out across the river. "An honorable profession and one that always intrigued me." He looked at Joseph. "I enjoy my little trips with Captain Goodman; he's a good man."

"That he is," agreed Joseph while noticing Mary's other brother approaching from behind Edward.

"Here you are," said Alex in a somewhat loud voice. "I've been looking everywhere."

Edward turned toward him with a grin as he winked at Joseph. "Apparently not everywhere. I was hoping we could make it to Florence first."

"Funny," Alex said without humor while forcing a smile for the stranger's benefit.

Mary introduced Alex. "Joseph, this is my other brother Alex, and this nice young man is Joseph Greene."

Alex was a year younger than Edward and stood only five feet six, but his height was compensated by a stocky build boasting a large, robust chest. He had the same McAlexander deep-set eyes under bushy eyebrows. Alex was hatless, and the slight breeze from the river played softly in his brown hair above a high forehead that bore a small scar. Joseph later learned he had received it while playing pirates with Mary as a child. Alex smiled, extending his hand. "My pleasure."

Feeling slightly uncomfortable with the attention, Joseph firmly shook Alex's hand. "I hope you have had a pleasant trip?"

Just then, the boat's whistle blew with a piercing shriek. Mary let out a small scream, as women do when startled, then placed her hands over her mouth and laughed, trying to hide her embarrassment.

Joseph looked upriver at the city of Florence in the distance. "That means work for me." Then he turned to Mary, smiled, and tipped his hat. "It was a pleasure talking to you, Miss." He turned and shook Edward's hand and then Alex's before he looked into Mary's brown eyes, turned, and walked toward the ship's bow.

Mary quickly called out. "Joseph."

He stopped and turned.

She hurried the short distance while her brothers waited beside the railing. She smiled and spoke softly. "If you have tomorrow off, there is a park near the river." She glanced back at her brothers and then looked at him. "I plan on being there around two."

Surprised yet pleased, he smiled. "I have tomorrow off, and I'm familiar with that park."

"Good," she said quietly, and then she smiled. "Till tomorrow." She turned abruptly and hurried back to her waiting brothers. Taking Edward's arm, she glanced back at Joseph over her shoulder as they walked away.

Joseph would keep that date and many more over the next two years.

Walking up the hill toward the church, Joseph saw Mary waiting by the closed front door, dressed in a dark brown dress with a matching waist jacket over a white lace blouse.

She waved excitedly, then waited while he walked through the gate of the picket fence and hurried up the walk. Her face wore a frown. "You're late."

He kissed her cheek and grinned. "You look lovely."

The frown turned to a soft smile. "Thank you, but you're still late, and I'm still upset."

Joseph opened the door, greeted by the singing congregation, and quickly closed it as they entered, finding seats in the pew behind her two brothers and their families. After they smiled their greetings to her brothers, they picked up a hymnal and joined the singing.

After a few more hymns followed by the Sunday sermon, the congregation filed out the front door, shaking hands with the preacher.

Mary and Joseph joined Edward, Alex, and their families as they visited while standing on the wooden walk beyond the white picket fence of the churchyard.

Joseph was preoccupied with his next trip and was only half listening.

Edward placed a hand on his shoulder. "Do you have the day off, Joseph?"

"I do."

Edward looked pleased. "Good, I wasn't sure what your schedule was. You seem to travel up and down the river so often."

Joseph grinned. "It does seem so. Tomorrow morning, we leave for Chattanooga."

Mary was talking to Alex's wife, Ella, when she noticed Edward and Joseph talking. Curious, she excused herself, walked over, and stood beside Joseph, taking his arm.

Edward smiled at his sister and then asked Joseph if he would join the family for Sunday dinner.

"He would love to," replied Mary.

Looking a little embarrassed, Joseph smiled at Edward. "I guess I would."

"Splendid." Edward pointed toward his waiting carriage. "You and Mary can ride with me."

It was not the first time Edward had invited Joseph for dinner, although the invitations were not often. Edward did not dislike Joseph but did not approve of the relationship. Understandably, both brothers believed their sister needed someone a little higher on the social ladder. Someone more suited to her needs, able to give her the way of life she had become accustomed to. However, Edward was also a realist, understanding that it was Mary's choice who she fancied and not his. Alex, on the other hand, had always been a little more protective of their sister.

Feeling out of place, Joseph thought about all this during the ride. The Negro driver turned the carriage from the cobblestone street onto a cobblestone driveway, guiding the horses between two large open wrought iron gates. Stopping at the veranda of a white, two-story home nestled among several trees, the driver jumped down and opened the door.

Joseph knew this house was something he could never compete with nor hope to offer Mary, but by now, he was certain of their love and confident that she would be happy wherever they decided to live.

Conversation during dinner was casual, centering on things like the house, farm, children, and fashions. Afterward, the men retired to the library behind closed doors for cigars and a drink to discuss the coming elections. Mary and Ella visited in the parlor, watching little Mary and Ella's children.

Once in the library, Alex sat on a small sofa facing a large fireplace with a small stack of wood awaiting a match while Joseph sat in a plush chair a few feet away. Letting his eyes wander around the library while Edward poured the drinks, Joseph took in the bookcase that filled an entire wall with all manner and sizes of books. A large dark cherry desk and a few straight back chairs occupied the far corner close to white framed glass doors leading to the veranda. Several paintings of horses, mountains, and a garden near a castle decorated the other walls. His eyes settled on a painting of Edward's late wife, Henrietta, above the fireplace just as Edward offered him a cigar and a glass of brandy. He straightened up in his chair and graciously accepted both. She took a sip of brandy before setting it on the table next to a photograph of Henrietta and little Mary, thinking that Edward must miss her.

Alex leaned forward in his seat and lit Joseph's cigar and then his own before throwing the dead match into the fireplace. He picked up his glass, sniffed the brandy, and then raised his glass. "Gentlemen," he took a small sip and looked at Edward as if waiting.

Edward puffed his cigar twice and then sat down while the smoke slowly drifted around his head before disappearing. He held the glass up, took a small drink, and then held it on his lap with both hands while staring deeply into it, lost in thought.

Alex watched his brother for a moment, then he turned to Joseph and asked about life on the river.

Fearing that her brothers may cause discomfort to Joseph, Mary excused herself from the parlor on the pretense of needing something from her room. Quietly, she stood by the doors, listening to the muffled voices inside, and upon hearing Edward laugh, she sighed with relief and continued up the stairs on her supposed errand.

Inside the library, Alex took a deep puff from his cigar, looked up at the ceiling while exhaling smoke, and then looked at Joseph. "What do you make of all this mess up north?"

Joseph had turned his attention to his glass and was thinking of Mary and tomorrow's journey upriver. Contemplating the question, he took a long drag from his cigar and then looked at Alex. "Which mess would that be?"

Edward was still staring into his glass of brandy as he laughed, finding humor in Joseph's response.

Alex, on the other hand, only smiled. "I agree. There are many messes up north and---"

Edward interrupted. "If this Abraham Lincoln gets himself elected in November, he will do everything in his power to abolish slavery."

Alex stood and walked to the liquor table, pouring another brandy. He picked up his glass and looked at his brother. "Where do you get such fine brandy?"

"I import it. Would you like a bottle or two next time?"

"Of course, I would. You know how much I like a brandy after dinner."

Edward smiled at his brother. "I certainly do. When it's my brandy." He turned his attention to Joseph. "And how about you, Joseph? Would you care for a bottle or two?"

Joseph considered the request for a moment but then shook his head. "No, thanks, Edward, but I appreciate the offer."

Edward gestured toward the cabinet. "Should you change your mind, please help yourself." He knocked the ashes from his cigar into an ashtray. "The South's only hope is that Vice President Breckenridge gets elected as our next President."

Edward glanced at Alex, pouring his third drink. "Not so fast, Alex," he softly scolded, followed by a small chuckle. "It's too early to pour your fat little ass in that small carriage."

Alex grinned at his brother, glanced at Joseph, and then filled his glass half-full. "You're right, of course." He took a small sip and sat down, winking at Joseph. "Forgive me, but I truly love my brother's brandy."

Joseph smiled while thinking about the upcoming elections, knowing that a wealthy family such as this took great interest in the North's politics and the issues discussed in Washington. Rather than speaking, he wisely chose to listen to what the two men may share with him.

Alex stood, walked to the fireplace, and leaned on the mantle with one hand holding the lit cigar and the other holding his brandy. Staring down at the small stack of wood that waited patiently for its match, he twirled the glass slowly with a troubled expression and took a quick sip. "If Breckenridge loses, the South is doomed." He looked at Joseph and then Edward. "The southern states may follow through their threats of secession if that happens."

Joseph took a sip of brandy while looking from one brother to the other.

Edward looked thoughtfully into his glass. "I fear Mr. Lincoln will be our next President." He looked at Alex. "As you said, dear brother, secession will follow."

"Do you really believe that?" asked Joseph.

Edward looked at him for a long moment with a sad expression. "Yes," he said softly. "And then, civil war will follow. And that is a war I'm not sure the South will survive."

Joseph's face filled with worry. "It would be a difficult war for the South," he said, gesturing with one hand. "The North is too powerful, their factories too numerous, and their Army already trained."

"Ah, poppycock," replied Alex, looking irritated. "The North hasn't the stomach for a fight with the South. And factories or not, the South is fighting for its way of life."

Edward looked at him with a concerned look. "Don't be so hasty, Alex. We may have the will, and we may believe we have the right, but there are a lot of northern men willing to fight this cause should the southern states follow through with their threat of seceding from the nation." He leaned forward, looking troubled. "It would be considered an act viewed as treason." He looked from Joseph to Alex. "We could all get hung."

Alex nodded in resignation. "I suppose you're right." Then he turned his attention to the fireplace.

Edward looked at Joseph thoughtfully. "Truly, Joseph, what are your opinions on this mess?"

Joseph had hoped he would escape that question and sipped his brandy while considering a response. "Quite honestly, I haven't come to any conclusions yet."

Alex scoffed while staring down at the pile of wood in the fireplace, waiting to be set afire. "I expected as much from a man who has not one thing to lose!"

Edward looked at Joseph apologetically, then at his brother. "Alex," he said as he stood, "Not every man knows what to make of this mess. There are a lot of men in Lauderdale County that don't own slaves or land or have a lot of money." He glanced at Joseph for a moment. "But they're still Southerners, and I'm sure that if asked, most men tonight, like Joseph, couldn't tell you what they'd do when the time comes." He sat down, shrugged, and shook his head. "That time is not yet upon us."

Joseph's face tensed with anger as he placed his half-empty glass on the table next to his chair and looked at Alex. "I don't own a slave, Alex, not one. No one in my family has ever possessed a slave. Nor do I have a lot of money, as you so eloquently said. However, I love the South, and I disagree with the North telling us how to live and run our affairs. And as far as nothing to lose, I beg to differ." He paused. "I, like others, have my life to lose."

Silence descended upon the room, and in the stillness that followed, Alex's expression was one of regret as he glanced at Edward while Joseph picked up his brandy and took a drink. "My remarks were in bad taste and uncalled for." He shrugged as he gestured toward the liquor cabinet. "Too much brandy, I suppose." Then Alex drew in a breath and let out a soft sigh. "Edward was right. What man knows what he'd do until the moment arises and the shooting starts?" He paused, gesturing with one hand. "Forgive me for speaking before my brain was engaged. Please accept my apologies."

Joseph nodded his forgiveness while Alex returned to his chair.

Edward broke the silence. "I'm afraid that if this comes to a shooting war, this country will have wounds and scars across our land that will never heal." He stood, walked to the open doors of the veranda, and looked out into the warm darkness of the night with his back to them. "Our beloved South," he said softly, "will be filled with graveyards of men not only from the North and South but from all over the nation. My deepest fear is that well-meaning men will dip their pens in ink and let loose monsters none of us have ever witnessed." He sipped his drink. "It will be a terrible, terrible ordeal."

Feeling tension in the room, Joseph glanced at Alex watching his brother, and then he looked at Edward standing in the open doorway.

"Mothers," continued Edward, "sweethearts and widows will never cease their wailing and crying." Edward paused to sip his brandy. "Brave men will fight and die in strange places with names most had never heard of, let alone able to read or pronounce." He took a drink. "I pray that this family will survive these terrible monsters."

A hoot owl somewhere in the darkness outside broke the silence while Joseph's mind filled with images of his father and brothers lying dead, perhaps on their farm. His father had spoken against slavery many times, and Joseph was sure that his brothers would fight with the North if war did come. His mind filled with thoughts of his brothers killing Edward and Alex, or they killing his brothers. Still, he had no answer as to what he would do.

Looking sad, Edward turned from the open doors, crossed the room, and stood beside Joseph, placing a hand on his shoulder. "I don't know what your family believes or which side holds their allegiance. But believe me when I say I sincerely hope that no harm comes to any of them."

Just then, the doors to the library burst open. Mary, Ella, her two children, and little Mary walked into the room complaining about being neglected.

Joseph stood while Mary smiled as she walked toward him. "Are you going to sit in here with my brothers getting drunk and talk about serious, boring things, or are you going to pay some attention to me?" She took his arm and smiled. "Take me for a walk in the warm night air and forget my brothers for a while."

Edward smiled as he gestured toward the veranda doors. "Go on, you two. It's a nice evening for a walk and simple things. Let's leave the world and its trouble for another evening of brandy and cigars."

Ella took Alex's arm and affectionately pulled herself into him.

He smiled as he whispered, "I know." He drank the last of his drink, set the empty glass on the mantle, and turned to his brother. "Edward, I believe it's time for Ella to take me home and put me to bed."

Edward picked up a tiny bell from the table and rang for his Negro housekeeper, Sophie. "A little too much of my good brandy?"

Alex grinned. "Guilty."

Sophie walked into the library and looked at Edward. "Yes, suh?"

"My brother and sister-in-law are leaving, Sophie. Please show them to the door."

Alex gently gestured her away. "We can show ourselves out, Sophie."

"Yes, suh," she replied, then she turned to little Mary, telling her it was her bedtime.

"I'll take her, Sophie," said Edward as he bent down to pick up his daughter, quickly adding, "Show my brother and his wife to the door."

"Yes, suh, Mr. Edward," replied Sophie, "can I gets ya anything else?"

"No, thank you, Sophie," he said. "After you show my brother and his wife out, you go on ahead and retire if you like; we'll just sit over here on the sofa listening to the night." He smiled at little Mary. "I'll tell her a story while she watches the fireflies blink at one another, and then I'll put her to bed."

Sophie turned to escort Alex and Ella to the front door.

"Goodnight, everyone," yelled Alex over his shoulder.

Edward said goodnight and then sat with his daughter on the sofa, watching the erratic blinking of fireflies beyond the open veranda doors.

Outside in the darkness and away from the light shining across the veranda from the open doors, Mary held Joseph's hand as they walked. "What were you talking about?"

He stopped and looked up at the star-filled sky and the full moon. "Politics." A soft breeze whispered through the cottonwoods, bringing with it the sweet smell of magnolia blossoms and other perfumes of the garden.

Mary looked away, disappointed. "Oh. I had hoped you were talking about us."

Joseph smiled, thinking how predictable she was. He stopped, turned her face gently with his hand, and looked into her eyes in the faint moonlight. "And why would you think that?"

Feeling embarrassed, she leaned against him and fussed with his tie. "I heard my brother's get a little loud once or twice."

"At the door, spying, were we?"

She smiled with embarrassment as she looked up at him. "I thought you had asked Edward for my hand."

Her perfume filled his head as he placed his hands on her waist and pulled her against him. "You know I love you, Mary, but we both agreed to wait." Then he kissed her.

Two

August 1860

The Southern Belle

In his room at the boarding house, Joseph folded the newspaper that told of Abraham Lincoln gaining support and increasing his chances of becoming the next President of the United States, defeating Vice President Breckenridge. He placed the paper neatly on the table, picked up a spoon, and thoughtfully stirred his coffee. Then he picked up the cup and took a drink as he watched the window curtains move slightly from the soft breeze coming off the Tennessee River.

He knew very well that the southern states would make good their threats of secession as he recalled Edward's words of treason and declaration of war the previous evening. Hearing the clock downstairs strike nine, he stood and walked to the closet, retrieving his dark blue jacket and neatly hung pants, having been pressed the night before by his landlady, Mrs. Powers.

Pulling a heavy black turtleneck shirt from the drawer of a nearby dresser, he removed his robe, slipped into the shirt, and then put on the pressed suit while thinking of someday having a tailored suit of clothes made when he had the money. The clock in the hall downstairs struck the half-hour, telling him that it was time to go. The Southern Belle would be leaving Florence soon, and Captain Benjamin Goodman would have his hide if he missed the trip. Locking his door, he hurried down the stairs to the kitchen, set his empty cup and saucer in the sink, and said good morning to Mrs. Powers, now busy over a hot stove. He thanked her for pressing his clothes and kissed her rough cheek, bringing a smile to her round, plump face.

Without turning from the hot stove and the noon meal she was preparing for the boarders, she wished him a safe trip.

The buggy drove along the pier, stopping several yards from the gangplank of the Southern Belle. As Joseph stepped down from the buggy, Negro men were loosening the ropes that had moments ago held the Southern Belle snugly against the pier. Realizing she was leaving early, he quickly paid the driver, grabbed his bag, and ran across the dock, jumping from the pier onto the boat's deck. Falling against a bale of cotton, he recalled the day he had first jumped on board as a young boy.

"Glad you could make it," shouted Captain Goodman from the bridge.

Joseph shaded his eyes with one hand, looked up while brushing off his suit with the other, and yelled, "I thought we were leaving at 11:30! A bit early, aren't we?"

"Depends," yelled the captain through the open window of the bridge.

"On what?"

The captain grinned as he yelled, "On whose clock you're looking at!"

Laughter echoed from inside the bridge, making Joseph feel foolish and angry.

"Well," yelled Captain Goodman. "Let's see if you can take us into deeper water and turn her toward Decatur without hitting a sand bar…or another boat."

More laughter from the bridge.

Joseph's anger rose a little higher.

Goodman looked down at him as he stood on the deck. "You gonna perform that little task from down there or up here on the bridge?"

Joseph looked up at the grinning face of Captain Goodman, looking pleased with his taunting, picked up his bag, and hurried toward the stairs, taking them two steps at a time. Entering the bridge, he dropped his bag and shouted orders to the helmsman. While ignoring the captain, Joseph walked to an open window, stuck his head out, and began barking orders to the deck crews below. As the big boat floated into the swifter current of the Tennessee River, he looked toward the rear of the boat and the red-painted sternwheel that slowly began to turn, pushing the Southern Belle gently downstream.

The aging Southern Belle was mechanically sound and had a clean appearance with a fresh coat of white paint and red trim. The 105 rooms could accommodate nearly 200 passengers who could enjoy a drink while gambling or fine dining while listening to the music of a small band.

"Well done," complimented the captain with a proud, pleased look. "You just may make a River Pilot one day, Laddie."

Joseph hated the term Laddie when he was mad at the captain, and the captain knew it, but that made the term all the more fun for the old man.

"It may take a few years, Laddie," said the captain. "But you might make it if you pay attention." Captain Benjamin Goodman was a big man, standing an even six feet tall on a big frame that he loved to push around when the opportunity presented itself. His face was tanned, lined, and leathery from the outdoors, but overall, he was still a good-looking man of fifty-plus years. A head of thick gray hair spilled from under his captain's hat. A neatly trimmed gray beard covered a warm, friendly face that could very quickly turn unfriendly. Bushy gray eyebrows sat above his wide-set dark green eyes, separated by a slightly crooked broad nose and a wide smile. He got up from his chair. "You have the boat, Mister. Take us to Decatur!"

Joseph nodded without speaking or looking back as his anger with the old man diminished.

The captain walked to the door, paused, turned, and chuckled. "I'd prefer you do that without hitting anything?"

Looking irritated, Joseph stared downriver. "I'll do my best."

"I'm sure ya will, Laddie," chuckled the captain. "I'm heading below to check out a few things, then to my cabin." He started to leave but paused. "You can join me for lunch if you've a mind to."

Joseph nodded that he would, then turned and climbed into the captain's chair. He sat back, hoping to enjoy a quiet, lazy journey as they sailed down the river. The passenger list Joseph examined showed 140 passengers, and looking down on the decks below, it appeared they were all enjoying a stroll around the decks in the sun. He settled back in the chair, enjoying the steam engines' constant quiet roar and the splashing sound of the giant red paddlewheel churning through the water. Jonah, the captain's slave of many years, was on the bow busy at some task, and as he watched the slave, Joseph recalled their first meeting.

June 1850

Joseph was dreaming of riding in a wagon down a bumpy road when he opened his eyes and looked into the face of a large Negro man of about thirty who was gently shaking his shoulder.

Looking worried, the Negro asked, "Ya's alright?"

Startled for a moment, Joseph looked for an escape, and finding none, he waited to see what the big man would do.

The big man smiled a friendly, warm smile. "Ask't if ya was alright?"

Deciding the man meant him no harm, Joseph grinned, looking embarrassed. "Guess I fell asleep."

Curious about the boy, the big man smiled. "Does ya mind if I sits a while?"

"Sure, go ahead."

The big man sat down on the hard deck next to him. "Yes, suh, I sho knows how dat is alright."

Joseph's family had never owned slaves, so he had never had the opportunity to say more than a few words to any Negro in his entire sixteen years. He studied the big man for a moment, finding trust in the friendly smile and taking a liking to him right away.

The Negro studied him a moment. "I was watching when ya's jumped aboard."

Afraid he would report him, Joseph stared into the dark eyes of this seemingly gentle giant.

"I s'pose I shud reports ya," said the Negro looking quite serious but friendly. Taking a liking to the boy, he smiled. "But don't s'pose ah will." Then, he surprised Joseph by asking if he was hungry.

Joseph smiled with anticipation. "Surely am."

"Well, den," the big man said, "yah waits right here whilst I runs an gets ya sumth'n ta eats." He started to leave but turned, looking worried. "Yah won't go no place now, wills ya?"

Joseph shrugged with a gesture. "Where would I go?"

The big man laughed, liking the boy's sense of humor. "Sho nuff," then he disappeared around the crates.

A short time later, Joseph heard two men talking. He recognized the deep voice of the big Negro, and then heard the sound of fading footsteps.

A familiar voice whispered, "Yah still in there?"

"Yeah," replied Joseph softly while peering between the crates at the big man's hands holding a plate of food. "Who's with ya?" he whispered.

"T'aint no one," the big man said as he crouched to his knees and crawled through the opening. "He were jus' a fren of mine. But don't ya go's worry'n none, he won't say nut'n." He held out the tin plate of beans and pork with one hand and offered a spoon with the other.

The aroma of the food rushed into his nostrils as he took the plate and spoon and began eating with enthusiasm.

The big man shook his head and chuckled. "Yah sure is hungry."

Embarrassed, Joseph paused to wipe his mouth on his sleeve and apologized for eating like a pig.

The big man grinned while telling him that he sometimes ate that way. "Dey calls me Jonah."

"I'm Joseph, Joseph Greene, Mister Jonah."

The Negro chuckled at being called Mister, figuring this boy hadn't been around many slaves.

"If'n I's you, Mistah Joseph, I's wouldn't go call'n me or no other colored man Mistah, no, suh."

Again, Joseph felt embarrassed but tucked it away in his memory, thinking he had a lot to learn. As he ate, he told Jonah of his home in Tennessee and how he had run away from his father. Then he described hiding behind these crates while watching his pa search the docks for him.

Jonah thought the boy wasn't like most white boys, and maybe it all came down to sharing a common desire to be free, something Jonah knew that he would never experience. As the two talked, they created an unspoken bond between them. Jonah told of his experience running away from a plantation owner in Georgia, only to be caught, whipped, and resold to Captain Goodman.

Joseph asked if the captain had ever taken a whip to him.

Jonah frowned and shook his head. "Ah no, suh, not da good Cap'n, no, suh." Then he nodded, looking serious. "The Cap'n, he's a kindly man for the most part. But that don't mean he couldn't lose his temper now and den, but he ain't never hit me." Then he smiled, saying the captain's temper was lost mostly on the passengers. "He's a fair man," Jonah said thoughtfully. "Leastways, he are ta me an dah others on dis here boat." Jonah grinned as he looked through the small opening. "Tells ya one thing tho, Cap'n Goodman has little use fer dese uppity passengers as he calls `em." Then he told Joseph he had to leave but would return later in the evening with more food. Then he backed his way out from between the crates.

Joseph moved some of the smaller bales and crates around, making his spot a little larger, and then spent the rest of the day looking out across the river between naps.

It was almost dark when Jonah returned with more food and water, apologizing for being gone so long. He pulled an old blanket from under his shirt. "Yah mite needs dis t'nites."

Joseph took the blanket, thanked him, and then took the food.

Jonah sat down in the cramped quarters. "Nice hiding place ya has here."

Joseph paused from eating, glanced around, and nodded in agreement. "Where you from, Jonah?"

Looking a little perplexed, the Negro said, "I don'ts rightly know."

Joseph took a bite of food. "What about your ma and pa?"

The Negro looked sad and thoughtful for a moment. "I don'ts recall dem a'tall, cuz I were tak'n away from `em and sold as a small boy."

Joseph thought of his mother and felt sorry for the big man, thinking it must have been terrible for him. The two talked for a while longer before Jonah left the hiding place for his cot somewhere on the boat. Joseph wrapped up in the blanket, sat on the hard deck against a bale of cotton, and listened to the soft sounds of the Southern Belle's bright red paddlewheel churning through the Tennessee River. He thought about the big man and was thankful they had met. In truth, he felt safer when he was around. The sounds of the river mixing with the soft music from somewhere inside the boat soon put Joseph to sleep.

It was dark when strange voices awoke Joseph. He crept out of his hiding place and stood in the shadows behind a bale of cotton. From there, he watched three men as they rolled some kegs next to a wooden crate to use as stools and then sat down. A big, heavyset man placed a lantern on the crate, then he and a freckle-faced man with red hair sat down on two smaller crates. The third was a tall, skinny man with dirty clothes who took out a stack of those stiff papers with the numbers from his pants pocket. He watched with curiosity as the man did something with them that caused a ruffling sound and then gently tossed one to each of the others and himself several times until each had a certain number of the papers.

Curious, Joseph stepped out of the shadows to have a closer look when the man with unruly red hair and freckles noticed him. "You have any money?"

The others turned and looked to see who the man was talking to.

Joseph eyed each one and then shook his head. "No, sir."

"Beat it," said the skinny man.

The man with freckles, who looked around thirty, motioned to Joseph. "Come have a seat, lad. You might bring me luck."

Joseph eagerly accepted the invitation, sat down on the crate behind Freckles, and then watched with fascination the shuffling of the stack of small papers, the game, and the exchange of money. Gathering a little understanding of the game as the men played and drank from a jug they passed between them, Joseph noticed they were getting a little drunker and belligerent as the evening wore on.

A fourth man in his fifties with dark hair and mustache dressed better than the others joined the game but refused to participate in the jug. Joseph became slightly concerned for the stranger whose winnings began to irritate the others.

Freckles became increasingly belligerent with each drink and blamed Joseph for his bad luck. "Can't ya sit somewhere's else, ya dang fool?"

Joseph didn't like being called a fool but knew he was no match for Freckles, so he decided to leave.

The man with the mustache said, "Sit over here, boy; you remind me of my little brother." Then he smiled. "He always brought me luck."

The others, looking unhappy, gave Joseph a mean look but said nothing. As the card game continued, the man who had called Joseph a fool lost the next several hands, and that pleased Joseph. It wasn't long before an argument broke out between Mustache and the other three. They accused Mustache of cheating, which he denied, and Joseph was sure he hadn't because he only dealt every fourth hand and won most of the hands the other three men dealt.

Freckles stood and looked at Mustache. "Get up."

Mustache smiled at Joseph while telling him to move away, and after Joseph moved, he punched Freckles in the groin and then stood, hitting him with an uppercut that sounded like a piece of wood breaking. The blow sent Freckles reeling backward against some cotton bales several feet away, ending up on the boat's deck. Joseph watched with wide eyes as Freckles wiped the blood from his mouth and nose. and then stood.

Joseph had never seen a brawl before and quickly backed away.

The big man stood to throw a punch, but Mustache landed a right cross on Big Man's cheek, knocking him back into Skinny. Before Skinny could get prepared, Mustache punched him in the stomach, followed by a right punch hitting Skinny in the nose, sending him sprawling backward onto the deck.

Joseph had never seen one man fight three at a time before and was amazed at how Mustache handled himself. While Big Man and Skinny were getting up, Joseph looked over at Freckles, seeing that he had pulled a knife from his boot. Joseph jumped Freckles and grabbed his arm without considering the consequences, trying to knock the knife loose. As the two wrestled, Freckles slapped Joseph across the face, knocking him against a cotton bale, and as Joseph was getting up, Mustache hit Freckles, knocking him backward and causing him to lose his knife. Mustache quickly pushed Joseph out of the way, picked up the knife Freckles had dropped, and tossed it overboard.

Big Man got up, tore a big piece of wood from a crate, and swung it at Mustache, who ducked and quickly stepped closer, landing a fist in Big Man's stomach. He followed that with an uppercut, sending Big Man reeling backward. As he fell, he let go of the club that also disappeared over the side of the boat.

Mustache turned to find Skinny, but he had ducked behind a crate while Freckles helped Big Man to his feet. As the two started walking toward Mustache, Skinny stepped from behind the crates. Big Man pulled a large knife from the sheath on his belt.

Acting quickly, Joseph kicked the knife from his hand, picked it up, and tossed it overboard.

Big Man gave Joseph a dirty look. "You little shit."

While Freckles and Skinny fought with Mustache, Big Man reached out for Joseph, who turned and started climbing up the crates. But Big Man grabbed his foot and pulled him down to the deck. "Come here, you little bastard."

Then Jonah appeared from out of nowhere, grabbed Big Man, shoved him against the railing, reached down, helped Joseph up, and pushed him behind himself to shield the boy from Big Man.

Having knocked out Mustache, Skinny, and Freckles stood next to Big Man, sizing up the big Negro. Freckles threw the first punch that Jonah blocked, and then Jonah hit Freckles in the nose, sending him back against the other two. Everything got so quiet that Joseph could hear the sounds of the big red paddlewheel churning through the water, and suddenly, he was very afraid for Jonah.

"You black bastard," said Freckles as he bent down and broke off a piece of wood from a nearby crate.

Skinny took a long, thin knife from his boot, grinned, and said, "We're gonna teach you a lesson about hitting a white man, you black son of a bitch."

"Like Hell you are," said Captain Goodman as he stepped out from the darkness with a pistol in his right hand. "Drop the knife."

Skinny stopped and looked at the man standing in the shadows but did not let go of the knife.

"I won't say it twice." The men were aware of Captain Goodman's reputation, and the sound of the hammer of the pistol cocking back seemed deafening in the stillness. Goodman smiled at the man holding the knife. "Your choice, Mister. Either you drop the knife, or I put a hole in that empty head of yours. But make it snappy, as I ain't got all day."

Looking defeated, Skinny dropped the knife, and then the captain looked at Freckles. "Toss that piece of wood overboard."

Freckles stared at Captain Goodman for a moment, considering his options, and then he tossed the wood overboard.

The captain gestured toward the railing with the gun. "Now stand over there, ya dang idiots." He shook his head in disgust. "Why do I always get the idiots on my boat?" Then he glanced at Jonah. "You alright?"

"Yes, suh, Cap'n."

Goodman glanced around. "Now, mind telling me what the hell's going on back here?"

Big Man pointed to Jonah. "That there black bastard hit a white man. That's what's going on!"

"That so?" asked the captain, considering the answer as he looked at Mustache lying on the deck a few feet away. "And what was it that fella did?"

The three looked back at Mustache, lying on the deck. "He cheated at cards," replied Skinny.

Joseph stepped out from behind Jonah. "No, he didn't. And Jonah hit one of `em 'cause they were gonna hit him."

Captain Goodman looked at the young boy. "And who the hell might you be, Laddie?"

"Name's not Laddie, it's Joseph Greene, and that man wasn't cheating."

Goodman looked at the boy, wondering what he was doing on his boat. "Is that a fact?"

Joseph nodded with a determined look. "Yes, sir."

"And I suppose you're some sort of authority on the matter of cards?" asked the captain.

Joseph looked humiliated. "Well, no..."

Amused at the boy, Goodman nodded. "Well then, Laddie, how in the hell would you know?"

Joseph stood a little taller. "I was watching them play, and these other three were just drunk and got mean cuz they's losing."

"I see," said the captain as he stared at the boy, thinking he had guts and admiring him for standing up against the others.

Freckles took a step closer. "You damn little liar." Then he looked at Goodman. "That man was cheat'n us, Captain, and we was about to handle the no-good when that there Black stepped in and hit me when I wasn't look'n." He paused and looked at Jonah. "We hang your kind for less than that where I come from."

Captain Goodman considered this with a nod. "I'm sure y'all do, ya damn dummy." His eyes narrowed as he pointed the pistol at Freckles. "But not on my boat and certainly not one of my men." He turned to Jonah. "Would you like to explain what the hell's going on back here and just who the hell this young boy is?"

Jonah told him he had heard the commotion and had come back to investigate. "Dat's when I seen one man lying on the deck, and it looked to me like the big man was gonna harm the young boy, so's I stopped him, Cap'n." Then he looked at Freckles. "And den dat one dun swung at me so's I hit him."

The captain considered this thoughtfully. "Would've done the same myself. Can't fault you for that." He looked at the three men for several moments. "The way I see things is, we can stop at the next town where I can send for the sheriff, who happens to be a personal friend of mine. Maybe this here boy and that man over yonder can file charges against the three of you for assault after I tell the sheriff you were drunk and disorderly on this here vessel." He grinned. "I'm certain he'd believe the three of you picked a fight with my man, who everyone up and down this here river knows is a gentle, good-natured fella."

Big Man frowned with a mean look. "You siding with a black man over three white men, Captain?"

"Yep." smiled the captain proudly. "I'd stake more claim of honesty in his word before the likes of y'all, ya dang idiots."

The three men looked at one another, considering their situation, and then Skinny asked, "We don't want to talk to no sheriff."

The other two nodded in agreement.

Big Man looked at the captain. "Is there another way to handle this?"

Captain Goodman grinned. "You can get off my boat right now."

The three looked around into the black night, and then Big Man looked at the captain. "Shit, we're in the middle of the river."

Goodman smiled again, looking please. "I gotta hand it to ya; you're a quick one."

Joseph looked at Jonah, unsure if he should laugh or keep quiet. A long minute passed in silence.

"Tell y'all what," said the captain as he gestured toward the shoreline with his gun. "There's a jetty up ahead, and just to show you three boys, I'm a kind and forgiving man, so I'll slow this old gal to a crawl while the three of you jump onto it."

Small sounds of dismay from the three filled the silence, thinking about the danger of such an undertaking. Just then, two other men stepped from the shadows. "Everything alright, Captain?" asked one, pointing a pistol at the three men.

Goodman chuckled. "I was just explaining to these three their options and how they might consider getting off my boat."

The two smiled, knowing exactly what their captain had in mind.

Captain Goodman told one of them to see what he could do for the man sitting up against the side of a crate and told the other to keep an eye on the three men. He turned and looked at the money lying on the crate. "The way I figure it, you three were losing, and that one there was winning, so just leave what's on the crate." Then he returned to the bridge, guiding the boat slowly toward the approaching jetty. When he had maneuvered close enough for them to jump to, he leaned out of the bridge window and yelled, "Jump for your lives, ya dumb bastards."

All three men jumped. Two made it, and one landed in the water.

Laughing, the captain looked down from the bridge at Jonah. "Jonah, bring the lad to my cabin."

Looking concerned, Joseph asked Jonah, "Are you in trouble?"

"I don'ts rightly knows. But dah cap'n, he a fair man an likes dah truth, so don't ya go lying none's to `em."

Joseph was a little apprehensive about seeing the captain as he followed Jonah through a doorway, down a dim passageway to a door where Jonah knocked and waited.

"Come in," came a voice from behind the door.

Jonah opened it, letting Joseph go in first, and then he followed, closing the door behind him. They stood in silence, staring at the captain sitting behind his desk, looking busy with some papers.

Captain Goodman sat back in his chair and looked at Joseph. "What's yer name, Laddie?"

Joseph disliked the term Laddie. "Same as I told you earlier, Joseph Greene."

The captain scowled at Joseph and then looked at Jonah. "It appears we have ourselves a smart ass." He looked at Joseph. "Tell me, Laddie, do you have passage on this boat?"

"No, sir," replied Joseph softly.

"Ha," said Goodman. "Didn't think so, Laddie. Yer not so smart now, is ya?"

Joseph glanced at Jonah and then shook his head. "No, sir."

"That's better," replied the captain, trying to decide what sort of lad this was and what he was going to do with him. "Now, sit down and tell me how the hell you got on my boat." Then he told Jonah to sit down as well.

Joseph sat down and quickly considered what to say when he remembered Jonah's warning about telling the truth, so he began to tell the captain about his father's farm in Tennessee and running away to Gasten. He told of hiding on the boat as she steamed out of Gasten, of Jonah finding and feeding him, and then about the men awakening him when they began playing cards.

Captain Goodman glanced at Jonah. "So, Jonah here fed ya, did he?"

Joseph suddenly became concerned over Jonah. "He ain't in any trouble, is he?"

The captain leaned forward, resting his elbows on his messy desk while looking affectionately at Jonah. "Ah, hell no." Then he sat back and grinned at Joseph. "Let me tell you something about Jonah, Laddie. I came by him seven years ago, and I trust him more'n I ever trusted anyone in this world. There's no place I'd go that I wouldn't take him with me. He's a fine Negro." He paused to look at Jonah. "Anything Jonah does on this boat is the same as me doing it." He glared at Joseph. "Understand?"

Joseph glanced from Jonah to the captain. "Yes, sir."

Captain Goodman opened the lower left-hand drawer of his desk, reached in, and pulled out a bottle of scotch and one glass. "You drink, boy?"

"Not really."

"Now, what the hell does 'Not really' mean?"

Joseph shrugged. "I used to sneak a drink out of a jug at my friend's house when his ma and pa weren't looking."

Filled with childhood memories, the captain smiled as he retrieved another glass from his desk drawer. After filling it about half full, he handed it to Joseph. "Here, try this."

Joseph took the glass, looked at the captain, then Jonah, and took a small sip. Feeling it burn as it went down, he coughed, bringing laughter from the two men.

"That's Scotch, Laddie," said the captain. "It'll put hair on that chest of yours."

Joseph wished again that the captain wouldn't call him Laddie, so deciding he wanted to show them he could handle the drink like a grown-up, he took a smaller sip, knowing now what to expect.

The captain sat back in his swivel chair, contemplating what to do with the boy. "So, you're running away from all that hard work back on the farm?"

Feeling the Scotch warm his stomach, Joseph nodded. "It ain't that I'm afraid of hard work. I just don't like farming."

Captain Goodman gulped his drink, set his glass down, and stared at the boy. "Would you like a job, Laddie?"

Joseph glanced at Jonah, who smiled and nodded yes. Joseph grinned with wide, innocent eyes as he looked back at the captain. "Sure. I mean, yes, sir."

"Alright," replied the captain. Then he looked at his Negro. "Jonah."

"Yes, suh?"

The captain smiled as he winked. "This here, young man, is about to join us. Seems the lad's in need of a job."

Jonah grinned broadly, showing his white teeth. "Yes, suh, Cap'n."

Goodman stood and walked from behind his desk.

Joseph stood, holding his half glass of Scotch with both hands.

The captain looked at him thoughtfully as he took the glass from the boy's hand. "You can't start at the top, boy," he warned. "The work will be hard, and the pay little. You may wish you were back on that farm by the time Jonah there gets done with you, but you'll learn a good trade." He grinned as he looked at Jonah. "Am I right, Jonah?"

Wearing a big, happy grin, Jonah nodded. "Yes, suh, Cap'n."

In the years that followed, Jonah and the captain not only taught Joseph about the river and how to navigate it, but Captain Goodman furthered the boy's education with books and an occasional tutor when time permitted. The two became very close, each earning the other's respect, and Joseph came to share the captain's love for the Southern Belle, but not the term Laddie.

The captain once confessed to Joseph that he treated the steamboat better than most men treated their wives. "There's no place for another female in my life," he once told Joseph. But then he quickly added, "Not that I don't like the company of an occasional lady, no sir. The truth is, I welcome it from time to time, but a wife waiting for me to come home, no, thank you. A thing like that robs a man of his freedom regardless of the niceties." Then he smiled. "The river's my home. This here boat's my wife, and she never turns away when I need comforting."

The whistle of a passing boat heading in the other direction interrupted Joseph's journey into memory just as one of the Negro cooks stepped onto the bridge with a big, dented gray coffee pot. Joseph slid out of the captain's chair, asking the helmsman if he would like a cup. The helmsman said he would, so Joseph poured him a cup, thinking it looked a little strong, and handed it to him. Then he poured another, and after taking a sip, he wasn't disappointed.

After dinner, Joseph silently walked the decks, stopping at a spot that overlooked the rear deck where he first met Jonah. He pulled a small tin from his pocket, took out one thin cigar, bit off the tip, spitting it over the railing into the night, and then lit the cigar. Blowing the match out, he looked back along the river at the big yellow harvest moon reflecting off the black water. The rhythmic sound of the Southern Belle's big red wheel churning through the water joined the soft music and laughter coming from the deck below. Imagining the players and their money exchanging hands at the tables, he rested his elbows on the railing and thought of Mary. Moments passed in silence, and then he considered a drink and maybe a card game before bed.

Two hours of cards passed with very little luck, so Joseph tossed in his hand, picked up his money, and made his way down the dim passageway to his cabin door. Stepping inside his cabin, Joseph found a lantern and put a match to the wick, filling the room with its soft yellow light. He sat on the edge of his bed, took off his shoes, turned the lamp off, and lay fully clothed on top of the covers. Listening to the river's sounds coming through the open portal above his bed mixed with the music and laughter from the casino above, he closed his eyes and thought again about Mary McAlexander.

Florence, Alabama

At that very moment, Mary was sitting on the window seat in her bedroom, hugging a large pillow while looking at the coble stone street beyond the iron gates of the driveway. The sound of a carriage on the street below brought to mind the image of it stopping and Joseph jumping out and running up the driveway. “A girl’s foolishness,” she thought as the sounds of the carriage faded into the distance. With her chin against the pillow she hugged, Mary looked out the window at the big yellow moon just as a star fell across the dark sky and wondered if Joseph had also seen it. Hoping he had, she made a wish, got up from the window seat, walked across the floor, dragging the pillow, and climbed into bed. As she closed her eyes, she hugged the pillow, wishing it was Joseph.

Three

August 1860-September 1860

The Tennessee River

The wake of another sternwheeler quietly making her way downstream nudged the Southern Belle ever so slightly against the wooden pylons of the piers of Decatur, Alabama. The slight motion was enough to cause Joseph to open his eyes in the darkness of his room, feeling tired. He lay still, listening to the sounds of the passing boat with its big paddlewheel thrashing in the water, growing ever fainter as it moved downstream. Sitting up, Joseph placed his feet over the edge of the bed and, in the dim room, reached for the dark image of the lantern sitting on the table next to his bed. Taking a match from the tin on the table, he lit the wick, filling the room with its soft light, and pulled his watch from his pocket, seeing it was 5 a.m.

A gentle knock came at the door, followed by Jonah's soft voice. "Mistah Joseph?"

"I'm awake, Jonah."

"Yes, suh, dah Cap'n sends me down ta git's ya, Mistah Joseph. Says he wants to see ya right away."

Still groggy from the drinks he had enjoyed while playing cards the night before, Joseph leaned forward, resting his elbows on his knees, his head in his hands, fighting the urge to go back to sleep.

"Yah's awake, Mistah Joseph?"

"Okay, okay, Jonah. I'm up. I'm up. Tell the Captain I'll be along shortly."

"Yes, suh Mistah Joseph."

Joseph looked at the door. "Jonah!"

"Yes, suh?"

"When did we dock?"

"I believes bout midnight Mistah Joseph."

"Thanks, Jonah. Tell the Captain I'll be along in a few minutes."

"Yes, suh."

Joseph cupped his face in his hands, listening to the big man's footsteps fade down the passageway. Standing, he stretched as he walked to the dresser and a pitcher of cold water. Pouring water into a small basin, Joseph splashed the cold water onto his face. As the water dripped back into the basin, he stared at his disfigured image in the broken mirror, thinking he could not feel any worse if he had been on a three-day bender. Then he picked up a cup with an old bar of soap inside and a small bristle shaving brush that he dipped into the water and started making a lather to shave.

Captain Goodman looked at Joseph as he stepped onto the bridge. "Thought maybe you died in your sleep." Then he pointed to a pot of hot coffee. "You look like you could use a cup."

Joseph picked up the pot and poured the coffee into a cup, wondering if it tasted as strong as it looked. Taking a drink, he burned his lip and tongue, cursing his own stupidity.

Goodman smiled. "A little hot, Laddie?"

Joseph was in a foul mood. "Don't miss much, do ya?"

Pleased with himself, the captain smiled proudly. "Not much, Laddie."

Joseph carefully took another sip, thinking of the way Jonah sounded when he was at his door. "What's so damn urgent?"

"Urgent?" asked the captain, looking curious.

Joseph nodded. "Jonah sounded as though something was urgent."

"Oh, Hell," chuckled the captain. "Jonah always sounds like everything's a damn emergency."

Joseph grinned, thinking that was true. "He said you wanted to see me."

"I thought you'd like to join me for coffee, is all." Goodman got up from his chair and slapped Joseph on the back, almost causing him to spill his coffee.

Irritated at the playfulness of the old man, he turned his attention to the window and the pier below as five men walked down the gangplank to a waiting buggy. "What's that?"

The captain turned from what he was doing and looked down at the men in disgust. "Oh, we had a bit of a problem last night while you slept." He paused, then added, "Damn, I wish we could have one trip without any trouble."

Joseph grinned. "It's the nature of the animal, Captain. What kind of trouble?"

Without looking up, the captain sighed. "The usual. Too much whiskey, I suppose. One fella got mad at the other and started a damn fight." He walked from the chart table to his chair, sat down, and scratched his beard with one hand. "You know, it's a mite peculiar, but we don't carry a whole hell of a lot of passengers on this here vessel." He paused. "Not like some of the other bigger boats, but it sure seems we catch the bad ones."

"It's like I said, Captain, it's the nature of the animal."

Goodman scratched his chin. "S'pose so."

Joseph turned from the scene on the pier. "Why didn't you send Jonah after me to help in the docking last night?"

"Think I need your help docking this old boat?" snapped the captain, looking irritated.

Joseph turned away, grinning at the old man's irritability. "No, but---"

"Good!" interrupted the captain.

Joseph knew the captain's moods all too well, so he wisely decided to let it go and turned his attention to the men working on the dock.

Moments of silence passed, and the captain shrugged his shoulders, his voice apologetic. "I didn't see any need in both of us being up here. I saw you were in the casino last night, and I figured you could use a good night's sleep."

Joseph knew this was as close to an apology as he would ever get. "I guess I did. I slept through the whole damn thing." Then, he noticed a well-dressed man walking across the boat's deck toward the gangplank. "Who's that?"

Goodman looked down at the figure and frowned. "According to the passenger manifest, the name's Charles Whittaker."

"Name sounds familiar."

"He's a gambler," replied the captain, looking annoyed. "Mr. Whittaker is not one to trifle with, Laddie. He's quick with a knife and just as deadly with a pistol."

"I'll remember that."

Goodman stared at the figure, walking down the gangplank to the pier. "Good thing to remember. A few years back, he killed a man in a duel in New Orleans."

"Maybe that's where I've heard the name."

"He's polite," said the captain. "And soft-spoken, but don't let that fool you. He's a dangerous man."

Joseph watched Whittaker climb into a carriage. "Where'd he board?"

"Florence," said the captain with a grin. "Something you'd have noticed had you been on time."

Joseph chose to ignore the remark. "Where was he during the trip?"

"In his room, I reckon. Stayed pretty much to himself the entire trip."

"Maybe he's hiding out," Joseph offered with humor.

"Possible," grinned Goodman. "Wouldn't be the first to do so."

Joseph nodded. "From the looks of his clothes, he looks like he belongs on the Memphis or New Orleans, where there's real money."

The captain shrugged with indifference. "Well, t'aint none of my business." He paused. "Maybe he's just looking for some peace and quiet."

After the buggy disappeared around the corner, Joseph turned his attention to the pier and the Negro men working. As he sipped his coffee, his thoughts went to the conversation with Edward and Alex on slavery. Jonah was working at some task, and as Joseph watched the big Negro, he wondered what Jonah or any of these other slaves would do if they were suddenly free men. Turning from the window, he placed his empty cup next to the gray coffee pot. "I better check on a few things below."

The glow of the dark red-orange sun hung low in the sky as Joseph walked down the gangplank to the pier. Stepping onto the crowded dock of crates, barrels, bales of cotton, and Negro slaves, he walked through the canyons of shadows cast across the docks by the late evening sun. He was thinking of Mary, smelling her perfume from memory, when a subtle movement next to some crates startled him.

"Didn't mean to startle ya, Laddie," said Captain Goodman.

Joseph paused and smiled. "Didn't expect to see you down here, Captain."

Goodman puffed his pipe, saying he was stretching his legs. Thinking Joseph looked tired, he asked, "Heading into town?"

Joseph looked along the dock toward town. "It's been a long day, and I need to stretch my legs as well, get a drink, and play a little poker."

The captain puffed his pipe, remembering the gaming tables when he was a younger man. "Change of scenery sounds good."

"Come along. I'll buy you a drink."

Goodman quickly considered. "Thanks, but I'll stick close to what I know. Good luck to ya, Laddie."

"Thanks, Captain. I can always use a little more luck." He paused to light a cigar, blew out the match with a puff of smoke, and tossed the match aside. "See ya in the morning."

Captain Goodman puffed his pipe as he watched the man he treated like a son disappear around the corner in the direction of gambling halls, saloons, and whore houses.

Away from the rough and noisy waterfront, Decatur was a pretty little town but one that Joseph seldom visited. He preferred the excitement of the waterfront bars with their gambling halls. It was there that Joseph felt at ease with life, feeding on the excitement and danger that the upper classes of towns could not offer. The bar he chose was not unlike the others he had been in over the years, and there was no particular reason he chose this one. Walking through the swinging doors into the noisy, smoke-filled room, Joseph made his way across the crowded room of tables and chairs where men played cards or eagerly sought a moment's pleasure with the whore they were drinking with. A woman screamed as she fell from the lap of a drunk, and as he helped her up and onto his lap, he said something to the others at the table, bringing laughter that Joseph couldn't hear. Reaching the bar, Joseph ordered a glass of brandy that he sipped while surveying the crowd, especially the gaming tables. A man with a cigar hanging from his mouth sat at a piano across the room, hunched over the keys and pounding on them as if trying to drown out the laughter and loud talking.

Another woman screamed, followed by a roar of loud laughter as she ran up the stairs with two men in hot pursuit. After all, three disappeared through a door on the second floor, he imagined the scene unfolding inside. He picked up his drink, took a small sip, and turned to glance over the crowded gaming tables. His eyes wandered the room before settling on a young, pretty girl talking to the man beside him at the bar. She had far too much makeup on in an attempt to look older, and he thought it ironic that young women want to look older, and older women want to look young. She smiled, which did not go unnoticed by the man next to her, as he turned and gave Joseph a dirty look. Deciding it was best to move away from the two, he picked up his glass and walked toward the gaming tables, looking for an empty chair. Making his way around the edge of the room, he stopped by a post supporting the balcony. Taking another sip of brandy, he noticed Charles Whittaker, the man he had seen leave the Southern Belle earlier that evening, playing cards at a table just a few feet away. He watched the other men at the table, trying to get a read from their mannerisms for a possible tell. Gamblers sometimes have an expression or other clue when holding a good or bad hand. From the size of the pile of money in front of Charles Whittaker, it was apparent he was winning. That came as no surprise to Joseph. After all, the man was a professional working his way along the Tennessee River.

Just then, one of the men stood, pushing his chair back, and said something to the others, gathered what little money he had left, and walked toward the bar needing a drink. Seizing the opportunity, Joseph quickly made his way through the maze of tables and chairs to the empty chair. "Mind if I sit in?"

"Okay with me, as long as you have money," one of the men said without looking up.

"Hope your luck is better than mine," said another half in humor.

Charles Whittaker nodded his approval as he gathered the deck of cards from the table.

Joseph pulled the chair away from the table and sat down. Taking some money from the inside pocket of his coat, he set it on the table in front of him in a neat pile. Waiting for the next hand to be dealt, he glanced at the men sitting around the table, letting his eyes pause momentarily on Charles Whittaker as he shuffled the deck.

The man on Joseph's left looked at him and asked, "You in?"

Joseph apologized, tossed the ante onto the table, and watched as Charles dealt the other players their cards.

The clock on the wall behind Whittaker told Joseph it was almost midnight. Several players had come and gone, and he was getting tired and sleepy. Knowing that was when men made their mistakes, he glanced at the others at the table and then at the money in front of him, thinking he had only lost a little of his money and that maybe it was a good time to call it quits. "Gentleman," he said while gathering his money and passing the deal to the man next to him, "I'm calling it a night."

"Yes, it is quite late," agreed Whittaker. "I'm afraid I will have to leave your fine and illustrious company as well, gentlemen." Whittaker picked up his money and followed Joseph across the room through the swinging doors and into the cool night air. Then he stopped and took a sniff of the night air. "Reminds me of New Orleans."

"What does?" asked Joseph, thinking of the story Goodman had told him about the duel.

"Why, that dreadful smell, of course." Whittaker gestured in the direction of the river. "That terrible river smell that reminds one of rotting fish. The same muddy smell of the Mississippi River that one just nevah forgets."

"Is New Orleans your home?"

"Lord no," said Whittaker with a disapproving expression. "Please, Suh, do not insult me." He stopped in front of a lighted window, offering an outstretched hand, "Sorry, Suh, we never formally introduced ourselves. Name's Whittaker, Charles Whittaker."

Joseph shook his hand and introduced himself. They continued along the boardwalk, passing through the dark shadows between lighted windows and doorways.

"To answer your question," Whittaker said, looking sad, "I hail from Arkansas, having the misfortune of being born to a poor family of sharecroppers with no land of our own." He paused in thought. "I don't think my poor father was ever smart enough to do anything but work hard for others."

Joseph thought of his father, remembering how hard he worked the land, although he had the satisfaction that it was his land.

Charles Whittaker was thirty years old, slender, and taller than Joseph by about an inch. A neatly trimmed reddish-brown beard and mustache partially hid his acne-scared face. He was smartly groomed and handsome in a rugged way. "And what about you, Joseph? Where are your roots?"

"A dirt farm up in Tennessee."

"I thought as much," grinned Whittaker, looking pleased with himself. "No offense, Joseph, but you still have the look of a farmer."

Joseph smiled. "No offense taken." Then he shrugged. "The truth's the truth."

"Never be ashamed of who you are," Charles said with a stern and tense face as he held one hand over his heart as if on stage, the other gesturing into the black night. "That's what my dear daddy said as I walked away from that muddy farm so many years ago." His expression suddenly changed to one of sadness. "Sometimes, I miss the old boy."

Joseph thought of his father once again. "Ever go back?"

He looked down at the boardwalk as if in shame. "No," he said softly. "I never returned." Then, a wry smile appeared on his face. "I don't think my daddy would approve of my profession. Don't get me wrong, he was a good man and a hard worker, but he would never have understood the life his son had chosen." After a moment of silence, he softly said, "Neither would my dear, dear mother, I'm afraid."

Joseph thought of his mother, dead these many years, and wondered what she would have to say about his life but decided it didn't matter. Not now, anyway.

Suddenly, Whittaker chuckled. "Strange thing is, I do miss them at times, and I have thought about going back for a visit, but hell, I'm not sure they're still alive after all these years."

"How long has it been?"

Charles considered the question. "Too many, I'm afraid, far too many." Then he looked at Joseph. "Tell me, Joseph, how long have you been working on the river?"

That surprised Joseph.

Seeing the look on his face, Charles smiled. "Saw you on the Southern Belle. I never forget a face." He stopped and pointed to the door of a boarding house. "This is my home for tonight, and I thank you for seeing me to my door." He grinned, tipping the brim of his hat. "Goodnight, Joseph Greene."

"Goodnight, Charles," said Joseph.

Whittaker stopped in the open doorway and turned, "Are you staying long in Decatur?"

"We leave in the morning."

Charles nodded thoughtfully. "Pity, but perhaps you and I will have another friendly game one day."

"Perhaps we will," smiled Joseph. "Goodnight." He watched Whittaker turn, walk across the empty lobby, and disappear up the stairs before he also turned and walked down the steps to the dirt street and his journey back to the Southern Belle. The warm night air filled his lungs with a mixture of sweet blossoms and the smell of the river. Thinking of his soft bed and sleep, he walked a little faster.

Joseph was dressed and shaven when Jonah called out. "Dah Cap'n wants ya on dah bridge Mistah Joseph."

Joseph opened the door. "Good morning, Jonah."

Looking surprised, Jonah smiled. "Why goods morn'n ta ya, Mistah Joseph."

Closing the door after he stepped into the narrow hall, Joseph gestured toward the door leading to the outer deck. "After you, Jonah."

Jonah grinned, thinking Joseph appeared in an extremely good mood. "Yes, suh."

Stepping into the morning sunshine, Joseph climbed the stairs to the bridge, where the helmsman and Captain Goodman greeted him. Pouting a cup of strong, hot, black coffee, he listened as the captain gave orders for getting underway. After the ropes holding the boat to the pier were untied and pulled back aboard, the Southern Belle slowly drifted away from the pier, the current pulling her into the river.

In deeper water, the big red paddlewheel slowly turned, pushing the boat toward Guntersville. Joseph drank his coffee, staring past the paddlewheel churning through the murky water at the town of Decatur considering Charles Whittaker. Although a little intrigued, he felt uneasy about the man. After a few minutes, however, his concerns over Charles Whittaker were left behind as Joseph turned and looked west along the river, thinking of Mary McAlexander.

The evening shadows were long when the Southern Belle slowly approached the piers of Guntersville. As the big sternwheeler settled softly against the big wood pilings of the pier, Captain Goodman stuck his head out of the open window of the bridge. "Jonah."

The big Negro turned, putting one hand next to his ear, and looked up. "Yes, suh?"

"Make sure we're secured good and tight."

"Yes, suh Cap'n."

While Goodman took care of the docking, Joseph left the bridge to mingle with the passengers, where he played the good steward by trying to look interested in their problems. After a while, he tired of the charade and sat on a small crate, lit a thin cigar, and watched Jonah go about his duties. The Negro's big arms poked through the sleeveless gray shirt unbuttoned to the waist and tucked into gray pants held up by an old, wide, black leather belt.

Joseph watched the big man, wondering how old he was, guessing he might be forty, give or take. He knew the captain had come by Jonah several years ago, and according to the captain, Jonah was the only slave he had ever owned. The other Negroes on board belonged to the owners of the Southern Belle. Joseph was and always had been intrigued by their relationship. There were times the captain became a little short with Jonah, but he never mistreated him, and Lord have mercy on the man who did.

He smiled, recalling the night Jonah accidentally bumped into a drunken man who had just boarded the boat. The man dropped his bag and slapped Jonah across the face calling him a dumb nigger. To the fool's surprise, the captain grabbed him by the seat of his pants and guided him down the gangplank to the pier, suggesting he take another boat. Yes, there was something special between Captain Benjamin Goodman and Jonah, the slave. Something that Joseph admired.

The night was slowly winning its battle against the daylight, and Joseph again felt the urge to visit the town and the gaming tables. After Jonah disappeared through a doorway almost too small for the big man, Joseph stood and walked toward the gangplank, pier, and town.

Lady Luck was a tease, letting him win the small pots while keeping the larger ones out of reach. Frustrated, he imagined her sitting on the lap of the man next to him whose pile of money grew, whispering into the man's ear as she laughed at Joseph. He had been drinking steadily through the night, and while he was not yet drunk, he was tired. As the next hand was dealt, he glanced around the table at the other four men. The man on his left was close to sixty, balding, gray-haired, clean-shaven, and wearing clothes old and worn. Joseph believed his profession was perhaps a laborer of some kind. Next to him sat a man who looked like a farmer, still dirty from the day's work, undoubtedly having little or no business gambling. Across the table sat a young man he guessed to be barely twenty, nervous and fidgety, irritating the man next to him dressed in a tailored suit. Joseph figured the man in the suit was a professional like Charles Whittaker.

However, unlike Whittaker, this man's mannerisms showed education and a privileged life with good breeding. He had broad shoulders, and while sitting down, Joseph guessed him to be about six feet and in his late twenties. He had light brown hair, brown eyes, and a square, clean-shaven jaw and appeared serious about his cards. During the evening, he often became irritated with the young man sitting next to him, and on several occasions, he told the young man to sit still, even accusing him of being a fool and looking into his hand.

Joseph glanced at the young, foolish boy, thinking he might not live to be much older. Picking up his cards, Joseph quickly decided to keep a pair of sixes and discard the others. He sipped his drink, waiting for three new cards that soon turned out to be the seven of spades, nine of clubs, and a jack of diamonds. Frowning, he threw them onto the table, pushed his chair away, and stood while picking up his money. "Gentleman, I have had enough for one night."

Getting no response from the others, he turned and walked to the bar, ordered a brandy, and watched as the bartender filled the empty glass. With his glass full, he tossed some money on the bar while considering his bad luck, unaware of the man beside him.

"Lady Luck has a way of going from one man to another," the voice said. "I'm afraid, much the same as a whore."

Turning, Joseph saw it was the man in the suit from the table. "Did that foolish young man drive you away from the table?"

The man ordered a drink and turned to look over his shoulder at their table. "You could say that, I suppose." Then he turned and looked at Joseph's reflection in the big mirror behind the bar. "I'm sure that one day someone will put a bullet through his head."

Joseph smiled, turned, and rested his elbows on the bar, looking across the smoke-filled room. "Best be careful what you say about Lady Luck. She could turn on you."

The man looked into his glass, considering the comment. "Lady Luck doesn't worry me." He smiled. "You see, sir, we know each other far too well, Lady Luck and I." He shrugged, wrinkling his brow. "All I have to lose is money."

Joseph found humor in the man's philosophy, already knowing the answer to his next question. "You from Guntersville?"

"Ah, hell no," the man replied with a frown. He turned, leaning against the bar on one elbow, motioning to the bartender to fill his empty glass. "Guess you might say the river's my home."

"A professional gambler?"

"Oooh," he said with a wrinkled brow. "That sounds terrible, but gambling provides a very good living. Or a hobby." He chuckled at what he had just said. "Not quite sure which one, though." He smiled and offered his hand. "Name's Colbert, Bob Colbert from Atlanta."

Joseph introduced himself as they shook hands.

Colbert pointed to an empty table a few feet away. "Shall we? Most everyone on this river is from someplace else."

Thinking that was probably true, Joseph followed him to the table.

Colbert pulled one chair from under the table, another for his hat and gloves, and then sat down. "And what about you, Joseph? What brings a man such as you to the river?" Then he smiled broadly. "The way you played cards tonight, I'm sure it isn't good luck."

Joseph grinned. "No, it wasn't luck. It was something else."

Colbert took a drink as he studied the man sitting across from him. "Let me guess. I'd say a muddy farm."

Joseph smiled, wryly remembering what Charles Whittaker had said. "Good guess. I've been told before that it still shows." He sipped his drink. "It was a poor mud farm in Tennessee and a Bible-thumping father."

"Ahhhh," nodded Colbert as he leaned forward, resting on his elbows. "I understand, my good Joseph, for I, too, am running away from my roots." Colbert sat back with a sad look. "However, it was not a poor mud farm but a valley of lush cotton, slaves, and a group of sniveling women. And one big bastard."

Joseph leaned back in his chair, his right elbow resting on the arm of his chair, his chin on his fist. "Your father?"

Colbert stared into his glass, pondering the question. "Afraid not. Like yours, my father was a Bible thumper, but it did him little good. His heart gave out one night while screwing one of the young Negro girls." He smiled into his glass of brandy. "I was only twelve at the time." He paused to take a drink. "My good mother, bless her poor dumb soul, married again a few months later." His face held a loathing look. "Of all the men in the valley, she chose the man who owned the plantation next to ours." He paused to take a sip of brandy. "A few years passed, and everything seemed to be going fine, but to make a long story short, my stepfather got a little too familiar with one of my older sisters."

Joseph sat forward in disbelief. "You're not serious?"

Colbert chuckled. "Oh yes, my good man, I'm dead serious."

"Didn't your mother suspect anything?"

"Ah, hell no," Colbert replied with a chuckle but looking irritated at the same time. "My poor mother was in heaven. The man was ten years her junior, and probably for the first time in years, she was getting more attention than the female slaves."

Joseph chuckled.

Looking somewhat embarrassed, Colbert quickly apologized. "Sorry, Joseph! I never really said that aloud before. Sounded a little crass, I suppose." He looked at his glass thoughtfully. "Must be the brandy."

Curious, Joseph asked, "So you just up and left?"

"Not right away." He shifted his weight in the chair and leaned toward Joseph, lowering his voice. "One night, I awoke to something outside, some sort of noise, I guess." He gestured with one hand. "I'm not sure what it was, but I got out of bed and looked out the window into the moonlit yard below. To my surprise, there was my sister in her nightgown running across the lawn, disappearing behind some bushes." He shrugged. "Well, I thought she must be walking in her sleep."

"Was she?"

"Not exactly. But like any concerned brother, I put on my shoes, hurried down the stairs in my nightshirt, and ran across the backyard looking for her. Being afraid that I would awaken and startle her, I quietly followed." Pausing for a moment, he took a sip of brandy. "As I made my way in the darkness through the bushes, I heard this strange noise and a man's voice. The words were unclear to me, so I stopped for a moment, and then I cautiously walked toward the sound, hearing someone moaning. Fearing my poor sister was injured, I ran toward the gazebo, and to my surprise, there was my sister on her hands and knees and my stepfather screwing the hell out of her from behind!"

Joseph put his head back and laughed.

Seeing the humor in his story, Colbert grinned and then laughed as he continued. "Well, I must have made a noise or uttered something, I'm not sure, but when my sister saw me, she got up, pulled her nightgown down over her privates, and ran toward the house."

Joseph wiped tears of laughter from his eyes as he let out a soft sigh of humor.

Colbert continued. "I was too afraid or shocked to move. The next thing I knew, he had me by the throat." Colbert's eyes were wide, demonstrating his fear. "All I could do was look past him at my sister pulling at her nightgown as she ran toward the house."

"What happened next?"

"Why, I was scared and almost pissed myself while my stepdaddy held onto my throat, telling me that if I ever told anyone, he would slit my throat and bury me where no one would ever find me."

Joseph sighed with humor. "So, what happened?

Bob Colbert sat back in his chair, touching his throat in memory. "He turned and walked away, leaving me with a bruised neck."

Joseph sipped his drink and waited for Bob to finish his story.

Colbert's face filled with hate, fear, and anger. "One night, several months later, I was reading a book in my room when the door opened and in he walked. He stared daggers at me as he slowly closed the door behind him. I was deathly afraid of this man. After all, he was much bigger. He crossed the room, picked up a chair, moved it close to mine, sat down, and looked me right in the eye, saying that he thought it was time for me to leave and make a life for myself elsewhere."

Feeling bad for Colbert, Joseph considered that for a moment. "Why didn't you tell your mother?"

His eyes grew wide. "Oh, dear boy, she would never have believed me." Then he took a drink and looked slightly wistful. "While my father was an educated man and somewhat intelligent, the son-of-a-bitch failed to leave a will, so everything went to my mother. Of course, when she married, both plantations became one: her husband's. That left my sisters and me out in the cold."

Joseph sipped his drink, feeling a little sorry for him.

"So," continued Colbert, "instead of 650 acres, the man now owned over 1,200 and a few more slaves to screw, not to mention the women in my immediate family."

"So, you just left?"

Colbert shot him a cheerful, sneaky look. "But not empty-handed," he said proudly. "You see, I was not as naive as my stepfather thought. After all, I was sixteen years of age, educated, and knew a little about life and such things, so I talked him out of a small fortune, packed my one bag, kissed my mother and sisters on the cheek, walked away, and never looked back." Gulping his drink, he slammed the glass on the table. "It's late. I'm getting drunk and starting to feel sorry for myself, so I'm walking across the street and up those winding stairs to my inexpensive room. There, I will lie down on my lumpy, spinning bed and probably throw up all over those nice clean sheets." He grinned as they stood. "With any luck, I will pass out and dream of some pretty, young thing who is hopelessly in love with me."

They walked out of the saloon into the night, saying their goodbyes on the wooden sidewalk. Joseph stood in the light of the saloon window, considering the story and the man named Colbert as he disappeared into the hotel across the street. Then he stepped off the boardwalk into the dark street and walked toward the docks and the Southern Belle. The sound of music from the bars faded, replaced by two cats fighting somewhere up a dark alley while a jealous dog barked, wishing he could join the fight. Soon, the only sounds in the darkness were his footsteps on the hard, rutted dirt streets of Guntersville, Alabama.

Climbing the boat's gangplank, he made his way through the dimly lit passageway to his cabin and undressed. His clothes strewn on the floor, he crawled between the cool sheets and lay his head on the cool, soft pillow. A bell on a nearby river buoy softly clanged in the stillness as a sternwheeler churned her way past the Southern Belle, making her way downriver. As the soft clanging of the buoy filled his cabin, his thoughts turned to Mary McAlexander and his hopes that he would be home by the end of September.

Florence, Alabama

Mary touched the library door with a nervous hand, hesitated, and then gently knocked on the door.

"Come in," said a voice from within.

Mary opened the door, stepped in, closed it, and walked toward her brother Edward, sitting behind his big mahogany desk, busy with his accounts.

He looked up and smiled as he stood to greet her. "Good morning, Mary." He walked around the desk, put his hands gently on her shoulder, and kissed her cheek. "And to what do I owe this morning's visit?"

Mary wore a troubled smile. "Edward, may we talk?"

Seeing her troubled look, he gestured to a small sofa. "But of course." He waited for her to sit down, then sat next to her, sensing that something of great importance was troubling his sister. While she fussed with her hands in her lap, as women do when nervous or afraid, he watched and waited for her to speak.

She looked at him, searching his eyes, hoping to find the understanding and gentleness she had come to know.

"What is it, Mary? What burdens my little sister so much that she fears speaking to her brother?" He placed his hand under her chin with a gentle touch as he looked into her eyes. "Tell me what troubles you."

Gathering her courage, she looked at him, "Why do you dislike Joseph?"

Silence descended on the library as a surprised Edward sat back on the sofa, wondering where she had picked up that idea. "I don't dislike him, Mary."

Looking regretful, she sighed. "Perhaps that was too strong."

"Indeed," he said with a stern look. "Quite the opposite. I think he's a fine young man. Whatever gave you the idea I disliked him?"

She looked down at her hands as they twisted a white handkerchief. "Fear, I suppose."

Understanding what she was trying to accomplish, Edward gently raised her head with his hand and smiled, trying to comfort her. "He's a fine man, Mary, but I'm not sure he's the man for you." He paused to smile at her. "Is that so bad of me?"

She smiled softly. "No, I guess not." She paused, staring at her hands and the handkerchief they held. "But I think he is the one for me." She looked up with a trembling voice. "Is that so bad of me?"

"Of course, it isn't!"

Mary placed one hand on Edward's knee and looked into his soft brown eyes. "If this is the man I choose, why can't you and Alex accept that?"

Edward had known that this day would come, but he had hoped it would have waited until after the war, which he feared would be coming to the South very soon. And on a day when she would have had more time to appreciate their wealth and realize what Joseph could offer. Feeling awkward at having to be a father instead of a brother, he smiled at her while wondering how he would handle things if this were his daughter. Edward stood and walked the few steps to the empty fireplace, thinking how to answer. Their world had changed so much over the past few months, and with the war looming, he was certain it was about to change even further.

Edward walked to the edge of his desk, where he paused to look down at some papers, and when he looked back at her, he saw something different in her face. Desperation, or perhaps it was love; he wasn't sure, but he remembered his desperation and emptiness when his wife had died. He gathered all the softness and gentleness he could into his voice. "You're no longer a child, Mary." He smiled gently. "You are a lovely young woman now." The smile left his face, replaced by sadness. "Neither Alex nor I can tell you whom to love or marry. Those days are long gone." He sat on the edge of the desk, picked up a metal object, examined it for a moment, and then looked at Henrietta's photo on a nearby table. Looking at his sister, he said, "Mary, who you chose to love, is your concern. But it is my duty as the head of this family to help you enter into a union that will not destroy you."

She started to protest, but he raised his hand to silence her.

"I can only advise you in such matters, and I'm certainly not blind." He smiled affectionately. "I've seen the two of you together, and what is in both your eyes as you look at one another." He glanced at the painting of his dead wife above the fireplace. "Not so different from mine and Henrietta's."

Mary looked at Henrietta's picture, remembering how happy they had been, especially during her pregnancy with little Mary, only to have it all end in tragedy. Edward put down the object he held, walked to the sofa, took her hand, and smiled. "Mary, if Joseph is the man you want, I will not stand in your way of happiness. I will support you in whatever you decide, and when the time comes that he asks me for your hand, I promise that I'll not turn him away."

Tears of joy filled her eyes as she stood and put her arms around his neck, kissed his cheek, and whispered, "Thank you, Edward."

He gently pushed her to arm's length, smiled, and then teased, "How do you know Joseph wants to marry you anyway?"

She laughed softly. "Oh, I know." Wiping the tears from her eyes, she stopped smiling, "But what of Alex?"

"Alex?" He put his arm around his sister, giving her a quick hug. "You let me handle Alex. Don't forget, I'm Alex's big brother also."

She rose on her toes and kissed his cheek. "Thank you, Edward; I shall never forget this."

He watched as she hurried across the room and out the library door. Hoping she wasn't making a mistake, he turned toward the liquor cabinet, thinking he needed a drink.

Her heart pounded with excitement and happiness as she hurried up the stairs to her room. Once inside, she rushed to the window seat, sat down, and stared past the trees to the green grass and flowers along the cobblestone street. Birds seemed happy in a nearby tree as they jumped from limb to limb, chattering. Beyond the iron fence, she saw a passing carriage with a man and woman talking and laughing, and she imagined she and Joseph in the carriage.

Four

August 1860 – December 1860

James Riley Chrisman

Tallapoosa County, Alabama

A rider and his big black mare stopped at the crest of a hill overlooking an ocean of cotton fields. The rider climbed down, letting the reins fall to the ground as he removed his hat, pulled a handkerchief from his back pocket, and wiped the afternoon sweat first from his neck, then his clean-shaven face, and finally, the inside of his white straw hat. Below the hill, men rode their horses at a leisurely walk between the rows of white cotton while Negro slaves picked the white, soft cotton bulbs, placing them in the long gray, dirty sacks they dragged behind them. Dirt roads separated the fields at determined intervals, filled with an endless procession of wagons kicking up small dust clouds on their way to and from the cotton barns. The slaves methodically picked the cotton, filled the long gray bags until they were full, and then lifted them onto the waiting wagons. After receiving fresh, empty bags, they continued their arduous, monotonous journey that proceeded slowly until the end of the day.

The rider stuffed his handkerchief into his back pocket, put on his white straw hat, and climbed back into the saddle of the anxious black mare. He gently rubbed her neck to calm her while calculating the potential days of harvest in his head, contemplating the need for more slaves. Owning but a few themselves, the family rented what they needed from Harper's Slave Trade in New Site, Alabama.

The rider was James Riley Chrisman. At sixteen, he found himself in his father's role of overseeing the fields instead of working in the barn with his younger brother, Davy. James, at five feet seven inches, was a handsome, dark-complexioned, half-breed. Coal-black collar-length hair framed his tanned face of brown eyes, thin lips, high cheekbones, and strong jaw. Young, powerful arms guided the big mare he affectionately called "the big black" down the hill.

An hour passed before James halted the mare again to wipe the sweat from his forehead and neck. As he wiped the inside of his hat, he glanced across the busy fields at a white two-story structure nestled among large trees full of hanging, green moss that offered shade from the late afternoon sun. White columns along the front porch supported a second-story balcony where the bedrooms were. Plants, shrubs, and flowers, the pride of his mother's labor, decorated the outside of the house, porch, and walkway leading to the driveway.

A figure stepped out of the front door, limped across the porch, and sat in an old wooden rocking chair. The figure was James's father, William Riley Chrisman. The rocking chair had replaced his horse last year after it stepped into a gopher hole, breaking a front leg while they were chasing a coyote. The horse had ended up on top of William, breaking his right hip. At forty-three, the hip was slow to mend, becoming arthritic and leaving him in constant pain, making it difficult to sit on a horse or wagon for long periods. These days, he spent most of his time in the rocking chair on the porch cursing the coyote and gopher hole that had claimed not only his favorite horse but also his right hip.

William Chrisman stood five feet eight inches, and his once dark brown hair was mostly gray. His brown eyes were not as keen as they were when, as a young man and a militia volunteer, he fought the Indians in Kentucky. A neatly trimmed brown and gray mustache occupied the upper lip of a weathered face whose deep age lines boasted of years in the wind and sun. Sitting back in his rocking chair, he looked out across the fields at the rider with pride.

As if the arthritic hip wasn't enough to endure, William rubbed his arthritic hands to ease their pain, contemplating the November elections while enviously watching his son ride up and down the rows of cotton. There were secession threats by Alabama and other southern states if John Breckenridge was not elected, and William knew that such a move would split the country and bring war.

William Riley Chrisman

William Riley Chrisman was born in 1817 on the frontiers of Kentucky. As a young man, he and his brothers worked hard on their father's farm when they were not volunteering in the militia during the Creek and Cherokee Indian uprisings. On one such occasion, the militia chased the Cherokee for several weeks until, tired and hungry, they finally surrendered. The militia was escorting them to a reservation, and it was then that William noticed a young, slender Cherokee maiden dressed in brown deerskin with dark skin and raven black hair hanging to her knees.

He soon discovered that she was the daughter of the tribe's medicine woman and was learning he mother's ancient ways. She quickly stole William's heart as he silently rode behind her and her mother, watching the young maiden's long black hair sway from side to side as she walked. He tried on several occasions during the trip to talk to this beautiful, dark-skinned girl, but she only showed her contempt toward the young man. But soon, she secretly smiled at his foolishness and giggled each time her mother, armed with a stick, chased him away or threw rocks, narrowly missing him, which brought laughter from his brothers and the other militiamen.

For the next several months after the Indians returned to the reservation, William would find excuse after excuse to visit the mission, hoping to talk to this young girl. His efforts were always in vain as she continued to ignore him, even refusing to make eye contact and letting him know that he was a man not worthy of her. On the other hand, the mother would always make eye contact, showing her contempt and hatred. The whole process was driving William insane. It didn't matter what he tried. She wouldn't look at him. Standing right in front of her didn't work because she merely looked at the ground, stepped around him, and kept walking. Hiding from her and jumping out at the right moment to startle her into looking at him didn't work either. After a certain period of frustration, he gave up and stopped visiting the mission. One afternoon, William's father told him to fill four crates with vegetables from their garden and kill four chickens to take to the Gorman family, the Christian missionaries working at the reservation's mission. William eagerly did everything his father told him to do, hoping for a chance meeting with the young girl before winter set in. Filled with hope and enthusiasm, he loaded everything into the buckboard and headed for the mission, arriving there late in the afternoon.

He searched for the young girl while he unloaded the wagon, and afterward, Mrs. Gorman invited him to stay for dinner. Happily accepting, he followed her to the back porch and a basin of water, where he washed his hands while several young Indian maidens walked by giggling at him, but not the one he wanted to see. He visited that wash basin three times before dinner, each visit a failure.

Wiping his hands for the last time, he walked into the house, finding Mr. Gorman sitting at the head of the table, the Gorman teenage boys on one side and their ten-year-old daughter across from them. Mrs. Gorman told William to sit next to the boys, and as he sat down, he noticed two extra places set at the table. Knowing one was for Mrs. Gorman, he wondered about the other.

Mrs. Gorman called out, "Lizbeth, time for dinner, dear."

William could have swallowed his tongue, but his heart got in the way as the girl he had tried so hard to talk with stepped into the room dressed in a light tan flowered cotton dress. Her long black hair was over the right shoulder, covering one small breast. Her face was long with high cheekbones, a straight nose, full lips, and large dark eyes. A glance from her made his heart jump.

She asked if Mrs. Gorman needed any help.

"No, thank you, dear. Go on ahead and have a seat across from young William there."

William could not take his eyes off the Indian girl. Then, as if coming out of a coma, he abruptly stood, knocking over his chair that crashed to the wooden floor in a terrible commotion, causing the three children to laugh. Embarrassed and feeling his face flush, William looked at the children, wishing they'd stop laughing, then at Mr. Gorman, who was scowling and apologized. Afraid to look at Lizabeth, he glanced at Mrs. Gorman. Fighting his urge to rush out of the house, he bent down, picked up the chair, and set it up right next to the table.

Elizabeth smiled. "Are you alright?"

William's face flushed again, but he managed a small smile and a quick nod as he sat down, making sure he did not look at the young girl.

Mrs. Gorman quickly scolded her giggling children. "Hush now, children. Y'all should take some notice from young William Chrisman on being a gentleman." Then she laughed, "Only do try not to break the furniture."

His face flushed again, but seeing the humor, he joined the laughter.

Mrs. Gorman placed a food dish on the table and then introduced their guests to one another. "William, this here's Elizabeth. She's been with us for several months now."

After all that time spent trying to speak to her, he fought to say the words that filled his mind but managed only a faint "Hello."

"This here's William Chrisman," said Mrs. Gorman to Elizabeth.

"I know his name. He was with the men that brought us to the mission."

William was glad that she remembered. "Do you live here?" Immediately, he thought that was a stupid question.

"Oh no," replied Mrs. Gorman, "she lives with her mother and father." She smiled at Elizabeth. "I'm teaching her to sew, so she spent last night with us. Ain't that right, dear?"

Elizabeth's dark eyes found William's. "Yes, ma'am."

Mrs. Gorman sat next to Elizabeth, took her hand, and smiled warmly. "Elizabeth was given a Christian name at birth. Shall we all join hands and pray?"

Jason Gorman surveyed the table, making sure hands were joined and heads bowed before he closed his eyes to pray.

William lowered his head, but instead of closing his eyes, he looked up, seeing Elizabeth looking at him. Embarrassed, he quickly looked down at his plate, missing the smile she gave him.

Mr. Gorman said Amen, and the kitchen filled with the sounds of dishing up the food and passing the plates around the table.

If asked later, William probably could not have told anyone what they had for dinner that evening or about the dinner conversation. There were times when Mr. Gorman had to repeat what he was saying because William's mind and thoughts were of the young girl across from him.

This did not go unnoticed by Mrs. Gorman as she watched Elizabeth and William, knowing the boy was a goner. Remembering her courting days with Mr. Gorman and his reluctance to make the first move, when dinner was over and the dishes cleaned and put away, she decided to take matters into her own hands by asking William if he would walk Elizabeth home. The boy could not believe his luck. He was finally going to be alone with her, and he silently prayed that she lived a good distance away. They excused themselves, and after William helped Elizabeth with her shawl, they left the Gorman house.

As they walked, they talked of many things, but all too soon, they were standing at the door of a small hut. Clumsily, William said goodnight, and as Elizabeth opened the door to go inside, she turned. "Why did you stop coming by the mission?"

William looked at her face, catching the light from inside the door, thinking she was beautiful. He shrugged. "You wouldn't talk to me, and your mother kept throwing rocks at me." He smiled wryly. "Sort of makes you want to stay out of range."

Elizabeth laughed quietly at this funny white boy. "By me not giving you the attention you wanted, you tried harder." She smiled softly. "But you gave up too soon."

His heart pounded at realizing she wanted him to try harder. He shrugged. "I thought it was useless." Then he grinned. "Besides, your mother's aim was getting better."

She laughed, recalling how he had nimbly dodged her mother's stones.

He glanced past her, looking worried, "By the way, where is your mother?"

"Inside," she said, motioning with her head. "Want me to call her?"

"No."

Elizabeth giggled, thinking he was funny and she liked that about him. He didn't seem like other white boys. She never heard him say bad things to the others, which made him different. "You did scare me when you jumped out at me."

William smiled, and his heart jumped. "Fooled me."

"I didn't want you to know. Do all white boys give up that soon?"

William shrugged. "I don't know. I didn't think I was getting anywhere."

She whispered, "Now you know different." With a small smile, she disappeared inside and closed the door.

He stared at the door for a moment until he heard movement and voices inside, knowing she was talking to her mother. Thinking of the rocks tossed at him, he turned away, walked back to the Gorman house, hitched the horses to the wagon, and made his way home, filled with thoughts of Elizabeth. After that, William Chrisman would visit the mission and Elizabeth at every opportunity. He made her laugh as they walked around the grounds, talking of all sorts of things, and as the weeks turned into months, even Elizabeth's mother came to like this white boy who made her daughter's heart laugh.

William's family was not at all pleased about the relationship, and the time came when his father forbade him to visit the mission, reminding him that it was the Indians who had killed his uncle. William's heart was torn between his family and Elizabeth. It wasn't her family that had killed his uncle, and he knew he could never give her up. He tried talking to his father, but his father raised his hands, not wanting to hear any more of what William had to say about an Indian squaw.

His mother knew he had fallen in love with this girl, but it was out of her hands. Against his father's wishes, William continued his visits to the mission until the spring of 1837. Then, at twenty years of age, he married sixteen-year-old Elizabeth Louisa Blackstone. Mr. Gorman performed the wedding ceremony in the mission chapel among a small gathering of her family and the Gorman's. The Chrisman family refused to attend, but William had hoped that his family would accept her once they were married.

After the ceremony, William and Elizabeth drove up to his father's house in the wagon, where his father stepped out from the house, demanding that William keep "that heathen squaw" in the wagon, and then slammed the door. Feeling hurt and embarrassed, William went inside, where he and his father argued terribly over his new wife. William pleaded with his mother, who only stood in silence, watching her husband and son arguing with such anger that it badly frightened her.

Mr. Chrisman told William to take his Indian and leave the county. But at the urging of his mother, his father gave him money and two slaves. An angry William took the money and packed the wagon his father gave them. Then he, Elizabeth, and the two slaves headed west. They settled in Tennessee, where their first child was born, and then on to Alabama, settling on land in Tallapoosa County near the Tallapoosa River.

Putting the past behind them, they raised five children.: Beth, James, Davy, Nancy, and Bonnie.

Having returned to the top of the hill, James wiped the inside of his straw hat, put it on, and stuffed the handkerchief into his pocket. Feeling thirsty, he yelled at the foreman as he gestured toward the big house. The man waved back, understanding his meaning, and then James rode down the hill and across the yard, stopping in the shade of a tree, where he dismounted. Giving the reins of the mare to a small Negro boy, he said, "Give her a good rubdown and plenty of oats."

"Yes, Suh," replied the boy.

Watching the Negro boy lead the black mare toward the livery, he stretched and then walked up the steps of the porch. "How you doing, Pa?"

William shifted his weight on the pillow he was sitting on, looking depressed. "Do'n alright, son. Looks a mite warm out there."

James removed his hat, wiped his forehead with the sleeve of his forearm, and sat on the porch railing next to his father's chair. "It's a warm one, all right."

William looked toward the outbuildings. "Seen, Davy?"

"No, I haven't, Pa. He's probably down at the bailing shed."

William grinned, looking skeptical. "Leastways, you hope that's where the little shit is."

James grinned as he set his hat on the small table next to the rocking chair. "Well, you never know about Davy, Pa."

"That's true enough, son," chuckled William, taking his pipe from his mouth. He looked up at his son. "How are things? We gonna get our cotton off to town soon?"

James considered that. "Think so, Pa." He grinned. "In spite of little Davy." Both men laughed, and then James looked a little more serious. "We may need a few more slaves from old man Harper, but I'll know more about that later in the week."

William put his pipe back in his mouth and thought about that. "Do what you need to do, son." He thought for a moment. " Maybe I'll go along and see if we can cut a deal from the old man."

"All right, Pa."

Just then, the front door opened, and James's older sister Beth walked out of the house carrying a tray of lemonade and two glasses. Beth, at twenty-one, looked like her mother had when she was young. She was thin with small breasts, the same dark skin, high cheekbones, long face, and big dark eyes as her mother. Her thick, long black hair hung past her small waist, swaying from side to side as she walked. She smiled at James. "Saw ya comin', thought you'd enjoy some fresh lemonade before dinner." She placed the tray on the table next to her father and poured a glass for each.

James took one, handed it to his father, and then picked up the second glass. "Thanks, Beth. What's for dinner?"

"Chicken."

"Chicken?" repeated William, looking disappointed. "What the hell's the matter with pork or beef? Hell, it ain't like we don't have neither around the place."

She stopped at the door and smiled at her Pa. "Ask Ma. She decides what's for dinner."

Just then, Davy burst out of the house, bumping into Beth.

"Hey! Watch where you're going, young man."

Davy turned with an apologetic look. "Sorry, sis." Then he saw the lemonade. "Can I have some?"

"Get yourself a glass," Beth told him just before disappearing into the house.

Davy followed her inside, returning moments later with a glass he filled with lemonade. Davy was only eleven years old but big for his age. He stood almost as tall as his brother James, which led people to believe he was older than he was. That led strangers to think he was a little slow in the head, and there were times his own family needed reminding that Davy was still a young boy with a childlike grin and childish ways. His complexion was dark, and, like the other children, he had the same dark brown eyes as their mother.

William watched Davy gulp the lemonade, then pour another glass. "Careful, Davy, you'll make yourself sick."

"Sorry, Pa."

James turned to his father. "Think Breckenridge or Lincoln will get elected in November, Pa?"

While William thought about the question, he struck a match across the railing and touched the flame to his pipe. As the cloud of white smoke slowly floated upwards, he looked at James. "Don't know, Son. But I fear there could be war if this Lincoln's elected."

Filled with childish excitement at that possibility, Davy grinned. "Think so, Pa?"

William glanced at the young boy affectionately, remembering he was still a child with childish thoughts. Then he looked toward the fields and the Negroes walking along the road toward their tiny cabins, having finished their day, and wondered what would become of them if the South lost such a war. Then he answered Davy's question. "Positive, boy." He considered the Negroes plight if suddenly set free with no place to live, such as a farm, or any of the simple things people needed to exist. "If the southern states secede, as they threaten, them fellers up north will come marching right down here, ready for war." Then he gestured out toward the land. "And we could lose all of this."

James looked at the scene before him of white men on horseback, wagons of cotton heading toward the barn, and the line of Negro workers heading for their huts and a night's rest.

William took a drink of lemonade and puffed on his pipe. "I've been afraid of what may come our way since that incident with that Brown fella and his boys."

James looked troubled. "They were all hung, Pa!"

"I know, Son, but all this talk up north about abolishing slavery and setting these Negroes free is sure to cause nuth'n but dissension between us and our Negroes. If Lincoln keeps preaching anti-slavery, I'm certain there'll be a lot more men thinking like that Brown fella and just itching to come down here to change things."

Davy laughed. "Hell, Pa, they'd just get killed."

William looked at Davy and started to scold him, but then he remembered he was only a boy and not old enough to understand the consequences of war. William stood and limped to the white porch railing, stood next to James, looked out at the land he had worked on most of his life, and then looked at Davy. "Them do-gooder, Bible-thumping bastards will come down here anyway, son."

James looked at Davy. "Ya see, Davy, people don't think about getting killed when they join a cause. They just want to be part of changing whatever it is they think is wrong, much like the Crusaders did in them books ya read at school. They think about killing others, not getting killed."

Davy frowned while he considered that. "But all this is none of their business."

James nodded. "That's the way most southerners feel, Davy, but that don't matter none to them up north." James looked toward the Negro slaves walking from the fields. "This has always been our way, Davy. Maybe it ain't right, but it's our way of life, and it should be up to us to change it."

Davy looked at James. "If war comes, you gonna join up?"

James glanced at his Pa, wishing Davy hadn't asked, and as he struggled for an answer, Beth stuck her head out the front door. "Dinner's ready."

"Come on, son," William said, putting his hand on Davy's head, rubbing it briskly. "Let's go eat some of your mother's good cooking."

James stood on the front porch, letting his dinner settle, listening to the sounds of the night while pondering the changes that would come in their lives if war came to the valley. Biting off the tip of his cigar, he took a wooden match from his pocket, scratched it against the porch pillar, touched the bright flame to the tip of his cigar, and puffed. He hadn't noticed his pa sitting in the darkness beyond the light from the window shining across the porch. A frog croaked somewhere in the yard, joining the monotonous singing of crickets.

"Loud little bastard, ain't he?" asked William.

Startled at his father's voice, James turned and looked into the darkness of the porch. "Didn't know you were out here, Pa."

"Warm one," William said. "Air's a bit heavy."

"That it is." James stepped off the porch into the front yard.

The front door opened, and Davy walked onto the porch and looked at his older brother. "Going for a walk, James?"

"Reckon."

"Can I come?"

"I guess." James turned to their pa, sitting in the dark corner. "Wanna come along, Pa?"

William wished he could but knew his hip would hurt. "No, you two go on ahead. I'll just sit here and enjoy the stars, my pipe, and the rocking chair." After his two sons stepped into the darkness, he followed the path of the cigar's red glow as the two walked into the darkness.

The brothers walked in silence for several yards, lost in their thoughts and listening to the crickets and frogs. Finally, Davy broke the silence. "Is Pa scared, James?"

James puffed his cigar as they walked up the dirt road away from the house, considering his brother's question. He stopped and looked up into the dark sky in awe at the number of stars and a large, yellow, new moon above the trees that lined the hills. It took a moment, but James found the Big Dipper, the North Star, and a few other shapes he remembered from school. He looked back at the porch, knowing their pa was sitting there rocking, his mind filled with thoughts of slavery and the South's future. "Let me tell ya a little about Ma and Pa, Davy. You probably know most of this, but I need to talk about it anyway."

"Okay," replied Davy, eager to hear what his big brother was about to say.

"When Pa was a young man and met Ma, Pa's family was completely against their relationship. Grandpa gave him $550.00 and two Negroes to start a new life someplace else because our ma is Indian, and their half-breed children wouldn't be welcome in their house."

"I know all about that stuff, James."

"I'm sure you do, Davy, but my point is that it hurt Ma and Pa more'n they'd ever admit. Pa's well-liked by most of the men in the valley, and he's helped most of `em one time or another. And there was a time when there were no doctors in the valley, and Ma took care of most people that were ailing, and they pretty much didn't care that she was an Indian." James puffed on his cigar and then slapped Davy on the back playfully. "So, people around here don't say much to us about being half-breeds Davy, leastways, not to our faces. I can't say what they say behind our backs, and it don't matter none, anyway."

"I never understood why Grandpa didn't like Ma."

"It ain't that he particularly disliked Ma," James said, "it was more about his brother being killed by Indians." James paused in thought. "People just naturally hate Indians, I guess, and it's hard to forgive a killing." James drew another breath of his cigar and then flicked off its ashes. "There'd been a lot of killing on both sides back then, and feelings run deep about such things. Even if Ma's family wasn't responsible, they were still Indians." James puffed on his cigar and blew the smoke into the darkness. "Shit, Davy, there's still killing going on out west between the Whites and the Indians." They stopped, and James looked back at the house, imagining their Pa sitting in the shadows on the porch. "Don't go saying anything to Pa about us talking about this. He wouldn't like it none."

"I won't."

James stopped and glanced around them as if he could see everything in the darkness. "Pa loves this place, and it's all he has. He and Ma worked hard and built this place, making a way of life for us, hoping we would take it over after they're gone. I guess he's a little afraid that a war would destroy it or a group of strangers will take it all away." James looked back at the house, imagining their pa sitting in the darkness. "And I guess he's afraid that I'll run off to Texas like I always talk about, and that scares the hell out of `em."

"Are ya go'n' James? To Texas, I mean?"

"No, I'm not going anywhere, Davy." James placed his hand on his brother's back and playfully guided him toward the house. "Leastways, not for a while."

Davy laughed.

"We best start back," said James. "I'm tired, and we have a big day tomorrow."

In his room, James walked through a moonlit replica of the window on the cold hardwood floor, took off his boots, undressed, and climbed into a bed of cool cotton sheets. He stared up at the dark ceiling, listening to the arguing of crickets, bullfrogs, and an occasional owl. A shoe landing on the floor, followed moments later by the other, echoed through the walls, and he pictured his pa getting ready for bed. James turned his thoughts to the fields and crops and his father's concerns over what would become of them if war came to the valley.

His thoughts turned to the slaves, their plight, and the difficulty his mother's family suffered. He knew all too well that it was his father's blood that separated them from a similar fate in the white man's world. Muffled words coming through the wall from his parent's room interrupted his thoughts, and as he listened, his eyes grew heavy, and his mind soon gave way to sleep.

James woke to a knock on the bedroom door. "I'm awake," he said as he sat up on his elbows, glancing around the room filled with the red glow of the morning sun. A rooster crowed amid dogs barking and yelping at play somewhere outside, followed by the voice of a Negro child calling them.

Throwing back the covers, he felt the early morning chill as he placed his feet on the small rug covering the wooden floor. Standing, he lit the lamp, giving light to the dim room, and then carried it to the dresser and the washbasin of warm water, soap, and towel; evidence of his mother's undetected visit followed by the knock on the door as she left.

Washed and dressed, he walked downstairs to the aroma of fresh coffee, eggs, and sausage rushing toward him from the dining room. His two little sisters, Nancy and Bonnie, aged ten and nine, were running around the table, slapping Davy on the back of his head with each passing of his chair. James grabbed a giggling sister under each arm and carried them to their chairs, setting them down and telling them to behave. Sitting between them, he understood his mother's seating order.

Just then, William limped into the room. "Good Lord almighty, what in heaven's name is going on in here?" Winking at the two girls, he smiled. "Sounded like a couple of roosters a fight'n." While the girls giggled, he turned his attention to James. "Don't forget about the trip to town."

"No sir," answered James as he lifted the china cup of coffee to his lips, feeling the hot steam against his skin. He watched as his father added two spoons of sugar to his coffee and wondered what was going through his mind, but quickly decided it was best left alone. He took a sip of coffee, and as he set the cup down on the saucer, he noticed Davy was staring at him. "You want something, Davy?"

"Can I go with ya?"

James looked at William. "Pa?"

"S'pose it'll be all right," replied William thoughtfully, and then he looked at Davy. "Be sure to get your chores done first."

James shoved a piece of bread into his mouth and looked at Davy. "I have a few things to take care of first."

James hadn't noticed his ma walking out of the kitchen.

She swatted him on the head. "Don't talk with your mouth full, James!" At the kitchen door, she turned to James, looking angry. "Taught you better'n that, James Riley. Because your Pa there does it, doesn't mean." She shot a glare at William before disappearing into the kitchen.

William rolled his eyes and then drank his coffee, accepting the blame for his son's table manners.

James shoved his mouth full of bread and eggs, then looked toward the kitchen before speaking softly with a mouth full of food. "Davy, I want you to find Bill and Eddie and tell `em they're needed in the fields while we're in town." James paused, turned, and saw his mother standing at the kitchen door, staring at him. He swallowed his food, "Sorry, Ma."

She shot him one of her famous glares and disappeared into the kitchen.

He turned to Davy. "Tell `em should something come up, to come see Pa."

It was a little past noon when James backed the wagon up to the dock of Langdon's Feed and Grain Store. After setting the brake, he jumped down and patted the two horses gently on the neck while Davy jumped down. James handed the list to Davy. "When you've finished loading, I'll meet ya up the street at Norton's General Store."

Davy looked confused as he took the list. "Where goin'?"

James turned and started walking while yelling over his shoulder, "To the saloon."

Davy kicked at the dirt, "T'ain't fair, James."

James grinned at his angry brother, then hurried across the street and walked into the saloon, paying little attention to the other patrons. James ordered a beer, took a sip, and licked the foam from his upper lip as he walked to a table next to the window that gave him a clear view of his little brother and sat down. He took another sip of beer, finding great pleasure in watching his brother, knowing he was fit to be tied, pissed off, and angry. Smiling in smugness at his cruel deed, he placed one leg on the seat of an empty chair and settled into his chair, getting comfortable.

"Howdy, James."

Turning from the window, he looked into the face of his old friend Allen Downs, whom he had not seen since school. Allen was tall and barefoot, wearing hand-me-down clothes that were a bit too big. He smiled as he pushed a chair from under the table with his foot. "Sit down and bullshit while I watch Davy works his ass off."

Allen sat down, leaned in his chair toward the window, and looked across the street, watching Davy. "How ya been, James?"

James sipped his beer. "Been all right, Allen. What can I do for ya?"

"Aw nuth'n," answered Allen shyly. "I's just sit'n over there with them other fellas talking when I saw ya come in and wanted to say howdy is all."

James glanced at the other men who he recognized from around town and then grinned at Allen. "Howdy, Allen."

The boy smiled with a childish grin as he settled back in his chair, scratched his freckled forehead, and pushed his bushy blond hair back with one hand to comb it. Allen's family lived on a small farm a few miles from the Chrisman place. He and James had known one another since early childhood and attended school together, often getting into various sorts of trouble. Allen had quit school much sooner than James to work full-time on his father's farm. William Chrisman had once prohibited James from seeing Allen, but of course, James, being the boy he was, ignored that rule at the expense of lectures and an occasional strap across the buttocks.

Allen adjusted his chair to watch Davy, and as the two talked, James briefly thought about helping his younger brother, not that he felt pity for the boy, but because he was briefly considering the possible lecture from their Ma. However, he decided his pleasure was worth the scolding and took a drink of beer. As he set his mug on the table, he noticed a nicely dressed young girl with an armload of packages walk out of a lady's apparel store across the street and continue down the wooden boardwalk. She stopped for a few moments to talk to Davy, then walked to a nearby buggy and placed the packages under the seat.

Allen grinned. "Well, well, if it ain't Martha Heard."

James looked at Allen with a surprised expression and then at the girl across the street. "That's Martha Heard?"

Allen grinned. "Yep, that's little Martha Heard."

James leaned forward in his chair and watched as she climbed onto the buggy seat. "Sure, don't look like Martha."

Allen nodded. "It's her all right, James. They live not far from y'all's place."

James frowned at Allen. "I know Martha and where they live, Allen." He returned to the window. "What happened to her?"

Allen chuckled. "She sort of grew up."

James lowered his voice. "What the hell ya mean sort of?"

Allen glanced at James, noticing the look on his face. "When was the last time ya seen her?"

James considered the question for a moment. "Last year at the pond when our families had a picnic." He paused. "But she sure didn't look like that."

Allen glanced around the saloon, leaned closer, and whispered, "Geez, James, a lot can happen in a year, but she's only fourteen, and that's what I meant by sort of."

James looked into Allen's grinning face. "Your teeth are gonna fall out, Allen."

Allen wrinkled his forehead, looking serious. "James, she still has a bit o' grow'n to do."

James lowered his voice. "Maybe so, Allen, but I'm only sixteen." He looked back at Martha as she took the reins of the horse. "She sure looks a lot older than fourteen."

Allen considered that as he turned from the window and stared at James, who had his full attention directed at Martha Heard as she turned the buggy in the direction of the saloon. Silence filled the table as Allen and James watched her drive past the window.

Looking straight ahead, Martha quickly turned and looked toward the window and smiled when Allen and James ducked down so she wouldn't see them.

"Why'd we duck?" asked Allen.

"Shit, I don't know, but did you see her smile at me?"

Allen chuckled. "Git serious, James. You were under the table."

James frowned. "I am serious." Then he watched the wagon disappear up the street before he looked across at Davy loading the wagon. "I wonder what it was that she said to Davy. Probably something about school."

"I doubt it was about school." Allen looked skeptical. "Old man Heard don't believe in educating his gals none."

James nodded thoughtfully. "Oh yeah. I remember."

"Yep," said Allen. "Old man Heard says no school fer the girls." Allen paused to take a sip of beer. "Yes, sir, old man Heard thinks it a waste of time and effort. Says they'll just git married and pregnant anyways, so why bother."

James got up from his chair, wondering what it was Martha had said to Davy. "What you say maybe so, but when Martha Heard is all grown up, you come and get me. Right now, I best help Davy. See you later."

Davy was mad as hell when James approached. "Where ya been?

James approached the wagon, looking apologetic. "Sorry, Davy. Tell you what, I'll finish this, and you can go on up to the general store and look around."

Davy grinned, looking happy, and quickly jumped down. "Can I get a jar of peaches while I wait?"

"All right, but just one." James put one foot on the side of the wagon to step up as he looked in the direction Martha Heard had gone. "Hey, Davy, what did you and Martha talk about?"

Davy looked puzzled. "You mean Martha Heard?"

James climbed onto the wagon, quickly glanced around, and lowered his voice. "Yeah, Davy, Martha Heard. What did she want?"

Davy walked backward as he yelled. "Oh, not much, but she did ask about you. I told her you were over in the saloon."

James wished Davy would stop yelling.

Davy stopped in the middle of the dirt street, looking thoughtful. "Oh yeah, she said to tell you hi.

Feeling his face flush, James looked toward the saloon, relieved that Allen wasn't watching. When he turned toward the feed store, Mr. Langdon stood in the doorway, smiling at him. Embarrassed by all this, James turned and continued loading the last of the supplies, wishing his loud-mouthed little brother would just shut up.

Davy yelled, "Are you sweet on her, James?"

Looking angry, James yelled, "No, I ain't Davy. I ain't seen her since the picnic." He glanced back at Mr. Langdon, who was still standing in the doorway of his store, grinning. James looked toward Davy and softly said, "Whenever that was."

Thinking James had said something else, Davy hollered, "What?"

Frustrated, James stood and yelled, "We'll talk on the way home, Davy!"

"All right!" yelled Davy. He turned and ran up the street, kicking at the ruts.

Martha Heard was a petite girl, barely five feet three inches tall and slender, with brown eyes, full lips, and shoulder-length light brown hair.

She was one of seven children of Richard and Susanna Heard, who lived on a small one-hundred-and-seventy-acre farm a couple of miles from the Chrisman place. The Heard clan consisted of several families living in neighboring counties whose grandparents had come from Germany around the turn of the century.

The William Chrisman and Richard Heard families had known one another for several years, attending the same church services, picnics, and other social events such as barn raisings or dances. James had paid little attention to Martha because she was a couple of years younger, while she, on the other hand, had quite a crush on young James. But as is generally the case, girls grow up a little faster than boys, and Martha Heard was doing just that, growing up a little faster than James Riley Chrisman.

He finished loading the supplies, retrieved his brother and the things on their mother's list from the general store, and headed home. James spent the time thinking of Martha while Davy lay in the back, curled up and sleeping.

Like most young men his age, he was a little shy when it came to girls, and the obvious method of getting acquainted with a girl had never occurred to him. So, over the next few weeks, he went through a painful ritual of finding or making up reasons to go into town, hoping for a chance meeting. The idea of riding over to talk to her was much too intimidating, not to mention terrorizing. Returning one day from another failure in town along the lonely dirt road, James was fearful that the summer would end before his plans could materialize. Deep in thought about more future foolproof schemes, he turned the wagon in from the road and drove the team to the back door. Sitting quietly on the wagon seat and talking aloud as if someone else were in the wagon, he argued over his lack of success with his well-thought-out plans.

His mother stood at the kitchen window, wondering who he was talking with.

James jumped down from the wagon and picked up the basket of things his mother had asked him to get. All the time, his lips moved, accompanied by various facial expressions.

Concerned over her son, Mrs. Chrisman turned and stood at the stove, waiting for him to walk up the steps and through the kitchen door. As if she weren't there, he placed the basket of things on the table, then turned and walked back outside, climbed onto the wagon seat, released the brake, and drove the team toward the barn.

Watching the boy, Elizabeth slowly shook her head and softly said, "Sure is acting peculiar."

William walked into the kitchen. "Who's acting peculiar, Mother?"

Turning from the window, she picked up the pot of coffee and nodded toward the window. "That son of yours, that's who." Looking baffled, she poured William a cup of coffee, placed the pot back on the stove, and sat at the table repeating herself. "That boy's acting awful peculiar."

"Which one?" William asked.

"James," she said. "The boy acts like he's love-struck."

William chuckled as he picked up his coffee. "Now, how would you know that?"

She smiled, remembering William as a young suitor. "He reminds me of his father prowling around the mission like a lost puppy searching for scraps."

William grinned, looking sheepish. "Well, you ought to know. You were the scraps I was after."

She blushed. "Oh, hush, Will, that sounds terrible." Then she slapped him playfully on the head as she got up and walked to the stove.

William sipped his coffee, digesting Elizabeth's comments as he stood and limped to the window, staring at the barn. "Come to think of it, the boy has been acting a little odd lately." He paused, "Been making a lot of extra trips to town."

Beth walked into the kitchen. "Y'all must be talking about James."

Elizabeth looked at Beth and then William. "See, even Beth's noticed. I tell you, Will, the boy is either sick or in love."

Beth laughed. "With his horse."

William chuckled. "You might be right about that, Beth."

With wide eyes, Beth blushed. "Pa!"

Elizabeth laughed softly at Beth's comment.

William turned to the window, sipping his coffee as Elizabeth and Beth went about dinner. Seeing his son walking toward the house talking to himself, he thought of what Beth had said and laughed, spewing coffee onto the window.

Elizabeth and Beth looked up from fixing dinner and laughed as Elizabeth wiped the window with a dishtowel.

James walked into the kitchen and, seeing everyone laughing, asked, "What's everyone laughing at?"

Embarrassed by his sudden appearance, they looked at James for a moment, then at one another. Knowing she would laugh, Beth turned and ran out of the room, unable to hold it back as she ran through the dining room. William began laughing as he sat down, trying not to spill his coffee, and while he wiped the tears from his eyes, Elizabeth buried her face in her apron in laughter.

Thinking they were laughing at him for some reason, James stormed out of the kitchen and up the stairs to his room, slammed his bedroom door, sat on his bed, and angrily tossed his hat against the wall. As the hat hit the floor, James lay on his bed and stared at the imperfections in the ceiling. A soft knock came from outside his door. "Who is it?"

Elizabeth opened the door and entered the room carrying a small pile of folded clothing. She glanced at the hat lying on the floor and then at James lying across his bed. She started to explain they weren't laughing at him, but that would have been a lie. "Are ya okay, right, James?"

"I'm fine, Ma."

She walked across the room to his chest, opened a drawer, put the stack neatly inside, and closed it. Looking at her son, she bent down and picked up his hat. After placing it on a nearby chair, she glanced at James, and aimlessly moved a few things on top of the dresser. She remembered her grandfather's advice: ' A journey on a well-worn path is better than getting lost in the woods.' She looked at her son and softly said, "Something's got you fast in its grip, James. Now, what is it?"

James continued to stare up at the ceiling. "T'ain't nothing, Ma; just got something on my mind, that's all,"

Elizabeth walked from the chest of drawers to the bed, sat on its edge next to James, and gently stroked his hair. "What is it, son?"

James looked into her soft, dark eyes. "I'm all right, Ma." Then he looked out the window.

"Is there something you want to talk about, James?"

He shook his head no as he stared out the window.

Deciding at last to leave her son to his private troubles, she gently slapped her lap. "All right." She stood, "Supper will be ready soon. Get washed up."

"Okay, Ma."

She turned away in silence, leaving James to himself, and went downstairs.

Elizabeth hummed while she and Beth worked in the kitchen preparing the evening meal.

Beth's thoughts were of James while listening to her mother's humming. "I think I know what's wrong with James."

Elizabeth stopped humming. "Really? And what might that be?"

Beth turned back to the stove, going from pot to pot as she talked in a low voice. "I ain't sure, but I think it's over Martha Heard."

Elizabeth looked surprised. "Martha Heard?"

"Shhh!" Beth said, glancing toward the door. "James may hear us."

"Don't shhh me, gal," scolded Elizabeth. "Now, what has this to do with Martha Heard?"

Beth hurried to the dining room door, pushed it open, took a quick peek into the dining room to make sure James was not around, and then hurried back to her mother. "Well, Davy was telling me that when he and James went to town a while back, she told him to tell James hi." Beth moved a pot on the stove, then looked at her mother, "Yah know Ma, sometimes we think Davy's a little slow, but now and again, he catches on to things we don't." She grinned, raising her eyebrows. "Davy thinks she's sweet on James, and I think that's why James keeps looking for reasons to go into town. Maybe have a chance meeting with her."

"Why on earth go to all that trouble?" Elizabeth said, gesturing with one hand while looking confused. "She only lives a piece down the road."

Beth giggled, moved closer, and lowered her voice. "That way, he wouldn't get embarrassed if she ignored him."

Elizabeth considered that and smiled affectionately, remembering William as a young man. "Like father like son." She paused in memory at the delight she and her mother had at William's expense. She shook her head. "Land sakes, that boy has about as much sense as his Pa." She did not want her son to go through what she and her mother had put William through, even if it had been enjoyable. She put her arm around Beth's shoulder, giving her a quick hug. "Let's not make a big deal over this. I'm sure James feels bad enough." Then she smiled. "These things have a way of working themselves out. Let's get dinner on the table."

James was very sullen and distant during dinner and had to be asked twice to pass a plate of food. After dinner, with his plate almost full, he excused himself and went outside to the front porch, where he stood on the steps watching the last of the evening sun. His mind was full of Martha Heard, and he did not hear the door open.

Elizabeth walked across the porch, stood beside him, folded her arms, and watched the sunset. "I love this time of day. The mornings are quiet too, just like this." She put her arm around him, squeezing gently. "It's always the same. When you wake up in the morning, you know you have a hard day ahead, but the evenings bring relief from the chores and hardships." She smiled, looking peaceful. "Maybe that's why I look forward to the evening so much."

I suppose," uttered James, watching the last of the sun dip behind the trees on the hill.

"I'm gonna say something, James," she said, sounding and looking serious. "And I don't want you getting all riled up and hateful."

Curious about what she was going to say, he stared at the western sky. "I promise, Ma."

She reached behind her with her hands, pulled her dress against the back of her legs the way women do, and sat on the porch's top step. She grabbed James's hand, pulled him down next to her, and looked out across the yard and the far-off hills turning dark with the coming of night. "All this is over, some girl, isn't it?"

"No," denied James, looking angry and embarrassed.

Elizabeth stared at him. "James, not only am I your mother, but I'm also a woman, and not so long ago, I was a young girl courted by your father." She paused in memory. "So he calls it." She chuckled, looking happy, then serious. "Some things just can't be changed or pushed away or hidden. They are what they are, and you have to deal with them." She held his hand gently between hers and looked at him as mothers do when they know their child is troubled. "Now, what's this all about?"

James sat in silence, agonizing over talking about Martha Heard to his mother.

Elizabeth smiled as she leaned her body into his shoulder. "Wouldn't be that Heard girl bothering you now, would it?"

James turned to the door, looking angry as he started to stand. "Damn you, Davy."

Elizabeth pulled him back down to the porch. "Now, don't get all riled up, James Chrisman," she scolded, looking angry. "Your brother Davy had nothing to do with any of this except mentioning to Beth that the two of you met her in town a while back." Elizabeth calmed herself, knowing that being angry was not going to help her son. She placed her arm around his shoulder and gave him a small, affectionate hug. "James, why don't you just ride over to the Heards and talk to the girl?"

The obvious was too frightening to him. "I can't just ride over there, Ma."

"Well, maybe not," she said, considering his dilemma. "Town's always neutral territory, I suppose."

James shrugged. "It seemed easier that way." He looked disgusted. "But she's never in town."

Elizabeth chuckled under her breath, smiled, and shook her head. "Well, James, for reasons unknown, girls aren't always accommodating. Besides, your way could take a year, maybe longer." She ruffled his hair with her hand. "Lord almighty, son, it's November."

"I can't just ride over there for no reason, Ma. Suppose she won't talk to me when I get there. What'll I do then?"

The vision of James standing next to the black mare in the Heard yard looking the way his father had so many years ago brought a smile to her face. "James, this is 1860, for heaven's sake, not 1760. Things are different now."

"Like how?"

Not sure how to answer that, Elizabeth considered that for a moment. "James, a girl like Martha doesn't just go around telling someone's brother to tell them 'hi' unless she's interested." She smiled. "Girls just don't do that. From what I understand, she made a point of telling Davy to say 'hi' to you, now, didn't she?"

James looked hopeful as he nodded.

She hugged him affectionately. "Coosa County seems a long way off, but it ain't that far away, and we visit them now and again, have gone on picnics together, and see them at church almost every Sunday." She softly laughed as she looked into his bewildered eyes. "So we ain't exactly strangers."

"I know," he said. "But this is different, Ma; I can't explain it none."

Elizabeth considered that. "No, I guess it ain't the same. I've been to their place many times when Mrs. Heard was ailing. They're a fine God-fearing family, so no one's gonna shoot ya if you ride up and ask to talk to Martha." She leaned her shoulder against his, adding, "What's more, I believe Martha is probably wondering what it's gonna take to entice you over there."

James smiled as his face flushed. "Still need a reason. I can't just go over there."

She shook her head, thinking this was going to be more difficult than she realized, believing this boy was too much like his father. "You're as stubborn as a mule, James. Land sakes, boy, you're gonna be a lonely man for a long time if you stay on this path." Then another idea came to her. "If it's a reason you want, son, I'll give ya a reason to ride over there."

He looked hopeful. "Like what?"

"I'll make up a batch of something with herbs and such like I did when she was ailing a few months back." She paused in thought. "You can take that over for Mrs. Heard, telling her that I was thinking about her and made up a fresh batch in case she was ailing again."

The door opened, and William walked onto the porch. "Not interrupting anything, I hope."

Elizabeth turned with a smile. "No, we were just talking." She got up, playfully messed James's hair with one hand, kissed William on the cheek, and went into the house.

Knowing enough to stay silent, William said nothing and walked to his chair in the corner of the porch to enjoy his pipe and the warm evening. His chair moaned as he sat down, breaking the stillness. "Got to get myself into town tomorrow and vote."

James pushed Martha out of his head and turned to his Pa. "Think Lincoln will win, Pa?"

"Don't know, son. I think Breckenridge has a chance, but he's from the South and supports slavery, something a lot of people don't, including a few Southerners."

James stood, walked across the porch, and sat on the railing. "How long before we know?"

"Oh, a month anyway, maybe longer."

"Want me to drive ya to town?"

"No, son, I'm riding in with some of the hands." Then, with a quick wink, he added, "Might just get a drink or two afterward."

James grinned at that, then stood and stretched. "Think I'll go on upstairs and read a bit, Pa. Don't feel much like talking."

"Go on ahead, boy. Sometimes, it's good just to sit out here and think about things without cluttering it all up with words."

"G'night, Pa."

"Goodnight, Son."

James went to his room and lay on his bed, trying to read, but his mind was full of Martha and what his mother had said. He placed the book on the table next to his bed, undressed, and turned down the lamp. Then he got into bed and shut his eyes, waiting for sleep he knew would not come easily.

The morning sun had risen above the hills in the east when James opened his eyes, realizing he had slept longer than usual. Tossing off the covers, he got up, and as he washed with the cold water that had been warm when his mother had left it earlier that morning, he wondered why he had not heard her knock. Washed and dressed, James hurried downstairs to an empty dining room of dirty plates and wrinkled cloth napkins. Hearing noises in the kitchen, he walked around the messy table and through the swinging door into the kitchen, finding his mother and sister Beth busy.

Elizabeth turned and smiled. "Hungry?"

"Some, I guess."

"Sit yourself down in that chair," said his mother with a nod.

James did as he was told while exchanging good mornings with his sister.

Elizabeth took a plate of food from the oven she had been keeping warm and placed it on the table in front of him. "Be careful. The plate's hot." She turned, picked up a small bottle, and sat it next to his plate. "Take this to Mrs. Heard and tell her that I would have come myself, but I had too many things around here to take care of."

James looked at the jar curiously and then at her.

Elizabeth sat down with a stern look. "Don't take anything from Mrs. Heard. She's proud and may try to give you something, but don't take it now. Do you hear me?"

Looking just a bit confused, James took a bite of breakfast. "Yessum."

"Don't talk with your mouth full," she scolded. "There's a note in that envelope. See, she gets it." She smiled, stood, and disappeared into another part of the house.

Beth sat down, looking apologetic. "James, I hope you're not mad at Davy and me. We didn't mean nothing."

James swallowed his food and smiled. "I know, Beth. It's, well, it's just a little embarrassing when people know about private stuff you don't want to talk about."

Beth smiled and placed a hand on his forearm. "For what it's worth, I think Martha's a sweet girl." Then she got up and left the kitchen, leaving James to think about his trip to the Heard place while he finished his breakfast.

James rode the black mare at a walk along the lonely county road toward the Heard place, thinking of Martha and what things he might say to her. The sun was warm, the air calm, except for a slight breeze moving the leaves of the trees and bushes along the road. The mare's hooves seemed loud against the hard ground as she walked indifferently toward her rider's destination. A few chirping birds flew across the dirt road in front of them, crows cawed in nearby trees, and grasshoppers buzzed and jumped from bush to bush. He looked up the road, seeing a buckboard turn from the Heard place onto the county road and head in his direction.

He guided the black mare to the edge of the road, pulled her up, and waited while Mr. Heard slowed the team as they approached, bringing them to a stop next to James.

"Well, howdy, James," said Mr. Heard.

Mrs. Heard smiled. "Hello, James, come calling on our Martha?"

Embarrassed and feeling his face flush, James lied. "No, ma'am, just doing an errand for Ma."

Mrs. Heard frowned in disappointment.

James forced a smile as he clumsily reached into his saddlebags, retrieving the jar his mother had given him, and held it up. "Ma wanted me to bring this to you, Mrs. Heard."

She stared at the jar, looking puzzled. "What is it?"

James frowned thoughtfully. "Not rightly sure, but she sent this here note along with it."

Mrs. Heard elbowed her husband. "Take it, Richard."

Mr. Heard leaned toward James, took the bottle and envelope, and gave both to his wife.

Susanna Heard examined the jar before laying it in her lap and then stared at James curiously as she opened the envelope and read the penciled words.

"Good morning, Susanna. I hope this finds you in good health. There's nothing in this jar but some kitchen grease. My boy's too shy to call on your Martha, so I'm helping him along. I'm sure you understand, and I hope you don't mind. Liz."

Mrs. Heard smiled as she folded the paper and looked up at James. "Since you've come all this far, James, why don't you go on down and visit with Martha? It's been a while since the two of you have talked." Then she elbowed her husband. "Best get going, Richard."

Richard Heard nodded at James. "Sorry to rush off, son, but we have to get to town so's I can vote." He slapped the horse with the reins, causing the buckboard to lurch forward along the empty dirt road.

James watched them for a moment as they traveled ahead of the small cloud of dust made by the buckboard, and then he turned and looked toward the Heard house in the distance. He sat in his saddle, trying to decide what to do. His mind made up, James nudged the mare toward the house at a walk while thinking of turning the mare and riding home. But something in him wouldn't let him turn, so he walked the mare through the gate and down the driveway toward the house.

Back on the road, Susana Heard re-read the words on the paper and smiled once again.

Richard Heard leaned toward his wife and asked what was in the note.

She folded the paper and glanced over her shoulder at James as he rode onto their property. "Oh," she said, smiling, "just woman stuff."

James considered things he might say to Martha as he rode toward the house and began practicing his greeting. "Howdy Martha," he said aloud, quickly deciding that sounded dumb. Then James remembered being told once that the proper way to greet a young unmarried woman was to put a Miss before her proper name. "Hello, Miss Martha," he said, and then he smiled, thinking that sounded much better, repeating it several times while adding hand motions.

Meanwhile, Martha was watching from the kitchen window, noticing he was talking to himself, often looking pleased with whatever it was he said and thought it was strange." She smoothed the front of her dress and pushed her hair away from her face while being curious about what brought young James a calling. She stepped away from the window, opened the door, and stepped onto the porch.

Seeing her, James wanted to turn and run like a fox with hounds on its heels but couldn't. He was trapped. Slowing the mare, he could feel his heart racing while he frantically tried to remember the greeting he had practiced or something else to say. Then he noticed her younger brother, Eli, chopping wood a few yards from the house and decided to speak to him instead. "Howdy, Eli."

Eli stopped and looked up at James with a puzzled look. "Howdy, James."

James looked at Martha with a grin. "Howdy, Martha," Suddenly, he realized he hadn't greeted her the way he had practiced and felt a little dumb, wishing he had never come calling.

"Hello, James," replied Martha with a curious expression. "What brings you all the way out here?"

"Ma sent me over with a jar of something for your Ma," his voice suddenly jumped two octaves. Embarrassed, he shook his head and coughed as if to dislodge whatever it was in his throat. Desperate for something to say, he nodded at her brother. "I saw Eli down here and decided to come and visit a spell." He glanced at Eli.

Knowing that James would never go this far out of his way to visit her 12-year-old brother, Martha decided to play along. "Ma and Pa just left." With one hand on the porch post, she swung off, stopped, and smiled shyly. "But if ya give it to me, I'll see that ma gets it."

Feeling the sweat on his forehead, he turned toward his saddlebags and remembered he had given the jar to Mrs. Heard. "Oh, …ah, ….I saw your ma and pa up the road and already gave it to her." He had reached the point where he wanted to turn and bolt for home. As his forehead and face filled with tiny beads of sweat, he smiled, thinking of how pretty she looked as he took off his hat, wiping the beads of sweat on his forehead and neck.

Becoming impatient, Martha decided to have a little fun at his pretense about seeing her younger brother. "Eli," she said, "why don't you stop chopping wood for a few minutes and visit with James?" She looked up at James. "After all, ya came all this way to visit with my younger brother."

"Guess I could," replied Eli. "What's on yer mind, James?"

James stared at Eli, trying to think of a reason that could make sense. "I saw someone down here cut'n wood and thought I'd come down and say hi and maybe get a glass of water."

Irritated, Martha stepped closer to the mare. "For heaven's sake, James, climb down and visit a spell. I'm sure you and Eli have a lot to talk about since ya haven't seen one another fer a spell."

James felt like a trapped rat. He couldn't run and didn't want to talk to Eli.

Eli just stared at him and waited for James to say something

James smiled. "Well, I guess while I'm here---"

Martha interrupted, "I'll go inside and get us all something to drink."

Looking confused, Eli decided it was easier chopping wood than trying to figure out what was going on, and he returned to his chore.

James climbed down slowly from the mare and brushed the dust from his shirt and pants, trying to act as indifferently as possible.

Still smiling, Martha pointed toward the big tree a few yards away that had a swing for two hanging from one of its limbs. "Go on over to the swing while I get us some lemonade."

"Water'd do just fine, Miss Martha."

"Sure, it would, James, but lemonade would be better."

He glanced at Eli, thankful he was busy chopping wood and wondered what was going through the boy's mind. 'Probably thinks I'm loony,' he told himself, then he turned and walked around the corner of the house to the big oak tree and the swing while the mare patiently followed. James sat in the swing for a few long minutes, enjoying the silence, and watched the black mare work on a clump of grass at the base of the tree. Hearing a door slam, he looked up just as Martha walked around the corner of the house, carrying two glass jars of lemonade.

He stood, took one of the jars, then held the swing for her while she sat down. Then he sat on the swing, careful not to let their bodies touch.

Embarrassed about the glass jars, she apologized. "Sorry about the jars, but they hold more than our glasses, and you looked a mite thirsty."

James smiled and nodded politely. “That’s all right; sometimes we drink from fruit jars because they do hold more, especially on hot days.” He knew the Heard family was poor, and like a lot of other folks around the county, they made do with what they had.

She knew that wasn’t true but took pleasure in his saying it. “How are your ma and pa?”

“Fine.”

“How’s Beth and the others?” she asked, trying hard to make conversation.

James sipped the lemonade. “Fine.”

She glanced at the small meadow beyond the yard, wondering what it would take to get more than ‘fine’ out of him. She scooted back in the swing while managing to move a little closer.

As their bodies touched, something strange stirred deep within young James as he caught a whiff of a sweet fragrance she was wearing. Then he noticed that when she had gone into the house, she had changed into a blue one that clung to her in all the right places. The two top buttons of her dress were unbuttoned, exposing her white skin and the edges of her breasts.

He looked at her. She smiled, and he knew she saw where he was looking. Embarrassed, he looked away and took a drink of lemonade.

“Is your pa voting today?” she asked.

James cleared his throat. “Yeah, he and some of the hands rode into town to vote and have a beer afterward.”

“Why didn’t ya go with `em?”

He shrugged. “Ma wanted me to bring something over for your Ma.”

“I’m glad she did,” smiled Martha as her face flushed.

James could feel her warm body against his, so he moved away just a little, thinking it was awfully warm for November. As Martha moved closer, something unfamiliar stirred again within him, and he felt the need to stand. “I think I best be getting back.” He handed her the half-empty jar, bent down, and picked up the reins of his horse.

Martha quickly stood up from the swing, looking disappointed. “Wish ya didn’t have to run off so soon, James.” Wondering why he was in such a hurry, she followed him and the black mare back around the house toward the porch.

James put one foot in the stirrup. “I better get home, Martha.” He started to mount but hesitated and turned. “Martha, would it be all right if I came calling sometime?”

Surprised but happy by the notion, she smiled and nodded her head. "I'd like that."

Proud of himself, James climbed into the saddle and looked down at her, thinking of how her breasts had looked back at the swing.

She looked up at him and smiled.

He felt embarrassed, thinking she knew what he was thinking, so he looked around for Eli, who was walking toward the barn. He looked back down at her. "I'm busy this Sunday, but maybe I'll drop by a week from Sunday after church…if that'd be okay?"

She nodded, looking happy. "Maybe we can go on a picnic if it's nice."

"I'd like that." He turned the mare and slowly walked her toward the road.

Martha walked alongside for a few steps, and suddenly, her eyes lit up. "Hope ya like fried chicken." Then she thought to herself, *'That was dumb. What man doesn't like fried chicken?'*

He grinned. "My favorite."

"See ya then, James."

"Bye." He tipped his hat, turned the mare, and trotted toward the main road.

Martha watched young James Riley Chrisman for a moment and began humming a song as she turned and walked back along the path to the house, looking forward to the picnic. Thinking how far off it was, she let out a heavy sigh as she walked across the porch. Pausing at the door, she turned just as James disappeared over the hill.

Five

August 1860-September 1860

Andrew Jackson Patterson

Anderson County, South Carolina

Andrew Jackson Patterson was 43 years old and stood six feet tall. He had blonde-gray hair in need of a cut and a neatly trimmed blonde and gray beard that framed a tanned face full of deep squint lines, trophies from long hours in the hot sun working on his farm in Anderson County, South Carolina. Cutting a handsome figure, he rode a light brown mare leisurely across his fields in the warm August sun.

In 1844, at 27, he married his childhood sweetheart Rachel Woods, and they settled on this farm. Rachel had given birth to four children: Aaron was fifteen and almost a man, Daniel eleven, Cora nine, and Naomi was eight. Tragedy struck in the summer of 1858 when an illness claimed Rachel's life at the age of 36.

The Patterson family's roots were deep in South Carolina history, having settled here from Sweden in the early 1700s at Long Cane Settlement. They remained there until around 1800 when the Cherokee and Creek Massacres forced the Long Cane Settlement to take refuge at Fort Boone. It was not until the end of these Indian wars that the Patterson family could set their roots down at Fork Township in Anderson County, South Carolina.

It was there in May 1817 that Andrew Jackson Patterson was born. He spent his childhood working on his father's farm and gaining a fifth-grade education, which was normal for most children in the early Carolinas. As a loyal Southerner, he believed that the North and Mr. Lincoln would better serve themselves and the rest of the country by taking care of the wage slavery of the North, leaving the South to resolve its own slavery situation. He was confident that the issue would eventually be resolved, knowing that no man could be a slave to another forever. History had proven that.

As he rode through the fields in the warm August afternoon, his thoughts lingered on these and other issues. Stopping his mount, he took off his hat, holding it up to shade his eyes while looking toward the house in the distance and then back to the workers and the bean crops. Putting his hat back on, he turned his mare and rode a few yards, stopping next to his hired hand and foreman, Jed Stattler. Jed nodded and gestured toward the crops with one hand. "Should be ready by next month, Andrew."

Andrew thoughtfully nodded as he glanced across the fields. "Yah might be right, Jed, leastways, I sure do hope so."

Being a man of few words, Jed didn't say anything more while considering the crops.

Andrew turned his horse and nudged her into a trot. "I'm head'n over to check on Matthew and John."

Andrew's two slaves, Matthew and John, and their six boys were hard at work when he arrived at the north portion of his farm. Matthew was walking behind the plow and, seeing Andrew, pulled at the reins, stopping the horse, and looped them over his shoulder so they wouldn't fall to the ground. He removed his hat and wiped his sweating forehead with his shirt sleeve. "How do, Mistah Andrew?"

Andrew dismounted from his mare and looked up and down the slightly crooked furrows left from Matthew's labor. "How are things going, Matthew?"

"Pretty good, ah reckon, Mistah Andrew." Matthew took a soiled handkerchief from his hip pocket and wiped more sweat from his forehead and neck.

Andrew removed his old hat, shaded his eyes, and looked up at the late afternoon sun. "It's a hot one, Matthew. Make sure you and your boys drink plenty of water."

"Yes, suh, we all is."

Andrew climbed back up onto his horse and took a quick look around. "After thinking on it, Matthew, maybe all of us should call it a day." He looked concerned. "No point in everyone getting sunstroke. Y'all can get an early start in the morning."

"Yes suh, Mistah Andrew." Matthew said, looking pleased. "Sounds plenty good ta me. I'll goes and tell John and his boys."

Andrew turned his light brown mare toward the modest yet sturdy two-story farmhouse in the distance. It needed fresh paint, along with many other things he kept putting off until he got the time. Three bedrooms occupied the upstairs: one for the boys, one for the girls, and the master bedroom. As he rode toward the house, his oldest son Aaron was chopping firewood, his oldest daughter Cora was at the coop tossing grain for the chickens, and little Naomi was carrying a basket Andrew hoped was full of eggs toward the house.

His younger son, Daniel, ran out the back door and sat on the ground, watching his older brother chop firewood. Andrew kept his children busy with plenty of chores, believing it was important that they found the meaning of an honest day's work. For that reason, he often worked them alongside the Negro children. Andrew knew the value of a good slave, believed in educating his slaves enough to read and write a little, and disapproved of anyone mistreating their slaves. For that matter, Andrew disapproved of the mistreatment of any man, White or Negro, making him a contradiction that some in the valley had a hard time dealing with.

Simply put, slavery to Andrew was a way of life, something he had grown up with. While there were times he questioned it like a few other Southerners, it was something that had always been a part of his life. While not a highly educated man, he was smart enough to understand that all of this may one day end. Life has taught him that it is full of changes, and most things in life do change. Some things naturally take a bit longer than others. He feared that if war did come, that day of change might come sooner than most realized. And like most stubborn men, he wanted the opportunity to let change come without having it shoved down his throat by politicians in the North.

Seeing his father riding toward the house, Daniel challenged his older brother to a foot race to greet their pa and then jumped up to get a head start on his older and faster brother.

Andrew pulled up and proudly watched the boys as they raced toward him.

Being bigger and stronger, Aaron soon overtook young Daniel, who, at losing the race, called his brother a cheater.

"Daniel," Andrew said with a stern voice and expression to match. "We've had discussions about cheating and winning, or, more importantly, being a good loser, have we not?"

Daniel kicked angrily at the dirt. "Yes, sir."

Aaron took the reins of Andrew's horse to steady her as his father dismounted while scolding his younger son. "It looked to me as though Aaron won fair and square. I saw no sign of your brother cheating."

"Yes, sir, I s'pose not," replied Daniel halfheartedly.

"If you challenge someone older and bigger, son, you must expect second place. Now apologize to your brother."

Daniel looked at his brother. "Sorry."

Aaron smiled, and as their pa turned his back, he stuck his tongue out at his younger brother.

"Pa, Aaron stuck his tongue out at me," tattled Daniel.

"That's enough, boys," said Andrew with a stern voice. "Seems to me neither of you has enough to do."

The boys looked at one another, making the usual distorted faces boys make, and then Daniel stuck his tongue out at his brother and ran toward the house in search of other things to occupy himself.

Aaron turned his attention to his pa. "How're the beans doing, Pa?"

"Good. It looks like we can harvest next month, maybe even a little earlier if this heat stays with us." He put his arm around Aaron and gently squeezed. "You need to give your brother a little room once in a while, son. He's younger, and unlike yourself, he's still more a child than a man."

"Yes, sir," replied Aaron, quickly changing the subject. "It's hot all right, Pa, doesn't even cool down at night. We all were wondering if we could sleep on the back porch again tonight."

Andrew looked thoughtful while considering the request as they walked into the barn. "I guess I see no harm in it, son."

"Thanks, Pa." Then Aaron unbuckled the saddle, lifted it from the mare with a grunt, and set it on the stall railing.

Andrew picked up an old rag and began rubbing down his horse. "Don't want a lot of arguing like there was last night."

"No, sir."

"You children kept me awake half the night arguing and slamming doors and such. I need my sleep, boy. Have the pigs been slopped?"

"Yes, sir. Daniel did it."

Andrew paused to look through the open barn doors toward the house and chuckled. "And what manner of threats did that take?"

Aaron grinned. "Not many." Then he grabbed another rag to help his father wipe down the mare.

Andrew hung the rag he was using on a nail, picked up a feedbag, filled it with oats, and slipped it over the nose of his mare. "We need to take some fresh vegetables over to the Davis family. They're not having such a good year with Jacob's down sick with the bad lungs and all." He paused, looking thoughtful. "I'm sure they could use a few extra chickens as well."

"Yes, Pa," said Aaron, "I'll take care of it tomorrow."

Andrew considered that. "No, son, I'll take care of it myself. You need to be in the fields with Jed. I have to go into town anyway, so I'll stop by the Davis place on my way." After the mare was rubbed down and fed, they closed up the barn and walked to the house while Andrew wondered what Alicia had for supper.

Setting back in his chair full of food, Andrew complimented the Negro cook Alicia on a fine dinner, and as he stood, he told her to leave the dishes for his children and tend to her own family. After he escorted her out the back door, he said goodnight and watched as she walked across the yard toward the small shack she and her family lived in. Taking the pipe from his shirt pocket, Andrew shoved it into his mouth, struck a match against the porch's post, and held it over the pipe. After blowing out the match, he tossed it to the ground and stepped off the porch. Andrew walked around the corner of the house to an old wooden swing suspended by ropes from a large limb. He and his dead wife Rachel had spent many evenings together in the swing before going to bed.

The old ropes groaned as he sat down, causing him to look up. He hoped they would last another summer as he carefully settled himself on the swing, resting his head on one arm and his feet on the other. As he puffed his pipe, the memory of Rachel and her laughter drifted through his mind. He missed her humor and laugh and the silly things she would do that caused him to join in her laughter. Emptying his mind of those thoughts that made him sad, he turned his attention to his pipe and this year's crop while watching the last of the sun disappear behind the trees. *'If the prices hold,'* he thought, *'we may have a little extra money to put aside for next year.'*

The sound of the back door slamming, followed by laughter, brought a smile to his worried face, and he knew the children had finished their chores and now fought each other for precious space on the back porch. Hearing footsteps and knowing it was Daniel, he waited for the boy's childish voice.

"Pa, you gonna stay out here all night?"

"Reckon not." Andrew sat up, putting his feet on the ground. "What seems to be the problem, son?"

Daniel tugged at his arm, looking anxious. "We're all wait'n for you to read to us, Pa, so's we can get bedded down on the porch for the night."

Andrew stood from the swing. "All right, boy, let's go into the house."

The children gathered around their pa's chair by the fireplace in the living room and watched as he opened his Bible and began reading. Occasionally, he would glance at each face, recognizing their apprehension and knowing they were anxious to return to the back porch to talk or argue before it got too late. Deciding it wouldn't hurt if they skipped a few verses, he told them they could get on with what awaited them. Sounds of joy filled the room as they got up, running into one another while heading for the back door.

Andrew sat in his chair and listened to their fussing with one another about this or that. Then he stood, walked into the kitchen, and picked up a piece of firewood from the bin next to the stove. After he placed it between the door and the frame to keep the door slightly open just in case, he blew out all the lanterns save one and made his way up the stairs, leaving the children to argue the night away.

In the darkness of his room, he lay in bed looking out the window at the white dots of stars against a black sky while the mumbled voices of the children drifted up through the open window. Recognizing Naomi's quiet giggle, he smiled and thought of his wife, Rachel. This was the part of the day he dreaded most because it was filled with the memory of how they had made love and then lay nude on the bed, holding one another until sleep came.

The moon crested the hill in the distance, spreading its soft light across the dark wooden floor. He recalled how she would always curl up next to him with her head on his chest as he held her. He could still smell her hair from memory, recalling how strong her frail arms were when they made love.

In the two years since her death, Andrew occasionally considered taking a wife for company on nights such as this, but there are not many single women around the valley. There were a few widows raising their children, and he wasn't ready for that. He missed the lovemaking and the lazy comfort of the bed the next morning, but another man's family was too much to ask, even for a soft, warm body on chilly nights. He turned from the window of stars to the dark ceiling, thinking of young Rebecca Davis, his friend's daughter. Remembering that she was only eighteen and a mite young for a man in his forties, he had to admit she certainly was a beautiful thing to behold.

He shook his head, thinking, '*You're an old fool, Andrew, to think of such things.*' After all, there were more important things to consider right now, such as the crops and the possibility of a war over slavery. His mind grew tired of thinking of his loneliness and politics, and suddenly, he realized the children seemed unusually quiet. That was not like them. As he turned toward the door, he raised his head from the pillow and listened, hearing their soft, muffled voices. As he laid his head back on the pillow, his eyes grew heavy with sleep, and his mind gave up Rachel and the day.

Andrew opened his eyes from a sound sleep and sat up, resting on his elbows, listening in the stillness for sounds coming from the children. Hearing nothing but silence, he glanced around the dark room, then at the empty pillow next to his, and wished Rachel was still alive. Lying back down, he turned to the window and thought about the crops, the Davis family, and his trip to town. The black sky outside his window turned to a light blue at the horizon, warning of the sun coming up.

Tossing the covers back, he sat up, placing his warm feet against the cold wood floor, and looked out the window into the early morning while Matthew's dogs barked somewhere in the yard. Reaching for his pants draped over the end of the bed, he put them on, and as he buttoned them, he watched the sun creep over the hill, casting its warm glow across the valley. A rooster crowed in the quiet morning, and he imagined it sitting proudly atop the hen house.

After putting on his shirt, he walked to the window and looked down at the two shacks his slaves lived in, wondering what went through their minds about the arguments up north. He was sure they knew about the coming elections, and as he pulled his suspenders over his shoulders, he noticed Matthew sitting in the morning sun by his front door while one of his dogs ran up to him with a stick in his mouth. Matthew took the stick and threw it across the yard, watching while both dogs gave chase. Andrew knew Alicia, Matthew's woman, was inside preparing her family's breakfast before coming to the main house.

Returning to the bed, he sat on its edge and put on his socks, then his boots. Standing, he walked to the basin of cold water on the small table by the window. As he reached for the soap and razor, the back door slammed, followed by running footsteps and laughter. The children were up.

After shaving, he wiped his face with the towel and looked at his dim reflection in the mirror. He turned his face, first to the left, then to the right, as he stuck out his tongue, having no idea what he was looking for. Turning from the mirror, he picked up his old hat and walked out of the bedroom, greeted by the smell of bacon and eggs rushing up the stairs, teasing his appetite.

Looking flustered, Alicia stood over the hot stove, shouting at the children to settle down. Ignoring her, they giggled as they chased one another around the table.

"SIT," ordered Andrew loudly.

The girls stopped and quickly took their places at the large oak table while Andrew apologized to Alicia for his children's bad behavior and lack of manners. Sitting down at the head of the table, he stared at the two girls squirming as they tried not to giggle. Noticing Daniel had fallen asleep on his plate, Andrew touched the boy's arm. "Daniel, sit up, son. This is a table, not a bed. What would your mother think?"

Daniel yawned as he sat up with sleepy eyes. "Yes, sir."

Aaron walked through the back door with his arms full of firewood that he carefully dumped into the wood crib next to the stove.

Andrew poured himself a cup of hot coffee while Alicia placed a platter of eggs on the table next to the plate of bacon and biscuits.

Meanwhile, the girls talked about the night on the porch and seeing ghosts and little fairies.

"There is no such thing as ghosts, children, y'all know that," said Andrew sternly. "Let us pray." After making sure the children bowed their heads and closed their eyes, he said the morning prayer.

Andrew gathered some fresh corn, string beans, and other vegetables in a basket and placed it in the back of the wagon with a crate of two live chickens clucking at one another. Climbing into the wagon seat, he took the reins and gently nudged the horses into a walk, thinking it would be another warm one. Turning the wagon toward the road, Andrew glanced at the fields, saw Aaron sitting atop his horse, talking with Jed, and felt proud of the boy. Hearing the door of the house slam, he turned.

Daniel came running after him. "Can I come along, Pa? Please."

Andrew looked down at his young son running beside the wagon and smiled, thinking he was a pitiful sight. He stopped the wagon, reached down with one hand, and helped Daniel up into the wagon seat.

"Where we going, Pa?"

"To the Davis farm first," Andrew said. "Then on to town."

"Why we stopping at the Davis farm?"

Andrew gestured with a nod toward the back of the wagon. "We need to drop these chickens and fresh vegetables off for the Davises."

Daniel glanced into the back of the wagon. "Don't they have any?"

"Yes, son," replied Andrew. "I'm sure they do, but sometimes it's neighborly to stop by and offer such things to your friends."

Daniel looked troubled. "Why?"

Navigating a turn at the fork in the road toward the Davis farm, Andrew hoped for silence, trying to control his temper, thinking it would be a long ride, and wondered if bringing the boy may have been a mistake. Then, feeling bad for getting angry, he smiled at the boy. "Well, son, Jacob Davis has been pretty sick with the bad lung disease, and I need to see how the family is getting on and if they need any help."

"What kind of help, Pa?" asked a curious Daniel.

Andrew frowned. "Do you have to ask so many questions, boy?"

"Sorry, Pa."

Andrew looked at his son, feeling sorry for his temper. "Sorry, son, I forget how curious a young boy can be." He placed one arm around the boy, giving him a quick hug. "Guess it's been a long time since I was your age and curious about what goes on around me."

Daniel smiled as he sat back in the wagon seat, deciding to be quiet and enjoy the ride.

Andrew guided the team from the road into the driveway of the Davis farm, and as he drove toward the two-story house, a woman he knew was Rebecca stepped out onto the porch, shielding the sun from her eyes with one hand. She waved with what appeared to be a towel, disappeared into the house, and reappeared moments later, minus the towel and apron she had been wearing. She walked down the three steps into the yard and waited.

Rebecca Jane Davis, Jacob's and Mattie's daughter, smiled as she waited at the bottom step. Rebecca stood five feet two, was slender with dark brown eyes and little wrinkles she called crow's feet when she smiled. A scattering of freckles had made friends long ago with her straight nose, and her full lips curled when she smiled, exposing small dimples at the sides of her mouth. Though her skin was fair and white, her arms and face were tan. As she stood waiting, the wind gently played with the long brown hair that hung to her waist.

Andrew stopped the wagon a few feet from the porch and tipped his hat, "Howdy Rebecca."

She smiled, looking friendly. "Hello, Andrew." Then she looked at Daniel. "Hello there, Daniel."

The boy smiled and pointed to the rear of the wagon. "We brung y'all some chickens and vegetables," he explained. Then he thoughtlessly added, "Pa said ya might need 'em."

Looking embarrassed, Andrew considered tossing his son from the wagon seat but managed a small, embarrassing smile instead. "The innocence of children."

She smiled at his dilemma.

"We were on our way to town anyway," said Andrew. "A family can always use a couple of chickens and some fresh vegetables."

Daniel proudly blurted out. "Pa said it would be neighborly."

Andrew gently kicked the boy's foot.

"Ouch, Pa, ya kicked me."

Rebecca smiled and started to ask them to come in when Mattie Davis, her mother, stepped onto the porch, gesturing with one arm. "Y'all come on in here. I just made a fresh peach pie that's been cooling in the window."

Beating Daniel to the punch, Andrew said, "Hello Mattie! Brought y'all some chickens and fresh vegetables." Then he climbed down from the wagon.

Mattie thanked him, stuck her head inside the door, and yelled for her son Robert to help with the chickens and vegetables. Mrs. Mattie

Davis was in her late fifties, a small woman, much like her daughter Rebecca. Her hair was brown mixed with gray and done up in a braid she wore in a circle atop her head, leaving tiny strands of loose hair dangling around her oval face. The apron she wore bore the evidence of her battles in the kitchen, and the sweet smell of hot peach pie cooling on the windowsill and freshly brewed coffee raced across the yard.

Daniel jumped down and ran past Andrew and Rebecca, up the porch steps, and into the house while Mrs. Davis followed him inside. Andrew started to scold Daniel, but he was thankful the boy was out of his hair for the moment. He smiled at Rebecca. "How's your pa?"

She looked concerned. "Not much better. Pa's been feeling poorly the past few days, gets better for a time, then feels poorly again. I'll sure be glad when all this is over and Pa's himself again." She managed a small smile.

"What's the Doc have to say?"

She shrugged. "Not much." They walked up the steps to the rear porch of the house, where she paused at the door. "All we can do is keep him in bed for rest and feed him lots of broth." She noticed the crate of chickens her brother was taking out of the wagon as she stepped inside the house. "Them additional chickens will come in mighty handy, Andrew. Thank you."

Andrew followed her into the house finding Mrs. Davis in the kitchen busy over a big pie.

She looked past Rebecca at Andrew, "Piece of pie, Andrew?"

He could smell the freshly baked pie, thinking it smelled delightful. "No thanks, Mattie, I'll just go up and visit with Jacob. I'm sure Daniel there would love a big slice."

Mattie smiled at Daniel. "How about a piece of pie, young man?"

Filled with anticipation, Daniel thought about the pies his mother used to bake. "Yessum."

Andrew put one hand on his son's shoulder. "Don't make a nuisance of yourself, son." Then, as he followed Rebecca up the stairs to her pa's room, he caught a whiff of the sweet fragrance she wore mixed with kitchen odors of soap and cooking. Noticing how snug her blue cotton dress fit as she walked up the stairs, he felt embarrassed and looked down at the steps, reminding himself she was his friend's daughter. Coughing from the room upstairs interrupted his thoughts of Rebecca, and as they reached the top of the stairs, he saw Jacob sitting up, resting his head against the headboard and pillows.

Jacob turned toward the door and smiled. "Look what the Devil done brung into my room."

Andrew smiled. “Morn’n, Jacob!”

Jacob coughed, then managed a smile as he pointed to a chair. “Bring that chair over here, so’s we can talk.” Then he coughed several times.

As Rebecca left the room, Andrew moved the chair next to the bed and settled onto it, looking at his old friend. Jacob was almost sixty, stood six feet tall, and weighed around 220 pounds with thinning gray. Even sickly, his blue eyes held warmth and friendliness. After several coughs, Jacob looked at Andrew. “How’s things at your place?”

“Things are pretty good. The beans seem to be coming in without no diseases, and if the prices hold, it should be a good year. And we’re start’n to plow the west fields for winter wheat.” Andrew gestured toward the north with a nod. “Providing the politicians up north don’t spoil it.”

Jacob’s grin was interrupted by several coughs. “Not too much to worry about yet. Leastways not until after the elections.”

Andrew sat helplessly in his chair, watching Jacob cough hard several times, struggling to breathe between coughs.

Jacob caught his breath and smiled. “And by then, your crops will have been sold and shipped.”

Nodding in agreement, Andrew stood. “Me and the boy best be get’n on to town Jacob. I’ve some business to take care of.” He slid the chair back to where it had been and looked at Jacob while trying to hide his concerns over his friend. “Just wanted to stop by and see how you was getting along.”

Jacob smiled. “Appreciate that, Andrew, I surely do.”

“How are your crops doing?”

Jacob coughed several times. “We’re get’n on all right, I guess. My three older boys are taking good care of the place.” He looked pleased. “I’m mighty proud of `em right now.” His expression suddenly changed. “Had two slaves run off a couple of days ago.”

“I didn’t know. Are you sure you can still get enough help to get yer crops in?”

“Oh, I’m sure we can manage. May have to rent a few slaves from Williams Slave Trade in town, but we’ll manage.”

Andrew reached down and squeezed Jacob's forearm. “Take care, old friend, and mind what the doctor says.”

Jacob nodded as he covered his mouth and coughed several more times.

Andrew turned and walked to the bedroom door, stopped, and turned. “If you have any trouble get’n help, don’t be too proud to send one of your boys to fetch me and mine.”

Jacob nodded. "I hear ya, Andrew." He coughed again several times. "If it comes to that, I'll send one of thc boys over."

"Be sure ya do just that." Then Andrew walked out of the room.

Downstairs, Andrew gathered his son, making sure the boy thanked Mattie for the pie, said goodbye to her, and followed Rebecca out the door and down the porch steps to his waiting wagon. He helped his son into the wagon seat, then climbed up and settled onto the folded blanket he kept on the hard seat. Taking the reins, he looked down at her. "Good day to you, Rebecca."

Shading her eyes from the sun, she said, "Drop by anytime, Andrew." Then she smiled, "I'm almost always here."

Pleased at her warm invitation, he swatted the team with the reins, and as the wagon lurched forward, he thought of how her cotton dress clung to her hips and the smell of perfume as he followed her up the stairs. When they reached the road, he turned, glanced over his shoulder, and wondered if she was just being friendly or asking him to come court'n. Turning to the road, his mind filled with the mystery of Rebecca Davis.

Aware of the distance they had traveled in silence, he glanced down at his son, who was staring along the road deep in thought. While he enjoyed the quiet of the trip, he realized that where Daniel was concerned, it just wasn't natural. "Something troubling ya, boy?"

"No, sir."

"I don't recall you ever being so quiet for so long. You feeling all right, boy?"

Daniel turned and looked up at him with a puzzled expression. "Do you like Rebecca?"

The question almost knocked Andrew out of the wagon. Pulling at the reins, he stopped the wagon in the middle of the road, set the brake with his left foot, and looked at his son. "Why on earth are you asking about Rebecca Davis, boy?"

Daniel frowned as he shrugged. "Don't know, Pa. Guess it's cause she's so pretty, and y'all seem so friendly."

"Son," Andrew softly said. "I'll soon be forty-four years old, and Rebecca Davis is just but eighteen or nineteen." Andrew suddenly felt silly talking to Daniel about this. "Hell boy, I've known her much of her life, ever since she was a small girl, younger'n you even." He shook his head, looked away for a moment, and then back at Daniel. "So, I guess we are friendly toward one another, but that doesn't mean nuth'n; we're just friends."

"All right, Pa."

"You understand, son?"

Daniel nodded. "Yes, Sir."

Andrew slapped the reins on the backs of the horses. "Get up there." The wagon lurched forward again, continuing its journey toward town, and in the stillness that followed, Andrew wondered if others might be thinking the same thing. *'Probably natural,'* he thought for his own self-reassurance. He glanced down at his son and then looked along the empty road up ahead. *'It's probably only natural for others to think things with me being a widower and her a single adult female. Probably a natural thing for folks to wonder.'*

But as he drove the wagon toward town, Andrew had to admit that he felt a definite attraction toward Rebecca Davis and quickly felt a little embarrassed. *'It's not as if she were a child,'* he told himself. *'After all, she's of marrying age, has been for some time now, and quite good-looking.'* His thoughts returned to her standing in the yard in her light blue cotton dress, waving goodbye, with her brown hair blowing in the breeze. Once again, his memory returned to the smell of soap mixed with perfume as he followed her slender body up the stairs to Jacob's room and suddenly, Rachel raced into his mind, and he was overcome with guilt.

The small town of Fork Township was busy with wagons, riders, and people making their way across the deeply rutted main street as Andrew guided the wagon to a stop in front of Bender's General Store. Andrew glanced around town and set the break while Daniel jumped down. Climbing down, Andrew put his arm around his son as they walked across the boardwalk into the store. Inside, Andrew told Daniel to pick out a piece of hard candy for himself and one each for the other children.

Daniel grinned with excitement as he hurried toward the glass cabinet of colorful treasures while Andrew went about the business of supplies. Daniel stood thoughtfully in front of the glass case, staring at the different kinds of candy, unable to make up his mind. Not far away, several men talked as they sat around a cracker barrel in front of a cold potbellied stove.

"Why the hell can't them northern bastard politicians just stay the hell out of our business?" one man asked.

Hearing the words hell and bastard spoken, Daniel's eyes grew large as he turned toward the men just as a bearded, short, heavyset man nodded in agreement. "Cuz they's nosey old men, that's why."

"That they are Jeb," chuckled another man. "Why, you don't see us going up there telling them bastards how to do things."

Daniel quickly turned back to the case, thinking that he should go find his pa, but the candy was just too tempting, so he carefully considered the candy while listening to the men behind him.

"No, we don't," said another man. "And if'n we did, they'd run us out of town."

Daniel turned to look just as one of the men spit, hitting the top of a spittoon next to his chair.

Tobacco still wet on the man's chin, he thoughtfully wiped it off and looked over at Daniel.

Embarrassed, Daniel turned to the glass case, wondering where his pa was.

"I agree with secession," said another, "if this Lincoln fellas elected President."

"That may mean war," replied another.

"So be it."

Not completely understanding what the men were talking about, Daniel returned his attention to the case and the candy that was of greater importance. His eyes roamed the clear china dishes overflowing with candy, thinking there were so many to choose from. Startled by a hand on his shoulder, he looked up into his father's smiling face.

Andrew knelt next to his son and looked through the glass. "Made up your mind yet, son?"

"Yes, sir." Daniel glanced at the men and then looked up at his pa. "I think the rock candy because it lasts longer."

"That'd be my choice." Andrew stood and looked at the store owner as he pointed at the candy. "Give us five of the rock candy there." Then, considering the six Negro children, he changed the number. "Better make that eleven, Charles."

Andrew climbed into the wagon and guided the team along the ruts of the main street, causing the wagon to bounce and sway gently. Silence rode with them as he guided the team toward the county road while both father and son were deep in their own thoughts. Andrew had thoughts of Rebecca and getting home in time for dinner.

Daniel watched the sun drift closer to the western horizon, thinking of the men at the store and the things they had said. He watched the silent battle between the day and the night as he held the bag of candy tightly in one hand. Leaning against his father, he wondered if they would ever get home. "Pa?"

"Yes, son?"

"What does suc, succession mean?"

"You mean secession?"

"Yes, Sir."

"Where'd you hear a big word such as that?" Andrew asked, looking puzzled.

Daniel watched two crows chase a hawk above a nearby field, interrupting its search for a late evening snack. "From them, men back at the store."

Andrew cleared his throat, considering the word. "What men?"

"The men sitting around the stove talking."

"Well, son," he said thoughtfully. "That's a word used by men who want the South to break away from the northern states and make their own country, with its own laws, government, and President."

"Would that be a good thing?" Daniel asked, looking a little troubled.

"Don't rightly know for sure, son. Guess I'll have to leave that up to the politicians."

Daniel looked up at his Pa. "One man said if we do, it'd mean war."

Andrew looked down at his son, thinking it was a heavy thing for a young boy to ponder. "Maybe, maybe not."

Silence held them for several moments, and then Daniel asked, "Pa?"

"Hmm?"

"Would you have to go away to war?"

"Don't rightly know, son," Andrew said, looking thoughtful. "It's possible, I guess."

Silence descended on the wagon once again, and feeling tired, Daniel curled his legs onto the wagon seat and placed his head on his father's lap. Still holding the bag of candy tightly, he closed his eyes and fell asleep.

The sun was low in the sky, and evening shadows of trees cut dark canyons across the county road and driveway of the Davis farm. Andrew looked beyond the trees and berry bushes that ran along the road, seeing the yard was empty, and the only movement was from the clothes hanging on the line that moved in the soft evening breeze. Disappointed at not seeing Rebecca, he looked at the road ahead and then down at his sleeping son. He gently stroked his son's blonde hair and thought how much it resembled the lock of Rachel's hair he kept in her favorite book of poetry next to his bed.

A few minutes later, the wagon bounced up and down as it crossed the ruts in the county road near and onto the road near their farm. Waking, Daniel sat up, feeling a little disoriented, but then he recognized the road that would take them home and to dinner. "I'm hungry," he said with a sigh.

Andrew smiled. "Me too, son." He turned onto his farm and drove toward the barn, promising they would eat as soon as they unloaded the wagon. After dinner, Andrew told Daniel to get the surprise they had brought back from town and then watched as Daniel sat on the kitchen floor, opening the brown paper bag. Slowly, almost teasingly, Daniel retrieved one piece of candy from the bag, giving it to Naomi, then a second piece to Cora. A third piece went to Aaron and a fourth to his pa while he took the fifth. Andrew placed his candy in his pocket for later in the swing. For now, he enjoyed the smiles on his children's faces. "Don't forget to take some out to the Negro children."

"No, sir," he said. "Should I go now?"

Andrew chuckled. "That might be a good idea while there's still some left!"

The boy jumped up with a grin, dashed across the kitchen, and ran outside, letting the back door slam. As he ran toward the two small houses, Andrew could hear him yelling the names of the Negro children.

Sleep eluded Rebecca Davis as she tossed and turned in bed, feeling that she would suffocate in the hot August night air. She tossed the covers back, sat on the edge of her bed, and looked out the window into the black night, barely making out the barn and other outbuildings. A slight breeze filled the open window, playing with the curtains. Knowing it would be cooler outside, she decided to take a walk and quietly made her way down the stairs and out the back door.

Stepping off the porch, she paused to feel the cool dirt beneath her bare feet. Her thin, pale-white nightgown moved slightly with the breeze clinging to her body and between her legs while she walked across the yard to the oak tree. Reaching the tree and the two-seat swing dangling silently from a large limb high above, she sat down. While holding onto the ropes, she leaned back, looked up through the leaves and limbs of the tree at the twinkling stars, and thought about Andrew's visit that morning. She wished he had stayed longer, but he had been in a hurry. *'After all,'* she thought, *'he's been a widower for almost two years. Too long for such a man.'*

Rebecca had secretly been in love with Andrew since her fifteenth birthday. Boys her age or slightly older competed for her attention, but they were only boys, full of boys' deeds and dreams, and she had never given them much consideration. On the other hand, Andrew was a man, mature in his years, and quite handsome. She pushed the swing backward with her feet, then settled back for the slow, easy ride as the cool breeze ruffled her nightgown past her knees. Listening to the groaning of the limb above her, she considered her mother, knowing she would say she was silly and filled with a young girl's foolishness for an older man.

But Rebecca knew she was no longer a young girl, and at eighteen, soon to be nineteen, she knew she was much more a woman than a girl. Her body and desires told her that much. As she floated back and forth in the swing, listening to the quiet creaking of the limb above her, she thought of the soft bed that awaited her upstairs and suddenly felt tired. She let the swing slow until she could stop it, get out, and walk across the yard, up the porch steps, into the house and bed. As she again lay in bed, Andrew Patterson was the last thing on her mind when sleep found her.

August soon turned to September, and fearing all the talk about the elections and possible secession of the South would bring prices down, Andrew was anxious to get his crops to market while the prices held. Wanting to beat that possibility, he rented several slaves from Williams Slave Trade.

But the prices held, and he had made his goal of putting a little extra money away for next year. It wasn't much, but it was something he took pride in. Sitting at the dinner table, he watched the children talk and laugh at silly things, and he wished Rachel were here to share this proud moment. His thoughts were interrupted by Alicia pouring more coffee into his cup. He looked up, smiled, and thanked her. "You go on and take care of your family, Alicia. Me and the children will take care of cleaning up."

"Thanks, ya kindly, Mistah Andrew," replied Alicia. She set the big coffee pot on the stove and hurried out the door.

The kitchen cleaned, the dishes put away, Andrew went outside and sat in the swing, going over the past several days in his mind. He thought of the children, the talk of war, Rachel, and, with a certain amount of guilt, Rebecca Davis.

Feeling a chill from the cool September evening air, a sure sign that fall and winter were close, he got up from the swing and walked beyond the garden to a small grove of trees and Rachel's resting place. He came here often to sit on an old chair he kept close to her grave so he could talk to her. He often told her stories about their children, things he wanted or needed to do around the farm, and any gossip he had heard. Tonight was no different. He talked about his fears and worries about the war and other things. He touched her grave marker, telling her how much he missed her and how lonely his life has been without her. The cool night air rustled the leaves above him, and as he looked up, he smiled, wondering if it was a whisper from Rachel telling him she understood his loneliness.

His visit over, he got up, placed the chair back in its spot next to the marker, and walked back to the swing where he lay down and stared up at the stars, wondering if she was looking down on them. A star shot across the dark sky and then disappeared. *'Someone's lost their Soul,'* he thought while remembering the story his father had told of men who died in sin and doomed to race through the night sky in search of their lost souls for all eternity. He sat up, thinking it was getting late, stood and walked into the house, up the stairs, and fell into bed. As he lay in the darkness of his room, his thoughts turned to the Davis family, and decided that he, his sons, and three of the Negro boys would spend two or three days helping Jacob.

Six

November 1860 - November 1861

Alex McAlexander and War's Reality

On November 6, 1860, Abraham Lincoln received 40 percent of the popular vote and 180 of the 303 electoral votes necessary to win the presidential election, defeating John Cabell Breckinridge. That defeat ended the hope for a peaceful solution to the slavery issue still being hotly debated in Washington and across the rest of the land. Many of the southern states were promising to make good their secession threats, and in response to those threats, President Lincoln argued that a government could not endure with its citizens half slave and half free.

A special convention was held in South Carolina on December 20, 1860, where those in attendance unanimously passed an ordinance of secession by South Carolina. The states of Georgia, Louisiana, Florida, Alabama, and Mississippi followed in January 1861, with Texas following on February 2, 1861. On February 9, 1861, those eight states elected Jefferson Davis, a West Point graduate and former U.S. Army Officer, as President of the Confederacy.

By the end of June 1861, Virginia, North Carolina, Arkansas, and Tennessee had joined the Confederate States, bringing the total number to eleven. One of the first duties of the newly formed government was to create an army of the Confederate States by immediately enlisting and training men sworn to defend this newly formed republic.

One of the first acts of President Lincoln was sending provisions to Fort Sumter in the harbor of Charleston, S.C. Upset by this move, the Confederacy sent an army under the command of General Pierre Beauregard to Fort. Sumter. At 4:30 AM on the 14th of April, 1861, he ordered his cannon to open fire. The Northern Army was bombarded into submission by the afternoon, and the Confederate Army proudly raised their new flag, the Rebel Stars and Bars.

The following day, President Lincoln issued a Proclamation calling for 75,000 militiamen and summoned a special session of Congress. During this session, General Robert E. Lee was offered command of the Union Army, which he declined to accept. Resigning his commission in the United States Army, he sadly said, "I cannot raise my hand against my birthplace, my home, my children." Lee left Washington for Richmond, where he accepted command of the military and naval forces of Virginia.

As the war planning continued in Washington, President Lincoln issued a Proclamation of Blockade against Southern ports on April 19, 1861. Since the rural South was dependent on receiving all its goods from seaports along the coast, Lincoln believed this action would cripple the South's economy and, thus, its ability to wage war.

Lauderdale County – April 1861

The McAlexander family

On the evening of April 20, 1861, Edward McAlexander was in his library, sitting comfortably in a chair by the fire, reading the Lauderdale Newspaper about the war. The thunder and steady rain beating against the windowpanes muffled the sound of the brass knocker on the front door. Edward did not hear the library door open or notice the Negro slave Sophie as she entered the room and stood next to his chair. "Mistah Edward, your brother Mistah Alex is wait'n ta see ya in the parlor."

Edward looked up with a curious expression. "Thank you, Sophie. Please show Alex in here." He folded the newspaper, placed it on his lap, and watched the flames in the fireplace while contemplating the war and the South's future.

Moments later, Alex walked into the library. "I hope this is not an inconvenient time." He paused at the liquor table. May I?"

"Why not?" smiled Edward, then jokingly said, "You usually do." He put the folded newspaper on the table next to his chair. "Pour me one while you're at it. God knows that after reading the newspaper, I could use a drink." He turned from the flames to watch Alex pour their drinks. "What brings you out on such a dreadful night?"

Alex didn't answer while he poured two glasses of brandy, and after handing one to his brother, he raised his glass in a toast, "To the Confederacy."

Edward raised his glass and started to take a drink, hesitated, and looked at Alex. "My God," he said, looking worried. "Don't tell me you've enlisted?"

Alex grinned proudly, looking enthusiastic. "I'm afraid I have."

Edward stood with a disapproving stare. "Have you lost your senses, Alex? This war will be over in a few months, one way or the other. Why in the hell would you put yourself at such risk?"

Disappointed by his brother's reaction, Alex walked to the fireplace, placed one hand on the mantle, and stared into the fire. "Because it will be over in a few short months is precisely why I enlisted." Alex looked at his brother, then returned his gaze to the fire, shrugged, and softly said, "Not that you'd understand, Ed, but I want to be part of this thing before it becomes history."

Edward did understand, as he had also considered joining, but current obligations prevented that, and at the moment, he was a little jealous of his younger brother. He sighed, walked to the fireplace, and stood beside Alex. Both stared into the flames in silence while Edward sipped his brandy thoughtfully. "What about Ella, your practice, and the farm?"

Alex turned away and sat in a nearby chair and rested his head against the back of the chair, holding his half-empty glass in one hand on his thigh. "The war won't last long. You just said as much. Ella and the kids can manage for a few short months."

Edward took a drink of brandy. "I'm in no position to take care of the farm, Alex. I've too many obligations of my own."

Alex looked at the back of his brother as he stood at the fireplace, staring into the flames that seemed to dance to the music of the rain and thunder outside. He sipped from his glass of brandy, hoping to avoid an argument, and then thought of how excited and enthusiastic he had been about going when he arrived. Now, Edward had robbed him of that, and it angered him. Wishing he'd never come, he took another sip of brandy.

Edward, on the other hand, was looking for an argument. "There's too much going on here, Alex," he said angrily. "I can't take care of my practice, your family, and the farm. Not yet, anyway."

"I don't ask or expect you to, and I didn't come here for that." He looked at Edward. "I came here to share this moment with my brother." He stood, looking angry. "I didn't come here to ask you to do anything, Ed, except understand and accept my decision." He paused and lowered his voice, looking apologetic. "Just as I would if this was your decision."

Edward sighed, finished his drink, and walked to the liquor cabinet. "Looking for that damn piece of glory we talked about as kids?" He picked up the bottle of brandy and began pouring a small amount into his glass. Holding up the bottle, he asked, "Another?"

"No, thank you!"

The room fell quiet as Edward gulped down his brandy, poured another half glass, and took a small, thoughtful sip. Placing the bottle on the table, he looked across the room at his brother sitting on the sofa, staring at the flames of the fire. Edward thought he looked defeated, raised his brow, shook his head, and smiled affectionately. "Alex, you're a dumb shit." Then he walked toward him. "This war is not going to be like the wars we played as children. Men will die, perhaps even you."

"I am aware of that."

A white flash of light burst through the windows, followed by a loud crash of thunder. The dark rain beat against the windows and veranda doors.

Edward glanced at the doors, waiting for the wind to blow them open, turned, walked to the sofa where Alex was sitting, and placed a hand on his brother's shoulder. "You're my only brother. When our mother died, and Uncle Edward took me away while you and Mary were sent to live with our grandmother, I missed the hell out of you."

Alex stared into the flickering flames, recalling those days.

"Now," Edward said softly. "Well… now… we have a different life. We see each other often. We make plans and share our dreams of a better life for our children and ourselves. I've come to know you."

The room fell silent again as the sound of far-off thunder and rain beating against the windows and doors roamed across the room.

Alex stood and looked at Edward, his expression troubled, his voice soft. "This is something I have to do."

Lighting flashed, followed by thunder rolling across the room, drowning out the blowing wind and rain that pelted against the windows. Edward once again turned to the doors of the veranda, expecting them to fly open, but the rain suddenly softened, gently playing its music against the glass. He nodded with an understanding expression. "I know." He half-smiled. "Just be careful and try not to get that big ugly ass shot."

Alex chuckled, looking relieved. "You've always had a way with words, but I intend on keeping my ugly ass out of sight."

Edward smiled. "What about the farm and Ella?"

Alex shrugged, looking confident. "Everything's arranged. Ella's sister will move in with her, so she won't be alone, and I've made arrangements with our foreman to handle things for a few months until I return. He knows to contact you if something unexpected should come up."

Edward reflected for a moment. Then he looked at his brother. "It sounds as though you've given this a great deal of thought."

"I have."

"I'll look in on Ella and the children from time to time."

"I know you will." Alex looked grateful as he grinned. "I counted on that."

Edward grinned affectionately. "You're such an asshole."

Alex chuckled. "Tell me something I don't already know!"

Edward put his arm around his brother's shoulder. "When do you leave?"

"In the morning. It seems they're in a bit of a hurry to build this new Confederate Army."

"In the morning?" repeated Edward softly, looking slightly puzzled. "Do you know where you're going?"

Alex shrugged. "Not yet."

Edward looked at him with a worried expression. "I hope you didn't join the Cavalry. That big ass would make too good a target atop a horse."

Alex laughed. "No. I joined the Infantry. That way, I can hide my big ass behind a tree when the shooting starts." He paused, looking solemn. "No matter what you think of me at this moment, I'm not an idiot."

Edward chuckled and shook his head. "That's a matter of opinion, little brother." He started to sip his brandy and, finding the glass empty, walked toward the liquor cabinet. "By the way, are you aware that our esteemed Uncle Edward O'Neal has joined the army and is with the 9th Alabama, holding the rank of Major?"

Alex looked surprised. "Isn't he a little old?"

"I would think so," chuckled Edward, but then he paused in thought. "Well, he is a leader, and that's what the Confederacy needs right now." Edward shook his head, sipped his drink, and sat on the small sofa before the fireplace, looking thoughtful. "Seems as though everyone is joining this fight but me."

Alex sat next to his brother, and together, they watched the flames of the fire leap above the wood and embers in silence. After several minutes passed, Alex spoke softly. "Edward, if it were not for little Mary, you would be riding off this very night in the damn rain."

Edward considered that and smiled wryly. "Maybe. But I can't, and perhaps I'm a little envious of you right now." He held his glass in a toast. "To Glory, may you have your share and mine."

The two drank and talked late into the night until it was time for Alex to leave. They shook hands hugged, and Edward watched Alex climb into his carriage. As it drove slowly from under the overhang, Edward stood at the door. He watched his brother disappear into the dark, rainy night, contemplating his brother's decision while praying he would safely return to his home and family.

The 4th Alabama and Alex McAlexander

In May 1861, Private Alex McAlexander was assigned to Company H of the 4th Alabama Infantry, serving with the Judge Advocate in Georgia. Three weeks passed while the army prepared for their march into Virginia to join other units and form one of the state's largest armies.

Having received their marching orders, Alex quickly wrote letters to his wife Ella and Edward, posting them before the army left.

The march to Virginia was without incident, and once there, the 4th Alabama proceeded to Harper's Ferry for further training and then on to Winchester. Within days, the brigade marched east from Winchester to Manassas, Virginia, arriving the second week of July 1861. The 4th Alabama and other infantry units set up camp, forming an army of several thousand men a mere sixty miles southwest of Washington, D.C.

Afraid the army would march on Washington, the Federal Army sent Union Brigadier General McDowell and a force of 29,000 men to Manassas on the 16th of July.

The Battle of Bull Run at Manassas

On the morning of July 21, 1861, the Union Army moved against the Confederates in an effort to cripple the newly assembled army at a place called Bull Run, near the city of Manassas. Union General McDowell and his Federals crossed the river at Sudley Ford, attacking the Confederate Army's left flank, the position held by the 4th Alabama.

Confederate Brigadier General Bernard E. Bee, realizing that the army's left flank was exposed, ordered the 4th Alabama to advance and plug the gap in the Confederate Army lines. After the 4th had moved into place, Alex took up his position on the firing line and awaited the advancing Union Army. He didn't have long to wait, and soon, the two forces engaged in heavy fighting for over an hour, with the 4th Alabama holding its position and repulsing several Union attacks.

This action gave the Confederate forces time to regroup for a crucial counterattack that turned out to be fierce and bloody. Hiding behind a fallen log with a small group of men, Alex fired and reloaded his musket rifle, never sure if any of his shots found a Federal soldier. He smiled briefly, thinking Edward would be proud of how he hid his big, ugly ass when he heard a thud. Turning, he saw the man on his left lying on the ground with blood pouring from a tiny head wound on the right side of his forehead.

Alex stared at the man who jerked and twisted while blood pumped from the wound. Then the man stopped moving, and never having seen a man die, Alex felt sick to his stomach. Fighting the urge to vomit, he turned away and aimed his rifle at a figure in the distance while rifle balls hit the stump he was hiding behind.

The Confederates had advanced several yards, only to be driven back under heavy fire where they hid behind trees, rocks, and old logs, taking cover against the barrage of Federal musket balls. The smell and sound of musket fire filled the air, mixing with the words of anger and agonizing screams of the wounded. Officers barked orders to keep firing, paying little heed to the dead or screams of pain from the wounded.

Alex fired his rifle, reached into the pouch attached to his belt, took out a paper cartridge containing a round bullet and premeasured powder, and shoved it down the muzzle. Using the ramrod, he shoved the cartridge down the barrel, cocked the hammer of the rifle, aimed, and fired, trying not to listen to the screams and cries of those wounded and in pain around him. He reloaded and raised his rifle to fire but paused as several of his comrades walked past, stepping over the dead and wounded while attacking the Federal positions. Almost hypnotized by the terror around him, Alex watched as some of the wounded tried to stand and advance, only to fall again. Others lay on the ground, their bodies contorted as they moaned or cried for help, while others lay still and silent. The smoky air was full of the smell of gunpowder, blood, and death mixed with the stench of body fluids that escaped from the dead. He saw a Federal soldier advancing toward him from the corner of his eye, so he turned and fired. The man's body jerked back from the impact of the rifle ball, and as Alex watched him fall, he thought, '*What madness.*'

The battlefield was filled with hysteria and insanity as Alex closed his eyes for only a moment, wishing he were at home. Then, looking up, he saw a Confederate officer mounted on a black horse in no man's land between the two armies. He was yelling and waving one arm, encouraging the men while urging them onward into the smoked-filled firestorm of musket balls. Alex reloaded and fired, then crouched behind the log, reloaded, and hurried a shot at a group of Union soldiers. As several fell, he could not tell if it was his or someone else's shot that claimed one of the victims. Tears of fear filled his eyes, blurring the barrel of his musket as Alex shoved another paper cartridge into the muzzle. Wiping the water from his eyes, he looked at the Confederate Officer on horseback, motioning the soldiers in gray onward. Suddenly, the horse reared up and tumbled onto its rider. Crouched behind the log, Alex watched the wounded animal as it tried to get up while the officer pushed against the saddle with one leg, trying to free his other leg. Alex could hear the horse screaming above men's yelling mixed with musket fire volleys.

Everything seemed to be in slow motion as the Federal troops advanced toward the fallen officer, who continued to fire his pistol while pinned beneath his injured horse. Out of nowhere, a group of Confederate soldiers dressed in gray gathered around the fallen officer and his horse, firing at the advancing Federal troops. After driving the

Federals back into a wooded area, the Confederate soldiers managed to free the officer's leg from under the wounded horse and, under fire, drag him to safety. Alex leaned against the side of the log and, having never heard a horse scream, watched the poor animal struggling to get up, wishing it would hurry up and die.

"Hell of a mess, hey, Alex?"

Alex turned from the horse to the young boy kneeling next to him. He knew the boy only as Billy. His eyes were red and swollen, his cheeks wet from fear.

Feeling sorry for the young boy, Alex returned to the animal that lay still on the battlefield. He turned to agree with Billy and heard a dull, soft thud. Feeling something wet and warm splash on his face, Alex watched as the boy slowly fell backward, eyes open, with a look of surprise and part of his skull missing. When he realized his face was covered with the boy's blood and brains, his stomach convulsed, and he stooped forward, vomiting. When he finished, he sat back, wiped his face with the sleeve of his jacket, looked down into Billy's lifeless brown eyes, and thought of the boy's mother.

The sound of men yelling and firing their weapons returned to him, and as his eyes welled with tears for the boy, he gazed across the smoke-filled expanse of the dead and wounded at the horse. The air was heavy with a haze of smoke that carried a terrible smell. Fear grasped him and held him tight as he hid behind the log, clutching his rifle, trying not to look into the lifeless eyes of the young boy. His thoughts turned to the letters he'd written to his wife and brother. Wondering if the words he had put to paper would be his last, he wished he had said so many other things in the letters.

A voice somewhere yelled the order to advance, and men around him rose, firing their weapons as they stepped out from behind trees, logs, and rocks. The sound of musket balls hitting them in the body or head had an unmistakable sound all its own that, for some reason, reminded him of when, as a boy, he threw dirt clods at outhouses. Some men walked, while others ran, stopping now and again to kneel and reload before continuing, repeating the process over and over again. Alex wiped the blood from his face, spit the taste of vomit from his mouth, and reloaded his rifle with trembling hands, wishing he was with Ella in the quiet of their bedroom.

His gun loaded, he watched his comrades run past him toward the Union positions, yelling and firing, some falling from the impact of a musket ball with that terrible thud. Cannonballs exploded, sending pieces of metal everywhere, killing and wounding men that he knew. Clutching his rifle, he stood and stepped over the log, feeling a sharp pain in his left hip. He looked down at his gray pants as they turned a crimson color, and he realized he was shot. A second shot found his right shoulder, knocking him back against the log he had used for cover. Alex lay on his back in eerie stillness, looking up at the blue sky through the tall pine trees as silent, blurry figures ran past him.

The sounds of battle slowly returned to him as cannon and rifle fire mixed with the yelling and screaming of men in battle. Propping his head against the log, he watched his comrades run past him, tripping or stepping over the bodies of the dead and wounded. Knowing he was going to die, his eyes found the dead horse, and he imagined riding him into heaven. He didn't want to die here on this muddy field covered in such destruction that God himself must have turned away. He looked toward the smoke-filled expanse before him as men continued their attack on the Federal positions, then up at the blue sky. Alex thought of Ella and the children, of his younger sister Mary, and of his brother Edward. Weakness and fatigue overcame Alex, and his eyes grew heavy as he looked at the two holes in his clothing and the blood draining the life from his body. He thought of home and the warm, sunlit fields he used to ride when his eyes once again found the horse. Feeling tired and cold, he closed his eyes.

Alex opened his eyes to a blurry figure standing over the man lying on a cot next to him. As his eyes cleared, he recognized the long white smock of a doctor and realized he was still alive. He gathered enough strength to whisper, "Did we win?"

The figure wearing the white smock turned and touched Alex's forehead, feeling his temperature. "Yes, you won."

Tears filled Alex's eyes and made their way down the side of his face and neck, finding the pillow. He was glad to be alive and managed a small smile. Then he thought of the men who had fallen, the horse, and the lifeless eyes of Billy. He wiped the tears from his eyes and cheeks as he looked up at the doctor. "Am I going to live?"

"You'll live," said the doctor. "But the war's over for you. You'll be going home in a few days."

Thinking of his wife, Ella, Alex closed his eyes and drifted into unconsciousness.

Seven

December 1860

James Riley Chrisman

Tallapoosa County, Alabama

James Riley Chrisman stood beside his mother in church, singing from the hymnal they shared while his father, Beth, and Davy shared another, with Nancy and Bonnie neatly tucked between William and Elizabeth. While James sang, he stared at the side of Martha Heard's face as she stood between her parent's two rows up and to the left. When the singing ended, she turned and smiled over her shoulder. He returned her smile but quickly looked away, then sat down.

A sharp nudge of his mother's elbow and a stern look warned him to stop flirting in church. For the remainder of the service, James fought the temptation to look at Martha, but she made no such effort, turning her head several times and smiling. Each time James would smile back, he would look at his mother, who was giving him one of her looks.

After the services, families gathered in front of the church to exchange pleasantries while James glanced around in search of Martha. Finding her just as her father was helping her mother into the wagon, he excused himself, walked his horse over to the Heard wagon, took off his hat, and smiled politely. "Hello, Martha." And without taking his eyes from hers, he said hello to Mr. and Mrs. Heard.

"Good morning, James," replied Mr. Heard.

"Good morning," smiled Mrs. Heard, noticing how James looked at her daughter.

Martha smiled shyly. "Good morning, James."

Holding the reins to the mare in one hand and his hat in the other, James carefully chose his words. "Martha…" he began but paused as he glanced at Mr. Heard, then Mrs. Heard before he looked back at Martha. "I was wondering…if I could come calling this afternoon?"

"I'd like that." She quickly glanced at her parents as if seeking their permission.

James looked up at Mr. Heard sitting in the wagon seat. "If that'd be all right with you and Mrs. Heard."

Mr. Heard gave James a long, stern look. "Suppose there'd be no harm if you were to come calling."

"I see no difficulty in that, James," said Mrs. Heard, thinking of the note from his mother. She glanced toward Elizabeth, watching from the seat of the Chrisman buggy, and they exchanged smiles.

James asked if taking Martha for a buggy ride would be all right.

"How about a picnic?" blurted Martha. Feeling embarrassed, she looked at her ma and then at James. "I can pack some food and stuff when I get home."

James grinned. "Sounds great!" He looked up at Mr. Heard, staring down at him, and politely asked, "If that'd be alright, sir?"

Mr. Heard liked James, always had, but still, he looked doubtful. "Don't rightly know about a picnic, James."

Mrs. Heard kicked her husband.

He gave her a surprised look but quickly understood. "Well," he said, "guess that'd be all right, James."

James grinned, looking relieved. "Thanks, Mr. Heard, Mrs. Heard. See y'all in a couple of hours with the buggy then."

Martha smiled with excitement as she quickly added, "And I'll have the basket packed."

The grin on his face left little room for anything else. He put on his hat, turned, and climbed into the saddle. Ready to burst, he tipped his hat, turned the black mare around, and chased after his parents' buggy.

William Chrisman was sitting on the porch in his rocking chair, enjoying his Sunday afternoon pipe while waiting for Sunday dinner, when James drove the buggy past the house, heading toward the county road. Elizabeth walked out of the house and stood next to the railing with one hand on the porch pillar, watching James reach the end of the driveway and turn onto the county road in a trail of dust.

William smiled wryly. "Hope he don't wreck our only buggy."

Elizabeth smiled. "Looks like that son of yours may have a little gal."

William blew a small cloud of smoke toward the road. "Yah mean other than that mare of his?"

She smiled at her husband's sense of humor, then turned away in silence and went into the house, leaving William to contemplate the mystery of his son. Before closing the door, she paused to look up the road, hoping Mrs. Heard hadn't become an expert rock thrower.

James turned the buggy from the road onto the Heard property and began searching the yard and porch for Martha. Seeing no sign of her, he guided the buggy to the front porch, stopped, and climbed down. Dropping the horse's reins, he walked across the porch, politely knocked on the door, and waited for what seemed a long time.

Mrs. Heard opened the door dressed in a grey housedress with a white apron, holding a big blue mixing bowl with the handle of a wooden spoon sticking out of it. "Hello, James. Come in." She smiled as she stepped away from the door.

James took off his hat and returned her smile. "Howdy, Mrs. Heard. Is Martha home?" he asked, immediately thinking that it was a dumb thing to ask.

"Of course, James," she said, looking puzzled. "Y'all are going on a picnic. Martha will be down in a minute." She nodded toward a chair. "Have a seat, and I'll get you a glass of water. I'd offer ya some lemonade, but I ain't made none yet."

"No, thank you, Mrs. Heard," he said, sounding nervous. "I'm not thirsty."

She wondered if he was polite or truthful. "Course ya are, James. Ya just don't know it. Now sit down, and I'll get ya some water." When she turned to put the bowl on the table and get him the water, she yelled, "MARTHA!" which startled James. Without looking back at him, she said, "Sit down, James, she won't be but a moment. For some reason, us gals like to take our time getting ready."

He thought about that as he sat down, watching Mrs. Heard get a glass from the cupboard and pour fresh water from a pitcher she had just filled from the pump. She handed him the glass. "It was awful nice of your mother to send that medicine over. Be sure to tell her how much I appreciated it and the note."

He swallowed, wondering when Martha would be ready, and set the glass on the table. "Sure thing, Mrs. Heard."

Martha walked into the kitchen all aglow, looking happy, her face a little flushed. "Hello, James."

He stood and grinned, looking nervous while playing with the hat he held in his hands. "Hello, Martha."

Mrs. Heard smiled at the two, remembering her first courting experience. Then she looked at James, giving him a stern look, then at her daughter. "I packed the basket while you were up changing. I expect you'll find everything y'all will need in there, girl." She looked at James as she spoke to Martha. "Don't stay gone too long."

James wasn't sure why he felt nervous, but maybe it had something to do with how Mr. Heard stared at him.

Martha sensed his uneasiness. "Thanks, Ma." She stepped a little closer to James. "Well," she said, trying to hide her excitement. "Shall we get going?"

He picked up the basket, thanked Mrs. Heard for the water, and opened the door. Martha walked onto the porch while he gave Mrs. Heard one last nervous glance as he closed the door.

Mrs. Heard smiled as she walked to the kitchen window to watch the two.

James placed the basket behind the seat, helped Martha into the buggy, and climbed into the seat next to her. Giving her a quick smile, he picked up the reins and turned the horse toward the main road.

Mrs. Heard leaned toward the open window and yelled after them, "Be back before it gets dark, girl, gets chilly once the sun goes down!"

Martha waved in response as she turned to James. "Where we going?"

He considered that for a few moments, and then he looked excited. "I'm thinking about the ruins at the old Rupert place."

"I know the place," she said, looking excited yet a little afraid. "My brothers used to ride out there and play before Pa made `em stay away 'cuz he said it was a bad place."

James chuckled. "Yeah, it was a bad place for the Rupert's."

Martha scooted a little closer, trying not to look afraid. "I'm not afraid if that's what you're thinking."

Looking skeptical, he looked down at her legs inches away from his and grinned. "You sure?"

She wrinkled her nose with a smile. "I think so!"

James slapped the reins on the back of the horse. "Get up," he said, smiling, "the Rupert place it is!"

They talked and laughed as they rode along the main road until they came to an old, overgrown trail that was seldom used, leading up a slope. James slowed the team and guided the buggy past fallen tree limbs and through an open rotted gate. Several minutes later, they drove past the ruins of the barn and house, stopping beside a two-foot-high stone wall once used as a fence.

"Welcome to the Rupert place," he told her while glancing around. Jumping down, he helped Martha from the wagon and picked up the basket and the blanket. Pausing to look around, he gestured with the hand holding the basket, "Over yonder."

She followed him to a shady spot under a big oak tree overlooking a small, grassy valley framed by trees. After he set the basket on the ground, she helped spread the blanket. "It's beautiful," she said as she sat on the blanket.

James turned and looked out across the small valley. "Sure is."

"What happened here, James? Pa never would say."

James sat on the blanket and opened the basket to see what was inside. Pleased with what he found, he closed the lid and looked around at the ruins. He considered her question for a moment and then looked at her, thinking how pretty she was.

She removed her red bonnet and fussed with her light brown hair that fell gently to her shoulders. "I'm still waiting for you to tell me what happened here." He gestured around the ruins, looking slightly mystified. "There are several stories, but Ma and Pa seem to believe the one about a stranger."

"A stranger?" she asked, looking puzzled.

He nodded, feeling quite the historian. "Think we could eat a couple of pieces of chicken first, Martha?"

She moved next to the basket to open it. "I guess we could if you've a mind to James." She lifted the lid. "Are you really hungry now? We just got here."

He grinned, looking a little embarrassed. "It just smells so good I thought we could eat while I tell you about the Rupert legend."

Martha smiled. "I guess so, but only if you tell the whole story." Her tone became serious. "And don't leave nuth'n' out!"

James agreed as he watched her remove the plate of chicken from the basket, then two empty plates. "Sorry, James," she said, looking embarrassed. "But I didn't bring anything to wash it down with. I guess I completely forgot about that."

James looked toward the buggy. "I think there's a canteen in the buggy. I'll run down to the creek and get some fresh water while you get things ready here."

She smiled. "All right."

He got up and returned minutes later with a canteen of cool water.

"Now sit and tell me about the Rupert's," she said excitedly.

James sat down, took the plate she handed him, and bit into a chicken leg. Then, licking his fingers, he thought the chicken was really good. "I can't believe you never heard the story about this place."

"Like I done told you, James," she said, looking nervous. "Pa would never tell us anything. My brothers heard stories at school about ghosts and Indians and such things as that, but Pa would never talk about this place." She giggled. "Like to see Pa's face if he knew we were up here."

James didn't want to think about that. "What'd you hear at school?" Immediately, he felt bad, remembering she was never allowed to go to school, and he wished he hadn't asked that question.

Looking embarrassed, she turned away. "I never went to school, James. I thought you knew that."

James felt awful. "Sorry, Martha, I forgot." He paused, looking at the back of her head. "I didn't mean anything by it. Really, I didn't."

Silence filled the air, but then she turned, smiling. "I know ya didn't mean anything, James. You'll just have to tell me the whole story yourself. That's better anyways."

Glad she wasn't angry, he grinned and took another bite of chicken, licking his fingers before wiping them on the napkin she handed him. Then he began. "Pa says the Rupert's was first in the valley. They say, Mr. Rupert, his wife, and two sons came here from someplace back East, heading for Texas. The story goes that this is as far as they got before Mrs. Rupert got real sick. After she felt better, they decided to stay, so he built this here place." He gestured toward the stream and valley. "People were starting to move into the valley about then, and the Indians had moved west, and the Rupert's were happy here."

James took another bite of chicken while Martha slowly ate hers, hanging on to his every word. He continued while gesturing at the stone wall. "Mr. Rupert built this here wall or started it anyways. Pa says he thinks Mr. Rupert was gonna build it all the way around the house. Like a fence."

Martha stopped eating and looked in both directions. "Land sakes."

"Anyways," said James, "the story goes on about this stranger that happened by on his way to Texas, they say. Mr. Rupert asked him to spend the night, and they got along so good, Mr. Rupert asked the man to stay on a few days and help him with the wall. One day, Mr. Rupert was down there in that valley plowing, and the stranger was up here working on the wall." James turned to Martha and lifted one eyebrow, looking devious. "That is, he was supposed to be working on the wall." He paused to take a drink of water from the canteen. "Well," said James, looking embarrassed, "Mrs. Rupert and the stranger…"

"What was his name?" interrupted Martha.

James looked puzzled. "Who?"

"The stranger," she said. "What was his name?"

James considered that. "Don't rightly know. Don't think anyone else does either." He leaned toward her, looking devious again as he lowered his voice. "Anyway, while Mr. Rupert was gone, Mrs. Rupert and the stranger…" he paused, letting the sentence die.

"What?" she asked, looking curious.

"Well," James said nervously, "...somehow...they got...you know?"

Not sure she understood what he was getting at, she stared at him with a troubled look and said, "No, I don't know."

James fussed for a moment, looking embarrassed. He didn't know how to say they were making love, so he took another drink of water. "Well," James paused for effect. "They got friendly," he paused again. "You know." He could see from her expression that she didn't understand what he was getting at. "They got, you know, real friendly."

Martha looked at him for a long moment, then giggled shyly. "You mean they went to bed together?"

"Yeah," replied James, surprised yet relieved at her response. "They went to bed together." His face flushed as he continued, "People think they must have fallen asleep in each other's arms, which is exactly how Mr. Rupert found `em."

Martha's eyes got big as her mouth hung open.

James could see the fear in Martha's face, so he leaned forward and lowered his voice. "Everyone says he went crazy, got his ax, and killed `em both; chopped `em into little pieces."

Martha dropped her piece of chicken and gasped.

James thought that might have been a little too descriptive as he watched her pick up the chicken pieces. "Some people say they never woke up, and others say they woke up just as he started. Some say she screamed and cried as he chopped at the stranger and then her."

Martha's face hadn't changed its expression.

James continued. "They say Mr. Rupert went crazy afterward and chased the children into the woods with his ax. The boys hid, and he called out their names clear into the night, both of `em afraid to answer, fearing he'd kill `em. Finally, Mr. Rupert set the barn on fire, and then the house with the stranger and Mrs. Rupert's bodies still inside. They say the children watched the place burn down and watched as their pa tossed a rope over that tree yonder." James pointed to a large oak tree several yards from the stack of rubble that was once the house by the fruit cellar. "Then he hung himself," he said, making as if he had a rope around his neck, pulling it with one hand while sticking out his tongue and making a choking sound.

Martha had not taken a bite of chicken for several minutes. She stared at the face James was making, then slowly turned and looked at the tree, imagining Mr. Rupert dangling from a rope as his children looked on. "How terrible!"

"Yep," said James matter-of-factly while reaching for another piece of chicken.

"What happened to the children?"

"Pa says the flames of the fire lit up the sky like crazy, bringing the Martin family from across the valley. Mr. Harry Martin found the two boys hiding in the fruit cellar scared as all get out."

"I reckon they were," said Martha with wide eyes.

"This happened about two years before Ma and Pa moved into the valley. Ma and Pa became good friends with the Martins, and Pa even helped him build a new barn the day Mr. Martin's son Bishop was born."

"Did you ever meet the boys?"

"The Rupert boys?" James shook his head, "Nah, never did. They ran off before I can remember, but Ma says they were a couple of strange ones."

"Who wouldn't be after that?" Martha asked, feeling a bit sorry for them.

"I guess," replied James thoughtfully. "Anyway, once they left, no one ever heard of `em again, although there were stories they lived in that old fruit cellar, but that's nonsense, according to Pa. It's just one of them stories people like to tell so's to scare little kids and all."

Martha glanced around, looking a little afraid. "You don't suppose they's still do live here, do ya, James?"

He chuckled. "Nah, they's long gone, Martha, have been for years."

"That must be why my pa calls this place evil."

"Lots of folks around the valley call this place evil cause of what happened here. Some say the place is cursed, and that's why no one has ever tried to fix it up, especially after that old man was found dead under the same oak tree yonder."

Martha's eyes grew bigger again. "What old man?"

"Some old man pa found dead under the oak tree. Pa said his old body just plain gave out, but people picked up on that and said that old man Rupert's ghost scared the life right out of them."

"Do you reckon that's true?"

James laughed and shook his head. "Heck, no, Martha, the man was just old. No one knows where he came from or where he was going. Pa said he must have stopped for the night and died in his sleep. Pa said he was really old." Seeing Martha was still caught up in the ghost stories and afraid she would want to leave, he smiled. "Stop thinking about ghosts, Martha. There's no such thing."

Embarrassed at her childish fears, she smiled and then laughed, realizing how silly she must appear to him.

They talked and laughed at other things while they enjoyed the afternoon sitting on the blanket, eating the food Mrs. Heard had prepared. Later, they walked around the ruins while James pointed out the three graves that Mr. Martin had dug, also pointing out that Mr. and Mrs. Rupert was buried together and the stranger a few feet away. They investigated the fruit cellar, not venturing too far in, and then they walked along an old footpath, one of the many trails made by curious children over the years.

Returning to the blanket, Martha sat down and leaned against the stone wall while James lay on the blanket with his head resting against the empty basket. They talked for another hour before James moved closer and sat against the wall next to her.

Their shoulders touched. "It's getting late," James said, feeling emotions he had never felt before.

Martha smiled, looking disappointed. "I know." Her heart raced as she looked into his eyes and at his lips.

Wanting to kiss her, he slowly leaned toward her until their lips gently touched for their first kiss. James quickly sat back, looking embarrassed. "Sorry, Martha."

She touched his arm with her hand and smiled. "I didn't mind, James. I've been curious about that for a spell now."

James felt his face flush. "Yah have?"

She giggled while nodding. "You're so brave, James, and yet so shy. I'm surprised you even kissed me."

He looked down at the blanket. "Been wanting to all day."

She touched his arm. "I'm glad you did."

Happy and relieved, he smiled. "Wasn't sure I ought to."

She put her hand under his chin, turned his face, and kissed his lips gently.

He clumsily put his arms around her, pulling her body into his, feeling her firm breasts against his chest, followed by a strong desire he had never felt before. He wanted her but was afraid of not knowing what to do and even felt a little embarrassed, so he sat back. "I think we better go."

"Probably should."

They got up and gathered up the dishes, basket, and blanket, putting them into the buggy, and then he helped her up onto the seat, walked around to the other side, and climbed up. As James guided the team around fallen limbs and tree trunks, they rode in silence until they turned onto the county road toward her house.

"Are you all right?" he asked while staring along the road.

She smiled and nodded. "I'm fine." She looked at the side of his face. "Why, you ask'n?"

"I don't know, just wondering."

Martha moved closer, put her arm under his, and pulled herself into him.

He could feel the warmth of her body. "I had a nice time today,"

She smiled. "Me too."

Comfortable with one another, they rode in silence, each busy in their thoughts about the day until they reached the driveway of the Heard farm. James stopped the buggy and looked at the farmhouse in the distance, with its thin line of smoke slowly creeping into the late afternoon sky. The late afternoon sun behind the trees cast long shadows across the yard.

"Can I come calling next Sunday?"

She smiled. "You better, James Riley."

They looked at one another for a moment, and then he dropped the reins, awkwardly put both arms around her, and clumsily kissed her. She felt soft and gentle in his arms, and there was no struggle as he held her warm body against his. Then he pulled away.

"What's the matter?" she asked.

"Your folks might see," he said, looking embarrassed.

She laughed. "So?"

He frowned. "I don't want anyone watching."

"For heaven's sake, James," she laughed as she glanced toward the windows of the farmhouse. "I'm sure Ma and Pa are just sitting at the window waiting for us to come down the road so they can spy on us."

Feeling foolish, he picked up the reins and drove the buggy to the front porch, only to stop at a safe distance where no one could hear. He glanced at the windows and around the yard, then took her hand. "Will you be my girl, Martha?"

She smiled, knowing she would break down and cry if she said anything, so Martha nodded.

Feeling happy and proud, he drove the buggy up to the house, stopping next to the porch, jumped down, helped her down, retrieved the basket from under the seat, and walked her to the door. "Here," he said, handing her the basket. "I had a good time today. Tell your ma the food was really good, and be sure to thank her for me."

"Me too." She smiled. "The best."

"Well," he said, wanting to kiss her as he glanced around, afraid someone was watching. "Guess I best be getting home."

They looked at one another in the stillness of the porch. Then James leaned forward and gently kissed her. She responded by putting her arms around him. The kiss was long and tender, and then they parted, smiled at one another, and then he turned and walked back to the buggy. She leaned against the porch post as he climbed into the seat, thinking about the kiss, and watched as he slowly drove toward the county road. As he disappeared over the hill, she turned and slowly walked across the porch to the front door.

Mrs. Heard was sitting in a chair by the stove, breaking the ends off of green beans she held in her apron-covered lap, dropping them into a pot of water sitting on the stove. She turned and smiled as her daughter opened the door and stepped inside, wearing a smile. "Have a good time?"

"Sure did."

"How many times you kiss that boy?" Mrs. Heard asked without looking up from the beans she was breaking apart.

Martha's face flushed and held surprise as she looked at her mother, then frowned with embarrassment. "Were you watching us?"

Her face held a smile. "Don't need to watch. I was young once myself, and you best be glad your pa weren't watching."

Martha considered that, while imagining her pa walking onto the porch as she and James kissed, and was thankful he was upstairs reading.

Mrs. Heard tossed a handful of beans into the pot and then thoughtfully wiped her hands. "Young James is a fine boy, comes from good stock. You could do worse."

"I know," replied Martha, looking sentimental, while taking a seat in an empty chair watching her mother work on the green beans. Taking a handful from her mother's lap, she broke the ends off and tossed them into the pot. "He's gonna come calling next week."

Mrs. Heard smiled with the knowledge that her daughter was in love.

"Ma?" asked Martha softly, tossing a handful of beans into the pot.

Hearing a troubled voice, her mother stopped what she was doing and looked at her daughter. "What troubles you, child?"

Martha looked worrisome. "You and Pa don't care that James is half Indian, do ya?"

Mrs. Heard stiffened in her chair, looking angry. "Why, child, whatever gave you the idea we did?"

Ashamed about asking, Martha shrugged. "Some in the valley do."

Mrs. Heard stopped what she was doing. "You should be ashamed for asking that of your pa and me."

Martha bit her lower lip and looked down at the floor. "Sorry, Ma didn't mean nothing. I was just wondering."

"Well, put those silly notions out of your head." Mrs. Heard paused, letting her temper and tone soften. "Your pa and me have known the Chrismans since before you were born. I remember the first time I met Elizabeth. She was carrying young James in her arms with Beth in tow, holding onto her mother's apron strings." Mrs. Heard smiled at the memory. "That child held on so tight I figured she was gonna tear the apron plum off Elizabeth."

Martha smiled as she placed her arms on the table, laying her head on them, looking at her mother, and listening as she talked.

"If it weren't for Elizabeth, I would have died once. She stayed with me day and night for a week, caring for me, cleaning, and feeding you young 'uns. I owe that woman a lot, so don't ever ask me if we care that she's an Indian or what her children are." Mrs. Heard wiped a tear from her eye and went back to work on the green beans. "Most people in the county feel the same." She stopped and looked at Martha. "The question is, child, does it matter to you?"

"No, it don't, Ma, it don't matter at all."

"That's all that matters, daughter. Now get cleaned up and help me get supper on."

Martha sat up, looking tired. "Yessum." She stood and thought joyfully about the kiss on the porch.

Eight

August 1861- December 1861
Alex returns – Edward leaves
Florence, Alabama

Hearing the whinny of a horse, Alex stopped beside a tree, placed one hand against it, and stared into the dense night fog. The horse whinnied again, and as Alex looked to his right into the dense fog and ghostly shapes of trees and bushes, a dark horse, with its saddle empty and reins dragging on the ground, stepped from the fog. He watched as it stopped and stared at him with its big dark eyes, snorted, jerked its head, and stepped back as if ready to bolt. Speaking softly, Alex reached out with his left hand as he stepped away from the tree toward the horse that snorted again as it stepped back, stopped, and stared at Alex. As he reached for the reins, the animal reared up, turned, and disappeared into the night fog.

Alex opened his eyes, looking up at Edward, standing beside the bed. Seeing the concern on his brother's face, he smiled. "Hello, Edward, what time is it?"

"Late," Edward said as he felt Alex's forehead, checking for a fever. "And about time you woke up. You've been home for over a week, and all you do is sleep."

Alex pushed himself up, sitting against a pillow resting against the headboard, thinking about his dream. "I've been shot. How long have you been here?"

"Not long," Edward held out a glass of brandy. "Your sleep didn't appear to be restful. Thinking of the horse?"

"Any fever?"

Edward shook his head. "Doesn't appear to be."

Alex took the glass of brandy and glanced toward the door like a child fearing an angry parent. "Ella would have my hide," he said, looking guilty, "and yours too if she were to catch me drinking this early in the morning."

Edward glanced at the door. "I'm your doctor, and I say it's good for you. It's almost noon and close to our drinking time anyway."

"Our drinking time is late afternoon, you big asshole." He sipped his drink and then looked at his older brother. "And why are you so full of shit? It isn't your birthday."

Edward chuckled, moved his chair closer to the window, and sat down. Propping his feet on the window ledge, he looked outside and sipped his brandy. Beyond the window, Alex's children played in the trees near a small pond, their laughter barely audible through the window. He marveled at their energy as he pulled a folded newspaper from his coat pocket and unfolded it.

Seeing the paper, Alex asked, "What news of the war?"

Edward looked at the bold type of the newspaper. "Mostly a lot of small battles or skirmishes so aptly named by those not fighting in them." Then he read the bold print, "Union Blockades Guard Southern Coastlines." He shook his head, looking glum. "It appears that both sides are waiting for the other to make the first move." He looked at Alex. "I've been reading about the battle you were in."

Alex looked unenthusiastic. "How exciting."

Edward fussed with the newspaper and grinned at his brother's sarcasm. "According to this article, it was very exciting." He returned to the article and read silently for a few minutes, then spoke softly and sadly. "A lot of good men died that day at Bull Run," he paused, "on both sides."

Alex turned to the window and watched his children playing in the yard as he listened to Edward begin to read.

"Over 4,800 men died at Bull Run," read Edward. "The North lost over 3,000 and the Southern Army about 1,800, including General Bernard Bee." He paused to look at Alex. "Did you know that, Alex?"

Alex shook his head no, looking sullen as he watched his children innocently playing as if nothing were wrong.

"It says," continued Edward. "The battle raged between the two armies of some 60,000 men." He stopped reading and looked at Alex once again. "Did you know there were that many men fighting at one time?"

Alex turned from the window. "No," he said, gesturing with both hands. "But it seemed most of them were running past me in one direction or the other." He forced a wry smile. "They were sort of a blur."

Edward chuckled. "Want me to stop?"

Memories of that day rushed at Alex. "No, it's all right. Go ahead."

Edward turned back to the newspaper. "A large Confederate Army of over 32,000 men met the charge of over 28,000 Union soldiers on a clear July morning, taking part in a battle that lasted into the late afternoon. Included in the horrific battle were the men of Lauderdale County Company H, 'The Dragoons', and part of the 4th Alabama Infantry." He paused to sip his drink. "The Fourth Alabama's gallant stand held its position, stalling the advance of the Union regiments, by repulsing several attacks, which gave the Confederate forces time to regroup and mount a counter-attack. The 'Dragoons" from Lauderdale County played a prominent role in the fighting that day, contributing to the Confederate victory. The 750 men of the 4th Alabama engaged the Federals for several hours, losing 38 brave men, including Brigadier General Bernard Bee and Colonel Marlow. The regiment lost every field officer and suffered 208 wounded, but still managed to help chase the Federals back to the safety of Washington D.C." Edward stopped reading, and the room filled with the rustling of the paper as he folded it on his lap. "I've been carrying this newspaper around for several days. I don't mind admitting that I am proud of you."

Alex looked at the pleasant scene being played out by his children beyond the window while thinking of Billy, remembering wiping the boy's splattered blood and brains off his cheek. He wanted to forget the boy's lifeless eyes staring at him. "I have nightmares."

Edward looked on with concern. "Ella told me."

Without turning from the window, Alex spoke softly. "I can't get the images out of my head, and they're worse in my sleep." He turned from the window, looking troubled. "You want to know what haunts me?"

Edward nodded, worried about his brother.

Alex's eyes welled. "Of all the men that died that day, I keep thinking about this horse, this poor damned horse." He paused to sit higher, struggling with the pillow to get comfortable. "I watched helplessly as he tried and tried to get up while men pulled his rider to safety, leaving the poor animal on the battlefield, kicking and screaming." He looked at his brother. "I've never heard a horse scream in death before." He turned back to the window. "That poor animal had no idea why the hell he was there, having had no choice in the matter."

"It was only an animal," Edward said, trying to console his brother.

Alex wiped a tear from his cheek and rested his head against the pillow, staring out the window. "I know that, but he was a living, breathing creature. I remember lying on the ground bleeding and thinking I was going to die while looking over the battlefield at the bodies of the dead and wounded men on both sides, smelling the stench of it all. I knew that some of the wounded who lay in agony crying for their mothers or sweethearts would not survive. In all that...," he paused a moment. "In all that tortured madness, my eyes found that poor animal lying across the meadow full of smoke, debris, and death." He closed his eyes and shook his head. "I knew he was dead, and I feared for my own life." He looked at Edward, paused, and gently gestured with his hands.

"Knowing he was dead and believing that I too was about to die, I imagined myself riding him up to heaven, passing all the dead men walking through the clouds, riding away to peace and safety." He wiped the tears from his red, welling eyes, his face crumpling. "I feel like a coward."

"You're no coward, Alex." Edward tried to imagine what Alex had gone through. "You're just a man with fears of dying like all men." He paused with a small smile. "Not quite the way it was when we were children, hey Alex?"

Alex remembered their argument that rainy night before he left. "No, it wasn't quite the same."

"I can't explain any of this," Edward said, looking uncertain. "The death and destruction of war are bound to affect one's mind while witnessing the horror that comes with war. That is bound to bring about dreams."

Alex looked troubled. "They say men who kill lose a part of themselves." He paused in fear. "Their souls, perhaps."

Edward half-smiled while looking skeptical. "That's what mortal men say. No man knows what's in God's plans." Edward shrugged. "What you have to do now is be my brother again, a father to your children, and a husband to Ella. Trust your soul to God, Alex. You're a good man."

Ella entered the bedroom carrying a tray of food. "You need your rest, Alex, and something to eat..." She never finished her sentence, noticing the partially filled glass of brandy on the small table beside the bed. "What are you doing with that drink?" She set the tray on another table, picked up the glass, and looked at Edward.

He smiled sheepishly. "It's good for him."

Her face flushed as she raised her voice in anger. "Good for him, indeed. It isn't good for him, and as a doctor, you should know that!" She handed the glass to Edward and went about adjusting and smoothing the covers around Alex. "You keep giving him brandy when I have asked you not to. You could kill your own brother, for heaven's sake."

Finding humor in her anger, Edward gulped the brandy, set the glass down, and retreated to the door, where he paused and looked at her. "That's not true, Ella," he said. Then he looked at Alex. "If I wanted to kill your husband, I would write to Union General McDowell telling him where he is. I'm sure he'd like to get his hands on one of the men who chased his army back to the safety of Washington!"

Ella stormed across the room, pushed Edward into the hallway, and slammed the door.

Edward stood alone in the hall, yelling through the door. "Doesn't she know I'm your doctor?"

"Go away!" she yelled.

Laughing, Edward yelled, "See you tomorrow, Alex!"

The Tennessee River

Captain Goodman was sitting at his desk, mulling over the cargo manifests, when a knock on his cabin door interrupted the menial yet important task of studying the words and figures on the paper. "Come in!"

The door opened, and Joseph stepped in. "Can I see you, Captain?"

The captain's frown of frustration turned to a grin. "Joseph, come in, Laddie." He stood up, looking glad to see him as he walked around his desk. "What's on your mind?"

Joseph closed the door and walked across the room. "I hope I'm not interrupting anything important."

Glancing back at the desk of papers, the captain chuckled. "Interrupting? Hell no, you just saved me from trying to make sense of these damn cargo manifests. Blasted things get harder each trip." He pointed to the pot of warm coffee on the potbellied stove behind his desk. "Cup of coffee or a drink, maybe?"

"No, thanks, Captain."

"Humph," grunted Goodman. "Suit yourself." He returned to his chair, settled back, and looked up at him. "What's on your mind, Laddie?"

Joseph nodded at a chair. "Mind if I sit down?"

"Course not," gestured the captain. "You don't have to ask, Laddie. Sit."

Joseph settled into the chair, looking troubled. "I've been doing some thinking, Captain."

Goodman looked curious. "That so?"

Joseph nodded. "Most of the men I know are off fighting this war, and…"

"And you feel a little guilty about Alex?" interrupted the captain, knowing Alex had been wounded in battle.

"I do. Not only about Alex but everyone heading off to fight in this thing."

The captain scowled as he stared at him. "Son, the same thing's eating at a few thousand other men that aren't marching off to fight in this politician's war."

Joseph shifted in his chair. "I'm sure you're right, but that doesn't change the way I feel. It just seems I should be doing more than riding up and down the river day in and day out while other men are off fighting."

The captain settled back in his chair, eyeing the unfinished manifests and thinking about what Joseph said. "I can't tell ya what to do, Laddie." He looked at Joseph. "If I was a younger man, I might feel the same." He stood and walked toward the nearest open porthole, gesturing for Joseph to follow. "Have a quick look out there, Son!"

Joseph stood and followed, glancing out the porthole, seeing crates filled with supplies for the Confederacy lined up on the dock. Young men dressed in gray uniforms waiting for the boat to take them North to the fighting were mulling around the dock.

Goodman placed his hand on Joseph's shoulder. "If it weren't for this old tub and the likes of you and me, those crates would sit there a long time, and the young men of the South might have to walk to get where they're needed." He paused, looking skeptical. "Oh, I'm certain both would make it one way or another, but damn it, boy, the fact of it is that you, me, and this here boat are the ones helping them get to where the South needs them to be. And to my way of thinking, that's a hell of a responsibility and a damn good way to fight this war."

The captain struck a match with his thumb, lit his pipe, and blew out the match with a breath of smoke. "We may not be in any of the shoot'n, but we're sure as hell involved in this here war."

Joseph knew the captain was right. What they were doing now and would do in the coming months was just as important. A sense of pride welled up in him. "You're right, Captain. I guess I felt the war was passing me by when, in truth, I'm right in the middle of it."

The captain smiled. "That's right, Son, smack dab in the middle." He returned to his desk and picked up his pen while staring at the words and figures written on the manifest. "Now get the hell out of here. We've both things to do."

Joseph grinned as he watched the old man turn and walk out of the captain's quarters into the warm sunlight. Pausing at the railing, he looked down at the men in their new gray uniforms, laughing and talking with one another. Joseph knew things would never be the same after this war. He took one last look at the uniformed men, turned, and walked down the stairs to the lower deck and the gangplank to the pier. It was time to have that talk with Edward.

Sophie greeted Joseph at the front door, escorted him into the library, and gestured to a chair. "Please haves yer self a seat, Mistah Joseph, while I tell Mistah Edward ya's here."

Joseph thanked her, and after she left the room he looked around at the familiar paintings and photographs, thinking of what he would say to Edward. Knowing that what he was about to ask would be a difficult thing in normal times, not to mention now. The war played an all too important factor for and against his reason for being here. He looked down at his hands and then the library doors, thinking this may not be the best time. He considered leaving when suddenly the doors opened.

Edward smiled, looking friendly. "Good afternoon."

Joseph stood and walked to meet him with an outstretched hand.

Edward crossed the room, grasped Joseph's hand, and firmly shook it.

"Hello Edward, how've you been?" asked Joseph.

"Fine," Edward said, nodding to a chair. "Have a seat." Then he asked, "And how about yourself? How are things with you and the Southern Belle these days?"

Joseph sat down. "Both busy."

"Yes, I can imagine." Edward gestured toward the liquor table. "Sherry or Bourbon, while you tell me your burdens."

"Bourbon sounds good," said Joseph, thinking a little bottled nerve wouldn't hurt right now.

Edward filled two glasses and handed one to Joseph, raised his, and said, "Cheers."

Joseph took the glass, repeated the toast, and took a quick sip. Instead of getting to the reason for his visit, he asked, "How's Alex getting on these days?"

"Alex is doing fine. " He smiled. "That's where Mary is."

"Yes, I know."

Edward looked worried as he sipped his drink and then stared into it thoughtfully. "He's gone through quite an ordeal, and well….," he paused. "Alex is a different man these days."

"I'm sure of it." Joseph tried to imagine his ordeal. "I've meant to see him, but the river keeps me busy these days."

Edward nodded, looking thoughtful. "Yes, the war. But I'm sure Alex realizes how busy you've been. After all, these are not easy times." Edward sipped his drink as he walked to a nearby chair and sat down, contemplating the reason for Joseph's visit. Normally, Edward would politely wait for his guest to bring up the matter of the visit, but he decided to hurry past all that. "Are you here to tell me you're going to run off to fight in this war?"

"In all honesty, I've been thinking about it a lot lately, but that's not why I'm here."

Surprised by the answer, Edward sipped his drink, wondering what sort of devils Joseph was fighting.

"I was going to enlist, but after talking to the captain..." Joseph let it trail off.

Edward nodded thoughtfully. "I'm sure the good captain had some pearls of wisdom."

Joseph grinned. "That he did."

Edward gestured at Joseph's glass, "You ready for another?"

"Not yet, thank you, Edward." Feeling nervous and hoping he didn't look it, he stood and walked to the bookcase, glancing at the rows of books while getting enough courage to say what had brought him here. "I've thought a lot about the war while carefully considering what may be the best or correct thing to do." He drank the last of the bourbon, looked into the empty glass, and then back at Edward. "I believe there'll be a big need for river pilots during this war, and that's where I'll be of the most use."

"I agree." Edward got up from his chair, taking Joseph's glass. "This war will not end soon," he said, walking toward the liquor table. "But until then, the South will need all sorts of help if she is to win. There are many ways to fight a war, my friend, and that includes ways to move men, munitions, and equipment." Edward shrugged. "Frankly, Joseph, I would have been disappointed had you made another choice. We've lots of young men to be soldiers and lots of older men to lead them, but river pilots...." he shook his head, letting the sentence trail off.

"I hope you're right."

"I am," boasted Edward with a confident smile. "Besides, I don't think the Army would have taken you anyway because of your occupation."

Joseph considered that. "Perhaps you're right, but that's something I'll never know."

"I know I'm right, Joseph," Edward said while pouring them another half glass of bourbon and sensing there was more to his visit than the war. "But this matter is surely your concern and needn't be explained to anyone, myself included." Edward studied Joseph while handing him the glass. "Now, my boy, what earthly matter is so important that it brings you here to see me instead of my sister?"

Joseph took the glass and another quick sip of bourbon. "This is not the best of times and, without question, the worst of all times to discuss this matter with you."

Edward sipped his drink and then sat down in a nearby chair while his eyes watched Joseph, suspecting the real motive behind his visit. "Have you come to ask for my sister's hand?"

Joseph looked surprised yet relieved. "Guess the cat's out of the bag, as they say."

Edward laughed. "I'm not blind, Joseph, nor a fool."

Joseph smiled, feeling uneasy. "Please accept my apologies for the timing, but these times rob us of doing things in the traditional or correct way." He shrugged. "So, we have to make do with what we are given, and that may put the acceptable or approved ways of doing things aside." Joseph smiled, looking sincere. "I love Mary very much."

"I'm sure you do. And you're right about your timing being bad. This war will eventually engulf the entire South and all that live in it." Edward paused, staring past Joseph out the veranda doors, as silence filled the room. Edward's voice softened, even sounding a little sad. "To be honest with you, I'm afraid for the first time in my life." Edward smiled, looking a little embarrassed as he shrugged. "I'm not afraid in the sense of the word. I'm not afraid of dying. My fear is that the South may not win this terrible undertaking." He sipped his drink and stared into the glass. "We will lose many good men. Peaceful, God-fearing men who want nothing more than to be left alone." He looked up. "You know how my brother and I have felt about your relationship with our sister from the start."

Joseph nodded, feeling uneasy. "Yes, we both did."

Edward stared at him sternly at first and then smiled warmly. "I appreciate the difficulty you faced in coming to see me, Joseph." He gulped the last of his drink. "Times change, and this is not last year or even last month. Who knows what the future has planned for any of us? I've watched the two of you over the months, and I know what's in my sister's heart, and I can only hope that what you say is truly in yours." A soft hush filled the library. "Last year, I might have said no and asked you to leave my sister to herself." He smiled wryly. "But that would have been a mistake. I believe she would have run away with you then, and I believe she would run away with you now if you were to ask her."

"I wouldn't allow us to make that fateful decision."

Edward smiled, looking pleased. "I know that." He picked up the newspaper on the table beside him and glanced at the headlines. "The news of so many men dying is disturbing." He settled back, resting his head on the back of the chair, and asked an unexpected question. "Do you dream?"

Joseph thought it a strange question. "At times." He watched the man across from him, who looked like a person carrying a heavy burden.

"I dream," said Edward, staring into his empty glass. "I dream of fire and death." He gestured around the room. "I dream of the death of this house. I see it in ashes, and I can't rebuild it. No matter how hard I try, I can't rebuild it because the fire keeps burning it down."

Joseph sat in silence, not knowing what to say as he watched him.

Edward looked up with a wry smile. "Of course, I don't know what these dreams mean." He shrugged. "Perhaps my dream is not about this house but the South." His expression turned grim. "You see, I'm not sure the South can win, and if we don't, well, the South we know will die. Another drink?"

Joseph thought about what Edward had just said. "No, thank you."

"Well, I need another." Edward stood and walked to the liquor cabinet, filled his glass, and took a drink. "I almost lost a brother, and I don't want to lose a sister, yet I believe that if I stood in the way of your love for one another, I would surely lose her." Edward smiled affectionately. "She waits for your visits, afraid you may not come." He looked at Joseph. "That's true." He smiled. "She loves you very much." Edward grinned and offered an outstretched hand. "You and Mary have my blessing."

Joseph shook Edward's hand, feeling and looking relieved, while fighting the urge to rush out the door to find Mary.

Edward sensed this urge and grinned. "I wouldn't wait too long. Your days of happiness may be short-lived."

"We've discussed getting married," confessed Joseph. "But, I haven't officially asked her. However, I will as soon as I ride out to your brother's."

"Well, then, my boy," Edward said, grinning, "you best get going. And if you're concerned about Alex, don't be. He and I will talk tomorrow when I check on him."

"Thank you, Edward." As Joseph turned toward the door, he had to force himself not to run.

After Joseph left to find Mary, Edward poured another glass of bourbon, walked to the veranda doors feeling a little drunk, and looked across the lawn, contemplating the South's future and Joseph's feelings about wanting to join the fight.

September 29th, 1861

A small group of family and friends witnessed Joseph Greene and Mary McAlexander's wedding on the back lawn of Edward's home. After the ceremony, the guests gave their congratulations, and while they visited with one another, Alex quietly coaxed Mary and Joseph into the pantry. After shutting the door, he placed his cane against the wall and uncovered three glasses and a bottle of Champagne he had hidden earlier. Alex opened the bottle, filled the three glasses, handed one to Mary and Joseph, and looked into his glass, waiting for the laughter from the dining room to subside. When it did, he looked at Joseph and Mary, thinking of the war. "It's good to see so much happiness at such an unhappy time."

Joseph and Mary smiled at one another.

Alex raised his glass, whispering above the inaudible words beyond the closed pantry door. "May the two of you hold on to your moment of happiness through these troubled times, never letting go."

Their glasses clinked. They took a sip, and Alex set his glass down, putting one arm around Mary and the other around Joseph. "Now, let's get back to the party before Edward accuses me of sabotaging his only party of the year."

"We'll be along in a moment," Mary told him.

Alex nodded, then gently pushed her closer to Joseph, picked up his cane, opened the door, and stepped out of the pantry.

After the door closed, Joseph kissed her. "Happy?"

She smiled as she wiped the tears from her eyes. "Very."

"I don't know what the world has waiting for us," he said. "But know that whatever fate holds for me, I shall always love you."

The door suddenly burst open. "I found them!" yelled Edward. He reached in and tugged at Joseph's arm. "Come on, you two; you're married now, so you don't have to hide in the pantry."

The room filled with laughter as everyone gathered around the table, taking their seats while Edward stood at the head of the table, waiting until the last person was seated. He lifted his fork and tapped it gently against a glass of wine. As the room became silent, he cleared his throat and looked at his sister sitting on his left and Joseph on his right, their hands stretched across the table, fingers touching.

"Not so long ago," Edward said sadly, "I lost the love of my life." He looked at Joseph, then at Mary warmly. "There was a time when Alex and I would have stood in the way of this marriage. But that would have been a mistake." He looked into the faces of the other guests, then at Mary. "It would have been a sin to keep you from this man." He paused to take a drink of water. "At times such as this, well-wishers are always full of empty wisdom and advice. I have found myself searching for the right things to say on this most important day, and I must confess the only words I have for you are to hold onto one another. God, in His wisdom, gives us many things during our short lives, but the most important and least appreciated is happiness." He paused, looked at Mary, and then at Joseph. "God bless the two of you, and may he carry us all from this time of war to a time of peace and happiness." Edward faced the guests and raised his glass. "God bless this marriage, and God bless the Confederacy."

Joseph and Mary accepted Edward's hospitality and moved into his house. Edward reasoned that it would be important for his daughter to have the influence of his sister and now a new uncle. However, in truth, he had selfish reasons. Edward feared that his loneliness would consume him. He didn't realize it, but Mary knew the reasons.

The days passed, and soon, the warm month of September gave way to a chilly October and that to November. The South went on about its business of training troops and building a new and separate country from the United States. With each passing day, Edward read the paper's account of the war, and in his heart, he knew the South would need every able-bodied man for its cause. Recalling his conversation with Joseph and his dilemma between the river and the army, Edward was also torn between his daughter's needs and the plight of the South.

On Christmas day, 1861, Edward succumbed to the need of the South. He was away on a pretense of business when, in truth, he was in Florence enlisting into the Confederate States Army. The following evening, Edward sat alone in the library, deep in thought about the future, watching the flames dance above the logs in the fireplace.

He heard the door to the library open and then close, followed by the familiar footsteps of his brother.

"Have you gone mad?" asked Alex, looking angry.

Edward continued to stare into the fire. "That phrase sounds familiar."

Alex tossed his coat across the back of a chair and walked toward the liquor table. "This is not the time to be funny."

"Help yourself to my liquor."

Alex reached for a bottle, paused, and then poured a drink. "Thank you. I believe I will."

Edward glanced from the fire as Alex gulped down his drink and then turned back to the fire with a smile, knowing what was coming.

Alex poured another. "After all the crap you gave me last year about Ella and the farm when I joined and all that other bullshit about my responsibilities, etc., etc., etc." Alex paused to take a sip of brandy. "How the hell can you enlist knowing what I went through?"

Before Edward could answer that question, Mary and Joseph walked into the library.

Alex turned to them. "Glad you're both here. Perhaps you can talk some sense into our brother." Alex downed his second glass of bourbon. "I need another drink."

"Easy, Alex," warned Edward without looking away from the fire. "You're on a short fuse."

Mary looked confused as she looked from Joseph to Edward. "What is he talking about?"

Edward stared into the fire. "I've enlisted."

"Oh, for heaven's sake," Mary said, "have you lost your mind?"

Edward did not look up. "Sounds a little like what your brother asked me a few moments ago, just before he decided to drink all my liquor."

"Funny," said Alex as he spitefully gulped another drink, disappointed that Edward ignored him.

Mary sat down next to Edward, putting her hand on his forearm. "Why would you do this after Alex almost lost his life? What will happen to little Mary if you go off to war? What of your patients and your practice?"

Having had enough of being lectured to, Edward stood and looked at Joseph. "Anything to add?"

Joseph raised his hands, gesturing surrender. "It's not my place, and I believe you already know how I feel." He turned to pour a drink, wisely avoiding a family argument.

Mary turned. "What do you mean, it's not your place? You are part of this family, and you love my brothers as if they were your own. It is your place. Now tell Edward he's foolish and irresponsible."

Joseph chuckled without humor and shook his head. "I won't do that, Mary. If I were not involved in trafficking war supplies and troops, I'd be going myself."

"Oh, you would?" she replied, looking angry.

Joseph looked at Alex and lowered his voice. "I have a feeling I'm going to need another drink before this night is over."

Alex nodded, managing a small chuckle. "We both will."

Mary turned back to Edward. "What of little Mary and your practice? You just can't leave everything and go off to some stupid war."

Edward continued to stare into the flames. "Everyone else is."

Mary became angry. "That's not funny, and no, they're not, and what about your practice? Who will take care of---

Edward interrupted. "All the necessary arrangements have been made." Determination filled his face as he looked at her. "This is not something I decided to do on a whim, Mary. I've struggled with this for some time." He stood and looked down at her. "And as far as little Mary, I had hoped you and Joseph would care for her until my return."

"Of course we'll care for her, Edward," she said in a choked voice. "You know that, but---"

"Enough, Mary," Edward said as he held up one hand, bringing silence to the room. Then, sorry for his outburst, he sat beside her and smiled warmly. "It's done, Mary. For God's sake, let it go."

Recognizing a lost battle, she settled back on the sofa in silence, wiping the tears from her eyes.

Edward took her hand. "I apologize for losing my temper, Mary. Forgive me."

She half-smiled as she wiped her tears with the back of her hand. "You're forgiven, and I apologize also."

Edward handed her his hanky and then turned to Alex. "If you don't mind, Alex, I'll pass on the liquor this evening and the next few days. I will need all my wits about me from now on."

"You couldn't talk me out of going," said Alex. "So, I'll not attempt to discourage you as much as I would like to."

Edward grinned and then looked from Alex to Joseph, "I'll ignore him and talk to you."

Joseph chuckled. "When do you leave?"

Edward poured a cup of coffee. "I've accepted an appointment as First Lieutenant with the 27th Alabama Infantry. I leave on the 28th."

"So soon?" Mary asked, looking worried.

Edward set the coffee pot down. "I'm afraid so; it seems the military waits for no man." He glanced at Alex and smiled. "Someone told me that once." Edward sipped the hot coffee, looking thoughtfully at Henrietta's painting, and then he turned and walked back to the sofa. "My regiment's already on its way to Fort Henry, somewhere on the Tennessee River in Kentucky. My orders are to proceed to Fort Henry at all haste."

"Of course, you're going as a physician?" asked Mary.

"No," Edward said. "I asked for a field commission, not a field hospital."

"But you're a doctor," Mary said, looking disappointed. "They'll need doctors."

Alex agreed with his sister while Joseph sat in silence, understanding Edward's reasoning.

"I don't want to fight this war from a damn field operating table patching holes, broken bones, and torn bodies of other men," he said sternly.

Mary stood. "But Edward…."

Edward felt angry, but as he interrupted his sister, he controlled his temper and spoke softly. "I've made my decision. It's done."

Alex knew it was time to let Edward go on his way and wisely interceded. "And with that settled, dear Sister, I will bid you all a good evening." He shook Joseph's hand, kissed Mary on the cheek, and asked Edward to walk him to the front door.

As they stepped into the cool December air, Alex looked up into the cloudless black sky of stars. "Beautiful night, even if it is a little chilly." He turned to Edward to shake his hand. "I'll come by before you leave."

Edward shook his brother's hand and smiled as Alex turned and climbed into the buggy. He stood in the doorway, watching the buggy as it went under the archway and out the open gate, turned onto the cobblestone street, and disappeared around the corner. His memory returned to another night when Alex disappeared around that same corner in the rain. It appeared that fate had laughingly brought back that moment, and it was his turn to go off in search of glory. He slowly closed the door, leaned his forehead against it, and contemplated his fate, wondering if he would be fortunate enough to return to his daughter.

Returning to the library, he found Joseph all alone, enjoying a cup of coffee in front of the fire. "Where's Mary?"

Joseph nodded toward the door. "She's upstairs tending to your daughter. I believe she's a bit upset."

Edward sat in a chair next to Joseph and stared into the fire. "I want you to know that if something should happen to me, I've made arrangements for my daughter to be with her mother's parents." Edward looked at Joseph. "Nothing personal, but you will have children of your own one day. And with her grandparents living next door, the transition will be easier." He rested his head against the back of the chair and closed his eyes with his hands resting across his stomach. "They're an influential family and can do a lot for a young lady."

"I think that's a wise decision."

Edward looked at him. "I have a favor to ask."

"Name it."

Edward looked worried. "Would you look in on Alex once in a while when you are in Florence? He hasn't been the same since he returned from Bull Run. He has become solitary and quiet, almost a recluse, and that worries me a great deal. I fear the memories of death and those he left there still haunt him." He looked into the flames. "Alex was not prepared for the horror he so innocently found." Then he paused and smiled without humor, "I wonder if I will be."

Joseph found no words of consolation for Edward but promised that he and Mary would visit Alex as often as possible.

Edward thanked him and stood, extending his hand with a weary smile. "You're a good man, Joseph. I believe my sister chose well." They shook hands firmly as he said, "Now if you don't mind, I have some things to take care of."

Joseph nodded. "Of course." He walked out of the room, closed the doors to the library, and thought of taking Mary to east Texas to escape the war.

Two days later, on December 28, 1861, Edward boarded a train, found an empty seat, and read the newspaper telling of President Lincoln's decision to send an army into the Carolinas. Unknowingly, Edward's journey would take him to a place where he and his unit would meet that army.

Nine

August 1861 - February 1862

Andrew Jackson Patterson

Anderson County, South Carolina

Daniel Patterson was sitting on the bottom step of the porch, anxiously awaiting his father's return from the Fork Township enlistment office. To pass the time, he tormented some chickens with the child's game of throwing pebbles at them, then grinning at how the hens darted around while frantically clucking as if warning one another. He reached for another handful of pebbles when he heard the sounds of a horse and wagon. Dropping the pebbles, he stood and waived to his pa, who ignored him as he drove the wagon toward the barn.

Daniel sensed something different about how his pa sat hunched over in the seat as the wagon stopped short of the barn door. Then he watched his pa jump down, unhitch the horse, and walk her into the barn. Daniel walked through the group of panicky hens into the barn, trying to hold back his excitement over his pa leaving to join the army. Wishing he, too, was old enough to go, he entered the barn just as his Andrew cursed a long line of profanities. Daniel stopped dead in his tracks when his father kicked a bucket, sending it flying across the barn and bouncing off the wall, startling the horses.

Andrew grabbed the reins of the horse he had unhitched from the wagon. "Whoa," he said gently to calm her, and then he told Daniel to calm the other two horses.

As he did so, Daniel considered heading back to the safety of the chickens, but as children often do, he decided to tempt fate. "What's got ya so riled up, Pa?"

"Haven't I told you to keep these damn buckets on the shelf where they belong?"

Daniel didn't remember using the bucket but quickly apologized. "Sorry."

Andrew turned back to the harness while talking to himself. "You're a mite too old, Mr. Patterson, the man says."

Believing his pa had lost his mind, Daniel stepped back, wishing Aaron was there.

Andrew gently took the bit out of the horse's mouth, slid the bridle down from its nose, and hung it on a bridle peg on the wall. He looked into the horse's big, dark eyes. "The Confederate Army has an age limit." He turned and looked at his son. "There's an age limit to fight in a damn war."

Daniel bent down, picked up the bucket, placed it on the shelf, and then picked up the harness, wondering if his father was drunk or had just gone mad. He had heard stories of people going mad for no reason, doing all sorts of crazy things, and talking to people who weren't there.

Andrew yelled some words the boy didn't recognize as he kicked the side of the barn, talking in that unfamiliar voice. "The age limit for enlisting is forty-four, says the man."

Daniel's eyes were the size of large eggs as he turned and hung the harness on the wall.

Andrew sighed and shook his head while putting the horse into its stall and gently patted the animal on the behind as he talked in that strange voice. "And since you're forty-four, Mister Patterson, we deeply regret having to turn you down." Andrew took a feedbag from a post, placed it gently over the horse's nose, and patted its neck. He looked down at his frightened son. "Close yer mouth, boy, before you catch a fly."

"Yes, sir." Afraid to move, Daniel watched his Pa.

"The nerve of the man telling me I'd better serve the Confederacy on my farm growing food." He looked at Daniel. "What the hell does that fat so and so know?" Andrew threw his hands up in the air. "Damned ignorant bastard!"

Surprised at hearing his dad cuss, Daniel stepped back toward the door and bumped into Aaron, who, upon hearing his Pa's ranting, had come to see what had him so angry.

Andrew looked at Aaron. "What's on your mind?"

He shrugged and explained, "I came to see how it went in town."

Andrew decided he had said enough, took a deep breath, let out a long sigh, and stared out the open barn doors, feeling the fool for acting crazy in front of his sons.

The two boys looked at one another, and instead of realizing that some things are better left alone, Daniel had to ask. "What did ya mean too old, Pa?"

Andrew looked at the boy, feeling bad about acting the way he had. "Never mind, son, I've some thinking to do." Then he walked out of the barn, heading toward the fields.

The boys stepped into the open doorway and watched him walk across the yard into the freshly plowed field, where he stood looking toward the west.

"Do you think Pa's old?" asked Daniel of his older brother.

Aaron didn't answer the question but asked one of his own. "What the heck was that all about?"

Daniel explained as much as he could, and the two deduced it was about the man at the recruiting office in town. Daniel repeated his question. "Do you think Pa's old?"

"No, I don't. But I ain't the recruiter." He tugged at Daniel's arm. "C'mon, we best get some work done b'fore supper so we don't irritate Pa no more than he already is. I think we ought to warn the girls about Pa's mood."

Daniel nodded. "Good idea."

Once inside the house, they warned Alicia and the girls, explaining that their Pa's mood had nothing to do with any of them and that it would be a very good idea if everyone kept quiet at dinner. Not understanding this, Cora and Naomi smiled and agreed.

Andrew walked into the kitchen, taking his usual seat at the dinner table, not noticing the children's rare stillness. The only thing moving on the children was their eyeballs as they glanced at one another. Andrew filled his plate and sat quietly at the head of the table, pondering his problem while he made designs in his mashed potatoes with his fork. The slave Alicia, having been warned by Aaron, made herself busy between the stove and sink, having already prayed to the good Lord to keep that small child Naomi from asking any questions.

Andrew sat forward in his chair, looking thoughtful with pursed lips. "I've been thinking," he said, staring at the wall.

The children's heads snapped in unison, their eyes staring at their father.

"We've some relatives up in Virginia." He paused as he thought further, and then he turned to Aaron. "Maybe I'll head up there in a day or two and see if I can join the Virginia army."

The children sat motionless, staring at him.

Alicia worked a little faster at the sink while silently whispering a prayer.

Aaron decided to speak up first since he was the oldest and bravest. "Ain't that a long way's, Pa?"

Andrew smiled, looking prideful at his decision. "It's a far piece, all right, Son, but not all that far." He shook his head slowly, then sat back in his chair, stirring his mashed potatoes with his fork, his appetite gone. He placed the fork on his plate and rested his elbows on the table, fingers entwined with an enthusiastic look. "Yes, sir, maybe I'll do just that."

Naomi quietly got up, walked to her Pa's chair, and stood looking up at him.

Seeing the girl, Alicia turned back to the sink and quietly whispered, "Please, dear Lord, guide that child's mouth."

"Pa?' asked Naomi.

Alicia closed her eyes and prayed faster.

Andrew looked down at his daughter and softly said, "What is it, Naomi?"

"If you go, who's gonna read to us at night?"

Andrew considered that. "Well, Daughter, I haven't figured that out just yet, but I will." He nodded with a smile. "I promise."

Naomi returned to her seat, and Alicia looked up and whispered, "Thank ya, sweet Jesus." Then, she continued scrubbing the pots and pans.

Andrew stared at the far wall as if speaking to it. "So, I'm a think'n. We have some cousins in Prince William County, Virginia."

The children looked from their father to the wall and back at Andrew, feeling slightly fearful.

Moments passed, the room became silent, and the children relaxed.

Andrew suddenly slapped the table with his hand. "Yep!"

Frightened by the sound of his hand on the table, the children's heads snapped back to him, waiting for him to speak.

"I'll just go up to Virginia, stay with them, and see about enlisting there."

The children looked at one another as he pondered his solution to the problem.

Alicia quietly took his plate and carefully hurried back to the sink.

"Thank you, Alicia," he said, smiling at her. "You can leave anytime; the children will finish up."

Relieved and wanting to leave the house, Alicia nodded, "Yes, suh." She turned and hurried out of the house, anxious to tell Matthew of Andrew's strange behavior.

Meanwhile, Andrew smiled and began telling them about his plans. Aaron would be in charge, and if they had any problems they couldn't handle, they were to go to the Davises' farm for help. "I'm not sure what'll happen when I get to Virginia," he said with a certain amount of humility. "But if I am taken into the Army, I'll send word so's y'all will know and won't worry none." He nodded approvingly to himself while the children digested what he had said. It took a few minutes before the two girls realized what was happening, began sobbing, got up from the table, and ran up the stairs to their bedroom.

Andrew looked at Aaron with a puzzled look, and Aaron shrugged his shoulders, looking puzzled himself. Andrew told the boys to start clearing the table, stood, and hurried upstairs. Reaching the girls' room, he knocked on their door, waited a moment, and walked inside. The girls were on their bed, embracing one another, sobbing.

Closing the door, he approached their bed, not sure what to say, as he smiled and sat on its edge, fussing with the quilt their mother had made. Then he spoke softly, "It's gonna be all right."

Cora looked up, her eyes red and welled with tears. "No, it's not Pa. Why do you have to go, anyway? I don't want Aaron in charge of me."

"Yeah," said Naomi with a furrowed brow, pursed lips, and tears streaming down her face.

"S'pose something happens to ya, Pa?" asked Cora as she wiped her eyes with the back of her hand.

"Yeah," repeated Naomi. "S'pose someth'n happens to ya?"

Andrew smiled. "Hey," he said as he wiped the tears from their faces, "This is your Pa, and I won't let anything happen."

"Promise?" sniffled Cora, wiping her tears with her dress.

He gently touched her head. "I promise. Now give us a big hug."

"But what about Aaron being in charge of me?" asked Cora.

"Yeah?" repeated Naomi.

Andrew fought the urge to laugh. "Aaron's the oldest, and someone needs to be in charge."

"I want you to be in charge, Pa," said Naomi, looking angry.

He smiled. "I know, but I won't be here, so Aaron will have to be in charge, so nothing bad happens to y'all while I'm gone."

The girls sat up and put their arms around his neck. He felt their wet cheeks against his and wondered if he could leave. "Now," he said, "you two need to get ready for bed." He kissed their foreheads and stood. "I'll be back later to tuck you in." He touched their heads once more, bent down, kissed their wet cheeks, and went downstairs. He wasn't worried about Aaron. He knew the boy had a good head about him and was not above asking their foreman, Jed Stattler, for advice or help when needed. On the other hand, Daniel was a different story, as he remembered how he was after their mother passed away.

Andrew walked into the kitchen, finding Aaron doing the dishes by himself. "Where's Daniel?"

Aaron nodded toward the back door. "Back porch."

"You okay with this, son?"

Aaron shrugged and nodded, looking unsure. "Guess so, Pa. It's a little scary."

Andrew felt a deep sense of pride in Aaron as he put his arms around him, giving him a quick hug. "I know it's a lot of me to ask of a boy just fifteen, but you're almost a man, and I'm proud as hell of you." He smiled proudly. "I'm proud of all my children."

"I know, Pa, but supposing I mess up and make a mistake about something?"

Andrew considered that for a moment. "You may be right about something happening. There's always that possibility, but you've been in charge when I've gone off before. I was gone two days just last month, and you were fine."

Aaron looked concerned. "That was only two days, Pa. This could be two years."

"Well," nodded Andrew thoughtfully as his smile faded. "I can't argue that. It could be a while, son, but we're at war." He paused with a serious face. "I know it doesn't make much sense, son. I've got to get into this thing and need your help. Understand, son?"

Aaron nodded. "I guess so, Pa, and like you said, if something comes up, I can always listen to Jed, and if'n I can't find him, I can ask Matthew for advice or run over to the Davis place for help."

Andrew patted him on the shoulder. "You'll do just fine, boy. Me and Daniel will be in to help with them dishes shortly."

"All right, Pa."

Andrew smiled, turned, and walked to the back porch, finding Daniel sitting on the steps, picking paint off the porch railing. "Daniel," he said in a soft voice.

Daniel ignored him and kept picking paint off the railing.

Andrew sat down next to the boy, seeing that he had been crying. "Stop picking at the paint, Son."

"Yes, sir'" Daniel quickly wiped his face with one hand.

"Hey!" Andrew leaned his shoulder against his young son playfully. "You gonna talk to your pa about all this?"

The boy sniffled, trying to hide his tears, "Ain't nuth'n' to talk about."

"Now that ain't true, Son, we have lots to talk about." Andrew placed his arm around the boy, pulling him closer.

Daniel looked up. "At first, I wanted you to go, but now I don't."

Andrew nodded thoughtfully. "I understand, boy, but sometimes things happen in our lives that we can't do much about."

"You can do something about this, Pa. You don't have to go." The boy's voice trembled. "The man in town even said you didn't have to go fight in this stupid war." Daniel sniffled, wiped his nose on his sleeve, and brushed the tears from his cheeks with his hand. "You don't have to go, Pa!"

"What you say is true, Daniel. I don't have to go. But you see, Son, the entire country is in a civil war, and I don't expect you to understand this now, but one day, maybe you will. When that time comes, you'll know I didn't have a choice." He smiled, thinking how much the boy resembled his mother. "I wish I didn't have to go, son, but this is something I have to do. There are men up north who want to change everything down here and stop us from living our lives as we see fit."

Daniel wiped his tears and looked at the shacks where the slaves lived, knowing that the reason for the war was to end slavery. "Is slavery a bad thing, Pa?"

"I don't rightly know, Son. It's been here since before I was born, and to be truthful, when I watch Matthew and John, I have mixed feelings." Andrew glanced at the two shacks. "We're poor farmer's Son, and I don't rightly know if we could make ends meet without the slaves. Never really thought much about it until all this talk about abolishing it came from up north." He shook his head thoughtfully and looked down at the ground. "I've never known another way to live, Son, but whether slavery is a bad thing or isn't, it's still our way of life. If change comes to the South, it's up to us to make those changes, not those stuffy politicians up north." He looked at Daniel. "You understand what I'm saying, Son?"

Daniel shrugged, looking unsure. "I guess so."

Andrew put his arms around him. "At times like this, I wish your mother were still alive."

"Me too."

Andrew looked toward her grave, beyond the lilac bushes, and wished she were still alive. Then, looking down at his son's wet, red eyes, he softly said, "Daniel, what I need from you right now is for you to be strong and help Aaron. He'll have a lot to do now that he's the man of the house and running this here farm." He smiled. "I need for you to promise that you'll do as your brother asks, especially with the girls, 'cause they're younger than you." He paused. "And try not to fight with them so much."

Daniel laughed. "Yes, Pa."

Andrew stood and lifted his son by the collar of his shirt, "Now, let's get inside and help Aaron with them dinner dishes."

Inside, Andrew picked up a towel and tossed it at Daniel. "We'll dry."

The boys laughed, and he knew that everything would be all right. When they finished with the dishes and the kitchen, Andrew tucked in the girls as promised and then joined Aaron at the kitchen table. After they went over the ledgers and made plans in the event he was taken into the army, Aaron said goodnight and went upstairs to bed for a sleepless night.

Andrew sat at the big oak table, looking down at the ledgers and the list they had made, making sure he hadn't forgotten anything. He set the list inside one of the ledgers, closed it, got up, and walked out onto the quiet porch. Andrew looked up at the star-filled sky and quarter moon, then across the yard at the lighted windows of Matthew's and John's houses. Faint laughter from within caused him to wonder if either or both would run north after he left. Andrew had known Matthew for almost twenty years and felt reasonably sure he would stay, but the slave, John, was another matter. He wasn't too sure about him, but since there were his woman and children to consider, chances were good that he would stay at least for a while.

Andrew turned from the shacks of the slaves and looked toward the light in the window of Jed Stattler's place. Jed was a quiet man who kept mostly to himself, but Andrew felt there was a bond between them, an unspoken trust, so to speak, and he knew that Aaron could count on Jed Stattler. Feeling the weight of the day settle around him, Andrew sat on the porch steps as laughter came from the girls' room upstairs. He worried that Aaron might run into difficulties with the girls, and then asking Rebecca Davis for help occurred to him. He looked into the darkness toward the Davis farm, thinking that maybe she could look in on them now and again. That would surely bring peace of mind while he was gone. He decided to visit the Davis farm in the morning as he stood and walked inside the house.

The next day, surprised to find Jacob Davis working in the fields with his two boys, Andrew pulled up his horse and smiled at Jacob. "Lord be Jacob, you're the last person I'd expect to see out here in the heat." Andrew climbed down from his horse, took Jacob's outstretched hand, and shook it vigorously. "No need to ask. I can see you're look'n a lot better than the last time I was by."

Jacob smiled. "I feel a whole lot better. Still a mite weak. But it sure feels good to be out here in the sunshine with my boys. What brings you by this time of day?"

"Oh, I was on my way to ask Rebecca a favor. How's them lungs?"

Jacob took off his hat and wiped his forehead with the sleeve of his forearm. "Lungs are fine. I guess I must be pretty near over whatever was ailing me. I've been out here working the past few days." Jacob suddenly looked curious. "You've come to ask a favor from my Becky?"

Andrew nodded, looking embarrassed. "That I am Jacob, if it'd be alright with you?"

Jacob scratched his head, considering that. "What sort of favor might ya be asking of my little gal?"

Not wanting at first to discuss his plans with Jacob, he frowned and looked down at the ground, but then, thinking Jacob was the girl's father, he guessed the man certainly had a right to know. "I'll try and explain as best I can, but I don't want no lecturing 'cuz I got all I needed from myself last night."

Jacob nodded, looking curious. "All right, Andy, guess I can listen like ya ask and keep my opinions to myself, so you go on and do the talking."

"I was turned down by the recruiter in Fork Township, saying I was too old."

Jacob looked at Andrew thoughtfully. "So, yer wanting to join this here fight?"

Andrew scowled as he held up one hand. "Yeah, I do, and hold on…"

Jacob interrupted. "I ain't saying nuth'n Andrew, just asking."

"Sorry, Jacob." Andrew slapped his hat against his leg and looked back toward the county road. "I can't explain it none, but I need to get in this thing."

Jacob considered that as he put his hat back on. "If I could, Andy, I'd be a get'n in this thing myself." He paused, gesturing at his two sons working a few yards away. "Afraid my two boys, there'll be a want'n to get into it, too." He looked back at Andrew. "Better if it was me. I'm afraid I won't be able to stop those two."

Andrew looked at the two boys and thought of Aaron. "Thanks for understanding, Jacob." He scratched his head, looking flustered. "I have this idea about going up to my cousin's place in Virginia and maybe joining this fight up there."

Jacob frowned as he considered his idea. "Sounds reasonable, but how'd ya know they'll take ya up there?"

Andrew shrugged. "I don't."

"Sounds a mite troublesome to me, Andy." Jacob looked puzzled. "Who's gonna take care of yer place while yer away?"

"Well, it may be troublesome, Jacob, but me and my boys have made a plan, and that brings me to the favor I need from Rebecca."

"If you don't mind me asking, what sort of favor might that be?"

Andrew took off his hat and scratched the back of his head as he looked at Rebecca hanging clothes in the back yard. "No, I don't mind you asking. You have a right to know. I was gonna ask Rebecca if she wouldn't mind look'n' in on the children while I was gone, especially my little gals. Aaron's old enough, and so's Daniel, but them little gals of mine are another thing." He looked worried. "They may need a woman's touch now and again."

Jacob chuckled, seeing his point. "Yeah, that could be. Want me to sort of look in on things once in a while as well?"

Andrew shook his head but looked thankful. "Don't believe so, Jacob. Jed's a good foreman, and I know Aaron will be all right with his help. Aaron knows to come running to you if he needs help."

Jacob considered that. "If the boys need help, I'll be most happy to oblige." He looked toward the house. "As for that favor of Becky, it'd be up to her, seeing as it's her time yer askin' fer."

Andrew extended his hand. "Thanks, Jacob, I appreciate that." They shook hands, and Andrew climbed back onto his horse.

Rebecca was hanging laundry on a line strung between the house and an old cedar tree and had already seen Andrew talking to her Pa. She laid a man's shirt over the clothesline, turned as Andrew rode up, and wiped her hands on her apron. Stepping toward him and his horse, she smiled while taking the reins and patting the horse's neck. "Good morning, Andrew."

He smiled. "Hello Rebecca, how are you this morning?"

She brushed the hair from her cheeks with the back of her hand. "Can't complain none, you?"

"No complaints." He glanced toward the fields and Jacob. "Good to see yer Pa's up and around."

She looked toward her father and nodded. "He's a lot better. Had us all worried for a while." She turned back to the task of hanging clothes. "I've got to finish hanging out this laundry." She paused, looking up at him. "You come to see pa or me?" Hoping it was the latter.

"Truth is, I came to see you, Rebecca."

She smiled at that.

He moved his horse closer. "I came to ask a favor."

She looked up with a curious face for a moment, wondering about the favor. Putting her hands on her hips, she asked, "Now, what sort of business would bring a man over here to ask a favor?"

Being a thinker, Andrew considered the question.

She waited, and when none came, she bent down for another piece of laundry, looking up at him as she placed it over the clothesline. "You gonna stay on that horse all day or climb down so's we can talk?"

Feeling the fool, he dismounted and took off his hat.

"That's better. Now I won't have to strain my neck looking up." She pointed to the basket of clothes. "Hand me them pants."

As he handed them to her, the smell of soap and clean clothes gave way to a slight whiff of perfume, bringing back the image of her climbing the stairs in her cotton dress. Suddenly, he recalled how feisty she could get and began to have second thoughts about the favor.

Perspiration trapped tiny strands of hair against her forehead as she smiled. Looking sassy, she took the pants, hanging them over the line. A slight breeze played with the clothes and her hair, carrying the aroma of her perfume. She turned and looked at him. "Andrew, you gonna tell me what brought you over here?"

Andrew felt uneasy. "I hate to ask Rebecca, but I need a favor."

She folded her arms and looked at him. "What sort of favor?"

He looked at his boots thoughtfully.

She patiently waited while enjoying the struggle he was having. He appeared a little lost and vulnerable, and she enjoyed that. It told her he was a gentle sort.

"Rebecca," he said, looking serious, "I'm going to Virginia in the morning to enlist in the Army…"

Angry and fearful at the news, she turned away as she interrupted, "You're a fool, Andrew Jackson Patterson!"

No man likes being called a fool, especially a man like Andrew Patterson. The comment took him off guard, and he didn't know what to say or do. He had certainly never expected her to react in such an angry manner.

She turned with her hands on her hips. "You've small children and a farm to run, Andrew. You've no business running off on some adventure that could get you killed."

Andrew knew she was feisty and high-spirited, but he had forgotten how outspoken she could be when upset, and she was certainly upset. He glanced at his horse, considering climbing into the saddle and riding out, but instead, he bristled in anger. "Don't expect you to understand, but I have to do this, Rebecca."

She turned away, staring at a group of trees beyond the barn for a few moments, then turned with her face flushed, "Oh, this is something you have to do?"

Still considering an escape, he knew he needed to get this settled. He looked into his horse's big black eyes, wondering who else he could ask but deciding that there was just no one else.

Rebecca told herself sternly that she had no right in saying the things she had, and after silent moments passed between them, she sighed, looking regretful. "I'm sorry, Andrew. It's none of my business or place to tell you what you should or shouldn't do." She picked up the empty basket, held it against her hip, and looked at him with a half-smile. "What's the favor?"

He nodded with a troubled look. "Ain't said nothing to me, I ain't already said to myself, Rebecca. Sorry if I got your dander up. Wasn't my intent." He paused. "As for the favor, I'd appreciate you looking in on the kids once in a while, that is, if you could find the time. Especially my two gals. It'd mean a lot."

"Of course I will. I would have even if you hadn't asked." She put the basket down and stepped between the clotheslines to separate a shirt fighting with a pair of pants.

He followed, standing behind her, watching as she untangled them, catching a whiff of her perfume.

She turned, looked up at him, and wondered what it would be like if he kissed her.

Seeing the desire on her face, he looked at her lips and her brown eyes and gently took her by the shoulders and kissed her. Letting go of her shoulders, he put his arms around her small waist, and she wrapped her arms around his neck.

Realizing what he'd just done, he stepped back. "I'm sorry, Rebecca; I had no right to do that."

She smiled. "You're such a damn fool, Andrew." She kissed him again and stood back with a smile on her face. "We best slow down, or we'll have these clothes lying on the ground."

Embarrassed, Andrew chuckled and stepped back, looking at the clothes. "That'd be a sight."

She looked toward the house. "Ma wouldn't be too happy about that."

"No, I guess not," he said softly. He looked toward the fields, glad to see that Jacob and the boys were busy. "Nor would your Pa." He looked at her. "I best be getting back to my place."

Hidden between the clothesline and his horse, she stepped closer, put her hands on his chest, and looked up at him. "Andrew, I'll watch the children for you, but only if I can sleep in your room."

He was puzzled. "Sleep in my room?"

"You heard me," she said, smiling. "I'll only do this favor if I stay at your place and sleep in your room, in your bed."

He looked at her, considering that. "What about your Pa…"

She quickly placed her hand over his mouth. "Pa's fine. You saw that for yourself. Besides, he has ma and the boys. I'm needed at your place more than I am here right now, Andy. I can always come over here during the day. Besides, I think the children will need me more in the evening than during the day, especially them gals of yours."

Andrew couldn't argue against that. "I'm giving ya fair warning. My room's a mess, and I'm leaving in the morning, so I won't have time to pick it up much."

"As if I ain't cleaned up after a man before," she said, looking irritated.

Thinking on that, he climbed onto his horse, settled into the saddle, and looked down at her. "Wish I'd kissed you a month ago."

She grinned. "Andrew, you're a coward, and you know it. You only kissed me 'cuz you're leaving."

Knowing that was true, he grinned as he backed his horse away.

She followed for a few steps, stopped, and said, "You come back from this war, Andrew Patterson. Ya hear me, you come back."

Andrew turned his horse toward the road, the smell of soap and perfume fresh in his mind, and as he rode along the county road, guilt over Rachel soon found him. He argued with himself, saying that she had been dead these two years, and he was lonely and would never have kissed another woman while she lived. Then, he remembered the night she died, when she told him to go on living and find happiness but asked that he never forget her.

He thought of the children and wondered how he would explain all of this to them. It had all happened so fast. As he considered his dilemma and what he would say, he knew he had to approach this carefully. He told himself that it had to be done correctly because once he was gone, it was out of his hands. He could only hope the children would be kind to her and give her a chance.

Sitting taller in the saddle, he nudged his horse ahead and decided he would tell them after dinner.

During dinner, the children seemed happy and talkative. Andrew hated to spoil all of that on his last night at home. He pictured the boys getting angry, especially Aaron, who would probably accuse him of not trusting him enough to take care of the place. Then there were the two girls. He envisioned crying, slamming doors, and going from this child to that one trying to explain things. Filled with anxiety, he ate very little, anticipating the scenes of tears and yelling.

As soon as the children had finished their dinner, he told Alicia she could go home and take care of her family, leaving the dishes for the children. He wanted to get on with the discussion, and after the kitchen was clean, he gathered the children in the living room, instructing them to find a place to sit on the floor. Anticipating a story, they were surprised when he told them they would have a family discussion about his going away the next morning.

Naomi's face wrinkled, looking puzzled. "We talked about that last night."

"Shhh," said Cora to her little sister. "Be quiet."

Naomi frowned at her sister. "But we did."

"All right," said Andrew. "Y'all hush now. Naomi, you're right. We did talk about this last night, but I have some good news."

"You're not going?" asked Naomi, looking hopeful.

"Yes, I'm still going," Andrew said, anticipating what was about to happen. "As you know, I'm leaving for Prince William in Virginia in the morning."

Naomi leaned against his leg, smiling up at him, waiting for him to tell them the good news.

He smiled at her and then looked around at the others. "I'm going there to see about joining the army." He paused to clear his throat while the children waited. "Well, other than my leaving, there's another reason I wanted to have this little talk."

"We know, Pa," said Daniel. "Aaron is in charge."

"That's right, Son, Aaron's in charge, but that's not what I wanted to talk to you about."

Cora moved closer, pushing Naomi away, prompting a squeal of anger and the proper angry face.

"Hush now, girls, please. The real reason I wanted to have this little talk is to tell all of you that I visited the Davis farm today and had a long talk with Miss Rebecca Davis about my leaving." Here it comes, he thought. "Seems she was quite concerned about all y'all here all alone and volunteered to stay here while I'm gone."

The children stared at him in silence, and he wondered if they had heard or even understood what he just told them. "Any y'all have anything to say?"

Naomi was the first to speak up, looking puzzled. "What was it you said about Rebecca?"

Andrew repeated the part about Rebecca staying with them. "I told her I would have to check with y'all first, but I thought it would be all right."

Cora looked at Naomi, and they began giggling as they got up and danced around the room, singing, "Rebecca's gonna stay with us. Rebecca's gonna stay with us."

Andrew grabbed their arms, telling them to sit down and be quiet, and then he looked at Daniel.

Daniel shrugged. "Okay, by me, Pa, she can help out with the girls."

Aaron nodded in agreement. "Okay, by me too, Pa. I was afraid of taking care of these guys anyway until you got back. This way, I can take care of the crops, and Rebecca can be in charge of the house and stuff."

"Can we go now, Pa?" asked Cora.

"Sure," he said, looking confused. "All y'all go on."

The children got up and left him sitting in the silence of the living room, trying to figure out what the hell had just happened and why they were so happy. Now, it seemed it didn't matter whether he left. In fact, he thought maybe they were glad he was leaving. Shaking his head in confusion, he knew this was something that only a woman would understand. "Humph," he grunted as he stood, wondering if he was in the right house. Thankful for silent blessings, he headed for the back door and his nightly talk with Rachel.

August – 1861

Having slept very little, Andrew sat on the edge of his bed, watching the arrival of his last morning at home. A narrow blue line separated the night sky from the black hilly horizon that grew steadily larger over the next few minutes. While he watched the disappearance of the night sky and stars and the arrival of the morning, he thought of last night and the children accepting Rebecca living with them while he was gone. The stars were gone, and the sun hidden behind the horizon of hills in the distance turned the sky a soft orange hue that soon would bring warmth to the valley. He thought about Rebecca, standing between the wet sheets hanging from the clothesline when he kissed her, wishing they had more time. He watched the sun rise above the hills, the rooster crowed on cue, Matthew's dogs barked in protest, and everything was as it had been for the past two years since Rachel's death. Andrew knew Matthew was sitting on his small porch, watching his dogs chase the stick he threw while waiting to go to work in the fields. '*Nothing's changed*,' he thought. All the plans Andrew had made over the years, the hard work, none of it made any difference in his leaving. Whether he was here, in Virginia, or anywhere else, for that matter, things would go on.

Believing that nothing ever really changes, he knew that no matter what happened elsewhere, things here in this valley, on this little farm, would go on. His children and the farm would be safe in this tiny, unimportant corner of South Carolina. He was sure it would be as it always was, and he thought of Rebecca and the softness of her body against his as they kissed. Suddenly, the aroma of fresh coffee from the kitchen made its way upstairs, reminding him it was time to get dressed. He stood, walked to the washbasin on the small table near the window, shaved and dressed. He picked up the old carpetbag he had packed the night before and looked around his bedroom, making sure he had everything. He stepped into the small hall, closed the bedroom door, and went downstairs.

The children were sitting around the table quietly eating while Alicia and Sadie went about their morning business. Sadie handed him a hot cup of coffee. "Yah sits down, Mistah Andrew, whilst we fixes ya some breakfast."

He thanked her, took the coffee, sat down, and sipped it as he looked at his children, wanting to remember their faces and this moment. He wanted to remember their last breakfast together as he listened to them talk of childish things accompanied by an occasional giggle.

Aaron finished first, saying he would get the wagon, got up, and walked toward the door.

Daniel got up without finishing his breakfast and quietly followed his big brother out the back door, but instead of following him to the barn, he headed around the corner of the house.

Andrew knew he was about to cry and thought it best to leave the boy alone. After eating, Andrew stood and looked around the kitchen, thinking of the hours his family had sat at this table. He turned and walked out the back door with Cora and Naomi gently hanging onto his pant legs. Outside, Andrew found Aaron waiting with the horses and wagon and the slave, Matthew, standing a few feet away. Andrew reached down and gently pushed the girls away, telling them to give him a moment, and he walked up to Matthew and placed a hand on the slave's shoulder. "You've been with me for a long time."

"Yes, suh," smiled Matthew. "Bin's a long time, Mistah Andrew."

Andrew had a worried look on his face. "Aaron's gonna need your help."

"Now, don't ya go worry'n none bout's dis here place, Mistah Andrew." Matthew's face lit up with a grin of white teeth. "Aaron's a good boy, smarter'n a whip. We all gonna do jus' fine, Mistah Andrew. Yes, sir, we gonna be jus' fine."

Andrew smiled, getting comfort from that as he extended his hand.

Surprised at the gesture, Matthew shook Andrew's hand firmly, telling him to be careful.

Andrew nodded. "Tell the others that Miss Rebecca Davis is gonna be staying until I return. She'll be sleeping in my room."

"Yes, suh, Mistah Andrew."

Andrew smiled at the big man, confident he wouldn't run off and leave his family. He couldn't explain it, but he knew he wouldn't run. Andrew turned, bent down, and said goodbye to the girls, giving them each a hug, and as he stood, he looked around for Daniel. Not seeing him, he wondered where his youngest was and climbed up next to Aaron. "Let's go, Son."

Aaron slapped the reins against the horses' backs, and the wagon lurched forward and rolled toward the county road. As they passed through the gate, Andrew looked back, waved at his daughters, and then looked again for Daniel. The boy appeared from around the house, running across the fields toward the road. Glad to see his youngest son, Andrew, stood and waved as the wagon turned away from the farm toward town. Daniel waved both arms while jumping up and down, yelling goodbye until the wagon disappeared around the bend.

Manassas, Virginia

Andrew arrived in Manassas on August 27, 1861, just one month after the first battle of Bull Run. Confederate soldiers were everywhere, raising his hopes that he would soon be wearing a smart, gray uniform. He walked through town and down a long and narrow dirt road toward the Patterson farm, which lay northeast of the city, arriving in time for supper.

On the morning of August 28, 1861, Andrew Jackson Patterson joined the Confederate States Army. It didn't matter that his enlistment was conditional, and he could only serve one year because of his age. Filled with the excitement of a child, he took the Oath of the Confederacy and was assigned to Company D of General Wade Hampton's Infantry Legions.

After reporting for duty, he was happy to learn that the legions were made up of men from South Carolina and had participated in the battle for Manassas at Bull Run the month before. Andrew Patterson was finally in the place he wanted to be, and now he had the chance to fight for the South. He was happy and excited yet homesick. His indoctrination over, he was issued a Confederate gray uniform that was a little big in places, a used rifle, and a backpack. Then, he settled down in a small tent where he wrote a letter to Rebecca and his children. Within days, the regiment broke camp to winter near the city of Richmond.

Anderson County, South Carolina

November 1861

Rebecca Davis caressed the pillow while watching the night lose its battle with the coming day. Her tears mixed with the pillow as she prayed for Andrew's safe return, wishing the war was over and that he was holding her in his arms, protecting her from the morning chill. The rooster crowed, and Matthew's dogs barked as they had every morning for the past several weeks since Rebecca moved in. She hugged the pillow, remembering the day Andrew came to their farm, seeking a favor, recalling their argument, and then their kiss. She didn't know her mother had been watching from the chicken coop and recalled their conversation later that night. Rebecca told her mother that she was in love with Andrew. Mrs. Davis had always liked Andrew, believing he was a decent, hard-working man, and she wasn't concerned about their age difference, telling her daughter that a man can only grieve so long. He needs a proper wife to cook, wash, warm him on cold nights, and give him children."

Rebecca sat against the headboard filled with those memories while watching the morning bring in a new day. She decided to visit her mother later in the afternoon. She lit the kerosene lantern on the stand next to the bed and opened a drawer, retrieving a small wooden box containing two letters from Andrew. Although sleepy, she opened the box, took out one of the envelopes, pulled out a piece of paper containing penciled words, and began to read.

Cora carefully opened Rebecca's bedroom door just enough so she could peer inside, seeing that Rebecca was still sleeping. Quietly creeping across the room, she sat on the edge of the bed, watching her sleep, and noticed the letters lying on the floor. Cora slid off the bed, picked them up, and examined each one, finding her name among the words she couldn't read, which pleased her. She climbed back onto the bed, leaned close to Rebecca's face, and gently shook her shoulder. "Time to get up, Becky. Breakfast is ready."

Rebecca opened her eyes and smiled at Cora. Then, as she sat up, rubbing her eyes, she realized she had fallen asleep. "Guess I fell asleep reading them letters from your pa."

Cora smiled, looking hopeful. "Will you read his letters to me, Becky?"

Rebecca yawned, took the letters, and placed them on the table next to the bed. "I already read them letters to you and the others. Right now, I've got to get up."

Cora giggled. "I like the part where he writes my name." She jumped off the bed, ran out of the room, and down the stairs, yelling, "Rebecca's up!"

Rebecca dressed and hurried downstairs, finding the children all seated at the table waiting for her. She paused at Andrew's chair, where Alicia handed her a cup of coffee. She thanked Alicia and then looked at Aaron. "Aaron, I think you're in the wrong place." She gestured to Andrew's chair. "Shouldn't you be sitting at the head of the table?"

Aaron looked surprised, as did the others. "Gee Becky, you're the oldest and have been sitting there."

Rebecca nodded, looking sincere. "Well, I've been thinking on that, and y'all's pa told me that you were taking care of things while he was gone, so I figure you should be the one sitting at the head of the table."

The other children silently watched Aaron, waiting to see what he would do. He glanced at the others and then at Rebecca, "Well, if'n you think I should."

"I think you should," she said, smiling. "So, pick up your plate and take your place at the head of the table. I'll sit here next to Daniel."

After Aaron sat down, he proudly looked at the others and began eating. Rebecca filled her plate, announcing that she would visit her ma and pa after the morning chores. The girls begged to go with her. "We'll see," she said.

Alicia bent over, leaned close to Rebecca, and whispered, "Matthew is in dah barn, Miss Becky, and needs ta talks wit' ya." She looked worried. "Tis purdy important."

Curious about why he wanted to see her, Rebecca excused herself and went looking for Matthew, finding him slopping the pigs in the sty behind the barn. "You wanted to see me, Matthew?"

He tossed the last of the slop, put down the bucket, and nodded. "Yessum," Then he took a rag from his pocket, wiped his hands, and frowned, looking worried.

She waited until he finished. "Something wrong, Matthew?"

Still looking worried, Matthew glanced around, leaned a little closer, and lowered his voice. "Miss Becky. Don't quite knows how's ta tell ya dis, but John's done up and ran away."

Rebecca looked at John's shack. "What?" She looked at Matthew. "Are you sure, Matthew?"

He nodded his head, eyes big, looking scared. "Oh, yessum, Miss Becky. He done up and left late last night, took some food, and all his stuff with 'im."

"How do you know all this?"

Matthew looked troubled. "Wells, Miss Becky, he nevah came out dis morn'n. So, I went to his place and found Sadie cry'n and looking real scared. Dat's when she told me John took some food and his clothes and left, saying he was head'n north. Dat's when I told my Alicia to tell you first thing." He paused. "I thought about telling Mistah Aaron, but since ya's dah oldest, I best tell ya, Miss Becky."

"He left his family?"

"Uh-huh! He sure did, Miss Becky." He gestured toward John's shack. "Dey's in dah house. Sadie bin crying most o' da morn'n. She's 'fraid what you and Mistah Aaron might do's to her."

"Ain't no reason for her to be afraid," Rebecca said. "She ain't done nuth'n wrong." Rebecca glanced around the farm full of worry, then looked toward the road, half expecting to see someone riding in asking about John. She started toward John's shack. "Come with me." Rebecca knocked on the door, glanced at Matthew, and waited.

The door opened, and Sadie stood in the dim doorway, looking frightened while holding a dishtowel against her chest. Her face was wet with tears.

Rebecca felt sorry for Sadie and could see she was scared as she stepped inside.

Sadie stepped back into the dim room, crying. "I's sorry, Miss Becky."

"You've nothing to be sorry for, Sadie," said Rebecca. "This ain't none of your fault, and it's gonna be alright. Now sit down." Rebecca looked around the room. A sturdy wooden table with three chairs and a long bench occupied a place close to the fireplace where Sadie did her cooking. Two wooden chairs separated by a small table and a lamp occupied a corner by the small window. Sadie's two boys sat on two narrow cots with their backs against the wall, staring at her and looking frightened. Next to the cots was an open doorway that led to a small bedroom. Rebecca told Sadie to sit down, and then she sat next to her. "Matthew says that John has run away, Sadie. Is that right?"

Tears rolled down Sadie's cheeks. "Yes'um. He done run for da North, for freedom, he say." Sadie glanced at her two boys. "Said he come back someday and buys us all back."

Rebecca glanced at the two boys in the dim light, unable to read their expressions. While Sadie buried her face in the dishtowel crying, Rebecca contemplated what she should do next. Feeling sorry for Sadie, Rebecca reached out and lowered Sadie's hands away from her face. "Sadie," she said softly. "Listen to me. This is important, and you must understand what I'm saying."

"Yes'um," sobbed Sadie, looking frightened.

"Y'all have nothing to fear." She looked at the two boys. "Y'all are not to blame for what John does. Do you understand that?"

"Yes'um," replied Sadie as the two boys nodded yes.

"Good," said Rebecca. "Because no one is going to send you away. All y'all still belong to Andrew."

Sadie said she understood but still looked worried and frightened. "What 'bouts John, Miss Becky? Dem slave hunters will be goin' aftah 'im, an dey'll beats 'im terrible when dey catches 'im!"

Rebecca squeezed Sadie's hand, knowing Sadie was probably right about that. They may even hang John now that there was a war to end slavery. She looked at the two boys, then at Sadie, wondering what to do when suddenly she realized what she had to do. She motioned for the two boys to come closer.

Rebecca looked from the boys to Sadie. "Y'all have to listen very carefully to what I am going to tell you." Rebecca glanced at Matthew, standing just inside the door, then looked at Sadie. "We're not going to say anything about this for a while. Not unless someone comes and asks, and then I'll do all the talking."

She looked at Sadie and the two boys. "Do y'all understand? This is important."

Sadie nodded. "Yessum."

The boys looked afraid, but each nodded that they also understood.

Rebecca turned and looked back at Matthew, "Do you understand?"

Matthew nodded. "Yessum, Miss Becky."

Rebecca stood, motioned for Matthew to come closer, leaned toward Sadie and the boys, and spoke in a low voice as if fearing someone would overhear what she was going to say. "If anyone comes to the farm and asks about John, y'all just tell `em to talk to me. Understand?"

Matthew nodded. "Yessum, I sho do, but what's do I tells `em, Miss Becky?"

"You tell `em nothing. Just say, 'Best ya see, Miss Becky.' That's all you have to say, do you understand?" She looked at Sadie and the boys. "Do you understand?"

All three nodded that they did.

Matthew was holding his hat, nervously turning the brim in his hands as he repeated, "Best ya go sees Miss Becky."

Rebecca looked from one to the other, wondering if she was doing the right thing. Fearing that with Andrew gone, the Home Guard may think that Matthew and the others knew that John was going to run and failed to tell anyone. She glanced at Sadie and then over Matthew's shoulder at the door, thinking they'd come looking soon. Then Rebecca thought of Jed Stattler. How could she handle this strange man who very seldom spoke? She had no idea where his loyalties lay, and suddenly Rebecca felt sick to her stomach. She looked at Sadie, feeling pity for her and the boys. Finally, she looked at Matthew, realizing she was putting all their lives in danger by not reporting a runaway slave to the Home Guard.

She was concerned that the Home Guard would take Sadie and the children away, accusing them of helping John run off. She thought that if Andrew were here, everything would be all right. But Andrew wasn't here to protect his slaves, and Aaron was just a boy. She considered going to her Pa, but that would mean more people knowing what had happened. No, this was the best way, she told herself. Rebecca didn't want the Home Guard poking around, scaring the slaves and Andrew's children. She needed to buy time until things settled down. She would report John after she had time to think. "I want everyone to go on about your work," she said. "We can't do anything about John now. He's gone, Sadie, and chances are you'll never see your man again, so best be getting used to the idea."

"Yessum," Sadie said, holding the towel to her face and sobbing into it.

Rebecca glanced at the boys and then at Matthew. "Matthew, you best get Alicia to help Sadie for the rest of the day."

"Yessum."

She followed Matthew outside. "Do you think John's boys will run?"

"No, ma'am Miss Becky, dey will stay here wit' their ma. Dey's still young and 'fraid of dem slave hunters."

Rebecca considered that. "That's good. We best make sure they stay afraid."

He nodded. "Yessum."

She returned to the house and told the children about John. After many questions, she finally convinced them she was doing the right thing and stressed the importance of not saying a word to anyone about this for the time being. The children wanted to know why, and Rebecca thought for a long moment. "I don't know. Maybe I don't want the Home Guard nosing around here asking all sorts of questions with Andrew gone. I'm not sure they'd believe that Sadie and the boys or Matthew didn't know he was going to run off and failed to tell us. Your pa's not here, and I'm not sure they wouldn't take her and the children off someplace."

"They wouldn't do that," replied Aaron, looking skeptical.

Rebecca's expression was fear. "I'm not too sure about anything these days, Aaron. You're probably right, but I'd just as soon see if we can get through this without them coming around."

Aaron nodded. "Okay, Becky, but what if they do?"

"You just tell them to see me."

The children went about their chores while she sat alone at the kitchen table, thinking of the Home Guard. She didn't want the Home Guard accusing her of trying to help a runaway slave and briefly reconsidered her decision. After a moment's pause, Rebecca decided that she had already started this, and she would see it to the end, remembering her father telling her she was too stubborn for her own good. Her thoughts turned to Jed Stattler, and she knew she had to talk with him now and find out what he would do about John.

She went outside to look for Jed, finding him behind the barn, greasing a wagon's axle. Seeing her, he politely stood, smiled, and wiped the grease off his hands with an already dirty rag. He nodded, "How do Miss Becky?"

Rebecca smiled, trying to look friendly. "Jed."

Jed Stattler stood six feet and was a thin, wiry man. His once-black hair was mostly gray and thinning on top but full on the sides and back, bulging from under his old gray hat with a floppy brim. He looked at Rebecca with soft, friendly, dark brown eyes framed by deep squint lines on a clean-shaven, leathery face.

Like the others, she wondered at his age, but no one had ever asked. No one knew much about him, and he never offered much about his past or his age. When Andrew had hired him fifteen years earlier, he did not ask Jed many questions about where he came from, and Jed never volunteered any information. Andrew pretty much took people the way they came, and while Jed appeared a mite slow, Andrew soon found out that he wasn't slow at all. He was a thinker who pondered questions more than most before answering.

Trying not to appear bossy, Rebecca said, “We need to talk about something Jed.”

Jed placed the dirty rag on the wagon seat while waiting for her to speak.

She told him about John and her decision to handle it while unable to hide her own emotions of fear and worry.

Jed took off his hat and scratched the top of his head with one hand, the other holding his hat against his hip, his face full of worry. He looked down at the wheel, leaning next to the wagon axle, then put his hat back on. “Bad situation, all right.”

Rebecca waited for him to say something else. When he didn’t, she said, “I know that, Jed.” Trying to hide her irritability, she asked, “But what about you? Will you help me?”

He looked at her for a moment, considering her question as he leaned against the wagon, looking thoughtful. “The way I see it, if Andrew were here, he might handle things a little different, but then again, he might not.”

Rebecca stared at him, thinking he wasn’t a lot of help. “Jed, will you help me? I’m not asking you to lie if anyone should come to you, especially the Home Guard. I’m asking you to say, ‘Best ya go talk to Miss Becky,’ and I’ll handle it from there.”

Jed frowned as he stared across the fields, apparently not too happy with what she asked of him. Several moments of silence passed, then he looked at her. “Let me tell ya something, Miss Becky. You probably know this, but then again, maybe you don’t, but I ain’t from around here.”

She wondered what that had to do with the current situation but listened anyway.

“I’m a runaway myself of sorts. I ran away from my home up in Pennsylvania after my pa nearly beat me to death over a mule I shot by mistake. I was aiming at a tree, and the damn fool animal stepped in front of me, and I shot `em in the head.” He bent down, picked up a stone, looked at it briefly, and then dropped it. “I ran away and never looked back. I’ve worked several places, harder than hell at times, hating everybody and every place I ever stopped.”

He looked around with a half-smile. “Till I got here.” He paused a moment, letting his happiness and contentment show. “Me and Andy, rather Andrew, well we hit it off, ya might say. He’s always been fair with me, pays me a decent wage, gives me that little place over yonder to live in, and don’t begrudge me getting drunk now and again or, excuse me for saying, taking a gal once in a while.” He smiled, looking embarrassed.

Rebecca pushed the images of that out of her mind, wishing he would say what he had on his mind.

He stood, looking stern and determined. "I'll back ya, Miss Becky, fer two reasons. First, 'cause I know Andrew would want me to no matter what, and second 'cause I ain't exactly fond of the damn Home Guard."

Rebecca smiled with relief. "Thank you, Jed."

He nodded and then returned to greasing the wagon's axle without another word, just as if she had already left.

Rebecca turned and walked away, thinking Jed was a strange man.

Jed paused in what he was doing and looked up. "Best, you be careful, Miss Becky. The Home Guard can be downright mean."

Rebecca stopped, turned, and looked at Jed as he worked on the wheel, considering his warning. Hoping she had done the right thing, Rebecca turned and walked across the yard and into the house.

The rest of the day passed without incident, and that evening, the family had a quiet dinner with no one speaking of John. As the evening settled in and Rebecca was alone in her room lying in the darkness, fear rushed at her, bringing with it visions of the Home Guard, and now she second-guessed her decision from the morning. Had she acted out of pity for Sadie and her children, or just plain stupidity? She told herself, whichever one it was, it was too late now. The pie was in the oven, as her grandmother used to say. She turned over and began to cry as she hugged Andrew's pillow, wishing he was there with her.

The weeks passed. Christmas came and went, and now it was mid-January 1862. There had been no word or sign of the slave John, and it seemed as if everything was going to be all right. The days that followed saw rain, and occasionally rain mixed with light snow, but never enough to cover the ground, much to the children's disappointment. At night, the temperatures dropped close to freezing, the fields were muddy, and the livestock was moved from pasture to pasture to what little grass there was. Other chores kept their minds occupied, and almost everyone forgot about John.

After a few weeks, the weather warmed enough for the children to return to school except for Aaron, who was running the farm in such a manner that Andrew would have been proud. He kept busy with the farm during the day, and in the evenings, after Rebecca helped the children with their lessons, he read stories from the Bible just as Andrew had done.

The days slowly passed while Rebecca waited for word from Andrew or news of the war. The nights were cold and lonely as she lay in bed, thinking of him and praying he was safe. Once late at night, she was awakened by thunder far off in the distance. She got out of bed and sat by the window, watching the flashes under the starry, black sky along the horizon, knowing it wasn't thunder but cannons. She thought of Andrew and wondered if he was taking part in the battle.

On the evening of February 23rd, 1862, Rebecca and the children had just finished dinner. They were talking about unimportant things when loud pounding at the back door interrupted. Startled, everyone stared at it in silence as Rebecca placed a finger to her lips, signaling quiet. Thinking of John, she whispered. "Let me do the talking."

Getting up from her chair, she walked to the door, reached up, and took down Andrew's musket rifle from above the door. The loud pounding continued, and she yelled, "Coming!" Glancing back at the children gathered around the table looking worried, she suddenly noticed that Aaron was not at the table, but with no time to worry, she opened the door just enough to peer outside.

Recognizing an old friend, Michael Evans, standing on the porch smiling, she opened the door a little wider. "Hello, Michael."

"Hi, Miss Becky," he said. "We need to talk to you about a matter of some importance. Mind if we come in?"

Rebecca had known Michael since childhood and heard he was with the Home Guard. She smiled as she stepped aside. "I suppose it'd be all right. Come in."

He took off his hat as he stepped inside, noticing the gun she was holding, and as the two men followed him inside, removing their hats, Aaron walked in from the other room carrying his pa's old pistol held tightly in one hand. Michael Evans looked at the old pistol and smiled.

Rebecca turned to see what was so amusing to Michael. "That won't be necessary, Aaron. I know this man, and he means us no harm."

She looked at Evans as she closed the door. "How's your family, Michael?"

"Everyone's fine, Miss Becky." He gestured at the gun she was holding. "We ain't looking for no trouble, just want to talk." He nodded at his two companions. "You know George Applegate, and this here's Randy Murphy."

Rebecca smiled at George, trying to look friendly. "Of course I do; hello, George."

He smiled politely and nodded, "Miss Becky."

Rebecca looked at the other man. "Hello, Mr. Murphy."

He was staring at the children. "Ma'am," he said without looking at her.

Rebecca looked at Michael. "You mentioned there was something of importance."

"Yes," he answered.

She gestured to the parlor door. "Let's go into the parlor where we can talk." She turned to Alicia. "Alicia, be a dear and bring these gentlemen some hot coffee so they can warm themselves."

"Yessum."

The men followed Rebecca into the parlor, where they sat down and waited for Alicia to pour the coffee. Michael Evans looked at the rifle Rebecca was still holding and smiled. "You gonna shoot us, Becky?"

The other men laughed while Rebecca blushed. Then she stood the rifle against the wall near the parlor door and waited for Alicia to pour the coffee. "Land sakes no, Michael. I didn't know it was you, or I wouldn't have been afraid."

Michael smiled, sipped his hot coffee carefully, and then asked, "Have y'all lost a slave, Miss Becky?"

Her heart jumped, but she remained calm. "Call me Becky, Michael. And yes, we have. Andrew's slave John up and disappeared a few weeks back."

"That so?" asked Randy Murphy.

Rebecca disliked him immediately, thinking he had cold eyes, and something unsettling about him bothered her. "Yes, it is," she replied matter-of-factly.

"If that be the case, Miss Becky," said George Applegate as he glanced first at Randy, then Michael, and then at her. "Why wasn't this reported to the authorities? Ya know we're trying to stop the Negroes from joining the damn northern army."

"Why no," Rebecca said, looking innocent. "I didn't know that." She smiled at Michael. "I'm only staying here to help Andrew Patterson with his children while he's off fighting in this terrible war." She paused, looking at each man. "As I'm sure all y'all would also rather be doing this very night."

George and Randy looked uneasy as they glanced at one another and then at Michael, who smiled, enjoying the way Rebecca handled herself, remembering her feistiness in school. She could always hand it out better than she ever got. He looked toward the kitchen. "What about the children? They'd surely know to report such things."

Rebecca leaned forward in her chair and looked through the doorway at the children sitting quietly at the kitchen table. Then, leaning back, she looked at Michael. "They're children, Michael, and they don't know the rules of war."

George leaned forward in his chair thoughtfully. “T’ain’t war we’re talk’n about, Miss Becky, it’s a runaway slave.”

Rebecca shot him a look.

George sat back in his chair.

She smiled. “I disagree, Mr. Applegate. To the children and me, they’re one and the same.”

Michael Evans smiled, knowing Becky had the better of Applegate.

George looked past her again into the kitchen. “But isn’t the oldest boy? What’s his name?”

“Aaron.” She replied. “His name is Aaron.”

Applegate looked at her. “Ain’t he old enough to know he’s supposed to report a runaway slave?”

Rebecca digested that, knowing she was in trouble, but then she glanced at Michael, deciding to go on the offensive by putting a little anger in her voice. “Oh, for heaven’s sake, George,” she said, looking angry. She paused for effect, getting the correct reaction from him. “Aaron is still a boy whose father is off fighting this awful war. Why he could be dead or wounded someplace up north for all we know.” She looked through the door at Aaron sympathetically. “Poor boy, he was charged with keeping this farm going, making sure the cows don’t run off or get stolen.” She looked back at the three men, her expression filled with sorrow. “He’s tries so hard to be both father and brother to the children, not to mention worrying about me.” She sighed, looking down at her hands and then at the men. “Do you have any idea what that boy’s gone through?”

The three men looked at Aaron thoughtfully while Rebecca stood and gathered their cups that still contained coffee and set them on the table while talking. “The poor boy is more worried about losing this farm, or one of the children getting hurt, or the cows dying, or a number of other things while his father’s gone.” She shook her head, looking despondent. “He’s more worried about those things than anything else, including what to do about a runaway slave.” She picked up the tray and walked into the kitchen, leaving the three sitting in the parlor. As she passed the table where the children were, she mouthed for them to go upstairs.

Daniel and his two sisters got up and headed up the stairs while Aaron remained motionless at the table, holding his pa’s pistol.

Rebecca set the tray on the kitchen table and turned toward the parlor and the three men. “I think the three of y’all would have more important issues to pursue than one runaway slave.” She looked at Michael. “Now, if y’all will excuse us, it’s getting late.”

Having dealt with Rebecca on other occasions, Michael knew not to waste his time. He turned to the others as he stood. "We're done here." Then, the three men walked through the kitchen to the back door. Michael smiled. "Nice seeing you again, Becky."

She forced a smile. "Nice to see you again, too, Michael. Be sure and tell your folks I said hello."

Michael returned her smile. "I'll do that. You take care now."

George stepped closer to Michael, glanced at Rebecca, and then looked directly at Michael. "Don't Andrew have a hired hand working the place? Maybe he knows something."

Rebecca's heart jumped.

Michael quickly considered that. "Have you ever talked to Jed?"

George shook his head. "Can't say as I ever have."

"Well," said Michael. "Let's just say it's late, and there's no need to bother old Jed. I'm sure he doesn't know anything more than Becky or the children here do, and besides, he's just a hired hand." He smiled at Rebecca. "Thanks for the coffee and your time, Miss Becky. We're done here for now."

She watched as they walked into the chilly night air to their waiting horses, climbed into their saddles, and rode away. As the sound of horses' hooves faded, Rebecca closed the door, resting her back against it, and looked at Aaron sitting at the table with the pistol in front of him. She closed her eyes and sighed, thinking about Michael's last words. "For now."

Ten

December 1861 - February 1862

Edward McAlexander

Fort Henry Kentucky

Fort Henry, an earthen fort standing on the Tennessee River's east bank, was under Brigadier General Lloyd Tilghman's command. Several old, outdated cannons were placed slightly above the high watermark. Because of its proximity to the river, the fort constantly needed repair from flooding during heavy rains.

Brigadier General Tilghman realized that if the surrounding hills fell into the Federals' hands, it would be impossible to defend the fort. That prompted him to build a secondary fortification across the river on the western bluff named Fort Heiman after the Colonel put in charge of its construction.

First Lieutenant Edward Asbury McAlexander first laid eyes on Fort Henry on a cold, wintry day of mild snow flurries on the 29th of December, 1862. He quickly joined the ranks of the 27th, Alabama, who had marched into the fort three days earlier, increasing the garrison's strength to 3,200 men. After reporting to the fort's commandant and then to the commander of the 27th, another officer escorted Edward across the snowy, muddy parade ground to the officers' quarters. There, he was greeted by many familiar faces from Lauderdale County.

The barracks was cramped and allowed little privacy. Cots lined the walls, separated by tall, narrow wooden closets. Three potbellied stoves radiated heat from both ends and the center of the room, each needing constant tending.

Edward followed the orderly to an empty cot at the far end of the barracks, where he placed his bag on the floor and sat on the edge of his cot, glancing around the room. His eyes settled on the man lying on the cot next to his, busy reading a book he held in front of his face.

Slowly, the book lowered, and the man smiled. "Hello, Asshole!"

Edward grinned with surprise. "Ethan, you son of a bitch."

The man was Ethan Hall, an old friend of Edward's. He was a big man standing almost six-one, boasting a big robust chest and muscular hairy arms whose large hands dwarfed the book he held. His friendly face needed a shave, and his unruly, curly, black hair needed a cut. Since their early school days, the two men had been friends, sharing in many deeds of mischief, often resulting in the use of a hickory stick by several teachers. After the usual greeting that consisted of a quick hug and handshake, they sat down on their cots and talked about old times and the fort's lack of amenities until late in the evening.

Over the next several days, the men of the 27th Alabama assisted in the work on Fort Heiman, returning across the river each evening for dinner and sleep. In the late afternoon of a day in the second week, Edward and Ethan were resting on their cots talking when an orderly approached, telling Edward that Colonel Hughes wanted to see him.

"Now, what've you done?" asked Ethan, who thoughtfully added, "You don't suppose he has a hickory stick, do you?"

Edward smiled. "I doubt it. Colonel Hughes doesn't seem the type." He buttoned his jacket while looking at Ethan. "Unlike you, I've kept my mouth shut."

Ethan grinned, looking skeptical. "That'll be the day, ya little shit."

Edward grabbed his hat and followed the orderly, chased by Ethan's yelling voice. "Some things never change Asshole. You're the one about to get your little ass spanked!"

Edward returned an hour later, brushing the light snow from his Confederate gray jacket. After tossing his hat on his bed, he sat on its edge, noticing Ethan had fallen asleep, and the book he had been reading since the day Edward arrived lay on the floor, inches from Ethan's open, outstretched hand. He smiled as he softly said, "You always were a slow reader." Then he gently shook Ethan's arm.

Ethan opened his dark eyes and sleepily looked up at Edward, sat up, put his feet on the floor, yawned, and combed his curly, black hair with one hand. "Why the big smile, Asshole? You get a little?"

Edward's face filled with a grin as he extended his hand, holding the new Major's bars.

Ethan peered into his hand and looked at him with disappointment. "Tell me you're shitting me."

"I've been promoted to Major, you sorry ass Lieutenant."

"Asshole." Ethan looked irritated. "Shit, if anyone around here should be promoted, it's me, not some fancy little kiss-ass."

Edward grinned. "Who in their right mind would promote you, Ethan? Hell, you're crazy most of the time. You even scared the shit out of your own mother."

Ethan frowned, considering the accusation. "That's true. I can't deny it." Then he smiled. "Never could scare my pa, though."

Edward chuckled. "Your pa knew you were crazy, Ethan. That's why he sent you away to school."

Ethan stood, grabbed Edward by the shoulders, and grinned. "A mere First Lieutenant on the 29th of January and a Major on the 30th." Then he frowned. "The way I figure it, you should be a general in three or four weeks." He shook Edward by the shoulders, jerking his head back and forth. "Congratulations, but this just makes you a bigger asshole." Suddenly, Ethan looked disappointed. "Guess I can't call you Asshole any longer. I ain't gonna like that much." He paused, looking sad. "Ah shit, this means I have to salute your little ass. What'll my pa say?"

"I imagine he'd say something like: the better man got promoted."

Ethan put his big arms around Edward, squeezing him so tight Edward couldn't breathe. "You little asshole, you can't talk about my pa like that."

Edward struggled to break free. "I didn't say anything about your pa."

Ethan let go of Edward. "You didn't?"

Edward laughed as he rubbed his shoulders. "No."

"Guess I misunderstood," he said, looking apologetic. "And to show there are no hard feelings, I'll buy you a drink."

Edward glanced around the barracks. "Where the hell you gonna get a drink around here?"

Ethan put his big hands on Edward's shoulders, turned him around, pushed him toward the other end of the barracks, and approached a corner cot occupied by a sleeping, skinny First Lieutenant. Ethan loudly cleared his throat.

The skinny First Lieutenant, Charles, opened his eyes, looked up, and softly said, " Lo Ethan."

"Howdy, Charles," replied Ethan. "This here's a friend of mine from back home."

"Uh-huh," replied Charles as he looked Edward over carefully before extending his hand.

Edward shook his hand.

Ethan whispered, "Got any stuff?"

The skinny First Lieutenant appeared uneasy as he looked from Ethan to Edward. "Maybe."

Ethan glanced around the barracks and then bent down, offering the skinny officer some money, which he quickly took and shoved under his pillow.

Edward couldn't figure out what all the cloak and dagger was about since everyone in the place probably knew he had smuggled in several bottles. The First Lieutenant slowly got up and nodded toward his closet. Ethan and Edward followed so closely that they ran into one another when he stopped. The skinny officer bent down, and when he stood, he held a small bottle of whiskey.

"Pretty small bottle," uttered Edward.

"Shut up," whispered Ethan as he shoved the bottle under his jacket, thanked the lieutenant, and grabbed Edward by the elbow, leading him back to their cots.

"Why the big secret?" asked Edward. "Everyone probably knows about the stash."

"Adds to the flavor, don't you know anything?"

The sound of reveille came too early for Edward and Ethan the next morning.

"Ah, shit!" came a moan from under Ethan's blanket.

Edward sat up, looking at the lump of covers. "Get up, Ethan. It's time. I have a meeting after breakfast."

The two dressed and walked across the muddy parade grounds to the mess hall, where they got in line for breakfast. Slowly making their way through the line, they sat at a table with other men when the same orderly that had taken Edward to see the colonel approached their table.

"Here comes trouble," said Ethan, nodding at the orderly.

"Major?" the orderly asked.

"That's him!" Ethan said, pointing at Edward.

"What is it, Private?" asked Edward.

"The colonel would like to see you, sir."

"Can't be another promotion," teased Ethan thoughtfully. "Even you aren't that good."

Edward ignored Ethan and gulped his coffee. "Shit, I forgot about the staff meeting." Then he grabbed his hat and followed the orderly out of the mess hall.

As Edward and the orderly walked away, Ethan shoved his empty plate aside, picked up Edward's plate, and began eating.

The cold January air greeted Edward as he and the orderly walked out of the warm mess hall. Pulling his collar up around his neck, he glanced at the gray morning clouds, wishing the sun would break through. Reaching the colonel's quarters, he knocked on the door.

"Enter," commanded a voice on the other side.

Edward opened the door and stepped inside the room filled with fellow officers.

"Good morning, Major," greeted Colonel Hughes.

Feeling a bit embarrassed at being late, he apologized for his tardiness.

The colonel gestured to the only empty seat, and while Edward sat down, the colonel filled a tin cup with water, took a small drink, and looked around at his men. "I attended a staff meeting with Brigadier General Tilghman earlier this morning." Hughes paused, looking concerned. "The general feels this old fort needs help, and I intend to see that the 27th does all it can to make the necessary repairs. Our big guns are old, but they're all we have, and while we can't do much about that, we can help in other ways." The meeting continued for almost another hour as the colonel repeated the general's fears of flooding by the Tennessee River should the weather change and heavy rains begin.

The colonel gave each officer their orders, saving the last for Edward. "Major," smiled the colonel. "The dirtiest job is always left for last, and since you were the last one through that door, I guess the dirtiest job is yours."

"Yes, sir," replied Edward, thinking of his men and how they would love him for this one.

"I want you to bring your men back across the river from Fort Heiman. Y'all have the task of working on the outer perimeter of the fort, building small walls with dirt and trees as dams to prevent further flooding." The colonel smiled. "Don't take it too hard, Major. The beavers seem to enjoy their work, and I'm sure your men will also." The colonel paused and added, "There'll be other times, Major, when I'm sure you won't be last."

"Yes, sir!" replied Edward, promising himself that he would never be last again.

By the 2nd of February, the mud dams were complete, so Edward and his men returned across the river to help build Fort Heiman. Around mid-morning, Colonel Hughes summoned all officers under his command to his quarters, informing them that President Lincoln had issued General War Order Number One to all United States naval and land forces. He looked sullen. "All Federal forces are preparing a general advance on the South." Hughes paused, looking at their faces. "The advance will begin no later than February 22nd. Since that is George Washington's birthday, it appears Lincoln has a sense of humor."

Light laughter filled the room.

The Colonel picked up a pointer and turned toward a large map of the area. "We believe the Federal troops will advance from two directions. Down the Tennessee River and another larger force by land."

Hughes turned from the map. "From what intelligence we have gathered, it appears General Ulysses S. Grant didn't want to wait for

George's Birthday." The room filled with laughter, and as it quieted, he continued. "It looks like the war is about to catch up to us, gentlemen, and it's imperative that we do all we can to see that our men and both forts are properly prepared." He tapped the map with the pointer. "We've posted scouts about a mile upriver, here, and here. Several men on horseback have been sent out searching for Federal troops to the east."

He looked away from the map. "We must complete as much work on Fort Heiman as possible." He paused. "I know this is asking a lot of your men, but we must have defendable positions when the Federals arrive. See to it. You're dismissed."

Edward returned to his quarters, gathering his pistol and sword before joining the other men crossing the river in small boats to Fort Heiman. Hours later, Edward and Lt. Colonel James Jackson, second in command of the 27th, walked around Fort Heiman, stepping in mud and icy water. They had known each other socially in Florence, so Edward felt at ease expressing his concerns about repelling any attack on this position.

"Colonel," began Edward. "As you know, we have over 200 men sick from the measles across the river in Fort Henry."

"Yes, I know, Major."

"Sir, that leaves only 550 tired, cold, and hungry men to defend this position; some of them are sick with bad colds."

"I realize that, Major. What's your point?"

"The Fort is nowhere near complete, and I don't feel we can hold this position very long if we come under attack."

Colonel Jackson stopped and turned. "Major," he said. "I understand your concerns, but we have our orders to build this damn fort, and if the Federals give us enough time, we will."

Edward recognized a lost argument. "Yes, sir."

Lt. Colonel Jackson turned toward the river, staring at it in silence for several moments. "We've split our forces between two mud forts, both attackable by the river and land." He looked at Edward. "I don't like it much, Major, but like all good soldiers, we have our orders to follow."

"Yes, sir."

Jackson nodded. "Now, if there's nothing else, we have a fort to build." He turned and walked toward the river just as a light rain mixed with sleet started falling.

"Great!" mumbled Edward as he looked up into the gray sky of falling snow. Thinking of a warm fireplace and a glass of brandy, he turned and walked toward his men working to enforce the dirt walls of Fort Heiman.

On the afternoon of February 4,1862, Edward and his men were still working on the mud walls of Fort Heiman when he received word that Colonel Hughes wanted all officers in his quarters in Fort Henry. Edward and Ethan entered the Colonel's crowded quarters, taking a position next to the stove as another officer entered the room. Edward found a small amount of relief, knowing he was not the last.

The Colonel began. "Our scouts have sighted seven Federal gunboats approaching from upriver." He turned to the fort's map and its surroundings, pointing to a spot on the map. "A large force is now landing a few miles upstream at a place called Baileys Ferry." The Colonel paused. "What General Tilghman fears, gentlemen," pointing to the map. "Is that the Federals will surely take the high ground around unfinished Fort Heiman by early morning."

One of the officers asked, "Are we to remain in that half-completed fort while they surround us, Colonel?"

"No, we are not," answered the Colonel. "General Tilghman has ordered the evacuation of Fort Heiman, deserting it to the enemy." The Colonel tossed the stick he had used to point at the map onto his desk. "Now, I suggest you get back across that river and gather your commands."

The men looked defeated as they glanced at one another. Noticing this, Colonel Hughes softly added, "I suggest you use haste, gentlemen."

The men at Fort Heiman were evacuated across the river to Fort Henry just as the dark gray clouds rained down a mixture of rain and snow, causing the temperature to drop severely.

Unaware that Ft. Heiman had been deserted, Union General Ulysses S. Grant ordered Colonel Smith and his men to flank and capture the fort, believing they would meet light resistance in the partially completed structure. Union Colonel Smith and his men were in position at first light, and as they advanced, they met no resistance and were surprised at finding the fort deserted. With Fort Heiman secured, General Grant ordered Colonel McClernand to take his command on a forced march south along the river to secure the roads to Dover and Fort Donelson no later than 11 a.m. the following morning, the 6th of February.

Grant planned to cut off any chance of retreat for Fort Henry's men, thus forcing an early victory. General Tilghman, anticipating Grant's move, called a meeting of all officers during the early evening of February 5th. As General Tilghman stood looking at the faces of his men, he contemplated their fate against a superior force. "Gentlemen," he softly said. "I believe we will be surrounded by mid-day tomorrow." Turning to look at the map behind him, he added, "We know Federal forces have occupied Fort Heiman, and the gunboats sailing down the river will be in position by early morning. If I were the commander of the Federal forces, I would send a force south to cut off our retreat to Fort Donelson." He paused, looking worried. "I'm positive this is already in progress."

"We can't hold out long against the Federals, Sir," said an officer, speaking up.

"I realize that," responded Tilghman while pointing again to the map on the wall. "I'm not about to surrender my men to Federal forces, this day or any other."

Another officer stood. "General, is there any chance of reinforcements from Fort Donelson?"

General Tilghman considered that as he turned from the map, looking at the young officer. "No, we will not be reinforced by Fort Donelson." He smiled proudly. "We are going to reinforce Fort Donaldson."

"Sir?" asked Colonel Hughes, looking surprised.

"Yes, Colonel?"

"Sir," said Colonel Hughes. "There's a lot of open ground between here and Donelson. If the Union army has already made plans to cut off our retreat, it will be impossible to get past the Federal positions without a fight!"

"True enough, Colonel Hughes," said the General. "But our scouts informed me moments before this meeting that the Federals are not in position." He looked at his men. "Seems they're having a bit of bad luck with the weather, and that is good luck for us. I believe they're still several miles from taking up those crucial positions." The general returned to the map and started explaining his plan for the withdrawal from the fort. "Colonel Heiman and the majority of the garrison will march to Fort Donelson shortly after midnight under cover of darkness." He looked at the faces of his officers. "A few chosen men and I will remain in the fort, and we will open fire on the Union gunboats in hopes of causing enough confusion to help the rest of you make good your escape."

The men listened to the plan, hoping it would take them to safety and create a larger force better equipped to fight the superior Union army.

Shortly after midnight on February 6, 1862, the garrison mustered on the parade grounds, where General Tilghman gave his officers last-minute instructions. Imperative that nothing slowed the army, their orders were to leave everything behind, including clothes, baggage, and blankets.

Lightly equipped, the army swiftly and quietly marched toward Fort Donelson, hoping to cover the 12 miles before the Union army could block their escape. General Tilghman accompanied his men for a short distance, and when he was confident the garrison would escape Grant's forces, he bid farewell to Colonel Heiman. "God's haste," he said, and then he returned to Fort Henry.

A few minutes before noon on the 6th of February, the first shot was fired at Fort Henry from the Federal flagship at a distance of about 1,700 yards, followed by volleys from the other boats. The volleys continued as they gradually drew upriver to within 600 yards of the fort. General Tilghman had been waiting for the Federal boats to get within range of his old cannon, and as they came within range, he ordered the guns to open fire. The distance between the fort and the gunboats narrowed with each passing minute, giving accuracy to both Federal and Confederate gunners.

A cannonball penetrated the boiler of the Union boat Essex, scalding several of the crew. At about the same time, one of the fort's guns was disabled by an 80-pound shell, causing a premature explosion of a 42-pound shell, killing three men and wounding several others.

At approximately 1:30 in the afternoon, Brigadier General Tilghman felt a sense of lost honor as he ordered the Confederate flag lowered and the white flag of surrender hoisted in its place. Escorted aboard the flagship Essex, he formally surrendered his sword and Fort Henry to the Union Army. The official report for the battle stated that the Union suffered 44 killed or wounded, and the Confederate losses were five killed, 11 wounded, and five missing. The bright spot of the day for Brigadier General Tilghman was the knowledge that he had General Ulysses S. Grant.

Eleven

February 1862 – April 1862

Edward McAlexander

Escape to Fort Donelson, Tennessee

The men from Fort Henry were tired, hungry, and cold as they marched along the narrow, muddy road. Entering Fort Donelson, they found another earthen fort whose walls of dirt and logs rose to a height of ten feet. Unlike Fort Henry, the walls and inner fort were above the high water line of the Tennessee River, with several batteries of newer cannons having complete command of the river in both directions. Trees had been cleared to about 100 yards from the rifle pits and trenches outside the fort walls, known as a killing zone. Branches of the fallen trees were sharpened into spear points and either left on the trees or placed in the dirt to impede any advancement up the hill.

Looking forward to rest and food, the men from Fort Henry anxiously marched between the open wooden gates toward the parade ground, where they waited while Colonel Heiman reported to Brigadier General John G. Floyd, Commander of Fort Donelson. Present at that meeting were Brigadier Generals Gideon Pillow and Simon Buckner. In his report, Colonel Heiman told of General Grant's army that now occupied Fort Henry and General Tilghman's decision to reinforce Fort Donelson while choosing to remain and cover the garrison's escape.

Brigadier General Floyd smiled after reading Colonel Heiman's orders. "The man always did have a flair for dramatics." The door opened, and an officer hurried across the room and whispered into General Floyd's ear. The General puffed his cigar, nodded, thanked the officer, and dismissed him. The General stood and walked to the window, looking across the fort. "Gentleman," he softly said, "I suggest y'all return to your commands and prepare for Fort Donelson's defense." He took the cigar from his mouth, stared at it a moment, then turned to his men. "An Army still feasting on the victory of Fort Henry is eagerly marching toward us, anticipating another quick victory. Something I hope to prevent." He told Colonel Heiman to quarter his men with the rest of the garrison, and he would receive orders within the hour regarding their positions in defense of the fort.

A group of soldiers sitting around a fire trying to keep warm watched as the men from Fort Henry inspected the small, dirt-floor log huts. A skinny, bearded soldier in a dirty, Confederate gray uniform with the look of a hardened warrior leaned against his hut, smiling with amusement. "Y'all won't find much heat in them little huts."

Another younger man laughed while taking a dead pipe from his mouth. "That's right, boys. The ground inside is colder than the ground outside. Them their huts keep the cold in, not out."

"All y'all are better off out here by the fire," offered the older soldier as he pointed to a nearby woodpile. "There's some wood yonder. Take what y'all need fer now. Y'all can replace it later."

The men from Fort Henry took what they needed, and once settled in, they told of their flight from Fort Henry and the fort's surrender.

On the morning of February 11, 1862, General Ulysses Grant's Union Army surrounded Fort Donelson and waited for the arrival of Flag Officer Foote's gunboats. As the garrison took up defensive positions, the 27th Alabama took up their positions outside the earthen walls in the muddy trenches of the outer defenses. There, they waited.

The Battle for Fort Donelson

Shortly after dawn on February 13, 1862, General Grant's cannons opened fire, beginning the assault on the Confederate outer trenches and Fort Donelson. Having just finished their meal of hot coffee and one slice of bread with beans, the Confederates moved to the edges of the trenches overlooking the expanse below. From these vantage points, they could see the Union soldiers coming out of the woods and up the slopes, slowly making their way through the fallen trees and their sharpened branches.

The Confederates waited until the Union soldiers were within range before opening fire with a barrage so heavy that Federal soldiers fell by the dozens. Edward thought of Alex as he fired his pistol, wondering if Alex had felt the same mix of fear and excitement that he was now feeling. The Federals moved from position to position, making their way up the hill, pausing only to fire and reload. Musket balls pelted the trenches like a swarm of wasps. Near misses splattered Edward and the others with tiny bits of dirt, while several found their marks with a dull thud, knocking Confederate soldiers back against the rear wall of the trenches, either wounded or dead.

Standing to fire, then ducking down to reload, the Confederates returned fire, killing or wounding many of the Federals in the open expanse below them. Sparks from Union muskets unintentionally set fire to the dried leaves of the fallen trees, quickly creating an inferno. Seeing that the Union's advance had slowed, the Confederate line yelled obscenities to the men in blue as they kept firing and pushing the Federals back into the woods.

Wounded or killed Union soldiers fell into the fires, some impaled on the sharp spears, and those that did not die screamed while being burned alive. Edward watched the scene below as he reloaded his pistol, remembering his oath as a physician to save lives. His heart pounded as he fired his pistol, unsure if he hit anything.

Several minutes passed before the Federals regrouped in the woods beyond the burning logs and launched another frontal attack that lasted for more than two hours. Finally, the Federals were driven back to the safety of the trees below the hill and out of Confederate rifle range, and the fighting subsided to an occasional shot from a sniper.

Edward looked at his trembling hands, and thinking of Ethan, he crouched down and ran along the trench, stepping over the wounded in his search, hoping he was still alive. After several minutes, he found him.

"Ethan!" he called out.

Ethan's grim and dirty face broke into a big grin. "Damn, Ed, am I glad to see you." They hugged one another with enthusiasm, and then Ethan said, "I was worried you got your ass shot off as I predicted."

"Not likely. Are you all right?"

Ethan jokingly glanced at his dirty gray uniform. "I guess. I don't see any holes, but I sure felt lots of near misses." He looked at Edward. "Shit, Ed. What the hell have we got ourselves into?" He gestured along the trench. "We were tripping over so damn many bodies we had to toss them down the hill, poor bastards."

Edward looked at the bodies strewn in front of the trench. "I know," he said. "We had to do the same."

Ethan looked worried. "I'm afraid a hell of a lot more of us are gonna die today."

"Just make damn sure you're not one of `em, Ethan."

A young boy of thirteen or fourteen approached from around the corner of the trench, carrying several tin cups on a string and a big pot of coffee and looking frightened. "Coffee, sir?"

Edward turned to the young boy. Thinking he should be home with his mother, he said, "You startled me, Son, creeping up on us that way."

The boy's voice was quivering. "Sorry, sir, didn't mean to." He held out the string of cups with a trembling hand, causing them to rattle against one another. "Coffee?"

Edward smiled. "Sorry, Son, guess we're all a little jumpy. Coffee sounds really good, and we appreciate you bringing it."

Ethan took two cups from the boy and poured them full of warm coffee. "Thanks, Son, you're a brave lad." Then he winked at the boy. "Keep your head down."

The boy grinned, "Yes, sir." He turned and made his way along the trench to the next soldier.

Ethan handed a cup to Edward. "Warm your hands, asshole."

Edward took the cup and sipped the hot coffee, surprised at how good it tasted. He held it in both hands, finding a little relief from the cold, and glanced down the trench at the boy giving a coffee to another soldier. The silence of the moment carried with it the sounds of rattling tin cups, moans, cries for help from the wounded, and an occasional shot from a Federal or Confederate sniper.

Taking advantage of the lull in fighting, they knelt, putting their backs against the trench wall, trying to keep warm. Edward looked into his cup. "I can't stay too long." He sipped the coffee again, enjoying the warm steam against his face. "I need to get back."

Ethan nodded while feeling the warmth of his cup against his hands.

Edward turned to Ethan and thought how tired his friend looked. "I just wanted to see if you were okay."

"What day is it?" asked Ethan softly.

"I believe it's the 13th of February. Why?"

Ethan looked up from his cup, staring at the dark walls of the trench. "Curious."

"Wondering what day we'll die?" Edward asked.

Ethan smiled. "Something like that."

Edward put a hand on Ethan's shoulder. "Don't think about it." He glanced up and down the trench, thinking of their friend Danny Smith. "Have you seen Danny?"

Ethan started to take a sip of coffee but saw his cup was empty, and staring into it, he gestured down the slope. "Today was his last day."

Edward stood with regret and looked down the hill at the bodies. "You sure?"

Ethan stood also and looked down the hill. "We were both loading and firing as fast as we could. I crouched down to load my pistol, and he fell on top of me." Ethan paused as he stared at Edward. "His eyes were still open, and he had this surprised look. When I lifted his head to see if he was alive, it was like holding a warm, mushy pumpkin." He paused. "The back of his head was gone." His face held deep remorse. "We just threw him down the slope, Ed, like you would a sack of cotton."

Edward thought of Danny's family, remembering that he was their only child. He wanted to say something, but he couldn't find the words. "The sun will be down in a couple of hours, and it's gonna get colder than hell. Guess I better get back to my men." He looked at Ethan. "We better send some men to fetch blankets for the night and stay close to one another for warmth."

Ethan nodded. "Wish I had that blanket I left back at Fort Henry. An extra blanket would come in handy right now."

"Several hundred of us wish the same thing, Ethan." Edward patted him on the shoulder and then turned to start back along the trench.

Edward sat on a stump he had placed on the damp floor of the trench and wrapped a blanket around himself, thinking of a warm fire in his library and a glass of brandy. He was tired, nearing exhaustion, and very cold. He pulled the blanket tighter, trying not to think of how cold he was as he closed his eyes.

When he opened his eyes a few hours later, it was still dark and cold. His feet were getting numb, so he stood and walked in a tiny circle, getting the circulation back into them while glancing up and down the trench at the dark figures of his exhausted men. Fearing frostbite, he walked up and down the trench, telling his men to walk and stomp their feet. The temperature had dropped below freezing, and he wondered how long they could hold out in these cold trenches with no fires and only one hot meal a day. He looked down the hill toward the Federal positions, seeing a fireless expanse, knowing they were not much better off.

He pulled his hat tighter onto his head, tugged at his collar, and pulled his blanket tighter. Returning to the stump, he leaned back against the dirt wall, taking short naps and thinking of what tomorrow would bring.

Canon fire broke the quiet of the cold, early dawn hours of February 14, startling Edward from sleep. Disorientated for a moment, he soon realized they were under attack and yelled for his men to take their positions. Looking down the slope, blanketed in light snow that had fallen during the early hours before dawn, Federal soldiers were making their way through the maze of fallen trees that yesterday had impaled many of their comrades. Their dark uniforms against the white background made excellent targets. *'Foolishness.'* he thought, ordering his men to hold their fire.

The Federals continued their slow assault up the hill, yelling and firing, only pausing long enough to reload. As he held his order to fire, Edward could see bayonets affixed to the Federal's rifles as they kept coming up the hill, getting closer and closer. Federal musket balls hit the dirt in front of and behind the trench, sending pieces of mud everywhere.

Edward held his orders to fire as he watched the enemy pass the fallen trees into the open territory of sharpened limbs sticking out of the ground. The Federals were 200 yards away, then 150 yards, and then at 100 yards, when the order to open fire was given. Puffs of smoke billowed out of the trenches following a barrage of musket balls of hot lead flying into the Federal lines. Killed and wounded men in their dark blue uniforms fell, some again impaled on the sharpened spears.

The Federals were relentless in their assault up the hill, taking cover behind those lying on the open ground or impaled on the branches. Edward had no idea how often he fired and reloaded his pistol or how many men he killed, some so close he could see their faces. `Forced to retreat, the Federals backed down the hill, only to regroup a few minutes later and charge up the hill, repeating this process until early afternoon and their final bloody retreat.

Cries of the wounded broke the silence as men tried to stand or crawl across the white snow, now turned to red and cluttered with men in blue uniforms, hats, and discarded weapons. Edward and his men watched in somber silence while Federal soldiers carrying white flags came out of the woods to gather their wounded, while men in Confederate gray did the same.

The scene was suddenly interrupted by the sound of cannon in the distance. Looking toward the river, Edward saw Union gunboats arriving from Fort Henry exchanging volleys with the fort's batteries. Men turned from the grizzly sight below to watch the battle from their bird's eye view as the gunboats and Confederate cannons pounded one another, with the gunboats taking the worst of the exchange. It wasn't long before the artillery bombardment from the Confederate positions located on Cumberland Bluff crippled many of the ironclads, forcing them to retreat to the Confederates' cheers. One battle ended, another began as the quiet hillside fell under attack again, continuing the land battle for Fort Donelson that lasted well into the evening hours.

After sunset, Generals Pillow and Buckner took two-thirds of the garrison under their command, advanced on Union positions on the opposite side of the fort, attacking and counter-attacking far into the late-night hours. They had hoped to break through, but both sides withdrew after several hours of fighting, each suffering many casualties.

Edward had dozed off while listening to the sounds of the Pillow and Buckner attack. When he awoke, he stood in silence and leaned against the trench wall, looking down the hill toward the Union lines, jealous of the campfires they enjoyed. In the darkness, Edward noticed the body of a Union soldier draped over the edge of the mound, half hanging into the trench a few feet away, and realized how close their position had come to being overrun. Looking farther down the trench toward Ethan's position, he hoped his friend was all right. He sat on his stump and closed his eyes, thinking of warm food, hot coffee, and a warm bed.

"Sir?" said the voice of a young boy, startling Edward. "Sorry, sir," he said. "I found this torn tent and thought a few of us could use it to stay warm."

Edward smiled at the boy. "Good idea, Son. Grab a few of those boys yonder and wrap yourselves up in it."

"How about you, sir?"

"I have to stay on my toes. You go on and wrap up with the other soldiers."

The soldier started to turn away but turned and handed Edward a blanket. "It's extra, sir."

He took the blanket, thanked the boy, and wrapped himself with it. *'If I don't freeze to death,'* he thought, *'I'll look for Ethan in the morning.'*

Saturday morning, February 15, started with a barrage of cannon fire from the Federal positions, followed by sporadic fighting. By evening, the men of the garrison had been fighting in the trenches with little sleep or warmth from fire for two days. The entire garrison was worn out to such an extent that General Buckner decided he could no longer ask his men to continue, and he talked of surrender.

General Forrest, commander of Forrest's Cavalry, argued against surrender. "Mr. Buckner, sir," he said, "I will not allow my men the ridicule of becoming prisoners."

Brigadier General Floyd silently listened to the argument between the two men and then sided with General Forrest.

General Simon Buckner stood silent, staring down at the floor deep in thought before looking up at Floyd. "These men cannot go on fighting in the cold without sleep or a decent hot meal."

The argument continued until, adamant about his decision, General Forrest declared that he and his cavalry would break out under cover of darkness. General Floyd advised General Buckner that he, too, would try an escape with his brigade.

"I wish you God speed and good luck, General," said Simon Buckner.

The three men shook hands, and under cover of darkness, Generals Forrest and Floyd, along with their men, some riding double, fought through the Union lines, making their way to Nashville but suffering heavy casualties. On the morning of February 16, 1862, General Buckner, now in command of the fort, called a meeting of all officers. In that meeting, he informed them of his decision to surrender Fort Donelson and told them that messengers had already been sent under a white flag carrying written terms of the surrender. Simon Buckner looked sadly at them, saying it was only a matter of time before the fort fell, and by surrendering, many lives would be spared.

A disappointed Edward carried the message to his men, who naturally showed their disappointment, but at the same time, he was thankful that those left under his command would not die in the cold trenches of Fort Donelson. "Corporal," he yelled, looking down the trench at a group of men huddled together.

"Yes, sir," the young man replied as he stood and ran toward him.

Taking a handkerchief from his pocket, Edward handed it to the young man, "Tie my hankie to the end of your rifle."

"Sir?" the boy said, looking puzzled.

Edward looked at the young man sternly. "We're surrendering, Corporal. Just do as I say and wave that damn white hankie. It's over!"

"Yes, sir," replied the young soldier looking disappointed. Then, with the handkerchief tied as ordered, he raised it above his head, waving it back and forth.

Edward stared at it sadly and looked out across the fort, seeing other flags of surrender as men climbed out of the trenches. At the bottom of the hill, Union soldiers walked out of the smoky tree line. They advanced up the hill slowly with weapons pointed toward the surrendering Confederates, ready for any sign of trickery.

Ethan was at Edward's side, looking defeated. "Hell of a note, huh, Ed?"

Edward looked at Ethan's scruffy face, relieved that his friend was okay, and then looked back down the hill at the advancing Federal troops, repeating Ethan's words. "Hell of a note. Maybe we should have stayed at Fort Henry and surrendered."

Ethan nodded. "Danny and the others would still be alive."

Edward heard Federal officers calling for them to throw down their weapons and step out of the trenches. He turned to his men. "Drop your weapons and place your hands atop your heads, men."

The young man with Edwards's hanky handed it to him. "Here's your hanky, sir."

Edward looked at it. "Toss it, soldier. I've no use for it now." After giving the order to climb out of the trenches, Edward and the other men of the 27th, tired and defeated, moved out together.

The three-day battle for Fort Donelson ended on February 16, 1862, with the official report listing 1,420 Confederate soldiers killed, wounded, or missing. The remaining 13,000 soldiers were sent to a prisoner-of-war facility at Fort Warren, Massachusetts. The Federal army, with its superior strength of over 30,000, listed some 2,500 killed, wounded, or missing.

March 21, 1862

Fort Warren Prison Camp

Edward and Ethan were sitting at a table talking when the door to the prisoner barracks opened, and a Union officer entered. "Pack up, Rebs. All of you will be transferred to Fort Monroe, Virginia."

"What the hell for?" yelled someone amid many words of profanity.

"Just get ready, Reb," said the Federal officer, looking angry. "You leave in two hours."

Ethan looked at Edward. "What the hell's going on?"

Edward considered. "Damned if I know. Fort Monroe seems like a strange place to send a bunch of southern prisoners. Shouldn't they be sending us up north?"

Ethan looked puzzled. "Wonder what's going on?"

Edward thought of the sickly Colonel Hughes. "I don't think Colonel Hughes can make the trip to Virginia."

Ethan nodded. "I looked in on him yesterday. He's still pretty sick."

They gathered what little belongings they had and joined the others outside, and within two hours, they were marching toward Fort Monroe in Virginia, arriving on the 25th of March. They took residence in a warm, comfortable barracks, receiving two meals a day. Having resigned themselves to spending the rest of what they thought would be a short war as prisoners, they settled in for the duration.

On the morning of April 2, 1862, Union officers divided the camp into several groups. While Edward and Ethan looked on, a Union officer climbed onto a chair and raised his hand, calling for silence. "May I have your attention?" Ignoring the profanities from the prisoners, he proceeded to tell them that many of them would soon be exchanged for Union prisoners. Cheering erupted throughout the camp, drowning out the Union officer's attempts to continue.

When the cheering ceased, the Confederate officers were instructed to report to the mess hall for further instructions. They would find the lists containing the names of those men in the prisoner exchange.

"Can you believe this shit, Ed?" yelled Ethan above the laughter. "We're on our way home."

Edward glanced around, looking skeptical. "Shit, I hope so. But if our names are not on the list, we may end up sitting out the war in some damn camp up north."

Ethan stopped dancing, and the smile left his face. "Ah shit, Ed, we gotta be on that list. We can't just sit on our asses until this thing's over."

"I know." Edward looked worried. "Ethan, get these men back to their barracks while I get the list of names. And see, they stay out of trouble. I don't want them doing anything that would change the Federal's' minds."

"Sure thing Ed, I'll keep `em quiet if I have to kick the shit out of a few."

"That's comforting." Edward smiled at his friend. "I am going to the mess hall for a copy of that list, and then I'll check in on the Colonel."

When Edward returned with the list, he warned the men that not all of them would be exchanged. After listening to the men's expected grumbling and expletives, he posted the list by the door. Edward took Ethan aside, telling him Colonel Hughes had succumbed to pneumonia.

Ethan shook his head, looking sad, saying it was too bad the colonel hadn't lived long enough to see his men exchanged. Then he asked if Edward knew who would replace Hughes.

"Lt. Colonel James Jackson," said Edward, adding, "Since he is second in command."

By April 4, 1862, Edward was exchanged for a Major Revere of the 20th Massachusetts Regulars, captured at the Battle of Richmond a few days earlier. Ethan was exchanged for another officer, and then the two of them joined the others, forming two companies of the 27th Alabama assigned to the 33rd Mississippi. Edward had been correct in his assumptions regarding Lt. Colonel James Jackson being promoted to Colonel and taking command of what was left of the 27th.

Several days later, Colonel James Jackson sent for Major Edward McAlexander. Edward knocked on the door.

"Come in," said a familiar voice.

Edward opened the door and stepped inside.

Colonel Jackson was sitting behind his desk. He smiled, looked pleased at seeing him, stood, and walked around the desk with an outstretched hand.

Edward smiled and shook Colonel Jackson's hand.

"Edward, you son-of-bitch. How the hell have you been?"

"Just fine, Colonel," Edward said quickly, adding, "congratulations on the promotion."

Jackson looked sad. "Damn, sorry business about Colonel Hughes. He was a good man."

Edward nodded in agreement and waited for the colonel to explain his summons.

Colonel Jackson returned to the chair behind his desk and paused, looking forlorn. "He was an extraordinary gentleman. The Confederacy will miss him." He gestured for Edward to sit down. "Ed, we've known one another for a long time. Our families have dined together and gone on church picnics. You and your Henrietta attended both my marriage and my father's funeral as dear friends."

That's true, just as you attended my wedding and my wife's funeral." Edward looked at the colonel in memory of those times. "I've always valued our friendship, Jack. I hope you know that." Edward was one of the few people who called him Jack instead of James, and he couldn't remember why or how that had come to be.

"I've always felt the same, Ed." The colonel reached for a small wooden box on his desk, extracting two cigars. "These arrived early this morning." Looking pleased, he offered one to Edward.

It had been a while since Edward had enjoyed a good cigar. "Why, thank you, Jack." He put the cigar under his nose, smelling it before biting off the tip and placing it in the ashtray. Then he searched his pocket for a match.

The colonel stood. "Allow me." He took a wooden match from a tin on his desk, and, striking it, he lit Edward's cigar and then his own. He glanced at Edward over the flame as he blew it out and then looked at his cigar with satisfaction. He took a long puff, tilted his head back, blew the smoke into the air, and then looked at Edward. "I'm sure you're curious as to why I sent for you, so let me get right to it." The colonel opened his desk drawer, retrieving an official-looking document.

Edward looked on in curiosity while the colonel walked from behind his desk and handed him the document.

As Edward unfolded the document and began reading, the look of surprise on his face gave the colonel a deep satisfaction.

"That's right, Ed. You're my second in command." The Colonel offered his outstretched hand., "Congratulations, Lt. Colonel McAlexander."

"I don't know what to say, Jack."

The Colonel laughed. "Thanks would be a good start."

Edward smiled, looking embarrassed. “Of course, Jack, thank you.”

Then Colonel Jackson’s expression became serious. “You deserve it, Ed. You’ve proven yourself, and I need someone I know I can count on.” The colonel walked to a small table behind his desk and picked up a bottle of brandy

Edward stared at the paper, re-reading it while the colonel filled two glasses.

Colonel Jackson handed one to Edward. “To the men of the 27th, Ed, and the South. With God’s help, may they both be victorious.” He gulped his drink and then placed his empty glass upside down on the table. “Now, for a bit more news.”

Edward took a drink of brandy and watched as the colonel retrieved another document from the top drawer of his desk.

“Leave, my friend,” said Jackson. “You’re going home for a few days.” He chuckled at Edward’s expression of an open mouth and wide eyes.

A bewildered Edward quietly took the paper, unfolded it, and read the orders that would take him back to Florence and his daughter.

“Several men have been granted leave until the army decides what to do with us,” explained the Colonel.

Edward looked at the paper again to be sure he was reading the words correctly and then asked. “Mind if I ask who the others are, Colonel?”

The Colonel sat on the edge of his desk, looking curious. “You aren’t concerned about that shithead Ethan Hall are you, Ed?”

Edward chuckled. “Yes, sir.”

The Colonel stood, placing his hand on Edwards' shoulder, and, turning him toward the door, said, “Well, don’t be. Major Hall, that’s right: Ethan Hall was also promoted, and he’ll join you on your trip to Florence. You both leave in the morning.”

“Are you returning to Florence, Jack?”

“Afraid not, Ed.” He grinned. “Seems I’m too important. Enjoy your leave. It’s early in the war, and there's no telling when you’ll get another.”

Twelve

April 1862 - May 1862

Andrew Jackson Patterson

Yorktown, Virginia

Confederate General Wade Hampton's brigade arrived at the edge of Yorktown, Virginia, on April 12, 1862, joining Major General Magruder's small force. They were unaware that a large force of Federal troops was approaching from the north as they pitched camp overlooking the Chesapeake Bay.

A weary Andrew Jackson Patterson settled into his bedroll shortly after a dinner of cornbread and beans, looking forward to a restful night's sleep. His thoughts were of home, his children, and Rebecca as he stared into the hypnotic flames of a campfire and fell asleep.

"Hey, old man, wake up!" yelled the corporal as he kicked Andrew's feet.

Andrew sat up, looked at the young corporal, and considered kicking his little ass, but instead, he glanced at the others rousted out of bed the same way. Andrew's mouth filled with a yawn. "What the hell's going on, Corporal?"

The corporal was a stocky man whose Confederate gray uniform fit a little snug, and Andrew guessed him to be in his mid-twenties. He had a full head of black hair and a short, trimmed, black beard. Andrew watched as the corporal kicked another man.

"Time to get up," said the corporal to the soldier. Then he looked at Andrew. "Somethin's a stir'n' on the other side of town."

The younger men affectionately called Andrew the "Old Man," which he didn't seem to mind. "What the hell do I care?" he asked, looking puzzled. "What time is it?"

"A little after four in the morning, I reckon," the corporal said. "And ya just might care if what I heard is true."

A skeptical Andrew asked, "And what was it ya heard, corporal?"

The corporal knelt, glanced at the others, and lowered his voice. "I don't rightly know fer sure, Andy, but I was told to get everyone up." Looking secretive, he leaned closer. "I heard tell some Union soldiers have done camped on the other side of this here city." The corporal stood. "So, get up, like I done said."

Andrew got out of his bedroll, pulled his suspenders over his shoulders, put on his jacket, and gathered his musket and backpack. He looked up into the black, star-filled sky and then at the back of the corporal as he walked away. "Mite chilly for a battle."

The order came to fall in, and as the sergeant waited, he glanced up and down the ranks. "Keep the damn chatter down. Y'all sound worse than a bunch of old women." The sergeant walked up and down the ranks, glaring at each face, and at the end of the line, he turned and walked back to the center of the line and glanced over the squad. "There's a Union army camped on the other side of the city."

'The corporal was right,' thought Andrew.

The sergeant spit tobacco juice onto the ground, wiped it off his chin with one hand, and then frowned with a squint. "We've been ordered to take up positions along this side of the river." Anticipating the next question, he said, "And there won't be time for breakfast, so don't ask for none." He turned his head, spit, and wiped his mouth again on the sleeve of his gray uniform. "The best y'all are gonna get this here morning's a hot cup of coffee and a dry biscuit." The sergeant turned, spit again, and smiled. "Then we're gonna shoot us some Yankee blue bellies."

Things didn't quite come to pass as the sergeant had promised. The Confederate forces dug in along the banks of the river southwest of Yorktown, and the two opposing forces probed for each other's weaknesses over the next few days. Meanwhile, the Federals were busy building siege fortifications and awaiting the arrival of their heavy guns, hoping to make quick work of the smaller Confederate army.

Realizing they were outmanned and outgunned, General Hampton wisely gave the order for a forced march from Yorktown northwest to Williamsburg, where he hoped to join forces with another Confederate army.

On the afternoon of May 4, 1862, the Union commander ordered a massive bombardment with his siege cannon. The barrage ended as quickly as it had begun when they discovered the Confederate army had slipped away during the night.

Williamsburg, Virginia

The twenty-mile forced march from Yorktown to Williamsburg had taken its toll on the Confederate army. By the time they camped at dusk on the 5th of May 1862, Andrew and the others were dog-tired and hungry. Most men just wanted to lie down somewhere and sleep, which is exactly what Andrew did.

It was dark, the ground cold and hard as Andrew snuggled down into his bedroll close to a small campfire next to a young private named Johnny Franks, who had recently joined the unit. The boy talked too much for Andrew's way of thinking, but for now, the boy was quiet, and Andrew was thankful.

The peace and quiet was short-lived, however. "Hey, Andy," the boy said. "The chow line's getting pretty long. Wanna go get something to eat?"

"I ain't hungry, kid," replied Andrew without looking at Johnny's young grinning face. "Go on and eat. All I wanna do is sleep some."

Johnny stared at Andy thoughtfully. "Want me to bring ya somethin' back, Andy?"

Getting a little annoyed, Andrew said, "Sure, kid," he answered, hoping the young lad would leave and allow him to sleep. As Johnny walked away, Andrew stared into the fire with heavy eyes at the red coals while his mind drifted back to Anderson County, to Rebecca and the children. His memory held her standing in the warm sun between the clotheslines just before he had kissed her, and he remembered how her body fit perfectly in his arms.

The fire popped, a log fell into the flames, and he regretted never having had the chance to make love to her before he left. Believing that thinking of such things would not do him any good, he turned away from the fire and thought of sleep, but his mind would not release her image. His thoughts suddenly turned to Rachel, and again, the guilt set in, so he turned back to the fire and stared once more into the flames and embers, trying to think of other things until sleep overtook him.

"Wake up, Andy," said a familiar voice. "Lookie here what I got. Beans and hot coffee."

Andrew opened his eyes and stared at the boy for a moment, and then, deciding he was hungry, sat up, took the tin of food and the cup of coffee, and crossed his legs, trying to get comfortable. "Thanks, Johnny." Andrew set his plate down on his lap, sipping his coffee as he watched the boy trying to sit down without spilling his food. Johnny Frank was a skinny boy with a childish, thin face of freckles and always seemed to be grinning about one thing or another. He was a likable young boy. "How old are you, Johnny?"

Looking embarrassed, he said, "Not rightly sure."

"You ain't sure?" Andrew asked.

"Nope. Ma says I's close to sixteen, so's I guess that's how old I am." He took a bite of biscuit, glanced at the others, leaned toward Andrew, and whispered, "I lied 'bout my age so's I could enlist." He stopped chewing and looked at Andrew with fear on his face. "Ya, won't tell, will ya?"

Finding innocent humor in the boy, Andrew smiled. "Nah." He watched as Johnny ate with an aggressiveness he had not witnessed since leaving his children. He liked the boy. "Where you from, Johnny?"

Johnny nodded toward the south. "Stephens County, Georgia, near South Carolina. My Pa's got a farm there."

"I know where Stephens County is!"

Johnny grinned, exposing a mouth full of yellow-brown teeth and food. "Sure 'nuff?"

"Sure do. Why I own a place in Anderson County, South Carolina, not far from Stephens County."

Still grinning, Johnny shook his head. "I'll be. Why I been to Anderson County with my pa to buy stock from some feller." The grin left his face. "Don't recall his name, though."

Andrew set his empty plate down, placing his empty cup on it. "Johnny, I've got to get some sleep. I'm not as young as you and the other fellas, and I need my rest." Andrew laid back, closed his eyes, and waited for sleep, trying to keep his mind away from things that kept him awake. He wasn't successful, and after a few moments, he turned back toward the fire, looking at Johnny, who was staring back at him. "What?"

"Well, I's jes' wonder'n Andy," Johnny said, looking curious. "How old is ya anyways?"

"Forty-three."

Johnny's eyes grew big, and his mouth fell open. "Golly gee, Andy, why yer almost as old as my Pa. How in thunder did ya get in the army when he couldn't?"

Andrew immediately thought of Daniel and his questions, thinking he and Johnny would get along just fine. He sat up, resting on his elbow, and looked at the young boy. "I joined in Virginia. It seems they weren't as particular as they was in South Carolina. Now, can I get some sleep?"

Johnny considered that a moment. "If I could write, I'd tell my pa to do the same." Seeing that Andrew had closed his eyes, Johnny laid down on his bedroll and quickly fell asleep.

The pudgy corporal visited Andrew the following morning, except this time, there wasn't any Union army and no forced march. The men spent the day cutting firewood, digging latrines, and performing chores their good sergeant could muster up. It wasn't hard work, but it kept everyone occupied.

When the day was over, Andrew was sitting by the fire with Johnny and some other men, enjoying the quiet evening, talking about home and other things to take away the boredom and loneliness.

The same corporal who woke them every morning knelt by the fire and began to warm his hands. "You boys best get a good night's sleep."

"Why's that?" asked Andrew, thinking this boy always had something to say.

The corporal stared into the flames of the fire and nodded to the north. "Cuz in the morning, we're marching north toward Barthamsville near West Point."

"Where's that?" asked Johnny, looking curious.

"It's a small farming town close to fifteen miles north of here by a place called Eltham's landing." replied the corporal.

Andrew looked at Johnny, anticipating his next question. "West Point's a school for officers."

Johnny grinned. "Gee Andy, I know'd that much."

A man Andrew knew only as Gideon because he couldn't remember his last name was sitting on the other side of the fire poking at the embers with a small stick, looking worried. "My place is but a few miles north of Barthamsville."

Knowing what was on his mind, Andrew thought of his family and hoped the good Lord would keep the war from them.

Eltham's Landing, Virginia - 1862

By midafternoon on the 6th of May, the Confederates made camp near Eltham's Landing, Virginia. Later that day, they joined two brigades under General Smith's command.

Johnny looked unhappy. "All we do is run away from them Yankees."

Andrew turned away from studying the embers in the fire. "You in a hurry for a fight, boy?"

"Guess so," replied Johnny. "I just wish we'd get into the fight'n Andy, sted of always running away."

"We'll get our turn soon enough," Andrew said softly. "Don't go wishing for something you may regret."

Johnny looked up from cleaning the gun that lay across his legs. "Just bored, I reckon."

Andrew was tired of walking away from the war, but he didn't want the kid to know. "Nuth'n' wrong with bein' bored in a war." But he knew it was hard to wait for the inevitable.

The sergeant knelt next to the fire and warmed his hands over the fire as he glanced at each of the five men. "Need three volunteers." He looked to be about forty, and it was rumored he had once been in the Union army and traded his allegiance to the South at the start of the war. He was a big man with a round face that wore a frown most of the time. His thick, red hair protruded from under his gray Confederate hat. He had bushy red eyebrows above green eyes and a scruffy red beard. And like the corporal, the sergeant's Confederate gray uniform fit a little snug.

Each waited for the other to volunteer while the sergeant continued warming his hands over the fire. Finally tired of waiting, he pointed at Andrew, Gideon, and another man from Georgia named Emmett Thatcher. "You, you, and you come with me."

Andrew and the other men glanced at one another, and then, as they reluctantly stood, they wondered what they had volunteered for.

The sergeant stood, put his hands on his hips, and shook his head, looking irritated. "Get yer damn guns!"

Feeling the fool, Andrew and the others gathered their weapons and followed the sergeant. "Where we going?" asked Gideon.

"Y'all are coming with me on a little patrol toward the river."

"Why us?" asked Emmett.

Andrew was wondering the same thing.

"Because y'all ain't doing nuth'n' but sit'n on yer asses." The sergeant looked angry. "B'sides, you boys are the oldest and probably have more experience hunting at night."

Emmett looked at Andrew. "Never thought that'd come in handy."

Andrew nodded with a small smile. "I never did much hunting at night."

A group of officers was gathered at a table in front of a tent next to a campfire as the four men approached. The sergeant stood at attention and saluted the captain. "Captain, sir!"

The captain returned the salute while glancing at Andrew and the others. "I see you have your men, Sergeant."

"Yes, sir!"

The captain looked them over quickly, showing his skepticism. "All right then, come with me!" The captain turned and started walking through the camp, followed closely by the others, all curious about this patrol and where they were heading, each man certain it would be dangerous.

The sergeant looked back at them. "Spread out a little, damn it, y'all gonna run me over, ya dang idjits."

The captain glanced back at them, considering the sergeant's choice of words and hoping they weren't idiots.

The small group soon found themselves in a wooded area about two hundred yards east of their camp. The captain raised his right hand as he slowed, then stopped and knelt to one knee beside a tree. As the three volunteers knelt and glanced around, straining their eyes to see into the darkness, the sergeant cocked his head to listen for any unfamiliar sounds that might be the enemy. But all they heard was Emmett's heavy breathing, the sounds of the forest, and a slight breeze rustling through the trees.

Andrew was startled by something running through a thicket to his left, imagining a critter of some kind, and wished he was back by the fire listening to Johnny talk.

The captain turned to the sergeant and whispered as he pointed to the dark sky. "The moon's up. We'll wait until that cloud covers it and then move toward the river."

"Yes, sir," whispered the sergeant, then he turned to the men and whispered. "Y'all heard the captain and keep quiet." Then he grinned. "Them guns loaded?"

Emmett and Gideon nodded, but Andrew believed it was a dumb question.

The sergeant chuckled. "Just checking."

The captain smiled at the sergeant's humor as he whispered, "Best take it easy. We may be here a while."

Andrew leaned back against a tree, looking toward the black sky filled with too many stars to count and the moon coloring white the edges of the dark clouds. He watched the white edges of an otherwise dark cloud slowly move toward the white, full moon, wishing it would hurry. He looked at the captain and wondered what sort of man he was and what was so important that he had to bring them out here into the wilderness at night. The captain was young and thin with blonde hair, blue eyes, and clean-shaven.

As a large cloud drifted over the moon, taking its dim white light away from the forest floor, rustling brush broke the stillness, followed by the cry of a screech owl that had just claimed its dinner.

Imagining an owl carrying off its dinner, the captain whispered, "All right, let's get moving. Stick close together, using the trees and bushes for cover. If y'all hear anything, stop, and for Pete's sake, try and be quiet until we know what it is." He stood with pistol drawn, crouched down, and carefully walked toward their unknown destination.

Hesitantly and slowly, the others followed in the same crouched position, listening for any signs of danger. Several moments passed, and the cloud moved away from the moon, covering the forest floor with soft white moonlight. The shades of grays and blacks of the trees and bushes played tricks on the men's eyes, causing them to slow and look harder into the night. Anxious to reach his destination, the captain had to prod the men along. Another cloud covered the moon, hiding the lighter shades of the trees and bushes as they continued their journey, only to pause now and again to wait for another cloud.

The sound of moving water from somewhere up ahead broke through the stillness, and they knew that Eltham's landing lay just ahead. Hearing muffled voices, the captain raised his hand holding the pistol, and the men stopped. Andrew was filled with both fear and excitement as he crouched down next to the sergeant and listened to the muffled voices of what he feared were Union soldiers, half-expecting to see a soldier step out from behind a tree. The captain motioned forward, and they slowly crept through the darkness toward the voices and the sound of the river.

The captain stopped raising his pistol, pointing it left and right, indicating for the men to take cover. He whispered to the sergeant, who nodded and silently crept off alone toward the voices. Andrew watched as the night swallowed the sergeant and then glanced at the dark figure of the captain and into the trees around them, wondering where the captain had sent the sergeant.

Minutes passed before the sergeant returned, sounding out of breath. Stopping next to the captain, he pointed in the direction of the river and whispered, "There's more damn Yankee soldiers up there than I can count, sir."

"Any idea as to their strength?" whispered the captain.

"No sir, but there's a hell of a lot of `em and more boats arriving on the river bank." He glanced back into the darkness. "Appears they're starting to make camp."

The captain considered that as he looked toward the sounds. "I need to take a look."

"Yes, sir," said the sergeant, "but be careful. The place is crawling."

The captain disappeared into the darkness as if he hadn't heard the warning, and the sergeant turned to the men. "Keep a sharp eye out fer the captain. We're getting out of here as soon as he returns."

That wouldn't be too soon for Andrew.

Minutes that seemed like hours slowly passed, and then the sergeant took out his pocket watch and held it up into the moonlight. "Captain's been gone almost 40 minutes." Filled with worry, he shoved the watch back into his pocket.

"Where do ya suppose he is?" whispered Gideon.

The sergeant shrugged his shoulders and whispered, "Damned if I know."

Emmett moved closer. "Yah think maybe we ought to get the hell out of here, Sergeant?"

Andrew couldn't see the sergeant's face but knew the question irritated him.

"No, I don't," replied the sergeant.

A crouching figure emerged from the shrubs and trees, stopped next to the sergeant, and lowered his voice. "Shit, Sergeant, if I'd been the enemy, y'all would be dead."

"Sorry, Captain," replied the sergeant. "What kept ya, sir? You were gone a long time."

The captain grinned foolishly. "I moved in a little too close and had to wait for an opportunity to sneak away." He gestured toward the Union encampment. "Several hundred men are coming into that camp by way of the river. My guess is they plan on attacking our positions at first light. We best get back as fast as we can."

"Yes, sir," replied the sergeant, then he turned to the others. "All right, let's be quick and quiet about this."

The trip back was uneventful, a little quicker, and when Andrew and the others reached the fire they had left earlier, a miserable-looking Johnny followed Andrew to his bedroll. "Where'd y'all go, Andy?"

"Patrol."

Johnny watched Andrew put down his rifle, take off his canteen, and lay on the hard bedroll. "See any Union soldiers?"

"No," replied Andrew as he closed his eyes, replaying the night over in his memory and wishing Johnny had gone instead so he wouldn't be plagued with the boy's questions.

Johnny had a forlorn look. "What happened, Andy?"

Thinking the boy was too much like Daniel, Andrew opened his eyes, giving in to the boy's curiosity. "Heard the Union soldiers making camp along the river. We couldn't hear anything but their mumbling and laughing. The only ones that got close to the camp were the sergeant and this captain we followed."

Johnny frowned and shook his head, looking flustered. "Wish I'd a been there."

"Me too. Now let me get some sleep."

"Time to get up," yelled the corporal. "Coffee's hot, and so's the sergeant." He smiled at Andrew, looking like he knew a secret. "He wants to see all of us."

As he sat up, Andrew wondered, 'What now?' He tossed his blanket to one side, wishing again that he had a soft bed or some straw to lie down on.

Johnny was still asleep, which irritated Andrew, remembering the boy's questions the night before that had prevented him from sleeping. He gently kicked the boy in the butt. "Get up, Johnny. The sergeant's pissed again."

"What's new"?" asked Johnny, his head still under the blanket. "He's always pissed 'bout something."

The two got their belongings, joined the other men of their squad by the fire, and watched the sergeant as he approached, looking angry. "Our orders are to break camp. We move out in ten minutes."

"Where we going, Sergeant?" asked Andrew.

The sergeant turned and walked away, talking over his shoulder. "Richmond."

"What about them Yankees?" asked Johnny, looking disappointed.

The sergeant just kept on walking as if he had never heard him.

Johnny kicked at the dirt. "Retreat'n again!"

Hearing that, the sergeant turned and walked back to Johnny, stood nose to nose, and glared at him. "That's right, and while we're retreat'n toward Richmond, General Smith's ordering two companies to mount an attack on Eltham's landing." He paused, looking at each man. "Poor bastards are gonna get it while covering our retreat back along the Barthamsville Road."

Johnny gritted his teeth and scowled. "We just come that way."

"Don't ya think I know that?" hollered the sergeant as he turned and walked away.

While the army marched along the Barthamsville Road toward Richmond, distant gunfire began behind them. Andrew looked back, feeling sorry for the small force left behind.

Johnny looked back along the road and then at Andrew. "It ain't fair, Andy. We should be back there fight'n with the rest of `em."

"I'm sure most of us feel the same, Johnny, particularly the sergeant." Andrew looked at the back of the sergeant walking alongside the column just up ahead. "I think he's a little pissed off right about now."

The army reached Richmond's outskirts in the late afternoon of May 7, 1862, setting up camp northeast of the city near the swampy lowlands between the James and Chickahominy Rivers.

Richmond, Virginia

The Confederate army enjoyed the next three weeks camped outside Richmond, and Johnny was beginning to believe that they never would see any action. But Andrew, being older, felt differently and enjoyed the peace and quiet, knowing that it would not be pretty when the fighting started. The soldiers were allowed to visit the city and spend what little money they had or walk through the streets taking in the sights, which was something Johnny didn't complain about.

May 31, 1862

When bugles sounded reveille, Johnny pulled his single wool blanket over his head and curled up under it.

Andrew grinned as he grabbed the cover, pulling it off the boy. "Get up, kid, b'fore the sergeant kicks your butt."

Johnny sat up with sleepy eyes as his face filled with a yawn. "Yah left a mite too early, Andy. We had ourselves a good time with them, ladies."

Skeptical, Andrew chuckled, "I bet!"

"No, Andy, really we did."

Andrew grinned, feeling doubtful. "I suppose you're gonna tell me you went upstairs with one and got a poke."

"Well, no," he said, looking embarrassed. "Twern't nothing like that, why we just sat and drank and talked, mostly about how things was afore the war."

Andrew figured Johnny had never been with a woman and decided to be kind and not challenge his manliness. "I'm glad you had a good time, kid."

"Andy?" asked Johnny, looking curious.

Andrew grunted as he looked around the camp.

"When we gonna get to fight?"

"Don't know." Then he tugged at the boy's arm. "Come on, kid, we'll miss breakfast."

The Battle of Seven Pines & Fair Oaks Fork

On the afternoon of May 31, 1862, the Confederate army got word that a large force was marching toward Richmond. After being told they were about to engage the Yankee army, Johnny's expression turned from frustration to enthusiasm. The Confederate army took up its positions southwest of the swollen Chickahominy River and waited for another two companies to reinforce their position.

The forces had crossed the Chickahominy River and marched toward Richmond when the Confederate commander was informed by his scouts that his reinforcements were marching along the wrong road.

Cursing the officer in charge of the lost unit and his bad luck, the commander knew that he would lose the element of surprise if he waited. Though outnumbered, he ordered his command to charge the positions.

Confederate officers rode up and down the lines waving their hats and shouting the order to advance across the road into the open fields. As they yelled encouragement, men stood, and as if in a hurry to catch a train, the line of gray uniformed men advanced on the Union positions along the river, yelling what had now become known as the Rebel Yell. The Federals watched in awe and opened fire on the gray wall before they were within range. Orders quickly flew up and down the Union lines to hold their fire until the enemy was within range.

Andrew had a hard time keeping up with Johnny's eagerness, as the boy ran as if in a foot race. "Looks like you got your damn wish," he yelled. "Hope you're satisfied, ya little shit!"

When the Confederate front lines were within range, the Federal troops opened fire, and as men fell, the Confederates knelt and fired at the white puffs of smoke coming from the Union muskets.

Andrew knelt next to Johnny, fired, took a paper cartridge containing a round bullet and premeasured powder from the pouch on his belt, and shoved the cartridge down the muzzle. Using the ramrod, he shoved the cartridge deep into the barrel, cocked the hammer of his musket, and fired at the puffs of smoke coming from the trees.

"Sure looks like we got us a fight, Andy," hollered Johnny, looking excited and without the fear Andrew felt for both.

Andrew fired, reloaded, and looked for Johnny, seeing him several yards up ahead, kneeling and firing his rifle and then quickly reloading. Cannon shells exploded, sending small pieces of metal into the gray mass of men while billows of smoke rose above the ground. Musket balls claimed man after man as the gray wall of yelling and screaming men continued their attack on the Federal's positions.

Volley after volley of cannon fire from both sides filled the air and the expanse between the two armies with thick smoke debris. Surrounded by gray uniforms, Andrew crouched as he ran, pausing to fire his rifle and reload while trying to keep an eye on Johnny, worried over his foolishness.

Reaching a narrow dirt road and an irrigation ditch, Andrew jumped into the ditch, landing in several inches of water and mud. Leaning against the damp wall of the ditch, he fired and reloaded while looking for Johnny. Seeing him a few yards ahead up the ditch, firing and reloading his musket with enthusiasm, it was apparent to Andrew that he was enjoying his chance to fight. Andrew crouched down and made his way along the ditch to the boy. "Ya all right, Johnny?"

As if he hadn't heard him, Johnny busily reloaded his rifle, fired, and reloaded. The air was full of musket smoke, making it difficult at times to see the Federals.

Andrew placed a hand on the boy's shoulder and yelled, "Keep your damn head down when you reload."

Johnny was grinning as he fired, but then he knelt to reload, looking disappointed. "Don't think I hit anything."

"That's okay," yelled Andrew. "Maybe you scared `em."

Musket balls made a thudding sound as they hit the ground, one splattering tiny bits of dirt into Andrew's eyes. Turning with his back against the damp wall, he knelt and wiped the tears from his eyes, dislodging the dirt, and as he blinked to clear them, he saw that the muddy water had a dark crimson color to it. Looking in both directions, he saw bodies of the dead and wounded filling the ditch and men still trying to fire stumbling over them. The first real fear he had of dying filled him as he stared at the bodies lying in the muddy ditch. He felt like running away from this carnage of death, but he looked at Johnny firing and reloading, seemingly absent of the fear that held him and felt ashamed. He stood and fired, reloaded, and fired again. The man beside him turned away from the battle, climbed out of the ditch, and started running. As that man got shot in the back, another climbed out, dropped his rifle, and ran, only to meet the same fate.

Andrew turned away, closed his eyes, and whispered a quick prayer as he rested his head against the barrel of his rifle, fighting the fear that held him. Bumped by another man who fell suddenly into the muddy water, he looked at the bloody face, stood, aimed his rifle at a dark Federal uniform, and pulled the trigger. The musket recoiled against his shoulder, and the figure jerked to one side and fell. Andrew knelt to reload when another Confederate soldier fell against him and slid into the bloody, muddy water, lying face down, the back of his head half gone.

Johnny bent down to reload his musket and looked at Andrew, staring at the man. "What's wrong, Andy?"

Andrew shook his head and looked away from the body, feeling embarrassed. "I'm fine, boy."

The boy looked concerned. "Ya, sure, Andy?"

"I'm fine," he said. "I was just saying a quick prayer."

"Sure hope He heard it over all this commotion," replied Johnny with a big grin.

"So do I."

The sergeant, hunched over, was running along the ditch, stepping over bodies and yelling. "Keep firing! Reinforcements are attacking from our right flank!"

Andrew grabbed the sergeant's arm. "Cartridges are getting low."

"Right there," replied the sergeant, pointing at the man lying at Andrew's feet.

Andrew looked at the sergeant and then bent down, taking the paper cartridges out of the dead man's pouch, trying not to look at his face.

Johnny knelt beside him. "Can I have some Andy?"

"Help yourself," he said, pointing at another dead soldier. "There's plenty to go around."

"They're pulling back," yelled the sergeant. "The damn Yanks are pulling back!"

Feeling hopeful it was over, Andrew rose just enough to see the Federal soldiers retreating into the Chickahominy wetlands. The sound of battle subsided with the last of the blue uniforms disappearing into the trees, leaving an occasional shot being fired somewhere in the distance.

Bodies in blue uniforms littered the expanse between the Union and Confederate positions. Wounded men were hobbling away from the battlefield, trying to help those too badly hurt to walk on their own. Several men with white flags emerged from the Union tree line to look after their wounded and care for the dead.

Andrew turned away from the sight and leaned over the ditch's back wall, fighting the urge to vomit. He closed his eyes for a few moments and then looked at Johnny. "You got your wish, Boy," he said softly. "How do ya feel now?"

Johnny was staring at the blue uniforms littering the expanse between the two armies, realizing that he had killed several men. Having never considered that in his eagerness to fight, he turned, leaned over the edge of the ditch, and vomited. Several moments passed before Johnny turned and looked at Andrew with red, watery eyes. "I…," he never finished.

Andrew felt regretful for what he had said. After all, Johnny had been a boy with boyish dreams of war and glory, and now Johnny was a man wishing he were still that boy. Andrew didn't know what to say, so he just turned and looked across the fields they had charged over to reach this muddy ditch. The ground was littered with gray uniforms, much the way the field behind him was with blue uniforms.

The stench of gunpowder and smoke from burning trees and bushes set afire by cannon shells mixed with burning grass, clothing, and skin. It clung to his nostrils, and though he tried, he couldn't free himself of the stench. He looked down at his boots in the dirty, bloody water. Feeling his wet socks inside his boots, he climbed out of the ditch and turned to Johnny. "C'mon, Johnny, let's help with the dead and wounded."

As the last of the day rushed to meet the night, the army bed down to eat and sleep where they had fought. Andrew and the others moved from the ditch to dryer-level ground behind it, huddling around fires in small groups for warmth. Small, peaceful campfires could be seen in both camps, separated by the quiet black expanse that had earlier witnessed the carnage of battle.

Andrew joined Johnny, Emmett, and the others around a small campfire, where he leaned back against a small mound and took off his shoes to dry his wet socks stained with the bloody water of the ditch. The lonely sound of a harmonica filled the stillness of the night, and as Andrew listened to the familiar song, he thought of God, the Bible, and the stories he used to read to his children before bedtime. Fearful of what tomorrow would bring, the cries of the wounded cursing God or crying out for their mothers filled his ears. He wondered how he would die and what words would pass between his lips, hoping he wouldn't curse God. Shaking his head to dislodge thoughts of dying, he checked his socks, and finding them dry, he put them back on, followed by his boots, and returned to staring at the flames of the fire. As the weight of the day's battle suddenly fell on him, his eyes grew heavy, and he dozed off. Then, waking with a start, having dreamt of those who had died in the ditch and fearing their ghosts may visit his dreams, Andrew fought a losing battle to stay awake.

Confederate cannon fire greeted the chilly early dawn of June 1, 1862, pounding the Federal positions with explosions of smoke, fire, and shrapnel as the Federal cannon responded in kind. The Confederate line was alive, with men scrambling for cover, and as Andrew jumped into the ditch, he was relieved at finding the bloody, muddy water gone. Small puffs of white smoke from Union musket fire filled the tree line in the distance, and knowing the Federals were out of range, he watched the puffs of smoke appear, disperse, and then reappear, wondering why they wasted their ammunition.

Andrew considered the distance between the puffs of smoke from the Yankee muskets and the ditch he was in and figured that one side would have to chance an advance on the other. He had a bad feeling that it wouldn't be the Federals after the beating they had taken yesterday. Whichever side dared to cross the open expanse between the two armies would walk into a nightmare of hell. His fear was short-lived as officers and sergeants up and down the trench yelled to fix bayonets. The air filled with the clang of steel on steel as men attached their bayonets to the ends of their muskets. Ordered to rise out of the ditch and advance across the open ground, Johnny looked from the edge of the ditch across the swamps of the Chickahominy wetlands that had been yesterday's killing ground. “They c’ain’t be serious, Andy. There ain’t no cover out there.”

Andrew shook his head, noticing that the puffs of white smoke in the distance had stopped, and knew the Federals would wait until they were in range. “Fraid they are Johnny. C’mon boy, let’s not tarry and get the sergeant pissed.”

Johnny watched Andrew climb out of the ditch. Then he glanced up and down the ditch at the others climbing out and forming two rows as they walked toward the Yankee positions. He climbed out and joined Andrew and the long gray line that slowly walked in a crouched position, fingers on triggers as they walked toward the swamp and trees where the Federals waited.

Minutes passed before the white puffs of smoke appeared again in the tree line, preceding the muskets' popping sound by a half-second. Musket balls hit the ground in front of the gray wall of soldiers as it advanced. As the Confederates got closer, the federal guns found their marks, and men began to fall. Some fell silent, some yelled, others cried like a small child, while others cursed the Yankees. Men from the second row quickly moved in to fill the gaps in the front row.

The gray wall paused to kneel and fire at the white puffs of smoke, reloaded, stood, and continued toward the enemy lines. Andrew’s heart pounded in his head, and his face felt warm and flushed while beads of sweat formed on his forehead and ran down his cheeks onto his neck, soaking his gray shirt. His mouth was dry, his palms and fingers wet and sticky. He began to pray for his and Johnny’s souls should they fall this day, but his prayer was cut short by the sudden thud of a musket ball hitting the man directly in front of him. As the man fell back, Andrew stepped aside and looked down at the blood spewing from a hole in the man’s head. Filled with a sudden, terrible fear of dying, he thought of his children and Rebecca as he looked at the tree line while the line started to walk a little faster.

There was no yelling or screaming like yesterday as the long gray line silently moved across the ground that yesterday was littered with dead men in blue uniforms. Then someone yelled, “Charge!” and another, “Give `em Hell!.” the men in gray began to run faster and faster, yelling and screaming with false bravery as the sound built into a roar of voices. As the distance between the two armies closed, men in gray were dropping up and down the line. Andrew slowed to look for Johnny, and seeing him up ahead, running as if he were trying to win a foot race, Andrew ran a little faster. But he couldn't catch the young boy as they ran across the wetlands of the swamp toward the puffs of smoke in the distant trees. The Confederates fired back across the field, sending their small lead musket balls across the expanse in search of a victim.

Moments later, without realizing he had made it, Andrew was at the edge of the trees, fighting his way into the thickets, unaware that the Federal troops were drawing them into the woods into an ambush. As if attacked by a hornets' nest, Federal musket balls, and he could hear the loud thudding as they penetrated both trees and Confederate bodies. The gray army continued their advance, stopping short of the thick undergrowth, where men took refuge behind trees, logs, rocks, and shrubs, trying to shield themselves from the barrage of musket balls.

Standing behind a tree, Andrew loaded and fired his weapon, repeatedly hoping Johnny was all right while men all around him fell. A musket ball hit the side of the tree he was standing next to, sending splinters into the side of his face. Dropping his rifle, he knelt to one knee, holding his face as the Confederate bugles behind them sounded the retreat. Andrew picked up his gun and started backing away from the trees in a slow retreat with other men while firing at the blue uniforms emerging from the woods. The next thing Andrew knew, he was in the ditch, firing at the Union army about to overrun their position. Someone yelled, "Retreat!" and the Confederates quickly climbed out of the ditch and withdrew under heavy fire to a wooded area where they took up defensive positions.

Exchanging musket fire with the Union army, the Confederate army drove them back past the ditch and across the road into the open. Then, sensing victory, the men in gray chased them back into the thickets beyond the wetlands, killing many as they retreated. Andrew found himself in the ditch once again, firing at the retreating Federals, and slowly, the fighting ceased until only smoke and bodies of both blue and gray again littered the battlefield.

In the eerie silence, Andrew sat down in the ditch, his back against the mud wall, looked down at his trembling hands, and thought of Johnny. Getting up, he glanced around at the dead and wounded in the ditch, fearful that Johnny may be lying among them. Men from both sides were mulling around the bodies, helping the wounded as Andrew climbed out of the ditch and began looking for him. He paused to help a wounded man with a drink of water when he heard his name. Turning, he saw Johnny giving water to another wounded soldier.

The officers of the Union Army were convinced that by taking Richmond, they could end the war. However, General Lee's Confederate forces inflicted such heavy casualties against the Union at Seven Pines that the Federal army withdrew. The Confederate capital and the Confederacy were both saved that day by the battle of Seven Pines, costing both armies 11,000 men: 6,000 Confederate soldiers and 5,000 Union men. The Confederate army pulled back from Seven Pines that night and would not see action again until June 27, 1862, at Gaines' Mill, near Boatswain's swamp, a few miles north of Richmond. It would be another bloody battle.

Thirteen

April 1862

Edward and Joseph

Florence, Alabama

The sternwheeler Katherine Ann needed a new coat of white paint and green trim, but she still cast a majestic figure floating down the Tennessee River. Black smoke drifted lazily from the twin stacks as the faded, green paddlewheel pushed her dull, red hull effortlessly through the murky waters toward her destination of Florence, Alabama.

Ethan slept in his cabin, resting peacefully for the first time in months. Unable to sleep, Edward walked the Katherine Ann decks, enjoying the quiet peacefulness of the river, anxious to get home to his daughter. Standing at the railing, he rested on his elbows, closed his eyes, and lifted his face toward the sun, letting its warmth caress his skin. As memories of Fort Donelson raced into his mind, Edward stared down at the murky water, thinking of the men who had fallen at his hand, men of his command dying, and the cold nights in the trenches. He looked up from the murky water to the riverbank with the knowledge and realization that this war would last a long time and that he and men like him were all responsible for the death of innocence.

"Here you are," said Ethan as he walked along the boat's deck toward him.

Edward turned and smiled. "About time you woke up."

Ethan's eyes looked tired. "I think I could sleep for a week." He joined Edward at the railing and looked across the river at the far bank lined with trees and a scattering of small, run-down shacks. "It's so peaceful, almost as if there was no war, no killing, and we were on holiday." He watched three small Negro boys playing in the mud on the bank of the river, seemingly oblivious to the war, and became jealous of their innocence. "Can I tell you a secret, Ed?"

Edward watched the three boys in silence.

"When the war first started, I couldn't wait to get into it, to stop the northern politicians from changing things in our beloved South. But now," he paused. "Now, I'm not so sure about things. Sometimes, I find myself wishing it was over, or more importantly, that it had never begun." He looked at Edward and smiled. "Guess that makes me a coward or a traitor."

Edward had a troubled look. "No, it doesn't, Ethan. This war we have ourselves in is a terrible thing, and I'm sure many men who have looked into death's mouth feel as you do, including myself. But as terrible as it is, I've resigned myself to its end." He looked at his open hands, fingers outstretched. "I'm a surgeon by choice, and I took an oath to save lives, but here I am, taking lives with the very hands that should be saving them." He shook his head, looking disgusted. "It's all very confusing at times." He paused. "I can't explain it, but I have to be part of this, however long it takes. And I'm afraid it will take a long time."

The sternwheeler slowly passed a woman on the far bank, busy washing her laundry, while another woman spread her wet laundry over bushes to dry in the warm sun. The scene was almost surreal in the peaceful morning as they talked of war and killing.

Filled with anticipation and excitement, Edward walked up the steps to the front porch of his home in the early afternoon of April 27, 1862. Finding the door locked, he lifted the brass knocker, tapped the brass plate, and waited. The door opened, and he was face to face with the Negro servant Sophie. Her expression was one of surprise, and then her face filled with a broad smile of white teeth as she placed her hands over her heart. "Mistah, Edward." Tears welled in her eyes. "Lord almighty Mistah Edward, it so goods ta sees ya." She backed away from the door, wiping the tears from her eyes and cheeks with the bottom of her white apron. "My heart's a beat'n so fast, Mistah Edward," she said, almost sobbing. "I thinks it's gonna explode."

Edward set his carpetbag on the floor, placed his coat and hat on top of it, smiled, and held out his arms. "Do I get a hug, Sophie?"

"Ya surely does, Mistah Edwards, ya surely does."

They embraced quickly, and then she stepped back, looking into his tired eyes, and with a choked voice, said, "It's so good ta see ya. We all worries about ya so." She paused, looking concerned. "Ya's alright now, ain't ya, Mistah Edward?"

"I'm fine, Sophie," he smiled. "But I have missed your smile and laughter."

Sophie was the daughter of two other slaves, willed to Edward by his mother, and like her parents, was educated in reading and writing. It was something the McAlexander family regarded as a necessity for their slaves, something that increased their value. When Edward was a small boy, Sophie's parents would often tell him stories of Africa and the vast expanses of land and animals he would later read about in books.

Sophie picked up his coat, holding it affectionately in her arms. "I'll sees ta ya bag n' things, Mistah Edward."

"Thank you, Sophie." He walked through the entry into the large hall, where he paused to look at each of the doors in memory of what lay beyond, and then his eyes found the staircase.

Knowing he was thinking of his daughter, Sophie smiled. "She's upstairs sleeping, Mistah Edward. She's such a sweet child, looks more like her dear mama every day."

Edward smiled at that. "It's good to be home, Sophie. I've missed this old house almost as much as I have your cooking."

Sophie covered her mouth with one hand as she laughed. "Mistah Edward," she said, her eyes big and happy. "Now don't ya go worry'n none cause Sophie's gonna fix somethin' special for dinner 'cause we gonna celebrate ya home com'n."

Hearing a door open, Edward turned to the library, looking into his sister Mary's surprised face, and smiled at her.

She called out his name and ran across the room into his arms. "I was so afraid we'd never see you again. We knew you were a prisoner, but not if you were injured or sick."

"I'm fine, Mary." He stepped back and looked down at her slightly round, firm stomach. "You're with child?"

"Of course," she said, blushing. "That usually happens when two people get married."

He laughed. "I suppose it does."

She took his hand. "Your daughter is upstairs sleeping." She led him up the stairs to his daughter's room, where they stood beside the bed, looking down at the tiny body lying crossways on the bed, pillow on the floor.

He stared at her for several moments, then whispered, "She's changed so much, so grown up."

"Yes, she has," whispered Mary.

"I'd forgotten how beautiful she is."

"Just like her mother," Mary whispered. "I'll leave you alone with your daughter; I'll be downstairs in the library."

He sat on the edge of the bed, took off his boots, and carefully lay on the bed next to his daughter, put his arm around her, closed his eyes, and slept.

Edward spent the next two days content in being part of his daughter's life of imaginary friends and listening as she told him things only a child would know. He was happy and, most of all, at peace with himself.

Mary stood next to the open doors of the library and watched Edward and little Mary. Stepping out onto the veranda, she walked into the garden and sat beside him on the white wooden bench. He was quietly watching his daughter chase a butterfly across the grass and laughed when the butterfly disappeared, leaving little Mary with nothing but bewilderment on her cute little face.

"Edward," Mary said. "Forgive me for interrupting, but you do need to see your brother. He's been by twice, and I can't make up another excuse. I know you want some time with your daughter, but you're hurting poor Alex's feelings."

Edward chuckled, looking skeptical. "Alex doesn't get his feelings hurt that easily, Mary."

"Yes, he does," she said, her expression filled with concern. "You should have seen him the last time he was here, and you told me to ask him to come back." Mary looked down, studying her folded hands, and grinned. "He looked like one of those boys I used to ignore in school. Sort of pathetic."

Edward chuckled while imagining Alex at the front door, looking forlorn. "He'll get over it, Mary. I'm just not ready to see anyone."

"Oh, Edward," said Mary irritably. "You are so dense at times. I could just shake you."

Edward looked at her, surprised at first, then he smiled. "Alex understands how I feel."

"No, he does not understand. When he came home injured, you were the first to see him and visited him every day. Sometimes twice a day."

Edward frowned thoughtfully. "That's true, I did. But that was different; he was injured and needed my professional help."

Mary shook her head. "Did you hear yourself? Why, you were worried sick about Alex, and you know it! And now, Alex is the one worried, and while he's not a doctor or surgeon, he is your brother."

Little Mary swatted at another butterfly, missing it and then watching as it flew off over the many-colored flowers. Edward chuckled and considered what his sister had said. "You're right, Mary. Perhaps I haven't been fair with Alex."

Mary placed her hand on his. "He doesn't want to hear about the horrors of war if that worries you. He knows of those already. He just wants to talk to you to see that you're all right."

He smiled, looked at her, and nodded. "Let's invite Alex and Ella for dinner tonight."

"I already have. Sophie's preparing dinner as we speak."

Edward laughed. "We needed your tactics at Ft. Donelson."

Mary wondered about Ft. Donelson as she stood to leave but paused. "I presume you still know how to dress appropriately for dinner."

He smiled affectionately as he watched her walk across the yard toward the house, thinking married life had been good for her. Then, hearing his daughter giggle, he turned to see what had made her laugh.

During dinner, Edward quietly ate while listening to his guests' conversation. The women repeated the town gossip while Alex and Joseph talked about the farm and the river, sidestepping conversation about the war. Edward caught bits and pieces of both conversations while he helped his daughter cut a piece of meat. Sitting back, he watched her eat, thinking it ironic that the simple things in life go on. He pushed the words of the conversations out of his mind and sat back, thinking that he and his family were sitting in the comfort of his home eating a nice dinner while men were killing one another a few miles away. *'My God,'* he thought, and then asked himself, *'Are we living in the same world?'* He looked around the table of half-empty plates of the delicious dinner prepared by Sophie. He remembered her at the front door only days earlier, happily greeting the man who was returning from killing the men who fought to free her. *'Is our way of life so wrong?'* he asked himself. The sound of his name interrupted his secret thoughts.

Sophie was standing behind Alex, wearing her usual big smile. “Can I gets ya anything else, Mistah Edward?”

He smiled at her. “No, thank you, Sophie. The dinner was delicious.”

Her face beamed with pride. “Why, thanks ya kindly, Mistah Edward.” Then she disappeared into the kitchen, and as she left, he couldn’t help but wonder how she felt about the war and all this killing for her freedom. Edward wiped his mouth with his napkin, looked at Alex, and then to Joseph. “Gentlemen,” he said, pointing toward the library. “Shall we?”

“Of course,” replied Alex, who turned to apologize to Mary and Ella, “Ladies, if you don’t mind, I’m in need of some of my brother’s fine brandy.”

Joseph kissed Mary on the cheek and started getting up when she tugged at his arm, leaned next to his face, and whispered in his ear. “I’ll try and wait up, but don’t let that hurry you.”

He grinned and winked as he stood and followed Edward and Alex into the library.

Mary turned to Ella. “Would you and your children care to join me in taking little Mary for a short walk before it gets dark?”

“He loves you very much,” said Ella, referring to Joseph as she got up from the table.

Mary blushed with a small smile, feeling pleased, and then looked toward the library in time to see the door close. “And I, him.”

Edward poured three glasses of brandy, giving one to Alex, one to Joseph, and then held up the third. "To the Confederacy."

"To the Confederacy," repeated Alex and Joseph as an awkward silence filled the room. Taking a sip of brandy, Alex and Joseph were apprehensive about discussing the war.

Edward was still processing his thoughts about Sophie and the war, and both seemed very confusing at the moment.

Alex sat on the familiar sofa where he often sat and watched his brother.

Joseph sat close by, glancing from one brother to the other, trying to think of something to say.

Alex sipped his drink. "I apologize for bringing up the war, Edward, but do you believe the South can win?"

Edward looked reflective. "No need for apologies, Alex, but to answer your question, I do not. Not if we can't do better than we did at Fort's Henry and Donelson." Edward sipped his brandy, stared into his glass for a moment, and looked first at Joseph and then Alex. "The northern armies are better trained, better equipped, and it seems like there's a hell of a lot more of `em."

"Something we discovered at Bull Run," said Alex

Joseph sipped his drink and watched Edward stand and walk the short distance to the liquor table to refill his glass.

Edward chuckled lightly. "I best be careful with my liquor; I'm not as used to this as I once was."

Alex laughed. "Nor I." He gestured toward the door. "Our sister hovers over your liquor like a vulture over its prey."

Edward grinned, imagining her standing in front of the table, preventing Alex from his brandy, then pushing at one another as they did when they were children. He took a small sip, returned to his chair, and stared into his glass. The room was quiet. "There were times," he said thoughtfully. "While in the cold trenches at Fort Donelson, I would have sold my soul for just one drink of brandy." Taking another sip, he turned to Joseph. "Have you had any word from your family in Tennessee?"

Joseph shook his head. "No, I haven't, but I'm going to make a quick trip home tomorrow morning." He glanced at the doors and then at Edward. "Something I've yet to tell Mary. I've booked passage on a boat to the town of Gasten, where I hope to rent a horse and ride out to my father's farm."

"Well," said Edward. "Let's hope you find them in good health."

"I haven't been home in a long time," Joseph said thoughtfully. "No telling what I'll find."

Alex considered that as he puffed his cigar. "When were you home last?"

Joseph considered the question, looking sad. "Many years ago. Many, many years, I'm afraid."

"I'm sure you'll find your family alive and glad to see you," said Edward hopefully. Then, changing the subject, he asked, "And how are things on the Southern Belle?"

"Busy," replied Joseph.

"And Captain Goodman?" asked Edward. "How is that ornery old son of a bitch getting on these days?"

"Cranky as hell," grinned Joseph, then he took another drink of brandy.

Alex watched his brother, realizing he, too, had come back a different man.

Edward chuckled, drank his brandy, and asked, "Have you and Mary picked a name for the baby?"

"Zachariah Edward Greene, if it's a boy," Joseph smiled. "After my father and yourself."

Edward looked pleased. "I'm honored, of course, and if it is a girl?"

"Julia Ann Greene," he glanced from Edward to Alex. "After mine and y'all's mother."

Alex smiled and took a drink of brandy.

Edward smiled. "Perfect for a young girl." Then his expression changed. "Terrible time to have children." He smiled a small smile. "Of course, I'm happy for the both of you, it's just this damn war, and I'm not sure Florence will escape it."

Alex had been sitting on the sofa quietly, watching and listening, but now he leaned forward. "Joseph and I talked about that very subject a few days ago."

"Oh?" replied Edward, looking interested.

Joseph cleared his throat nervously. "I may take Mary and the baby away from Florence after the child is born."

Edward frowned. "To where, if I may ask?"

"East Texas," replied Joseph.

Edward's expression turned angry. "What in heaven's name gave you the idea to take them to east Texas?"

Joseph thought he should have seen this coming as the room fell silent. He did not want to argue over something he and Mary had already discussed and settled. "I don't believe the war will reach there," he said. "But I do believe Florence will not be so lucky because of its proximity to the Tennessee River." Joseph paused and glanced at Alex, hoping for support. "Captain Goodman…"

Edward scowled in anger. "Ah yes, of course, good old Captain Goodman, and what the hell would Captain Goodman know about what's best for your family?"

Angered by that, Joseph managed to control his temper, believing this was not the time to lose it, so he settled back in his chair and calmly said, "As I was going to say, the captain and I have traveled to Shreveport and East Texas, and both are crawling with new business."

Edward stared into the flames in silence, sipping his bourbon, angry over Joseph and Mary's decision.

"For the past several years," continued Joseph. "Boats have traveled from the Ohio and Tennessee Rivers, down the Mississippi, up the Red River to Shreveport, then into the great Caddo Lake that pours into east Texas and then branches into other waterways." Joseph paused to drink his brandy. "Why the city of Jefferson on the Big Cypress that flows between Caddo Lake and Lake of the Pines has become one of the largest inland ports in Texas, second only to Galveston."

Edward looked up. "I know all that, Joseph," he said flippantly. "I read the papers." He stood and walked to the liquor table, poured another drink, took a sip, thinking he had probably overstepped, and then looked at Joseph. "You put up a convincing argument."

"I know the area around Shreveport and Jefferson," Joseph said. "I've been there many times and have seen many boats the size of the Southern Belle and larger. I would have no problem getting employment."

Edward sipped his drink and looked into his glass, then smiled, looking apologetic. "Forgive me, Joseph. I have no right to question your decisions regarding such matters when it comes to your family. You're probably correct in your assumptions about Florence and East Texas, possibly even Shreveport. Perhaps I should send my daughter away." Shrugging, he turned back to the fire. "But where in would I send her?"

Alex looked at Edward. "To be honest, Edward, I too have considered sending Ella and the children away, but as you so eloquently asked, where to? I can't just up and leave no more than you can."

Edward turned to Joseph. "I'm afraid I was being selfish. I've grown accustomed to Mary and you living here, and honestly, the two of you keep the loneliness at bay, and if you leave, I may never have the opportunity to see my new nephew or niece." He returned his gaze to the flames in the fireplace. "I suppose each of us has to do what he believes is best for his family in times such as this." He turned to Joseph, smiled, and nodded. "You have my full support, whatever your decision."

Joseph quickly considered an alternative. "When you return to the war, maybe it would be best if little Mary came to stay with us until the war is over."

Edward quickly considered that. "Thank you, Joseph, but no, I want her to stay here, in this house, near her own things, the things she's used to, and then perhaps she won't be afraid at night. Little Mary loves and trusts Sophie."

The sound of women's laughter invaded the library through the closed doors, and when they opened, Ella, Mary, and a young woman entered, talking and giggling like children.

The men stood with their drinks in their hands.

Mary held up the hand of the young woman. "Look who's here, everybody, it's Sarah Koger."

Sarah Koger was the younger sister of Edward's deceased wife Henrietta and had been away at a finishing school in Savannah, Georgia, for the past few years. The dark green silk dress and sheer white blouse exposing just enough skin did much for her figure, and she seemed to glide across the room. "Hello, Edward," she said, holding out her hand. "It's so nice to see you again." Sarah had grown up a lot since Edward last saw her. She was a beautiful woman that any man would proudly escort around Florence or New Orleans.

He smiled, taking her hand. "Hello Sarah, what a pleasant surprise. I had no idea you were in Florence. Are you staying next door with your parents?"

"I'm afraid so," she said, looking depressed. "With this terrible war and all, the school decided the girls would be safer at home, so they closed it and boarded up the windows until the war is over." She turned to glance at the others. "This dreadful war ruins everything."

Alex noticed the way his brother was watching Sarah. "How long will you be in Florence?"

"Forever, I guess," said Sarah, her expression filled with despair. "Or at least until this horrible war is over."

Ella stood next to Alex and took his arm. "Let's pray that won't be too much longer!"

Mary moved next to Joseph, taking his arm. She and Sarah had been friends for many years. "You remember Joseph?"

Sarah smiled. "Why, of course, I remember your nice young man. Hello Joseph, it's been a while since I've seen you."

"Yes, it has. Good to see you, Miss Sarah."

Sarah looked at Mary. "I truly regret that I was unable to attend the wedding, but congratulations." She looked at Joseph. "You are a very lucky man, Joseph. Mary and I often talked about you before I went off to boarding school." She winked at him. "I know all your secrets."

Embarrassed, Joseph forced a smile.

Mary laughed, remembering how good Sarah had always been at making men feel uncomfortable. "Sarah, dear, you promised you would never tease Joseph."

"I guess I did," she smiled. "Oh well, then, I do apologize."

Edward gestured to the sofa as he offered her a glass of sherry.

"A small one, please," she said while extending her thumb and forefinger, indicating an amount. At twenty, Sarah Koger was a beautiful, slender girl of five feet three inches with light brown shoulder-length hair, looking a little frail. This was a misconception because she was much stronger than her appearance. A small, straight nose separated her blue-green eyes, and full red lips carried a warm smile when she looked at Edward.

He was captivated, and Alex knew it as the group settled in comfortably and talked the evening away. Alex and Ella were the first to say goodnight, followed by Joseph and Mary as they retired upstairs. The library was suddenly quiet and awkward for Edward, so he offered Sarah another sherry, which she refused, saying it was late, so he offered to walk her home.

She smiled with humor. "I just live next door."

"I know, but it's late and dark outside, and if anything were to happen to you, well, I would never forgive myself."

As they walked in the warm night air, she told him of her adventures at the finishing school, repeating how sad she had been when it closed. Unknown to Edward, she had experienced quite the crush on him when she was younger, and as she grew, that crush had blossomed into a secret love, even before Henrietta's death. Of course, she locked these feelings deep in her heart, never admitting or discussing her secret with anyone, not even her best friend, Mary.

"I'm probably in the minority," said Edward with a smile. "But I'm thankful the school did close. If it hadn't, we might not have seen one another for who knows how long."

She blushed. "How long will you be in Florence?"

"Ethan and I must return to our units in about eight days."

Looking surprised, she stopped. "Do you mean Ethan Hall, that terrible boy you were always with?"

"He wasn't so terrible," laughed Edward in his friend's defense.

"You may think not, but I remember a few things I heard Daddy tell Momma." She laughed, shaking her head. "The two of you were a little wild if I remember correctly."

"We were no different than a lot of other boys our age."

"Oh, I'm not sure that's entirely correct," she said, letting the evening silence walk with them while she thought about his leaving. "Eight days is not a long time. Where will you be going?"

"The 27th Alabama is somewhere in Virginia. I'm not sure where, but when we're ready to leave, we'll check with the recruiting office in Florence. They should be able to tell us."

Reaching the front door of her home, she turned, leaned against it, and looked into his eyes. She could barely see in the pale light of the moon. "If I were to write to you, would you answer my letters?"

"I'd like that, but they may not find me for weeks, even months."

"Just the same, I'd like to."

"I'd be honored to receive your letters, Sarah."

Her face was soft now in the white light of the big moon, and he wanted to kiss her but knew that would be inappropriate.

"Goodnight, Edward," she said. "I had a lovely evening."

He kissed her hand, said goodnight, and waited for her to close the door before he walked across the porch and down the steps to the sidewalk with his mind full of Miss Sarah Koger.

Edward sat on a white wooden lawn chair with his eyes closed in that restful period one experiences of half-sleep, half-awake. The water of a nearby stream gurgled and bubbled over rocks that tried hopelessly to slow down the path that had long ago cut through Edward's backyard. A robin called to its mate, followed by the soft fluttering of wings. Bees in the flower garden hummed, busy pollinating his garden, ensuring next year's flowers and their food supply of honey. As the breeze softly played with the leaves of the tree he sat under, the sun's rays occasionally found his eyes as the leaves rustled above him.

While enjoying this serene symphony, his memory took him back to the days before the war and happier times, and when she approached, he was unaware of Sophie's presence.

"Mistah Edward," she said softly.

He did not open his eyes. "Yes, Sophie, what is it?"

"Dat Mistah Ethan Hall's in the parlor," she said, sounding irritated. "Does ya wants me to shows him out here or to the library?"

Ethan's voice blurted out, disrupting his mood. "Never mind, Sophie." Ethan walked past her, sat in a lawn chair beside Edward, and grinned at him. "How are you doing, asshole?"

Edward grinned without opening his eyes. "Sophie, would you mind getting my rude friend and myself some lemonade?"

Ethan frowned. "Lemonade? What the hell happened to brandy or bourbon? Or even rum?"

Edward opened his eyes and sat up, glancing at the unread book in his lap, then looked at Ethan with a scowl. "It's a might early, Ethan."

"It's after one o'clock in the afternoon."

Edward placed the book on the table next to his chair, turned to Sophie, and smiled. "Lemonade, if you please, Sophie."

"Yes, suh, Mistah Edward." She gave Ethan a disapproving look for disturbing Edward and then turned and walked toward the house to get the lemonade.

Edward laid his head back against the wooden chair and closed his eyes again. "What's on your mind?"

Ethan settled back, looking around the yard, momentarily taking in its serenity, and then placed his right elbow on the armrest, his chin in his hand. "Edward, I truly love my Lori, but I had to get away."

Edward opened his eyes, looking curious. "What's wrong?"

"She can't keep her hands off me."

Edward burst into laughter. "You should be so lucky, you big mule!"

Sophie returned with a tray containing a pitcher of lemonade and two glasses, placing them on the table next to Edward. Clearly, she disapproved of Ethan disturbing her Edward from his rest, and Ethan knew that but grinned at her anyway. He had known Sophie almost as long as he had Edward, and he was all too familiar with her facial expressions.

Edward thanked her, picked up the pitcher, and filled two glasses, handing one to Ethan and picking up the other. He sat back and took a drink. He told Ethan about Joseph's plan to take Mary to east Texas after she gives birth.

Ethan took a drink of lemonade, wishing it was brandy, and stared at the small stream running through Edward's property. "I, too, would like to get my family out of Florence."

Edward was surprised by Ethan's remark. "I can't say I blame Joseph. Florence may not escape the war, and truthfully, I would like to send little Mary somewhere. Even Alex has considered taking his family away."

"Alex has too much responsibility," said Ethan thoughtfully.

Edward took a drink of lemonade. "That's true. Alex has the farm, his practice, and my affairs to watch over." Edward grinned.

"Serves the little shit right for getting shot at the beginning of this war. The dumb bastard should've waited."

Ethan chuckled. "My family originally came from east Texas, not far from Shreveport."

Edward looked at him. "I had forgotten that. Didn't your family move back there recently?"

"My father feared a big war was inevitable, deciding east Texas would be better than Alabama." Ethan sipped his lemonade. "He bought a small farm near my uncle's place, not far from the city of Jefferson." Ethan looked at his half-empty glass, considering Texas. "I would prefer Lori and the children go there until this war is over."

"Jefferson's where Joseph plans on taking Mary."

"You don't say?" said Ethan, looking surprised. "Don't suppose I could get a glass of brandy?"

"No," replied Edward.

"Didn't think so." Ethan took a drink of lemonade, thinking of Joseph and Jefferson, Texas. "My parents' place is just a few miles from Jefferson." In the silence that followed, Ethan thought about Joseph. "Do you think Joseph would entertain the idea of Lori and the children tagging along?"

Edward considered that for a few seconds and then shrugged. "I guess that's possible, but you'll have to ask Joseph."

Ethan looked worried. "Joseph should leave as soon as possible. The waterways won't remain safe much longer, and it's a long trip down the Tennessee, Ohio, and Mississippi rivers." He glanced around. "Where is that river rat anyway?"

"He left early this morning, before dawn." Edward went on to tell of Joseph's concerns after Shiloh's battle, explaining that his father's farm was not far from there.

Ethan looked concerned. "I read about Shiloh in the newspaper day before yesterday, and I guess it was pretty bloody. Over 23,000 men died there." Silence descended as they tried to imagine the battlefield strewn with bodies wearing gray and blue, and then Ethan asked, "Any idea when he'll return?"

Edward shook his head. "Not really, but I expect he'll return in a couple of days, three at the most."

Ethan placed his empty glass on the tray, stood, and stretched. "I hope everything is all right with his family." He looked down at Edward with a mischievous grin. "I'm sure Lori's worried, so I'd better get." Then softly sang, "She loves me so."

Edward grinned. "You're an asshole, Ethan. I'm sure you can show yourself out." After Ethan left, Edward closed his eyes and returned to the quiet peacefulness he had enjoyed before Ethan's visit.

The Greene farm in Tennessee

Joseph sat atop the horse he had managed to rent in Gasten, looking down at his father's farm and remembering that morning so long ago, just before sunrise. He was thinking that the scene had not changed all that much as he took in the barn, chicken coop, pigsty, outhouse, and other outbuildings. Then his eyes found the space where his mother's garden had once flourished, and he visualized her on her knees, planting or weeding while humming to herself. A thin trail of smoke escaping from the chimney and floating toward the cloudless blue sky was the only sign of life.

Gently nudging his horse, he started down the hill, thinking it strange that his brothers weren't in the fields. Catching a whiff of the dark soil only a farmer would appreciate, he rode down the hill and across the fields, studying the green haze of young seedlings breaking through the dark, rich soil. As he approached the house, the front door slowly opened, and a figure with a rifle he recognized as his father stepped onto the porch.

The old man raised one hand to the brim of his hat, shading his aging eyes from the bright sun in the sky behind Joseph. Then he stepped off the porch, pointing the rifle at him. "Hold it right there, Friend."

Joseph's heart raced with excitement at being home, yet he felt apprehensive, wondering what sort of welcome he would receive after all these years. "It's me, Pa. It's Joseph."

"Joseph?" the old man repeated. Straining his old eyes, he stepped closer to the edge of the porch.

Joseph rode up to the porch, dismounted, and looked into the face of the man he had run away from twelve long years ago. His once full head of dark brown hair and beard were mostly gray, and he seemed thinner and shorter than Joseph remembered, or perhaps Joseph was a little taller. His face showed the lines of age and days in the sun and cold weather. The years had taken their toll on the once strong body of the man, whose temper was still quick, but his body was now old and frail-looking. Joseph recalled the day when he was only seven that his pa had knocked a stranger right through the general store window over some argument.

Zachariah silently stood frozen in place, looking into the face of the son he had not seen in so many years. His eyes turned red and then welled with tears as he looked at his son as he stepped off the porch. "Good Lord almighty, son. I'd given up ever seeing you again, feared maybe you were dead." After they hugged one another, he stepped back with tears in his eyes. "Damn, it's good to see ya, son," Zachariah said, looking joyful. "Thought a lot about you over the years." He gestured toward the hill. "Many a day, I'd glance toward that hill yonder, picturing you riding over it, coming back, coming home." His face suddenly held sadness. "As time went by, I didn't look as much, and one day, I just gave up, thinking maybe you were dead." He looked away in silence, trying to hide the tear he wiped away with one finger. Then he turned, smiling again. "The good Lord's answered my prayers, sending you back so this old man can ask your forgiveness."

Joseph smiled affectionately. "There's nothing to forgive, Pa. I was just a foolish boy wanting more than this old farm could give. It had nothing to do with you."

Zachariah nodded, looking relieved, then turned toward the house and yelled, "Daughter, come out here and see who the good Lord brought back to us."

Joseph looked past his father to the door just beyond the porch.

His younger sister, Sissy, stepped out of the house, stopped at the edge of the porch shading her eyes with a dishcloth she held in her right hand.

"Don't just stand there, girl," said Zachariah. "This here's your brother Joseph, who's come home."

Sissy stepped off the porch, hesitantly at first and looking unsure, then walked over and stood next to her father, staring at Joseph, thinking of how much he had changed. "I was only about six when ya left. Hardly remember you."

"Guess that's true enough," said Joseph, looking regretful. "It's been a spell, but I remember you." Then he smiled. "You sure are pretty. Look a lot like Ma."

She looked down at the ground with a shy smile. "That's what everyone tells me."

Joseph smiled. "I bet Pa has to chase off all the boys in the county."

Still blushing, she looked up, smiled, and stepped back, glancing at her pa. "Just one. Stevie Miller."

Joseph remembered the Miller family was one of the first families to settle in the valley. Their farm bordered his pa's, and he recalled a young boy about Sissy's age. Then he thought about his brothers. "Where are Lester and Billy?"

Zachariah looked worried. “Gone,” he said, nodding toward the eastern horizon.

Joseph looked concerned. “Gone, where to?”

“Off to war,” Zachariah said as he gestured around the place. “Like most other young men in the valley, they’s anxious to get themselves into this damn war. I’s afraid they was at Shiloh earlier this month, but I got a letter from yer brother Lester a few days back say’n he and Billy are up in Virginia’s someplace with the Confederate army.”

Joseph frowned, “I thought they would go the other way, as much as you preached against slavery.”

Zachariah nodded thoughtfully. “I don’t agree with slavery of any kind, Son, but I disagree more with them high and mighty Northerners telling us how to run our business.” His eyes narrowed, his lips tightened. “We didn’t like the King of England telling us what to do, and a war ended that. So, it seems to me the question of slavery ought to be our problem to settle without the help of Mr. Lincoln and his thugs. Next thing they’ll be do’n is com’n’ down here telling us what crops to grow.”

He turned to his daughter. “Sissy, how bout fix’n’ me and yer brother here something to eat while we talk a bit more?” He turned to Joseph. “Come on, son, let’s go inside, and you can tell yer pa where ya been all these years.”

“I could use a bite to eat,” said Joseph. Then he chuckled. “Seemed like the ride from Gasten is a lot longer than I remembered.”

Zachariah looked at him with a wry smile. “It’s a mite longer still with a stubborn horse in tow.”

Joseph grinned, knowing his father was referring to him bringing back the horse he had ridden into Gasten. He followed them into the house, where Sissy busied herself at the stove while he and his pa sat at the same table Joseph remembered sitting at as a boy. He glanced around the familiar room that had changed very little and watched Sissy working at the same black iron stove his mother had used for cooking. It was hard to believe that Sissy was now eighteen, while in his memory of her, he recalled a little girl. She was all grown up, wearing her long, blond hair in a ponytail that swayed as she walked while unruly strands hung down the sides of her face. She was barely five feet and slender but deceivingly strong. He recalled her temper as a child, remembering she was never one to back away from her brothers. Joseph smiled, wondering if Stevie Miller knew what he was getting into.

She turned. “Coffee?”

Joseph smiled. “Coffee’d be fine, Sissy.”

“How long can ya stay, son?” asked Zachariah.

Joseph told them he could only stay the night.

The old man nodded, looking disappointed. “You in this here fight?”

Joseph shook his head. “Not in the shooting part.” He told of his life on the river, the Southern Belle, the Captain, his marriage to Mary, her being with child, and their plans to move to east Texas.

When Zachariah stood to get more coffee, Joseph noticed that he favored his left leg and asked if he had arthritis.

Sissy turned from the stove with a big grin and said that a mule had kicked their pa a few months back.

Joseph grinned, remembering his Pa’s temper. “Is the mule still alive?”

Zachariah grinned, looking a little embarrassed. “Hell,” he said. “T’weren’t the dang mule's fault. I guess I lost my temper.” He glanced at Joseph. “I’m sure you remember how that was?”

Joseph grinned. “I recall running toward the barn to hide from you time to time.”

Zachariah’s laugh was half embarrassment and half affection as he looked down at his coffee cup. “Oh,” he said. “I’s upset over something or other, and I up and slapped the mule pretty darn hard on her ass, so she up and kicked me against the horse.” He paused in thought. “Guess I’s lucky the horse never kicked me.”

Joseph laughed.

Zachariah’s expression changed, his smile gone. “As I lay there on the barn floor, I thought about kill’n `em both, but I knew I deserved it.” He shrugged, gesturing toward the barn. “They’s just a couple of animals fight’n back, but I swear, Son, as I lay in bed that night hurt’n like the dickens, I heard them two out there in the barn laugh’n.”

Joseph smiled with a chuckle. “Maybe they were, Pa.”

Sissy turned from the stove. “Pa quit losing his tempter pretty much after that. Dinner’s about ready. You two better wash up.”

After dinner, Joseph helped Sissy with the dishes while they talked about the past and her hopes for a future with Stevie Miller. Joseph asked if Stevie had asked for her hand, and Sissy smiled, saying she believed he had started to once or twice but chickened out. She grinned. “Guess maybe I’ll have to do the ask’n.”

When the dishes and kitchen were clean, Joseph put the horse away in the barn and joined their pa by the fire. Recognizing his pa’s old Bible, he remembered the nights the family sat around this very room. He remembered them watching the flames dance above the burning wood and hot coals, imagining what hell would be like.

Zachariah closed the Bible and held it on his lap with both hands while they talked. Joseph saw a side of his father he had never seen growing up. He felt sad about missing that part of his life, regretting many things he had said and thought over the years.

The night wore on, Joseph grew tired and went to bed in his old room. The bed felt strange, yet it was like an old friend as he recalled every friendly lump and crease in the worn mattress. The smell of the house and bedding set free memories he had pushed deep down within himself. In the room's silence, he stared at the glow of the fireplace in the other room reflecting its way between the cracks of the closed door.

Movement in the other room interrupted the tiny lines of light, and Joseph knew his father was walking back and forth across the floor, reading his Bible. The soft murmured words mixed with Sissy's soft humming while she was busy with something. Sleep stalked him like a hunter, and soon, his eyes grew heavy while his mind drifted in and out of sleep. The door opened, and for one reason or the other, he pretended to be already asleep.

Zachariah slowly approached the bed, stood over his son for a moment, then bent down and gently adjusted the covers like Joseph's mother had always done. He turned and quietly walked out, leaving the door partly open as they had when he was a child.

Joseph felt sorry for his pa and sorry for the hurt he must have left behind when he ran away. He wanted to tell him he was sorry but did not know-how. He thought of how lonely his pa must have been all these years without the woman he loved, and then he thought of Mary, and he wanted to hurry home.

Sissy's humming suddenly stopped. The house became quiet, and the lamps went out in the other room, leaving only the fireplace's dim light. He imagined Sissy in her room, pa in his, and then he closed his eyes and thought of Mary and their child, promising himself that he would be a good father.

Joseph woke to the smell of hot coffee, eggs, and bacon rushing through the cracks of the bedroom door. He dressed, stood at the bedroom window, moved the curtains back, and looked out at the freshly painted picket fence around his mother's grave. Feeling an emptiness he had not felt in a long time, he let go of the curtain, turned, and walked out of the bedroom and into the kitchen.

"Morn'n," Sissy said, turning from the stove. "Have a seat, and I'll get ya some coffee."

"Where's Pa?"

She nodded at the door. "Git'n more eggs for breakfast."

Joseph sat down and looked at the familiar cup she placed on the table.

Sissy smiled and said softly, "Makes ya think of Ma, don't it?"

Joseph nodded, remembering it had been her cup. "Ma's grave looks good."

"Pa replaced some of the pickets in the fence and whitewashed it." She paused, looking in the direction of the grave. "He spends a lot of time out there these days."

Joseph got up, walked to the window, and looked toward the barn. "How are things around the place, Sissy?"

She considered that a moment. "We're doing okay, Joseph. The Miller boys come over and help out some, as does the Jackson boy down the road."

The door opened, and Zachariah walked in with a small basket of eggs.

"Morn'n, Pa," said Joseph.

"Morn'n Son." Zachariah set the basket of eggs next to the stove, poured a cup of coffee, and joined Joseph at the table. "What time ya leaving?"

"Reckon as soon as I eat. I gotta get back."

Zachariah nodded thoughtfully. "You be careful, Son."

"I will, Pa."

Sissy placed a platter of eggs, bacon, and bread on the table and sat next to Joseph. Zachariah cleared his throat as he always had before praying, then said grace, asking for the end of the war, his son's safe return, and Joseph a safe trip back.

The sun was well above the eastern hills as Joseph stood in the shade of an oak tree at the fence surrounding his mother's grave. The smell of the fresh coat of whitewash still lingered as it mixed with the scent of a small bunch of wildflowers placed next to the wooden marker. A slight breeze played with the leaves of the oak tree, and it felt like a peaceful place. One that his mother would have picked. His heart began to ache, something he had not felt in a long time. His eyes welled, and tears made their way down his cheeks as he wiped his face with the back of his hand. A hawk's cry as it circled high above, a squirrel chattering, and birds chirping filled the quiet morning.

Joseph smiled. "Looks like Pa and Sissy are taking good care of you, Ma. Sorry for being gone so long, but the road I took was long, and I can't stay long." Glancing back at the house, he saw Sissy sitting on the porch steps next to their Pa, holding the reins to his horse. Joseph turned back to the grave. "I misjudged Pa, and I don't have the words to tell him, so if you don't mind, I'll leave that up to you when you next see him. I miss you, Ma."

He turned away, walked toward his horse, took the reins from his father, extended his hand, and smiled, "Good to see you, Pa."

Zachariah looked down at Joseph's hand, pushed it aside, and hugged him for a long moment before stepping back.

Surprised at that, Joseph smiled at the old man. "Sorry I took so long to come home."

"I'm just glad you made it, Son."

Sissy's eyes were tearing as Joseph put his arms around her tiny body, holding her tightly against him. "I'll be thinking about you, Sissy, and when this war's over, I want you to get married and have lots of kids." He looked down at her and smiled affectionately. "Name one after me."

She nodded, forced a smile, and wiped the tears away with her hands. "I promise."

Joseph climbed into the saddle and looked down at them. "I'll write." He tipped his, looked at them for another moment, turned his horse toward the hill, and nudged it into a lope. At the top, he stopped to look back, feeling deeply satisfied that he had made the trip and promising himself he would return after the war. With that, he waved and disappeared over the hill.

Fourteen

April 1862 – June 1862

Edward and Joseph

Alabama to Texas

Mary McAlexander Greene was worried about Joseph as she sat in the window seat of her bedroom, looking out the window. The sun had long since given up the day to the dark, clear sky of moon and stars, and as the clock in the hall tolled ten, she looked down at the ghost-like archway and gate at the end of the dark driveway, wondering where her husband was.

The lamplighter had already visited the posts along the cobblestone street, giving yellow-orange life to the street lamps. The book she had used unsuccessfully to occupy her time lay neglected among the window seat pillows. Weary from the stress of waiting, her eyes grew heavy, longing for sleep, so reluctantly, she left the window for the comfort of bed, closed her eyes, and fell asleep.

She opened her eyes from a restless sleep and sat up listening to the clock in the hall, tolling midnight, fearing something may have happened to her husband. Lying back down on the bed, she pulled his pillow into her and began to cry. At last, she heard the lonely sounds of a horse's hooves faintly echoing along the cobblestone street, growing louder and then stopping. Sitting up, she looked toward the window, got out of bed, and whispered his name as she hurried to the window seat. Seeing the dark images of a horse and carriage beyond the gates at the end of the driveway beneath the street lamp, she watched as a figure with a carpet bag closed the carriage door and paid the driver. As the carriage drove away, the figure turned and walked through the wrought iron gates and up the driveway toward the house.

Joseph quietly opened the front door and entered the foyer, thankful for the small lantern Sophie had so thoughtfully left. He slid out of his coat and then took off his hat. Placing them on a small table under a large mirror on the wall, he picked up the lantern and his carpetbag and walked out of the foyer toward the stairs. As he stepped onto the first step, he looked up, seeing Mary in the dim light at the top of the stairs waiting for him. He raced up the stairs, stopping one step below her, dropped his bag, set the lantern on the step, and took her in his arms.

She put her hands on the back of his head, gently pulled his head against her soft breasts, and kissed the top of his head. "I've been worried."

He could feel the warmth of her body through the soft nightgown and hear the fast beat of her heart. A small nudge from her stomach pushed at him. He looked at the bulge, smiled, and whispered, "I think we woke him."

Filled with relief, he was home, she smiled. "We've missed you terribly."

He bent down, picked up his carpetbag of dirty clothes and the lantern, and followed her into the bedroom. She climbed into bed and waited while he set the lantern on the dresser and his carpetbag on the window seat. After getting undressed, he blew out the lantern and climbed into bed, lying on his back, staring at the dark ceiling, thinking of his father and sister.

She nestled against him, resting her head on his chest, and asked about his trip. As he talked, she closed her eyes and tried to fight sleep but couldn't. She was happy and content listening to his calm, familiar voice, and as the minutes passed, her soft, shallow breathing told him she was sleeping.

Looking at her dim face in the darkness, he smiled and stopped talking, and as he lay in the stillness of their room, he thought of his pa of Sissy and his brothers, wondering if he would ever see them again.

Early the next morning, while Mary slept, Joseph quietly dressed, slipped downstairs, and walked into the dining room.

Edward glanced up from the newspaper with a happy expression. "Good morning."

"Good morning, Ed."

Edward smiled and gestured toward a silver pot of fresh coffee. "Help yourself to a cup of coffee?"

Joseph sat down and poured himself a cup.

Edward picked up the plate of biscuits and handed it to him. "Sitting at a table with clean linen, fine china, and good food feels a little strange."

Joseph took the plate. "I can only imagine."

Edward put the paper down. "There were nights I could see the Union fires flickering through the trees across the expanse we called No Man's Land. Often, we could smell what it was they cooked, causing my stomach to growl, and I often thought of Sophie's biscuits and gravy for some reason." He smiled at Joseph. "So I asked Sophie to fix breakfast biscuits and gravy for breakfast. It's a simple meal but one of my favorites. I hope you don't mind."

"Not at all," replied Joseph as he took two biscuits, placed them on his plate, picked up the gravy boat, and poured hot gravy over them.

Edward sipped his coffee and watched Joseph's fork cut through a biscuit, methodically stirred it through the gravy, and put it into his mouth. "I need to talk to you about a matter of some importance. It concerns your plans on leaving Florence."

Joseph looked at Edward, hoping they would not argue over his decision.

Edward shifted, getting comfortable. "I find myself in the awkward position of having to ask a favor."

Curious, Joseph stopped eating and looked at him. "What sort of favor?"

Edward raised his brow, looking embarrassed. "Ethan has the same fears as you about his family."

Relieved it did not concern him taking Mary and the baby away, Joseph stabbed at a piece of biscuit with his fork. "I would imagine so."

"I had forgotten that Ethan's parents had moved back to east Texas a few years ago. It appears his father shared your fears that Florence would feel the ravages of war." Edward paused to look at his hands folded on the table in front of him, and then he looked at Joseph. "Ethan wants desperately to get his wife and children out of Florence to Texas." He paused and gestured with both hands. "His obligations to the Confederacy make it impossible for him to deliver them himself, and the other men he might trust are already off fighting in this damn war." He pushed his chair back, took the napkin from his lap, and put it on the table next to his plate. "While you were away, Ethan dropped by and asked about you. I told him where you were and of your plans." He paused and added, "I hope you don't mind."

Joseph looked at Edward. "Of course not." Having his suspicions where this was leading, he decided to remain silent and let Edward talk.

Edward studied Joseph while waiting for his reaction. When none came, he continued. "Ethan is going to ask you to take his family with you and Mary to Jefferson. Ethan's father's farm is but a few miles from there." He paused. "This is a big favor to ask, but if you could manage this, I would forever be in your debt." Edward leaned forward, looking uneasy. "The importance and enormity of such a responsibility is almost overwhelming. Both Ethan and I would respect and completely understand your reasons for declining."

Joseph chewed his food and swallowed. "I barely know Ethan, yet he would place his family's safety in my hands?"

Edward wished Ethan was there to do his own asking. "Desperate times call for desperate measures, Joseph." He smiled warmly. "Besides, I trust you with my sister."

Joseph grinned as he considered the request. "It's a long journey, and a lot can happen, especially in a time of war." Silence descended on the room as he looked at his half-empty plate, thinking about all that could happen and wondering what Mary would say. "If Ethan is willing to entrust his family into my hands, I don't see how I could refuse."

Edward let out a long, relieved sigh. "Thank you, Joseph. I'm in your debt.

"Besides," said Joseph. "I'm sure Mary will welcome the company of another woman."

Edward considered that. "I'm sure she would. We can discuss the particulars with Ethan after dinner tonight." He stood. "Now, if you'll excuse me, I have to take a long walk next door and ask a certain young lady if she will honor us with her presence at dinner."

Joseph smiled, looking eager. "Good Luck!"

Edward walked along the winding stone path between the grass and flowerbeds to the Koger house's front porch, thinking of Joseph's words, 'Good Luck.' Reaching the front door, he paused, thinking it was more than luck he needed as he removed his hat and pulled the cord. The bells chimed within the house, and moments later, the door opened, and Sarah greeted him with a friendly smile. "Good morning."

Surprised at her opening the door instead of the Negro maid, he smiled. "Good morning. I wasn't prepared for you to open the door. I'm afraid you caught me off guard."

She smiled at his embarrassment. "I can't imagine anyone catching you off guard, Edward. Are you here to see Daddy or me?"

He looked down at his hat and then into her green eyes. "I'm here to ask you a favor."

Standing in the open doorway, she smiled, looking curious. "A favor?" Then she gestured to the white wooden chairs on the porch. "Would you care to sit out here or in the parlor?"

Edward looked at the chairs thoughtfully. "Uh….that would be fine."

"Which?" she asked.

"Pardon?"

She smiled, "The parlor or the porch?"

Edward's face flushed. "The parlor, if you don't mind."

Sarah stepped back, and after Edward walked inside, she closed the door and showed him to the parlor, where he waited for her to sit. After she was comfortable, he sat down in a chair across from her.

"What is the favor?" she asked.

"I'm having a few close friends over for dinner tonight, and I would be honored if you would be gracious enough to be my guest."

She hesitated with a surprised look and then smiled. "I couldn't think of a better way to spend an evening."

Looking relieved, he smiled and told her Alex, his wife Ella, Joseph, and Mary, as well as Ethan and his wife Lori, would join them.

"Sounds fun," she said, looking pleased.

"I can't guarantee that it will be fun," he said, "but with you sitting next to me, I certainly won't be bored by my brother all evening."

She laughed as she folded her hands on her lap. "I'm sure Alex is anything but boring."

"Perhaps not, but it will be nice to have you at my side just the same." Feeling awkward, he stood, took her hand, and helped her up. "I hate to rush off, but I have business in town."

"Don't you want to tell me what time you'll be calling for me?"

"Yes, of course; how about seven-thirty?"

"I'll be ready."

They walked to the front door, and as he started to open it, he turned, "Perhaps I should call for you around seven so we could have a little time together before the others arrive."

"I would enjoy that very much."

He opened the door, stepped out onto the porch, and smiled. "Until seven." He turned and walked down the steps toward the street.

She watched him for a moment and slowly closed the door, thinking of her sister, when suddenly, guilt found her. Sarah turned with her back against the door and closed her eyes. *'This is your dead sister's husband,'* she told herself, and as she walked upstairs to her room, she argued with herself in silence about accepting his invitation. In her room, she lay across her bed, looking at her sister's photo sitting on her dresser. She closed her eyes and whispered, "Forgive me, Henrietta."

Sophie gently touched Edward's shoulder, waking him from his nap. He opened his eyes and sat up, saying he must have dozed off while reading the paper.

"Mistah Edward, it's almost seven o'clock."

He glanced at the grandfather clock in the corner. "I told Sarah I would call for her at seven." As he stood, the newspaper dropped to the floor.

"Yes, suh," Sophie said, looking worried. "Ah knows, Mistah Edward, that's why I woke ya."

He thanked her as he reached down, picked up the newspaper, folded it, placed it neatly on the table, and retrieved his coat from a nearby chair. Imagining Sarah waiting for him, he slipped into his coat as he hurried from the parlor nervously, tugging and smoothing his vest as he ran out the door.

A middle-aged Negro woman dressed in a white dress and apron opened the door and smiled. "Good evening, Mistah Edward."

"Good evening, Eunice. And how are you tonight?"

"I's fine, thank ya kindly." She stepped back so he could enter. "Do come in and have a seat in the parlor." She made sure he was settled in a chair. "I'll go up and tell Miss Sarah you're here."

Edward waited for several minutes before Sarah appeared at the parlor door, smiling a warm, friendly smile. "Hello, Edward."

He stood thinking how lovely she looked in her red dress, and then he smiled. "You look lovely tonight, Miss Sarah."

"Well, thank you, Edward. I must apologize for taking so long."

He smiled, "It was well worth the wait." Then he took her arm, putting it on his. "Shall we?"

Edward was pouring a glass of sherry for Sarah and a bourbon for himself when the library door opened, and Mary stepped inside.

"Sarah," greeted Mary as she walked toward her.

Sarah stood, returned the hello, and they embraced.

As she stepped back, Mary said, "I was thrilled when Edward told me you were his guest for dinner. Please, do sit down."

"Thank you," Sarah said, glancing at Edward and then back at Mary. "The truth is I'm a bit nervous."

Mary smiled, looking surprised. "Why, Sarah, whatever for?" She glanced at Edward. "The truth is I'm happy someone has finally gained Edward's interest."

Edward could feel his face flush, wishing his sister would keep her thoughts to herself.

Sarah had never confessed her feelings for her brother Edward, even though she and Mary were best friends. On the other hand, Mary had suspected Sarah's feelings for several years. And of all the women Mary knew, she felt that only Sarah could make her brother fall in love again. One of Mary's greatest fears was that Edward would live without the love of another woman. She placed her hand on Sarah's arm. "If you will excuse me, I believe Joseph is about to declare war on his tie."

During dinner, the conversation was about fashion, the latest gossip, children, and anything else but the war. The men smiled and politely listened to the women. They interjected a thought here or there, but for the most part, they let the women enjoy the evening, knowing it was important for them to forget the war, even if for only a few hours. Nearing the end of dinner, Edward brought up Ethan's request for Lori and his children. Decisions were discussed, plans were made, and after several minutes, it was settled. Joseph would take Lori and the children with him, Mary, and their child to east Texas, seeing them safely to Ethan's father's farm. The conversation then moved from the dining room to the library, where they talked and laughed about other things.

During the evening, Edward found it difficult to keep his eyes off Sarah and often thought of his sister's words about finding someone who gained his interest. As he watched Sarah, he thought of holding her in his arms and wondered what it would be like to kiss her. Then, the reality of the war filled his mind, and he knew there was no time for a proper courting of Miss Sarah Koger. But he promised himself sincerely that he would see as much of her as time allowed.

The voices of Joseph, Ethan, and Alex discussing the trip to Texas, mixed with Sarah's as she talked to Mary, Lori, and Ella, gave Edward a sense of not belonging. Feeling the need to get up and go outside, he fought the urge and sat quietly, thinking the world was different now as it rushed toward self-destruction. Sarah's laugh brought him back from the terrible places his mind had ventured.

Mary had been watching Edward, knowing that whatever haunted him had made him a different person, just as the things that haunted Alex had made him a different man. She glanced at Joseph, who was talking to Ethan, and was glad he was taking them far away to the safety of east Texas. There, he would be safe and not experience what Edward and Alex had. She did not want the war to change or take him from her.

Edward kept the promise he had made to himself and spent most of his time with Sarah, taking long walks or buggy rides into town or along the river, and each day, his love for her grew. He often thought of his dead wife Henrietta and their deep love. Guilt often found him, and he was unaware of Sarah's guilt, yet neither had any reason to feel guilty. Henrietta had been dead for almost five years. He wrestled with his feelings during every waking moment until the afternoon that he visited her grave. Kneeling beside it, he talked to her ghost, and when he left her grave, he knew that Henrietta understood.

Sarah was in her room, sitting in the window seat, looking out the window, thinking of Edward when she turned and looked at Henrietta's picture. She missed her kindness and laughter, remembering how they had teased one another as little girls. She stood, walked to her dresser, and picked up the picture. "I don't know if I can be with him, Henrietta. I love him terribly, but I'm afraid the memory of your love may destroy us."

Caressing the picture, she began to cry, wishing someone would tell her what to do. Then, thinking of Mary, she put the picture down, hurried out of her room, down the stairs, and out the front door. Knocking on the door of Edward's house, she asked Sophie if she could see Mary.

Moments later, Mary walked into the room where Sarah waited and saw the concern on her friend's face and in her eyes, suspecting that it had something to do with Edward. She put her arm around Sarah, and together, they walked outside to the gazebo, where they could talk in private.

Sarah told Mary of her feelings toward Edward and her fear of Henrietta's ghost.

"Does Edward know how you feel?"

Sarah looked down at her clasped hands. "I'm not certain. I have never given him cause.

Water cascaded softly over and around the rocks in the small stream, filling the silence as Mary smiled at her friend and put her hand over Sarah's clasped hands. "I've watched Edward when you are together, and I think he feels more than just friendship, Sarah."

She looked at Mary with hope in her eyes. "Really?"

"Yes, I do, and you both have to remember that Henrietta has been gone for over five years. The dead don't begrudge the living their happiness, and I'm certain that Henrietta would be sad knowing that the two people she cared for walked through life without the love and happiness they could share. Now, you best go before Edward returns and thinks we are conspiring against him."

Sarah laughed. "Wouldn't want that, would we?" She wiped the tears from her eyes as she and Mary walked through the yard to the front gate. Mary watched her friend hurry home and thought of how much she loved her.

Edward drove the buggy home from the cemetery, his mind full of arguments against his feelings for Sarah. The war could last for years, he may not survive, or he could return a cripple as so many others had. There was their age difference to and little Mary to consider. As he rode along the streets of Florence, he suspected that Sarah had feelings for him, but how deep they went or how strong was something he had yet to discover.

Sarah Koger was sitting in the window seat of her bedroom, chin resting on her forearm, staring down at the big, black, ominous iron gates guarding the driveway while she also dealt with the uncertainty of the future. Edward would be leaving very soon, and the fear of him never coming back frightened her. She wanted to be with him, to spend her life with him, to give him children. However, war and his duty to honor his commitments could very well rob her of his love and a life together.

Hearing the sound of horses and a carriage, she looked out the window, seeing him drive the carriage up the driveway and disappear under the overhang. She turned and looked at herself in the mirror, wiped the tears from her eyes, and waited eagerly for the familiar ring of the doorbell.

Edward was sitting in the parlor, staring out the window and deep in thought, when she walked into the room. He turned and smiled.

She paused and returned the smile, hoping he wouldn't notice she had been crying.

He stood, took her in his arms, and gently kissed her. "I've wanted to do that since the evening you walked into my study with Mary and Ella."

She looked up into his brown eyes. "I've thought of little else since the first night you walked me home." She turned and sat down on the small sofa they had come to share over the past days. Taking his hand, she looked at him, murmuring, "What are we going to do?"

"I've had several arguments with myself about that very thing."

"I think I'm in love with you, Edward."

He sighed. "You have no idea how happy that makes me."

She started to speak, but he put a gentle finger to her mouth and smiled. "We both know that until this terrible war is over and our lives once again belong to us, we have no choice but to wait."

The room grew heavy with silence.

"Then we'll write our letters," she said. "And put our faith in fate, praying she'll be kind to us. And if we feel the same after the war....?"

Edward interrupted. "Sarah, I love you, and perhaps it's madness to think of such things right now, but I can't put my feelings aside."

She looked down at her hands, then into his eyes. "I feel guilty, Edward."

"Over Henrietta?"

She nodded yes in silence.

He sat back. "I visited her grave today."

Surprised, she looked at him. "You went to the cemetery?"

He took her hand and held it tightly in his. "I don't believe Henrietta would begrudge us our love and happiness, Sarah. It is not as though she was alive, and you and I were in love and seeing one another behind her back. You must know that I loved her very deeply." He paused, looking down at their hands, and then he looked at her. "But she has been gone these five years. It's time I moved on and found happiness with whatever time I have left in this world."

"Come," she said as she stood pulling him from the sofa. "We have today and tomorrow, and you promised me a buggy ride."

In the early morning of April 25, 1862, Edward held Sarah's hand as they walked along the station platform in silence. Ethan and Lori quietly talked to one another while the children waited a few feet away. The engine hissed, spewing steam across the station platform, reminding Edward of the fog at Fort Donelson, the sounds of musket fire, and the killing.

Sarah squeezed his hand, pulling him back from those memories. "What are you thinking of?"

"Nothing," he said, not wanting to share those memories. "It's not important." He knew the train would soon move along the tracks toward the death and destruction of a war that awaited him and Ethan. He looked at her face, wanting to remember the way she looked these last few minutes.

Sarah looked into his dark, sad eyes while an endless river of words filled her mind that she could not speak. The fear of crying held her as she bravely forced a silent smile, but she could not stop her eyes from welling. Turning away, she looked at the other people dealing with their goodbyes.

The bell on the engine clanged, mixing with the hissing steam of the engine and rushing across the platform of voices that seemed to talk faster. They looked into one another's eyes in silence, listening as others said their goodbyes. Women were crying while clinging to their husbands or sons, who gently forced themselves free, then hurried up the steps of the railcars, disappearing inside.

The whistle blew, and Sarah reached out, taking Edward's arm as she glanced toward the engine that would take the train and him away. Her eyes welled again with tears as she looked up into his dark eyes. "Come back to me."

Taking her in his arms, he kissed her. "I promise."

The train whistle sounded again, the train lurched forward with a loud, thunderous noise, and the conductor yelled, "All Aboard!" for the third and last time.

Edward glanced at the conductor, then at Ethan holding Lori, and then he looked back at Sarah. "I love you." He turned and stepped up onto the slow moving railcar. Ethan kissed Lori and his children and then ran after the train, leaping onto the steps next to Edward. Giving a last wave to Sarah and Lori, Edward and Ethan disappeared into the rail car.

Sarah and Lori stood at the edge of the train platform and watched as the train got smaller and smaller as it followed the rails toward the war.

Joseph and Mary Greene

On the night of April 29, 1862, with Joseph by her side, Mary gave birth to a healthy boy named Zachariah Edward Greene. While Mary and the child slept, Joseph sat at a nearby table writing a letter to his father, pausing now and then to marvel at his wife and child.

The Southern Belle quietly slipped through the Tennessee River's waters, heading southwest toward Guntersville, Alabama. Joseph stood in an open window of the bridge, looking at the moon's reflection on the river while Captain Goodman sat in his captain's chair, puffing on his pipe.

The bridge filled with idle conversation as they enjoyed the warmth of a peaceful June evening. During a lapse in conversation, Joseph thought of Mary and his son, Texas, and points beyond and away from the war. Glancing at the dark figure of Goodman puffing his pipe, he wondered what thoughts ran through the old man's mind, deciding they were best left alone. Goodman cautioned the helmsman to mind the sand bars up ahead. The helmsman acknowledged him, turned the wheel slightly to the left, and maneuvered around a wide bend with the white moonlight reflecting across the water. Musket fire broke out, followed by musket balls hitting the bridge. Joseph and the helmsman ducked while Goodman slid out of his chair, taking cover on the floor. Hidden in the corner of the bridge, Joseph peeked out the window, watching the flashes of gunfire as musket balls passed through the side of the bridge and windows. He turned to check on Captain Goodman, kneeling next to the wounded helmsman.

Joseph grabbed the wheel and quickly corrected the Southern Belle's course into deeper waters. Confederate soldiers who were traveling onboard returned the gunfire, aiming at the flashes on the bank while Joseph steered the Belle around the bend. As both sides stopped firing and silence returned to the river, the only sound he could hear was the big paddlewheel thrashing through the water, pushing the Southern Belle downstream. Glancing out the bridge's open window, Joseph saw several Confederate Soldiers standing on the deck, with muskets pointing toward the riverbank. As the soldiers returned to their spots on the deck, Joseph looked at Goodman as he tended to the helmsman. "How's he doing?"

"It's superficial," replied the captain. "Bastards," he said as he stood and looked toward the bank in the darkness. "Fools could have killed innocent passengers."

"We were lucky this time, Captain," Joseph said, continuing to steer the Belle along the calm waters.

Agreeing silently, Goodman helped the helmsman to his feet, telling him to go below and send up another helmsman. "I'll be down in a bit to patch that wound." Then he turned to Joseph. "Damn lucky we had some of our soldiers on board. Hope they shot a few of them Yankee bastards."

The shooting war had found them. Joseph knew this was just a prelude of things to come, realizing that the longer the war went on, the more this would happen. He thought of the cities along the river, Florence in particular, and worried about Mary and young Zachariah. River cities would be targets for the northern armies, and he had to act fast if he was to get his and Ethan's family out of Alabama. "Captain, we need to talk."

As another man walked onto the bridge, taking the wheel, Goodman looked at Joseph, knowing what was on his mind. "Let's go below. I need a drink."

In his cabin, Goodman offered Joseph a drink, which he refused. "Suit yerself," replied the captain as he poured from the bottle he kept in his desk drawer. He picked up his glass and asked, "What's on your mind, Son?"

Joseph sat down, looking troubled. "Things are getting complicated, Captain." He paused and watched as Goodman took a sip of whiskey. "I'm afraid I'll need those letters of introduction you promised and my final pay when we dock at Florence."

Goodman took a drink of whiskey. "I been expecting this since that son of yours arrived."

Joseph looked worried. "Tonight's just the beginning, Captain. The war is getting closer each day, and Florence is right in its path. I need to move now while the waterways are still passable. I have a promise to keep."

"I know," said Goodman softly. "You gave your word to that Ethan fella."

"That I did, Captain, and I aim to keep it."

"And so you shall, Laddie." Goodman took a drink and looked at him. "One's word is an important thing." He gulped the last of his drink, turned his glass over, and set it upside down on his desk. "The letters and pay will be ready when we get to Florence."

Relieved yet feeling remorse mixed with guilt about leaving, Joseph stared at Goodman for a moment and extended his hand. "Sorry, Captain."

Goodman shook his hand and then gestured toward the door. "You go on now while I get those papers ready." Feeling a great loss already, he watched the door close as Joseph left his cabin. When the Southern Belle docked at Florence, the captain made good his promise by handing Joseph the letter of introduction, his wages, and a little bonus.

Joseph accepted a final drink, shook Captain Goodman's hand, said goodbye, and walked out of the captain's cabin.

Goodman's tired eyes welled as he stared at the closed door, knowing he would never see Joseph again. "Take care of yourself, Laddie."

On the afternoon of July 17, 1862, Joseph, his family, and Ethan's family boarded a sternwheeler that would take them from Florence, Alabama, north up the Tennessee River to the Ohio River. They changed boats and headed west to the Mississippi River, heading south, avoiding the city of New Orleans that had fallen to Union forces in April. They sailed up the Red River to Shreveport, then across the great Caddo Lake and Big Cyprus River. After a nine-day trip, they arrived at the bustling east Texas town of Jefferson. Joseph made good on his promise by delivering Ethan's family safely to the Hall farm, some twenty miles northeast of Jefferson. The trip was long and arduous for Mary, and she was tired, giving Joseph cause to worry over her and the baby. He knew the city of Jefferson was a busy, sprawling city full of noise and an occasional shooting or stabbing, and he was having second thoughts about his decision to bring Mary and his son to such a place.

As if reading his mind, Del and Janice Hall (Ethan's parents) suggested that Mary and the baby stay with them. "We've plenty of room," said Janice.

At first, Mary refused and protested against the suggestion, but finally, she agreed to stay until the baby was a little stronger. A few days later, satisfied his family would be safe on this peaceful farm, Joseph said goodbye and left for Jefferson, Texas, in the wagon he had rented in Jefferson along with a horse and saddle he had borrowed from Del.

Fifteen

June 1862 – August 1862

Rebecca Davis

Anderson County, South Carolina

A rooster perched proudly atop the Patterson farm's hen house as the sun crested over the far-off hills. Stretching his neck and flapping his wings, he let out his piercing screech.

Waking to the sound, Rebecca Davis rose onto her elbows, turned her head, peered through the open window at the sunrise of pinks, oranges, and purples, and thought about killing Mr. Rooster. Sitting up, she stretched, tossed back the covers, and put her feet over the edge of the bed. Looking down at her feet, she saw the letters from Andrew. Realizing they must have fallen from the bed when she fell asleep, she reached down to get them. And as she gathered them up, she felt a sudden movement of the bed. Turning, she saw the lump of covers and Cora's head resting on the other pillow. Smiling at the girl, she picked up the letters, placed them on the nightstand, got back under the covers, and put her arm around Cora, who responded by snuggling up against her. Cora's breathing was soft and steady, apparently happy in her dreams, and smelled of the lavender soap Rebecca had used to wash both girls' hair the night before. Rebecca closed her eyes, thought of Andrew and his letters, and wondered when another might come. Pots and pans that seemed to beckon from the kitchen downstairs interrupted her thoughts of Andrew and the letters. Careful not to disturb the sleeping bed jumper, she got up, quietly dressed while considering a trip to town for supplies and headed downstairs.

The slave, Alicia, was busy over the stove, preparing breakfast, when Rebecca walked into the kitchen. They said their good mornings, and Rebecca set the table while they talked idly about unimportant things. It wasn't long before the children joined them, taking their usual places around the table. Rebecca had quickly learned to enjoy the mornings when the children were too sleepy to argue. As she ate her breakfast, she watched the children eat and decided to take Cora and Naomi to town with her, knowing that Aaron would be busy in the fields with Matthew and Jed Stattler, leaving Daniel to his chores.

The trip to town was uneventful, and as they returned with the supplies, Cora and Naomi giggled while singing a silly song they'd heard long ago. The spring sun felt warm, and the air was still and quiet except for an occasional bird or the sound of grasshoppers. The girls' giggling stopped as a rider darted onto the road from the bushes, startling the horses and causing them to rear up and bolt. Cora and Naomi screamed while Rebecca yelled for them to hold on as she fought to pull back the reins, shouting, "Whoa!" at the horses. Pulling with her small arms as hard as she could, she managed to bring the team to a halt. Making sure the two girls were all right, she turned to the rider with an angry look. "Are you just plain crazy, or are you trying to get us killed?"

The rider sat hunched in the saddle as his horse made a blowing sound while nonchalantly kicking at the dirt road with a front hoof.

Rebecca stared at the figure while the girls sobbed in fear. "Be still now."

"Who is he, Miss Becky?" asked Naomi.

Wishing she had a gun, Rebecca whispered, "Shhhh, be quiet now."

As the rider sat motionless in his saddle watching them, Rebecca gripped the reins tightly in both hands, ready to run if necessary. The rider nudged his horse toward them, and then she recognized Randy Murphy, one of the men who had accompanied Michael Evans the night they came to the farm asking about the runaway slave, John. She watched as he guided his horse to the girls' side, stopping beside the wagon.

He leaned on his saddle horn with one elbow, looking first at Naomi, then Cora, and finally at Rebecca. He grinned. "Didn't mean to scare y'all." He took off his hat and smiled an unfriendly smile. "Name's Randy Murphy, Miss Becky, you may not remember me…"

"I remember," she interrupted coldly.

He expected more fear in her face. "Sorry, ma'am, already said I didn't mean to scare y'all none, we sorta came upon one another sudden like."

There was something about Randy Murphy that Rebecca didn't like. She couldn't put her finger on it, but she disliked him. "But you did scare us, Mr. Murphy. And I don't appreciate it any." She nodded toward the girls. "Just look at these two girls. They're scared half to death."

"Said I's sorry, ma'am," he said in an irritated voice. And like I done told ya, we sorta came onto one another by accident at the bend back yonder." Randy turned his attention to the girls. "My apologies, young ladies." He reached out to touch Naomi on the arm, but she quickly moved closer to her sister. Settling back in his saddle, he grinned. "My, my, aren't we a couple of pretty little things this morning? I truly didn't mean to scare ya none."

Rebecca did not much care for the way he looked at the girls. "It looked to me that you purposely bolted your horse onto the road to scare us, Mr. Murphy."

He took his eyes from the girls and stared at Rebecca with narrow eyes as he backed his horse to the rear of the wagon. Leaning from his saddle, he lifted the tarp covering the supplies. "What ya got back here?"

Rebecca met his stare with defiance, trying not to show him any fear. Angered at his rudeness, she said, "Ain't none of your business what's under there."

He looked up, letting go of the tarp. "Now that ain't exactly true, Miss Becky." He grinned while pointing at the crude homemade star on his coat. "This here gives me the right to do a lot of things." The smile left his face. "Like looking fer runaway slaves, deserters, and such."

"You won't find any runaways or deserters under my tarp," Rebecca said. She nodded at his star. "That homemade star you're wearing don't give you the right for nothing."

Feeling belittled, Randy sat up in his saddle with an angry look. "Seems to me, a woman ought to be careful how she talks way out here with no one around."

Rebecca felt a stronger fear, and longed to get back to the safety of the farm. "Is that a threat, Mr. Murphy?" She sat tall in the wagon seat. "If you want to do something worthwhile, I suggest you join up and go fight the Yankees and leave us women and children be."

Cora leaned close to Rebecca and whispered. "Let's go, Becky."

Suddenly, Randy dug his spurs into his horse, sending her around the wagon in a cloud of dust, stopping next to Rebecca and giving her a hateful look. His hat had fallen from his head onto the road, but he didn't seem to notice. His dirty fingers combed the unruly, bushy brown hair away from his ears and eyes.

Seeing the meanness in his cold blue eyes, Rebecca feared for the girls.

Cora tugged at Rebecca's sleeve and whispered, "Let's go, Becky, I'm scared."

Afraid to take her eyes from Randy's, she ignored Cora's plea.

He glanced at the two girls as he settled back into the saddle, looking comfortable, and lowered his voice. "Seems to me, ya need to remember your manners when talking with someone from the Home Guard."

Deciding she'd had enough, she defiantly said, "Ain't nuth'n' wrong with my manners." Then she slapped the horses with the reins and yelled, "Get up!" The wagon lurched forward and quickly picked up speed along the dirt road toward Andrew's farm, leaving a cloud of dust between them and Randy Murphy. Afraid to take her eyes from the road and look back at him, she asked the girls, "What's he doing?"

Cora looked back. "He's picking up his hat."

"I'm scared," cried Naomi.

Rebecca glanced over her shoulder just as Murphy turned his horse in the opposite direction. Then, bouncing the reins on the backs of the horses to urge them on, she said, "Don't be afraid; we're almost home." It took several minutes for her to calm down enough to slow the team to a trot, and as she did so, she glanced behind them once more to make sure he was not following.

Cora frowned. "I don't like him."

"Me neither," said Naomi.

Fear left Rebecca as quickly as it had come, replaced by her humor at Naomi's expression. "I ain't too fond of him either, Naomi."

But believing that the man still posed a threat to them, she told Aaron, Daniel, and Jed about the incident, warning them to be careful and watchful while in the fields or doing their chores.

July-1862

Three weeks had passed since the incident on the road involving Randy Murphy, but the images remained etched in Rebecca's memory, making her edgy. At times, she felt as though someone was watching her but discarded the feeling as a case of bad nerves. When it came time for her to make another trip to town, she decided to let Aaron accompany her. As they passed the place in the road where Randy had jumped out at them, she stiffened in the seat.

Aaron could not help but notice and placed a reassuring hand on her shoulder. "I brought Pa's pistol."

She smiled, knowing the boy meant well, but cautioned him. "You be careful with that thing, Aaron."

He smiled proudly. "Pa showed me how to use it, and I got pretty good."

Rebecca thought about that. "Just the same, you be careful. I don't need you going to jail for shooting someone."

As it turned out, there was no sign of Randy Murphy or any of the Home Guard in town or on the road. That evening after dinner, Rebecca busied herself, making sugar candy near the kitchen window. Movement outside caused her to look up just as Daniel strolled past, carrying a small bunch of wildflowers. Curious, she watched as he walked across the yard and through a row of apple trees, disappearing behind a group of berry bushes to visit his mother's grave. Rebecca smiled, thinking how sweet it was, and then, seeing that the sugar candy was almost ready, she decided to let it cool while she visited the hammock where Andrew used to spend his evenings.

Rebecca sat alone in the hammock, lost in thoughts of Andrew and the war, wishing it was over and he was home. A noise startled her, and as she sat up, she saw Daniel walking toward the house, more interested in the ground than where he was going. "Are you all right, Daniel?"

He stopped and looked up. "Just visiting my ma."

"That's sweet, Daniel," she said. "I'm sure your ma's quite happy about the flowers."

He then walked to the hammock, sat beside her, and looked down at the ground. "She liked the wildflowers that grow out past the barn. She used to pick `em for the kitchen table."

"You miss your, Ma, don't you?"

He glanced in the direction of the grave, looking sad. "I guess. I mean, sometimes I do, a lot, even more now that Pa's gone."

She put her arm around him; her voice was soft and low. "I'm sure she misses all of her children, Daniel."

He looked up at her. "Pa says she's always watching over us. Do you believe that Becky? That she's always watching, I mean?"

She smiled, giving him a quick hug while considering the question. "I don't know." She looked puzzled. "I don't rightly know where people go after they leave us, but I suppose they may come and visit sometimes because they miss us the same as we do them."

That pleased Daniel, and he smiled. "Pa used to visit Ma every night after dinner about this time."

"I know," she said, looking in the direction of the grave. "Your pa told me."

"I didn't want her to get lonely since Pa's gone. That's why I brung them flowers."

She smiled at him. "That was special of you, Daniel."

"Candy finished?" he asked.

"The candy," she said, jumping out of the hammock so fast she fell. Getting up and laughing from embarrassment, she grabbed his hand, and they ran toward the house. "I plum forgot all about the candy. It must be cooled by now."

August – 1862

In the weeks following the incident on the road, Rebecca was still leery about venturing too far from the farm without Aaron or Jed Stattler in the seat next to her. Even then, she was in constant fear and always vigilant on trips to town or her ma and pa's place, keeping an eye on the gullies or the underbrush alongside the road or the trees just beyond. When she did venture into town, Rebecca always checked the lists of casualties posted at the General Store, relieved at not finding Andrew's name and saddened at the names of men or boys she had known.

It was late August, and Rebecca and Jed Stattler were returning from one such trip when they saw Randy Murphy again, sitting on his horse alongside the road, one leg draped over the saddle horn.

Jed saw her stiffen in the seat. "Gonna be all right, Miss Becky."

Sitting with one leg relaxed around the saddle horn and one foot in the stirrup, Randy moved into the center of the road, blocking their path. Jed pulled the wagon to a stop.

Randy took off his hat, nodded, and smiled at Rebecca, ignoring Jed. "How do Miss Becky?"

"Mr. Murphy," she said without expression.

"Yer blocking our way, young fella," said Jed in a friendly tone.

Murphy removed his leg from the saddle horn, put his foot into the stirrup, and nudged his horse closer to Rebecca, ignoring Jed. "You sure look purdy today, Miss Becky, and where are them sweet little gals?"

Rebecca ignored the question and looked straight ahead down the road, wishing he would ride away. "Please let us pass."

Seeing that she was too afraid to look at him, Randy smiled as he moved his jacket enough to show his homemade star. "In due time, Miss Becky." He grinned, then added, "In due time."

"What do you want, Mr. Murphy?" she asked.

"You may have fooled Michael and them others with that story about the runaway," he said, "but I'm not too sure about all that. I'm thinking someone at your place helped him."

Jed looked at him. "Why don't ya just let us pass, young fella?"

Murphy's eyes narrowed, his lips drawn tight against his teeth. "When I'm ready, Old Man." They glared at one another for a moment, and then Randy turned his head and spit tobacco juice onto the road while recognizing the clicking sound of a pistol. When he looked back, Jed was indeed holding a pistol aimed at Randy's belly. Knowing that at this range, the bullet would rip his spinal cord apart, he raised his hands. "Now, hold on, Old Man. That thing may go off."

Jed stared at him. "Now that's a damn fact."

Rebecca looked at the gun, which seemed big, being so close to her, and sat back in her seat with wide eyes, wondering if Jed would shoot Randy.

Murphy stared back at Jed, contemplating his next move, wondering if the old man had enough sand in him to pull the trigger. Deciding it was something he could not afford to find out, he smiled, looking friendly. "Didn't mean no harm," he said. "I's just doing my job, Old Man, and trying to have a little fun."

Jed looked Randy in the eyes. "How `bout you stop calling me Old Man and let us pass?"

Randy considered that quickly. He knew very little about Jed, where he came from, or who he was. He had heard he was a little slow in the head, but a miscalculation now could be costly.

Fearful, Rebecca seized the moment. "Jed, I don't want any trouble."

"Won't be no trouble, Miss Becky," said Jed as he stared at Randy. "Will there, Boy?"

Being called a boy angered Randy to a fool's bravery. "Best listen to the lady, Old Man." Then he lowered his hands and leaned forward in the saddle. "You don't want no trouble with the Home Guard."

"Mr. Murphy, just let us pass," Rebecca said, feeling fearful. "We don't want no trouble."

He ignored Rebecca and concentrated on Jed Stattler, but he couldn't figure the old man out. He didn't appear to be afraid of him, and he certainly wasn't backing down by lowering the gun. Randy had never killed a man before, never even shot at one, but he wasn't so sure about this old man who appeared ready to do both.

Buzzing grasshoppers and birds joined the creaking of Randy's saddle as he shifted his weight. He glanced at Rebecca, looked at Jed, and backed his horse away from the wagon.

Jed held the pistol in one hand while he picked up the reins from his lap with the other. Keeping his eyes on Murphy, he tapped the team with the reins, feeling the slight jerk in the wagon as they began to move past Randy.

Rebecca stared at Randy as they drove by and watched until he turned and rode in the other direction. When he was out of sight, she angrily turned to Jed. "He could have shot us both."

Jed looked straight ahead at the road and shoved his pistol under his belt. "A man like young Murphy is a coward, Miss Becky. He won't do nuth'n' less he's sure how things are gonna turn out." He smiled apologetically. "Didn't mean to worry you none, ma'am, and sorry if'n I scared ya, but I just couldn't let the little fool bully us no more."

Rebecca glanced back, then looked at Jed and started laughing nervously, unsure if it was her fear or the expression on Mr. Murphy's face she had found funny. She pushed at Jed's shoulder with one hand, "Damn, good thing I didn't have that gun. I may have just gone ahead and shot the idiot."

Jed chuckled and spit tobacco juice into the road. "I'd a loved to have seen the surprise on that boy's face if'n ya had, Miss Becky."

The wagon and road filled with their laughter, and Rebecca was damn glad that Jed had stood up to the bully but wondered what Michael Evans would have to say about all this.

After that incident, Jed made it a habit of keeping his pistol tucked in his belt when he was in the fields. He had known men like Randy Murphy, and while they were usually cowards, they were prideful, making them dangerous.

Sleep escaped Rebecca as she lay in the darkness of Andrew's bedroom, filled with worry that he may be hurt, dying, or dead on some muddy field. She closed her eyes once more, trying to think of more pleasant things, but unable to do so, she sat up, hugging her knees. She thought of Andrew's first wife, remembering the two of them driving past her Pa's place on their way to or from town, always laughing and looking happy.

Rebecca was no fool; she knew she could never replace Rachel and was willing to accept what love Andrew could give her because she loved him. The thoughts flowed through her mind like water from a broken dam, and she became irritated at her inability to sleep. She got up, knelt at the open window with her chin on her arms on the windowsill, and looked up into the black sky of stars, wondering if Andrew was looking up at this moment. Then she looked at the dark silhouettes of Matthew, Alicia, and Sadie's shacks, barely visible in the dim light of a half-moon. A light in Jed's window made her curious, and she wondered what he was doing up so late. Maybe he was reading or fell asleep while reading, she thought, and suddenly she felt sadness for him, wondering if he was lonely and if he had ever loved a woman or had ever been loved by one.

Of course, she would never ask for fear of embarrassing him because there are some things you never ask. She thought of what Michael had said about him being slow and remembered how irritated she became at Jed when talking by the barn about John, the slave. But she liked Jed Stattler and wished she knew more about him. Something moved in the shadows by the barn, and suddenly, Rebecca was afraid. Holding her breath, she stared into the darkness, waiting for it to move again, but after several moments, she decided the night was playing tricks on her. She glanced at her closed bedroom door and thought about the back door, wondering if Aaron had secured it after bringing in the firewood. She turned to the window and stared into the darkness at the black images of the barn and outbuildings, waiting to see if anything moved. Her mind revisited the back door, and she knew that she wouldn't be able to sleep unless she went downstairs to make sure it was locked. Getting up from the windowsill, she quietly opened the bedroom door and crept along the hall, grimacing with each creak of the floorboards. She paused at the top of the stairs to listen to the children's steady breathing while gathering enough courage to tiptoe down the stairs to the back door. Finding it locked, she leaned against it with a sigh, hurried up the stairs, jumped in bed, and pulled the sheet around her neck. The crickets and the owl outside played their evening songs, and suddenly feeling tired, she turned her thoughts to Andrew and closed her eyes.

Rebecca opened her eyes, again finding Cora's warm little body fast asleep beside her. She smiled as she turned to the window and the faint light of the sky above the hills where the sun was hiding. Matthew's dogs barked while the sentry rooster waited for the exact moment to announce the new day. She got up carefully so she wouldn't wake the bed jumper, walked to the open window, and looked up at the last of the stars in the dim light that comes just before dawn. She could see Matthew sitting on his porch petting one of his dogs while the other barked either at the barn or Mr. Rooster. The black dog turned, relieved itself against a tree, and ran back to Matthew with its tail wagging. She looked at the lights coming from the windows of Sadie's small house and felt sorry for her and the children, knowing that she must be lonely and fearful for her man. Jed's place was still dark, and she imagined him sleeping.

Glancing back at Cora, she decided to visit the hen house for the eggs this morning and let the girls sleep in a little longer. She put on her robe, walked downstairs to the empty kitchen, and built a fire in the stove for either Alicia or Sadie to prepare breakfast. Then she picked up the egg basket and walked out the back door toward the chicken coop in her bare feet, noticing the vigilant Mr. Rooster perched on the roof of the hen house.

Matthew's dogs raced toward her, and he quickly called them back with his deep, commanding voice. As the dogs retreated, she and Matthew waved good morning. Reaching the gate of the small, wire-fenced yard around the hen house, she opened it and entered the coop. The hens clucked and jumped about as if a fox were after them while

Rebecca spoke softly, "It's okay, y'all, it's okay." The hens settled down a little while their tiny heads tilted in little jerky motions, their big eyes watching as she gathered several nice-sized eggs. She thanked them politely and calmly and left the coop, making sure the latch of the door was in place. While Mister Rooster, on top of the hen house, fluttered his wings, getting ready for the sun to peek over the eastern hills, a noise in the barn got her attention. Turning, she noticed the door was slightly ajar, and first, one of the horses in the barn snorted nervously, then another. A fox, she thought, but then dismissed that, knowing a fox would cause the horses to raise a bigger fuss. She turned back to call Matthew, but his chair was empty, and she figured that he must have gone inside, so she decided to check the barn herself. She walked the short distance to the barn door and pushed it open, deciding to talk to Matthew and the others later about making sure the barn doors were locked at night.

She glanced back at Matthew's place, seeing he had returned to his chair on the small porch of his shack, and then stuck her head inside. In the dim light of the barn, she could see the dark images of the heads and necks of the four horses and the single mule, all in their stalls. They appeared calm, so she stepped inside, greeted by the smell of hay, horse urine, and manure. The morning sun crested the eastern hills casting eerie, small lines of dusty orange light through the slits and knotholes of the east wall. As she walked toward an empty stall, Mister Rooster crowed on cue.

All appeared to be quiet and calm in the barn as she reached up and touched the forehead of one of the horses and spoke to it in a soft, calm voice. Suddenly, the horse raised its head, snorted, and shied away. As Rebecca stepped back, someone grabbed her, covering her mouth so she could not scream, and dragged her into the empty stall. Dropping the basket of eggs, she struggled to get free and grabbed the side of the stall. Unable to hold on, she was thrown onto the hard dirt floor, hitting her head on the side of the stall. Dazed, she tried to get up, and as her head cleared, she found herself lying face down on the hay strewn, dirt floor, with someone's hands forcing her robe and nightgown above her hips. Feeling the weight of his body on her and his warm, foul breath against her face, she struggled and began to cry, unable to scream.

"Keep quiet, you little bitch," he whispered. "Or I swear I'll cut your damn throat and then kill them little ones you care about so much."

Knowing what was about to happen, she closed her eyes. Suddenly, he went limp with the full weight of his body on top of her. She rolled over, slowly pushing him off, and crawled away until she was against the wooden wall of the stall.

"Ya all rights, Miss Becky?" asked Matthew as he knelt beside her.

Seeing the hammer in Mathew's hand, she looked up into his dark eyes and sobbed as she curled up, pulling her nightgown and then her robe down around her thighs.

Matthew gently touched her shoulder and again softly repeated, "Is ya all right, Miss Becky?"

It took her a moment to stop sobbing as she stared at Randy Murphy lying on the dark barn floor. Then she looked up at Matthew, wiped the tears from her eyes, and nodded. "I think so."

"I'll go gets my Alicia," he said, dropping the hammer as he hurried out of the barn.

When Matthew returned with Alicia, Rebecca was still curled up against the corner of the stall staring at Randy Murphy's body. Alicia knelt beside her. "Is ya okay, Miss Becky?"

Rebecca's face was dirty and wet from tears, her hair a mess. "I think so." Looking up at Matthew, she began to cry again. "If you hadn't come along when you did, he would of…" She let the sentence die.

"Don't ya's go think'n bout that stuff, Miss Becky," said Alicia. "Yah gonna be alright, we's here now."

Matthew knelt next to the body, looking scared. "I thinks I done kilt `im, Miss Becky."

"Good!" said Rebecca, and then she spit on the body. "I hope he rots in hell!"

Matthew's face filled with fear, and his eyes held terror as he looked at Alicia, "Dey's gonna hangs me fer sure."

Knowing Matthew spoke the truth, Alicia buried her face in her hands and began to cry.

Feeling sorry for Alicia and Matthew, Rebecca sat up on her knees, wiped the tears from her face, put one hand on Alicia's shoulder, and looked up at Matthew. "It's gonna be all right."

"No, Miss Becky," he said, "Dey's gonna hangs me. I done kilt a white man and a Home Guard at that." He looked at the bloody hammer lying on the ground and then at Rebecca as his eyes welled. "Oh sweet Jesus, dey's gonna whup me terrible, and den hangs me fer sure."

Alicia looked at Rebecca with red, teary eyes. "What's we gonna do now, Miss Becky?"

"I don't know. But we can't let them find him here." Wiping her eyes with the sleeve of her robe, she stood up, straightening her robe and gown while trying to think of what they should do. Her head hurt where she had fallen against the stall, and when she touched it, she had blood on her fingers. Getting angry, she kicked Murphy in the side. "You bastard!"

"Dat ain't gonna do no goods, Miss Becky," said Matthew.

Rebecca's face had a mean look. "Hell, it won't." Then she turned to Matthew, "No one else has to know about this, ya hear me?" She looked from one to the other. "I mean no one."

"Yessum," replied Matthew. "But what's we gonna do?"

Alicia softly cried as she stood beside Matthew, gripping his arm. She looked at Rebecca. "Dey's gonna drag my man to jail anyway, fer sure, Miss Becky."

Feeling sorry for them, she did not want to argue with them anymore and didn't want the children, her parents, or anyone else to know. She ignored Alicia, walked to the barn door, and looked toward the house. "The children aren't up yet." She turned to them. "I'm gonna go up to the house and get dressed." She told Matthew to hitch up the wagon and bring it to the back door of the barn. Then, thinking of Jed Stattler, she told him to do it quietly.

Alicia sobbed. "What's we gonna do, Miss Becky?"

Rebecca looked at Alicia, considering that very thing. "Matthew and I are gonna get rid of the body." She pointed to a tarp in the corner. "We'll cover him with that tarp after we load him in the wagon." She started out the door but then stopped and turned. "Alicia, you need to get dressed and get up to the house. I want all of us to act like nothing's wrong. Ya hear me?"

Alicia wiped the tears from her eyes, "Yessum, if'n I can."

Rebecca gently but firmly grabbed Alicia by her arms. "You've got to. Your man's life and mine may depend on that. If anyone asks where we are, you say Matthew drove me to my ma and pa's house." She paused a moment. "I'll think of a reason later. And don't wake the children. Let `em sleep."

"Yessum," said Alicia. Then she hurried out of the barn toward their shack to do as Rebecca had told her.

When Rebecca returned to the barn, Matthew sat on the wagon's front seat, looking hopeless. "It's done, Miss Becky," he said softly. "Just like ya told me."

Afraid of getting caught, Rebecca climbed into the wagon, feeling sorry for Matthew. "We've got to hide this body. Maybe we should bury it on the farm someplace."

Matthew shook his head, looking skeptical. "No, ma'am, da dogs or raccoons will dig `im up. B'sides what about his horse yonder?"

Rebecca snapped her head, seeing Randy Murphy's horse tied to the tree next to the barn. "Damn," she said, looking tense. "I didn't think about his damn horse." She jumped down, got the horse, tied it to the rear of the wagon, and then climbed back up on the seat next to Matthew. "Head toward the county road and try not to make any noise."

"Yessum." Matthew slapped the horses with the reins and drove away from the barn with Randy Murphy's horse in tow.

Seeing Jed's shack was still dark inside, she said, "Be quiet going by Jed's."

"Yessum, Miss Becky."

It was still early, and Rebecca felt they had a good chance no one would see them on the road, hoping that if they were seen, it would not be by the Home Guard. It would be hard to explain the horse in tow, which would certainly lead to the discovery of his body under the tarp in the back of the wagon. The fear of that brought visions of Matthew beaten and then hung, with her stripped naked and hung next to him with a sign on her reading "Nigger lover." Pushing those images from her mind, she glanced behind them and wished Matthew would drive a little faster. "Hurry, Matthew."

"Yessum, Miss Becky, but where's we go'n'?"

"There's an old road not far from here." She looked at him. "And Matthew, you needn't always say, Miss Becky."

"Yessum." He prodded the team along the dirt road while Rebecca diligently looked behind them, across the fields, and along the road up ahead. After a few minutes, she told Matthew to slow down and pointed at an old dirt road almost hidden among the underbrush. "Turn here." She nervously checked the road in both directions as he turned the wagon onto the trail. "There's a cliff, and some falls up ahead."

Matthew drove on in silence while tiny beads of sweat formed on his forehead. He was thinking of being beaten and then hung by the Home Guard. Glancing at Rebecca, Matthew knew that she would not be able to stop them from hanging him from a tree and setting it on fire. He could see the fear and desperation on her face and knew what they would do to her.

Rebecca touched his arm. "Slow down, Matthew." Then she pointed. "There, over there by those trees."

Matthew stopped next to a small group of birch trees, set the brake, and looked around. A slight breeze rustled through the leaves and branches of the trees, a few birds chirped, and others darted past them in flight. A crow called out from high in a tree, joining the soft roar of a waterfall. He jumped down, turning to help Rebecca, but she was already walking around the back of the wagon from the other side. He followed her to the edge of a cliff, where they paused to look at the waterfall crashing onto the rocks some two hundred feet below. Rebecca stared down at the rocks and water below for a few moments and said, "Listen."

While Matthew listened, she glanced around at the trees and shrubs, then back down the trail to see if anyone was watching. They strained their ears listening but heard only the sounds of the falls, the wind in the trees, the birds, and the crow above them. "Hurry," she said, gesturing to Matthew as she started toward the wagon. They uncovered the heavy body, pulled it out of the wagon, and dragged it to the edge of the cliff, where they struggled to stand it upright between them. She looked down at the bottom of the falls with its mist-covered rocks and closed her eyes. "Now!" and then they pushed the body over the edge. Opening her eyes, she looked down at Randy Murphy's broken body lying on top of the rocks next to the stream. Turning away, she put her hands to her mouth and began to cry.

Matthew stared down at the white man he had killed to protect Miss Becky. He looked around, fearful of being discovered, and then he looked long and carefully at her. "Best be get'n back, Miss Becky."

Rebecca wiped the tears from her eyes that were not for Randy Murphy but for her and Matthew and what they had done. They hurried back to the wagon, where she untied Randy's horse and tied it to a nearby tree. Rebecca started toward the wagon but stopped, looked back at the animal for a moment, and then untied it. She looked at Matthew as she climbed into the wagon. "I think we better leave the horse untied. If we tie him up, mountain lions or wolves could get him, and I wouldn't want that. But if we let him loose, he'll head home, and maybe a search party will eventually find the body."

"Yessum," said Matthew, approving of the idea, and then looked up at the blue sky. "If not, dah buzzards will show `em where's ta look." Rebecca considered that. "I'll drive back." They climbed into the wagon, and she drove back down the trail toward the county road, where she pulled up hidden by the bushes several yards from the road. Standing in the wagon, she looked in both directions. Hearing something behind them, they turned, seeing Murphy's horse trotting toward them. They watched as it trotted past and continued down the road toward town. She watched the horse for a moment, thankful that it was trotting in the other direction, and then she slapped the team with the reins. "Git up."

Jed had just poured a cup of coffee and was starting to sip it when he heard the sound of a wagon and walked over to the small window of his cabin. He looked out, seeing Miss Becky and Matthew driving toward the barn, then disappearing behind it. Turning from the window to the eggs he was frying on his small potbellied stove, he thought it strange they were up and about so early and wondered where they had been.

While Matthew unhitched the team and put them in the barn, Rebecca pulled the tarp out of the back of the wagon, letting it drop to the ground while she stared at the bloodstains.

Matthew was beside her. "We best burn it, Miss Becky."

She nodded. "See to it, Matthew, and the sooner, the better, and be sure you bury the ashes." She paused. "I don't want any reminders of today."

"Yessum, Miss Becky."

She thought again of Jed Stattler. "If Jed asks what you're doing, tell him you're burning some trash." She knew Matthew was scared. "It's gonna be all right, Matthew." She looked into his worried eyes. "As long as you, Alicia, and me say we never saw him. It's that simple, Matthew. We never saw Randy Murphy."

"Yessum, Miss Becky." Matthew looked skeptical as he stared down at the tarp.

"Matthew, this is important. Both our lives depend on this. I do not want you or Alicia trying to add anything or make up any kind of story. We never saw him. You hear me?"

"Yessum." Then he turned to get a shovel from the barn.

Rebecca hoped he understood and then turned and walked toward the house. Walking into the kitchen, she found the slave Alicia at the stove cooking, and the children were nowhere in sight.

Alicia ran up to her with fear in her eyes and whispered. "Where's Matthew, Miss Becky?"

She glanced toward the hall door and whispered. "He's in the barn putting everything away. Are the children up yet?"

"Dey's just now got up, Miss Becky."

"No one's come downstairs?"

"No, ma'am, nary a soul."

"Thank God," said Rebecca. Giving Alicia the same instructions she had told Matthew, she took a big pot out of the cupboard, poured water into it, and then put it on the stove. Pouring herself a cup of coffee, she considered putting a little whiskey in it, but not being a drinker, decided against it. She stood next to Alicia at the stove and whispered, "Don't forget Alicia: Randy Murphy was never here."
Alicia nodded, looking scared. "Yessum." She started to say something, but at that moment, the girls ran into the kitchen.

Rebecca and Alicia performed their charade admirably as though nothing was different, considering that Rebecca had been nearly raped, a man had been killed, and she and Matthew had tossed the body over a cliff. The pot she had placed on the stove began to boil, so she picked it up, excused herself, and hurried upstairs to her bedroom. Setting the pot of hot water on the floor, she undressed, knelt on the floor, dipped the washcloth into the hot water, and washed away the stench of Randy Murphy.

When she finished washing, Rebecca gathered her robe and nightgown from the morning and the clothes she had worn to the cliff and stood looking at them. She briefly considered burning everything. Instead, she got dressed and took them downstairs to launder them. The children were finished with breakfast when she returned to the kitchen carrying her clothes, so she told Alicia to go home, leaving the dishes for her and the girls. She needed to keep busy to push the images of the day out of her head.

The hours of the day crept by as she continually paused to look out the window toward the road, relieved each time at not seeing any riders, and then telling herself to calm down. Finally, the day was ending, but she knew the darkness would follow, bringing with it shadows and other fears for Rebecca Davis. She ate very little at dinner, and afterward, she sat in the swing thinking of Andrew, unaware of Jed's presence.

"Miss Becky."

The soft words startled her. "Why, Jed, you startled me."

"Sorry, Miss Becky. Didn't mean to scare ya none."

She smiled, looking relieved. "Didn't expect anyone is all."

Jed took off his hat as he stepped closer, and while his hands played with his hat, he glanced around at the colors of sunset as if thinking of something to say.

She could see he wore a troubled face, and fearing what he may say, she patiently waited for him to speak, remembering how others said he was a mite slow.

Moments passed before he spoke. "Miss Becky, I just want to tell you how sorry I am for what happened to you earlier this morning."

Surprise filled her face; fear gripped her heart as her eyes got wide, and her mouth hung open.

"I saw you and Matthew returning in the wagon earlier this morning." He gestured toward the barn with his hat.

She closed her eyes and sat back in the swing fearing for her and Matthew's lives. Staring down at the ground beneath her feet, her eyes welled as tears found their way down her cheeks.

Jed moved a little closer to the swing. "I found Alicia crying behind the shack." He started tapping his hat against his leg. "I saw you and Matthew leave this morning with a strange horse in tow, and it weren't with ya when y'all came back. It didn't dawn on me till later that it looked like that young fella Randy Murphy's horse." He gestured toward the barn. "Then later, I saw Matthew burning and bury'n trash out behind the barn."

She stared at the ground. "What did Alicia tell you?"

"All of it," he said softly. "No need for details."

She bent over, hid her face in her hands, and began to cry as the day's terror rushed at her like a hot July wind. She thought of Andrew, and the children of Matthew, and her own life, wondering what the Home Guard would do to her. Jed watched her in silence. "I ain't gonna say nuth'n Miss Becky, if that's what's worrying ya."

Feeling afraid yet relieved, Rebecca raised her head and wiped her tears with her hands. "If Alicia broke down with you," she said in a quivering voice, "she'll break down if Michael Evans or any of the Home Guard talks to her."

Jed considered that. "No, she won't, Miss Becky. She only told me cuz she knows and trusts me. B'sides, she's a pretty strong little gal, and as the days pass and she's had time to collect herself, she'll do just fine."

"I'm not so sure." Rebecca forced a smile. "And what about you Jed, can I trust you?"

"Mind if I sit with ya a spell Miss Becky?"

She nodded, moved her dress so he could sit down, and wiped the tears from her eyes and cheeks.

He sat next to her, looking thoughtful as he watched the last of the sun disappear behind the trees in the distance leaving everything a dark hue of reds and oranges. His fingers played with the brim of his hat. "I don't much like men like young Murphy."

Rebecca looked into his weathered, lined face and then into his eyes that were soft and gentle. She wondered where he had come from and how old he was, thinking he was still a good-looking man. His voice was soft and calming, much like a father's voice talking to his daughter, and she wasn't afraid anymore.

Jed stared at the horizon in silence for a moment. "I have been with Andrew a long time, Miss Becky. The years have come and gone, too many to count. Andrew trusted me when no one else would and gave me a chance, my last chance, I reckon."

Rebecca thought he was a strange man, one that seemed to blend in while remaining different, choosing to be alone. "Ever think about going home?" she asked.

He shook his head, grimacing. "No, not for many years now. What was left of my family's surely dead by now, same as my past, and it's best left that way." He got up lazily and looked down at her. "Don't worry none about this here mess, Miss Becky. I have a feeling it's gonna be alright."

She looked skeptical. "I hope you're right."

"It will," he said, then he put on his hat. "Goodnight, Miss Becky." He turned and disappeared into the darkness toward his cabin.

Rebecca stared after him feeling confident that he would never give up her secret, and suddenly she was tired and thought of bed and sleep. She got up from the swing and went inside, telling the children that she didn't feel well, and then went upstairs to her room. After she undressed, she climbed into bed and closed her eyes, trying to find sleep. But visions of the barn, the cliffs, and Randy Murphy's body lying in the ravine kept her awake. She tossed and turned, thinking of the danger for Jed and Matthew, and she began to cry, wishing Andrew was here. After a few minutes of crying, she dried her eyes on the sheet, got out of bed, walked to the window, and knelt on the floor. She put her forearms on the windowsill and rested her chin on them, looking out at the chicken coop and barn, regretting what had happened. Not for the bastard that Matthew killed, but the consequences for her and Matthew.

The light in Jed's shack went out, and she found small comfort in his knowing about it all. She wished she could tell her father, but feeling the guilt of what had almost happened to her, she knew she never would. She cursed Randy Murphy as she tried dealing with the conflicting emotions of hate and remorse and the fear of being found out. She looked at Matthew and Alicia's dark shack, thankful for the brave man that had saved her from a terrible experience, thinking now that maybe they should have taken him into town and explained what happened. But she knew in her heart that no matter what they said or how they tried to explain it, Matthew would be beaten and hung, and she could not let that happen. She thought of Alicia and hoped Jed was right about her being strong.

Returning to her bed, she lay in the darkness, thinking of Andrew, wishing the war was over, and he was home. Her mind flooded with visions of the children sleeping across the hallway, and suddenly, she sat up, looked at the window, slowly pushed back the covers, and got out of bed. She walked to the window and knelt again on the floor with her arms on the windowsill. Rebecca stared across the moonlit yard at the dark figures of the coop and barn. Shivering, she whispered, "Cora and Naomi." She paused in terror. "He was after one of the girls." She felt sick to her stomach. "You son of a bitch," she whispered, thinking of the horror for the girls had he found one of them that morning, knowing that either Cora or Naomi usually gathered the eggs. "You bastard!" She looked in the direction of the falls and was glad Matthew had killed him, and she was glad it was she and not one of the girls. She sat on the floor at the window for a long time staring at the dark image of the barn. Then feeling tired, almost to exhaustion, she stood, walked to the bed, lay down, and hugged her pillow as tears filled her eyes until sleep overtook her.

Rebecca lived in fear during the days that followed and kept a close watch on Naomi and Cora whenever they went near the barn or the chicken coop. Randy was safely dead, but the fear of what had nearly happened would not leave her. Neither she nor Matthew or Alicia ever spoke of that morning, but its memory was always just below the surface, and although there were times it seemed more like a bad dream, she knew better.

She and Cora were hanging laundry in the mid-morning sun when Cora paused and pointed toward the road. "Someone's coming, Becky."

She turned and shielded her eyes from the sun with one hand while staring at the lone rider, and then seeing who it was, she handed the shirt she was holding to Cora.

Curious about the rider, Naomi ran from the porch and stood next to Rebecca. "Who is it?"

Not answering, Rebecca started walking to meet Michael Evens, figuring this was not a social visit. She knew Matthew was in the fields with Aaron and the others, while Alicia and Sadie were in the main house working.

"Can we come?" asked Cora.

"No. Finish hanging the clothes." She walked toward the rider, hoping to keep him far enough from the girls so he wouldn't talk to them.

Pulling his horse up a few feet away, he smiled. "Good morning Becky."

Rebecca forced a smile, trying to act casual. "Good morning Michael." Then she looked past him. "Where's your friends?"

"Not sure," he said, stepping down from the saddle looking serious. "That's partly why I'm here."

"That so?"

He waved at the girls. "Morning, young ladies."

They waved back. "Morning."

She turned to the girls. "You girls finish hanging that laundry." Then she turned to Michael. "Care for a cup of coffee and a piece of pie?"

"No, thanks, Becky, but appreciate the offer."

She was curious about his visit but did not want to appear anxious or afraid, so she just smiled and waited for him to tell her.

He took off his hat, wiped his brow, put his hat back on, and glanced around at the yard, the house, the barn, and the other outbuildings. "Place looks pretty good, Becky." Then he smiled. "Andrew would be proud of y'all."

She smiled as she tried not to look at the barn and coop.

Noticing the bruise on her face, he asked, "What did you do to your face?"

Having forgotten the bruise, she thought quickly and gestured at the back porch, looking embarrassed. "I fell off the porch, acting silly around the girls." She forced a grin. "Guess I should grow up."

He smiled. "You grew up just fine and better'n most."

She smiled and glanced at the girls as silence grabbed the moment.

"Haven't seen Randy Murphy, have ya?"

"Randy Murphy?" She turned from the girls trying to look puzzled and innocent.

"He was with me the night we dropped by asking about the runaway."

Rebecca paused for effect. "I remember." She turned and started walking toward the corral, away from the girls while talking over her shoulder, hoping he would follow. "Is he missing?"

"His horse returned a few days ago," replied Michael.

"How awful," she said, looking worried.

"Several of the boys have been out scouring the county, but it appears no one has seen him lately."

Rebecca placed her hands on the top railing of the corral and stared staring at a young colt playfully teasing his mother. "Maybe he's hurt someplace." She looked at Michael. "Or maybe he just went away."

Michael considered that, looking worried. "Hurt, maybe. Don't think he would just up and leave." Then he gestured at the colt. "Has some real pretty markings."

"Yes, he does." Wishing Michael would leave and wanting to talk about something other than Randy Murphy, she smiled. "May I ask you a personal question?"

"I suppose," he said, looking curious.

"When the war started, why didn't you join up?"

He smiled, looking disappointed. "One leg's a bit shorter than the other, so they wouldn't take me."

"Were you born that way?"

"No. I broke it when I was a kid in school."

Remembering the accident now that she had forgotten about, she laughed. It felt good to laugh. "I remember. You were trying to sneak out the back window of school and fell through the cellar door."

His face flushed as he chuckled. "Never bragged on being the smartest kid in that one-room school." He turned to climb into his saddle, saying he'd best continue his search for Murphy, and as Michael settled in his saddle, he glanced around. "Sure, be glad when this war is over."

Rebecca nodded, thinking of Andrew. "I think we'll all be glad when it's over." She looked up at him. "Hope you find Mr. Murphy."

"I'm sure we will. You take care of that bruise now."

The sound of horses caused them to turn toward the road, seeing several riders galloping toward them. Rebecca's heart skipped, and while Michael was looking toward the riders, she glanced toward the girls, motioning for them to stay where they were.

As the riders stopped in a cloud of dust, George Applegate called out. "We found Murphy!"

"Where?" asked Michael.

Applegate pointed toward the hills. "Up Coyote Canyon. Looks like he fell."

Michael turned to Rebecca. "I best be getting on, Becky." Then he turned his horse and rode away with the others.

She watched as they rode off in a trial of dust, and as she turned, she saw Matthew standing by the barn door. She yelled for the girls to get inside and then ran around the corral to Matthew. "They've found Randy Murphy."

"Yessum," he said. "S'pected they had when I saw dem ride'n in so fast."

Rebecca stepped closer to him as she looked back, making sure the girls were heading for the house. "Remember: he was not here. That's all we have to say. He wasn't here, and we never saw him."

He looked skeptical. "Yessum, I only hopes dey believes us."
She nodded, looking confident. "Why wouldn't they? I'm sure the others didn't know he was coming out here to rape me."

A few days later, Rebecca returned from visiting her ma and pa, enjoying the quiet, peaceful afternoon as she drove the wagon along the county road. She was thinking about Andrew's last letter as she made the bend in the road. Seeing a rider sitting in the middle of it, her heart pounded, thinking of Randy Murphy. As she got closer, Rebecca recognized Michael Evans. She slapped the horses with the reins and drove the team toward him, and put on a friendly smile as she pulled up and set the brake with her left foot. "Hello, Michael."

He nodded and tipped his hat. "Afternoon Becky. Have a few minutes so we could talk?"

"I reckon," she said, and then wrapping the reins around the brake handle, she smiled and sat back with her hands folded in her lap.

Michael nudged his horse next to the wagon, stepped from the saddle into the wagon, and sat next to her. "How are things at Andrew's place?"

"Fine," she said, forcing a smile to hide her fear. "You startled me sitting in the middle of the road like that."

"Sorry, Becky, these are hard times, and I didn't mean to scare you none. I had stopped by to talk to you, but Cora told me you were visiting your ma. I thought I'd just wait around this here bend until you came along, so's we could have us a little talk." He shrugged, "Didn't think I'd scare you, but these days with the war and all, I guess I should have waited for you at Andrew's place."

Glad he had not, she smiled. "I'm just a little jittery these days." She shrugged as she lied. "Don't know why."

He studied her for a moment as he considered that, then took off his hat, wiped his brow, and put his hat back on. "We're gonna have ourselves a little talk right now, Becky."

Her heart pounded in her head, and she felt faint. "About what, Michael?"

"We found Randy's body at the bottom of the ravine up Coyote Canyon, not too far from here."

"I heard that the day you came to Andrew's place," she said.

"Found some interesting things up there."

"Really," she said. Then she blinked, smiled, and waited for him to tell her.

"Wagon tracks," he said as he glanced at the wheels of her wagon. "Found several sets of footprints as well, none belonging to Murphy."

She fought the need to jump from the wagon and run, but where would she go? Then the image of Matthew beaten and hanging from a tree ran through her mind. She wanted to know if Matthew was ok, but all she could do was sit next to Michael and wait for him to tell her Matthew was dead.

"Found a couple of small boot tracks belonging to either a boy or a woman." He glanced down at her boots. "About the size of your boots, and a pair of working shoes, like the Negroes wear."

Her face flushed as her heart pounded against her chest, and her head felt like it was going to explode. She felt faint while trying to think of something to say, remembering her own advice about not volunteering any information or making up a story.

He settled back in the seat, put one boot on the front railing, and stared at it. "My boys made quite a mess of the area trampling out most of the tracks. I stayed behind while the others took his body to town, nosed around a bit, and found me some more tracks." He paused and shook his head. "Things just didn't add up. I'm not the smartest fella around here, but it just looked a little odd to me." He paused. "Looked to me like something heavy, like maybe a body was drug across the ground, disturbing the moss around the edge of the cliff."

Rebecca glanced around, trying not to show that she was nervous, wishing she had thought about the drag marks before she and Matthew had driven away from the falls.

Wondering what was going through Becky's mind, Michael looked at the team of horses, then at the road that disappeared around the bend behind a grove of trees. "After Cora went into the house, I walked over to the barn and went inside."

Her heart stopped, and she couldn't catch her breath.

"I found a small amount of dried blood on the post of one of the stalls with a bit of hair and what looked like a dark, dried-up puddle on the floor of the same stall under some hay."

Wishing she had thought about that, she sat in silence and waited.

"I don't know what happened in that barn, Becky," he said softly and without emotion. "And maybe I don't want to know." He looked down at his hands and turned them over, examining first the palms and then their backs. "I've known your family ever since I was a kid. I remember pulling your braids in school and having dinner at your house when my folks would come to visit."

She forced a smile. "I remember."

Michael looked baffled. "Something bad happened out here; I'm right sure of it, in fact." He studied his muddy boot. "The thing is, Becky if I do what I'm supposed to, is that really the right thing to do?" He paused thoughtfully. "And if I do, is that gonna change anything?"

"I don't know, Michael," she said. "I'm not sure what---"

"Me neither," he said, interrupting her. A heavy silence hung in the wagon as he sat next to her contemplating what he should do. He reached down with one hand, picked at the mud on his boot, and tossed it away. "Randy Murphy wasn't a very nice fella, Becky. He done some things he shouldn't and some things I should've jailed him for, but with the war and all…" He let it trail off and looked toward a grove of trees in the distance. "Randy was…well…he was different than most men. I'd had some complaints about him from some folk around the county, not particularly liking the way he looked at their young daughters." He paused, shifting nervously in the seat.

Rebecca listened in fear for Matthew, the man who had done the only decent thing he could to protect her from something too terrible to imagine. She wanted to know how Matthew was but was afraid to ask. She watched as Michael picked at another piece of dirt on his boot, wishing he would get it over with.

"Randy was a bad seed, all right. But I can't lock a man up just for looking." He looked into her eyes as if searching for something deep within. Guilt, perhaps, maybe deceit, forgiveness, or the truth.

Her heart raced, and she knew that he knew.

Michael took a deep breath and sighed. "Like I said b'fore, something bad happened out here, and I've a thought or two what it was."

Her heart pounded. She felt faint again as fear raced through her every bone and muscle. Why doesn't he just get it over with, she asked herself.

He sat back, looked at her, and did something she never expected. He smiled. It was not a hello smile or a good day smile, but a warm, friendly, understanding smile. "The way things are, there's a hell of a lot of bad in this old world right now, so why destroy something good?" His expression was warm and easy. "Let's just say that somehow those tracks and footprints up there will disappear, the dried blood will fade, and the moss will grow back." He handed her the strands of hair he had pulled from the post in the barn.

Taking it she watched as he stood, and stepped from the wagon onto his saddle.

"I don't understand."

He settled comfortably in his saddle and smiled. "I think you do, Becky." He paused, then smiled again. "I hope Andy comes home soon, and y'all have a good life together." He started to turn his horse but stopped and looked back at her. "That bruise seems to be healing. Most bad things do heal over time, and most are soon forgotten." He tipped his hat. "Take care, Rebecca Davis."

She was confused yet relieved as she watched him ride toward town, knowing Matthew would escape the wrath of the Home Guard, and she, her terrible fate. "It's over," she whispered, feeling as though the world had forgiven her. She held her hand out to her side, dropped the hair, and as it fell to the dirt road, she reached down, untied the reins from the brake, looked over her shoulder at Michael, and then gently tapped the team, driving them toward Andrew's farm.

Sixteen

May 1862 – August 1862

James Riley Chrisman

The War beckons

The sun was behind a row of poplar trees that lined the Heard's property, making a broken pattern of long finger-like shapes across the yard. James Chrisman rode down the driveway toward the house, passing in and out of those shadows thinking of Martha Heard and wondered how she would take the news.

The front door opened, and Martha stepped onto the porch and waved. Grinning like the young boy he was, James nudged the black mare into a trot toward Martha, who waited impatiently on the porch. When he dismounted, she rushed from the porch into his arms with such force it pushed him back against the black mare.

The mare turned, looked at them with her big dark eyes, snorted, then looked away.

"Careful," James said, glancing at the house, looking embarrassed. "S'pose your pa and ma see us?"

Martha smiled. "You fool, James. Don't ya think they already know how we feel about one another?"

"I don't know if they do or not. Besides, that's not the point."

She giggled. "What is the point?"

"I don't want anyone looking at us," he said, sounding flustered.

Martha laughed while taking his hand, thinking he was being silly. They walked around the corner of the house toward the big oak tree and the swing while the mare followed, tail swishing gently with each step, seemingly understanding her place.

"It ain't funny, Martha."

She let go of his hand, took his arm, pulling herself into him as they walked. "Honestly, James, it ain't as if they don't know we already kissed."

The weathered wooden swing they had come to know the past two years hung motionless from a large limb high in the tree. James held the swing steady while Martha sat down, then he sat next to her and pushed backward with his legs. The large branch creaked and moaned as they slowly swung back and forth, giving James concern on whether it would hold.

She curled up against him, her head on his shoulder. "I wish this darn war was over. Have you heard from Allen?"

"Ma says his folks got a letter last week. He's still in Alabama somewheres," James said, looking thoughtful.

Silence filled the swing while Martha watched the black mare nibble on a clump of grass. "You ain't thinking about joining up, are ya, James?" His silence told her what she feared the most. "Darn it, James, ya done joined up, haven't ya?"

He nodded. "This morning."

Filled with fear and anger, she sat forward in the swing dragging her feet to stop it, got out, and walked the short distance to the mare, placed her hand on its nose, and looked up into its big dark eyes.

Knowing he had upset her, James sat in the swing quietly, watching, afraid to say anything for fear of starting an argument.

She hugged the mare's neck, closing her eyes, remembering the first time she had ridden her by herself. Then she took hold of the bridle and kissed its cold nose. Instead of looking at James, she looked into the mare's dark eyes. "You're not even twenty yet, James."

"I will be next month."

"And that makes you old?" She sighed and asked when he was leaving.

James got up from the swing and stood behind her with his hands on her shoulders. He put his cheek gently against the top of her head, smelling her hair.

She relaxed against him, touching his hands with hers, fighting the need to cry. "When do you leave?"

"Tomorrow morning," he said softly.

She had not planned on this. She didn't want to cry or argue or beg him not to go, so she stood in silence, looking into the mare's dark eyes that seemed to understand her fear and sadness.

James gently turned her with his hands and looked into her soft brown eyes.

She forced a smile as her eyes welled with tears that found their way down her cheeks. "I don't want you to go." Her voice quivered. "I'm afraid."

He wiped the tears from her wet face. "I'll be careful, Martha," he said, trying to give comfort. "The recruiter says I'll be joining the 47th Alabama, the same one as Allen." He half-smiled, letting his forehead touch hers as he looked into her eyes. "Allen and me can look out for one another."

She pushed away, turned, and looked at the plowed fields growing darker with the coming of evening.

Mrs. Heard called from the back porch. "Time for dinner, Martha," then quickly added, "You can stay if you've a mind to, James."

Martha wiped her face with her apron, turned from the fields, and looked up at him. "Can ya stay, James?"

"Best not," he said, looking sorry. "I think Ma plans a big dinner, this being my last night and all."

Looking disappointed and filled with emotions she had never felt before, she held his hand as they walked in silence toward the house with the mare following a few yards behind.

"You know I never got no school'n," she said.

"Yeah, I know."

"My pa didn't think I needed no learning."

"Lots of people feel the way your pa does about their daughters."

She stopped and looked down at the ground and feeling embarrassed. "Since I can't read and write, how we gonna keep in touch? Why you could be gone for months, even years, so's how can I write and tell you what I feel, or read what you're feeling?"

He thought about that a moment. "I have an idea," he said, looking hopeful. "I can send my letters to my sis Beth, and she can read `em to you and then write back what you tell her."

Martha shook her head, looking skeptical. "That would be too embarrassing."

"Why?"

"I don't want Beth to know I can't read or write."

"Beth's a good person, and she likes you a lot. She even told me so. Besides, she'd never tell anyone what's in our letters."

"She'd laugh at us."

He shook his head, looking determined. "No, she wouldn't. Beth's not like that."

Martha looked uncertain. "You sure 'bout that, James?

"Positive!"

Martha considered that for a few moments and then smiled. "Alright then, Beth, it is."

"Beth, it is," repeated James. "I best get going. I'll be late for supper." He glanced at the back door and quickly kissed her. He started to say goodbye when she threw her arms around his neck, held him tight, and then kissed him.

Surprised at her strength, he looked at the back door and window, wondering if anyone had seen them.

Martha giggled. "You're so funny, James."

Feeling embarrassed, he climbed into the saddle. "Will you be at the station in the morning?"

She began to cry. "Don't know right now, James."

He leaned down from the saddle. "I sure wish ya would."

She looked up at him with welling eyes. "Can't say right now. It hurts too much, just thinking of you leaving."

He bent down, took her chin in his left hand, kissed her, and turned the black mare toward the county road and home.

May 13, 1862

The train depot was crowded with families saying goodbye to their sons, husbands, and fathers. James was only half-listening to the words his mother spoke while searching the crowd for Martha, fearing she would not come and say goodbye.

Elizabeth Chrisman glanced at the other mothers' faces, seeing in them the same sadness that she felt. "Never saw so many people in one place at the same time." Taking James by the arm, she pulled him closer while pondering the faces of the other young men. To her, they all seemed so casual about going away to terrible places, unaware of the complete sadness they brought to their mothers and wives. She remembered the times of long ago when the women's wailing in her village filled the night with songs of the young men that never returned. The train whistle blew, and she looked into her son's eyes, fearing he may not come back to her.

The conductor gave the call, "All aboard!"

"It's leaving early," said James searching the crowd again for Martha.

Elizabeth put her hand on his chin and turned his face toward hers. "You be careful out there, James."

James looked into his mother's dark, sad eyes. "I will, Ma. I promise."

William pushed his way between them and gripped his son's shoulders with his strong hands. "Don't go doing nothing foolish, boy."

"I won't, Pa." Then he searched the crowd once more for Martha.

Knowing what was bothering her son, Elizabeth held his face gently in her hands. "I'm sure she tried, Son."

He smiled with disappointment, knelt to one knee next to his little sisters, and told them goodbye. He then stood, turning to Davy, who held out his hand. James pushed it aside, hugging his brother. "Take care of the mare, Davy."

Davy nodded, his eyes welling. "I will, James. Keep yer head down."

He nodded that he would, then gave his mother another hug while looking into Beth's big dark eyes while she stood behind her mother, waiting to say goodbye. Knowing she was about to cry, he let go of his mother and hugged her.

"I love you, James," said Beth. Then she whispered. "I'll tell Martha you said goodbye."

"Thanks, sis, tell her…" he let it trail off.

Beth's eyes welled as she nodded knowing what he wanted to say.

A soldier dressed in gray yelled at James to board the train. Steam rushed from the engine farther up the depot tracks, and then the whistle blew, the train lunged forward, and cars jerked and clattered along the track. As the train began moving very slowly, the soldier yelled for James to get on the train.

James glanced at the soldier, gave his mother one last hug, said goodbye to his Pa, and jumped onto the steps of a passing railcar, waving as the train slowly moved along the tracks. The train whistle blew, the train jerked again, and he almost lost his balance. The engine's big wheels spun rapidly and then slowed, gripping onto the steel tracks pulling the train slowly out of the depot.

As he stood on the step, James heard Martha yell his name, and as he searched the faces of the crowd, he saw her running past his family along the platform, one arm holding her dress off the platform, the other waving at him as she chased after the train. James leaned from the step. "I thought ya wouldn't make it!"

"I know. I wasn't going to," Martha yelled, chasing after the train. "I was afraid."

"Of what?" he yelled.

She laughed, shaking her head. "I don't know. Ma said I was foolish." She laughed again. "I never knew Pa to drive a team so hard."

The train was picking up speed. "I'm glad ya came."

"Me too," she yelled. Stopping at the end of the station platform, she raised both arms above her head waving goodbye until the train disappeared around the bend.

Cedar Mountain, Virginia

August 7th, 1862

James and the 47th Alabama camped near the Southern capitol of Richmond on the morning of August 7, 1862, not far from a place called Cedar Mountain, Virginia, a place historians would one day call Slaughter's Mountain. James was sitting on the ground, his back against a tree looking across the fields thinking of home and Martha when Allen Downs plopped down next to him.

"Still ain't no mail," Allen said, looking disappointed. Not getting a response from James, he leaned a little closer. "Didn't ya hear me, ain't no mail again today."

James was staring at the trees in the distance, still thinking of Martha. "We've been moving around a bit, Allen; I doubt mail will be catch'n up for a while. Sure do wish it would hurry up, though."

Allen nodded in agreement as he leaned his back against the same tree and closed his eyes, also thinking of home.

James returned his attention to the distant railroad tracks beyond the open field, running parallel to the tree line. It was getting warm, and he imagined drinking some of Beth's lemonade when laughter from a group of men interrupted his daydreaming. Listening to their words of home or a girl, images of Martha on the station platform filled his mind.

The others laughed again, disturbing his images of her, so he tried to shut the noise out, and as he stared at the train tracks, he thought of the black mare. He closed his eyes, imagining riding her across the fields of his pa's farm, and hoped Davy was taking good care of her. The warm sun made him tired, and looking at Allen, seeing he was already sleeping, he rested his head against the tree, pulled the bill of his hat down over his eyes, and slept.

James was dreaming that he was sleeping at the dinner table, and his pa was calling him. "James, wake up. James, wake up. It's time to eat."

Opening his eyes, he looked up at Allen Downs, not his pa.

"You awake?" asked Allen.

James blinked as the reality of where he was came back to him, and he felt homesick. "I ain't hungry right now, Allen."

Allen glanced around, leaned closer as if he had a secret, and whispered, "Yah best eat something James. I heard we're moving out early in the morning." He paused to point toward the hill beyond the cornfield, railroad tracks, and trees in the distance that James had been staring at earlier. "To that hill yonder."

James sat up and looked in the direction Allen was pointing. "How'd ya know that?"

Allen glanced around again. "Hear'd some fellas talk'n."

James looked past him at a group of soldiers. "What fellas? And what makes you think they know what the hell they's talking about anyways?"

Allen frowned, looking offended as he gestured toward a group of men. "I don't, I reckon." Then he shrugged. "But one fella over there said he heard a couple of sergeants talk'n."

James looked at Allen with skepticism, then at the men sitting around the fire talking. Seeing they were the same men whose laughter had interrupted his thoughts of Martha earlier, he considered moving.

Allen leaned closer. "One of `em said that all of us are gonna climb that hill over yonder, behind them trees to a place called Cedar Mountain."

"Today?"

Allen shook his head, looking frustrated. "Nah, James, tomorrow."

James grinned as he stood, helped Allen up by his arm, and then pushed him playfully toward the mess area. "Let's eat, ya big horse's ass."

August 9, 1862

The 47th Alabama men were rousted from their bedrolls a couple of hours before sunrise, fed breakfast, ordered to break camp, and by noon they were marching in the hot, August sun along the main road toward a town called Culpeper, Virginia. Two hours into the march, they received orders to take up positions alongside the dusty dirt road for a fifteen-minute rest.

Thankful, they had stopped, Allen took off his backpack, sat down next to the road, and laid down, resting his head on his pack.

James took his backpack off, laid down next to Allen, and closed his eyes, letting his mind fill with thoughts of Martha. Hearing a commotion further up the road, he sat up, seeing a soldier on horseback approaching a group of officers. Looking excited, the soldier pointed toward the bend in the road as the officers huddled around the colonel. Moments later, one of the officers started running along the road in their direction, quietly yelling that the Union army was just beyond the bend and to form a skirmish line in the creek bed across the road. Filled with both fear and excitement, James and Allen grabbed their gear and raced across the road, jumping into the dry creek bed. Kneeling behind a dead log near some scrub bushes for cover, they laid their guns across the log and waited while the other men of the 47th took cover. Unbeknownst to James, they were at the edge of the cedar forest at the base of a knoll below Cedar Mountain. They had a clear view of the road, cornfield, and a line of trees behind the cornfield.

Confederate artillery from the knoll behind them and those on Cedar Mountain opened fire on the tree line beyond the cornfield where the Union Army had taken up positions. James watched the explosions of cannonballs sending flames and dirt skyward, some downing trees. After the first Confederate volley, puffs of smoke burst from the trees in the distance as Union cannon returned the barrage, pounding the road, creek bed, and trees behind the 47th. Exploding shells of fire and smoke sent pieces of shrapnel in all directions. Men up and down the line yelled profanities while others screamed in pain from shrapnel wounds or from having legs or arms blown off.

James closed his eyes and covered his ears as he and Allen lay curled up on the ground, huddled next to the log. When the noise stopped twenty minutes later and the smoke cleared, they looked at one another with eyes that gave away their fear. They sat up, looking up and down the line at men, wounded, or dead, being glad they weren't among them. It was eerily quiet as a soft breeze played in the leaves of the trees above him and moved the corn stalks on the other side of the road ever so slightly. Men around him were yelling for help, crying and moaning, the sounds all mixing with the buzz of grasshoppers in the hot, quiet afternoon. He felt his heart pounding in his head, and he could hear his own heavy breathing. Beads of sweat trickled down his face, gathering at his shirt collar. Hearing a low roar coming from the battered tree line beyond the cornfield that moments earlier had been the target of rebel cannon, he rose enough to look toward the sound, curious as to what it was.

"What's that noise?" asked Allen, staying below the log.

"I don't know."

As the roar grew louder, Union infantry emerged from the trees yelling false braveries as they ran into the cornfield from the safety of the trees.

"Hold your fire!" someone yelled.

James pulled back the hammer of his musket, hearing the click, click, click, and then watched and waited for the mass of blue uniforms as they closed the distance between the two armies. James raised his rifle tightly against his shoulder, took aim, and then remembered the order to hold his fire. Relaxing his grip on the rifle, he wiped the sweat from his face and stared at the blue wall of men racing through the tall, green stalks of corn that would soon be in range. Suddenly, he was afraid. Afraid to die, afraid to kill another man, and afraid he would run. He wanted to turn and run, but it was as if his legs weighed 1000 pounds. He wiped the sweat from his face and secured the rifle firmly against his shoulder, his cheek on the wood stock as he looked down the barrel, wondering if he could kill another man.

Off to their left, Union cavalry rode from the tree line, racing past their own infantry, and then turning to attack the Confederate cannon at the edge of the cedar trees. When the Confederate cannon opened fire, men and horses fell amid the explosions of fire and shrapnel, kicking up dirt and smoke. James turned from the terrible, gruesome scene to the noise of the blue wall racing through the cornfield and waited for the order to open fire.

The Federals didn't wait, and opened fire, filling the air with small white puffs of smoke, the cracking sound of exploding powder and musket balls pelting trees, the log, and dirt like a swarm of hornets. Some found their targets of men, knocking them backward with the sound of a dull thud.

Someone yelled, "Fix bayonets!"

James remembered how they had playfully practiced the art of hand-to-hand combat, never dreaming it would become a reality. Fear consumed him; sweat filled his forehead and face, his palms were wet, his mouth dry. He thought of the water in his canteen as he took the long bayonet from its scabbard and attached it to the end of his rifle barrel. He looked across the road at the mass of blue uniforms running through the cornfield, getting closer and closer while yelling, pausing to load, and then firing their rifles. Union officers rode their horses, yelling orders of encouragement, urging the men dressed in Union blue onward.

The Confederates didn't know they were outnumbered that day but stood their ground waiting for the order to open fire. When it came, the air suddenly filled with one loud explosion as hundreds of rifles fired almost simultaneously. On the knoll behind them, the Federal cavalry inflicted heavy casualties against the Confederate cannon positions before turning their horses to support their infantry charging the creek bed.

The air filled with crackling sounds as muskets fired from both sides. James fired, not knowing if he hit anyone, then reloaded by shoving a paper cartridge containing a round bullet and premeasured powder down the muzzle. Using the ramrod, he shoved the cartridge down the barrel, cocked the hammer, aimed, and fired at a man whose head jerked back as he fell, tripping the man behind him. He reloaded in time to see the blue wall crossing the dirt road, and as he raised his rifle pulling the trigger, he hit a man in the chest just a few feet away. The Federals were among them now with bayonets, yelling and screaming senseless words. James thrusted his bayonet into a soldier's stomach, feeling it go deep against the spine. He looked into the surprised face of a boy that was not much older than he, and he felt remorse for killing him.

Stepping back, he pulled the bayonet out of the boy, watching him fall forward, landing face down on the ground in front of the log. The scene was blue and gray, like salt and pepper on a plate of potatoes. Bodies of arms and legs locked in fierce combat, while men cursed profanities at one another, screamed, and yelled; some cried and sobbed while fighting not to die. The god Chaos was everywhere instructing the battle while men struggled to kill the other so they could live another day.

Men were on the ground, hitting one another with their fists or rocks, or anything they could grab, as they poked at eyes, pulled hair, bit off ears, screamed and yelled, anything to kill and live. James got caught up in a struggle between a young Confederate and an older Union soldier. As the three wrestled on the ground, James pushed himself free only to see the older Union soldier cut the younger Confederate soldier's throat, spraying James's face with blood. James screamed with anger while filled with horror as he stood with his rifle, clubbed the older Union soldier, and turned in time to drive the butt of his rifle against another Union soldier's face.

Seeing another, he stepped forward, thrusting his bayonet into the man's chest, feeling it go between the ribs. The man looked at him with eyes wide and mouth open as he slowly dropped to his knees. The scene around him was indescribable. The shooting was sparse during the fierce hand-to-hand combat, neither side having time to reload their guns. James forgot his fear as he stood behind the log, yelling and screaming while using his rifle as a club. Swinging wildly from side to side with such force, he almost lost his balance. After hitting a man dressed in blue in the face with his rifle, he got knocked to the ground. Dazed, he looked up and seeing the man was about to bayonet him he quickly rolled away. As he got to one knee, he looked into the soldier's eyes then saw a bloody bayonet come out from the Union soldier's stomach. The young boy stared at James as he slid off the bayonet on top of him. James pushed the soldier off and tried to get up when another Federal soldier, much older than he, was on him with his hands around James's neck, squeezing.

James stared into the angry man's eyes, gasping for air as he tried to pull the man's hands from around his throat and push at him to get free, but the man was too strong. He could feel his eyes bulge, and the figures struggling around him became blurry. Suddenly, the soldier released his grip and fell on top of him. Coughing and gasping for air, James pushed the dead soldier off, silently thanking the man who had saved his life a second time. Men of blue and grey were locked in fierce combat all around him as he tried to get up, only to be knocked down by another man who fell on top of him. Angry and screaming in frustration, he wrestled with the man only to discover he was already dead. Pushing him off, he stood, picked up a rifle, and swung it at a Union soldier. Missing, he lost his balance and fell, and as he got to his feet, a much bigger man grabbed him in a bear hug. James stared into the man's mean, hateful eyes while he pushed the man's head back with his one free hand. Then, the man's grip suddenly relaxed, and they both fell to the ground. When he looked up, Allen was standing over them with his rifle butt covered in red blood. He looked at James for only a moment and then turned to hit another man in the face with the butt of his rifle.

James got up off the ground, grabbed a rifle, and stood back to back with Allen, both of them swinging their guns wildly at whatever moved. The Southern lines collapsed toward the trees of the knoll, men tripping over bodies of the dead and wounded from both sides as they fought bravely, trying to hold their ground. Confederate reinforcements joined the melee from the trees, saving the day for the Confederate army. The Confederates pushed the Union ranks into the creek bed where they took temporary shelter, then retreated across the road into the cornfield, disappearing into the tree line. The battle that had lasted just over thirty minutes was over.

James and Allen stood with the others among the dead and wounded, listening to the cries and moaning of both Confederate and Union soldiers. Exhausted, James collapsed onto his knees, covered his face with his hands, and cried. When he looked up, he could see Allen sitting next to a tree, his tears leaving lines down his dirty cheeks. James looked around at the bodies, turned away, and vomited. Spitting to cleanse his mouth, he sat at the base of a tree staring at the blood on his pants and hands. Noticing his shoes were stained with mud and dirt, and for some reason, James thought about cleaning them. Feeling pain in his arm, he realized a bullet or bayonet had grazed him. He didn't know which. His uniform was dirty, the sleeves of his jacket torn, his pants torn, and his knees bloody. He touched the torn pants and thought that his ma would give him hell for looking so dirty. He laughed at that while tears filled his eyes and rolled down his dirty cheeks.

The moments passed while he and Allen sat together against the tree, and then Allen noticed that James was wounded. Concerned, he got to his knees and quickly examined his arm, then relieved, said, "Yer just grazed."

The only sane emotion left for them was laughter, and it suddenly consumed them both. When they stopped laughing and returned to reality, Allen looked around them at the bodies. "I don't wanna do this no more, James. I wanna go home."

Tasting salt in his mouth from tears, James turned away, leaned over the rock, and vomited again, while sporadic gunfire in the distance suggested others' deaths.

Allen closed his eyes at the frightful sounds and then looked at James. "Yah all right, James?"

James sat up and wiped the vomit from his chin with his sleeve. "I'll never be all right again."

A veteran sergeant in his late thirties, wearing a day's growth of beard, face dirty and sweaty, stood near a tree watching the young boys. Recalling his own first taste of battle filled with fear and terror and the aftermath of emotions that followed, he stepped closer. "Either y'all wounded?"

The boys looked up with surprise. "He is," said Allen as he pointed to James.

"Just a flesh wound," corrected James, feeling a bit embarrassed.

The sergeant guessed these two young pups to be fresh off the farm, and from their looks, he figured they had made a pretty good accounting of themselves this day. He knelt. "Let's have a look, Lad."

James moved the material of his shirt so the sergeant could see his arm.

The sergeant leaned forward to examine the wound. "It ain't bad, boy." He grinned, thinking if this had been an older man, he would have told him to forget it, but he knew these two young boys needed to get away from the dead and dying for a few minutes. "I think you're gonna be all right, but it might be a good idea if you were to get yourself back to the hospital tent and let someone take a look."

"Which way's the tent?" asked James.

The sergeant stood, pulled him up by his shirt collar, and pointed toward the trees to the east. "Just walk in that direction, ask someone from time to time, and you'll find it." He looked at Allen. "You go along too, so's he doesn't get lost." He watched as they picked up their muskets, and then the sergeant pushed the two in the direction he had pointed, and told them to tell the doc that Sargent Winslow had sent them. He watched them for several moments before turning to the arduous task of helping the wounded and gathering the bodies of the dead.

The Confederate army withdrew from Cedar Mountain a few days later with the Union army in pursuit. Reaching Manassas's outskirts on the evening of August 27th, 1862, Confederate General Stonewall Jackson, having grown tired of retreating, swore that he would not withdraw any further. Giving the order to dig in, he declared his army would make a stand at Manassas. Then he waited for what history would call the Second Bull Run at Manassas.

August 27, 1862

Manassas, Virginia

The Battle of the Second Bull Run

In the early evening of August 27th, 1862, the Confederate army was camped near Manassas when the Union army arrived, making camp on the other side of the city. The 47th Alabama was camped in a wooded area that overlooked a large, open pasture. Beyond the pasture lay a stream that ran parallel to another wooded area several hundred yards in the distance where the Federals were camped.

Smoke from campfires of the Federal troops floated above the tree line as James and Allen watched the Federals move about the small stream and disappear into the trees. The August sun hung low in the west, its light not as bright or warm as it had been a couple of hours ago. James let his mind drift toward tomorrow and the battle that was sure to come with the dawn. Glancing in the other direction, he knew they would have the advantage of the sun at their backs.

As the sun dipped below the western horizon bringing darkness, campfires glowed on both sides, like stars in the black, moonless sky above the two armies. Men on both sides went about their tasks, trying not to think about the battle they would fight in the morning. In a surreal setting, the two armies cooked, ate, and slept within sight of each other's camps.

"Smell that?" asked James casually.

Allen raised his head and smelled. "What ya smell'n?"

"Black, rich soil, and livestock, the smells of a farm. Smells like home."

Allen chuckled. "Shit James, all I can smell are campfires and cooking." He turned onto his side, staring into their small campfire. "Tell ya one thing, though, sure wish I's home right now sitting at the table smelling Ma's cooking and listening to Pa pray'n."

James rolled onto his back, propping his head against his backpack. "Yeah, that'd be nice, all right. I wonder how long this here war's gonna last?"

"Don't know," Allen said, throwing a small stick into the fire and watching the flames feed on it. "When I joined, they said it would only last a few months."

James rolled onto his side, propped his head in his right hand, and looked at Allen while considering that. "I think it's gonna last a lot longer. Possibly a year, maybe longer."

Allen glanced around, looking secretive, and whispered. "You ashamed of the other day?"

James whispered back. "Cuz we cried?"

"Uh, huh."

James looked at his young friend, thinking he looked a little older. "I don't reckon we were the only ones who felt that way."

"I'm scared," Allen said, looking ashamed. "Scared of dying. I keep seeing the faces of the men I kilt, and I can't get the sounds of the screaming and yell'n out of my head." He glanced around to see if anyone was listening, but the others were occupied with their own fears and haunting memories. Then he whispered, "I ain't sure I can take another year o' this."

"We don't have much choice." James nodded toward the Federal positions. "No more'n those fellas across them fields do."

Allen looked up from the fire toward the Union campfires, considering the thought. "I wonder what they's talking about."

James pulled his blanket up over his shoulders and his cap down over his eyes. "Probably the same as us: home, the war, and killing. We best get some sleep."

"If'n I can," Allen said thoughtfully.

Bugles in the early morning hours of August 28, 1862, rousted both camps. The sun had not yet crested the horizon behind the Confederate camp, but the light blue and pink sky warned of its coming. The sergeants moved up and down the line making sure every soldier's gun was loaded and bayonets affixed. James watched as the sunshine touched the tops of the trees where the Federals camped beyond the pasture. His thoughts returned to Cedar Mountain and the roar that had preceded the Union army's charge and the terror that followed.

As the Confederates waited with anticipation, the quiet hours of morning slipped away into the late afternoon. The men became restless, fearfully waiting for something to happen, for the battle to begin, yet hoping that either the Federals or they would move back, preventing an all-out charge. A sergeant made his way up and down the lines telling them to keep a sharp eye and to take turns eating and napping while they had the chance. The hours quietly passed, and in the late afternoon, sounds of bugles, cannons, and small arms fire from somewhere in the distance interrupted the silence.

"Someone's catching it," whispered Allen.

James nodded in silence, imagining the chaos, hoping their side was winning.

The hours passed, and with sunset came the silence and relief that there had been no battle this day, but the fear of tomorrow lingered in everyone's mind. The moonless night saw the return of small fires in the distance. James was staring across the open pastures at the campfires thinking of Martha and was oblivious to the sergeant kneeling next to him.

"Private," said the sergeant.

Startled, James turned. "Yes, Sergeant."

The sergeant found humor in the boy's expression. "I want you to make yer way into them fields about a hundred yards or so."

James looked at the sergeant, turned and looked into the darkness, and then back at the sergeant with skepticism. "You crazy?"

The sergeant chuckled, enjoying the validity of the question. "Probably."

"What the hell am I supposed to do out there all by myself?"

The sergeant placed a hand on his shoulder. "Stand guard. You won't be alone, Private. We've a dozen or more men out there spaced every fifty yards or so. We wouldn't want anyone sneaking upon us in the dark now, would we?"

"Oh boy," said James looking doubtful. "A dozen of us. That ought to scare the shit out of them Yankee's."

Thankful it was James and not him, Allen chuckled.

The sergeant found no humor in James's comment. "Don't give me any shit, Private. Just get your little ass out there, like I said. If you see anything, try and get back here without getting shot." The sergeant turned and spit tobacco juice into the fire, then gestured at Allen. "I'll send your skinny little friend to relieve you in a bit." Then he pushed at James's shoulder. "Now, get out there and stay awake."

James looked at Allen. "Hope to see ya soon." He gathered up his gun and blanket, crouched down, and started walking.

The sergeant looked at Allen. "Get some sleep, boy. Your little ass is gonna relieve him in about four hours."

James trotted into the darkness, counting steps until he thought he was about a hundred yards from camp, he sat down. He wrapped his blanket and slicker around his shoulders, leaned against a large rock and looked back at the campfires, picturing Allen nice and warm. Looking west, James could also see the Federal campfires and wondered where their lookouts were sitting. Settling in for the duration, he looked around, finding it impossible to distinguish between the black ground and black sky if not for the stars and campfires. Looking skyward, James recognized the big and little dippers and a few other constellations, naming them in his head to pass the time. He noticed the Federal campfires were disappearing, and getting concerned, James looked back at the Confederate camp, seeing theirs were also disappearing.

He held his right hand in front of his eyes. 'Shit," he quietly said. "Can't even see my hand." His newly found friend, fear, was with him, and he began to imagine all sorts of things moving about in the darkness as his hand slid along the rifle butt to the trigger. With his musket lying across his lap, he stared into the black night toward the enemy camp and then looked skyward at the stars, recalling the evenings he and Davy had walked along the driveway after dinner.

A hoot owl gave its evening greeting, and James turned toward the sound, imagining it sitting safely in a tree watching him. Wishing he too were safe in a tree, instead of out here on the cold ground, he returned to his vigilant watch over the woods in the distance hidden by the black night.

The minutes slowly passed as he strained his eyes and ears for the enemy while fighting sleep. Seeing the vague shape of something in the darkness, James cocked the hammer of his rifle.

"James," whispered a voice.

"Who is it?"

"It's me, Allen. Where are you?"

"Not so loud…I'm over here."

"Where?"

"Over here."

Allen made his way to where James was sitting. "Sure is dark out here."

"No shit," replied James sarcastically. "Bring your slicker?"

"Got it right here." Allen watched as James gathered up his stuff. "Can't ya stay a while?"

"Hell, no," replied an irritated James. "I've been out here long enough. It's your turn." And with that, he turned and started walking, hoping he was going in the right direction.

By the time the sun crested the eastern hills, the 47th Alabama had moved farther back into the woods, taking up new positions that gave better protection while maintaining an excellent view of the Federal positions and the killing fields in between. Sergeants made their way up and down the ranks informing the soldiers that their orders were to hold this position at all costs, meaning that there would be no retreating.

James knew that meant but one thing, and that worried him.

Coffee and dry bread was the morning meal, and as James bit into the hard, dry bread, he thought of the food his ma used to have waiting for him each morning. Suddenly those pleasant thoughts were interrupted by the sound of bullets pelting the trees, accompanied by sounds of gunfire and tiny white puffs of smoke in the tree line across the expanse.

"Snipers!" someone yelled.

"Stay down!" yelled another.

A few men fired back at the puffs of smoke in the distant trees until the sergeant yelled, "Hold your fire, ya idiots, them snipers are plum out of our range."

Another bullet hit a tree, then another, and James couldn't get any closer to the tree next to him, but that didn't stop him from trying. Confederate snipers returned fire at the puffs of smoke while he raised his head, looked at the tree line in the distance, and thought he saw movement. Moments later, men in blue uniforms emerged from the trees into the sunlight, walked across the narrow creek, and entered the pasture's green haze. He watched as the Federalists continued to come toward their position, and then, under cover of Federal snipers, they started to run with the same low yelling roar he had heard at Cedar Mountain.

The sergeant yelled, "Stay low until them snipers stop shoot'n!"

James and Allen watched as the dark blue wall ran toward them, getting closer, ever closer, yelling inaudible words.

The sergeant raised one hand. "Get ready."

James's heart pounded inside his head as sweat rolled down his forehead, face, and neck. As the blue wall came closer, he saw the United States flag waving on a pole carried by a soldier and realized for the first time that he was at war with his own country. He had never really thought about it before, and it gave him a strange feeling of mixed emotions. The blue wall came closer and closer, as the yelling grew louder and louder, and then he heard the order to pick their targets but hold their fire.

James aimed at a figure and waited.

"Easy, men!" yelled the sergeant.

Allen moved nervously, bumping against James's left elbow.

'Take it easy, Allen,' thought James. He glanced at Allen, wondering if he was thinking the same thing he was, that they should get up and run!

Federal cavalry suddenly appeared from behind the blue wall that opened its ranks, letting the men on horseback through. He watched as they attacked the Rebel lines some 200 yards to his left, bringing back memories of Cedar Mountain. Bullets started whizzing past, thudding into the trees by the hundreds. Hearing an unfamiliar sound, something splattered the right side of his face, and when he looked at the man on his right, he was slumped over his rifle, blood pouring from a head wound. He wiped the side of his face, looked at the blood on his hand, wiped his hand on his tattered pants, and looked at Allen on his left. Relieved he was okay, he looked back at the bloody head, closed his eyes, and fought the urge to vomit, wishing someone would give the order to fire.

"Get ready!" yelled the sergeant.

James set his rifle down and picked up the rifle belonging to the dead man on his right, took aim, and then waited for the order to fire.

When he heard it, James, pulled the trigger. His musket kicked against his shoulder, and a white puff of smoke rushed from the barrel following the tiny musket ball. The man he was aiming at jerked, dropped his rifle, and fell. James reloaded and fired again, repeating the process mindlessly over and over as the warm, August air filled with the smell and haze of rifle smoke. He loaded his musket, looked up, seeing the soldier carrying the United States flag fall to his knees. Another man grabbed the flag, raising it above his head, and then he too was hit by a musket ball. And as he fell, still another man behind him grabbed it and raised it above his head, waving it back and forth. He took aim at the man with the flag but changed his mind, aimed, and fired at the man next to him.

The Federal cavalry had stopped their advance, having encountered heavy Confederate fire from the trees, rocks, and bushes. Horses rose up on their hind legs, some getting shot and falling on their riders, others losing their riders, while still others ran in different directions as the gods of War, Confusion, and Chaos ruled. Finally, the cavalry retreated, followed by the Federal infantry stopping its advance, turning, and retreating behind the cavalry under the relentless volley of Confederate rifle fire. Confederate officers and sergeant stepped from the woods waving and yelling encouragement to their men, ordering a charge against the retreating Federals. The Confederate line, filled with the sense of victory, gave the Rebel Yell as they stood and charged after the retreating blue uniforms.

Now, it was the Confederate roar the Federals heard chasing after them. Federal cannon opened fire, sending bursts of smoke and shrapnel all around the advancing Confederate army. One shell burst so close to James it knocked him to the ground, where he lay stunned and dazed for several seconds. He slowly sat up and shook his head, trying to clear his mind. Standing on shaky legs, dazed and unable to hear anything, he glanced around at the blurry figures running past.

Seeing his rifle on the ground, he knelt to pick it up when someone bumped into him, knocking him back to the ground. As he got up to one knee, a small group of Confederate cavalry rode past him in pursuit of the Federals. His eyes began to clear, and his hearing returned, so he bent down, picked up his rifle, and started walking while weaving to the left and then to the right in the direction the cavalry had ridden.

Upon reaching the tree line, he took shelter behind a fallen tree, realizing he had lost his cap. Deciding he would look for it later, he loaded his rifle and fired at, but missed, a blue figure backing into the trees. Union soldiers had momentarily taken shelter behind trees and logs, and now they fired and backed away to another position. The Confederates followed, yelling and firing their weapons, taking shelter behind the same trees the Federals had deserted for other shelters.

Suddenly and eerily, it was over. The Federals were gone, and the Confederates stopped their pursuit. Kneeling beside the fallen tree, James looked through the haze of smoke, hearing an occasional musket fire somewhere in the distance. The stillness filled with men moaning in pain or calling for help, and the forest floor was littered with bodies of the wounded and dead, as were the fields they had run through. Looking around, he thought of Allen, stood, and rushed from body to body. Wounded men from both sides cried for help or water, some missing arms or legs from cannon fire. A few tried to get up while others screamed in pain. James came upon a man trying to push his intestines back into his stomach with his hands.

Feeling sick, James looked away, thinking he had to help him, but how? When he looked again, the man was dead. Glancing around at the horror through tear-filled eyes, James saw a figure walking out of a group of trees, but as hope filled him, James saw that it was not Allen. Frantically, he walked deeper into the woods, stepping over body after body, stopping now and again to offer water to wounded Confederate and Union soldiers alike. He had to find Allen, and he walked on in desperation. As he stepped over a fallen tree, he tripped over the body of a dead Confederate soldier, his eyes still open as if staring into the distance, and he could see that part of his head was gone just above the left ear, exposing his brains. James turned and convulsed into a vomit of an empty stomach, then got up, and as he hurried away, he tripped and fell. Getting up as he looked back at the dead body, he ran again, searching for Allen.

He came upon two Confederate soldiers, one sitting against a tree, the other lying down with his head in the other's lap. Not knowing if they were dead or alive, he slowly approached the two when the man sitting against the tree opened his eyes.

"Y'all okay?" James asked with concern.

The man sitting against the tree looked up; his eyes were red, and tears left small lines on his dirty face. "I am." Then he looked down at his friend. "He's dead."

James looked down at the dead man, seeing he was just a young boy, not so much younger than Allen. Maybe it was pity he felt for the two men, or maybe it was the fear of finding Allen dead, but whichever it was, James felt compelled to sit next to them. James leaned his back against the tree and sat in silence for several minutes, watching the man gently stroke the hair of his dead friend. Minutes passed in silence, and then he said. "I'm sorry about your friend."

The man just stared at the face of his dead friend in teary silence.

"I'm look'n for my friend. Ain't seen him since we started chasing them, Yanks."

The man sat in silence while staring down at the boy's bloody face as if he hadn't heard James.

"Sorry, Mister, but I have to find my friend."

Without looking up, the man said, "I hope you find him."

James stood, looked down at the two men, and then disappeared into the bushes, wanting to get away from the sorrow, fearing that he would find Allen dead. After several yards, he saw Allen sitting against a tree, holding his head in his hands. James called out, "Allen!" Then, he ran toward him.

Allen looked up, stood, and called out, "James."

They hugged one another for several seconds as they cried tears of joy, each thankful the other was still alive. They sat down and leaned against the tree, and James reached up to take off his cap but remembered he had lost it. That made Allen laugh, and he pushed James playfully, who pushed back like a small child would. All too soon, the aftermath of the battle interrupted their brief moment of innocence. Their smiles left as quickly as they had come, and James Chrisman and Allen Downs spent the rest of the day helping to bury the dead and care for the wounded. James thought it was a strange and eerie scene to experience to watch men wearing gray and blue uniforms walking side by side on the torn battlefield, each side gathering up their dead and wounded.

Evening found James and Allen unable to eat a dinner that looked more like pig slop, reminding James of the brains and guts he had seen earlier in the day. Tired, with appetites gone, they curled up next to a small fire and slept between nightmares.

Waking up after one such nightmare, James sat up and looked at Allen, who was staring into the fire, unable to sleep. Wanting to be alone and rid his mind of the images of war, James picked up his rifle, stood, and wandered around camp aimlessly. He didn't know how long or far he had walked when a voice called out to him. "Find your friend?"

James recognized the man from the tree who had been holding his dead friend, sitting by a fire with two other men. "Yeah, I did."

Then, he motioned in the direction of his camp. "He's resting by the fire."

The man smiled, looking glad. "That's good." He held up an open hand. "Andrew Patterson, South Carolina."

James shook the hand vigorously. "James Chrisman, Alabama."

Andrew pointed to one of the other men. "This here's Morgan, and the friendly one there's Gideon. This here's the young fella I was telling y'all about."

James shook their hands.

Andrew gestured to a vacant spot by the fire. "Sit down and visit a spell."

James did as asked and sat down, feeling the warmth of the fire.

Andrew smiled at James. "I reckon after today, I shouldn't call you or anyone else in this army a young fella."

James grinned, feeling proud. "What was your friend's name?" Then, feeling bad about asking, he apologized.

"No need to apologize," said Andrew, looking reflective. "He was Jonathan Albert Frank, but everyone called him Johnny."

"He from South Carolina?" asked James.

"No," replied Andrew, poking the fire with a stick. "He was from a small farm in Georgia." Then Andrew grinned in memory. "We first met when he joined our unit, same as Morgan and Gideon here." He looked up from the fire, reflecting on that day. "He was only sixteen and couldn't wait to fight." Silence fell on the four men, and Andrew wiped at a tear, shook his head, and grinned again in memory as he tossed the stick into the fire. "I'm gonna miss the little bastard."

Silence fell around them as James stared into the fire for several moments and, without looking up from the fire, asked, "How long y'all think this thing is gonna last?"

"Don't know," replied Gideon, and then he pointed at Andrew. "I only know it'll be over for the old man there soon."

Andrew nodded with a big grin. "True enough." He looked at James. "It's my age, Son. They'd only let me sign up for one year, and that year was up when this here damn battle started."

Gideon slapped Andrew on the shoulder, "Yep. Old Andrew, there'll be going home soon." He paused. "Wish we all were."

"Lucky bastard," laughed Morgan as he playfully kicked Andrew's foot.

Andrew chuckled as he looked at James. "Want to know what's so damn strange about all this?"

James nodded with a curious look.

"Just a few short miles from here is Manassas, where I enlisted."

James stared at Andrew, feeling happy for him, grinned, and then chuckled. "Looks like you made the round trip."

The others laughed.

"Nice of this old war to bring ya back, Andy," teased Morgan.

Andrew frowned. "It's a trip I wish none of us would've ever made."

The men spent the next hour talking about home and families before James realized how late it was. He stood, thanked them for their company, and shook their hands, shaking Andrews harder while wishing him a safe journey home. Then he picked up his musket, turned, and quickly disappeared into the night.

When James returned to his camp and bedroll, he found the fire needed wood, so he quietly placed a couple of logs on it and then turned to his bedroll. Surprised at seeing the empty space where Allen should have been, he glanced around at the others sleeping. Then James saw a folded note stuck between his backpack and bedroll. Fearing what was in the note, he quickly unfolded it, leaned toward the dim fire, and began reading. *'I've kilt enough. Allen'*

He glanced around to see if anyone was watching, crumpled the note, tossed it in the fire, and watched it burn. He looked into the darkness, hoping he would make it home, then got into his bedroll for a sleepless night, anticipating the next morning and the sergeant's questions.

Heavy rain fell the next morning as James and the others lined up for roll call. The sergeant paced up and down the ranks several times before stopping and glaring at James. "Where's yer little friend Soldier?"

Filled with fear for Allen, James hesitated before answering, "Don't know, Sergeant. I seen `im last night before I took a walk."

Lightning flashed, followed by a sudden crash of thunder that rolled across the ground as the sergeant stepped closer. James could feel the toes of his boots against his own, their noses almost touching. "Was he here when you got back, Soldier?"

James was scared and nervous. "I got back pretty late and went right to bed after stoking the fire with wood. I never noticed if he was there or not."

The sergeant glared at him looking skeptical. "You sure about that, Private?"

Lightning flashed again, followed by thunder.

"Yes, Sergeant."

The sergeant looked angry. "Where the hell were you last night, anyways?"

The rain made little streams of water as it poured from the bill of the sergeant's cap, spilling onto James's coat, and he wanted to get out of the rain. James told him about his evening walk and meeting some other men from South Carolina.

The sergeant listened to his story and appeared satisfied that he knew nothing about Alan's disappearance. Then clenched his teeth. "Well, Private, yer little friend's a deserter, and when young Private Downs is caught, he'll hang and then his body thrown into an unmarked grave."

James looked at the sergeant, thinking, *'You stupid fool Allen, you stupid, stupid fool.'*

The sergeant dismissed the men and then stomped toward the captain's tent to report one of his men's desertion.

Charlie Hogan, one of the other men of the 47th, stood next to James while the rest of the men walked toward the mess tent and breakfast. He placed his hand on James's shoulder. "I know he's your friend and probably not a bad sort, but he sure bought himself a bunch of trouble."

James nodded in agreement as he looked through the rain in the direction Allen would have taken.

Charlie glanced in the direction he was looking. "If he gets past the Union lines, he'll have to hide from the Home Guard in every county along the way home, if that's where he's headed. If he gits lucky enough to make it home, he'll have to hide fir the rest of his life, or git hung."

James nodded as he stared off into the distance, imagining Allen running away. "I know, but there ain't nuth'n I can do about that."

Charlie put his arm around his shoulder, "C'mon James, let's get something to eat. Sorry about Allen."

As was the first battle on July 21, 1861, the Second Battle of Bull Run was a significant tactical victory for the Confederates and another blow to Union morale. Union casualties were about 14,000 killed and wounded out of 62,000 engaged, and the Confederates lost about 1,000 killed and 7,000 wounded out of 50,000 engaged.

Seventeen

September 1862 – October 1862

Andrew Jackson Patterson

Manassas to Anderson County

On the morning of September 28th, 1862, Andrew Jackson Patterson was sitting on a hard, wooden bench inside Manassas's dimly lit train depot. He had occupied that same bench for two days, reading his discharge papers countless times while awaiting transportation through the war-torn country to South Carolina.

"Mister Patterson?" shouted the old man behind the ticket window.

"That's me," replied Andrew, grabbing his bag and running to the ticket counter.

"You're in luck, Soldier," smiled the scruffy ticket agent, dressed in a dirty, white shirt that was slightly too big. The old man smiled, displaying the few teeth he had left in a mouth framed by a stained, white, unruly beard. "Sorry, this here's taken so long, soldier, but maybe we can get you out of Manassas 'round midnight."

Andrew smiled, looking relieved. "Thank the good Lord."

"However," said the old man. "That all depends on whether the incoming trains on time and if'n them damn Yanks don't attack Manassas fer the third time. If not, then we might get the train out of town." He smiled and winked. "Other than that, it looks like yer all set."

Andrew looked hopeful. "Let's hope them Yanks have had enough fight'n for a spell."

The ticket agent smiled, filling his face with deep wrinkles. "Only thing is," he said, looking apologetic. "We can only get you as far as Richmond. From there, it depends on how the line is farther south. Ya might have to wait a day or two."

Andrew grinned with excitement. "Richmond's fine. It's closer to home than this place."

The ticket agent chuckled. "Now, that's a fact." He handed Andrew his tickets, advising him that the train was due in about 30 minutes, and warned him not to go wandering off.

Andrew grinned. "Not much chance in that, Mister." He returned to the hard, uncomfortable bench to wait for the "All Aboard".

The hours on the train seemed to pass slowly. Andrew tried passing the time napping, but every bump woke him and made him wonder if they were under attack. When the train finally pulled into Richmond, with the bell clanging and steam spewing from the engine, he gathered his belongings and hurried off the train. He went inside the depot to the ticket counter, and asked about the next train. The man behind the counter informed Andrew that Union soldiers had destroyed the tracks farther south. After cursing the Union army, he asked the agent if he knew how he might find transportation south. The agent thought for a minute, then remembered a Confederate medical unit leaving for Petersburg, Virginia, camped on the other side of town.

Andrew thanked him, ran out of the station, and down the street, soon finding the unit. Somehow he convinced the officer in charge to let him tag along as far as Petersburg, where he hoped to catch a train into North Carolina and then transportation south to Anderson, South Carolina.

The train slowed as it approached the outskirts of Anderson a day later. Andrew looked out the window at the familiar buildings as they slowly passed the passenger car window. Thinking the town had not changed much, he waited anxiously for the train to stop at the small depot. It was late afternoon; the sky was gray and the air was chilly. A typical October day, he thought as he stepped from the train onto the platform. He walked toward the depot, past soldiers and passengers in a hurry to board the train. A rush of warm air hit him from the potbellied stove sitting in the center of the room as he entered the depot. After warming his hands, he watched people scamper about, saying hello to those that had just arrived or goodbye to those about to leave. With his hands warm, he ventured back into the cold afternoon and walked toward the livery, hoping old George would rent him a horse, but found the building now boarded up and deserted. Curious about old George and disappointed at not getting a horse, he stood in the cold October air mulling over what to do next. It would be dark in a little while, and Andrew still had over ten miles to go and too far to walk this late in the day. Glancing up the street, he saw the familiar sign of Bender's General Store. Looking up at the gray clouds turning darker, he headed up the street contemplating a hotel for the night after visiting with Charles Bender.

He walked up the steps, across the boardwalk, opened the door, and walked into Bender's General Store to the familiar sound of the tiny bell above the door. The proprietor, Charles Bender, stopped what he was doing, turned, and looked toward the door in the dim light, not recognizing the figure dressed in Confederate gray approaching the stove and cracker barrel. It took Bender a moment, but then he thought the figure looked a little like his old friend Andrew Patterson and he hurried from behind the counter. "I'll be damned. Is that really you, Andrew?"

Andrew smiled as he warmed his hands. "'Fraid it is, Charles."

Charles laughed as he turned his head, yelling over his shoulder. "Jessie, come see who's home from the war!"

The two men embraced and stepped back just as Jessie Bender pushed her way through two heavy, dark curtains hanging in the doorway of the storeroom. Recognizing Andrew, she hurried toward him with arms open. "Andrew." They hugged, then she stepped back, looking worried. "You're not shot or hurt, are ya, Andy?"

"No, just tired, Jessie, tired and anxious to get home."

Charles moved a chair closer to the stove. "Sit down, Andrew. How's bout a cup of coffee, with a little whiskey in it?"

"I could use the coffee, not sure about the whiskey. It's been a while since I ate."

Bender laughed. "Nonsense Andy, it'll warm your insides." He turned to his wife. "Jessie, would you mind getting Andrew and me here a cup of coffee while I get the bottle from under the counter?"

Jessie nodded with a smile. "Be only too glad to." She hurried to the kitchen with her husband close on her heels, heading for the counter and a small bottle of whiskey he had hidden. Retrieving the bottle, he hurried back to Andrew and the warm stove. "Shit, Andy," he said, grinning. "I can't believe you're home."

"Me neither, Charles, me neither." Andrew looked tired. "Sure seems like I have been gone a hell of a long time."

Charles noticed his tattered and dirty uniform. "Looks like that uniform has seen a few things."

Andrew looked down at his uniform, thinking it surely had.

Jessie arrived with a coffee in each hand, giving one to Andrew, the other to her husband.

Charles set his cup down, opened the bottle, and poured a little whiskey into their cups, complaining, "Hell woman, ya didn't leave no room."

Jessie frowned. "Oh, shut up, Charles." She turned her frown for Charles into a smile for Andrew. "He hasn't changed any, still thinks he runs things."

Andrew smiled, and as he started to taste the coffee, the warm fumes from the whiskey caught him off guard; he coughed and then took a small sip.

Charles laughed. "Sip a little more Andy, need a bit more room for the whiskey."

Andrew smiled at Jessie while Charles poured a little more whiskey into his cup.

"There," said Charles, "that'll warm you up better'n any pretty gal."

"Charles, mind your manners," scolded Jessie.

The three talked for more than an hour about the war, followed by news and gossip of the county. Charles told Andrew that most of the young men around the county were in the army or getting ready to enlist.

Jessie told him that his family had been in just a few days ago for supplies, then she leaned closer, winked, and smiled. "Rebecca was with `em."

Charles gave her a look she ignored, and then she sat down on the nearby chair, telling him that everyone in the county knew Rebecca was staying at his place.

Andrew took another drink, trying to hide his embarrassment.

Jessie looked at him. "Imagine her out there taking care of the children." She smiled, clasping her hands over her heart. "She's such a sweet girl." Then she leaned forward, placing one hand on his knee. "You should marry that one, Andrew."

Andrew felt warm and flushed, but not from the whiskey. He closed his eyes, letting the warmth of the whiskey fumes and hot coffee mix with the heat from the stove, wishing Jessie would keep quiet about Rebecca. He began to feel relaxed and warm, and thought it was good to be home. While Jessie continued, Andrew's memories turned to young Johnny and the sadness his death had brought. A quick silence came, and he looked at Charles. "I stopped by the livery and found it all boarded up."

"Aw, that one's a shame, Andy, a real shame." Charles started to pour a little more whiskey into Andrew's cup, but he placed his hand over it, so Charles put the cork back into the bottle and set it on a nearby table. "The Army came through here two, maybe three months ago, and took all his horses and mules. They wiped him out. Pert near killed old George." Charles looked sad. "That place was all he ever had. His pa left it to him when he died back in '45.

Andrew shook his head thoughtfully. "I remember." He drank the last of his whiskey coffee. "Did they pay for the livestock they took?"

"Oh, they paid him in government vouchers for the livestock all right Andy, but not near what they were worth, and if the South loses the war, those vouchers will probably be worthless." Charles leaned closer, looking disgruntled. "He had some pretty fine animals down there."

Andrew nodded. "I remember. What became of George?"

"He lit out on a train for Mississippi, said he had a brother out there."

"Sister," corrected Jessie. "It was a sister."

Charles gave her a stern look for correcting him and then leaned a little closer to Andrew. "You sure you don't want no more, Andy?"

Andrew shook his head. "No, thank you, Charles." He set the cup on a barrel next to him. "I have to find a room for the night and a way out to my place in the morning."

"Shit," said Charles looking embarrassed. "Jacob Davis is across the street, having a beer." He stood and walked across the room and looked out the window while talking. "Plum forgot about old Jacob. Why that's his rig right outside the store."

Andrew stood, walked to the window, and looked outside, recognizing the wagon. "Hell, I walked right past it and up them steps. Must've been so damn tired I didn't see it." He looked toward the saloon up the street as someone walked out of the saloon door. "Here he comes now."

They watched Jacob Davis walk across the street, stumbling in a wagon rut, and then turn to curse it. Andrew chuckled, knowing Jacob was cussing like a muleskinner. Stepping back into the dim light, he grinned at Charles.

Moments later, Jacob opened the door, ringing the tiny bell, and stepped inside. "Bit chilly out there, Charles." Jacob turned, closed the door, ringing the tiny bell once more, and then turned, walking toward the stove.

Charles stood next to the stove, grinning as Jacob walked across the room, rubbing his hands together. Jacob sat on one of several kegs that visitors used to sit on while gossiping, put his hands in front of the stove, flexing his fingers, and looked Charles with a puzzled look. "What the hell ya grinning at Charles? You look like the mule that kicked Lincoln."

Jacob looked at Jessie. "He lost his mind, Jessie?"

Still grinning, Charles pointed toward the door.

Jacob turned just as a figure stepped out of the dim light from the corner next to the door. He slowly stood with a surprised look. "Well, I'll be damned."

"Howdy, Jacob," smiled Andrew. "Hope your Rebecca ain't spoiled, my children."

"Andrew, you son of a bitch," Jacob said, and then he turned to Jessie. "Apologies, Jessie."

She smiled and waved a dismissive hand.

"Damn, it's good to have you home," said Jacob as he started to walk toward Andrew.

They hugged one another and sat by the stove while Charles poured Jacob and himself a drink to celebrate. The three men visited for a short time, and then Jacob and Andrew said their goodbyes to the Benders and left. During the long ride to Andrew's place, Jacob told him how things had been in the valley, including Andrew's slave John running off and the mysterious death of one of the Home Guard.

"Becky wrote about John," Andrew said, looking puzzled. "But not about the fella with the Home Guard, who was he?"

"He was a no-good by the name of Randy Murphy."

Andrew considered the name. "Don't believe I knew him, he from around these parts?"

Jacob shook his head. "He was a no good who worked some odd jobs around town, probably one of them fellas ya see but pay little if any attention to."

Andrew nodded, trying to put a face to the name, but quickly gave up.

"Did Rebecca tell ya about the Home Guard visiting her?" asked Jacob.

Andrew could not remember that in any of her letters. "No, she failed to mention any of that, was everyone all right?"

"They scared the hell out of her and the children. Said they's looking for that slave of yours?" Jacob smiled, looking proud. "My Becky's a tough little gal. She told `em all what for."

Andrew smiled, remembering her temper. "I can imagine." He pictured her letting loose on the Home Guard and them backing away, and then he asked about his other slave Matthew.

Jacob told him that Matthew, his family, and the other Negro woman and her two boys were all working hard around the place, as was Jed and Andrew's children. He went on to say that he ought to be proud of `em all.

Andrew knew that was truthful and sat back, proud of his family.

Jacob broke the silence. "Ain't none of my business Andrew, but I'd like to know what your intentions are with my Rebecca?"

Surprised at that, Andrew looked up the road, considering Jacob's words and Rebecca's letters.

"Sorry, Andrew, it's just that I know my gal has a lot of feelings for the children, and her ma tells me she's always had feelings for you."

Andrew shifted nervously in the seat. "Well, truth is, I was never really sure about all that. Remember, I've been gone a spell, and while we did write, we never discussed anything permanent. Not that I hadn't thought about it over the months, mind you." Andrew paused, glanced at Jacob, and then back at the road. "Jacob, you been a good friend of mine for a long time, and to be truthful, I do have feelings for your Rebecca, and well, I just never knew if it was a proper thing or not."

Several moments passed in silence, and then Jacob reached over and patted Andrew's knee. "It's proper if it's ok between you and Rebecca. Personally, there ain't another man in the county I'd rather see her with, if that means anything."

Andrew grinned. "Means a lot, Jacob. Means a hell of a lot, and I thank you for saying it." Andrew looked up the road, wishing Jacob would slap the horses on their backside and get him home faster.

It seemed to Andrew that the ride was taking forever, but in time, they reached the driveway to his farm. "You don't need to go any further, Jacob."

Jacob pulled the team up and set the brake. "You sure, Andy? I can take you right up to your door."

"I need the walk." Then Andrew held out his open hand.

Jacob took it and squeezed. "Glad to have you home, Andy."

"Don't fret none about Rebecca," Andrew said as he got down and gathered his belongings. "She's not the only one's got feelings."

Jacob grinned, gently slapped the team with the reins, and drove away. Andrew stood at the end of the driveway for a few moments watching Jacob guide his wagon along the dirt road just as light snow began to fall. The sun had set, and it was getting dark as he turned and started walking toward the house, thinking the place looked different. Andrew was not sure if it had changed, or he had, but everything seemed different in some way, and he didn't know how or why. As he walked through the gate onto the driveway toward the house, the snow became heavier. He glanced around the familiar fields and outbuildings, and then his eyes found the trees that shaded Rachel's grave, and he decided he would visit her in the morning.

The falling snow lightly covered the fields that Daniel had run across while chasing him and Aaron the day he had left for the war. Looking at the house in the distance with its yellow and orange windows that threw reflections on the thin layer of snow, it looked warm and inviting. Approaching the house, shadows moved back and forth across the lace curtains. Moments later, his head and shoulders covered with snow, he stood at the porch listening to the laughter inside, able to pick out Daniel's voice yelling at his older brother. He smiled, thinking that some things never changed. Afraid to knock, he listened a moment longer to the sounds coming from within as if to prepare himself. His heart pounded with anticipation as he took a deep breath, blew it out in a sigh, and knocked on the faded door of peeling paint.

Rebecca opened the door and stood in the doorway, staring at him. Tears welled in her eyes as she looked at Andrew's familiar unshaven face and the snow on his shoulders. She said his name just above a whisper, threw her arms around his neck, and yelled. "Y'all's pa is home!"

As he stepped inside the house he had left so long ago, the children gathered around him, with each one fighting for a hug. He grinned as they pushed at one another, arguing whose turn it was. He closed the door, shutting out the war and the rest of the world for a while, and looked at Rebecca. Wanting to tell her so many things, he listened instead to his children as they fought for his attention.

Eighteen

September 1862

James Riley Chrisman

Harpers Ferry

With the end of The Second Battle of Bull Run, the Union army withdrew from Manassas, Virginia, while the Confederate army marched north into West Virginia. At a place called Harpers Ferry, Confederate and Union forces fought bitterly from September 12 through September 15, 1862, in some of the campaign's fiercest fighting. Despite suffering heavy losses of 8,000 men, the Confederate army pursued the retreating Union forces from Harpers Ferry to Sharpsburg. As both armies dug in near a place called Antietam, James thought about Allen and his friend Charlie Hogan who had died at Harpers Ferry.

Battle of Sharpsburg

September 17, 1862

A chilly dawn of gray clouds greeted September 17, 1862, as Confederate and Union armies engaged in bitter fighting that lasted for two days. The battle for Sharpsburg, at Antietam, Maryland, was the first engagement fought on Union soil and became a turning point of the war. It was a battle so bitterly fought that it unsettled and shocked both sides and proved very costly to both armies.

The 47th Alabama suffered heavy losses with every commissioned officer and 115 enlisted men killed by mid-day of September 18, 1862. James and sixteen other men, led by the only sergeant left alive, fought gallantly near Miller's cornfield until late afternoon. Weary, hungry, and out of ammunition, they found themselves surrounded, having no recourse but to lay down their weapons. They raised their hands and surrendered, tasting the bitterness of defeat.

On the morning of September 20, 1862, a prisoner exchange made it possible for James and the others to rejoin the Confederate army that was ordered to the Rappahannock River in Virginia for rest. The 47th would be reinforced to full strength by January 1863, and in mid-February 1863, the 47th Alabama marched into Suffolk, Virginia, and saw little or no action for several months. During this time of rest, James became very ill with a fever in March 1863 and was placed in a field hospital.

Tallapoosa County, Alabama

March 1863

The Chrisman Farm

March 1863 was a wet and muddy month on the Chrisman farm, and after a hard day's work, his supper eaten, and his chores done, Davy Chrisman was in the barn rubbing down James's black mare as he had promised James when he left for the war. The sun had long since set, and the barn was quiet except for an occasional appreciative snort from the mare and the soft sound of the brush in Davy's hand making its way along the mare's neck and back.

A noise somewhere outside caused Davy to turn and peer out the big open doors into the night, straining both eyes and ears. After several seconds of hearing only silence, he returned to the brush and the mare. He was thinking of James, hoping he was all right, when he heard his name called in a whisper. He stopped, turned toward the door, placed the horse brush on a nearby ledge, and cautiously walked out of the barn into the cool, night air. Standing just outside the door in the light of the lantern inside, he strained his eyes, searching the darkness. "Who's there?"

"Hey Davy," came the whispered voice once again.

Davy stepped back, thinking of the pitchfork on the wall near the open doors. "Who's there?"

"Davy, it's me, Allen Downs."

Surprised, Davy took a few cautious steps toward the sounds, searching the darkness. "Where are ya, Allen?"

"Over here."

Davy looked in the direction of a nearby oak tree just as Allen Downs stepped out from behind it. Surprised at seeing Allen, he ran the short distance. "What the hell you doing here, Allen? You're supposed to be with James in the army."

Allen glanced around, looking frightened. "I ran away, Davy."

Davy looked worried. "You deserted?"

Allen nodded, looking ashamed. "Yeah." He sat down with his back against the tree.

Davy glanced around, feeling worried and thinking of the Home Guard, and then sat down next to him. "When?"

"A few months back, sometime in August."

"August," said Davy looking perplexed. "Where the heck you been these past months?"

Allen told him how he had managed to hide from Union and Confederate soldiers, stealing food and sleeping under bushes, in barns, or anywhere he could. Of being afraid of everyone and every sound until he got home, and even then, he was still afraid. His ma and pa had hidden him in their fruit cellar, but his pa was afraid the Home Guard would find him and possibly hang them all. So, they decided he should hide out in the fruit cellar at the old Rupert place.

Davy knew the spot, remembering how he and some of the other boys used to ride out there searching for ghosts before the war.

Allen glanced around, searching the darkness. "Yah can't see the place until yer right on top of it." He paused and looked at Davy. "Have any of them Home Guard been around here looking fer me?"

Davy glanced toward the house, the barn, and then into the darkness of the fields. "They ain't been on the place in a while, but we see `em riding by once in a while." Davy grinned. "Pa sure hates `em, says they're nothing but a bunch of cowards too afraid to fight unless it's against old men, women, and children."

Allen chuckled. "I can just picture your pa saying that." He glanced around, looking fearful. "I best be get'n back, Davy. I only stopped by to see if'n y'all have heard from James, and if'n he's all right."

Davy glanced around once again. "Pa got a letter just the other day saying he was someplace in Virginia resting. Said he and some other fellas ran out of ammunition and were captured last September but got traded for some Union soldiers."

Allen smiled, looking happy as he picked up a rock and threw it. "Good, he's still alive." He looked up into the night sky and stars, feeling remorse. "Sure wish I'd stayed with James."

Davy looked puzzled. "Why'd you leave Allen?"

Allen shrugged, looking ashamed. "Got scared, I guess. I never saw so much kill'n, b'fore, Davy!" He paused. "I never thought it'd be like that. It was terrible."

Davy could see the fear in his eyes, even in the dim light.

"Men were screaming, yell'n and cussing at one another," said Allen. "The ground was covered in blood and guts, and everyone was trying to kill the other. Damn, Davy, it were awful."

"Why don't you just go back?"

"I thought on that, but it's too late. They'd jist hang me anyways, and I surely don't wanna get hung."

Davy took pity on him, knowing he must be afraid of staying all alone up at the Rupert place. "Maybe I can come to see you now and then."

"No," said Allen looking scared. "Don't ever come out there. You might be followed." He sat up, looking afraid. "Promise me you won't come out there."

"But I could bring you some fruit and stuff, or even news about James," argued Davy.

Allen slapped his hands against his legs, feeling afraid as he looked at Davy. "No! Ya got to promise me you won't come out there."

Davy could hear the fear in his voice. "I promise."

"I best get back," Allen said as he stood from the tree. "Don't go telling anyone ya saw me, not even your ma and pa."

"I won't," promised Davy, and then he watched Allen disappear into the darkness.

The month of March gave way to April, and Davy kept his promise to Allen. On the other hand, Allen kept regular late-night visits with Davy at the Chrisman barn, where Davy would give him food and news about James.

May 1863

Davy Chrisman and his friend Emmett Heard (cousin to Martha Heard) were sitting on the Chrisman front porch enjoying a lazy Sunday afternoon talking about things young boys talk about. Emmett's family owned the land next to the Chrisman's, so the boys naturally spent a lot of time together, especially during the summer months. Louisa Heard had brought the boy over to spend a week with Davy and had decided to stay for Sunday dinner and visit with Elizabeth. William Chrisman sat in his rocking chair listening to the two boys, remembering his own childhood on lazy Sunday afternoons with his brothers back in Kentucky. It was times such as this that he missed his family, though the bitterness of his leaving still hung heavy in his memory.

The peaceful afternoon on the porch was interrupted by two riders who turned from the county road onto the Chrisman property and rode toward the house at a slow trot. William got up as fast as his hip and body would allow and stood next to his chair, telling Davy to go inside and get his pistol from the library.

Davy did as he was told and handed the pistol to his Pa. "Who's that Pa?"

William spit into the rose bush next to the porch. "Damn, Home Guard. Everyone be quiet, I'll do the talking."

Davy thought of Allen as he and Emmett stood next to William.

As the riders approached, Elizabeth, Beth, Emmett's mother Louisa, and her other two children stepped onto the porch and watched them in silence.

William yelled, "Be careful about the bushes and plants there, Bishop!"

The two riders halted their horses just short of the lawn and shrubs and sat in silence until their dust settled around the horses' hooves. The smaller of the two turned to the other, telling him to mind the flowers, and then he turned to Elizabeth. "Sorry, Mrs. Chrisman, howdy Will, Davy." Then he nodded at Emmett.

"What's on your mind?" asked William.

As if he hadn't heard William, he looked at Beth. "Good afternoon Beth."

She nodded in silence.

Then he looked at Mrs. Heard. "How's yer husband?"

"All right, I reckon," said Mrs. Heard coldly.

These days the men of the Home Guard were accustomed to such greetings.

Not in the mood for conversation, William asked, "What's on your mind, Bishop?"

Bishop Martin was a small man standing just over five feet four inches, a little heavy around the chest and gut. Unfriendly, dark eyes peered from under bushy eyebrows, and his heavy, dark brown beard hid most of his acne-scarred face. Greasy, dark hair bulged from under a broad, dusty brown hat that had seen better days. If he wasn't so mean and dirty looking, he might be on the comical side. But then there was nothing comical about Bishop Martin, and Will thought Bishop was nothing like his late pa, who had been his best friend.

Martin leaned forward, resting his forearms on the saddle horn. "Still looking for that young Downs boy." He glanced around the yard and outbuildings, looking thoughtful. "We figure he's holed up someplace close to home."

Will looked at the two with a puzzled face. "Y'all figure the boy's hiding out on my place?"

Bishop grinned. "Yah never know, Will. Ya may not even know it."

William spit into the rose bush. "I think I'd know if someone were hiding on my place, Bishop. I ain't stupid."

Bishop grinned. "Never said you were Will." Then he looked at Davy. "You ain't seen `em, have ya, Davy?"

Davy's heart skipped a beat.

"The boy doesn't know anything," responded William.

Bishop gave him a dirty look. "Twern't ask'n' you, I's ask'n' the boy there."

William met Bishop's dirty look with one of his own. "I told you the boy doesn't know anything."

Bishop gave William a long gaze and then looked at young Emmett Heard. "How about you, boy, seen any deserters hiding around these parts?"

Emmett shrugged, looking innocent. "No, I ain't seen none."

Bishop looked at Davy. "How old are you, boy?"

"Fifteen," Elizabeth answered while stepping closer to her son and putting her arm around his shoulders. "You should know that much, Bishop. He's gone to school with your little cousin, Jessica."

"Didn't mean no disrespect Lizabeth," Bishop said with a nervous laugh.

"Could be the boy's older and just a mite slow," said Ben Rogers, the other Home Guard.

"The boy's fifteen," responded William. "And I'm sure he's not as slow as you, Ben."

Ben Rogers stopped laughing and stared at William as he moved his horse closer to the porch. "Careful there Will." Ben Rogers was the bigger of the two, standing just over five feet nine, scruffy-looking with red, bushy hair flowing frantically from under an old, dirty, beat-up military hat. He leaned forward in his saddle, forced a smile, exposing a gap between his front teeth, his dirty freckled face in need of both a washcloth and razor.

William gestured toward the yard. "Told you boys to stay off my missus' bushes."

Bishop settled back in his saddle, enjoying this, and waited to see what Ben would do next.

Beth walked to the porch railing and looked at Bishop Martin. "You're a brave one, Bishop." She had hated Bishop Martin ever since school when he and some other boys had chased her home, calling her a dirty filthy Indian. She placed both hands on the porch railing and leaned forward with a mocking smile. "But if I remember correctly, you and them others always were brave until James had that little talk with y'all."

He remembered all right. "James ain't around now, is he?"

William had quietly lifted his gun over the railing and pointed it toward them. "No, James ain't here right now, Bishop, but I am."

"He's got a gun," warned Ben Rogers, backing his horse up a few steps.

Bishop raised his hands. "Hold on, Will. We were just having a little fun. All we're trying to do is our duty, which is looking for deserters and runaway slaves. We happen to know that Allen Downs is a friend of James, and we thought---

William cut him off. "What's that got to do with my place?"

Ben looked at the gun, considering the man who held it, and grinned. "Hell, Will, we just think he may try and hide out on familiar territory, that's all, and maybe Davy there's seen `im."

William chuckled without humor. "Your duty. My wife done told both y'all, our son here doesn't know anything." He paused. "And I'll tell you one more thing, Bishop: if Davy here were old enough, he'd be with his brother James this very day and not pissing away his time riding around the county aggravating old men and scaring the womenfolk." The clicking of the hammer was loud in the stillness of the porch

The two men looked at the pistol in William's hand, wondering if he'd pull the trigger.

Beth put her arms on Davy's shoulder and gently pulled him away from their father while Elizabeth did the same with Emmett.

Ben Rogers smiled as he raised his hands. "Take it easy, Will. We didn't come out here to start no trouble. We's just asking some questions and having a little fun."

William gestured toward the county road with his gun. "Funs over, now get off my land."

Bishop Martin looked at William with a nervous smile. "All right, Will, no hard feelings." He and Ben backed their horses away from the porch and turned them toward the county road.

Elizabeth was furious with William as she walked across the porch. "You could have gotten us killed with that damn gun."

He glanced at her and then back at the two riders. "Not likely, Mother," he said softly. "Not likely. They's a couple of cowards."

Elizabeth shook her head in anger, turned, and followed Mrs. Heard into the house.

Beth watched the two men until they rode off the Chrisman property and onto the county road, then turned and looked at Davy before she went inside.

Wondering if Beth knew about Allen, Davy looked at his father as he slowly let the hammer down on his gun and set it on the table next to his rocking chair. As William sat down, Davy felt a sense of pride in his pa, wishing James had been here to see how their pa handled the Home Guard. Looking back toward the road and the dust they left, Davy worried about Allen being all alone at the ruins. "Be back in a minute," he told Emmett. "I'm going upstairs."

Emmett watched Davy disappear into the house then sat down on the porch railing next to William. "Think they'll be coming back, Mr. Chrisman?"

"Can't say for sure, Emmett, but it ain't likely, leastways not for a while."

Upstairs in his bedroom, Davy looked out the window in the direction of the old ruins, thinking that he had to warn Allen.

Beth walked in, closed the door, walked across the room, stopped next to Davy, and looked where he was staring.

Davy turned from the window and looked at his sister. "What's wrong, Sis?"

Beth's dark eyes looked accusing. "You know something about Allen. Now, what is it?"

"I don't know anything, Beth."

She could tell he was lying. "Davy," she said, stepping closer. "I know you better than ya know yourself. I always could read you and James like a book."

His shoulders slumped as he sat down on the edge of his bed, staring down at the floor. "I know where Allen is."

Scared for her brother, she sat on the bed next to him. "What? Where is he?"

Remembering his promise, he stared at the floor, refusing to talk.

Beth put her hand under his chin, turned his face toward her with an understanding look, and spoke in a soft voice. "Davy, where's Allen?"

"I can't tell you, Beth," he said, looking afraid. "I promised."

"Davy, you have to. Is he all right?"

"Yeah, he's all right. He's hiding in the fruit cellar of that old place up in the woods."

"The old Rupert place?" she asked, looking surprised.

Davy nodded. "He's scared, Beth."

She looked out the window in the direction of the ruins, considering that, and the Home Guard. "He's got a right to be scared." She looked at her brother. "And so should you. Does Emmett know?"

He shook his head. "No."

"How long has Allen been home?"

"Don't know for sure. He was hiding in the cellar at home, but his ma and pa were afraid the Home Guard would find him and kill `em all. So, they made him hide out there all by himself." He looked sorrowful. "Has nothing to do out there except sit and wait until his ma takes him food and stuff."

"Have you ever gone up there?"

He shook his head no. "Allen comes to that old oak tree by the barn sometimes at night, and I give him some bread and what news I can about James."

Beth looked irritated as she stood. "I can't believe this. I have to go downstairs and help ma with supper." She started toward the door, stopped, and turned. "You stay away from Allen. You hear me, Davy, stay away from him."

"You gonna tell where Allen is?"

She considered that. "No need worry'n' ma and pa about this right now. They've enough on their minds worrying over James getting killed in this damn war."

May 1863

The 47th Alabama

Somewhere in southern Virginia

James walked into the captain's tent, saluted, and then stood at attention. "You wanted to see me, Captain?"

The captain returned the salute, eyed him for a moment, and said, "That I did, Private, how ya feeling, boy?"

Curious as to why the captain had sent for him, he nodded. "Better, I guess, sir, still having a hard time keeping food down. Can't seem to shake whatever it is I have."

The captain pointed to one of two folding canvas chairs. "Sit down, Son." He waited for James to sit down. "When was the last time you were home, Private?"

James thought a moment. "A year ago, sir, when I enlisted."

The captain looked at him thoughtfully, noticing the darkness under his eyes. "The doc's been talking to me about you and a few others, and he's of the mind that some home cooking's about the only thing that'll get rid of whatever it is that's ailing you."

"Sir?" replied James, not fully understanding.

The captain smiled as he took two steps to a small folding table that was substituting for a desk, picked up some papers, and looked at James as if considering what to do next. "At the good doctor's request, I just signed some orders giving you three weeks at home." He paused for a reaction, and seeing James was surprised, he smiled. "We're moving out tomorrow, and so's the hospital. It seems the doc thinks you and a few others are in no condition to come along on a long, forced march. Thinks you might be a burden."

James considered that in silence, wondering if he could manage a long march.

The captain handed James a train pass and papers that included a pass through the Confederate lines. He extended an open hand. "Good luck, Son."

Feeling a little confused but glad to be going home, James stood, took the papers, and shook the captain's hand. He turned to leave but paused and turned, looking worried. "How'll I know where to find the unit, sir?"

"When you're ready," said the captain. "Check with the local authorities to see if they know where we are; I'm sure they'll know. I suggest you go pack. You have a train to catch."

Tallapoosa County

The Chrisman farm

Elizabeth paused from her cooking. "Nancy, go tell your brother and Emmett to come down for breakfast." Then she shook her head, looking flustered. "Them two boys would sleep the day away if we let `em."

Nancy turned and ran upstairs, knocked on Davy's door, and waited for a response. When none came, she knocked a little harder, waited a minute, and slowly opened the door, calling his name. Finding the room empty, she ran downstairs. "Ma, they's gone."

Elizabeth turned from the stove, looking worried. "What do you mean, gone?"

"Gone, Ma," she said, looking perplexed. "Davy's room is empty."

Beth was overcome by fear as she looked out the kitchen window knowing that Davy had broken his promise and had taken Emmett with him to warn Allen. She headed for the kitchen door. "I'll check the barn. They may be taking care of James's horse."

Elizabeth stood at the window gripped with fear, and watched Beth as she ran down the back steps and across the yard toward the barn.

Just then, William walked into the kitchen. "What's so important out the window, Mother?"

She turned with fear on her face. "Emmett and Davy's gone."

"Maybe they're somewhere's outside," he said, trying to ease her fear. "The barn, maybe."

For reasons she could not explain, Elizabeth was uneasy as she saw Beth run out of the barn toward the house. "Here comes Beth." Then she turned to her husband. "It ain't likely those two are in the barn."

Worried, William walked to the window. "Where would they be?" He stood next to his wife, looking out the window at Beth as she hurried toward the house. "Now, Mother," he said softly. "Let's not let ourselves get worked up until we know something. They's just boys, and you know how boys can be."

"Ain't like them boys to miss breakfast before doing chores. Something's not right here, Will. I can feel it."

William knew Elizabeth was not one to fret about things, and he also knew it wasn't like Davy to miss out on breakfast and figured they went off somewhere. Trying to hide his concerns, he sat down at the table, poured a cup of coffee, and waited.

Beth ran into the house. "The black mare's gone, and so's your red roan, Ma."

Elizabeth looked at William with a worried look. "Something's wrong, I tell ya."

William stood, thinking his wife may be right. "Where could them boys be off to this early?"

Beth took off her apron. "I think I know." She placed her apron over the back of a chair. "I'll change into a pair of pants and ride out after them." Then she hurried past his chair.

He turned in his chair, "Where to?"

"I'll explain later, Pa," Beth cried out, looking over her shoulder as she disappeared upstairs to her room.

Elizabeth hurried out of the kitchen, following Beth.

William took a quick sip of coffee, got up, and followed as fast as his hip would allow. By the time he got to Beth's room, she had on her riding pants and was tucking in her shirt while her mother was asking where she was going.

William stood in the doorway, looking puzzled. "Just what in the hell's go'n' on here?"

Elizabeth turned to him. "Stop yelling! That's what I've been trying to find out, but your daughter won't tell me anything."

William calmed down and softly said, "My daughter?" He closed the door and stood in front of it so Beth could not leave. "You're not going anywhere, young lady, until you tell your ma and me what the hell's going on around here." He glanced at Elizabeth and then at Beth, who just looked at him, refusing to answer. Unable to control his fear and anger any longer, he raised his voice. "Where's Davy and Emmett gone off to?"

Beth's eyes welled with fear as she sat on the bed, looking worried. "I think Davy and Emmett are with Allen Downs."

William became furious. "What?" He looked from Beth to Elizabeth and then back at Beth. "How the hell would Davy know where he was?"

Elizabeth raised her hand to silence him and, in a calm voice, asked, "How long have you known Allen was home?"

Beth wiped the tears from her face with the backs of her hands as she looked at her mother. "I only found out that day Ben Rogers and Bishop Martin were here. Davy looked like he knew something, so I confronted him in his room after they left."

"How long has Davy known?" asked Elizabeth.

Beth shrugged. "I'm not sure, Ma, a couple of months, I guess."

"You guess?" William asked, moving closer to the bed. He raised his voice in anger. "Where the hell are they?"

Elizabeth looked at him once again while raising her hand, gesturing for silence. "William, stop yelling. Please." She placed one hand on Beth's shoulder, looking sympathetic. "Where are they, Child?"

Beth looked at her mother, sniffled, and wiped her cheeks. "Allen's hiding out at the old Rupert place. Davy says he's been staying in that old cellar."

William threw his hands up and turned toward the window looking in the direction of the Rupert ruins. "Good Lord almighty girl, why didn't you tell us?"

Beth looked up at him with a regretful face. "I wanted to, Pa, but we didn't want to worry you and ma none with the Home Guard coming around." She wiped her face with the back of her hand as she looked at her mother. "I made Davy promise he'd stay away from there."

William knew she felt bad and was not so sure he wouldn't have done the same. He turned from the window, sat on the bed, put his arm around her, and held her. "It's all right, Beth, I guess you did what you thought was best, and I can't fault you for that. It's gonna be all right, girl." He took his arm away and looked into her big, brown, welling eyes. "But right now, go saddle my horse and go after them, boys." He paused. "I'd go myself, but I can't ride hard, and we need to find them fast before someone else does." His face filled with determination. "When you do find `em, you get their little butts back here."

"Yes, Pa," Beth stood, grabbed her riding jacket, ran out of the room, down the stairs, and out of the house to the barn where she saddled William's Chestnut and rode toward the Rupert ruins.

Nineteen

July 1862 - June 1863

Joseph Samuel Greene

Jefferson, Texas – July 1862

Jefferson, Texas, was a thriving river community that sprang up soon after the Louisiana Purchase of 1803, boasting several thousand inhabitants. Like the Big Cypress that flowed into Lake Caddo, Jefferson and its rivers resembled Louisiana and Missouri more than it did the rest of Texas. Large cypress tree forests rich with Spanish moss, tall pines, and hardwood trees housed eagle's nests high above the waterways that were as abundant as sparrow or robin's nests. The city had become an important river port and was often referred to as the river port to the Southwest. Large, bulky bales of cotton grown in neighboring counties lined the docks waiting for transportation by boat to other ports, some destined for Europe. With the great civil war, Jefferson had become the supplier of cotton and meat, hides, food staples, munitions, and leather for the Confederacy.

It was dark when Joseph drove the wagon with Del's saddled horse in tow along the dusty streets of Jefferson, Texas, taking in the view of the Big Cypress River and wharves crowded with cargo and boats. Whistles from the boats and the Big Cypress River's smell brought back memories of the Southern Belle, the Tennessee River, Captain Goodman, and Jonah. Reaching the livery, he pulled up, set the brake, and jumped down from the wagon, looking around for the owner.

A young, skinny man with red hair and dirty clothes walked out of the livery's big open doors. Wiping his hand on a dirty cloth, Josh Harris, the owner, smiled. "See, you made it okay."

"I did." Then seeing that Mr. Harris noticed the horse in tow, Joseph smiled. "Belongs to a friend. Hope you have an empty stall."

"I think we can manage."

Joseph untied the horse and walked it past Josh, who was unharnessing the team of horses from the wagon.

Josh nodded toward the livery. "Any empty stall will do." Then he led the two horses into the livery, putting each in an empty stall.

When Del's horse was unsaddled, and safely in a stall, Joseph turned to Josh Harris and asked about a boarding house.

He thought a moment. "There are several nice places, and if I were looking, I'd head up the street away from the river and the noise of the saloons."

Believing that was good advice, Joseph asked Josh to see his horses got plenty of oats, gave him money for the boarding, said goodnight, and walked out of the livery into the night, engulfed by the sounds and smells of the city. Four blocks later, he happened upon a painted sign hanging over a large paned window reading Manor House. Another sign with bold black letters on white paper hung in the window, reading 'Vacancy.' It had a clean yet inexpensive look about it, and he decided that this one would do. He stepped inside to the sound of a small bell above his head. He closed the door, stood in the deserted lobby containing the usual chairs and small tables, and seeing a counter a few feet away, he walked over and rang the tiny silver bell sitting on the counter.

A plump, middle-aged woman with a kindly face, soft, graying black hair, and friendly green eyes, stepped from between the dark curtains. She was dressed in a black dress with a white shawl over her shoulders. She smiled. "Good evening."

"Good evening to you Madam, I'd like a room."

"I think we can accommodate you, Mr. ..." As she let the sentence die, she gave him a careful look, trying to determine what sort of man he was.

"Greene, Joseph Greene."

She folded her hands on the counter and laid out the rules. "I've a nice place here, Mr. Greene."

He smiled. "I'm sure of it, madam."

"I don't allow drinking or girls upstairs." Her eyes narrowed. "Not that I mind a man having a drink at one of them establishments or playing a game of chance now and again if he chooses to waste his hard-earned money with such things." She paused, waiting for his response, and when none came, she continued. "That's as long as he behaves himself when he's under my roof, and if you've a lady friend, you both stay down here in the parlor just beyond them curtains over there." She pointed toward the parlor across the room. "Gives you and your lady friend enough privacy to talk."

He glanced toward the parlor and then back at her with a serious expression. "Let's see. No drinking upstairs and no ladies either." He smiled. "I'm a married man Mrs. ..." he let the sentence trail off.

She smiled approvingly. "Oh, sorry. Name's Trudy, Trudy Hansen. Married, are ya?" she asked, sounding pleased.

"Yes, ma'am."

Turning the register so he could sign it, she asked, “Where is the Mrs.?”

Picking up the pen, he dipped it in the ink well and signed his name in her register while explaining that his wife and child had stayed with some friends east of town. Setting the pen down, he said that he hoped they would join him later after he found work.

She turned around to a wall of small wooden boxes, each containing a key or set of keys and some letters or notes. “Hmm,” she muttered thoughtfully, more or less to herself. “I think this one here’ll do nicely.” Taking a key from one of the small wooden boxes, she picked up a lantern and walked from behind the counter. “This way, Mr. Greene.”

Joseph bent down, picked up his carpetbag, and followed.

As they walked toward the staircase, she talked over her shoulder. “If I ain’t too nosey for asking, what’s your profession?”

The light from the lantern she carried rushed ahead of them up the dark staircase while Joseph explained his occupation. She answered that her deceased husband had worked on the river, but she offered no explanation of what he had done. She did volunteer that he had died some years ago, not giving the particulars of his death, and Joseph thought it best not to ask. He followed her along the dim, second-floor hallway with its creaking floorboards.

She stopped at door she unlocked and opened. She stepped inside as the room filled with the orange-yellow light of the lantern she held. Mrs. Hansen walked to a small table with one chair, set the lantern down, and lit another lamp.

Joseph stepped into the room, finding a neatly made bed against the far wall separating a chest and dresser. A small stove whose belly was empty sat in one corner by the window with a small bin of firewood. A wardrobe closet stood in the opposite corner, and it all looked very tidy. Seeing but one chair, he understood why no visitors were permitted.

“’Tain’t much,” she said, “probably not what you’re accustomed to, I’m sure, but the bedding’s clean and gets changed once a week. A pitcher of warm water is delivered each morning at your door in a basin with clean towels.” She pointed to the bed. “There’s a mug under the bed for your business if necessary during the night. It gets emptied and cleaned each day.”

Joseph finished his tour of the room and smiled. “Looks fine, Mrs. Hansen, much better than some I’ve stayed in.”

She smiled with pride and then looked toward the window. "I decided you'd prefer a room in the front overlooking the street. Breaks up the boredom a bit, I expect."

"Yes, ma'am, I expect so. Thank you." He set his carpetbag on the bed.

She handed him the key. "I almost forgot. Two meals a day are included in the price of the room. Breakfast is served from 6:30 to 7:30, and dinner from 6:00 to 7:00. Miss them, and you go hungry." She turned toward the door, only to pause with a stern look. "There'll be no cooking on that stove; it's for warmth only." She walked into the hallway and closed the door.

Joseph listened to her footsteps fading down the hall while he looked around the room and then unpacked, got undressed, and climbed between the covers, thinking of tomorrow and about finding a job.

The days turned into weeks while he looked for work between visits to the Hall Farm. He had met with several boat captains presenting the letter of introduction from Captain Goodman, and while several showed an interest, none hired him. As the summer gave way to the shorter days of October, he was still out of work, and when boredom set in, he spent his nights playing poker and drinking. He was lucky at cards, winning enough to keep his stay in Jefferson pleasant, thus not having to worry about his room or meals. He had not been home for several weeks, and the absence of a job made him feel uncomfortable facing Mary, deciding it would be easier to write of his failures on paper, and explaining that interviews and job possibilities kept him in Jefferson. During the evening of October 5, 1862, after having several brandies and winning a rather large sum of money, Joseph announced to the others at the table that he was calling it a night. He pushed his chair away from the table, ignoring their disapproving remarks while he gathered his money.

One of the men leaned forward, placing one hand on Joseph's as he pulled his winnings toward him. "You got an awful lot of our money there, Mister."

He looked at the man. "I believe that's the idea." He pushed the man's hand away. "It's late, and I'm tired!"

The man settled back in his chair, looking angry. "I'd like a chance to win it back."

Joseph pushed his chair under the table with a friendly expression. "Look, friend, you had your opportunities this evening, the same as me. If the cards don't fall, they don't fall." He smiled wryly. "There's always tomorrow night, gentleman. I'm not leaving town, and you'll find me right here. Maybe y'all's luck will be better than mine tomorrow." He turned and handed some money to the waiter, telling him to bring the men at the table a bottle, and then walked toward the door, shoving the money into his inside pocket.

The night air smelled of October as he walked along the empty, wooden sidewalks looking for a dark, empty doorway. Finding one, he looked behind him before stepping into the darkness, where he took most of the money out of his coat pocket, and stuffed it into the tops of his boots. He folded what little he had left into some folded paper that he carried in his coat pocket so that it felt and looked like there was more money than there really was. Then he looked in both directions before stepping into the street beneath a black, star-filled sky and a large October moon. He adjusted his coat around his neck to keep out the chilly night air and crossed the dirt street, careful not to trip in one of the many wagon ruts. Reaching the other side, he scampered up the steps to the wooden sidewalk and paused to glance back into the empty street. The money he had won tonight would allow him to ride home and see Mary and Zach. He smiled, imagining the scene of welcome he would receive.

Aware of footsteps on the boardwalk behind him, he crossed the street without looking back, but as he stepped up onto the boardwalk, he glanced over his shoulder, seeing two figures behind him keeping to the shadows. Fearing it was the two men from the table, he hurried around the next corner, seeing the dim lights of the boarding house lobby just up the street. Reaching the street corner, he quickly glanced back, seeing the street and boardwalks were empty and wondered where the two men were. Breathing a sigh of relief, he jumped from the boardwalk into the street, twisting an ankle in a wagon rut. Getting up, he cursed the wagon rut and never saw the two men until they were on him, hitting and pushing him to the dirt street. He tried to get up, but one of them kicked him in the face, and as he lay stunned, one of them kicked him in the back while the other reached into his coat pocket and took his money. Lying in pain, he watched through blurry eyes as they ran across the dim street and disappeared into an alley.

Thinking they would be back when they discovered just a few bills and blank paper, he slowly got up and limped toward the boarding house. Holding his sore side, fearing he may have a broken rib or two, he hurried up the street. Reaching the steps of the boardwalk in front of the boarding house, he leaned against the post for a moment catching his breath, then managed the three steps to the door only to find the door locked. Remembering Mrs. Hansen telling him she always locked the door at midnight, but the key to his room would also unlock the front door, he fumbled for his key, unlocked the door, and stepped inside the dim lobby. After locking the door, he pulled the curtain back and peered outside. Not seeing anyone on the street or boardwalk, he turned in pain, walked to the stairs and up to his room.

"Mr. Greene," yelled Mrs. Hansen from the hallway. She waited and then knocked again. "Mr. Greene, you awake in there?"

Joseph opened his eyes, glanced at the door, and then sat up on one elbow. "Just a moment, Mrs. Hanson." He tossed the covers off and painfully turned to sit on the edge of the bed, bent over in pain.

"You okay in there?" called out Mrs. Hansen.

"Just a moment, Mrs. Hanson." He slowly stood on wobbly legs, holding onto the bed with one hand, his ribs with the other. The pain in his lower back and spine made it difficult to stand upright, but he managed to walk to the door and open it just enough to see Mrs. Hansen's face.

"Breakfast is ready." Upon seeing his bruised face, she grimaced. "Glory be Joseph, are ya sure you're alright?"

"I'm fine, Mrs. Hansen."

"Would you like me to fetch Doc Bradley and the Sheriff?"

"No, I'm just a little sore, that's all. I'll be all right, but thanks all the same." He started to close the door, but she pushed her way into the room. Wearing only the bottoms to his long underwear, he was embarrassed, but he was in no shape to resist. "I'm not exactly dressed."

"I've seen men in their underwear or stark naked more times than I can remember, so put that thought out of your head." With one hand, she took his chin and moved his face from one side to the other, making those titch, titch sounds women make while shaking her head. "Now see here, Joseph Greene," she said, looking concerned. "You're hurt." She turned his face toward the window for a better look and then gently pushed him toward the bed. "Now sit down here, and let me take a better look at you,"

"I'm all right," he persisted. "Really, I am."

"Sure ya are," she said, looking skeptical. "Now you listen here, Joseph. I'm always right in my own house." She gestured toward the window. "Out there it may be different, but in here, I'm always right."

He was tired, sore, and recognized a lost argument, feeling a bit like a child getting a scolding from his mother. So, he sat on the edge of the bed while she had herself a look at the cuts and bruises.

She fussed over him for several seconds, smelling of soap and breakfast mixed with cheap perfume. She shook her head, making that titch sound again with her mouth, and then walked through the door to retrieve the pitcher and towels that had been placed outside in the hallway. She carried them to the dresser and poured some water from the pitcher into the basin. She dipped a towel into the water and began gently cleaning his face of dried blood. "You bled all over my pillowcase and sheets, young man."

"Be glad to pay for the trouble."

Insulted by the offer, she paused. "Did ya hear me asking to be paid?"

He looked at her with one eye, the other being swollen shut. "No, ma'am."

"I've cleaned up worse messes than this one. Besides, there's something in ya that reminds me of my late Lyle."

"He get beat up and robbed too?"

She laughed, finding humor in that. "Several times, I'm afraid." She paused in memory. "Yes, sir, my Lyle was robbed more than once over the years." Her cloth filled hand returned to the chore of cleaning off more dried blood. "Mind telling me what happened?"

"Not much to tell."

"Hmm," she said, looking doubtful. "From the looks of you and your clothes, there's a lot to tell."

Joseph looked up at her kindly face filled with resolve for the task at hand. "Got robbed," he said with a shrug.

She stopped and looked at him with a frown. "I know that much." She continued looking through his hair for more blood. Finding none, she tossed the towel onto the table and sat down in the room's one chair. "Jefferson used to be a nice place to live," she said thoughtfully. "But then, the town started growing and became enterprising, and with that came the riff-raff, all looking to make a quick fortune. Somehow they all manage to stay out of the war, which if ya ask me is where they belong." She picked up a clean towel, stood, and gently patted the dampness from his face. "Know who they were?"

"Not sure, as it was too dark, but I've my suspicions."

"How much they get?" she asked, then quickly apologized. "Maybe I'm getting too nosey for an old lady."

"I hid most of it inside my boots, so all they got for their trouble was some blank paper I always carry wrapped with a few dollars."

She chuckled. "Smart."

Thinking of Captain Goodman, Joseph said, "Something I learned from an old man on the Tennessee River a long time ago."

"Hmm," she said thoughtfully, "My Lyle came home one night, all beat up and robbed. A lot worse off than you, I'm afraid." Sadness filled her face. "I thought I'd lost him for sure, but he was a tough one." She smiled proudly. "Yes, sir, took more than a beating to do him in." She gestured toward Joseph's boots. "Too bad he didn't think about putting his money in his boot, but then again, I don't suppose he was as worldly as you are, Joseph." With that, she stood, pushed the chair under the table, and looked him over, seemingly satisfied with her nursing deed. She picked up the towels and pan, and then walked to the door where she paused. "You hungry?"

"Some."

"Now, you just stay put; I'll bring ya up a plate and some coffee. Don't reckon you're much in the mood to answer a lot of questions from the others."

"Not particularly Mrs. Hanson, and thanks for cleaning me up."

"Ah, that twern't nothing," She smiled. "Breaks the morning routine a bit. The truth of it is I ain't had to do that since my Lyle." She winked. "I enjoyed the memory. I'll bring up the morning paper, such as it is, with your breakfast."

After she closed the door, Joseph lay back on the bed, thinking of the previous night. As his thoughts turned to Mary and his son, he decided he would leave for home as soon as possible. Joseph got out of bed, put on his shirt and pants and sat down on his bed with his back against the brass headboard, and waited. Several minutes passed, and then came a knock on the door, and before he could speak, the door opened.

Mrs. Hansen entered with a tray of food and the morning paper which she set on the table. "After you eat, I'll gather up your dirty clothes and see what I can do with `em."

"Thanks, but you needn't bother."

She shook her head, looking annoyed. "You men are all alike. You go out, get drunk, get beaten up, and then turn down the help offered by those who care. Tain't no bother Joseph, that's what we women do: clean up after you men." She picked up his coat and looked at the pocket thoughtfully. "I ain't so sure I can patch this tear. It looks like it goes right down the lining."

"It's an old coat anyway, Mrs. Hanson." He looked over the breakfast of eggs and potatoes, smelling the aroma of strong coffee.

"It won't kill ya, Joseph, go on and eat." She sat down on the edge of the bed. "I cleaned up after my own man for many years before he died." She paused a moment in memory, looking down at Joseph's coat lying across her lap. "Lyle got his chest crushed, and his lung punctured out there on the Big Cypress."

Joseph paused from eating, looking surprised and not sure what he should say.

Suddenly she stood, opened the door, and looked back at him. "As I told ya earlier, something in you reminds me of my Lyle. Like you, he was a damn stubborn fool." She smiled again in memory. "Right till the end. I'll be back for them dirty clothes."

Joseph ate his breakfast, shaved, dressed in clean clothes, and went downstairs, finding Mrs. Hansen in the parlor sitting on the sofa, putting the last stitch on the inside pocket to his coat.

She looked up. "Just about finished," she said, looking proud, then bit the thread in two. "Good as new almost, or close to, anyways. You're lucky it's on the inside and not all that noticeable." She stood. "Looks like you're on your way out, so I'll just go up and get the rest of your clothes and see they're cleaned along with this here coat."

"Thank you. I was wondering if we could have a few words."

"Sounds a mite serious." She pointed toward the sofa. "Have a seat." After they sat down, Mrs. Hanson folded her hands and looked at him the way women do when you're about to confess something. "You're going home for a spell, aren't you?"

He nodded and smiled. "For a few weeks."

"Good," she said, looking pleased. "You're a smart man Joseph, smarter than most anyways. I'm sure your Mrs. will be glad to get you back. When are you planning on leaving?"

"Tomorrow morning, I hope."

"I'll be sure and have your clothes back by then. Are you coming back?"

He nodded. "Yes, ma'am."

They chatted a little longer, and then he excused himself, saying he had to run some errands. After he visited the bank, he passed a little shop, seeing a shawl in the window and thinking Mary would like it, but the shop was closed.

The next morning, Joseph made a quick trip to the livery asking Josh Harris to have his horse ready around noon, and then he visited the dress shop again for the shawl. When he got back to the boarding house, he finished packing, glanced around the room, making sure he had everything, and hurried downstairs with his bags finding Mrs. Hansen standing behind the counter.

She looked up and smiled. "All set to leave, are ya?"

"That I am, Mrs. Hansen."

"Your room will be waiting."

He shook her hand, thanked her for her kindness, and turned to leave, but stopped. "Mind if I ask you a personal question, Mrs. Hansen?"

She looked at him curiously. "I'm not sure, Joseph, just how personal you plan on getting?"

He laughed. "Not that personal, Mrs. Hansen."

"Now that's a bit of relief," she said. "Go on ahead and do your asking."

Joseph dropped his carpetbag on the floor and then leaned on the counter. "You said that your late husband had his lungs crushed."

"That I did."

"Mind if I ask how that happened?"

She stopped what she was doing and filled her lungs, letting out a long, sad, thoughtful sigh. "The riverboat Lyle was working on hit a sandbar, and a crate pinned him against a bale of cotton. He was pretty close to death when they brought him to the little house we had on the other side of Jefferson." She paused, remembering that night while sadness filled her face and eyes. "Poor Lyle," she said affectionately. "He suffered terribly for three days, coughing up blood and wheezing for breath." She paused, looking as if she were about to cry but didn't. "Died in these very arms, he did."

"Sorry, I asked Mrs. Hansen. I didn't mean to bring back any bad memories."

She looked at him and smiled. "Don't be sorry, Joseph. Why Lyle and me, well, we had a good life together, and while we buried three children between here and Pennsylvania all before they was four, our life was full of love and happiness. Each day was filled with wonderful memories, so don't be sorry for asking about a good life." She looked down at what she had been doing. "Now you go see that family of yours. Your room will be waiting for you when you return."

Joseph picked up his bag. "So long, Mrs. Hansen." Then he turned and walked out the door into the October afternoon. The air was unseasonably chilly, and the streets were filled with people going this way and that. He hurried along the boardwalk toward the livery, walking with a slight limp and favoring his twisted ankle. The cut above his eye was a line of dried blood, the skin dark and bruised, the gash on his cheek still oozed a bit, and he briefly considered Mrs. Hansen's advice about seeing a doctor, but there was no time.

Arriving at the livery, finding his horse saddled and ready as he had asked, he tied his bags behind the saddle, thanked Josh Harris, climbed onto the saddle, and rode north toward the Hall farm.

The sun was below the horizon, and darkness gathered around him as he turned from the dirt road toward the familiar house in the distance. Riding up to the front porch, he dismounted, anxiously stepped onto the porch to favor his ankle, adjusted his clothes, and knocked on the door.

Mrs. Hall pulled the window curtain back, peered out, smiled at Joseph, and yelled for Mary, telling her Joseph was here. She opened the door, and as he stepped inside, Mrs. Hall noticed the bruises on his face. "Heavens Joseph, are you alright?"

Before he could explain, Mary hurried in from another room and ran into his arms, kissing one cheek and then the other. After a long hug and tears welling in her eyes, she saw the cuts and bruises on his face. "My God, Joseph," she said, looking worried. "What happened to your face? Are you all right?"

"I'm fine," he told her with a reassuring smile. 'How's Zachery?"

"He's sleeping," replied Mary.

After exchanging greetings with Del and Janice, he admitted being tired after the long ride. He sat at the kitchen table and asked Del if his grandson, Teddy, would take care of the horse.

Del yelled upstairs for his grandson, sat across from Joseph, and looked at his bruised face. "We're all curious about what happened."

Mary poured him a cup of coffee while listening to the story of the robbery and beating.

Del shook his head and puffed his pipe thoughtfully as the smoke floated lazily above his head. "Jefferson's got a little mean since the war began."

Joseph thought of Mrs. Hansen. "So, I've been told."

Janice stood, looked at Joseph, and smiled. "I bet you're starved."

He yawned. "I'm more tired than hungry, Mrs. Hall." Then, noticing that Ethan's wife was missing, he asked, "Where's Lori?"

"Up in her room, sleeping," replied Del. "She hasn't been feeling all that good lately."

Joseph looked concerned. "Nothing serious, I hope?"

Janice shook her head and looked toward the stairs leading up to Lori's room. "I think she worries too much about Ethan if ya ask me." She looked at Joseph. "Much the way your Mary worries about you. Now you sit here, and I'll get you a piece of pie and another cup of coffee."

Joseph protested, but Janice ignored him and went about the business of slicing the pie and refilling his cup.

Mary stood closer and examined the cuts and bruises on his face. "These need cleaning."

Reluctantly, he settled back and allowed Mary to clean the small amount of blood that had dried around the wounds during his ride from Jefferson.

Janice set a small plate of pie on the table in front of Joseph

Joseph took another drink of coffee and then cut through the thick crust with his fork and took a bite, enjoying the flavor. As he ate, he talked about Jefferson, saying he liked the city.

Mary looked surprised. "How can you say that after being beaten and robbed?"

"There's always a few idiots, Mary. Even Florence had its share." Then he told Mary about the many boats on the lakes and rivers and his surprise at the difficulty in finding a position on one.

The conversation turned from his wounds and Jefferson to the war, and when he finished the pie, he sat back in his chair and pushed the empty plate away.

Realizing that Joseph looked tired, Del looked at Mary. "I think you best get that man of yours upstairs to bed."

Joseph apologized for being tired, thanked Janice for the pie and coffee, said goodnight to Del, and then followed Mary upstairs.

Joseph opened his eyes, looking at an unfamiliar wall, glanced around the room, and remembered he was at the Hall farm before looking at the empty pillow next to his. Wondering where Mary was, he put his head on her pillow that still carried her favorite perfume and thought of her warm, soft body as they had made love the night before. An unfamiliar rooster crowed good morning as Del's dogs barked, and the cows argued, interrupting his thoughts of Mary.

The dull sound of footsteps and muffled voices below made their way upstairs, accompanied by the smell of breakfast. Memories of his father's farm with its hard work, disappointments, and hardships crept into his mind, and he hoped everyone back home on the farm were okay.

Mary walked into the room carrying a cup of coffee, and as she handed it to him, she cautioned that it was hot. Then she smiled. "Don't get used to this."

He grinned as he took the coffee. "Why not?"

"I only wanted to show you that I've missed you."

Still grinning, he looked at her. "I got that message last night."

She raised her brow and whispered, "You almost fell asleep and missed my message."

Taking a sip of coffee, Joseph set the cup down and pulled her down next to him. "I'm not as tired as I was last night. Besides, I was awake long enough."

"Really," she said, looking serious. "Not for very long, and be quiet. Someone will hear us." She got up from the edge of the bed. "You've things to do, Mister Greene, now get up."

Joseph glanced around the room, looking a little confused. "I know I was tired last night, but didn't I have a pair of pants on when I got here? I swore I left them on that chair."

She nodded toward the closet as she started for the bedroom door. "In the closet, where they belong."

"Guess the honeymoon's over," he whispered to himself as the door closed.

In the days that followed, Joseph helped Del prepare for the long winter that lay ahead. Del had no slaves, so he and his grandson Teddy and two other teenage boys named Billy and Ward Jenkins worked the land. The Halls had taken in the two boys about a year ago when their father, who owned the farm next to the Halls, joined the Confederate army. Their mother had died while giving birth to the youngest boy, and their pa had never remarried. Both farms' acreage was small enough that Del and the boys had little problem working both places.

Del and Joseph were busy cleaning out the stables and barn when Joseph told Del that he was considering a small farm after the war. Surprised at first by Joseph's plans, Del told him about a couple of small places that he could probably buy at a reasonable price with the war and all.

Joseph considered the idea for a moment. "Afraid I'm not quite ready yet, Del. This war has to end first. I can't just sit it out. I'm either going to have to join the fight or find something on the river. I don't feel good about just sitting around while others, like your son and Mary's brother, are off someplace fighting."

Del paused, wiped the sweat from his forehead, and looked at Joseph. "I understand yer feelings on that. Hell, I'd go myself if they'd have me, but I'm too damn old. Even the two Jenkins boys are talk'n about going, but I won't let `em." He returned to what he was doing. "Promised their pa I'd keep `em here, and I aim to do just that."

The barn cleaned, they walked outside into the bright sunshine. Joseph wiped his brow, rested his arms on the corral fence, and put one foot on the bottom rail, looking thoughtful. "This whole thing has been weighing pretty heavy on me, Del. Seems I'd best make up my mind pretty soon." He paused to look around. "Don't want to have to explain myself to any recruiter."

Del stood beside Joseph and watched two mules in the corral sleeping in the sun resembling statues. "Taint none of my business, but if you're looking for a little advice---"

"Nothing wrong with a little advice now and then," interrupted Joseph, being glad for any encouragement he could get.

Del retrieved his empty pipe from his shirt pocket, placed it in his mouth, and sucked air through it. "Speak just the same as I would to Ethan if he were here."

Joseph turned, leaned his back against the corral, and looked out across the land.

"No one knows how long this here war's gonna last," Del said. "But once it is over, people are gonna have to get on with their lives. Make a living, having kids." He shrugged. "Same as before the war." He began filling his pipe. "I don't rightly know what's right or wrong. You seem like a levelheaded sort, and you're the one that has to figure out what's best for you. There's plenty of land out there for sale you could pick up cheap now and work it after the war."

Joseph knew Del was right. "Money's the problem. Ain't no one gonna make me a loan with this war going on."

"And ya might be right about that." Del struck a match on the corral post and then touched it to the tobacco in his pipe, and as he puffed it, small clouds of white smoke floated up past his head. Holding the pipe between his teeth, he looked at the two mules that hadn't moved. "You know your Mrs. is welcome to stay with us whether you stay in Jefferson or join up? Mary's good company for Lori and my Mrs. has taken a real liken to that son of yours."

"Thanks, Del," Joseph said, looking appreciative.

Del looked at him, "Guess what I'm trying to say is you do what you think best." Then he started walking toward the barn. "Best check on that horse you'll be needing later if you decided to return to Jefferson."

Joseph slept very little that night, replaying his and Del's conversation over in his mind. Tired of his turning and tossing, Mary sat up. "What's bothering you?"

"Just thinking," he said, staring up at the black ceiling.

"About what?"

He sat up, resting against the headboard, staring into the darkness. "I can't just stay around here and do nothing. Eventually, someone's gonna start asking questions about why I ain't in the war."

Mary pushed herself onto her elbows. "There's plenty of men I bet that aren't in the war."

"I don't care about them, Mary. Besides, most have legitimate reasons."

"I don't want you off fighting in this war, Joseph. I'm sorry, but I can't see where one more life will make any difference."

"It's not that simple, Mary."

"Wouldn't farming be a good enough reason for not going?"

He thought about that as he stared into the night beyond the window. "The problem with that line of thinking is we don't own a farm; we're staying with friends."

She considered that. "Well then, what about the boats and the river?"

"Mary, I've been looking for work, and there just ain't any right now."

The room filled with silence while their minds overflowed with solutions, but none seemed to solve their problem. Joseph turned and took her hand. "I'll ride back into Jefferson and try the river again. But if I don't find a boat, I'll have to join up. I can't sit around while others like your brother and Ethan are off somewhere getting shot at."

She sat up thinking about all that. "You could go to Florence and ask Alex for a loan against my inheritance. In six months, I'll turn twenty-five."

Joseph considered that but quickly decided against the idea. "Even if Alex was agreeable, I don't want to ask for a loan on your inheritance. That wouldn't change things right now anyway because we're still in this damn war."

Mary thought about that. "Maybe you're right," she said, shrugging. "I'm not sure how Alex would accept such a visit. He can be very funny at times." She frowned, shaking her head. "Especially about family money." Then she chuckled. "Can't you just picture the look on Alex's face while you asked him for money from my inheritance?"

Joseph laughed as he mimicked Alex puffing on a cigar and then taking a drink of Edward's brandy. They laughed, and then Joseph put his arm around her, and they huddled together on the bed in the darkness. Each was busy with their own thoughts, his of work, and hers of fear of losing him to the war. The room was silent, peaceful, and dark, the bed soft and warm, as was Mary's body. He kissed her, she put her arms around him, and they melted into one another under the warmth and safety of the covers.

Jefferson, Texas

Joseph returned to Jefferson on the 19th of November 1862, finding work as the second mate aboard the sternwheeler, Isabella. She was not the Southern Belle, and the captain, a man the crew called Iron Mike because of his stubbornness, was no Captain Goodman, but it was a job. During the next several months, the Isabella sailed from Jefferson, along the Big Cypress into Caddo Lake and the port of Shreveport. A few other Confederate boats would risk the voyage south along the Red River to the Mississippi, and then turn north, avoiding New Orleans, which was still under Union control.

Joseph missed Mary's twenty-fifth birthday because of the Confederate army's need for the supplies that the Isabella carried. But he kept his promise to be home when she gave birth to their next child. On the 8th of June 1863, Mary gave birth to a baby boy they named Joseph Samuel Greene Jr. During his stay with Mary and his children, he and Mary decided it was time for a visit with Alex, something Joseph did not look forward to as he left the Hall farm a few days later.

Twenty

May 1863

Tallapoosa, Alabama

The Ruins

Davy Chrisman told Emmett Heard about Allen Downs while they saddled their horses to ride out to the ruins. Riding across the clearing, they slowed to a walk as they rode into the woods near the ruins. Minutes later, Davy stopped and raised one hand with his finger against his lips, signaling Emmett to be quiet.

Emmett nodded his understanding, but still filled with worry, he glanced around.

Davy cautiously nudged the black mare deeper into the woods and soon heard what seemed like angry voices coming from Allen's camp. He pulled up, reached out his hand to stop Emmett. They looked at one another, hoping it was Allen's pa and not the Home Guard. Davy dismounted, waited for Emmett to dismount, and then they led their horses slowly toward the voices, fearing they were about to see the Home Guard. The two boys stopped next to a tree to listen to what sounded like arguing. Davy handed Emmett the reins to the black mare and took a few steps closer to the voices while Emmett quickly tied both horses to the tree and then followed Davy.

Bishop Martin and Ben Rogers were standing over a kneeling, sobbing Allen Downs, who had his hands tied behind his back. Ben slapped Allen's face, calling him a coward, and then Bishop put a boot on the boy's chest, pushing him backward to the ground.

Angered at that, Davy ran into the camp. "Leave him alone!"

Martin turned, surprised at first and then angry. "Thought you didn't know anything, you little bastard!"

Allen yelled a warning. "Get out of here, Davy!"

Rogers turned to Allen. "Shut up ya little deserter."

Bishop saw Emmett Heard standing by the trees a few feet away. "Well, well, there's another liar. Thought ya didn't know anything."

Rogers looked from Emmett to Davy. "I s'pose the two of you just happened along and didn't know this here deserter was camped out here."

Allen's nose was bleeding as he managed to get back up to his knees and look up at Rogers. "They didn't know I was here."

Ben Rogers turned to Allen. "Then what the hell are they doing here?" He looked at Emmett, and then at Davy. "Well, boys, what's y'all's answer to that?"

Davy thought fast. "We were riding up to look around and heard voices." He turned to Emmett. "Ain't that right?"

Afraid to speak and wishing he hadn't come along, Emmett only nodded.

Bishop looked at the two boys. "You boys expect me to believe that?"

Davy was scared and wishing his pa were here. "It's the truth."

Ben Rogers grabbed Davy by the collar of his coat and threw him down to the ground.

Emmett grabbed Ben by the arm. "You got no call to do that."

Bishop hit Emmett over the head with the rope, knocking him to the ground, and then both Rogers and Bishop drew their guns.

"Just sit tight," warned Bishop.

Emmett sat up, looking afraid as he rubbed his head where the rope had hit him.

Davy feared for his Emmet and wished he had not brought him along while he tried to think of a way out. "What are you gonna do to Allen?"

Ben Rogers grinned. "I'm taking him in, the same as y'all, and locking all y'all up for helping deserters. Now stand up so's I can tie yer hands."

As Davy got up, he thought of running, but turned his back, extending his hands behind him. "Wait till my pa finds out about this."

Bishop Martin began tying Davy's hands. "I'll deal with your pa when he comes to town to watch ya hang for helping deserters." Finished with Davy, he turned to tie Emmett's hands, but the boy suddenly pushed Bishop down and ran toward the horses. Ben Rogers got off two quick shots, hitting the boy twice in the back, and killing him instantly.

Davy's eyes grew wide with horror as he yelled, "You killed Emmett!"

Allen looked on in disbelief. "Why'd ya go and do that?"

"Ah hell Ben," yelled Bishop as he ran to the boy, knelt, and turned him over. Seeing he was dead, he turned to Rogers. "The boy's dead." He got up, walked back to Davy, lifted him by the collar of his coat, and slapped him hard across the face. "This is all your fault."

Allen yelled, "Stop it. You got no cause to do that!"

Bishop pushed Davy back to the ground, turned, and glared at Allen. "Shut up." Then he looked at Ben Rogers. "Now what the hell we gonna do, ya damn fool?"

Ben Rogers looked at Bishop considering just that, and then he looked at Emmett's body lying a few feet away, at Allen, and then at Davy. Without warning, he stepped toward Davy, pulled out Allen's old pistol from his belt that he had taken from him earlier, and shot him in the chest. The force of the bullet at this range knocked Davy backward. As blood spewed from the small hole in his chest, Davy had a surprised look on his face as he struggled to get up, and then lay still.

Allen cried as he yelled, "Davy!" He watched helplessly as the blood oozed from the corners of Davy's mouth and then looked up at Ben Rogers. "You had no cause to do that, you bastard."

Bishop knelt, looked into Davy's lifeless eyes, and felt his neck for a pulse. He turned to Ben. "You crazy fool, what the hell ya kill the Chrisman boy for?"

"He saw me kill the other boy."

Bishop took a deep breath and exhaled, looking at what they had done. "Yah damn fool," he said, looking scared. "Damn it, Ben, now what the hell we gonna do?" He looked worried. "Will Chrisman will kill us both."

Allen was sitting on his knees, his hands tied behind his back, crying as he looked at the two men. "Yah didn't have to kill `em."

Bishop Martin turned and slapped Allen in the face. "I told you to shut up!"

Allen looked at Bishop with hate in his eyes. "Damn you to hell."

Rogers knelt, grabbing Allen's collar. "This is all yer fault. If'n you'd stayed with yer damn unit instead of desert'n, these other boys would still be alive." He slapped Allen across the face, stood, and looked around. "We can't just leave `em like this."

The two stood in silence for several minutes, considering what to do next. Both knew they couldn't just leave the bodies and take Allen into town. He would tell everyone what happened. Bishop Martin saw the knife and scabbard on Davy's belt, bent down, took the knife out of its scabbard, and stood, giving Ben a long look.

Rogers wondered what Bishop had on his mind.

Martin suddenly turned to Allen and plunged the knife into his heart.

Wide-eyed, Allen gasped for breath, stiffened from pain, and fell backward, jerking like a fish out of water. Then he went limp.

Bishop took out his own knife and cut Allen's ropes, did the same to Davy, stood and looked at Ben. "They killed one another." He took Allen's pistol, fired four shots into the air, and then placed the gun in Allen's hand.

"What about the knife?" Rogers asked.

Bishop looked down at the knife and considered it. Then he told Rogers to put it in Davy's hands. "I doubt they told anyone about the deserter. Stands to reason they could have stumbled on his camp, got into a fight, and this happened." He looked around thoughtfully. "The deserter there shot that one over yonder as he ran to warn the Home Guard. Davy here, pulled his knife and stabbed that one, and got shot in the process."

Ben Rogers looked around at the three bodies. "Might work."

Bishop Martin smiled, looking pleased with himself. "Who's to say different?"

Rogers scratched his chin as he grinned at Bishop. "Ain't no one around ta say any different."

"That's right," said Bishop. "And neither were we. Now let's get the hell out of here and put us a story together."

They climbed up on their horses and rode out of camp past the black mare and the roan, leaving them tied to the trees just as Davy and Emmett Heard had left them.

When Beth approached the clearing Davy and Emmett had ridden across earlier, she slowed the Chestnut to a walk, stopping at the edge of the trees, and glanced behind her, making sure she hadn't been followed. She started to nudge the Chestnut slowly into the clearing when she heard the sound of approaching horses and quickly backed her horse into the trees to hide.

Two riders burst from the trees across the clearing, galloping as if something awful were chasing them. Beth rubbed the Chestnut's neck to keep him calm, and as she watched the two men ride past, she recognized Bishop Martin and Ben Rogers. She wondered if they were coming from the ruins and suddenly became frightened for the boys. Fighting the urge to bolt across the clearing, Beth waited until the two men had disappeared around a grove of trees, and the sounds of their horses had faded. As the clearing became quiet, filled only with the sounds of the breeze, crows, and grasshoppers, she nudged the Chestnut into the clearing at a walk, glancing back after Bishop Martin and Ben Rogers. Afraid they might come back for some reason, she paused to take one last look, put her spurs to the Chestnut, and galloped across the quiet clearing to the sound of the horse's heavy breathing and its hooves pounding on the hard dirt floor of the clearing.

Slowing the Chestnut to a trot, she entered the tree line while keeping a vigilant watch in all directions, and after a few yards, she pulled up and let the horse walk toward the ruins. She stopped to listen in the eerie silence as a slight breeze played in the trees, and a bird chirped here and there. A large crow frightened her as it cawed while springing from the branch of a fir tree, flapping its wings and disappearing in flight. Beth held her breath to listen for some sounds of danger, but hearing only the breeze and other forest sounds, she nudged the horse forward at a slow walk.

A horse neighed somewhere up ahead, causing Beth to pull up. Hearing only the leaves rustling in the slight breeze and the sound of water from the creek at the ruins, she nudged the horse forward, and as it walked slowly toward the sound of water, the smell of a campfire filled the air. Seeing her mother's horse and the black mare standing by a tree, Beth nudged the Chestnut toward them. Wishing she had brought her pistol, her heart pounded with fear as she moved slowly toward her mother's roan and James's black mare. The black mare turned its head, stared at her for a moment, shook its head rattling its bridle, snorted, and looked away. She guided the Chestnut slowly toward the other horses, telling herself there should be voices. Reaching the big black, she stopped next to it to listen. Hearing nothing but the breeze and water, she nudged her horse into the small clearing not far from the stone wall. Smoke from the smoldering campfire caught her attention first, and then she saw the three bodies lying on the ground a few feet away.

Terror held her as she looked from one to the other, knowing who they were, and that they were dead. She glanced around into the woods, thinking of the ghost stories of this terrible place, and half expecting to see old man Rupert walk from behind a tree. Fearful, she climbed down from the Chestnut, and while she held the reins in one hand, she walked over and knelt next to Davy, seeing the knife in his hand, the blood on his jacket. As her eyes welled, she dropped to her knees, put her arms around him, and softly called his name. After a few moments, she sat up and noticed the bloody knife that James had given Davy in his hand. Then as she stood, she glanced at Emmett and then at Allen. Confused over what had happened, Beth held onto the reins of the Chestnut and slowly walked over to Allen and knelt beside him. She looked into Allen's bloody face with tearing eyes, and then Beth saw the stab wound in his chest. She glanced back at the bloody knife in Davy's hand and then at Emmett lying a few feet away. Knowing he too was dead, she wiped the tears from her eyes and cheeks, slowly got up, glanced once again at the three, and climbed up into the saddle. Still wondering what had happened here, she glanced from one body to the other, and then having the presence of mind to do so, she untied her mother's roan and the black, knowing they would follow her, and rode as fast as she could away from the terrible place.

The sound of horses brought Elizabeth to the kitchen window, and looking out, she saw Beth and the two riderless horses. Fearing something terrible had happened, she called out to William, who was in the library. "Will, come quick, Beth is back." Then she rushed out the back door, stood on the small back porch, and waited for her daughter.

As Beth reined in the Chestnut, she jumped down and ran into her mother's arms, crying, "They're dead, Ma, they're all dead!"

Afraid of what her daughter was saying, Elizabeth held her daughter. "Who's dead, girl?"

Beth's rambling made no sense as she tried to tell her about Davy, Allen, and Emmett.

Elizabeth took her by the shoulders and looked into her face, seeing something terrible in her daughter's red puffy eyes. Then noticing the blood on Beth's clothes, she feared the worst.

William stepped out of the house and slowly and painfully knelt on his bad hip. Fearing the worse, he asked, "Where's Davy and Emmett?"

Beth collapsed to her knees, sobbing, "Davy's dead."

Elizabeth's eyes welled as she looked at Will.

William saw the blood on his daughter's clothes. "What the hell happened?"

Elizabeth looked up at him with tears in her eyes. "She says Davy's dead."

Filled with disbelief, he looked at Beth. "Davy's dead?" He waited for an answer, and when none came, he put one hand on her shoulder and asked again in a louder voice, "Is Davy dead?"

Beth never answered as she held onto her mother and sobbed.

William slowly stood then reached down to help them up. "Let's go inside."

As they got up, William yelled at two of his ranch hands who were watching from the barn to take care of the horses, and then he helped Elizabeth and Beth into the house.

Beth was still sobbing when she sat down at the kitchen table, resting her head on her arms, muttering words about Davy neither Elizabeth nor William understood.

William knelt next to her chair, put his hand on her knee, and spoke softly. "What happened, girl?"

She looked up at her ma and then at William. "They're dead, Pa. Davy, Emmett, and Allen. They're all dead."

Elizabeth held onto the edge of the table and slowly lowered herself to her knees, where she wailed in sorrow, saying her son's name over and over again.

William put one hand on his wife's back, wanting to comfort her. He looked at his daughter, stood, pulled out a chair, sat down, and looked into her red watering eyes. "What happened, girl?"

She wiped the tears from her eyes with a dishtowel that was sitting on the table and looked down at her mother sobbing on the kitchen floor. Finally, she looked at her pa. "I ain't sure Pa, but Davy's dead, and so are Emmett and Allen. They're all dead!"

William's eye welled as he reached out and tenderly touched the back of his wife's head, wishing he could comfort her where there was no comfort.

Several moments filled with grief passed, and when he looked at Beth with red, teary eyes, he said, "Girl," he softly said. "Tell me what you found out there."

It took a couple of seconds for her to stop crying enough to sit up and wipe the tears from her eyes and cheeks with the dishtowel she was holding. "I'm not sure, Pa. I was pretty scared when I found them." She stopped and looked down at her mother, sitting on her knees, sobbing while softly calling out Davy's name.

William looked into Beth's tearing, red eyes. "Are you sure they're all dead?"

Beth nodded that she was, and then she got out of the chair, sat on the floor next to Ma, and put her arms around her. William watched them cry as he wiped his wet cheeks, but then after a few minutes, he tugged at Beth's arm. "Tell me everything, girl. Everything you saw from the time you left here until the minute you got back."

She wiped the tears from her eyes, and while holding her mother in her arms, she told him how she had seen saw Bishop Martin and Ben Rogers ride past her as if being chased by the devil. Then of finding the black and the roan tied to a tree, and of creeping through the woods and finding the three boys.

"Think back, girl. Tell me exactly what you saw."

"Not sure what I saw, Pa. It all looked so confusing to me. Emmett had been shot in the back. Allen's gun was lying on the ground next to him, and Davy was shot in the chest." She paused. "Pa, it appeared that Davy stabbed Allen before he got shot."

William shook his head, looking skeptical. "That don't make no sense, girl. Makes no sense at all. You sure of what you saw?"

"Pretty sure, Pa. It looked like Allen was stabbed with the knife James gave to Davy for his 10th birthday. The one he always carried on his belt?"

William put one hand on the table and stood to look out the kitchen window towards the barn while considering all she had told him. Then he softly said, "Makes no sense. Makes no sense at all." He turned from the window to Beth. "Davy wouldn't stab anybody, especially Allen, and Allen surely wouldn't just up and shoot Emmett." William paused in thought. "And why were Rogers and Martin in such a hurry?"

He bent down, gently took her by the shoulders, and helped her up. "Wash your hands and face, girl, and then go down to the barn and have the boys saddle you and me a fresh mounts fresh mounts, and three packhorses." His eyes welled again as tears made their way down his rough face. "You're taking me to them boys."

Elizabeth looked up from the floor, her eyes red and puffy, full of sorrow, and her cheeks wet. "You can't ride Will. Your hip!"

William reached down, helped her to her feet, and held her wet face in his rough hands, looking into her red eyes filled with all the sadness of the world. Their son was dead, and William wanted to scream at God but held it in. "I'm riding today, Mother. We'll go slow." He wiped the tears from her cheeks and around her mouth, then looked into her dark eyes filled with a sorrow he could not take away and tenderly kissed each one.

She placed her hands on his face. "Bring our boy home."

He nodded that he would, kissed her forehead, and brushed away the tears from his cheeks as he turned and took his coat from a hook behind the door. He and Beth stepped out of the house into the yard, and as William limped toward the barn, Beth held her pa's hand.

A thin trail of smoke drifted aimlessly from the small pile of burnt wood and ashes from Allen's still burning campfire. The ride to the ruins had been slow and painful for William Chrisman, and as they sat in silence looking at the three bodies, the realization of his son's death hit him like a shovel in the face. William stared at his son's body for several moments and cried without shame, drowning out the slight breeze that moaned in the fir trees. Beth's quiet sobs mixed with her father's.

Then William wiped the tears away, and like an old hunter, he moved his horse forward a few steps while surveying the scene, pausing to look at each of the three bodies before he asked Beth to help him down. She dismounted, and after helping her father down, William stood next to his horse as he looked at Emmett's body, then Allen's, and finally Davy's. He gestured with one hand. "Is this the way you found `em?"

Beth nodded as she wiped the tears from her face. "Yes, Pa."

William gestured to Beth. "Stay put, daughter." Then he quietly walked around the camp, looking everything over carefully before he walked over to Davy's body and stared down at his son. "Davy didn't kill Allen, girl," he said softly. "And Allen never shot him, or Emmett."

Beth's voice quivered. "How'd you know, Pa?"

William didn't answer, but instead, he slowly walked around the camp, looking at the tracks in the dirt. Putting his hand on a nearby tree, he bent over and looked at the signs. "Several things." He pointed to the ground. "Them small boot prints, they'd be yours. The slightly bigger ones that are worn on the insides would be Davy's. Emmett and Allen's would be those there, there, there, and there. Bigger, heavier, men made these others." He paused. "Men like Ben Rogers and Bishop Martin." He looked from his son's body to Allen's. "Someone did a heap of walking between these two boys." William painfully got to his feet and looked down at Davy. "Another thing is yer brother's not left-handed."

Beth looked down at her brother. "I never noticed the knife was in the wrong hand. Guess I was too upset."

William nodded, "That's okay, Daughter, took me a moment too." He paused in thought. "Ben Rogers is left-handed."

Beth looked at her father. "You think he killed Allen with Davy's knife."

William stared down at his son without answering, and then with the help of a slender tree, knelt next to Davy, affectionately fussed with his jacket, gently touched his face, and with his fingertips closed his son's eyes.

Beth's eyes welled again as she watched her Pa lean down and whisper something into Davy's ear that she couldn't hear.

William noticed the rope marks on Davy's wrists. "Beth, go check Allen's hands and see if he has rope burns on his wrists."

She rushed over and knelt next to Allen. "Yes, there are, Pa."

He looked at Emmett's body, figuring that he had tried to make a run for it. "These two boys were tied up at one time." With the help of the tree, he slowly straightened in pain. "Help me get these boys on the pack horses. We need to take them all to our place so's their families can come take care of their boys."

The two of them managed to load the three bodies onto the spare horses, gather Allen's horse, and then ride through the trees and across the clearing toward home.

The ride home was long and quiet, with neither speaking. When they reached the back porch, Beth jumped down from her horse, ran into the house and up the stairs to her room. William stared at the closed door wishing Beth had not witnessed such a terrible thing.

Three men came running, and as William slowly climbed down from his horse, he told one of the hands to ride to the Heard's place, then to the Downs' place, telling them that their sons were dead. "Do it easy, mind ya," he warned. "This is gonna be hard on them folks." Then he and two other hands carried Davy's body up the stairs to his room, where his mother waited.

She watched as they placed her son on his bed. "Careful," she whispered.

"Yes, ma'am," softly replied one of the hired hands, trying not to make eye contact, and then he and the other man left the room with their eyes on the floor.

Elizabeth sat on the edge of the bed with red, welling eyes, looked at the bloody clothes and the hole in her son's jacket. She bent down and gently kissed his cheek and whispered his name.

Knowing there was nothing he could do to ease his wife's pain, William reached out to touch her but hesitated and withdrew his hand. He watched as Elizabeth lay on the bed next to Davy, held him in her arms, and talked about his life. Unable to watch any longer, William turned, walked out of the room, and closed the door. He stood in the hall, staring down at his hand on the doorknob, thinking of the way Davy laughed or how he had gulped his food. Eyes filled with tears, he looked across the hall at James's room, walked over, opened the door, and looked inside, wishing James was here. Closing the door, William walked down the hall past Davy's room and hesitated at Beth's closed-door, hearing her crying inside. He thought about going inside and holding her in his arms to comfort her, but knowing she couldn't be comforted, he went downstairs to the library.

Alone in the library, sipping a glass of brandy while remembering the life of his dead son, he thought of James and hoped he was safe, and prayed that God watched over him, knowing that Elizabeth couldn't bear the loss of both sons. The big clock in the corner tolled five p.m., and thinking it would be dark soon, William wondered what was keeping the Heard and Downs families.

As William sipped his drink, his thoughts raced upstairs to his dead son and the day that he was born. Memories spilled into his mind like pages from a photo album, remembering how James would tease the boy unmercifully. His memories were interrupted by a knock at the door. Suspecting who it was, he drank the last of his brandy, placed his empty glass on the table, and stood, feeling unbearably tired. He walked to the front door preparing for what lay ahead, feeling the aches of the years in his old body, and thinking no one should outlive their children.

Opening the door, his eyes fell on Louisa and Henry Heard, and he saw their eyes, like his, were swollen and red. "Come in." He stepped aside, motioning them in. "We can talk in the library." William pointed to a small sofa for Louisa and Henry to sit on. After they sat down, he offered them a drink, thinking that they both could use it, but both refused. William told them how Beth found the boys, came back for him, and how together they had brought them all back. Then he told them that he believed someone had killed the three and made it look like Allen had shot their son Emmett, Davy stabbed Allen in the heart, and Allen had managed to shoot Davy before he died.

Silence filled the library. Louisa looked at him with sad eyes. "Where's my boy, William?"

He stood, took her small hands in his, and helped her up. "Can't tell ya how sorry I am, Louisa."

"I know, William. You're a good man and a dear friend." Tears welled in her eyes and rolled down her cheeks. "I know Allen didn't kill my Emmett no more than Davy killed Allen. Where's my boy?"

William nodded toward a closed door. "He's in the next room, Louisa, lying peaceably on the table."

She nodded with a half-smile, then turned and walked toward the door, hesitated, then turned back. "How's Elizabeth?"

"Holding on, Louisa, just holding on."

"If you would, please tell her," (she paused) "tell her I asked after her."

"I'll do that, and she'll appreciate it." After Louisa left the room, William sat down and looked at Henry Heard with anger. "Someone killed both our boys, Henry." They talked briefly about what had taken place at the ruins, and Henry asked if he had any idea who would have done such a terrible thing. William did not want to tell Henry what he suspected, fearing that he might take revenge and get hung. "I've my suspicions, Henry. But they's just that, suspicions."

Louisa's soft sobbing escaped from the other room. Glancing at the door, Henry stood, offering an outstretched hand to William. "I best go be with my wife."

"I'll help you with your son when you're ready."

Henry forced a smile, looking appreciative. "Thank you kindly, Will, but if you don't mind, I'll take care of my son myself. I know you mean well, and I don't mean to disrespect you in your own home. It's just the way I want it."

William knew he would have done the same. "I understand, Henry." While Henry walked into the other room, William poured another drink and sat down in a leather chair listening as the Heard's carried their son to the wagon waiting outside. He waited until he heard the door close and the wagon leave, and then he sipped his drink and waited for the sound of another wagon followed by a knock at the door.

Davy Chrisman was laid to rest on the 8th of May, 1863. After the funeral, the family and a few close friends gathered at the Chrisman farm for food and drink, honoring the memories of Davy Chrisman, Emmett Heard, and Allen Downs. The long day ended in silence after William said goodnight to the last guest. Elizabeth, declaring she was tired, went upstairs to sleep in Davy's room, and William decided to leave her to her sorrow. He sat alone in his big chair in front of the fireplace watching the flames consume the logs, while in the other room, Beth and the girls rattled dishes as they cleared the table. No one spoke.

Twenty-One

May 1863

James comes home

In the days that followed Davy Chrisman's funeral, Elizabeth spent most of her time in Davy's room with the door closed, going through his things and remembering his life. At night she cried herself to sleep in his bed where his smell lingered. This weighed heavily on William. He had always tried to protect her, but this was something for which there was no protection, and he felt helpless. He missed his wife and the friend that she had become, but he respected her grief and left her to the privacy she wanted and needed. It had become a lonely time for him, and he missed his wife.

William sat in his chair on the porch in the early evening, thinking about Davy and filled with worry about James. At some point, he closed his eyes and drifted into a light sleep, awakened by the sound of a horse and wagon. Sitting up, he peered over the porch railing into the darkness with sleepy eyes as the wagon stopped several yards from the porch. As a figure dressed in gray climbed down from the wagon, William whispered, "James." He stood and yelled, "James is home!"

James shook the driver's hand, thanking him, and turned, hurrying to meet his pa limping down the porch steps. They embraced, and William's eyes welled with happy tears as he held his son's shoulders tightly in his hands.

Beth and the girls ran across the porch and down the steps. Beth being the fastest, ran into his arms while the smaller girls fought each other for position around his legs until he knelt and hugged them.

Elizabeth stood at the edge of the porch with happy tears. "James," she said just above a whisper as she hurried down the steps and into her son's arms.

William and the others stood by quietly watching, hopeful that she would return to the family now that her oldest son was home.

James looked into his mother's eyes, thinking she looked tired and somewhat sickly. "Everything all right, Ma?"

William put a hand on James's shoulder, looking sad. "We need to go inside, so's we can talk, Son."

James glanced around. "Where's Davy?"

William bent down and picked up James's carpetbag. "Let's go inside, son."

Sensing something serious had happened to his brother, James followed them up the steps and into the house. Once inside, Elizabeth told Beth to take the girls upstairs to their rooms, causing protests, since she needed private time with their brother. He knelt to one knee, smiled, and promised that he would look in on them later. Satisfied with that, they went with Beth.

James watched as his mother sat down on the sofa and stared down at her folded hands, with sadness on her face. It was then he noticed she was wearing black, a color she seldom wore, and he feared the worst. Her face was swollen, her eyes were puffy and red, and the skin under them was dark.

William handed a glass of bourbon to his son.

James took the glass. "What's going on, Pa?"

He told his son to sit down, and then he sat next to his wife on the sofa, put his hand on hers, and looked at James. "There ain't no easy way to tell you this son, Davy's dead."

James stared at his pa in disbelief. "What? How? What happened?"

Elizabeth buried her face in her hands and began crying.

Beth walked back into the library, sat down next to her mother, and put an arm around her, knowing they had just told James about Davy.

William took a sip of his drink and told James all that had happened. He told of Allen hiding out at the old Rupert place, of Davy knowing he was there but keeping it a secret from the rest of the family. About the Home Guard stopping by, prompting Davy to take Emmett Heard with him to visit Allen, probably to warn him.

Beth told him of riding out to find Davy and Emmett and seeing Bishop Martin and Ben Rogers riding from the direction of the old Rupert Place. Then she told of how she found the bodies and came home to tell their ma and pa.

James recalled the day he and Martha had their first picnic at the Rupert place. Then he looked at Beth. "You sure you saw Bishop and Ben riding from the old Rupert place?"

Beth nodded. "I'm sure of it, James."

Hate and anger filled James. "Bastards." Then he looked at his ma, quickly apologized for the language, took a drink of bourbon, and looked at his Pa. "Have ya gone to the sheriff?"

William frowned, gesturing with one hand dismissively. "There is no sheriff, boy. He and his deputies are off in this damn war, same as you. The damn Home Guard is the only law we have, and we can't go to them." He paused and then raised his voice. "They're the sons-of-bitches responsible!" He looked at his wife. "I'm sorry for yelling, Liz."

She gave him an understanding smile as she wiped the tears from her face with her handkerchief.

James considered everything quickly. "Damned if we can't, Pa! They can't all be like Bishop and Rogers. Someone has to pay for Davy and the others."

William scowled, looking angry, and raised his voice to meet James's. "Don't you think I know that Son?" But I'm just a crippled old man, and we can't just go kill someone b'cuz we want to."

James stood. "I've been killing men for months, Pa, and I can sure as hell kill these two bastards."

Fear for both her husband and son gripped Elizabeth as she stood raising her hands, her eyes welling with tears. "Enough!" she shouted, bringing silence to the room.

James felt ashamed. "Sorry, Ma."

She wiped her eyes with a hankie, told James to sit down, and then she sat down with William and looked at James with a pleading face. "For God's sake, I just buried one son, James. I know you mean well, son, but listen to your father."

James set his glass down, slid out of his chair, knelt in front of his mother, and took her hands in his. "I'm sorry, Ma. Don't worry. I won't take revenge against Bishop and Ben. I promise. At least not now, but I can't promise on later."

Elizabeth wiped her eyes, and then her nose with her hankie, turned to William and smiled a half-smile. "I'm tired. I'm going back up to Davy's room."

James stood and helped her up, feeling sorry for his mother's grief.

Beth hugged James, said she was glad he was home, and then she helped Elizabeth upstairs.

After they were gone, William looked at James. "We can't do anything right now, son. It'd be too obvious, but I promise everyone in this here house, the day will come when Bishop Martin and Ben Rogers will pay for killing my boy and them other two lads."

James knew his father meant what he said. They talked a while longer, and then James said he was tired and went upstairs to see his two little sisters, leaving William alone in the library, not wanting to go upstairs to a lonely bed.

James opened his eyes and quickly looked around, remembering that he was home in his bed. In the faint light of morning, he looked across the room at the table near the window and saw the pitcher of warm water with steam rising above it and the clean towel left by his mother. In the stillness of his room, James watched the sky turn light blue and thought about last night. Memories of Davy and Allen raced through his mind, and he wanted to scream at someone, anyone, for the injustice of it all. He got out of bed, shaved, washed, got dressed, and then walked down the stairs, finding his mother busy setting the breakfast table. William was at the head of the table, keeping a cup of coffee company. They exchanged greetings, and James sat down and thought about last night, watching as William poured him a cup of coffee.

Beth entered the room, and as she passed behind his chair, she flipped his hair as she had always done. "When you gonna see Martha?"

He watched his mother disappear through the swinging door into the kitchen, sipped his coffee, thinking that it tasted a lot better than the army coffee he had been drinking. "Thought about going over this afternoon, after I visit the cemetery."

Elizabeth came out of the kitchen carrying a platter of eggs, placed them on the table across from James, and looked at him, her face filled with concern. "James, you look thin, son. Are you all right?"

He told them about being sick and in the hospital, and when the army was ready to move out, how the doctor had informed the captain that he was in no condition for a forced march, let alone a fight, and so he was given leave to rest and get his strength back.

Elizabeth smiled. "I don't care what brought you, home son. You're home, and that's all that matters." She paused while looking at him. "Your ma will put some meat on them bones."

The morning sun was warm, the air crisp and quiet. Grasshoppers buzzed in the fields, and birds chirped and darted here and there in search of their breakfast or food for their babies. The black mare's hooves clomped lazily on the hard, dirt road as she steadily walked toward their destination. James enjoyed the quiet that was unlike the camps and battlefields. A crow flew from a nearby tree, cawing as it flew across the field. A curious squirrel paused halfway across the road, stood on hind legs, looked at the solitary rider, and then dashed through the underbrush. In the stillness, his head filled with noisy battles, faces of the dead men he knew, and of Allen's grin. He remembered Davy's look of worry at the depot and his promise to look after the black. James was afraid of returning to the army and the killing but couldn't let on. He had no choice but to return, or he'd end up like Allen. "Stupid war," he said aloud.

Before he realized it, he was riding along the road next to the church and cemetery that held his brother. Turning from the road, he made his way past the church to the weathered picket fence surrounding the graveyard. Stopping at the open gate of the graveyard that was clinging to the fence by one hinge, he climbed down.

Knowing the black mare would not run off, there was no need to tie her to the old fence, so he let her reins drop freely and stepped through the opening left by the broken gate. He paused a moment while he searched for the two fresh graves of Davy and Allen. He made his way between the weathered wooden markers, some fallen over having rotted from time and weather, others leaned to this side or that, straining not to fall. A sparse number of markers stood tall, resisting time and the elements. Some graves were so old, they had no markers at all, lost to time, or perhaps by mischievous children.

The spot reserved for the Chrisman family was covered in the shade by a large oak tree standing on the other side of the fence. Holding his hat between the fingers of his hands, James stood next to Davy's grave, knelt to one knee, and looked at the wooden marker through watery eyes. Slowly he traced the lettering of William. David Chrisman with the fingers of one hand and wiped his eyes with the back of the other. "Ah Davy," he said in a soft, choked voice, looking at the partially wilted flowers left by their ma. "I should've been here." He wiped his eyes and nose with the sleeve of his shirt, then bent down and picked up a small amount of dirt, letting it fall through his fingers over the grave. His hand empty, he looked toward the hills in the direction of the Rupert ruins, remembering his and Martha's picnic. Trying to imagine the terror Davy and the others had gone through at Ben Rogers and Bishop Martin's hands, his mind filled with hate and anger. He looked back down at Davy's grave. "Thanks for taking care of the black. She looks really good." He began to cry, and after a minute or two, he looked at the marker. "Me and Pa don't know for sure what happened that day, Davy, but we know you and Allen didn't kill one another. But I know pa, and I promise he'll find out what happened. If not, I will after this damn war's over. I swear it, Davy."

He wiped the tears from his face, stood, and walked to his friend's grave, where he touched the marker and smiled. "I miss you, Allen, and I don't blame you none for any of this. You couldn't help yourself. This war's a terrible thing. I ain't ashamed to admit that I wanted to run away myself, just couldn't find the courage." Putting on his hat, he turned and walked toward the opening in the fence toward the mare nibbling on some weeds. Climbing into the saddle, he turned her away from the weathered fence and rode at a canter toward the Heard place and Martha.

James turned from the county road onto the Heard place, thinking that it had not changed much. The door opened, and Martha walked onto the porch, looking up the hill at the rider. Recognizing the black mare and who rode her, she waved as she ran off of the porch. Nearly falling when she stumbled, she managed to catch her balance and never lost a step as she laughed, then cried, and then laughed again, calling out his name.

He pulled the mare up, jumped down, and ran to meet her. Their bodies crashed into one another, entangled in hugging, kissing, then laughter and tears. James held her fast in his arms, not wanting to let go of her soft body, and then he looked at her red, watery eyes and smiling face.

"James," she said softly with love in her eyes.

Mrs. Heard yelled, "Kiss her again!"

James looked at Mr. and Mrs. Heard, who were standing on the porch watching them.

Martha glanced back at them and giggled as she looked at James. "Well, James, ya gonna kiss me again?"

His face flushed, he grinned as he looked at her ma and pa and then gave her a small kiss.

Mr. Heard yelled, "You call that a kiss, James Chrisman?"

James lifted Martha off the ground and kissed her to the cheers of her ma and pa. Feeling embarrassed, he held her hand as they walked toward the house.

Richard and Susana Heard hurried from the porch to greet James. After exchanging hellos and the Heard's saying how sorry they were about Davy, Mrs. Heard asked him if he could stay for dinner.

James nodded. "Yes, ma'am," he said happily. "I'll just see to my horse."

After dinner, while Martha's sisters helped with the dishes, James asked Mr. Heard if he could give his mare some oats before he saddled her for the ride home. Martha's brother Eli quickly said he would do it, but James said that he and Martha would, hoping it would give them some time alone. Martha accompanied James to the barn where he filled a feedbag with oats for the mare, and while she ate, he put the blanket and saddle on her. When she had finished, he put the bit in her mouth and led her to the front porch, where he and Marth sat for a while on the edge of the porch, talking of things that were of little importance, enjoying one another's company.

Realizing it was getting late, he stood and walked the mare to a nearby trough, letting her drink as he stroked her neck. "I should be heading home soon."

Martha stepped off the porch, took James by the hand, and led him around the corner of the house to the swing while the mare leisurely strolled behind them patient as always. As they walked, Martha asked

James if they had any idea who would have killed Davy, her cousin Emmett, and Allen Downs.

He lied. "No, we don't."

"Good," she said, looking distraught. "We don't need any revenge killing."

He held onto the rope while she sat down in the swing and then sat next to her while the mare, patiently waiting, watched them with big dark eyes.

Martha put her hand on James's chin, turned his head toward her, and kissed him. "I've missed you, James Riley." She smiled and kissed him again, then grinned. "I really missed you."

They looked at one another in silence, and then he stood and took her hands in his, helped her up from the swing, took her in his arms, and slowly kissed her. His strong hands slowly moved down her back to her small waist, pulling her into him, remembering the times he thought of her when he was afraid. Neither one could hold back the passion they had for one another; it had become too strong and too consuming for both.

He slid his hands down her arms grasping her hands, and led her into the woods to a grassy glen beyond the swing. In the stillness of the glen, they looked into each other's eyes as they knelt, and as they kissed, he gently lowered her onto the soft grass. Filled with desire, his hands fumbled with the buttons on her dress while the mare stood like a voyeur in silence, watching the two lovers.

The full moon cast its white light onto the road and countryside as James rode the mare at a slow walk up the driveway from the county road. His mind returned to the grassy glen by the swing, and he wanted to do it all over again. James stopped, turned in the saddle, and looked back at the house and its windows of orange-yellow light. As he sat atop the mare staring at the house, a flood of thoughts rushed in and out of his mind. He loved Martha and did not want to go through life without her. He cursed the war, knowing that all too soon, he would have to return to the sounds of battle and of men dying, fearing that he would be one of those poor souls. A star fell across the sky above the Heard house, and he remembered his mother telling him stories of how the spirits would help those lost by marking the path for them in the night sky. Suddenly he felt excitement for life he had never felt before, turned the mare, and rode back to the Heard house. Jumping from the saddle, he hurried up the two steps, across the porch, and lightly knocked on the door.

Moments later, Mrs. Heard opened the door looking puzzled. "James, is everything all right?"

Looking somewhat determined, he asked if he could talk to Martha.

Mrs. Heard considered that a moment then stepped aside. "Won't ya come in?"

"No thanks, Mrs. Heard," he said, fighting the old urge to bolt and run.

"Well then," she said, looking curious. "Wait here, and I'll fetch her."

Several minutes later, Martha, wearing a faded robe, opened the door and stepped onto the porch. She looked worried. "James, what is it?"

He took her hand, led her to the edge of the porch, and stared into the darkness.

She placed her hand under his arm, pulling her body against his, and waited.

He stood in silence, feeling Martha's warm body against his as he looked at the black mare in the moonlight, and then he turned to her. "Marry me."

Martha's expression was a mixture of surprise, skepticism, and pure joy, but she still held the fear that he could change his mind. "You sure that's what ya want, James?"

"As sure as I am about anything these days." He took her hand and stepped off the porch. "Walk with me."

They walked along the driveway toward the road, hidden in the darkness with the mare following. He sucked in a large amount of air and then let it out in a soft sigh. "I almost died in that hospital from whatever it was that made me sick." He paused in thought. "Things aren't the same anymore, and I'm not the same as before I left. I feel different somehow, different inside." He stopped and squeezed her hand, looking into the darkness of the night instead of at her. "The world's gone crazy," he said thoughtfully. "Men I never saw before are trying to kill me at places too terrible to talk about. Instead, I've killed them or most of them, anyway." He paused in memory. "I can't forget their faces and the screaming as they died. I think that's what drove Allen to run away." He stared into the night. "Men are angry and killing one another, and I'm part of that anger. I can't get rid of the hate I feel inside, and I can't undo the killing and other terrible things I've done." He looked at her. "You're the only thing that makes any sense to me anymore, and if I make it through this war, I want to spend my life with you."

Tears filled her eyes as she put her hand on his cheek. "I'll marry you, James, tonight, even if that's what you want."

He grinned. "I wish we could, but we can't, so I guess it'll have to wait till I get back." He took her in his arms, kissed her, climbed up onto the mare, and held out his hand. "Want a ride back?"

"I think I'll walk. It ain't so far." She looked up at him. "When you gonna talk to my pa and ma?"

James hadn't considered that before. "Tomorrow, first thing after I talk to my folks." He bent down, kissed her, turned the mare, and rode away.

She wrapped herself in her arms, watching him disappear into the darkness, hearing only the mare's hooves on the hard ground fade before she turned and walked back to the house. Filled with a young girl's dreams, she wished they were already married.

James slowed the mare to a walk while the day raced through his memory, wanting to marry Martha before he left. Then he thought about the war lasting months, perhaps years, and never coming home again, leaving Martha a young widow.

"Damn war," he cursed aloud. He was so sure when he was with her, but now out here on the lonely road at night, he got confused and felt hurried. He blamed himself for that, wishing they had more time, but that was something neither of them had, and soon he would return to the 47th, the war, and maybe even death. He wished Allen were alive so that they could talk. "Damn war!"

The lights of his home shone in the distance, and he knew his ma had left a lantern on the kitchen table for him. Imagining her still awake in Davy's room, he wondered if he should talk to her tonight but decided to wait until the morning. His mind returned to the arguments inside his head. '*What if he died in some far- off place being buried in a mass grave, never to see home again or Martha.*' The image of himself lying dead or dying on the cold, wet ground in some stranger's plowed, muddy field could become a reality. Still, he loved her and wanted her for his wife, and he wondered if that would be fair to her.

Riding into the barn, he dismounted, groped in the dark for the lantern, and lit its wick. The flame filled a small portion of the barn with a dim orange light, leaving the rest of the building dark and shadowy. He unsaddled his horse, put her away for the night with some fresh hay, blew out the lantern, and walked to the house, surprised at finding his mother sitting at the kitchen table. "Ma," he whispered as he knelt beside her. "You didn't have to wait up, Ma." Then worried about her, he asked, "You feeling all right?"

She smiled affectionately. "I'm fine, son." She placed a hand on his cheek. "I wanted to be sure you got home, all right."

James sat in a nearby chair. "Sorry, Ma. If I'd known, I'd have hurried home."

She pulled her shawl tighter around her shoulders. "No need for that, son."

"You're cold, Ma." He looked at the stove. "Want me to build us a fire?"

"Won't be necessary, son," she said, smiling at him. "You been at the Heard place all this time?"

Nodding his head, he sighed, "Yes, Ma."

Seeing he looked troubled, she asked, "Trouble got his hands on you, boy?" Before he could answer, she asked, "You want to marry that gal, James?"

Embarrassed, he smiled as he looked into his mother's tired eyes and grief-stricken face, knowing she already knew the answer. He thought she looked a little older than he remembered, or maybe it was the death of Davy she carried with her. Her long, raven black hair had a hint of gray, and her face showed the sorrow death brings with it. He felt the urge to move from his chair and kneel on the floor, placing his head on her lap as he had as a child.

She looked down at him as she stroked his hair with gentleness.

"I don't know what to do, Ma. I want to marry Martha."

One hand gently held the side of his head while the other stroked his hair. She looked at the flame in the lantern thoughtfully. "You love that little gal, James?"

"Yes, I do, Ma."

Silence filled the kitchen while she moved her fingers through his hair, remembering the young Indian braves she knew as a child. Her memory drifted to another place in the distant past when a young Cherokee girl was in love with a young white boy. With her heart aching from the desire to be with him, she had sat with her head in her mother's lap, hearing of the obstacles and hatred she would face. Now, all these years later, she smiled at the memory of the love she and William had shared. "When your father and I decided to get married," she said softly. "We knew that we could endure the hate, the looks, and even the cruel words that could come from others."

She paused, letting her fingers comb through his hair. "But we knew our love and passion were strong like the winter wind blowing so hard that tall trees fell. We believed that nothing could separate us, even in death. We endured a lot over the years, but we never weakened. Our love was strong like a big oak tree." She lifted his head, held it in her hands, and looked into his eyes. "Don't let your happiness and love float away on clouds of rain and thunder, James. If you do, you will die an unhappy man and live alone in the place of the spirits. This will happen either in the war or after. It will be the same sad death without the one who loves you to mourn your passing." She kissed his forehead, gently pushed him away, stood, and picked up the lamp, admitting she was tired.

James followed her up the stairs, digesting all that she had said, and when they reached his bedroom door, she placed one hand on his face and kissed his cheek. "Get some rest. You'll need a clear head when you talk to Martha's ma and pa tomorrow morning."

Twenty-Two

May 1863 – November 1863

James Chrisman and Joseph Greene

The evening was unusually warm for the end of May, or perhaps it was James who felt unusually warm as he waited for his bride. His father, William Chrisman, stood proudly beside him as best man, a role once saved for Allen or Davy, and Beth was matron of honor.

The hymn ended, the choir looked toward the doors, and all heads turned as the choir began a soft melody. Martha wore a simple white dress, carried a small bouquet of spring flowers, and wore her light brown hair in a braid encircling her head, with three white flowers over her right ear. She smiled at her proud father as they walked down the center aisle. Then, seeing James as he nervously waited for her at the altar, she smiled.

Martha and her father stopped at the front pew. James stepped forward and held out his right elbow. Mr. Heard kissed his daughter on the cheek, shook James's hand, placed her hand on James's forearm, and stepped back.

They exchanged their vows and love for one another, and it seemed to Martha that it was over too quickly, while James thought it would never end. With the last "I do," the church filled with applause, cheers, and laughter as the happy couple hurried outside, chased by well-wishers amid the laughs, cheers, and confetti. James helped Martha into the buggy and climbed in beside her as someone yelled, "Give her a kiss, James!"

Without hesitating, he kissed his bride, bringing another multitude of whistles, cheers, and laughter. Deciding to help his son, William slapped the horse on the rear, sending her trotting toward the road and the couple's first and final night together at the Chrisman farm. The Chrisman family would visit with the Heard family until late evening, giving the newlyweds time to settle in and get acquainted.

James stopped the buggy next to the gate and helped Martha down as the young Negro boy ran to greet them and care for the horse. James took her arm and helped her up the stairs of the porch to the front door. After opening it, he kissed her, picked her up in his arms, and carried her inside.

"Don't drop me," she giggled.

"Never," he said, managing the door with one foot, and once inside, he paused to look around. "Sure is quiet."

"Feels a little funny," she said with a wrinkled nose and a shy smile.

James smiled, thinking it did feel strange as he lowered her feet to the floor and glanced nervously up the stairs, thinking of the bedroom.

She looked at him. "I love you, James Riley."

He took her hand, led her up the stairs to his bedroom, and closed the door to their private world. He lit a lantern and saw the pitcher of honey cider and two glasses that Elizabeth had left.

Martha smiled at the thoughtfulness, poured a small amount into each glass, and handed one to James.

He raised his glass. "To us," he said, then put his glass to her mouth while she put hers to his. Each took a small sip, smiled, and set the glasses on the table. He took her in his arms and kissed her, feeling the warmth and softness of her body against his. As he held her in his arms, she could feel his breath in her hair and smell the lotion he wore on his clean-shaven face. They looked at one another for a moment, and then she stepped away and unbuttoned her dress, pushing it over her shoulders letting it fall to her waist. He looked at her white skin and small, firm breasts as she stepped closer and unbuttoned his shirt, pushing it over his shoulders. Pulling his hands free of the shirt, he pulled her against him, feeling her warm skin against his. She turned the lantern down, and in the dim light of the room, they awkwardly helped one another off with the rest of their clothes. Standing naked, he took her hand, and they climbed under the covers where they embraced in love, shutting out the war and the rest of the world.

They lay in the silence of his room, each filled with their secret fears of his leaving, both trying desperately to shut it out of their one night together. Martha did not want to cry on their wedding night, so she kissed him and held his naked body against hers. She tried hard, but cry she did while James held her in his arms.

Their time together passed all too quickly, and as his family returned, they listened in silence while the others quietly found their bedrooms. Then, trying to crowd a lifetime of love into one night, James and Martha would not sleep on their last night together.

The following morning, James and Martha made love, dressed and then joined the family for breakfast. While the others were talking about unimportant things with an occasional laugh or grin, the two lovers smiled secretly at one another. All too soon, the time came for James to leave. William carried his bag while James helped Martha and his mother into the wagon. Beth climbed onto the back seat with James and Martha, and the two girls sat between Elizabeth and William.

The ride from the Chrisman farm to the train depot was filled with small talk and silence. James and Martha held hands, each squeezing the other's firmly. Arriving at the depot, Martha squeezed James's hand one last time before he jumped from the wagon to help her and Beth down. William tended to Elizabeth while the two girls giggled as they jumped from the wagon.

With Martha safely on the ground, James reached for his bag, but his father quickly picked it up and escorted Elizabeth to the platform.

"Got your papers, Son?" William asked over his shoulder.

"Right here, Pa." James patted his Confederate gray uniform jacket.

Stepping onto the depot platform and the waiting train, Elizabeth brushed imaginary dirt from the shoulders of James' uniform. "You look handsome in your uniform." She was proud yet afraid as she stepped closer and whispered, "The spirits of your ancestors will guide you, son."

He smiled at her. "I know, Ma. I'll be careful, I promise."

She forced a smile that couldn't hide her fear for the son she might never see again.

Seeing her distress, William put his arm around her shoulder and gently hugged her.

James looked into his father's red eyes and nodded, needing no words as they shook hands. He kissed his mother's cheek, then her forehead, and did the same to Beth and his younger sisters. He took Martha by the arm and walked a few feet farther down the depot platform. Her eyes were red and watery. "Don't know when I'll be coming back." He was trying to look unafraid.

She wiped at her tears with one hand and forced a smile. "I know. Just be careful."

He looked into her soft eyes. "I don't know what to say."

"That you love me," she said.

"You know, I do."

With tears streaming down her face, she looked into his eyes and, in a choked voice, said, "Promise me you'll come back, James."

The conductor yelled, "ALL ABOARD!"

James looked at the conductor, then at Martha. "Time to go. I'll write when I can, just as before, to Beth."

The conductor yelled a second time. "ALL ABOARD!" James looked at the man and took Martha in his arms. "No matter what happens, wait for me. No matter what, you have to wait for me."

Tears rolled down her face. "I will."

The conductor yelled for the final time, "ALL ABOARD!" The train jerked forward, then jerked forward again as it slowly moved along the tracks toward the war.

James kissed her, and as he held her in his arms, he whispered. "I'll come back. I promise. Believe in that." He looked into the faces of his family, picked up his bag, and ran along the platform, jumping onto the steps of the passenger car. Holding onto the side railing, he waved until the depot disappeared around the bend before he stepped inside to find a seat.

June 1863

When James arrived at Guntersville, Alabama, he gathered his belongings, stepped from the train, and hurried through the streets toward the river. He was anxious to catch the next boat that would take him up the Tennessee River to Knoxville and then north to the 47th.

The Southern Belle was docked alongside the pier at Guntersville, having only recently arrived from Florence, Alabama. She looked old, worn out, and badly in need of a fresh coat of paint and was not exactly what James had expected.

Onboard, he pushed through soldiers and other passengers to find a place to stow his gear and relax. The number of travelers surprised him as he walked her decks, noticing the bullet holes in the cabin walls, evidence that the war was not that far away.

"Lower away," yelled a voice from the bridge.

James looked up in the direction of the voice, seeing a bearded man dressed in black who he believed was the captain, and then he turned to watch as the men raised the gangplank. The loud shrillness of the Southern Belle's whistle startled him, and he dropped his bag to cover his ears until it stopped.

"Loud, ain't she?"

James turned, facing a man dressed as the one on the bridge but much younger. "That she is," agreed James, pointing at the bullet holes. "Looks like you had a run-in or two with the Yanks."

The man smiled wryly. "A couple of times, but no one was seriously hurt."

"Looks like you have a bit of luck riding with you."

The man glanced at the bullet scars and shrugged with a small smile. "In more ways than one. If you'll excuse me, I better get up to the bridge before the captain has a conniption." The man touched the short bill of his cap. "Enjoy your stay, soldier; we'll be in Chattanooga around ten tonight."

"Thanks." James watched as the man disappeared up a staircase, then picked up his bag and continued his search for a quiet place to rest.

The war saw an increase in the number of civilians and soldiers traveling up and down the river, leaving a scarcity of cabins. Like most Confederate soldiers traveling under military vouchers, few got the luxury of a private cabin or a shared one. They spent their time roaming the decks, sitting, and sleeping on the cargo. James soon found himself on the boat's stern, where the big paddlewheel churned through the water, pushing the boat easily along the river. Finding a vacant spot on a crate, he made himself comfortable using his bag for a pillow. Enjoying the warm afternoon sun, he thought of Martha and their last night together as he drifted in and out of a lazy sleep.

Opening his eyes, he lifted his head, seeing the sun was almost behind the western horizon. While his stomach growled with hunger, he sat up, considering his complaining stomach. As he looked around, he noticed several other soldiers holding tin plates of food. When asked about the food, they nodded toward a door, telling him about a group of women dishing up food below. Moments later, he was in line, getting a plate of food from a woman with a kindly face. He thanked her and found a secluded place to eat while looking for a familiar face he would never find.

His stomach full and content, James roamed the boat half-listening to the soldiers' talk of home, a girl, or the war. An older soldier with a harmonica sat cross-legged on the deck, his back against the wall, playing a soft, sad song as a small group of soldiers listened, each deep in thought of either home or their girl. The minutes passed, and James soon found himself standing in front of the crate with two soldiers keeping his belongings company.

"This here your stuff?" asked the bigger man eagerly, puffing a pipe.

James thought him to be around twenty years old, and noticing the new uniforms, he nodded. "It is. What outfit you fellas with?"

"Sixth Alabama Infantry," answered the big man. "You?"

"47th Alabama Infantry."

The bigger man took the pipe out of his mouth, blowing smoke into the air, and extended his empty open hand. "Name's Jacob." He pointed to the other man with the hand holding the pipe. "That ugly fella, there's Willie."

Willie looked a little younger, and James thought of Davy. Willie nodded and grinned from a freckled, friendly face. "Howdy." As he and James shook hands, Willie said, "We're heading up to Virginy. Our outfit's supposed to be round there somewheres."

James thought they looked fresh off the farm, probably much the way he had not so long ago. The man named Willie looked at James's faded gray uniform. "Looks like you been in for a spell. We just finished our training."

"Figured as much," said James.

Willie grinned at Jacob and then looked at James. "It's these here new uniforms, ain't it?"

James grinned. "Dead giveaway,"

Jacob stood and tugged at Willie's arm. "C'mon, let's take a walk around this here boat." He turned to James and asked if they could leave their belongings with him, explaining neither one had ever been on a boat before.

"I ain't going anywhere." James watched the two walk away, then laid back on the crate, resting his head on his bag, closed his eyes, and as he began to think about Martha, a voice interrupted his daydream.

"I see you found a comfortable spot," said the man he had met earlier

James sat up, grinned, and nodded. "Took a bit of looking."

The man gestured around them. "Pretty full these days with all you soldiers moving about the country."

"When did you say we were get'n to Chattanooga?" asked James.

"Around 10 o'clock tonight," the man said. "Chasing your unit?"

"Yeah. I've been home on leave."

The man leaned against the crate, looking thoughtful. "How'd you manage that? I didn't think they'd be passing those out."

"Well, they aren't," James said, "but I took ill up in Suffolk and ended up in the hospital. When the army was ordered on a forced march taking the hospital with them, they sent me home." He grinned, looking happy about that. "Doc said I was too sick to travel and thought some home cooking would fix me up."

The man chuckled. "Looks like the doc was right." He extended an open hand. "Joseph Greene."

James responded with a firm grip, "James Chrisman. I'm still a mite thin, but my ma tried her best."

Joseph chuckled. "They'll do that. Where's home?"

"South of here, little place along the Tallapoosa River, not far from the town of New Site."

Joseph recognized the name. "I know the place."

D4Pleased that someone knew of New Site, James smiled and proudly announced that he had gotten married while home.

Joseph congratulated him with a handshake and sat down on the crate next to James, listening as he spoke of Martha and his concerns about the war finding New Site and their farms. Joseph said he had much the same concerns about Florence, believing the cities along the river were vulnerable to that very possibility. As they talked, Joseph told him of moving his family to a farm in east Texas.

James perked up at that news, saying that he had wanted to go there ever since reading about the Alamo, Jim Bowie, Davy Crocket, and the others when he was in school. James was full of questions about Texas, eager to find out what it was really like.

Joseph told him of the good land, rolling hills and thick forests for good lumber, and the waterways carrying people and supplies for the war.

"If I ain't too nosy, what are you doing back in Alabama?"

"There was some personal business I had to take care of." Then he gestured at the boat. "I sailed on the Southern Belle for many years and decided to take one last voyage with Captain Goodman before I headed back to Texas." Noticing the lights of Chattanooga up ahead, he stood. "I best be on my way. I'm getting off as soon as we dock so I can catch the next boat back to Florence, then make my way back to Texas." They shook hands, wished each other well, and Joseph hurried through the doorway.

Joseph knocked on the captain's door and waited.

"Come in."

He opened the door and stepped inside the captain's cabin.

Goodman was frowning. "Where the hell ya been?"

Joseph grinned at his foul temper. "Talking to a young soldier. You look like the South just lost the war."

The captain considered that for a moment. "Well, they may be." He gestured at a chair. "Sit down, so's I can tell you why I wanted you along on this trip."

"All right," Joseph said, looking curious. "I've been wondering about that."

Goodman cleared his throat. "I could use a drink." He pulled a small bottle of whiskey out of his coat pocket and gestured toward two glasses on a nearby chest. "Get yourself a glass, Laddie. You're gonna need this as much as me."

The captain's troubled mood concerned Joseph as he got the glasses and then waited while Goodman poured two drinks. He was anxious to find out what was on the captain's mind, but he waited until the old man had finished his ritual of pouring the drinks.

Goodman handed Joseph a glass and then took a hefty drink of his.

Watching the captain, Joseph sipped his whiskey.

"This war's brought a lot more trouble than we ever realized, Laddie." Goodman's expression was worrisome. He gulped the rest of his drink, stared into the empty glass, and then put it on the table. "I know you have your own set of problems, Joseph, and the last thing you need is for someone to ask a favor of you."

Curious about the favor, Joseph watched the captain, thinking he looked worried and a little afraid. "You know all you have to do is ask, Captain."

Goodman grinned at him. "Don't ya think you should find out about the favor b'fore accepting?"

Joseph smiled. "It can't be that bad."

"It's Jonah. I need a favor for Jonah."

Joseph looked surprised. "What's happened to Jonah?"

"Nothing's happened to him." Goodman looked uneasy and flustered. "It's what I'm afraid might happen if this war goes on much longer."

Joseph looked confused. "I don't understand."

The captain settled back in his chair, thinking of how to explain it. "I want you to take Jonah back to Texas with you."

Joseph looked surprised. "To Texas?"

Goodman nodded. "That's right."

Joseph frowned and shook his head. "He would never leave you and this boat; he'd be lost without you and the Southern Belle."

The captain digested that with a nod. "Don't ya think I know that?"

Joseph looked at him in silence as Goodman stared at the floor.

"It's hard for me to put this into words, Laddie." He looked up from the floor.

James thought he saw his eyes begin to well.

"Do me this one favor."

"Of course, I will, Captain, but I don't rightly understand why."

Silence filled the cabin as the captain looked at him. "I'm afraid that if he stays here with me, he'll get himself killed." He sat back in his chair with a worried face. "Other than you, Jonah's all the family I have, and I want him someplace safe." He paused with a sad look. "I need this favor, Laddie."

"He won't leave you, Captain."

"He'll go, Laddie. If I tell him to, he will."

"That'd be a might cruel, Captain. He won't understand."

"If I tell Jonah you need him, he will," said the captain. "He likes you, always has, ever since he found you hiding among them crates all those years ago."

"I remember," replied Joseph recalling that day long ago. "All right, Captain, if this is what you want, but you'll break Jonah's heart."

The captain looked sad. "Better, he suffers a broken heart than end up dead." Goodman got up, shook Joseph's hand, looking grateful, walked to the door, opened it, and looked back at him. "I'll have his papers ready by the time the two of you leave the boat."

Joseph set his half-full glass back onto the table and walked toward the door.

Goodman looked at Joseph as he walked past him and into the hall then glancing up and down lowered his voice. "Promise me one thing."

Joseph paused in the hall.

"We're no fools," he said. "We both know how this war's going to end. Jonah will be a free man for the first time in his entire life, and he'll need your help."

"Don't worry about Jonah, Captain. I liked Jonah from that first day; after all, he saved my life."

Soon after the Southern Belle docked at Chattanooga, Joseph walked down the gangplank with Jonah close behind, looking confused and worried and carrying an old carpetbag of clothes. As they stepped onto the dock, Joseph glanced up at the bridge, expecting to see the captain in his usual spot, but the window was empty, and as they walked away, he wondered if he would ever see Captain Goodman again.

"Have a good trip, Joseph," someone cried out.

Joseph turned, expecting to see the captain, but saw James Chrisman leaning on the Southern Belle's railing, smiling down at him.

Joseph smiled, waved, and then he and Jonah disappeared into the crowd.

James Chrisman

James caught up with the 47th Alabama in time for their march north into Pennsylvania and a place called Gettysburg. The Confederate army engaged the Federals in a battle that lasted three days before retiring, defeated, into Georgia, resting for two months. On September 18, 1863, the 47th engaged Union forces again in a battle that lasted two days in what became a costly Confederate victory, losing over 18,000 men. In the end, the weary Confederate army marched into Tennessee and a place called Browns Ferry, near Wautachie, Tennessee, and on October 28, 1863, they surprised a Union battalion and suffered light casualties.

After a few days of rest, the James and the other Confederate soldiers marched farther into Tennessee, engaging in several small skirmishes until the battle at Armstrong's Hill, on the Holston River, near Knoxville, Tennessee.

The battle at Armstrong's Hill was a two-hour battle that started on the morning of November 25th, 1863 and was fought mostly hand to hand, with such savageness, that when it was over, Generals and officers from both sides stood in awe at witnessing such brutality. A few days later, the Confederates mounted a spirited assault on the slopes of Little Round Top that, in years to come, would be the subject of stories and poetry. In the late afternoon of that day, James and the others sat on the ground and wept. James leaned back against a broken tree that had also become a casualty and glanced around at the bodies littering the terrain, feeling tired to the point of complete exhaustion. As tears filled his young eyes, he looked at his bloody hands, asking God's forgiveness and for Him to end the war. But that was not in God's plans, for the war would last another two years.

Twenty-Three

June 1863

William Chrisman

In the months that followed James and Martha's wedding, little changed in the Chrisman household. The hours Elizabeth spent in Davy's room were a mystery to William, and he couldn't understand her inability to let her dead son's ghost rest. Davy was gone, and nothing would ever bring him back. Their son would never laugh or walk the floors of the Chrisman house again. William wanted his wife and friend back in his life to take away his loneliness and ease his pain from Davy's death, but he did not know how to accomplish that.

Beth and the girls spent much of their spare time at the Heard place, visiting with Martha while Beth helped her write letters to James, or visited other households in the valley that were having happier moments. To deal with his loneliness, William rode his Chestnut through the rows of crops until the pain in his body forced him to the front porch, leaving the fields to the foreman, hired hands, and slaves. In his solitude on that familiar porch, he considered Elizabeth and her sorrow, knowing there was nothing he could do. William missed the closeness they had shared over the years and kept telling himself that Indians grieve differently than white women. He gave up trying to get close to her; she would move away, leaving him to his lonely silence. It was a sad house, and the laughter that once echoed within its walls had been replaced by the creaking of walls, floors, and roof.

Having spent one morning in the fields, he sat on the porch alone, enjoying a glass of lemonade while remembering James and Davy talking and joking on this very porch. A horse-drawn buggy turned from the main road onto his property, and though his eyes were old and tired, he knew immediately it was Martha. Hoping she had a letter from James to share that would bring a little cheer to his wife, he called out to her. Before Martha could climb down from the buggy, Elizabeth and Beth were waiting on the porch.

Martha climbed down from the buggy, looking excited. "Got a letter from James." She hurried across the yard, and up the porch steps hugging Elizabeth and then Beth.

William stood from his chair and smiled. "What about this old man?"

She grinned, hugged him, and then held up the letter. "Got a letter from James."

"I heard," William said, looking anxious.

Martha smiled shyly and then handed the letter to Beth. "You can't read the private parts, only the parts about the war." Her face flushed as she smiled and sat down in the chair offered by William, who sat in the chair next to her. Elizabeth sat in another chair looking anxious, while Beth took the folded letter from the wrinkled envelope and sat on the top step of the porch leaning against the pillar. She read in silence as her mouth formed the words James had written, picking out the parts saved for Martha while the others patiently waited.

When she finished, she read the letter in which James told of his trip up the Tennessee River, joining the 47th Alabama in time for a long march to a place called Gettysburg.

William nodded with a frown, having read about the battle in the newspaper and the number of casualties on both sides, and thanked God his son was still alive.

Beth glanced at her mother, then read the part telling her mother not to worry about him, that he was feeling better, even gained a little of his weight back. Elizabeth smiled with pleasure at that news. Beth went on to read that he hoped his Pa's hip wasn't bothering him too much, promising that when the war was over, William could sit on the porch while James rode the fields.

The moment of joy was disturbed by the sound of horses in the distance. Seeing who it was riding along the country road, Elizabeth stood and walked to the edge of the porch, staring at the riders and the dust they left. William got up from his chair and joined her at the railing, while Beth looked toward the riders, recognizing the two men and wishing they hadn't ridden by and spoiled the moment.

Martha asked who they were.

Williams's face filled with anger. "Bishop Martin and Ben Rogers." He leaned over the railing and spit on the ground as if getting a bad taste out of his mouth, then put one arm around Elizabeth and watched the two until they disappeared over the hill.

"Bastards," whispered Elizabeth. "Ain't fair, those two are still alive."

Silence fell on the porch like a heavy July heatwave as William looked at the side of his wife's face, seeing it filled with so much hate it unnerved him. He looked at the empty road wishing he were a younger man.

Elizabeth forced a smile and turned to Beth. "Please continue, dear."

After Beth finished reading the letter Elizabeth thanked Martha for allowing them to share her letter, asking if she could stay for dinner.

Martha thanked her but declined. "I have to get home, so's I can help ma get our dinner on the table."

Elizabeth smiled. "Another time."

Martha and Beth walked to a flat rock near the flower garden several yards from the house, where Beth read the rest of the letter to Martha. William sat alone on the porch, watching them, but his mind was inside the house with his wife and her hatred.

A Good Day for a Ride

William lay in bed, looking out the veranda doors toward the dark crimson dawn, waiting for the sun to peek over the hills beyond the cotton fields. In an already crowded mind filled with Elizabeth and Davy, he thought of James and the letter Beth had read the day before. For fear of waking Elizabeth, he lay perfectly still, feeling the warmth of her body next to his, hoping her dreams were of happiness and not of sorrow. The horizon slowly grew to a lighter shade of reds and oranges against a light blue sky as the dawn and night fought with one another.

His thoughts went from the sun peeking over the hills to Davy lying beneath the cold ground, deprived of having the chance to grow old, then of James, off somewhere fighting in a war that could rob them of another son. Wanting to forget such thoughts, he turned his mind to the morning, deciding it would be a good day for a ride. A rooster crowed somewhere outside, greeting the new day as it had every day before the sorrow and unhappiness had come to visit and refused to leave.

Elizabeth turned, placing one arm around him, then nestled her head against his shoulder, something she hadn't done for a long time.

Believing she was asleep, he lay still, enjoying her presence, feeling the warmth of her familiar body that he missed. He longed for her touch and tenderness as her fingers traced the creases of his ear and softly touched his gray hair.

Elizabeth knew she had neglected the man she loved for too long, and now it was time to bury the dead and love the living. Thinking he needed a haircut, she kissed his shoulder, rose to one elbow, turned his face with her hand, and looked into his red, puffy eyes, knowing he was thinking of their dead son as well. She placed her hand on the side of the weathered and wrinkled face she had loved for so many years. "I love you."

Knowing his wife had returned from that sad, lonely place, he smiled. "And I you."

She moved closer, kissed him tenderly, got out of bed, put on her robe, and pulled her long black hair from under it, letting it fall down her back to her waist. She turned and smiled. "I'm going downstairs to start the coffee and breakfast."

He watched her leave and then turned back to the day, realizing the dawn had changed to a bright new morning, an important morning. He sat up, placed his feet on the cold floor, stood, and reached for his pants hanging over the back of a nearby chair. He dressed, then walked across the room to a large chest of drawers by the window and opened the top drawer. With one hand, he pushed aside the clothing until he found the large hunting knife that was a wedding present from Elizabeth's grandfather nestled in the back of the drawer. The old man had told William of the days when he was a young brave, and the red-haired, white man that had tried to take his scalp with that very knife. The old Indian smiled as he moved his hands, mocking the fight, telling of his skills as he fought and wrestled on the ground with this angry white man. The old Indian once more lived his victory as he knelt to the ground showing how he plunged the knife deep into the man's heart. William remembered the old brave's smile as he boasted that it was he who won the knife and took the white man's red hair. Then, as the old man handed William the knife, he said it was big medicine.

William had put the knife away, thinking he would give it to one of his sons, and he had decided long ago that it would go to Davy. With both hands, he slowly and gently lifted the knife and scabbard from its hiding place, then examined the carved bone handle. With a timelessly-honored ritual, William slowly pulled the knife from its crafted leather scabbard, touching the small strand of long, red hair hanging from it. He lightly touched the shiny blade, and finding it still sharp, he slowly shoved it back into the leather scabbard, unbuttoned his shirt, placed it next to his skin, and buttoned the shirt back up.

The smell of fresh coffee greeted him like an old friend when he walked into the kitchen, pleased at seeing Elizabeth busy at the stove, humming a familiar tune. Beth also appeared in good spirits as she smiled and said good morning while she carried plates into the dining room. He poured himself a cup of coffee, telling Elizabeth he wasn't hungry and was going out for a ride.

"You ain't going to church?" she asked, looking surprised.

"Not today, Mother," he said softly. "I have a lot on my mind."

"I know," she said. "You kept me awake."

He took a drink of coffee. "I didn't realize I was tossing that much."

She smiled without looking away from the hot stove. "You don't have to move for me to know you're not sleeping."

He smiled, thinking it was the Indian in her. "Anyway, I ain't hungry."

"You haven't missed breakfast in 30 years." She turned the eggs, motioning toward the dining room with the greasy spatula. "You need your breakfast, now go sit down."

He did as he was told and waited patiently at the long, empty table, imagining his sons arguing about one thing or another, and in his memory, he could hear Davy laughing as he chased his little sisters around the table. The plate of eggs, potatoes, and bacon that Elizabeth set in front of him interrupted those happy memories.

"More coffee?" she asked.

He nodded yes, watched the coffee pour from the spout into his cup, and then watched her disappear into the kitchen through the swinging door. Footsteps of children running and their muffled screams and laughing upstairs caused him to look up at the ceiling, wondering what those two were doing. He hurried through breakfast, glad that Elizabeth had made him eat, knowing he would not get another meal until that evening. He wiped his mouth with the napkin, dropped it on the plate, stood, picked up his cup of coffee, and walked into the kitchen. Drinking the last of the coffee, he placed the empty cup on the kitchen table and glanced at his coat hanging behind the door.

Elizabeth paused from her cooking, thinking of his bad hip. "When will you be back?"

"Not sure." He paused, looking at her. "Late, maybe."

They looked into each other's eyes for a long moment in knowing silence, and then she turned back to the stove to prepare breakfast for the girls. As she hummed a familiar tune, William walked to the door and his coat hanging from a peg on the wall, hiding the holster and pistol he had hung there the night before. He quickly slung the holster around his waist, buckled the belt, and adjusted the holster against his leg. He slipped into his coat and pulled the ends of it down over the gun, trying to hide it.

Elizabeth turned from the stove and her cooking, looked at her husband, his gun and holster, and quickly turned away.

He buttoned two of the four buttons of his coat that bulged over the holster and pistol, took his hat from a peg on the wall, and opened the door. He paused in the open doorway to look back at his wife busy with the children's breakfast, put on his hat, walked outside, and closed the door behind him. He walked down the steps into the crisp morning air as his hands felt the morning chill. His hip hurt like hell with each step toward the barn, but he felt alive and full of resolve. Refusing the help of a hired hand, he saddled his Chestnut, climbed up into the saddle in pain, and rode out of the barn past the corral and the big oak tree where Davy and Allen used to meet at night. He turned the horse toward the county road, knowing Elizabeth was watching from the kitchen window, which gave him comfort.

Hidden in the trees of a small wooded area, William sat on the Chestnut quietly, staring at a small rundown house on the other side of the open field of tall, brown grass. It was mid-morning, and smoke rose lazily from the chimney carrying with it smells of wood, bacon, and coffee. He glanced around as he moved the Chestnut cautiously along the trees into a deep gully of rocks and a small stream, stopping in a spot that placed the barn between him and the house.

He dismounted, ignoring the pain in his hip, tied the Chestnut to a small bush, patted her on the neck, and made his way out of the gully. Careful to keep the barn between him and the house, he made his way to the back of the barn, opened the narrow back door, stepped inside, and waited for his eyes to adjust to the dim light. He slowly walked through the dusty rays of sunlight shining through the cracks between the boards that made thin lines of light across the dirt floor. One of the horses gave out a nervous snort and then uttered a low, soft whinny while the other horse looked at him with big, black eyes. William spoke to them with gentle, soft words until they decided he meant them no harm and went back to their morning meal of hay. He made his way to the big doors in front of the barn, and in the silence of the barn, he peered through the cracks of the closed doors toward the house across the yard. His thoughts returned to the Rupert ruins and the lifeless bodies of Davy, Emmett, and Allen, and then of the Rupert murder-suicide so long ago, and the day Harry Martin took in the two Rupert boys, who later ran off.

William looked at the dark, weathered wood of the door and gently touched it in memory of the day he and Harry Martin had hung the large doors a few days after Constance Martin died giving birth to Bishop Martin. He thought of the day Harry Martin died, knowing it was a day he lost a good friend, and thought about how it seemed like such a long time ago. A noise jerked him back from the past, and his eyes returned to the crack. Bishop Martin closed the back door of the house and walked toward the barn while adjusting his hat and his belt. The chickens in the yard darted frantically in front of him, clucking warnings to one another.

With his heart pounding in his chest and ears William stepped back into the shadows while sliding the pistol from its holster. The door opened, and Bishop Martin walked into the barn, pushing one door out of the way, unaware of William's presence, until he turned. Seeing the figure before him, Bishop jumped back, startled at first, and then seeing it was William, he smiled. "Shit Will. You darn near gave me a heart attack!" It never occurred to him to ask what he was doing in his barn until he saw the gun.

William stepped toward Bishop. "There's a debt to pay today, Bishop."

Fear set into his face as Bishop realized what William meant, and asked the question he already knew the answer to. "What are you doing with that gun, Will?"

William's cold, angry eyes stared deep into Bishop's eyes, searching for some small sign of good that would give him mercy; but he found none. "It's time to pay for little Davy, Emmett, and Allen."

"What the hell ya talking about, Will?" He took a step back toward the open door, remembering that his gun was still in the house, and then, hearing the clicking of the hammer of William's gun, he stopped.

William stepped closer. "You know what the hell I'm talking about, you bastard. It was you and that damn Ben Rogers who killed them boys, at the old Rupert place."

Bishop had fear in his eyes as he backed into the door, glanced back at it quickly, and then looked at William. "I heard what happened, Will, and I swear, we weren't near the place."

"Liar!" shouted William in anger. "Beth was hiding in the woods as you two rode by, looking like the devil himself was chasing you both."

Martin thought about running for the house and his gun, but knew he would never do it. "It wasn't me, Will, honest,"

William tensed full of hate. "Liar!"

Bishop's face filled with tiny beads of sweat. "It was all a mistake Will. We were arresting Allen when Davy came running at us with a knife. Ben shot in self-defense." He looked at the gun in William's hand. "Please, Will. All we's doing was having some fun with the Downs boy before we took him in."

William considered that, knowing his son would never attack anyone, and quickly decided it didn't matter. "I want to know what really happened out there, Bishop. Who shot my boy, and who shot Emmett Heard?"

Bishop quickly blurted out, "It was Ben Rogers. He killed `em all, I swear, Will." Bishop put his hand toward William in a pleading way. "It was Ben Rogers, Will." He paused, looking as if he were about to cry. "Please, Will."

William looked at the pitiful sight begging for mercy where there was none. He was going to kill Bishop Martin, but he wanted to know what had happened before he did. "Get down on your knees."

Bishop Martin began to cry. "Please, Will."

William motioned to the floor with his gun. "On your knees!" After Bishop was on his knees, he asked, "What the hell happened out there?"

Bishop looked up with welling eyes as tears streamed down his face and softly whimpered, "Please, Will."

William wondered if Davy had the chance to cry before they killed him, and as he filled with rage and hate, he put his foot on Bishop's chest and pushed him back against the door, ignoring the shooting pain in his hip.

Martin sat up and began to explain what happened. "As I said, Will, Davy ran toward us, and Ben turned and shot him in self-defense. I checked Davy and could tell your boy was hurt." He looked hopeful. "He was still breathing, and I said we needed to get him to town, but Ben told me to shut up." Bishop wiped the tears from his eyes. "Ben picked up Davy's knife and stabbed Allen in the heart. It happened so fast I couldn't stop it."

William stepped back and pointed the barrel of the gun at Bishop's head. "You're going to hell with a lie on your lips."

Bishop hung his head and cried, sobbing tears of fear.

William raised his voice in anger, "I knew your father." He gestured at the barn. "I helped build this damn barn you're gonna die in." William's head pounded with each heartbeat, and it felt as though it was going to explode before his gun as he yelled, "You two killed them three boys."

Bishop cried as he held out his hands and shook his head, pleading for his life. "No, Will, please."

William's voice turned soft and gentle. "Stand up, Bishop."

Bishop stared down at the dirt floor of the barn as he whimpered and pleaded for his life. Then as he slowly got up, he looked into William's eyes, searching for mercy. "Please, Will, it was Ben."

"There were marks on their wrists Bishop." Then William screamed, "Their damn hands were tied. They were defenseless young boys!"

That was the last thing Bishop heard as William pulled the trigger, felt the gun jump in his hand, and watched as the concussion of the blast knocked Bishop's head against the barn door. As the smoke cleared, William watched Bishop slide down the door, leaving a trail of brains and blood on the weathered door. He stared down at Bishop for several seconds before he heard the frightened horses jumping and kicking in their stalls.

Adrenaline filled his body with strength and power he hadn't felt since the days he rode with the militia during the Indian Wars back in Kentucky. Looking out the door at the chickens scrambling around the yard trying to fly while clucking warnings at one another, he turned from his vengeance to the frightened horses. Limping into the stall, he softly said, "Whoa." He gently stroked their noses and necks to calm them. After they settled down, he returned to the gully without looking back, and once in the saddle, he considered Ben Rogers. Though his hip hurt like hell, William felt alive as he rode out of the gully, knowing that Rogers would figure it out as soon as he heard about Bishop. He was certain that he and the other men of the Home Guard would come after him, and knowing that Rogers lived alone, he prodded the Chestnut with his spurs into a trot.

The ride had been long and painful for William, but now he stood next to a tree, half-hidden behind a large bush watching the small house of Ben Rogers. The Chestnut stood a few feet away, busy with the grass beneath a tree. The pain in his hip and back when he had dismounted reminded him that surprising Ben Rogers was out of the question. The fleetness of foot had left with the arrival of age and arthritis and getting close enough to ensure getting off the first shot before Rogers saw him, looked skeptical at best. It was stealth he needed now, the stealth he remembered from his militia days as a young man fighting Indians on the Kentucky Frontier.

Bishop Martin had always been a coward and a loudmouth bully, but Ben Rogers was different. He was downright mean and calculating. William looked down at the gun neatly tucked away in the leather holster he wore, then at the house, calculating the distance and the time it would take to cross the open yard. His hand moved from the pistol grip to the bone handle of the big hunting knife in the scabbard attached to his belt. The morning sun had moved across the sky toward noon, and it was getting warm, so he took off his coat and hung it over the saddle. After patting the Chestnut gently on the neck, he stood next to a tree behind a small bush, and considered his options.

Hearing a door open, he looked up and saw Ben Rogers walk out of the house and begin chopping firewood from a stack of wood near the house. As he watched Ben toss the pieces of wood onto a nearby woodpile, William calculated the wind and direction, thinking that if this were the old days, he would chance a shot, but he had used his pistol very little over the years and had never thought about bringing a rifle with him. Besides, he needed to get close. He wanted to look into Ben

Rogers' eyes as he died. But how? The distance was too great, and he was too slow, but with patience as his ally, he waited.

The minutes passed, and Rogers stopped chopping, placed the ax against the chopping stump, and walked a few feet across the yard to the outhouse. As he disappeared inside, William saw his chance, took the knife from its scabbard, and quietly made his way across the open space, hiding behind a thick blueberry bush a few yards from the outhouse. Even at this distance, he could hear Ben coughing and grunting while doing his business. Not thinking about the cracks in the outhouse walls, he moved around the berry bush and stood next to the door.

Ben saw a shadow. "Who's there?"

Realizing his mistake, William held the knife in his right hand with his body tense, ready for the door to open. As it slowly opened, Ben Rogers stuck his head out, and at seeing William, surprise filled his face. "Will, what the hell you doing here?"

William lunged at him, plunging the knife deep into his chest, and leaning into Rogers, he covered his mouth with one hand as they fell back inside the outhouse, onto the seat and against the back wall. Ben's big hands found William's face and shoulder, trying to push him off, but William used his legs to brace himself against the walls for leverage. He looked into the surprised, fearful eyes of Ben Rogers. "This here's for my son and them boys, you son-of-a-bitch!"

Ben struggled to move his head from side to side, his eyes wide with terror, staring into William's dark, hateful eyes, then he bit down on Williams's hand.

Ignoring the pain in his hand, William put his face next to Ben's ear. "I'm sending you to hell with Davy's knife, you bastard." Then he pulled the knife out, leaned back, and cut Ben's throat. Blood spewed out of the gash onto Williams's shirt and against the sides of the outhouse. William stood back with his free hand on Ben's bloody chest, listening to the gurgling sound of blood filling Ben Rogers' throat and lungs. There was one last quick struggle, and it was over.

Pushing himself off of Ben, he looked at his hand, seeing the teeth marks left from Ben Rogers during their struggle. With the front of his shirt and sleeves covered in blood, he stared at his terrible deed for a long moment and then slowly backed out of the outhouse. He walked painfully to the nearby water pump, washed the knife and then his hands.

It was late afternoon when William rode into his barn, dismounted, and unsaddled his horse. The day hung heavy and silent as if the end of the world was nearing. He walked across the yard with as limp, up the back steps, and into the house through the back door. Finding the kitchen empty, he hung his coat on the same peg he had removed it from that very morning, followed by his hat. He unbuttoned his bloody shirt, took it off, and stuffed it into the stove, and while the shirt burned, he washed his hands with soap and water. He splashed water onto his face, dried both face and hands, and then wrapped his left hand with a towel to cover the bite marks of Ben Rogers.

The sound of his footsteps seemed loud as he walked with a slight limp across the creaking, wooden floor from the kitchen through the house to the library. Once inside he unstrapped his gun, shoved it into the bottom drawer of his desk, and set the hunting knife on top of it. Feeling tired, he walked to the liquor cabinet, poured a brandy, and sat down in his black leather chair at the desk. Taking a sip, he stared at the knife, remembering the fear in Ben Rogers' eyes as he was dying. William thought about Bishop Martin, his good friend's only son, as Bishop begged for his life in the barn that he had helped Ben's father build. Taking another sip of brandy, William's eyes welled as he silently asked for Henry Martin's forgiveness. Then he wiped his eyes, gulped down the rest of the drink, picked up the knife, slowly stood in pain, walked out of the library and up the stairs.

He paused at the top, wondering where his wife and his daughters were, and remembered they had planned visit Martha, and he was glad they weren't home. He opened the door to his bedroom and stepped inside, surprised at finding his wife lying on the bed sleeping. He quietly walked to the chest, opened the top drawer, and put the knife back. He set the towel on the dresser, looked at the bite marks on his hand, and then sat in a nearby chair and took off his boots. Placing them neatly beside the chair, he stood, and carefully lay on the bed next to his wife.

Feeling the bed move, Elizabeth opened her eyes, turned, and looked into her husband's red eyes, noticing the red stains on the front of his white, long underwear. With eyes welling, he took her in his arms and held her against him while remembering the terrible things he had done in vengeance. William wanted to confess to someone, but to who? He turned away and looked out the veranda widow wanting to sleep, to rid his mind of the images of this day and his terrible secret. Elizabeth put one hand on his shoulder, and gently turned him over. Putting one hand on the side of his face, she caressed his cheek as she looked into his red, puffy, watering eyes. Then as if understanding, she kissed each eye tenderly and wrapped her arms around him, holding him as she would a child.

Twenty-Four

June 1862 – April 1865

Edward McAlexander

By the first of June 1862, Edward and Ethan were back with the 27th Alabama, wintering at Port Hudson, near Baton Rouge. They would remain there until taking part in the battle of Champion Hill, Mississippi, also known as The Battle of Bakers Creek, on May 16, 1863. It was another Union victory, costing the Confederate army over 4,300 men.

Fighting in small skirmishes over the next several months, the 27th Alabama, would not take part in another major engagement until July 9, 1863, when they joined another 32,000 Confederate soldiers that had dug in near Jackson, Mississippi. Engaging in a seven day battle against a far superior Union army determined on taking the city, the badly outgunned and outnumbered, Confederate Army, low on supplies, slipped away under cover of darkness on July 16, 1863.

In the weeks that followed, the battles fought by the 27th Alabama, continued to be one-sided, favoring the Union army that claimed victory after victory. The 27th Alabama left Mississippi and marched into Georgia, in early October 1863, for rest and reinforcements. Edward received a letter from his sister telling him she had given birth to his nephew, Joseph Samuel Greene Jr., on the 9th of June, 1863. Two days later, he was summoned to the Colonel's quarters and given a dispatch marked urgent. The dispatch told of his daughter's serious illness. Granted an immediate leave, he left for Florence on October 23, 1863.

October 30, 1863

Florence, Alabama

It was dark when Edward stepped from the train onto the Florence, Alabama, depot platform. His once smart gray uniform was slightly tattered and soiled, his face unshaven, and his hair was long and dusty under the wide-brimmed, dirty, light gray hat. There were no greeters eagerly waving; no one shouted his name, kissed his cheek, or hugged his neck. The days of glory and excitement, while men young and old eagerly hurried off to fight had ended long ago. Edward walked down the wooden platform stepping onto the cobblestone streets of Florence, oblivious to those with whom he shared the boardwalks. The better part of a half-hour passed, and now he stood at the iron gate looking at the big house at the end of the driveway. A yellow-orange glow in the windows seemed friendly, inviting, and warm. Standing in the darkness beneath the archway of the gate, he remembered how the death of Henrietta had left the house and its rooms cold and lonely.

Now, he feared an even greater emptiness if his daughter had passed away. For the first time in Edward's life, he didn't know what to do as he leaned against the brick pillar supporting the archway and gate. His eyes were red and watery as he silently prayed for his sick child.

"May I help you, sir?" came a woman's voice.

Startled out of his prayer, he looked up and smiled. "Hello, Sarah."

She gasped with surprise. "Oh, My God!" She put her hands over her mouth and began to cry.

He took off his hat. "My apologies Sarah, I never meant to frighten you."

She was in his arms in an instant, kissing his bearded face and lips, and then she looked up into his eyes, asking if he was hurt.

He shook his head and smiled, telling her he was just tired, having slept very little since the dispatch about his daughter. "How is she?"

Sarah smiled, saying that his daughter was fine. "The sickness left her three days ago, and at this very moment, she's upstairs sleeping."

Feeling as if a large weight had been lifted from him, he said, "Thank God."

"I posted a letter to you just two days ago telling you that she was all right."

"I had already left by then."

She looked into his tired eyes, touched his face with her fingers, and smiled. "I'm sorry if I worried you. But I'm so glad you're home." And even though he was dirty and bearded, it was the face she loved, and he was home. "Come." Taking his hand, she led him up the driveway.

He glanced toward the Kroger house. "I thought she was staying at your house."

"She was, but as she got better, she missed her own bed and things, so I brought her back here. I hope you don't mind, but I moved into your room so I could keep an eye on her."

He smiled. "Of course, I don't mind."

They hurried up the porch's steps to the front door, and as they stepped inside, the slave Sophie walked out from the kitchen. At seeing him, she stopped and stared at them as if she had seen a ghost.

Seeing her, Sarah laughed. "It's Edward."

Sophie clasped her hands over her heart. "Lord almighty, Mistah Edward." Then she hurried across the room, seeing how dirty his clothes were. "Looks what they's gone and done to ya, Mistah Edward." She paused to look at him as tears made their way down her dark cheeks. "Ya's ain't hurt or nothing?"

"I'm fine, Sophie." Edward gently took her shoulders in his hands and smiled. "I've missed you."

Looking worried, Sophie wiped at her tears. "Yah looks too thin, Mistah Edward." Then, she smiled, looking determined. "But ol' Sophie's gonna take care of that in the morn'n."

Edward laughed as he took off his coat.

Sophie reached for it, then took his hat, draped the coat over her arm, and affectionately brushed it with one hand. "I'll clean dis for ya, Mistah Edward. Now you go see that child of yours."

Sarah took his hand. "Come, Edward." She led him up the stairs to little Mary's room, where he found his daughter sleeping peacefully. He sat down in the chair next to her bed, and in the stillness of the room, the war seemed unimportant and far away. There were no guns here, no screams of pain, or sounds of men dying, only the soft breathing of an innocent child. Sarah bent down and whispered that she would be in the library.

Sarah changed into a nightgown and robe and waited for what seemed like hours in the library. She was staring into the fire, filled with memories of times before the war when the library doors opened. She stood in anticipation and waited while he closed the doors.

He walked across the room, took her in his arms, and kissed her. Then he looked into her soft eyes as he held her and said, "I must smell terrible."

"Like a man," she said affectionately. "But you're home, and that's all that matters."

They sat on the large rug in front of the fireplace, backs resting against the sofa, his arm around her as they stared into the fire.

She turned from the fire and kissed him as he gently lowered her to the rug, where his hand fumbled at her robe, touching her smooth, warm skin. Moments later, her nightgown, robe, and his clothes were lying on the floor.

The restful sleep that held Edward gently let go as he opened his eyes, and wondering where he was, he remembered he was in his bedroom. He turned to look at the empty pillow next to him, disappointed at not seeing Sarah next to him, and sat up with his back against the headboard. He sat in silence thinking of last night while watching the birds outside his window scampering from perch to perch in the tree, chirping at one another, arguing. There were no bulges sounding muster for the morning meal, and Ethan wasn't telling him he was an asshole. There was only a peaceful silence.

He turned to the empty pillow where Sarah's head had rested. Laying his head on her pillow, he smelled the fragrance of her, closed his eyes, and played the scenes on the rug by the fireplace over in his memory. A soft knock at the bedroom door interrupted those images. "Yes."

Sophie's familiar voice called from the other side. "Mistah Edward, when ya's ready, I'll fix ya a hot bath."

"I'm more than ready."

"Yes, suh won't be but a few minutes."

He sat up, reached for his robe lying on the foot of the bed, and as he put it on, he was surprised at finding a hint of Sarah's perfume on it. He smiled, imagining her wearing it around the bedroom, with sleeves rolled up. He looked down at the unmade bed and thought of her next door in her bed or taking a bath. She should be here with him, but for now, she needed to be in her bedroom, in her father's house. Tying the cloth belt of his robe into a loose knot, he walked across the hall to the big metal tub Sophie had filled with hot water. A fresh bar of soap, washcloth, and towel sat on the chest next to the tub, as did another pot of hot water, steam rising from the spout. Finding a razor, brush, and soap dish under a towel, he shaved before bathing.

Bathed and shaved, he returned to the stillness of his room, finding the birds had disappeared, and walking to the window to inspect the empty tree, he thought of Ethan, hoping he was safe. A horse and buggy trotted along the quiet, cobblestone street below, looking surreal in a world of war and killing. He turned to his closet to consider the many suits, thinking it had to be something that made him feel good. After carefully examining each one, he chose a light brown suit with dark brown piping along the lapel and pockets.

Dressed in the suit of his choice with a white silk shirt and brown shoes, Edward proceeded downstairs, stopping first at little Mary's room, disappointed she wasn't there. He walked past the hall clock, pausing to compare it to his pocket watch and seeing it was a few minutes past nine-thirty, thinking his was slow, or the big clock fast. Continuing down the stairs, he was greeted by the smell of biscuits, gravy, and fried pork.

Walking into the dining room, he found Alex sitting at the table reading the morning newspaper and eating breakfast.

Alex looked up, chewed, and swallowed. "Good morning. I tried to wait, but I decided to hell with you."

Pleased at seeing his brother, Edward smiled. "That doesn't surprise me. I'd expect you to treat my food as you do my brandy."

Alex laughed. "They are both excellent." Then he stood, walked to his brother, and they hugged one another.

Edward gripped Alex by the shoulders. "How the hell did you know I was home?"

He shrugged as he returned to his chair. "Sophie. She sent word first thing this morning, telling us you were home."

Edward smiled. "I should've known." He looked toward the kitchen. "Sophie wastes little time."

Alex was concerned over his brother. "You've lost weight."

Edward nodded. "Our meals in the field aren't quite up to Sophie's standards, as you should recall."

"Yes," said Alex. "I remember." He turned to the kitchen door. "Sophie, you have a skinny man out here in need of your cooking."

Moments later, Sophie entered the room carrying fresh coffee and a boat of steaming hot gravy. Placing them on the table in front of Edward, she gave Alex a quick, worried look. "Now, Mistah Alex, ya leaves these for Mistah Edward, I needs ta fatten him up a bit." She laughed and then turned to Edward. "Miss Sarah had come by earlier and done took little Mary next door so's you could sleep." Then she disappeared into the kitchen.

Edward fixed a plate for himself as Alex talked about the farm and his interest in politics. Surprised at that, Edward smiled, imagining his brother campaigning for State Representative around the county, all puffed up in his black suit and asking for votes. Secretly he believed Alex would make a good Representative in the new government. While Edward ate, Alex told him of the surprise visit from Joseph.

Edward looked at him with interest. "When was that?"

"Early June," said Alex. Then he went on to tell of the letter he had received from Mary asking for her inheritance now that she had turned twenty-five.

Edward thought about that for a few minutes and then shrugged. "It's her money, and best she has it now because no telling what things will be like after the war. I hope you gave it to Joseph?"

Alex nodded. "Of course. Joseph said they were going to buy a farm near the Hall's in east Texas."

Edward smiled, knowing Mary was happy, and that she, Joseph, and their sons were safe. After breakfast, Edward saw Alex to the front door, said goodbye, and then watched Alex climb into his buggy and disappear around the corner. He stepped inside and started to close the door when he heard his daughter call him. Stepping back onto the porch,

Edward saw her running up the driveway, followed closely by Sarah. He hurried across the porch, down the steps, and knelt to one knee, catching his daughter as she ran into his arms. He hugged her tightly and then looked at her smiling innocent face. "Look how big you've grown."

"I know, Daddy," she said, grinning. "I'm five now."

Edward picked her up. "Daddy missed you." Then he hugged her.

She frowned, looking very serious. "Are you going to stay home now?"

"For a while, little one." He thanked Sarah for occupying her while he got ready and had breakfast.

Sarah laughed. "There was no keeping her when I told her you were home."

He grinned, looking pleased, gave his daughter another hug, put her down, and took Sarah's hand in one hand, his daughter's in the other, and walked up the steps into the house. Inside, little Mary bolted up the stairs to her room only to return a short time later with a doll. "Here it is, Daddy. Here is the doll you sent me."

Edward knelt to one knee to examine the doll and then looked up at Sarah.

She smiled and winked.

Edward looked at his daughter. "I hope you like it."

"She's my favorite."

"I have some errands to run," said Sarah. "So, I will leave you two to get to know one another again."

Edward stood. "Will you have dinner with me tonight?"

"I'd love to."

After Sarah left, Edward and little Mary spent the remainder of the day together until finally, too tired to go on, she fell asleep on his lap while he was reading to her.

In the days that followed, Edward managed his time between his daughter and Sarah, and while Sarah had fallen deeply in love with Edward, she was not as sure about his love for her. At night, the library became their world of love and passion, both growing ever stronger, and she feared the day he had to leave. Tonight was no different. They had made love and were sitting on the floor of the library covered by a blanket, their backs against the sofa, watching the flames dance as the fire consumed the logs in the fireplace.

The room was quiet and peaceful, interrupted by the occasional pop of a burning log. Sarah leaned forward, taking most of the blanket with her, folded her arms on her knees, and looked into the fire. "When do you leave?"

He looked at the side of her face, thinking she was beautiful. "In two days."

"That's awfully soon."

"I know," he said, staring into the flames.

She sat back and looked at the fire. "I don't want you to go."

He put his arm around her, pulled her to him, and kissed the top of her head. "I know."

Suddenly she sat forward, filled with excitement. "Let's do something special tomorrow."

"Such as?"

"Oh, I don't know," she said thoughtfully. "You think of something."

"It was your idea."

She smiled. "It may be my idea, but you have to think of something."

He chuckled. "Now that makes sense." He stared at her for a few moments, thinking of how much he loved her. "I have an idea."

Her eyes lit up with excitement. "What?"

"Let's get married."

Sarah stopped smiling and gazed into his brown eyes. "Don't joke about that, Edward."

He put his hand on her cheek affectionately. "I wouldn't joke about such a thing." Then he took her hand and kissed it. "Will you marry me, Miss Sarah Kroger?"

She stared at him, thinking of her answer, already knowing what it would be. There was the war to consider, which may last for years, her parents, the issue of her taking the place of her sister Henrietta in his and little Mary's life.

"Well, Sarah," Edward said, waiting for her answer. "Will you marry me?"

Her eyes welled as tears made their way down her cheeks. "If you're sure that's what you want."

"If it wasn't," he said, smiling. "I wouldn't have asked."

She smiled, looking happy and excited. "I can make plans while you're away."

"I don't want to wait."

Looking surprised, Sarah asked, "When then?"

Edward considered the question for only a second. "Right away." Then he looked at the clock in the corner, seeing it was 10:30 in the evening. "Tomorrow."

"Edward, we couldn't possibly. Tomorrow's Saturday, and you leave Monday." She sat back, staring at the fire, looking disappointed.

Edward digested all that for a moment, but then excitement filled his face. "I know a judge, and he owes me a favor."

Hope filled her face. "Do you truly think we can?"

"Of course," he said. "Or I wouldn't have suggested it."

She thought about everything very quickly. "Are you sure this is what you want?"

"I've thought of little else this past year." Then he looked at the fire with a sad face. "While I was cold and hungry and at times afraid of dying, the thought of you gave me the strength to endure the unendurable." He turned and smiled, taking her hand. "Sometimes, Sarah, I believe the thought of making love to you is all that kept me from going insane."

"I'd be honored to marry you, Edward Asbury McAlexander," she said with a big smile. Then she stood, taking the blanket with her while he grabbed for something to cover himself.

"I best go home. I'll need a few hours of sleep if I am to be married in the morning."

Edward grabbed at the blanket, but Sarah stepped backward, laughing. "You'll have to wait until our wedding night, young man." Then she giggled, but before she could move away, he took her hand and gently pulled her down to the floor.

It was eleven Saturday morning, November 12, when Edward and Sarah stood on a porch unfamiliar to her. Edward smiled as he pulled the cord, ringing the bell of Judge Jacob Pratt's home. Sarah giggled as if a young schoolgirl. Moments later, the door opened, and they looked into the eyes of an elderly and slightly built Negro woman dressed in a long, neatly pressed, black dress with a white apron.

Not used to having visitors on a Saturday morning, she glanced at them curiously. "May I helps y'all?"

"Hello Bertha, is the Judge home?" Edward asked politely.

"Yes, suh, he is," she said, recognizing Edward. "How is you, Mistah Edward?"

"I'm fine. Please tell Jacob that Edward McAlexander," he glanced at Sarah. "And a friend is here to seek his assistance in a very important matter."

"Yes, suh." She gestured with one hand to come in, and after Edward and Sarah stepped inside, she escorted them to the parlor and a small sofa. "Please ta have a seat whilst I go tells the Judge y'all' are here."

Edward and Sarah waited in the stillness of the big house nervously smiling at one another, and after several minutes they heard heavy footsteps.

A tall, heavyset man walked into the parlor, wearing a smile with a big outstretched hand. "Edward, is that really you?" They shook hands. "My dear boy, what in the hell are you doing here? The last I heard, you were off someplace killing them bastard Northerners." Before Edward could answer, the Judge apologized to Sarah. "I am very sorry, my dear, please forgive my vulgarity."

"Quite all right," smiled Sarah. "I fully understand."

The judge turned to Edward looking curious. "Bertha mentioned something about needing assistance with an important matter?"

"Yes. I, or that is we, do, Judge."

The judge considered that a moment. "Can't be too serious old boy, as you're both smiling."

Edward laughed. "No, not serious, but it is important."

"Hmmm." The judge gestured toward the door. "In that case, let's go to my study. The parlor is no place for important matters."

They stepped into a study filled with expensive furniture, walls of paintings, and shelves of books not much different from the ones in Edward's library. The judge politely pointed at two heavily stuffed chairs in front of a large, dark wooden desk. "Please, have a seat." He waited for them to sit before settling into his chair behind the desk. He smiled at Sarah as he took some papers out of the top drawer, placed them neatly on his desk, reached for the pen in the ink well, and looked at Edward. "Now, dear boy, in what way may I be of service?"

Edward took Sarah's hand in his and squeezed it gently. "We want to get married."

Looking surprised, the judge considered that as he placed the pen back in the ink well and sat back in his chair, looking disappointed. "This is quite unexpected. I thought you were in some sort of trouble."

Edward grinned. "You always did have a keen memory Jacob, but it's not trouble I'm in."

Jacob laughed robustly. "You must admit, you and that Hall fella were a bit of trouble to a teacher or two." He leaned forward, frowning. "And let's not forget the Dean."

Edward chuckled and glanced at Sarah, feeling the heat from the blood flushing his face. "You make it sound as if Ethan and I were terrible young men."

"No worse than a few others," said the judge, grinning. He looked at Sarah, raised his brow, and nodded. "Edward, my boy, I can't say I blame you for wanting to marry this beautiful creature."

Sarah blushed at the compliment with a shy smile.

The judge looked at Edward sternly. "If you are both sure this is what you want, I would be most happy to perform the ceremony." He stood and walked around the large, dark desk, stood in front of Sarah, took her hand, and gently kissed it. "It would be my pleasure." Then he turned to Edward and shook his hand. "I suppose congratulations are in order. When is this big event?" he asked as he walked to his chair, talking over his shoulder. "I need to prepare for such an occasion."

Edward grinned. "Today."

Jacob looked surprised. "Today? My word, man, these things take time, preparations, etc., etc., and on and on." He looked at Sarah. "You should know that, young lady."

Edward chuckled. "Yes, Jacob, today. We want to get married right now."

The Judge was without expression, his mouth wide open.

Edward and Sarah smiled at one another and waited.

Finally, the judge blinked and smiled, knowing it was no use arguing, but continued anyway. "My boy, my dear Sarah, the two of you need to plan for such things. A party, a reception, invitations to write and send out, and all the other things one does for one of the most important events of their life."

Edward frowned while considering all that. "We know. But we no longer have those kinds of luxuries." He smiled wryly. "If we did, we wouldn't be sitting in your study."

The judge sucked in a big breath, blowing it out in a big sigh, looked at them for several moments, and then turned to the window and looked out at the flower garden in silence. Even sitting down, Sarah thought he looked big. Judge Jacob Pratt stood six foot three and weighed 270 pounds, with black curly hair, a clean-shaven face, and friendly, gray eyes. Without turning away from the window, he spoke softly. "I suppose this war has changed our lives." Then he waved his large hands frantically. "Everyone is in such a hurry these days." He turned from the window and looked at them. "You're both sure about this?"

They looked at one another, smiled, and nodded.

Jacob smiled, looking skeptical. "This is just a joke, isn't it, Edward?" His eyes narrowed. "You're simply paying me back for some trick I pulled on you in school."

Edward laughed. "No, my old friend, this is not a joke." He smiled at Sarah and then turned to Jacob. "We truly want to get married before I leave."

"And when is that?"

"Monday morning."

The judge stared at him, sat back, and folded his hands on his round stomach, letting his thumbs play with one another. After a moment, he slowly got up from his chair, touched the top of his desk with the tips of his fingers, and looked at Edward and Sarah. Then he walked to the door of his study, opened it, and stuck his head in the hallway. "Josephine!" he yelled, then glanced back at Edward and Sarah with a smile and yelled once again. "Josephine! Can you come down here?"

A voice from somewhere in the house yelled back, "I'm busy!"

The judge turned to Edward and smiled, looking embarrassed. "If you remember, Josephine is not one to put forth a lot of words in a conversation." He stuck his head into the hall once again. "I need your assistance in the study."

"Can't it wait?" she yelled back.

The judge stepped into the hallway. "Just come down here, please." Stepping back into the room he smiled looking embarrassed.

Moments later Josephine appeared in the doorway in an apron covered in flour and grease. "Oh," she said, looking surprised. Josephine was a small woman of slight build. Her dark brown hair was in a reckless bun atop her head and had the look of a cook busy with a meal for forty men. "You should have told me we had company, Jacob." Then recognizing Edward with a warm and happy expression, she hurried across the room. "I'm a mess," she said, extending a very small hand to Edward. Then looking at Sarah, asked, "Who is this charming and beautiful young lady?"

"Josephine," Edward said, "this is Sarah Kroger."

Josephine smiled. "Hello my dear, so nice to meet you, are---"

Jacob quickly cut her off, took her by the arm, led her to a spot across the room by his desk, and lowered his voice. "They want to get married."

"How wonderful," she said while clasping her hands over her heart as she turned and smiled at them.

The Judge scowled as he cleared his throat. "Josephine, will you please wait until I am finished talking?"

She smiled at her husband. "If I did that, I would never get to say anything." She turned and nodded proudly at Edward and Sarah.

"Now is not the time," warned the judge quietly.

Josephine raised her eyebrows and smiled at him. "Yes, dear."

Edward and Sarah fought the urge to laugh but smiled at one another.

Jacob paused, giving his wife an irritating look. "The point, my dear wife, is they want to get married today and----"

"How wonderful," she interrupted, looking at Sarah and then at her husband. "Sorry, dear, you were saying?"

Jacob frowned as his voice deepened with authority. "Now, as I started to explain," he said, forcing a smile. "We need you for a witness and one other person."

She looked at him with a raised brow, eyes wide, and smiling mouth, waiting for him to tell her who the other witness was. When he didn't, she said, "I would be happy to be a witness, dear, and who else are you planning to use?"

Jacob shook his head and looked down at the floor with pursed lips, his face tense. He forced a smile. "Well, dear," he said softly. "I had hoped that perhaps you knew of someone we could get…like now?"

"Bertha," she blurted, startling everyone in the room.

"Bertha?" repeated Jacob, looking skeptical.

"Of course," she said, frowning. "What's wrong with Bertha? She's alive, and what's more, she's just upstairs."

Jacob looked thoughtful as he rubbed his forehead, considering the suggestion. "A little irregular," he said more or less to himself.

Josephine rolled her eyes, looking disgusted with her husband. "For heaven's sake, Jacob. Bertha will do just fine."

Jacob frowned, looking unsure. "I'm not sure this is legal. I've never done this sort of thing before."

Josephine closed her eyes, shook her head, and then looked at him. "For heaven's sake, Jacob, do you always have to be so damn proper?" She smiled at Edward and Sarah. "From the looks of these two, we better hurry."

Sarah blushed, and Edward chuckled.

Jacob scowled. "That was not funny, my dear." He looked at Edward and Sarah, slapped his desktop, and grinned. "All right, Josephine, get Bertha, and we'll marry these two."

Josephine returned within minutes with Bertha in tow, instructing her to stand beside herself and the Judge. Edward did his best not to laugh while Sarah thought it was wonderfully romantic, if not the most interesting wedding she had ever attended.

November 14, 1863

The bedroom was still dark when Edward opened his eyes, escaping from the nightmare of lying wounded and bleeding on a smoke-filled battlefield. He turned to watch Sarah sleeping and wondered if they had done the right thing. What if the nightmare was a vision of the future, and he never came home, never held her, never made love to her, or never just sat and talked with her again? Watching her sleep, he marveled at her face in the dim moonlight coming through the window, smiling at how she hogged the covers, her discarded pillow on the floor, now owning his. As he watched her sleep, he decided that if he were to die on some bloody ridge or drown in a dirty swamp, and these moments were all they would ever have, it would be enough. Sarah would care for little Mary and keep his memory fresh in his daughter's mind.

Slowly and carefully, he got out of bed, put on his robe, and tiptoed across the hall to his daughter's room, stood beside her bed, and watched her sleep. He had been there for several minutes when Sarah put her arm around his waist, her head against his shoulder, as they watched the child sleep.

The morning air was cool as they stood on the depot platform waiting for the "All Aboard" call. Edward wondered why the trains he took always left in the early morning instead of the evening. He took off his hat, holding it with the fingertips of his left hand. "I'll write when I can,"

"I know," she said softly. "And I'll write every day." She brushed his hair to one side with her fingers. "Try not to worry about us. Little Mary and I will be fine."

He smiled. "She likes you."

"I've come to love her as well. She'll be very angry when she finds out you left, but I'll tell her you were in her room earlier. She'll like that."

He started to say something when he saw Alex and Ella getting out of a carriage and knew their moments alone were gone. "I love you."

"Edward!" Alex yelled as they hurried up the ramp toward them. "I was afraid we would miss you. Hello Sarah." Then he grinned. "I mean, Sister."

Sarah blushed and smiled. "Alex, hello, Ella."

The train whistle blew with a piercing shrill, followed by that familiar "All Aboard!" They turned toward the conductor as he walked up and down the platform, lantern in hand. "All aboard," he repeated while waving the lantern back and forth.

Seeing the signal from the conductor, the engineer pushed a lever forward, and the big wheels spun. Steam hissed and spewed across the platform as the engine jerked, and the cars down the line sounded like rattling thunder.

Edward turned to Alex's outstretched hand and shook it firmly. Neither spoke while sharing a knowing look. Each understood. Then he kissed Ella goodbye on the cheek. He turned and took Sarah in his arms, kissed her, and held her tightly as the railcars slowly started moving, their sound almost drowning his whispered words, "I love you."

On the verge of tears, she couldn't speak as she looked into his eyes. He smiled, then turned and ran after the train, jumping onto the bottom step, turned, and waved. She threw him a kiss, then waved.

Edward pretended to catch the kiss, smiled, and disappeared into the railcar.

Twenty-Five

June 1863

Joseph and Jonah

The trip from Florence had taken longer than expected, so Joseph was tired and a little irritable when he guided the rented buggy off the county road through the gate, onto the Hall farm, and toward the house. Thinking of Mary and the children, he put the reins to the horse, prodding it a little faster toward their destination. "We're almost home, Jonah."

Jonah had been looking toward the hills and remembering the Southern Belle and Captain Goodman. "Yes, suh," he said sadly.

Having told Jonah the truth about why he was with him in Texas, Joseph glanced at him, knowing he must miss the captain and the Southern Belle. "I feel bad about this. But the Captain did it for your own good. It was a hard thing for him."

Jonah stared at the far-off hills. "Yes, suh. I 'spect it were, but now I worry's bouts dah Cap'n all by his self."

"I worry about the old boy too, Jonah, but ain't much we can do about that right now."

"No, suh, expect nots, but I surely do miss `im."

Joseph nodded with a small smile. "So do I, Jonah, and I know he misses us, but the captain figured you'd be safer with us here in Texas."

"Yes, suh, I knows all dat, and I unerstans it all, I guess, but I's jus wishes dis war had nevah come along." He looked at Joseph. "Can's I ask ya sumthin' Mistah Joseph?"

"I reckon."

"Does ya b'lieves things'll really be any bettah fer us colored folk after dis war's ovah?"

Joseph considered that. "I can't answer that, Jonah."

"No, suh. S'posen ya can't," Jonah said, sounding disappointed.

Joseph looked at the old Negro, feeling sorry for him, wishing he was still back with the captain where he belonged instead of with him here in Texas. But for now, and until this war was over, there was nothing he could do but take care of Jonah like he had promised the captain. "All I can say right now is that no matter what happens, you'll always have a place with Mary and me." Joseph shrugged his shoulders. "That's about all I can promise. This damn war has changed a lot of things for a lot of people."

He nodded. "Yes, suh, dat it has." Then he returned to his memories of the Belle and the Captain.

The day was lingering as dusk slowly spread its dark shadows across the land by the time Joseph guided the horse to a stop alongside the porch of the Hall farm. The door opened, and Mary hurried from the house just as Joseph climbed down, looking tired.

"Did everything go all right with Alex?" she asked, and then she noticed Jonah. "Why is Jonah with you?" That was followed by the logical question, "Where's Captain Goodman?"

"I'll explain later," Joseph said over his shoulder while retrieving the bags from under the seat. "Everything with Alex went just fine."

Jonah climbed down and stood next to the front wheel, looking lost and bewildered as he took off his hat and held it with the fingers of his hands. "Hello, Miss Mary."

She gave Jonah a curious smile. "Hello, Jonah. I didn't expect to see you."

"No, ma'am, I spect not."

Needing an explanation, Mary looked at Joseph. "Is Captain Goodman all right?"

"He's fine, Mary. As I said, I'll explain it all later. Right now, all I want to do is get this horse and buggy put away and go inside."

She stepped closer and whispered, "Did Alex give you everything?"

Joseph lowered his voice as he glanced around. "No, not everything." Then he changed the subject. "How are the children?"

"They're fine." Curious about his answer, she stepped closer and spoke softly. "What do you mean not everything?"

The door opened, and Del walked out of the house, saving Joseph from an argument. "I thought I heard a horse and buggy." Then he noticed the Negro standing next to the wagon. "Who's that with ya?"

Joseph looked at Jonah and then at Del. "This is Jonah. I'll explain later."

Del figured from Joseph's tone that he didn't want to discuss it, so he let it go. "All right, need some help with the horse and buggy?"

Joseph shook his head, saying they could handle it, and then asked if he could borrow Del's horse again in the morning to return the horse and buggy to the livery. Del agreed while sensing Joseph and Mary had something going on between them and, wanting to keep out of it, went back inside.

Joseph waited until the door closed, and then he glanced at Jonah, looked at Mary, and lowered his voice. "It's complicated, Mary. Let me put the horse away and get Jonah settled, and then we'll talk."

Seeing that he was tired and short on patience, Mary apologized and asked if he was hungry. He said no, but Jonah might be, so Mary asked Jonah. He smiled and said he was, so she told him to wait where he was while she fixed him a plate of leftovers. Joseph led the horse and buggy next to the barn, unhitched the horse, and put it into a stall.

A few minutes later, Jonah walked into the barn carrying a plate of food, setting it down on a barrel. "Mistah Joseph, let me takes care of dat horse. Ya go on in and visit wit' Miss Mary."

Tired, Joseph agreed and then showed Jonah a room attached to the barn with a cot, explaining they would fix it up later. "Eat your food before it gets cold, Jonah. Then you can worry about the horse and buggy."

Mary was on the bed playing with Joseph Jr., and when Joseph walked into the bedroom, she smiled and looked at the baby. "Here's your pa."

Joseph grinned as he sat on the edge of the bed. "Looks like his brother."

"No, he looks like you," corrected Mary, then she smiled. "They both do."

That pleased him, and as he played with his son, he told her about his trip and the money in the two bags lying next to the door, one containing half the money in U.S. currency and the other bag with its half in Confederate. "Alex wanted me to be sure and tell you that you still own a third of the farm, and he'll settle accounts with you after the war." Joseph shook his head and frowned. "Times are bad for the South. We're losing the war, and Alex said the Confederacy has taken most of the livestock, stored food, and cotton from the farmers around the county and is still asking for cash donations." He paused in thought. "Alex hasn't sold anything in over a year. Says if the war lasts another few years, y'all will be broke."

Mary looked confused. "But won't the Confederate government pay us for what they've taken?"

Joseph smiled wryly. "Oh, they gave Alex a voucher, the same as they do to everyone, but the Confederacy is almost broke. They need the money to pay their soldiers and buy arms from France and England."

"What about after the war?" she asked, looking hopeful.

"If the South loses, which Alex thinks they may, and I have to agree with him, those vouchers won't be worth the paper they're written on. The Confederate government will be abolished, and no one will be held accountable for the money lost in support of the war. Certainly not the United States politicians. I can guarantee that."

"What about the Confederate money?"

He looked worried. "I'm not sure. Perhaps the Federal Government will trade dollar for dollar, but my guess is they won't. We best spend the Confederate money first." Then he lay back against the headboard, his hands folded across his stomach, and smiled. "That brother of yours is a shrewd one." He chuckled. "He's hidden most of the money around the farm instead of keeping it in the bank. He told me he hedged his bets before the war started and stashed a lot of US Currency and gold coin just in case." He looked at the bags by the door. "I have to find someplace to hide that."

Mary stood to put Joseph Jr. to bed. "We'll find a place. What about the acreage you and Del discussed? Can we still buy it?"

Joseph shrugged. "It'd be a good investment." Then he paused, considering the land. "After the war, we might even be able to sell it for a profit." He suddenly felt tired and closed his eyes.

She stood, picked up her son, and put him in his bed next to his brother. Then she got into bed and nestled against her husband with the hope that a farm would keep him close to her and the boys. "Will you stay and work the land?" There was no reply, and seeing he had drifted off to sleep, she got up, took off his shoes, covered him with a blanket, and lay beside him, listening to his soft breathing. She was happy once again.

Two roosters outside were yelling in competition when Joseph opened his eyes to the morning sunlight. He sat up, looked at the empty pillow next to him, and then out the window at the sun bursting over the hills. A slight breeze flirted with the curtain in the single window of the room, and from downstairs came the muffled sound of kitchen noises mixed with voices and the smell of food and coffee.

Realizing he still had his clothes on, he sat on the edge of the bed, lit a thin cigar, and thought about his trip, Captain Goodman, and Jonah. He carefully considered the things Alex had told him and what Mary had asked about working the farm while he pretended to be asleep. It was a question he had no answer for at the moment, remembering the hard work that came with a farm, small or large. He put out the cigar, walked across the floor to a basin of freshwater, washed, shaved, changed clothes, and joined Mary and the Hall's downstairs.

After the idle conversation had come and gone over breakfast, Joseph talked about buying the twenty acres he and Del had previously discussed.

Surprised and delighted, Mary looked at him with a questioning expression. "Are you going to work the land?"

He digested the question, knowing she would be disappointed, and took a drink of coffee. "I have obligations to the Confederacy until this war is over, Mary. We will buy the land and hold onto it until after the war, and then I'll decide. But right now, I need to get back to Jefferson and do what I can for the South until this war is over." He shrugged. "I really have no choice."

She smiled, knowing that was true while hiding her disappointment.

November 10, 1873

Caddo Lake

The chilly wind of November 1873 blew across the lake, creating small white caps on almost every wave. Heavy rain fell out of the dark, gray clouds, pounding against the rough waters and across the decks of the Isabella. Joseph shivered as he stepped from the galley into the rain, chilly wind, and fine spray from off the lake. He adjusted his hat and coat collar, and then lowering his shoulders into the wind and driving rain, made his way to the hall that led to his cabin. Once inside, he closed the door, found a lamp, and as the Isabella rolled to and fro in the rough waters of Caddo Lake, he struck a match and touched the flame to the lamp's wick. The lamp flickered with a small flame that grew into a soft, orange light that filled his cabin. He repeated the process with a second lamp, making sure both lamps were secure so that they would not fall onto the floor. He built a fire in the small potbellied stove, and while he waited for the room to warm, he opened a drawer, took out a bottle of brandy and one glass, filling it half-full. The boat rolled to one side, knocking him against the wall he was standing next to, spilling some of the brandy. He took a good drink, felt the warmth in his throat as it went down, took another drink, added some more brandy to the glass, and returned the bottle to the drawer.

Careful not to spill his drink, he carefully made his way to his bed, and sat down with his back against the bulkhead, his legs sprawled in front of him. He picked up the book that lay on the table next to the bed and opened it to the marked page. Several minutes passed, as did the drink and pages he scarcely remembered reading. His eyes grew tired, so he replaced the marker between a new set of pages, set the book down next to the empty glass, took off his boots, closed his eyes, and fell asleep with his clothes on.

November 21, 1863

Mary Greene

A Place of Strangers

Mary, Lori, and Janice talked about life after the war while cleaning the kitchen of dinner dishes and dirty cookware while Del read aloud from the Bible in the other room. The children sat around the fireplace in silence, staring into the fire's glow while their mind's eyes imagined the characters of the story Del was reading. He paused and listened to what sounded like thunder, and realizing it was horses, he put the Bible down and hurried into the kitchen, finding the frightened women looking out the window.

As the sound of horses nickering and men's voices came through the closed back door, Del hurried toward it and reached for the loaded rifle above it. Janice took a pistol from a nearby drawer, hiding it between the folds of her apron. Mary picked up a butcher knife and held it in the folds of her dress as she stepped closer to Lori. The racket outside quickly quieted, followed by heavy footsteps across the porch and then pounding on the door.

These were dangerous times, and Del did not know if the men outside were Union or Confederate soldiers or deserters looking for money, food, and possibly women. "Who's there?"

"Captain Beale of the Third Texas Cavalry."

Del turned to the women and motioned for them to step back. Then cocking the hammer on his old musket, he placed one foot close to the door and cracked it open just enough to see a Confederate Officer standing on his porch. "You feller's lost?" he asked.

The man smiled. "No, suh just tired. My apologies if we frightened ya and your family. Name's Captain Seth Beale."

Del cautiously opened the door, stepped back with his rifle pointed halfway between the floor and the man dressed in dusty Confederate grey calling himself Captain Beale.

The captain cautiously stepped inside, seeing the women by the table looking frightened. "Apologies, ladies. I didn't mean to scare y'all." He offered an outstretched hand, which Del shook while looking past Beale and out the door to the others still in their saddles. "Name's Del Hall, Captain, some of those fella's look hurt?"

Beale looked tired and worried. "Got our butts kicked day before yesterday north of here along the Red River by some Union boys."

"Didn't realize them Yanks was this close," said Del.

Captain Beale turned and looked at his forty men with a worried look. "I've seven wounded. A couple of them pretty bad." He looked at Del. "Suh, we're cold, and we're hungry." He nodded toward the barn looking hopeful. "We'd be ever thankful if ya would allow us to bed down in your barn for the night and tend our wounded."

Del stepped past Beale onto the porch and then into the yard to look at the other men, seeing they were tired, and several were wounded. He turned to Captain Beale. "See no problem in that, Captain, if you're sure them Union soldier's ain't close behind." Del grinned. "Don't want no damn war fought on my place, scaring the hell out of the hens so they won't lay any eggs, not to mention the women and children."

The Captain chuckled at Del's sense of humor. "I won't lie to you, suh. I don't know what, if anything's chasing us, but I'll send a man back a ways as a lookout to give us fair warning so we can get the hell out of here if we need to." He stared back along the trail, looking worried. "To be honest, though, could be the Union Cavalry's sniffing after us, or could be them hounds from hell the devil done let loose in this here war." He grinned, looking friendly. "The only thing I'm certain of right now is that we chewed them Union infantry boys up pretty good and did some damage to their cavalry. I'm hoping they're all holed up lick'n their wounds like the bunch of stray dogs they are."

Del grinned, appreciating the captain's choice of words as he turned his head and yelled. "Janice, you can put that pistol away now. Looks like we got us a bunch of soldier boys that need a place to stay!" Del looked to the captain. "Don't know about the food, Captain, leave that up to the womenfolk, but you and your men are welcome to stay as long as ya like." Del grinned proudly. "My own son's someplace out there with the 27th Alabama, and I hope someone would do the same for him if they needed someplace to stay."

Beale smiled appreciatively. "Thank ya kindly, Mr. Hall. I hope's son is safe and comes back real soon."

Janice, Mary, and Lori were on the porch staring at the men in their dirty gray uniforms sitting silently and weary in their saddles while some soldiers helped the wounded to stay in their saddles. Janice stepped toward Captain Beale. "Hello, young man," she said. "You and your men look like a hot meal would do some good."

Beale took off his hat, smiled, and nodded politely. "Yes, ma'am, we surely could use one, but we don't' want to be any trouble." He glanced at his men, gesturing with the hand holding the hat. "We have a cook, ma'am, just no pots and pans." He chuckled amusedly. "We had to leave in a bit of a hurry." He held out one hand and introduced himself. "Name's Captain Seth Beale ma'am, at your service."

Janice took his hand, shaking it gently, then wrapped her shawl more tightly around her shoulders and stepped past him to the edge of the porch, looked at his men, and then turned back. "Y'all are welcome to use our kitchen Captain, and I think we can afford a few chickens and some eggs." She stepped off the porch and smiled warmly at a young man who looked too young to be fighting. "We just baked some fresh bread today," she said, looking into his eyes.

The boy smiled, looking grateful. "Thank ya, ma'am, sounds right delicious."

"We appreciate the kindness, ma'am," said Captain Beale. Then he told his men to corral their mounts, and keep the fuss and racket at a minimum, and to remember they were the Halls' guests.

Janice quickly glanced around at the men before going into the house to get things ready.

Beale turned to Del and asked, "Any others on this place besides the four of you?"

Del nodded. "Some children inside, and a Negra by the name of Jonah living in a small room in the back of the barn. He's a good man."

"I'll see the men don't bother him none."

Janice stuck her head out the door. "Mr. Beale, soon as you get your men settled, you're welcome to come in for a cup of hot coffee."

"Right nice of you, ma'am, thank you." He turned and followed his men to the barn while Janice led the Confederate cook into the warmth of her kitchen, and together they prepared a meal for the forty hungry soldiers.

After the men in the barn had consumed their meal, Mary and Lori walked among them offering refills of coffee. Inside the house, Del puffed on his pipe between sips of coffee, listening to Captain Beale talk of the battle.

"It was after dark," began the captain. "We had just made camp on the Big Red when a small Confederate infantry unit made camp on the other side of the river. Figuring they'd ford the river at first light and join forces with us, we watched them as they made camp and settled in for the night as well." He paused to take a drink of coffee. "We were just getting ready to eat when we were jumped by Union infantry, while across the river them infantry boys were attacked by Union cavalry." He paused. "Those boys didn't have a chance. I lost seventeen men in the first few minutes and knowing we were outnumbered and soon to be outflanked, I gave the order to mount up, and then we fought our way out and rode like hell until we got here."

Del puffed his pipe, shook his head, and looked at Beale. "Lucky you got out when you did."

Gloom filled the captain's face. "I only wish I could have helped those poor souls on the other side of the river, but there were just too damn many Yankees."

Del broke the momentary silence. "Sounds to me, you didn't have much choice."

Beale nodded with a dismissive grunt. "Maybe, but I wasn't about to get myself and my men captured."

Mary knelt beside a young man that she believed to be no older than fifteen or sixteen burning with a fever. Using a damp cloth, she gently wiped his forehead and face while cleaning the dried blood from the corners of his mouth. He opened his eyes and smiled as Mary carefully checked the bloody bandages covering the oozing hole in his chest. Never having seen a man wounded before, she felt a little faint, but she forced a smile and looked around for the doctor, seeing he was quite busy with another soldier. She looked back down at the young man and asked his name.

"Wayne Shipley, ma'am," he said. Then he turned his head and coughed up a small amount of blood.

Mary gently wiped his mouth, knowing he was badly hurt and felt helpless, wishing the doctor would hurry. Having little medical experience, she tried to comfort him as best she could until she could get the young doctor's attention. "Where you from, Wayne?" she softly asked while wiping the perspiration from his forehead and the blood from his mouth.

"San Antonio, ma'am." He grinned up at her. "Ever been there?"

"Afraid not, I'm from Alabama."

"Good Lord ma'am," he said, looking puzzled. "What the hell ya doing clean out here?"

"Staying with some friends until this war's over."

The boy closed his eyes, stiffened with pain, and coughed up another small amount of blood. When he opened his eyes and looked at her, his breathing was labored. "Your man off fight'n somewheres?"

She smiled, being thankful he wasn't. "No, he works on a riverboat along the Red River supplying the Confederate army."

The young man considered that. "My daddy took me on a riverboat once."

"Did he now?" she asked, wishing she could help in some way. She checked again for the doctor and seeing he was still busy with yet another badly wounded soldier.

Wayne stopped smiling, and his eyes grew heavy. "I'm a mite tired."

He either fell asleep or passed out, she wasn't sure which as she felt his fevered forehead, and then she sat back and looked at the young face not yet shaven and thought of the boy's mother. She glanced back at the man tending to another a few feet away, got up, and walked to him, tapping his shoulder. "Excuse me, are you the doctor?"

The man turned, and to Mary's surprise, he was not much older than Wayne Shipley.

"No, ma'am. The Doc got kilt yesterday." He pointed to the bag next to him. "This here's his stuff. I used to help him some." He paused, looking around the barn at the wounded. "I don't know what to do. They need a real doctor."

What's your name?" Mary asked.

"Name's Grant, ma'am, Corporal Grant McKee, from Lubbock, Texas."

"Are all of these men wounded, Mr. McKee?"

"Yessum."

Mary pointed to Wayne and whispered, "Mr. McKee, what about that young man over there?"

The corporal looked at Wayne and then leaned close to Mary and whispered, "Wayne? He's pretty bad off. Got shot in the left lung, and if he goes with us, he'll probably drown in his own blood." He looked regretful and quickly apologized. "Sorry, ma'am, I didn't mean to be so coarse."

"War is coarse, Corporal. Is there anything you need?"

He glanced at the other men considering that. "Do ya have any bandages? It seems I lost them somewhere."

"No, but we have some sheets."

"That'd do nicely, ma'am. I could tear `em into bandages."

"No need for you to do that. I'll do it." She turned and hurried to the house, going upstairs to a trunk in her room filled with things she was saving for her own home. Removing two sheets and pillow cases from the trunk, she cut them into several strips and returned to the barn, where she and Lori spent the rest of the night helping the corporal care for the sick and wounded.

Wayne's coughing woke Mary from a restless sleep of bad dreams about Joseph and her brother Edward. She watched as Corporal McKee kneeled beside Wayne checking his bandages and feeling his forehead for a fever.

The Corporal looked at Mary with a worried face. "He's burning up with fever."

She looked down at Wayne's pale, gray face wet with perspiration and reached for the cloth in a small pan of water next to her, wrung it out, and gently patted his face.

The corporal touched her hand. "I'll tend to Wayne for a while, ma'am, best you go rest a spell."

Mary was tired, too tired to argue, and without saying anything more, she handed the damp cloth to McKee, stood, and walked out of the barn, stopping just beyond the doors to stretch. It was still early, the sun barely above the trees along the eastern hills, and a white, eerie morning fog covered the fields. The soldiers were already up and gathered around small fires for warmth when she walked into the house, greeted by the smell of fresh bread. Seeing Janice at the stove, looking as if she had been awake all night, Mary started to go upstairs and check on her children. Pausing at the living room door, she looked inside at Del, Captain Seth Beale, and four other officers drinking coffee and talking. Seeing her, they stopped talking, stood, and said good morning. Walking into the room, she smiled at each one and then looked at Captain Beale. "Your men look like you're preparing to leave."

Captain Seth Beale shrugged. "We can't take the chance on getting caught here. We'll be leaving within the hour."

Mary expressed her concerns for the sick and wounded. "You have some young men that are pretty sick."

Beale said he appreciated her concerns but told her they needed to get the wounded to a field hospital. She nodded her understanding but looked skeptical. "Forgive my asking, Captain, how far must you travel?"

Hearing a horse, Beale never answered as he stepped out of the room and into the kitchen, watching the back door. Footsteps raced across the porch, the door opened, and a veteran looking sergeant saluted the captain. "Union Cavalry, a few miles back, Captain."

"How long?" asked Beale.

"Thirty minutes," reported the sergeant. "Maybe less."

Beale turned to the four officers. "Get the men ready while I check on the wounded." He took a drink of his coffee, set his empty cup down, excused himself, and hurried out the door.

Concerned about the wounded men, Mary followed, and as she entered the barn, Beale was talking to Corporal McKee.

"How are the men doing, Corporal?" asked the captain.

McKee looked doubtful. "A little better."

Beale knelt next to Shipley. "How you doing, son?"

Wayne managed a small smile. "I'm all right, Captain." Then he turned his head and coughed.

Seeing blood on the boy's hand, Beale felt his forehead, finding him burning with fever. Then he stood and looked at the others. "Can they travel?"

"I believe so, Captain, but---"

"But what?" interrupted Beale.

"It's just that I ain't no doctor."

Captain Beale considered that for only a moment. "You are today, Corporal." Then he turned, and at seeing Mary, and walked over to her looking worried as he lowered his voice. "Private Shipley's in no condition for a hard ride."

"He can stay here," offered Mary.

Del was beside her. "As many as you want to leave behind, Captain."

Beale turned, looking grateful, and looked at each wounded man, considering his options and chances for survival, and after a moment, he knelt down to one. "Can you ride, Soldier?"

The man looked tired and sickly, with shadows under his eyes. "I think so, sir."

Then the captain asked the next man. "How about you, soldier?"

"Yes, sir," replied the second man, looking about the same.

Beale asked each sick and wounded man the same question, and all gave the same reply. He stood up, considering each man carefully, and then turned to Del. "Can I leave three men?"

"Why, hell yes," replied Del.

Captain Beale glanced around the barn with a worried look while he tapped his dusty, gray hat against his dirty pants leg, looking much older than his twenty-five years. He was not a very tall man, standing just five feet seven. Beale was thin, and his dirty blonde hair was badly in need of a wash, comb and scissors while several days of beard growth covered his tanned, handsome face. His gentle, blue eyes looked tired and in need of sleep as he turned with a worried face to Mary. "Will you see to `em, ma'am?"

"Of course I will, Captain."

He looked into her soft, sad eyes. "Do what you can for Private Shipley. He's a good, brave lad." He paused, looking exhausted, and lowered his voice. "I don't think he's gonna make it."

Mary put her hand on Beale's arm. "I'll do what I can, Captain."

He smiled appreciatively, turned, gathered his officers, and within minutes, the Confederate soldiers were saddled and ready to ride. Beale shook Del's hand, thanked the women for their kindness, and then looked at Mary.

Seeing he was worried, she smiled reassuringly. "We'll take care of your men, Captain."

“Thank you, ma’am.” Then he turned to mount his horse when suddenly Mary grabbed his arm and kissed him on the cheek. “God speed, Mr. Beale.”

He smiled at her. “Thank you, ma’am.” Then he climbed into his saddle, tipped his hat, turned his horse, and nudged it into a gallop, leading his men to the southwest and away from the farmhouse.

As their dust settled and the sound of their horses disappeared, Mary and the others walked toward the barn and the wounded.

Hearing horses, Mary stood from tending one of the soldiers, walked to the open barn doors, stopped, and put one hand on the weathered doorframe.’

Del burst from the house, holding his old musket, looking worried. “The Union cavalry’s here.” After telling everyone to stay inside, Del stood in front of the two open doors of the barn next to Mary. Best you go back inside with the others.”

A group of seven Union cavalrymen led by a seasoned sergeant rode across the yard, stopping short of the barn. The sergeant saluted. “Sergeant Skinner, United States Cavalry.”

Del nodded as he moved the barrel of the gun up and down in a mocking salute. “What can I do for ya, son?”

The sergeant examined both the gun and the old man and then smiled, trying to appear friendly and posing no threat. He looked at the barn, and other outbuildings and the many horse tracks in the yard, and then looked at Del. “How long they been gone?”

Del looked puzzled. “Can’t say fer sure.”

Figuring he wasn’t about to get any information from the old man, the sergeant smiled. “Mind if we have some water?”

Del pointed to the pump. “Help yerself.”

The men got down from their horses and took turns drinking while the sergeant asked again how long the Confederate soldiers had been gone.

“Can’t say for sure.”

The sergeant grinned, knowing this was not going to be easy, and then took another drink of water.

Del considered his options and quickly decided he didn’t have too many, figuring they would probably search the place. “There are three wounded men in our barn. They’re all pretty bad off, and I doubt one of them’s gonna make it through the night.”

The sergeant nodded, looking regretful, then politely asked, “Mind if I take a look, sir?”

“Reckon it’d be alright.” Del turned and yelled over his shoulder. “Ladies, don’t be afraid, I’m coming in with a Union sergeant. I don't want anyone getting hurt, so keep them guns away from them wounded men." Then he led the way into the barn.

The sergeant knelt and examined each of the Confederate soldiers' wounds, then frowned, and looked up. "They're in pretty bad shape, all right."

Mary approached the sergeant. "Could you and your men help us get them inside where they'd be a little more comfortable?"

Sergeant Skinner turned to his men. "Help get these wounded men inside."

They had just moved the three men inside when the sound of horses announced the arrival of the rest of the regiment. The sergeant glanced at the three men, looked at Mary as he stood, and hurried out to the porch in time to greet his colonel with a salute.

The colonel dismounted and returned the salute. "Report, Sergeant."

"The main force has ridden out, Colonel, but there are three men inside, all in pretty bad shape."

"I see," replied the colonel eyeing Del and the gun he held across his body. "Can they be moved, Sergeant?"

"Don't believe so, sir, they're pretty bad off."

Standing next to his horse and still looking at Del, the colonel yelled, "Captain Brock!"

"Yes, sir," replied Captain Brock as he dismounted with his black medical bag.

"Three wounded inside, Brock, the sergeant doesn't seem to think they can be moved." He nodded toward the house. "Take a look."

"Yes, sir." Captain Brock hurried inside.

Colonel Eugene Bradford introduced himself and asked Del a few questions that Del said he couldn't answer. The colonel studied Del and the gun he held for several moments, thinking that he probably could give them answers but wasn't planning to.

Inside the house, Mary knelt beside the doctor as he examined the men, and when he finished, he took her to one side. "Sorry, ma'am," he said softly. "But I don't think they'll make it till sunset." He looked down at the men, feeling remorse, and handed her a small bottle telling her it was a narcotic called laudanum, and that it would help with the pain, and help them sleep a little easier. After giving her instructions on how to use it, he gave her some clean bandages. "Wish I could do more." He tipped his hat and walked back to the porch, reporting what he had found to the colonel.

"Very good, Brock," said the colonel looking regretful. Then the colonel took a cigar from his pocket, bit off the end, lit it, and puffed vigorously. Smoke billowed around his head and trailed after him as Colonel Brock walked toward the far end of the porch. Stopping at its edge, he stood with his hands clasped behind his back, occasionally releasing a hand to puff the cigar as he looked out across the fields toward the trees and hills in the distance. Moments passed before he turned, looking at his tired men sitting tall in their saddles, anxious to continue their pursuit. He turned from them and looked out across the farm in silence for a very long time, watching the Negro man doing something next to the barn.

Del studied this scholarly looking man in his dusty, dark blue uniform and muddy boots that revealed too many days away from camp. He was a good-looking man with deep-set brown eyes, dark hair, and a neatly trimmed beard. He had gentle mannerisms and a soft voice, giving the impression of a thoughtful man, unlike the usual cunning warrior intent on the hunt.

More time passed while the colonel stood alone at the edge of the porch smoking his cigar while his men quietly awaited their leader's orders. Finally, he took a final hefty drag and blew smoke into the tip of the cigar, causing it to glow. His decision made, he turned and walked back along the porch and smiled at Del as he gestured toward the land with the hand holding the cigar. "Reminds me of my place."

"Where might that be?" asked Del.

Colonel Bradford puffed his cigar while organizing his memory, and then with the smile gone, he looked into the distant north. "A long way from here, I'm afraid." His eyes met Del's with another smile. "Yes," he said, "quite a long way from here." He offered an open hand, which Del took, and then they firmly shook hands. "Thanks for your politeness, sir."

Del nodded.

The colonel walked across the porch to his waiting mount, took the reins from the young corporal holding it, and started to climb up when he paused and looked back at Del. "Under different circumstances, you might have invited me in for a drink or cup of hot coffee."

Del smiled. "Under different circumstances, Colonel, I'm sure I would have."

There was nothing further for either man to say, so the colonel turned to the sergeant. "Mount up, Sergeant."

The sergeant yelled his orders and then looked at the colonel. "We going after them, Reb's, sir?"

The colonel settled in his saddle and looked in the direction of the horse tracks. "No, Sergeant, I believe we've come about as far as we should. No sense in getting caught this far south." Something soft in his expression replaced the look of determination as he looked down at Del. "Good luck with them wounded. Such a pity men so young have to die so far from home." The colonel glanced around and smiled. "But it's peaceful here, and there are worse places for men to die." He tipped his hat, turned his horse, and led the regiment back north.

The three men left behind soon died, and Del and his grandson Teddy buried them on a hill overlooking the Hall farm, with wooden crosses bearing their names and the date of their death. When Wayne Shipley died, his eyes were swollen with tears as he confessed to Mary that he was afraid, wishing his ma was with him. It was Mary who held Wayne Shipley when he drew his last breath. Having found out where each was from, Mary promised herself that she would write to the three mothers describing their final resting place after the war, hoping in some small way it would bring them comfort.

December 24, 1863 - The Hall Farm

The room was still dark when Mary opened her eyes and looked out the window at the soft glow of the coming dawn just above the eastern horizon. The house was quiet, still filled with the night's chill, and while she knew she should get up, Mary chose to stay in bed a little longer with Zachariah on one side and little Joseph on the other. She lay between her two children listening to Zachariah's soft breathing with an occasional period of snoring that reminded her of Joseph. Her heart yearned for her husband, wondering where he was and if he was all right, wanting him with her on this day before Christmas. The room became lighter with each passing moment as the sun got closer to the horizon, and then sounds from downstairs told her that Lori or Mrs. Hall, and perhaps both, were busy in the kitchen.

Mary kissed each child on the forehead, quietly got out of bed, dressed, and went downstairs, finding Mrs. Hall setting the table. They exchanged good mornings, and Mary helped with the breakfast, asking if Lori was still asleep. Mrs. Hall paused to glance at the stairs and said she thought she had heard her moving around in her room earlier. Hoping Lori was okay, Mary began the process of cracking eggs against a bowl for scrambling.

Lori walked down the stairs, chasing a yawn while stretching. "I could have stayed in that warm bed a little longer."

Mary nodded in agreement.

Mrs. Hall asked Lori to help with the potatoes.

Lori began working on the potatoes, only to pause and look out the window. "I wonder what Ethan's doing right now?"

"Hopefully," replied Janice Hall. "He and Edward are both eating a good breakfast."

Mary paused in what she was doing. "Wouldn't it be nice if he and Joseph were to walk through that door right now?"

Lori glanced toward the door. "Yes, it would."

"Amen to that," replied Mrs. Hall without looking up from her task.

Lori looked at Mary with a questioning expression. "Do you suppose Joseph will make it home for Christmas?"

Mary paused to consider that while continuing with what she was doing. "Don't know, Lori. I don't even know where he and the Isabella are. She could be in Shreveport or on the Mississippi." Mary looked up at the door. "I hope he makes it home soon."

Christmas 1863

Mary sat in a chair holding Joseph Jr. as she watched young Zachariah and Lori's oldest boy lying on the floor, staring into the fireplace while Del read a story from the Bible. While Lori held one daughter, Mrs. Hall was thinking of her son Ethan, wishing he were home and the war was over. It didn't matter to them at this moment which side won, so long as it was over. Del's soft voice was interrupted by a loud pop of the fire from the sap on a piece of wood, shooting sparks in the air, startling everyone and yet bringing nervous laughter. That laughter turned out to be one of the few joyful moments the families found on this Christmas Eve.

By nine that evening, Del had read several passages from the Bible, and the children were asleep on the floor. He put his book down and looked at the children. "I think it's time for these rascals to get to bed. It appears to me they're plumb tuckered out."

"Sure, you ain't speaking for yourself?" asked Janice as she stood to help with the children.

Mary tucked the two boys in their bed and then returned downstairs to the fireplace, sat down on the floor, watched the dancing flames, and thought about Joseph. It was not long before Lori and Janice, having the same idea, joined her on the floor where they sat in silence watching the flames consume the wood, each in thought about the men in their lives.

Ethan and Edward were at that very moment in Mississippi, sitting around a campfire with other men remembering past Christmases and better times. Joseph and the Isabella encountered light rifle fire from scattered Union forces along the Red River north of Shreveport. They suffered two casualties and several more holes in the ship's bulkheads, one narrowly missing Joseph's head.

Christmas of 1863 passed without further incident at the Hall farm. The children enjoyed fruit and homemade candy as presents. Lori's boys' each got a wooden toy gun Del had hand-carved, and the girls received button-eyed rag dolls that Mrs. Hall had made with Del's old socks. The best present would have been the return of Ethan and Joseph, but that didn't happen, and Christmas was just another day for those caught up in the war that cut its blustery path across the South.

Most men barely noticed the coming of the New Year as they lay on the cold ground, in dirty ditches, or field hospitals. On the Hall farm, the women continually looked toward the road, hoping for the return of their men as their heads filled with wishes and dreams of peace.

In the early morning hours of January 1, 1864, Mary knew she was carrying her third child who would arrive in late July or early August. She stood at her window, caressing her belly with one hand, and watched the sunrise, thinking of Joseph. Mary leaned against the window, feeling the cold glass against her face, and wondered why he hadn't written. As tears welled in her eyes and ran down her cheeks, she slowly slid down the wall to the floor and cried.

Twenty-six

January 1, 1864, to June 1864
Joseph Greene – Shreveport January 1864

When the Isabella's captain heard of a boat capsizing during the storm on Caddo Lake and the resulting drowning of 190 passengers and crew, he cautiously decided to wait one more day before crossing into Texas. Understanding but disappointed with the captain's decision, Joseph changed clothes and visited the waterfront saloons of Shreveport to welcome the New Year. Occupying a chair at a table in the corner of a saloon, he nursed a glass of brandy that he filled from a bottle. The noisy crowd was a mixture of old men left out of the war, a few crippled men unable to fight, and several young soldiers looking too young to drink but not too young to die.

Shreveport's women came in all sizes and all ages, and all were wearing too much makeup. It was a strange mixture of people who roamed the bars these days, thought Joseph as he watched a short, stocky man at the piano enthusiastically guiding his fat fingers across the black and white keys playing something unfamiliar to him. The piano player held a cheap cigar between his teeth and tilted his head to keep the smoke out of his eyes as he swayed before the keyboard.

No one seemed to notice him and the skinny man standing beside the piano, guiding the bow of his fiddle just as enthusiastically while tapping one foot in time with the music. Joseph had just taken a sip of brandy when the crowd suddenly erupted, yelling Happy New Year, drowning out the piano and fiddle. While a few drunks danced on tables, the mixture of Shreveport citizens and guests displayed the age-old ritual of hugging, kissing, slaps on the back, and if you were a woman, a pat on the butt.

A young woman was standing next to Joseph. "Buy me a drink?"

Looking up into the face of a pretty blonde woman holding an empty glass, he nodded to an empty chair. "Why not?"

She smiled as she settled into the chair. "They call me Mona. That's short for Ramona."

Joseph doubted that, knowing that few girls used their own names. "Hello Mona, I'm Joseph." Then he filled her glass with brandy.

She thanked him, took a small sip while looking at him over the rim of the glass, and then set the glass down and looked around at the drunks. "People seem to go just a little crazier this time of year."

Joseph glanced around at the near-riot and chuckled. "Most people are crazy the better part of the year."

She laughed, thinking that was funny, and then tasted the brandy. "Are you crazy most of the year, Joseph?"

He shrugged. "Sometimes, I think I am." Then thinking of the war, he said, "But most everyone is these days." Letting her think about that, he sipped his drink, wishing she would visit another table.

"It's been a while since I've seen you at the tables gambling," she said.

That surprised him. "Other things seem to occupy my time these days."

She sipped a little of her drink. "Those other things wouldn't be the river and a boat? You have the dress of a riverman."

He glanced at his clothes and smiled. "Those would be two."

"Strange," she said. "If not for your clothes, I would have guessed you were a gambler."

"I may not be a gambler by trade, but I enjoy the game."

She smiled. "Most men enjoy the excitement of the game first, and then the enjoyment of life's other little pleasures after."

Knowing where she was going, Joseph chuckled. "I'm sure you're right."

She shifted in her chair, sipped her brandy, and asked what he did on the river. Joseph said he worked on a sternwheeler, but he was stuck in Shreveport for a day or two because of the storm on Caddo Lake.

"My sister and I used to ride the steamboats up the Mississippi before the war," she said. "My father owned a business in New Orleans that took him up river every couple of months, and once in a while, he would take us with him." She smiled in reflection. "I used to enjoy the slow trips up and down the river, especially the dinners and music at night." While she stared into her empty glass in memory, Joseph poured her another drink. She thanked him, took a small sip, and smiled, looking embarrassed.

He felt sorry for her. "What brings you to Shreveport?"

She sipped her drink and then looked down at it in thought. "The war." She looked at him. "Just before New Orleans fell to the Yankees, our father gave us money and arranged safe passage to Shreveport." She frowned, looking sad. "When the money ran out, we started working in places like this."

"And where's your sister now?"

She shrugged with a small smile. "My sister didn't like Shreveport very much. This gentleman she met talked her into going to

San Antonio." She paused to take another drink and then changed the subject. "Your work sounds fun and exciting. Always traveling, seeing all sorts of cities, and meeting all sorts of people."

"It used to be enjoyable," he said softly, almost sadly. "But that was before the war." His mind quickly traveled back to Captain Goodman, the Southern Belle, and the stillness of a calm Tennessee River in the warm sun. He remembered dinner at Edward's house on Sundays and the quiet afternoon walks with Mary in the park.

"Yes, the war," she said, looking sad. "Everything used to be fun b'fore the damn war."

As he listened to her, he thought she was probably in her late teens, but he wasn't sure. Most women in her business tended to grow old quickly, and imagined her in five or ten years. He had known many women like her up and down the southern waterways before he met Mary. They were all the same, looking for that one man who would rush them off to another city and, hopefully, a better life. As she talked about herself, he looked into her expressive eyes that widened and narrowed with each gesture of a hand as she talked. Her breasts were full, pushed up by the low-cut silk, dark blue dress that complemented her blonde hair and blue eyes. A painted mole under her left eye stood out of her heavy, rouged cheeks. He wondered what it would be like to take her upstairs, but then thinking of Mary, he looked at his pocket watch. "It's after one." He gulped the last of his drink, pushed his chair from away from the table, and stood. "It's time for me to leave."

Looking disappointed, she said, "I have a bottle in my room at the hotel across the street."

He thought of her soft skin and warm body against his as she got up and walked around the table, and as she stood close to him, he could feel her firm breasts against his chest and smell her cheap perfume. "Another time."

She looked disappointed. "Too bad." Then she turned and made her way through the crowd, finding a young soldier in a brand new uniform. Joseph smiled as he turned and walked toward the swinging doors, thinking that the young lad was about to have the ride of his life. Stepping outside, he was greeted by the chilly night air and took a deep breath to clear his head of the perfume and desire that held him. He was thinking of Mary and how her warm body felt when they were together when a drunk bumped against his shoulder. The man smiled, apologized, wished him a Happy New Year and then staggered along the boardwalk. Hoping the man made it to his destination, Joseph headed toward the Isabella and sleep.

East Texas

Dark, gray storm clouds warned of another rain as Joseph walked down the Isabelle's gangplank chased by a chilly March wind that blew across the Big Cypress River. Stepping onto the pier, he adjusted the collar of his coat and headed for the muddy streets of Jefferson as he walked through a puddle that filled his shoe with cold water, soaking his sock. Cursing the puddle, he found a nearby post where he paused to shake the mud and water from his shoe and then continued across the muddy street, avoiding the other puddles.

Reaching the boardwalk, he hurried up the creaky steps to the wooden sidewalk and stomped his feet to clean the mud off, then pushed his way through the swinging doors. Surprised at the number of empty tables, he placed his bag on an empty chair and eased himself into another, realizing it was still early afternoon. A heavyset, middle-aged woman, wearing too much makeup and looking like she had stayed too long in her profession, asked what he wanted in an unfriendly tone.

He ordered a brandy to take away the March chill, and while he waited, he thought of Mary and the miles he had to travel. Moments later, the same heavyset, unfriendly barmaid set his drink on the table. "Know how to read, mister?"

Thinking it a strange thing to ask, he looked up at her plump face, messy black hair and then noticed the newspaper. "Yes, I can read."

"Interested?" she asked.

Hoping she meant the paper, he quickly took it from her outstretched hand, thanked her, and while she returned to the bar where she continued talking to an elderly man, he opened the paper and began reading of the war and Union victories. Hearing the heavyset woman laugh, he looked up for a moment, and when his eyes returned to the newspaper, he thought of Edward and Ethan. He took a quick sip of brandy and glanced through the paper for some mention of the 27th Alabama, then remembered he was in east Texas. It stood to reason that all, if not most of the news would be about Texas units, so he folded the paper and set it on the table.

Remembering the letter in his pocket from Mary, he took it out, pulled the letter from the envelope, unfolded it, and smiled as he read again about the news of a baby that would be born in late July that Mary was hoping to be a little girl. She wrote about the Confederate soldiers stopping at the farm and the three young boys that had died and were buried on the hill overlooking the creek.

He didn't see the heavyset woman approach his table. "Another?"

Looking up at the barmaid, he asked, "Can I order something to eat?"

She shook her head. "The cook's not in yet, and I can't leave the bar." She gestured toward the door. "There's a café just down the street."

He thanked her, put the letter away, picked up his bag as he stood, and headed for the door and café before going to the livery for his horse.

The Hall Farm

Mary and Lori Hall cleaned up the dinner dishes and talked about life after the war when the door opened and Joseph walked in. Realizing he had just scared the hell out of them, he chuckled, "Hello ladies."

They laughed with relief as Mary ran across the room to greet him with a hug and kiss. "We expected you yesterday."

While still holding her in his arms, he exchanged hellos with Lori just as Del rushed into the room. After saying hello to Del, Joseph explained why he was late, and another boat's sinking on Caddo Lake. "The captain decided to stay in Shreveport another day." Then glancing around, he asked, "Where are the children?"

"Asleep," replied Mary.

Just then, Janice Hall hurried into the kitchen. "I thought I heard your voice, Joseph." She smiled as she gave him a quick hug and kiss on the cheek. "Glad you finally made it home. Mary's been worried. Are you all right?"

"I'm fine, Janice, thank you."

Mrs. Hall smiled warmly. "Can I pour you a cup of hot coffee?"

"I'll get it," said Mary.

While Joseph pulled a chair from the table and Mary turned to get him a cup of coffee, the others sat down at the table, asking questions about the war. Joseph told them that the war was not going well for the South, and Sherman's march through Georgia, Mississippi, and parts of Alabama, quickly assuring Mary that Florence was untouched by the war. Catching a lull in the conversation, Joseph asked if they had any news of Edward and Ethan. Del told him that the last they had heard, both were somewhere in Virginia.

The time passed quickly, and Joseph drank the last of his coffee and asked about the Confederate army mentioned in Mary's last letter. Del told the story with occasional interruptions from Janice, who made sure he told the story correctly, which irritated Del. Mary sadly told of the wounded boys she and Lori had tended. Del told about the Union cavalry and their doctor doing what he could for the three young men.

He shook his head, looking sad, saying that the good Lord had taken all three in the end. Then he smiled as he told Joseph about the Union Colonel who seemed a nice enough fellow, even if he was a Yankee.

Having a feeling that Mary and her husband would like to be alone, Janice Hall grabbed Del by the arm, telling him to say goodnight, and then quickly ushered him and Lori upstairs, leaving Mary and Joseph alone in the kitchen. As silence filled the kitchen and the muffled sounds of voices upstairs made their way down from upstairs, Mary stood to pick up his cup and saucer. Joseph put his arm around her waist, pulling her against him.

She giggled. "You'll make me drop these!"

"You won't." Then he smiled. "You're too careful."

She smiled and patted her round, protruding stomach. "Does this look like I was careful?"

"I see your point."

She set the cup and saucer down, put her hand on the back of his head, pulled it into her breast, and kissed the top of his head. "You look tired." She combed her fingers through his hair, thinking how much she had missed him

"I am tired," he said, feeling the weight of the trip. Then thinking of Jonah, he asked how he was getting along.

"He seems all right," replied Mary. She got up from his lap, picked up the dishes, set them on the counter, took his hand, and led him upstairs to their bedroom. Quietly closing the door behind her, she leaned back against it, watching Joseph as he stood over their children's beds. "They look so innocent," he said, and then he grinned. "But, I know different."

"I've missed them almost as much as I have you," he said, and then he took her in his arms, feeling her slightly protruding stomach against him, looked down, and smiled. "Ummm. I seem to remember being able to get a little closer."

She smiled with a worried look. "Do you mind?"

"About the baby?"

She nodded.

"Why would I mind? I love children."

She took his hands and held them at her side as she looked into his eyes. "I was afraid you'd be upset."

"Why on earth would I be upset?"

Feeling a little foolish, she turned down the bed.

He made the necessary trip across the room, put his arms around her, and smiled. "That's nonsense, and you know it." Then he grinned. "Now, we won't have to be careful for a few months."

She smiled as she pushed him back. “You’re impossible.” Then she undressed, put on a nightgown, sat down on the stool in front of the mirror, and began brushing her hair.

While she was busy with the brush, he undressed, climbed into bed, and looked at her image in the mirror. “That going to take long?”

She looked into the mirror at his image, set the brush down, stood, blew out the lantern, got under the covers, and lay next to him with her head on his shoulder. She put her arm around him, feeling content and whole once more. The house was quiet and peaceful, the soft breathing of their children played to the sounds of the creaking house, and in the dim light of their quiet room, they found one another.

Mary’s contentment would last only a few days. Joseph had to return to Jefferson and the Big Cypress River. He said his goodbyes to Mary and his sons, kissed Lori and Mrs. Hall on the cheek, and then turned to Del, who held the reins to his horse. After shaking Del’s hand, he climbed into the saddle and rode toward Jefferson.

February – 1864

Edward McAlexander

Meridian, Mississippi

General William Tecumseh Sherman and his Union Army of several thousand men were busy destroying the southern railroads on their march toward Meridian, Mississippi and were looking ahead to Selma, Alabama, and then the city of Mobile. Confederate General Polk was sent to stop Sherman’s advance but quickly realized his small army was no match for Sherman’s larger force. On the 14th of February 1864, General Polk evacuated his army from Meridian, leaving the city and the rail center to General Sherman.

After suffering heavy losses fighting against Sherman’s army, the 27th Alabama camped near Canton, Mississippi. It would remain there until early April, when it received orders to march to Tuscumbia, Alabama, just fifteen miles from Florence. Arriving in Tuscumbia in late April 1864, the 27th made camp and awaited supplies and reinforcements.

Edward received permission to visit his family, so on the 30th of April, he said goodbye to Ethan and rode out of camp toward Florence. In the early dawn hours of May 1, 1864, Edward climbed down from the saddle and stood at the gates of his home in Florence. The spring sun eclipsed the eastern hills, spreading its warm light on the roof and second story of the big house. It was quiet, and only a few early birds were busy chirping while foraging for their morning breakfast. His mare bobbed her head and whinnied softly, saying she was tired and hungry. He stared at the house as he patted her on the neck. "Soon, old girl," he said softly, then led her through the archway, past the open iron gates, and up the driveway to the porch. Slipping the reins of his horse through the black ring attached to a wooden post, he glanced around, thinking to himself that things hadn't changed, then walked up the steps and across the porch, followed by the sound of his own footsteps.

Wondering what he would find beyond the big oak door, he pulled the cord, hearing the familiar ring of the bell inside, and after waiting for what seemed a long time, he pulled it again. The door opened, and he looked into the slave Sophie's surprised eyes.

She clasped her hands over her heart as her eyes welled with tears. "Mistah Edward, thanks, the Lord ya's safe."

Edward smiled at the familiar friendly face as he stepped inside. "Hello, Sophie. How is everyone?"

"Everybody's jus' fine, Mistah Edward," she said, looking happy. "Dey all's just fine."

"And how about you?" he asked, looking concerned.

"Why ya knows me, Mistah Edward." She gave him a big smile. "Ol Sophie jus' keeps on go'n."

Edward smiled. "Indeed, you do, Sophie."

She fussed with the front of her red robe. "I bet ya's a bit tired and hungry."

He nodded, looking weary. "I rode most of the night."

"Den Mistah Edward, ya go on ups ta bed, and I'll fix ya's some good breakfast after ya wakes up."

Edward took off his coat, handed it to her, and told her to have someone take care of his tired horse waiting in the driveway. As he started up the stairs, he looked up, seeing Sarah standing at the top in a white nightgown. As a smile filled her face and tears filled her eyes, she raced down the stairs into his arms, almost tripping on her nightgown.

She felt soft and warm in his arms as he whispered. "I've missed you."

"Oh, Edward," she said softly. "I've missed you terribly." She looked into his tired eyes. "I thought I heard voices and was curious who would come calling at this dreadful hour. I was afraid it was your brother with bad news, and when I saw you, my heart stopped. How long can you stay?"

"Not long, only one day."

"One day?"

"And one night," he said, smiling. Then he asked about his daughter.

"Little Mary is fine. She misses her father and talks about you constantly, asking every day when will you come home." She took his hand. "We haven't long," she said. "Let's make the most of it." She gently pulled him up the stairs and into the bedroom. Closing the door, she giggled as she ran, jumped onto the bed, sat on her knees, and waited for him. He stood in silence for a moment, looking at her, then walked across the room, leaving a trail of clothing. Standing at the edge of the bed, he pulled her nightgown up over her head and tossed it on the floor, and then took her in his arms and lowered her onto the bed.

Edward opened his eyes from sleep and looked into the face of little Mary standing next to the bed staring at him. He smiled warmly. "What're you doing?"

She leaned against the bed and touched his face with the tips of her tiny fingers. "Watching you sleep."

"How about a little kiss?" he asked.

She giggled, threw her arms around his neck, kissed his cheek, and held him very tight in her small arms. "I've missed you, Daddy."

"And I've missed you." He pulled his head back and looked at her. "Look how you've grown."

"Sophie says I'll soon be all grown up." She touched his face again, looking quizzical. "Are you going to stay home now?"

He propped himself up on one elbow while resting his head in his hand he said, "No, daddy has to leave early tomorrow morning."

She leaned on her elbows, her head in her hands looking sad. "But I don't want you to leave."

He forced a smile. "I know, Sweetheart, but I promise that one day soon, daddy will be home for good."

Sarah felt the tears begin to well in her eyes, raised her head, looked over Edward's shoulder, and smiled at little Mary. "How about some breakfast?"

"I already had breakfast," boasted little Mary.

"You did?" asked Edward with a childish grin.

Little Mary nodded. "Uh-huh."

Sarah touched little Mary's nose with one finger. "But your father and I haven't had breakfast yet, and we're both very hungry. Why don't you run downstairs and tell Sophie that your daddy is ready for his breakfast?"

"Okay." Then she ran out of the room, yelling, "Daddy wants his breakfast, Sophie!"

Edward looked at the clock. "Maybe we should have a late lunch or an early dinner since it's almost two in the afternoon." He lay back, putting his arm around her, and pulled her into him.

She giggled. "Almost time for bed." Pushing him away, she sat up. "Get up; your daughter's waiting."

The day passed all too quickly, and after enjoying a quiet dinner with Alex and his family, they said goodbye, and as Edward closed the door, he contemplated his leaving tomorrow morning. Walking back toward the library and thinking of a drink, he saw little Mary at the top of the stairs asking if he would read to her. Thinking the drink could wait, Edward rushed up the stairs to perform the delightful chore that ended too quickly with her falling asleep. Careful not to wake her, he adjusted her covers, bent down, kissed her on the forehead, and looked down at his daughter, trying to burn the way she looked into his memory. He blew out the lantern, and after leaving the bedroom door open slightly, he walked across the hall, opened the door, and stepped into his bedroom.

Sarah was sitting in bed wearing a pale, blue, flimsy robe with her back against the pillows when he walked in. Putting the book down that she suddenly had lost interest in, she smiled bravely, not wanting to cry. "She asleep?"

He smiled. "She didn't last long."

"She was probably tired. It has been a big day for her."

Edward looked at Sarah for a long moment wanting to remember her just as she was. Then he sat down on the edge of the bed, feeling tired and wishing the war was over.

Sarah leaned forward and combed his hair with her hand, thinking he needed a haircut. "Come to bed."

He undressed, climbed into bed, took her in his arms, and kissed her. After they made love, they lay in each other's arms, enjoying the stillness of the big room and thought about tomorrow morning and all the mornings that would follow without one another. The clock in the hall struck the hour; and the ticking clock on the dresser seemed unusually loud while Sarah silently cursed them both.

It was still dark when Edward and Sarah stepped out of the house onto the porch the next morning, greeted by a chilly, white ground fog. He adjusted his long gray coat and she, her robe as they walked down the porch steps holding hands. A few feet away, a young Negro slave looking sleepy held the reins of Edward's horse. Taking the reins, he thanked the young boy and turned to say something to Sarah when the anxious mare nudged him in the back, signaling she was ready. He turned to the horse. "Don't rush me."

He turned back to Sarah, put one arm around her, and while holding the reins to his horse, they walked down the long driveway toward the big iron gates and fence barely visible in the chilly fog, marking the end of her journey. Reaching the archway and the open gates, Edward took Sarah in his arms and kissed her.

Sarah fought a losing battle with her welling eyes but forced a smile, looked up, and said she loved him. "Please come back to us."

Seeing her eyes full of tears, he softly said, "I promise." The horse nudged him in the back again, and Edward grinned, "I guess she's in a hurry."

Sarah wiped her tears with her hand and looked at the horse, and softly said, "Bitch."

Edward chuckled at that, took Sarah in his arms, kissed her, then turned and swung up onto the mare. Settling in his saddle, he looked down at her welling eyes and wet cheeks, leaned over, and touched the side of her face. "I'll write when I can." Sitting back up, he nudged the mare toward the street.

Sarah clung to his leg, looking up at him with tears in her eyes as they passed under the arch and through the open iron gate. Letting go when they reached the street, she watched as the fog swallowed them, leaving only the sounds of the mare's hooves against the cobblestones. Sarah stood at the iron gates, staring into the dense fog until there was only silence. Wrapping herself in her robe, she wiped her eyes and cheeks as she walked back through the gates toward the big house.

James Riley Chrisman

The 47th Alabama marched into Tennessee in April 1864, where they made camp along the Tennessee River, not far from Chattanooga. Learning they would be there for a few weeks, James asked for and was granted a ten-day leave. He wasted little time heading home aboard a boat headed for Guntersville, Alabama, and then he boarded a train for the last 90 miles.

He stepped from the train and hurried to the livery to rent a horse, only to find that the army had taken all but a couple of mules. Disappointed, he started walking the ten plus miles home, hoping he could catch a ride, but the dirt road remained deserted as he followed the wagon ruts in the road toward home. To pass the time, he threw an occasional rock, whistled, or hummed a tune, and thought a lot about Martha.

The time seemed to pass slowly as he ran, then walked, then ran again, but finally he crested the familiar hill and paused to look down upon the Chrisman farm. A scattering of Negro slaves was in the fields, livestock in the pastures were feeding, and a few Negro children played by the barn. His heart pounded with the excitement of being home, and he hurried along the road, looking for William in the fields or barn. Not seeing the familiar Chestnut, he looked toward the empty porch and walked faster.

Stepping off the road into the driveway and walking toward the big, two-story house, he fought the urge to run. A woman came out of the front door, stood at the edge of the porch holding a hand above her head, and shielding her eyes from the sun. Knowing it was either his mother or his sister, Beth, he waved and called out, "Hey!"

The figure waved back excitedly and then hurried down the steps, across the yard to the driveway, with her long black hair trailing behind her. James knew it was Beth, and as they approached one another, he dropped his bag just as she exploded into his arms, almost knocking him down.

Looking overjoyed, Beth asked, "Why didn't you tell us you were coming?"

"Didn't have time, Sis. I probably would have beaten the letter here anyways."

Beth stepped back and playfully slapped him on the shoulder. "We've all been worried."

Laughing, he picked up his bag and took Beth's hand as they walked toward the house while he asked how everyone was.

Elizabeth walked out of the door, and seeing who Beth was talking to, she yelled her son's name as she stepped off the porch. She raced across the yard holding the front of her dress above her ankles, and moments later, she was in his arms. "Are you home to stay, son?"

He shook his head. "No, Ma, just a few days."

"How many?" Beth asked.

"I have to leave in six days."

Elizabeth's expression was disappointment, but she quickly pushed that aside, took his face in her hands, and looked into his eyes. "You look wonderful. Not sickly like last time."

James grinned. "I feel better too, Ma."

"You gonna go see Martha right away?" asked Beth.

"In a bit," he said. "After we all visit a spell. Where's Pa?"

Elizabeth pointed. "Down at the barn."

James looked worried. "How is he?"

His mother smiled as she took his arm while they walked. "The same." Seeing William, she gestured toward the barn. "There, he is now."

James waved and then ran to his father, giving him a long hug.

William stepped back, grabbed his son by the shoulders, and looked him up and down. "You ain't hurt, none, are ya, boy?"

"No, Pa, I ain't hurt."

As the family walked toward the house, Beth walked backward to look at James while telling him about Martha sharing her letters. Seeing him blush, she laughed. "Don't concern yourself, James. I skipped over the mushy stuff so Ma and Pa wouldn't hear any of it."

Feeling his face flush again, he changed the subject by mentioning the livery in town, the army taking horses, and asked about the black mare. William told him they had to do some quick thinking and hide the mare with the plow horses and mules, knowing the army wouldn't take any of those from the farmers. When they reached the front porch, Elizabeth told him to sit with his father while she and Beth went inside for some lemonade.

As the door closed, James looked at his pa. "Bishop and Ben still riding around picking on people?"

William considered the question. "Bishop Martin was found with his head almost blown off in his barn, and someone took a knife to Ben Rogers while he was doing his business in the outhouse."

Elizabeth and Beth walked out of the house with a tray and four glasses of lemonade.

William looked at his wife. "James was just asking about Bishop and Ben Rogers, Mother."

Elizabeth never looked up while pouring the lemonade. "Someone in this valley done the world a favor that day." Then she glanced at William with a small smile and handed him a glass while Beth gave one to James. Elizabeth sat on a chair beside William, tasted her lemonade, and smiled, looking happy. "You best be getting over to see that wife of yours. I expect you'll be spending the night."

"I guess so, Ma. Is that all right?"

She smiled. "You two are married, James. I'd think it a little strange if you stayed here."

He nodded, feeling embarrassed. "Martha and I will come by tomorrow." Feeling the need to hurry, he gulped his drink. "I best go saddle up the mare. I sure hope she remembers me."

"I'm sure she will, son," replied William as he got up from his chair. "I'll come along and help."

James thanked his mother and Beth for the lemonade, gave each a hug and a kiss, and followed his pa down the porch steps toward the barn, thinking about Ben Rogers and Bishop Martin and his pa's old hunting knife.

Elizabeth walked to the edge of the porch filled with happiness, leaned against the post watching her son, and thought of Davy, wishing he was here to greet his big brother.

James walked up to the stall inside the dim barn where the mare was and spoke softly.

The mare looked at him with big dark eyes, and recognizing his familiar scent, she shook her head and neighed.

"Hello, girl," he said, stepping into the stall as he patted her on the rump, sliding his hand over her back and up her neck as he walked toward her head. Looking into her big, dark eyes, he spoke softly. "You're not mad at me for leaving, are ya, gal?"

She snorted softly, her ears perked, as she looked at him with big black eyes. James laughed and then hugged her neck, knowing she had missed him. William put the blanket on her, then James the saddle, and William cinched the saddle while James put the bit into the mare's mouth. As if the mare knew he would soon be upon her, she jerked her head and pranced in the stall.

William chuckled. "She wants you in the saddle, son. The mare wants to show you how much she's missed you." William patted the mare on the neck and stepped back as James led her out of the barn and swung up into the saddle.

James looked down at his pa. "Have any ideas who could have done in those two bastards?"

William patted the mare, looking into her eyes instead of his son's. "No, I sure don't." He paused. "Could've been almost anyone. Those two weren't exactly anyone's favorite Home Guard."

James considered that for a moment, thinking he knew who it was. "Yeah," he said. "Could've been anyone, I reckon." Then he turned the mare and galloped toward the Heard's' place.

The once white pickets of the fence around the cemetery looked weathered and gray, with the paint peeling. James pulled the mare up next to the fence, noticing that several boards had fallen on the ground and were lying in the weeds while others hung loose or crooked. He dismounted, thinking the war was claiming another victim, and walked through the wobbly gate to Davie's grave. James stood looking down at the grave before he knelt beside the weathered, wooden marker, seeing the evidence of his ma's last visit beginning to wilt.

He touched the marker with one hand and looked at the name. "I miss ya, Davy. Pa says Rogers and Martin got killed last year." James thought about that for a moment. "My money's on pa." Then he stood, glanced toward Allen's grave, and looked back at Davy's marker. "If you see Allen, tell him I miss him." He walked over to Allen's and knelt by another bunch of the same familiar flowers. He spoke softly to the marker bearing his friend's name. "Wish you had stayed, Allen. Sure, do miss ya."

Filled with regret and despair, he sat on the hard ground, folded his legs, and looked around at the other markers, thinking of the other men he once knew who were dead and buried in unfamiliar places. He wiped the tears from his welling eyes. "Wish this damn war was over. I'm tired of always being afraid before each battle and sick after. I just wanna come home." He looked out across the peaceful valley at the cotton fields and trees in the distance as he listened to the quiet. "I ain't told anyone this, Allen, but I gotta tell someone." He wiped his eyes again. "There was this small boy, maybe nine or ten, that must've been watching the fighting. Jesus, Allen, I saw someone move from the corner of my eye, and I turned and fired. I didn't see him till it was too late."

James cried for several minutes, then wiped his cheeks. "I see that boy in my sleep, Allen." He wiped his eyes again, got up, and looked down at the grave. "If ya see the boy Allen, tell him I'm sorry, and would you take care of Davy for me? I know y'all are together." James reached down, touched the weathered wooden marker, turned, and slowly walked back to his horse.

Martha was busy in the kitchen when she looked out the window, easily recognizing the black mare and knew the rider was James by how he sat in the saddle. Uttering his name, she stopped what she was doing, raced out of the house, across the porch, and flew over the steps, landing on the ground at a dead run. James pulled the mare up, wrapped the reins around the saddle horn, and jumped down.

Martha ran into his arms, kissing his lips, cheeks, forehead, and eyes, then his lips again. He laughed and tried talking to her but gave up and let her kiss him. She hugged him. "Oh, James, I missed ya so much." She looked at him and began to cry. "Why didn't you tell me you were coming home?"

"I didn't know until the last minute. The 47th's up by Chattanooga waiting for replacements."

Feeling fearful, she asked, "Yah didn't run away like Allen, did ya, James?"

He smiled, told her no, and then explained that he had been given a ten-day furlough and had to leave in a few days. Hearing a door slam, James looked up, seeing Mr. and Mrs. Heard as they hurried from the porch.

"James," greeted Mrs. Heard as she hugged him. "We've all been so worried. Are ya home for good?"

"No, ma'am, just a few days." He shook Mr. Heard's hand, telling him hello, and with the mare following, they walked toward the house. James explained his leave, where his outfit was camped, the boat ride, the railroad ride, and his walk home. Reaching the porch, James tied the mare to the railing and followed the family inside, where they talked for the next hour while Martha and her mother prepared dinner. As the women talked, James only half-listened to the things Mr. Heard was telling him. James's thoughts were of the men he had killed and his friends lying dead on the battlefields.

Mrs. Heard's voice interrupted his thoughts. "You're staying for dinner, James, no arguing about it."

James pushed the face of a small boy out of his mind. "Yes, ma'am." Then he stood. "I best put the mare in the barn."

James only half-listened to what Mr. Heard said as they sat at the table after dinner. He was busy watching Martha help her mother clean up and was more curious about what the two were quietly discussing.

Mrs. Heard stopped what she was doing and looked at James. "Of course, y'all will be staying here tonight?" She smiled at him, then at Martha, who shyly smiled back. "Only proper now that you're man and wife." She had a stern look about her. "Won't take no for an answer. For now, y'all stay here in Martha's room. After all, she still lives here. What the two of you do after the war is between you and Martha."

James thought things were suddenly very confusing.

Mrs. Heard walked to the table, sat beside her husband, and smiled at Martha, knowing she wanted James for herself. "Your pa and me will finish the dishes while you and James take a walk. It's a nice evening outside; the fresh air will do you both good."

Richard Heard didn't look too pleased but didn't argue.

Martha looked happy as she took James by the hand and led him outside. As the door closed, he let go of her hand, walked to the edge of the porch, and looked up at the night sky, thinking again about the men he had killed in battle.

Martha stood next to him. "James?"

"Yeah," he said, staring up at a thousand stars.

"Are you all right? You seem different."

He looked at her face reflecting the dim light from the window. "How do ya mean?"

"You're quiet, almost sad-like. Ma had to ask ya more than once if ya needed anything during dinner."

Feeling embarrassed, he turned away. "I'm all right, Martha."

"Then what's wrong? Is it staying here tonight that concerns ya?"

"Gosh, no, Martha."

She placed her hand on his arm, looking worried. "Then what's wrong?"

He shrugged and turned back to the night sky. "I don't know. Everything's just a little confusing for me right now. I can't explain it, none."

Her heart was sad, her face fearful. "Try James," she said softly. "I'm starting to think you don't want to be with me like we was before ya left."

That wasn't true, but he kept staring at the black sky in silence.

"James," she said softly, holding back the tears.

He turned and looked into her eyes and wondered how he could tell her what terrible things he had done. How the constant fear of dying or the fear of having to kill someone kept him awake at night, fearing the nightmares more than the loss of sleep. "I've changed, Martha. Inside I've changed. It's difficult to explain."

Tears made their way down her cheeks. "I thought so."

"I don't mean about us."

"What do ya mean then?"

"Where I've been and what I've done and seen has taken something from me." He paused and gave her a troubled look. "All I can say right now is that I want to be with you tonight. I need to feel you next to me, to feel you breathing when we lay next to one another. I want to feel the warmth of your body."

She looked into his troubled face, trying to understand, but he seemed so far away. She wanted to hold him and make it better if she could. She took his hand. "Let's take a walk."

They walked in the dark away from the light of the windows with neither speaking. When they stopped, James let go of her hand and looked up again at the moon and stars. "When I would stand guard late at night, I'd try and pick out the ones that might be over my pa's place and here."

Martha put her arm around him, rested her head against his shoulder, and looked up. "It's getting late."

"S'pose it is," he said, glancing back at the closed door and lighted windows. "Just seems a little strange, is all."

"Well, of course, it does, James,' she said. "Feels a mite strange to me, too." She let go of his arm and looked up into his eyes. "I want the same things, to lie down and feel ya next to me all night, and to open my eyes in the morning and see it weren't just a dream." She took his hand in hers and walked toward the house.

When they entered the kitchen, Mrs. Heard was folding her dishtowel, and as she laid it on the counter, she smiled. "It's good to have you home safe, James. It seems like it's been a long day." Then she walked over to Martha, kissed her on the cheek, did the same to James, and said goodnight. They watched as she paused at the door to the living room. "You've got some reading to do, Richard, and me some sewing." Moments later, Mr. Heard walked out of the living room with his book and followed his wife upstairs.

James and Martha stood in the kitchen, staring at the empty staircase and then at one another, each anticipating their night together. In the stillness of the kitchen, they heard her mother and father's bedroom door closing, shoes dropping, her pa coughing, and then silence. Martha blew out all of the lamps but one, and that one she handed to him so that would guide them upstairs to their sanctuary. Inside her room, Martha took the lamp, set it on the dresser, blew the flame out, returning the room to darkness, and then she walked to James, waiting at the foot of the bed. Standing in the white moonlight from the window, she undressed, letting her clothes drop quietly to the floor, and then stood in silence and waited while he undressed.

James spent the next several days working at the Chrisman farm during the day and sleeping at the Heard's place each night. Elizabeth and Martha both wanted James with them full time, but each knew the other's needs, so they settled for what he could give them. His time home was short, and the day arrived to say goodbye and return to the war. He and Martha spent their last night together in his old room at the Chrisman place, sleeping very little.

The morning sunrise Martha had feared was here, and James was up early getting ready. She was in bed sitting up against a pillow at the headboard, watching him put on his clean yet somewhat ragged gray uniform that his mother had washed. After he packed his carpetbag, he sat on the edge of the bed and held her hand as he looked into her sad, red and welling eyes. "Time to go."

"I know," she said, trying to be brave by forcing a smile.

They looked at one another in silence, each filled with words they could not speak. There was so much they wanted to say but no time to say it. James turned away to the window and the clouds above the horizon that were a palette of oranges, pinks, and purples, wondering if he would ever see her again.

For some unexplained reason, Martha suddenly knew she was carrying his child and wanted to tell him, but knew that would only worry him. So she kept the secret and prayed that God would grant her prayer of bringing him back to them.

He stared out the window at the colors. "I don't want you to come to the station this morning."

"But, James…"

"Martha, please," he interrupted her looking upset. "It's too hard."

Looking disappointed, she argued. "For you, maybe."

"My minds made up." Then he turned to kiss her.

She turned away in anger. "Fine," she said, tossing the covers back and getting out of bed. She put on her robe, opened the door, stepped into the hall, slammed the door, and went downstairs.

James sat on the bed for a few minutes wondering why she didn't understand and finally understood what his pa meant when he had said marriage is hard work. He stood from the edge of the bed, picked up his carpetbag, and looked down at the unmade bed thinking about last night, turned, and headed for the bedroom door, wondering what he would find downstairs.

William sat in his usual place drinking coffee while waiting for breakfast, wondering why Martha was sitting where Davy used to sit instead of the chair next to James.

All of this seemed a bit odd to Beth while she glanced from James to Martha, then at her pa, who raised his eyebrows, acknowledging her curiosity. Beth stepped into the kitchen to help her mother and warn her that things weren't quite right between James and Martha. Elizabeth paused, considering that, and quickly decided it was a matter between James and Martha and told Beth to help get the food on the table. Elizabeth entered the dining room carrying two platters of food, paused to look around the table, and commented on how quiet it was. She set the platters on the table, folded her arms, and looked at James and then Martha with a stern look. "Something going on here?" Neither answered, then she noticed that Martha still had her nightgown and robe on. "Why aren't you dressed, girl? We have to leave for the station right after breakfast."

Martha stared at James with an angry look. "James doesn't want me to go."

Elizabeth looked at James. "Why on earth not?"

James glanced at his father, looking for help, but William, being the wise man he was, started eating his breakfast. Realizing he was on his own, James turned to his mother to explain. "I just don't want everyone to go, Ma, that's all."

Elizabeth gave him one of her looks. "James Riley, that makes no sense at all."

Martha's voice quivered as she fought not to cry. "That's what I thought, Mrs. Chrisman."

Then Beth sat down at the table and looked at her brother. “Ain’t no one gonna stop me.”

James gave his sister a quick look.

Elizabeth smiled at Martha, then lightly patted her on the shoulder. “You best go back upstairs, girl, and get dressed.”

Martha looked defiantly at James with a triumphant smile as she pushed her chair back, got up, and hurried out of the dining room.

James glanced up at his ma and then stared down at his plate, aware that he had lost the argument.

Elizabeth almost felt sorry for her son. “Eat your breakfast, James.”

By the time the train whistle blew its third and final warning, James had told everyone goodbye more than once. The engine spun its wheels, jerking the cars one by one back to the caboose toward the end of the station platform, and someone yelled, “All Aboard!” James kissed Martha one last time, said he would write, told her not to worry, and jumped onto the steps of a passing rail car.

Hanover Junction, Virginia

James and the 47th Alabama fought in two major engagements. The first was Parkers Store, Virginia, which became known as The Battle of the Wilderness, where the Confederate Army suffered over 11,000 casualties. That engagement was followed by a bitterly fought battle at Spotsylvania Court House, costing the Union army over 18,000 casualties and the Confederates another 11,000.

Undeterred by the losses, Union General Ulysses S. Grant led his army into Virginia, while the 47th Alabama made its way from Spotsylvania to North Ann and Hanover Junction. Weary from the long battle at Spotsylvania, the 47th rested until the 24th of May, 1864, when an overwhelming force of Union infantry attacked them. On May 27th, 1864, the third day of fierce fighting, James and several others were captured. They would spend the remainder of the war in a prisoner of war camp at Elmira, New York. It was a camp that history would prove a terrible place with crowded conditions, sickness, and shortages of food, clothing, and medicines. Of the over 12,000 Southern prisoners incarcerated at Elmira, over 3,000 would die slow, agonizing deaths. When the war ended in April 1865, those who survived were mere skeletons of their former selves.

June 12, 1864

Tallapoosa County

Martha Chrisman and Beth went to New Site for a little shopping and lunch, trying to forget the war and worrying about James. They walked along the boardwalk, talking when they saw a crowd gathering in front of the general store. Knowing that was where they posted the dead, wounded, and missing list, they made their way across the street and up the boardwalk steps.

Martha pushed her way past the others and stared at the letters of names she could not read, then turned and looked questioningly at Beth, whose eyes were beginning to well. "What is it?" asked Martha.

As her tears rolled down her cheeks, Beth put her arm around Martha. "It says James Chrisman is missing in action."

Martha's knees buckled, Beth caught her, and as Martha cried, Beth helped her into the buggy and then hurried around to the other side and climbed in beside her. Martha looked at her with red, welling eyes. "I'm carrying James's baby."

Surprised at the news and hoping her brother was not dead, Beth put her arms around Martha and held her for several minutes. Then wanting to get Martha home, she picked up the reins and drove to the Heard place. Martha Heard Chrisman would give birth to a son in early December 1864.

Twenty-Seven

June 27, 1864 – June 30, 1864

Edward McAlexander

Battle of Kennesaw Mountain near Marietta, Georgia

The battle of Kennesaw Mountain began at 8:00 a.m. on June 27, 1864, as 200 Federal cannons opened fire on Confederate positions located on Kennesaw Mountain. At 8:30 a.m., the Federal army moved toward Kennesaw Mountain, dealing with dense thickets, steep rocky slopes, and a lack of knowledge of the terrain. By 10:30 a.m., the fighting ended with the Union suffering over 3,000 casualties and the Confederates a little over 1,000. Although the battle was a tactical victory for the South, it was nevertheless another useless slaughter.

During the final day of that battle, Colonel James Jackson, commander of the 27th Alabama, was seriously wounded and due to his injuries, later lost his right arm. Three days later, on the afternoon of June 30, 1864, Lt. Colonel Edward Asbury McAlexander was promoted to full Colonel, taking command of the 27th Alabama Infantry.

August 1864 – November 1864

The Hall Farm

Mary was all alone in a boat floating down a river on a hot afternoon searching the shoreline for Joseph when suddenly her back hurt, and the boat began to fill with the lake's clear, warm water. Waking from the dream, Mary sat up, pushing the covers back and knew that her water had broken, and that she was about to give birth to her third child. Fighting the pain in her lower back and between her legs, Mary managed to sit on the edge of the bed and put her feet onto the cold, wooden floor. Taking deep breaths, she looked down at her wet nightgown and sheets, and then at her sleeping children a few feet away. With one hand under her bulging abdomen, she held onto the bedpost with the other and slowly stood. Resting for a moment while a contraction came and went, she made her way to the closed bedroom door, opened it, and walked across the hall to Janice Hall's bedroom door. Pausing with her damp forehead against the door as another contraction came, she tapped on the bedroom door and softly called to Janice.

A sleepy-eyed Janice opened the door, looked at Mary, and knew what was happening. "Looks like this child is not going to wait." She stepped out of the room, closed the door, and helped Mary across the hall and into bed.

Mary apologized for getting the sheets and bed wet.

Janice smiled, saying they were going to get a lot wetter. "You've done this before, so you know what to expect." Janice helped her to bed and then squeezed Mary's hand with a reassuring look. "You're going to be just fine. I'll get Lori."

Lori took Mary's children to her bedroom and put them to bed while Janice dealt with Mary. Having been through this before, Del hurried downstairs to build a fire in the cooking stove and fill several pots with water to boil.

Mary's face was wet with perspiration as she gripped Lori's hand, looking afraid. "Where's Joseph? Why isn't he here?"

"I don't know," Lori said softly as she wiped Mary's forehead.

Janice scrambled around the bed, placing more sheets under her and adjusting pillows for the arrival of a new life. That done, she hurried downstairs to the kitchen, pushing Del away from the stove to check on the water. Del watched until she disappeared up the stairs and then stoked the fire, listening to the sounds of footsteps hurrying across the floor above him. Believing it would be a long night and morning, he decided to make a pot of coffee.

The water began to boil, so Del hurried upstairs and tapped on the door. "Water's boiling."

Footsteps approached the door, and as it opened, he glanced inside, but Janice pushed him back, stepped outside, closed the door, and hurried toward the stairs at the end of the hall.

Del watched as she quickly disappeared down the stairs, glanced at the closed door, and then followed his wife down to the kitchen. As she poured hot water into a smaller pan, he asked, "Is there something I can do?"

"Yes," she said as she hurried past. "Stay down here and keep the fire going. I'll call if we need more hot water."

Wondering if she thought he was mindless and wouldn't have thought of that himself, he sat down at the table, picked up the cup of coffee he had been enjoying, and took a sip, imagining the scene upstairs.

Janice hurried into the kitchen. "Put down the damn coffee Del. We need more towels."

In the instant it took him to look toward her, she was already rushing up the stairs yelling, "Just knock on the door. There's no need for you to come inside!"

He sighed and shook his head, remembering when he and Janice had delivered their own child Ethan in the dead of winter. This whole thing seemed a bit dramatic to him as he took another drink of coffee, gathered several towels from cupboards and drawers, and headed up the stairs. Del raised one hand to knock when Mary let out a small scream. He stared at the door, recalling what Janice had told him about not coming in, knew that he was better off on this side of the door anyway, and knocked.

Janice opened the door, took the towels without so much as a thank you, and slammed the door shut.

Del returned to the kitchen, added more wood to the stove, checked the water in each pot, poured another cup of coffee, and sat back down at the table, stuffing tobacco into the bowl of his pipe. Cries of the new life suddenly made their way down the stairs, and he paused with a smile imagining the tiny life upstairs, struggling with its first taste of a harsh world. His pipe packed with tobacco, Del bent down to the wood box next to the stove, tore a slender piece of wood from a piece of firewood, lit it in the stove, and put the flame to the bowl of the pipe. A small, sparse cloud of smoke gathered around his head as he sat back in his chair, hoping it was the little girl Mary had wanted. His peaceful moment was short-lived. Janice opened the bedroom door and yelled downstairs that it was another boy. Del placed his thumbs in his suspenders and proudly sat back in the chair as if he had managed this whole affair himself.

Upstairs, Janice cleaned the infant, wrapped him in a swaddling blanket she had made for the occasion, and handed him to his mother. Even though she was exhausted from the ordeal, Mary radiated the wonderful glow of a new mother as she smiled and helped her son find his first nipple for the first time to suckle.

"Appears he knows what to do," smiled Lori.

Mary watched her son feed. "I wish Joseph were here." Then she smiled. "He looks like his father." Then she softly laughed. "My God, they all do."

Lori and Janice laughed, and Lori leaned closer to the baby. "Oh, I don't know, I think I see a little Edward in this one."

"Really?" smiled Mary, looking pleased.

Janice sat on the edge of the bed and watched the wonder of new life suckling from its mother. Her mind found the memory of the day she and Del had brought Ethan into the cold wintry world. Her eyes turned red and then welled with tears of worry for her only son. "Have you thought of a name?"

Mary thought for several moments. "Edward, I think," she said, looking at her child. "Yes, Edward Joseph Greene would be a fine name." Then she looked at Janice and asked if she would mind getting her Bible from the drawer next to the bed. Janice retrieved the Bible with the generations of McAlexander names, along with Mary's two children. "Would you like me to do it for you, Mary?"

Mary said yes and then watched as Janice wrote: Edward Joseph Greene, Born August 29, 1864. When she finished, Janice held it so Mary could read the words. Mary thanked Janice and then settled against the pillow, looked down at her sleeping child, and turned toward the window. Seeing the first light of a new day, she thought of Joseph's promise that he would be home in time for the child, and she worried where he was.

August 29, 1864

Jefferson, Texas

Joseph's shoulder ached and throbbed with pain as he stumbled beneath the searing sun of the hot desert. Thirsting for water, his dry and swollen tongue touched his parched lips, and unable to go any farther, he stumbled and fell, waiting for death.

Opening his eyes, it was chilly and dark, and when he looked up, the sky was starless and black, and the sand beneath him was hard. Looking around, he realized he was lying on the floor of his room, having fallen out of bed. Hot from fever, he managed to sit up and pull himself up onto his knees next to the bed. Burning up and thirsty, he pulled himself up onto his wobbly legs. Taking two steps toward the table, he collapsed, knocking the chair, pitcher of water, and glass onto the floor.

The sound brought Mrs. Hansen rushing into the room, finding Joseph on the floor trying to get up. She rushed across the room and knelt beside him. "For heaven's sake, why didn't you call me? You're a stubborn fool, ya are."

He looked up at her with sleepy eyes, managing a small smile. "Thought I could get it, Mrs. Hansen. I didn't want to be a bother to you and your boarders."

"Well now," she said. "That didn't work out so good now, did it?" She helped him onto the bed, put his feet up, propped his head against the pillow, and reached for the covers, deciding he only needed a sheet. "You needn't worry about being a bother," she said, looking worried. "You should have called out." She tossed the covers over a chair then covered him with a sheet. “As for the other boarders,” she said sternly, “I suggest you let me do the worrying about them.”

She felt his forehead, shook her head, and stepped back in thought. “Still got your fever.” She glanced at the stove. “I’ll get some water after I stoke the stove up a bit and get some heat in this room. Don’t want ya catching pneumonia on top of everything else.”

“It’s hot in here,” he complained.

“Nonsense,” she said. “That’s the fever talking. You’re going to get the chills with shivers between sweats, so keep the sheet around yourself.”

Joseph closed his eyes, wanting sleep while listening to her work on the stove with kindling and wood, followed by the sound of a match. He opened his eyes just enough to see the flames grow as she shut the small, iron door of the potbellied stove.

Satisfied with her work, she hurried out of the room, returning minutes later with a pan of water, a new pitcher, and a towel draped over her arm. “That’s better,” she said. “It’s already getting nice and warm in here.”

“It’s too hot,” complained Joseph.

“Nonsense,” she said. “It’s like I done told you; that’s your fever talking.” Picking up the pieces of the pitcher and the glass, Mrs. Hanson set them on the nightstand. Then she sat on the edge of his bed with a pan of cold water and a washcloth and looked at him with a worried face. “You owe me a pitcher,” she said with a smile, and then she dipped the washcloth into the water, wrung it out, and placed it on his forehead.

“Afraid I got your floor and part of that rug wet,” he said with a proud half-smile. “Managed not to break the chair, though.”

She scowled. “That old rug’s had worse things on it, and that chair’s tougher than you are.”

He considered that and managed a small smile as he closed his eyes, thinking the damp cloth felt good. “Never did get that drink of water I was after.”

She laughed softly and shook her head. “Plum forgot about that.” Leaving the cloth on his forehead, she poured a glass half full and helped him take a drink. “Reckon I should send you home to that wife of yours where you can get some real care.” She placed the glass on the table, and then checked the wound in his shoulder. “I need to change them bandages and apply that salve Doc Bradley left. He said it’d help fight any infection.” She hurried from the room, returning in a matter of minutes with fresh bandages and the salve, and then began working at taking off the bloody bandages. "Think that wife of yours has given birth yet?" she asked as she worked.

"I hope so," he said, looking regretful. "It's past due." He paused. "I promised I'd be there."

She paused from what she was doing and looked at him with an understanding smile. "Now, it wasn't any fault of yours that this happened." She took the top off the jar of salve. "Besides, and I'm speaking from experience, you would've just been in the way. Most men are at such times, so don't go fretting none about that right now." She raised her brow and nodded. "I'm sure she's plenty worried about you like any good wife." She paused, sat back, and looked at him with a stern look. "However, you have some explaining to do once she sees the way you look." She had a worried look as she began to apply the salve to the wound. "You're lucky that knife didn't do more damage."

Joseph grimaced and cringed when she began with the salve.

She stopped for a moment. "Don't be such a child, Joseph. You should ask your wife what real pain is. My guess is she'd tell ya."

"I'm not about to get any sympathy, am I?"

Her eyes narrowed as she considered that. "None." When she finished with the salve and fresh bandage, she stood. "I think you'll live. All you need is a little rest and some nourishment. I'll return later with some warm broth."

His voice was soft, sounding tired. "I can hardly wait."

"Don't get uppity," she said, looking insulted. "Now, close your eyes and get some rest."

The days passed, and thanks to Mrs. Hansen's nursing abilities, Joseph was well on his way to recovery. Sitting by the window in the only chair in the room, he watched the people on the boardwalk below. A woman walking by reminded him of Mary, and he missed her very much. He knew that by now, she had received the letter he had paid a man to deliver to the Hall Farm, telling her that he was sick and would be home as soon as he was able to travel.

A knock on the door interrupted his thoughts.

He turned from the scene below to the door. "Come in."

The door opened, and Mrs. Hansen backed in with a tray of freshly baked bread and a plate of fried chicken and mashed potatoes. She closed the door with one foot, set the tray on the small table, and smiled. "Thought ya could use some lunch."

"Thanks, Mrs. Hansen, but I could've made it downstairs."

"I think you're better off up here for a spell longer." She fussed with the tray and plates. "How's that shoulder?"

"A few more days, and I'll be good as new." He stood, moved the chair to the small table, and sat down and grinned at her. "I'd ask you to sit, Mrs. Hansen, but you only allow one chair in the room."

Her expression was without humor as she placed a napkin on his lap and sat on the edge of the bed, looking curious. "Some men have been by asking about you."

He stopped eating and looked at her. "Did they leave their names?"

"They did," she said, looking deep in thought. "But I don't remember. One man was dressed like you. Black clothes and hat, a riverman I expect. He was a big man."

"Sounds like Iron Mike."

She considered that for a few moments and thoughtfully said, "Interesting name. The other looked like a drummer." She winked as she smiled proudly. "I ran the likes of him off."

"Why would a drummer come to see me?"

She nodded. "That's exactly why I run him off."

Joseph was curious about the drummer as he began working on a piece of chicken, and as he wiped his mouth with the napkin, he asked, "What did he look like?"

She stared out the window, thinking how best to describe the man. "Thirty, I reckon, not sure. Slender build, blond hair, a handsome looking man. Had a slight limp and walked with a cane."

"Sounds like Bob Colbert, but the cane doesn't fit." Joseph took a bite of the freshly baked bread and grinned. "If it were Colbert, I'd love to tell him you thought he was a drummer. Are you sure about the cane?"

"Sure as I saw him limping. What does this Colbert do for a living?"

"He's a gambler."

Her eyes narrowed, looking troubled as she leaned forward. "Is this Colbert the one that stabbed you?"

Joseph chuckled. "No, it wasn't Colbert. That's not his style."

Mrs. Hansen stood, said she had chores to do, and left him to contemplate Bob Colbert and the cane.

Finished eating, Joseph returned to the window and quietly watched the people in the street below, looking forward to the day he would run into Charles Whittaker. But for now, Whittaker would have to wait. He had more important things to do, like getting home to Mary and the children.

Joseph sat on the edge of his bed and watched with interest as Doc Bradley looked at the bandages and the skin around the two wounds. "When do you think I can travel, Doc?"

Doc Bradley paused at what he was doing and glanced at Joseph over the rim of his glasses. "Know more about that after I finish, young fella." Looking at the bandages he was carefully removing, he asked, "You in a hurry to get someplace?"

"Yeah, I am Doc."

Doc Bradley held the bloody bandages close to his nose, smelled them, tossed them on the floor, and then examined the two cuts on Joseph's chest that he had stitched up several days ago.

"How's it looking, Doc?"

"Seems to be healing nicely, them bandages smell okay, and there's no sign of infection." He adjusted his glasses on his nose. "The flesh around the stitches appears to be healing nicely." The doc pressed on the wounds. "That hurt?"

Joseph flinched. "Does a chicken shit, Doc?"

Doc Bradley chuckled as he sat back in his chair. "You shouldn't use that arm much for a while. You could tear loose what those stitches are trying to hold together and possibly get one hell of an infection. Whoever did this came a little too close to your heart and lungs." Doc's face turned serious. "An infection, there would be fatal."

Joseph nodded, understanding although disappointed that he would be in town a little longer. He settled back against his pillow so the doctor could apply more salve and re-bandage the wounds while he thought of Charles Whittaker.

Finished with new bandages, Doc examined the cut above his eye and the one on the side of his neck that had narrowly missed his jugular. "These others will probably leave scars." Bradley stood. "But they're healing nicely."

Joseph sat up, tossing his legs over the bed, and reached for his shirt. "So, I have to stay put for a while." He struggled with his shirt. "When can I travel?"

The doc helped him with his shirt. "Depends."

"On what?"

The doc smiled. "On how far and by what means of travel."

"A little farm twenty or so miles north of here, and I'd be riding my horse."

Bradley looked concerned. "What's the big hurry, Son?"

"My wife was expecting our third child and should have given birth by now."

The Doc smiled. "Well, well, congratulations, but that still doesn't change the fact that a ride that far could bust something open, letting an infection set in." He paused, putting one hand on Joseph's shoulder. "The body needs time to heal, or that new child of yours won't have a pa."

Joseph finished tucking in his shirt. "I have a promise to keep…"

The doc cut him off, sounding angry. "All right, young man, I can see you're in a hurry, and I can't say I blame you none." He turned and began packing his equipment into his black bag. "Five, six days should do the trick." Then he closed his bag and sat on the edge of the bed. "I'll have the stitches out by then, and while you'll have some soreness, the skin should have healed enough for a long ride." The doctor scowled as he pointed to the bandages. "You were pretty lucky, son. Whoever did that meant to kill you."

Joseph thought of Whittaker. "I know."

"That six-inch gash across your breastplate came damn close to your heart. The second wound between your ribs and shoulder just missed the top of your lung."

Joseph considered that as he watched Doc Bradley shrug into his coat.

"You're a lucky man Son," the doctor said as he picked up his little black bag. "Whoever he was, he must've been in a hurry, and that's probably why you're still alive." The doctor put on his hat and walked toward the door talking over one shoulder. "I'll be back in a couple of days. We'll get you home to that wife and child of yours as soon as I think it's safe." He paused at the door. "Don't be reckless, boy. You wouldn't want to be on that farm with an infection and no doctor."

Joseph nodded. "Okay, Doc, five days it is."

Doc Bradley smiled wryly and winked. "Just pay the bill."

Joseph smiled as Bradley walked out of the room, then he moved back to the window, and as he watched the street below, he thought about the Doc's words regarding the intent to kill him. A quiet knock on the door interrupted his thoughts of that night. "It's open."

The door opened, and a big man having the look of authority filled the better part of the doorway stepped into the room. As the man closed the door, Joseph noticed the bulge in his coat. "I'm Sheriff Bill Parker, and I'd like a word or two with you. That is, if you're up to it."

Joseph started to get up, but the sheriff motioned him to stay put with the wave of his big hand. He looked around the room for another chair, which Joseph found a little humorous while he grinned and nodded toward the door. "Mrs. Hansen only allows one chair per room, Sheriff.

But you can sit on the bed if you want." He thought the man looked a little old for a sheriff and guessed his age to be close to fifty, maybe fifty-five, which was a little old for most men in his profession. This was the first time Joseph had met the man, but he was familiar with his reputation of being a no-nonsense sheriff.

Settling on the edge of the bed that moaned with his weight, the sheriff glanced around the room as he took off his hat, setting it next to him on the bed. A thick head of gray hair hung past his ears and collar, he was clean-shaven except for a long, handlebar mustache and bushy brown and gray eyebrows set above intense, dark brown eyes. Sheriff Parker had spent most of his life as either a deputy or sheriff in, Arkansas, and the Texas panhandle before taking two .44 slugs in the chest that had almost taken his life. He was a man already well known to the Jefferson City Council when they had persuaded him to leave Fort Worth and come to Jefferson a couple of years ago. Despite his age, the people of Jefferson had soon learned he was a man to be taken seriously. Parker studied Joseph for a moment and then nodded toward the door. "Saw Doc Bradley downstairs, he said you want to get out of town as soon as possible." The sheriff paused and smiled. "Says you're pretty anxious to see that new baby."

"Yes, I am," smiled Joseph. "But according to the doc, that may not be for a few days. What's on your mind, Sheriff?"

Parker studied him for a few moments. "I was wondering if you got a look at the fella who did this?"

Joseph frowned, remembering Whittaker's face, and then shook his head. "Sorry, Sheriff, wish I could help, but it was dark, and it all happened pretty fast."

Parker pursed his lips, looking troubled. "Figured as much." He paused in thought. "Often, people see more than they realize. If you were to look at some posters, you might recognize the face."

Joseph shook his head. "Sorry, Sheriff, but I never saw his face. He came at me from behind, and the only thing I saw was the knife. I wasn't much interested in the man's face at that point, and like I said, it was dark."

Sheriff Parker looked disappointed. "That's too bad. I sure would like to catch this one. Its fella's like that give this town a bad name."

Joseph shrugged. "Sorry I can't be of more help, Sheriff."

Parker picked up his hat and stood. "If you think of anything or happen to see this fella before ya leave town, you come and see me."

"I'll do that, Sheriff."

Parker walked to the door, opened it, and turned. "Hope you get home safe to that wife and baby, Mr. Greene."

Joseph smiled, thanked him, and after the big man stepped through the doorway, closing the door behind him, he turned back to the street below. As he watched the sheriff walk across the street, Joseph remembered the look in Charles Whittaker's eyes reflected in the dim light from the window that shone onto the street as they fought.

On November 11, 1864, Doc Bradley told Joseph he was well enough to travel, so he packed his carpetbag, said goodbye to Trudy Hansen, and headed northeast out of town.

East Texas – Hall Farm

It was almost dark when Joseph turned his horse from the county dirt road onto the Hall farm. Anxious to see Mary and the children, he nudged the horse into a trot. Reaching the front porch, he pulled up and jumped down, feeling the jar from that mistake in his healing wounds.

The door opened, and Mary stepped out of the house and ran across the porch into his arms. "Where have you been?"

Just like a woman, he thought, happy as hell to see you, but when the greeting's over, they want an explanation. "I told you in my letter."

She looked at the scars on his face. "Are you all right?"

He smiled. "I'm fine. Still a little sore, but I'm all right."

She gently touched the still healing scars on his face and neck. "My God, Joseph, what happened to you?"

He looked apologetic. "I didn't want to worry you with the new baby and all. But I was stabbed and robbed."

Looking worried, she asked, "Are you sure you're all right?"

He smiled. "I'm fine, Mary."

Looking relieved, she said, "Teddy, can take care of your horse. Come inside, supper's almost ready."

Inside the house, Mary got a better look at the scar on the side of his face that disappeared into the hairline above his left ear and another one on his neck. "Are you sure you're all right?"

He nodded. "I'm fine."

"I swear, Joseph," said Mary. "Sometimes, I don't know what to say to you."

He grinned. "I should live so long."

Mary scowled. "That's not funny."

Del and Janice's grandson walked into the kitchen from his room upstairs. "Welcome home, Joseph."

Joseph smiled, "Thank you, Teddy. Would you mind taking care of your pa's horse?"

"No, sir, not at all."

"Go easy on it. He's had a long ride."

Teddy grinned as he walked outside, talking over his shoulder. "Yes, sir."

Del, Janice, and Lori walked into the kitchen, and after a quick exchange of hellos and before anyone could ask about his face, Mary rushed him upstairs to see their new son and reunite him with the other two boys. Zachariah jumped up from the floor where he was playing and ran to his father. Joseph knelt, picked him up, and hugged him. Joseph Jr., on the other hand, sat on the floor, holding a wooden block between his hands, looking afraid. Joseph gave Zach another quick hug, put him down, knelt, and smiled at Joseph Jr. as he slowly and gently picked him up.

The boy looked like he was about to cry, but then he smiled. Joseph bent down, picked up Zach, and with a child in each arm, he walked to the small bed in the corner of the room and looked down at his new son, Edward Joseph Greene. "Looks just like me."

Mary smiled. "I told Lori they all do, but she insisted this one had a little of Edward in him."

Joseph looked down at his son sucking on the fingers of one hand. "Really? I hope he doesn't have those bushy McAlexander eyebrows."

Mary quietly laughed while looking down at their son. "Would that be so bad?"

Joseph put the boys down and watched as they went back to what they were doing while he turned and smiled at his new son. "Hello, little man, I'm your pa. Would you like bushy eyebrows when you grow up?" The baby looked up with legs, arms, and hands flailing. "See," said Joseph. "Even he doesn't like the idea."

Mary laughed softly as Lori's voice from beyond the door told them dinner was ready.

"We'll be right down," said Mary through the door.

Questioned about the scars on his face by Del during dinner, Joseph retold the story of the robbery, leaving out the name Charles Whittaker, and answered their curious questions about his wounds.

Mary lay in Joseph's arms with her head on his chest, listening to the sounds of their children sleeping. She was content as she stared out the window across the room, feeling complete once again, something she hadn't felt since he left all those months ago. A screech owl somewhere outside broke the silence as Mary turned and accidentally touched the bandaged shoulder, causing Joseph to flinch. "I'm sorry."

"It didn't hurt. I'm just a little jumpy."

She snuggled against him and ran her fingertips along his lips, down his cheek, to his neck. "You need a shave."

He turned and kissed her.

"Your shoulder," she whispered.

"It's fine."

A bedroom door closed somewhere in the hallway, followed by muffled voices as he pulled her closer and kissed her neck as his hands found her breasts.

She smiled. "You said you were tired?"

His eyes searched for hers in the dim light of the room. "I was, and the keyword here is "was"."

She muffled her giggle with one hand and then pulled him on top of her, surprising him with her strength.

"Ouch!" he whispered.

She giggled. "Sorry."

Another door shut.

Joseph whispered, "Wish to hell they'd all go to bed."

Del's shoes hit the floor, and Mary giggled, enjoying Joseph's frustration. She whispered. "I love you."

"I know, and I love you." Then he glanced toward the door. "I'd certainly like to make love to you if only they'd stop with all the noise."

Mary muffled another giggle as another door shut.

"What is it with these people?" he asked, glancing at the door. "Are they always this noisy?"

"I don't know," she whispered. "I never paid any attention."

The mood gone, he sat up against the headboard, looking frustrated.

Still giggling, Mary sat up next to him. "Giving up?"

"No. I thought we'd wait until everyone got settled."

One of the children let out a small cry in his sleep.

"Great," he said.

Mary laughed quietly. "That's just sleep noise, don't worry about it." She looked at the side of his face in the dim light. "I'm worried about you going back to Jefferson."

"Why?"

She sat forward. "Damn it, Joseph, this is twice you've been robbed, and this time you almost died."

He sighed and shook his head. "I could get kicked by a mule in the barn and die as well."

She looked out the window into the darkness. "That's a poor comparison, and you know it."

"I don't want to return to Jefferson," he admitted. "But I have no choice. I don't see how this damn war can last much longer."

"Then why return to it?" she asked.

"It's something I have to do." He shrugged. "I can't explain it."

"I don't understand the point of going back. You said the South is losing the war, so what does going back prove?"

He digested that for a few moments. "The point of it is, we are still in a war, and I can't ignore that fact and look the other way. The work I do is important and needed by the Confederacy."

She sat back, wrapped her arms around her legs, rested her chin on her knees, and looked out the window into the darkness. "I just wish it would hurry and get over."

He put one arm around her and gently pulled her back into him as she rested her head against his shoulder. He kissed the side of her head. "When this thing's over, I'd like to try my hand at farming that little piece of land we bought."

Excited at a more positive subject, she leaned forward, looking relieved. "Really, Joseph, are you sure?"

He covered her mouth with one hand and whispered: "Shhhhh, not so loud. You'll wake the children."

She looked toward the children and smiled. "A boat whistle couldn't wake those kids." Then she looked back at him, her eyes filled with the hope of a brighter future. She smiled as she pulled him to her. "Now come here, Mr. Farmer."

Five days later, Joseph kissed the children goodbye, told Mary that he loved her, and rode south to Jefferson, the Isabella, and the war.

Twenty-Eight

April 1865 to August 1865

Surrender of the Confederacy

Edward was still in command of the battered and hungry 27th Alabama, now a mere skeleton of the original command as it marched into the Carolina's in search of food. The once proud regiment was forced into the role of scavengers of the land and the dead for ammunition, clothing, and boots. Even so, the 27th continued its useless fight against the Union Army.

Joseph

The Isabella came under fire more than once as the Union Army closed its mighty arms around the southern states. Joseph escaped injury several times during small skirmishes with Union patrols. He worried about Mary and the Halls, recalling the previous Union army's visit, wondering if the next visit would be peaceful and friendly. He considered going home more than once but stayed on out of a sense of obligation to the South.

Martha Heard Chrisman

Months passed before Martha knew that James had been captured and held as a prisoner of war in Elmira, New York. But although happy he was alive, she was unaware of the terrible conditions he and the others had to endure there as prisoners. Although Martha's young son couldn't understand most of what she said, she would tell him a story each night about his father. She couldn't understand why James never wrote, but just the same, she and Beth continued to write him letters, never knowing if he received them. Still, Martha never gave up hope.

Sarah

Sarah received letters from Edward when he had the time to write, and she worried between them, wondering if he was dead, alive, or badly hurt. Little Mary was getting bigger and was almost seven years old, having spent very little time with her father over these past five years. Like everyone else, she waited for the war to end and the return of her father.

Mary

Mary waited at the Hall farm, getting an occasional letter from Joseph that brought little relief from the loneliness that burdened her. The letters were a comfort but only left her to worry until the next one arrived. Their children were growing up without their father, but she talked about him every night so that they wouldn't forget him. In her heart, she knew it was only a matter of time before the war ended. So filled with patience and hope, she waited for her Joseph. Several times each day, she would walk outside and look toward the road, and at the end of each day, she turned to her children to forget her loneliness.

April 9, 1865
Appomattox, Virginia
General Lee's Surrender

On April 9, 1865, Confederate General Robert E. Lee's army was surrounded by a larger, better equipped, and better fed Union Army led by his old friend and adversary, General Ulysses S. Grant. General Lee had looked upon his men as he rode the ramparts contemplating his next offensive. As he looked into their faces, he came to the realization that his brave army could no longer endure the taste of battle. General Lee knew they were willing, but his conscience would not let another brave man die for a lost cause. With tears in his eyes, he told his aide that the South's cause was over. The more agricultural South had relied on foreign trade to supply its men with guns, food, and clothing, but it was no match for the rich and industrial North. General Lee wisely surrendered to General Grant in the deserted McLean House in Appomattox, Virginia, finally ending the long war.

April 10, 1865

Edward Asbury McAlexander

Greensboro, North Carolina

Edward Asbury McAlexander performed his last duties as Colonel and Commanding Officer of the 27th Alabama Infantry on April 10, 1865. Under the watchful eye of his friend Ethan Hall and the others under his command, he surrendered his sword and the 27th Alabama to Union forces at Greensboro, North Carolina, thus ending their war. Shortly after that, Edward and Ethan started their arduous journey home, Edward to Florence, and Ethan to east Texas.

The roads were full of defeated Confederate soldiers having pledged their loyalties to the United States, and all in a hurry to get home, fearful of what they may find. Not only were the roads full of men, but the trains and boats were also overcrowded with men trying to get home.

Every train depot and dock was utter chaos as men fought for space in lines or auctioning off their tickets. Fights broke out; men stole horses, mules, buggies or wagons, anything and everything to get home.

On the second day of the third week after surrender, Edward and Ethan stepped from the decks of a battered and damaged Southern Belle onto the docks of Florence. Edward waved goodbye to his old friend Captain Goodman, took one last look at the old boat, thinking what a pity that it, too, had become a casualty of war. Captain Benjamin Goodman had become a disappointed and heartbroken man over the outcome of the war. The Southern Belle owners could no longer pay for its needed upkeep, so the boat was finally left to rot on a lonely part of the river near Florence, Alabama. Captain Goodman packed his belongings and headed west, hopeful of finding Joseph and Jonah.

May 1865

Florence, Alabama

Edward walked with Ethan to the ticket office and waited while he purchased a ticket on a boat that would take him up the Tennessee River to the Ohio River, west to the Mississippi River, and then south to New Orleans. From there, he would board another boat for Shreveport, and a third into Texas and the town of Jefferson by way of Caddo Lake.

Ethan walked away from the ticket window holding his ticket up for Edward to see. "My boat leaves in a couple of hours."

Edward gestured toward town, feeling sad. "One last drink?"

Ethan looked surprised. "I figured you'd be in a hurry to get home and see your daughter and wife."

Edward grinned as they walked off the pier onto the street. "Time enough for that." He motioned toward a saloon across the street, and several minutes later, they were sitting at a table in the corner by the window with a bottle of brandy and two glasses. As Ethan poured the drinks, Edward glanced around the large room, surprised at the number of men and women drinking this early in the morning. "I don't think I've ever been in here before."

Ethan glanced around, understanding why, and then he picked up his drink. "Here's to you, Asshole."

Edward smiled, knowing he was going to miss that, raised his glass, and drank. Each slammed their glass onto the table, and then Edward poured another. He smiled with amusement. "We better take it a little easy here, Ethan. You have a long trip, and I don't want to be drunk when I see Sarah and my daughter."

Ethan looked a little sorrowful as he settled back in his chair, running his index finger around the top of his glass. "I suppose you're right." He looked up from the glass. "But damn, it sure would be fun to get drunk one last time."

Edward's thoughts returned to the days before the war and the carefree days of college when both men were innocent and more than a little rowdy. He looked across the table at his friend, knowing those days were gone forever, and then thought of those they had left behind on battlefields who would never have the chance to remember the old days. Suddenly he felt forlorn, realizing that he would probably never see Ethan again after today.

Ethan stared into his empty glass, thinking about Edward and the trip home. Again, remembering the battles, he asked, "Think it was worth it, Ed?"

"The war?"

Ethan looked up with a sad expression. "Yeah, the war. Do you think the dead were worth the effort?"

Edward thought about that for several moments. "I don't know, Ethan. I guess you'd have to find a way to ask them."

Ethan nodded in thoughtful silence. "It'd be interesting to see what they had to say."

Edward poured two drinks. "I don't think it matters if people such as I believe it was worth it." He looked around the room at all the other people trying to forget the death of the old South they had known and loved. He gestured around the room. "I suppose if you asked five men in this place, most would say it was." Edward picked up his glass. "Here's to you, Asshole."

They gulped down their drinks, and then Ethan filled both glasses again and looked around the room. "I suppose you're right. No one wants to admit all those men died for nothing." He looked at the clock on the far wall and then at Edward.

Edward glanced at the clock, knowing it was time, and stared back at Ethan, again feeling a deep sense of loss.

Ethan stared at his friend. "I better get going, Ed. I wouldn't want to miss my boat. The next one doesn't leave for two more days."

Edward downed his drink, and as the two stood, he picked up Ethan's bag and then his own. "I guess we better get down to the docks."

The two men walked mostly in silence to the pier, having already said the important things to one another, neither looking forward to the end of their journey, and knowing that words would only clutter up the moment anyway. They walked along the crowded wharf's wooden platform to the sounds of boat whistles, people yelling goodbyes, and vendors selling their goods. A waiting steamboat has the same special sound a train engine has of steam and pumps that seem to belong in a dream or even a nightmare.

They stopped several feet from the gangplank where Edward set his bag down and then Ethan's worn carpetbag next to it. He glanced around at the other people then looked at his friend. Already knowing the answer, he asked, "Think you'll ever get back this way?"

"Never can tell. I might surprise you one day." Ethan offered an outstretched hand that Edward pushed aside as he embraced his friend firmly, and then stepped back.

As they shook hands, and Ethan looked into the tired, red eyes of his friend, knowing his were just as red, and managed a smile. "It was a hell of a way for a couple of guys to spend four years together."

Edward grinned with a chuckle. "Yes, it was a hell of a way, old friend, a hell of a way indeed."

The sound of the boat whistle blew, announcing the end of their journey with cold finality. These two friends who had killed men they never knew, froze in the cold trenches of Ft. Donelson, scavenged for food like animals, and witnessed the end of their beloved South, were about to say goodbye. The whistle sounded, and the man at the ramp yelled for last minute borders while men on the pier untied the big ropes that held the boat. As the ropes fell into the water, the men on the boat pulled them out, laying them on the deck while several other men struggled with the gangplank.

Edward reached down, picked up Ethan's bag, and handed it to him. "You best get going. Tell Mary and Joseph I said hello, and I'll write soon."

Ethan grinned, took the bag, and ran up the gangplank, where he turned and yelled, "Maybe we didn't win, Ed, but we scared the hell out of `em!"

Edward shouted back, "We sure as hell did!" He waved. "Good luck!"

Ethan waved as the boat drifted into deeper waters, where the boat's big paddlewheel slowly started churning the water, gathering speed away from the pier and Florence. In a final gesture, Ethan took off his gray officer's hat, waved a final goodbye, turned, and walked inside to find his cabin.

Edward watched the steamboat until it disappeared around the bend toward the Ohio River, feeling a heavy emptiness inside. With the steamboat and Ethan gone, he turned and headed for the streets of Florence, walking past the familiar church that he, his sister, and Alex had once attended. Then Edward hurried down the hill past houses he had never really noticed before with the bright May sun warming his back. His mind filled with images of the men he had left behind on unknown landscapes, occupying mass graves, or left dead on frozen, cold winter ground. He thought of Ethan, and his face warmed with a smile, knowing his friend and he had made it through a terrible ordeal. He would miss being called Asshole.

He stood before the large iron gates guarding the driveway to his home, remembering a year ago when he had stood at these gates in the chilly morning fog, saying goodbye to Sarah. The gates, in need of repair, squeaked on rusty hinges as he pushed them open, stepped inside, and walked up the driveway. It was quiet and peaceful, and he noticed that the yard and flowers needed tending. Then the silence was shattered by Sophie's shrill voice yelling for Sarah and little Mary, telling them that he was home. Moments later, Sarah rushed out of the house, across the porch, and down the three steps, holding her dress above her shoes with both hands so she wouldn't trip, all the while yelling his name.

He dropped his bag, and his faded, dusty, gray coat, tossed his gray hat down, and took her in his arms. They kissed and held onto one another, and Sarah looked up into his tired, brown eyes and smiled, thinking his face looked thin and drawn. With one hand, she fussed with his long, dark brown hair that now carried a little gray. His bearded face was tanned and lined, having the look of an old warrior at the end of a hard battle. Sarah thought he looked more like a beggar than a respected surgeon, but none of that mattered, now because he was home, and she knew that in the days and months to come, he would never leave her again. Not for the rest of their lives. She took his hand, and they hurried up the driveway to his daughter and Sophie, waiting at the door.

July 30, 1865

James Riley Chrisman

Tallapoosa County, Alabama

William Chrisman sat in his rocking chair in the shade of the porch on the early Sunday afternoon of July 30, 1865, while Elizabeth and the girls were inside preparing dinner. William's thoughts were of his son, James, who had yet to return from the war as had the other men in the valley. The family had received word that he had survived the camp at Elmira and had been released in April, but yet he had still not come home. He looked out across the fields, remembering James atop his black mare, riding up and down the rows of cotton, and then riding up to the porch for lemonade or cider along with young Davy. Turning his eyes from the fields, he looked toward the chair where Davy had often sat while James sat on the porch's railing, and he imagined them laughing while James teased his younger brother.

He looked from Davy's chair to the county road beyond the driveway just as he saw a figure cresting the hill. Doubting his familiar emotions of falsely hoping he would see his son among the other travelers on that road these past weeks, he watched this particular figure walk down the slope of the road toward the driveway. Slowly standing from his chair, ignoring his pain, William recognized something familiar about the figure as it continued along the road. He stepped to the edge of the porch, leaned on the weathered, paint peeling railing with both hands, and strained his old eyes to see if it was his son. William watched in silence, his heart and head pounding with anticipation and hope, absolutely refusing to call his wife until he knew for sure it was James. He watched in silent vigil as the figure came up to the Chrisman driveway, turned toward it, walked through the open gate, stopped to remove his hat, and waved.

"James," uttered William softly, and then he turned in joy toward the house. "Elizabeth, it's James! It's really James! Our boy's home at last!" William hurried to the steps and limped down them into the yard.

The door behind him opened and then slammed shut, followed by footsteps across the porch. Elizabeth ran past him, followed by Beth as the figure in the distance hurried his steps too weary to run to meet them. Elizabeth ran as fast as she could up the driveway toward her son, but Beth, being younger and fleeter of foot, raced past her mother and into her brother's arms. Reaching her children, Elizabeth pushed Beth out of the away, took her son in her arms, and held him as she had never held him before, all the while scolding him. "Where have you been? The war's been over for months!"

Beth looked at her brother. "Don't matter none, Ma. He's home now." Beth wiped her eyes with her apron, touched his arm and then his hair as if making sure he was real and not a ghost.

James smiled wearily, his eyes red and welling. "I just needed a little time Ma."

Curiously Elizabeth brushed the hair on his forehead to one side and looked into his tired eyes. "Time for what, James?"

"I just needed time to sort things out, Ma."

She looked at his thin face, not sure what he meant, but knowing for sure how thin and sick he looked, much like the time he had come home after they buried Davy. She thought he looked older, much older. But being the wise woman she was, Elizabeth held his face in her hands, kissed his lips, and then his eyes, saying, "You're home now, son; let the ghosts be free of your dreams. Give them to heaven."

"I'll try, Ma." Then he looked at his pa limping up the driveway. "Pa," he yelled and ran to his father.

William grabbed his son by the shoulders, looked at him for a long moment, hugged him, and then smiled. "We were worried we might never see ya again, Son."

James looked regretful. "I know, Pa." Then he turned and put one arm around his mother and his sister Beth, and they all started toward the house. As they walked, James was silent while Elizabeth told him about his son and Beth related the day Martha had fainted when seeing his name on the list of missing soldiers. William explained that it had taken several weeks for them all to learn that he was a prisoner and even longer to learn where he had been taken, but that they had just been thankful he was alive.

James glanced around, asking where his younger sisters were. Elizabeth said they were at a neighbor's and would be home in time for supper. She asked why he never wrote, and he explained how the guards read their mail and then teased them. She asked what sort of place would allow people to be so cruel, but James shrugged and never answered her, nor would he ever talk about it in future years. Reaching the house, James sat on the porch's railing where he had sat so many times in the past. He looked out across the fields at the crops, buildings, and livestock, thinking of the days before the war. James felt as if it had all changed somehow, but because he couldn't see what had changed, he knew that everything was different.

Beth told him that his son was the spitting image of himself, and that brought a smile to his face as he glanced in the direction of the Heard place. "How's the black mare?"

"Just as ya left her Son," replied William. "Beth's been riding her, so's she wouldn't go wild on us."

James smiled at Beth. "Thanks, Sis."

Elizabeth placed her hands on her son's shoulders. "Go see your wife and son."

The Heard farm

Martha and her mother were working in the garden on their hands and knees, pulling weeds and repairing what the night creatures had dug up or trampled the night before. Martha knew in her heart that James was alive, but she couldn't understand why he hadn't come home with the other men or at least written. As she worked, she talked to her mother about other things, but as usual, her mind was always on James, fearing that their son may never know his father.

Susanna Heard slowly stood, feeling her age as she held onto her lower back. "Get'n too old for this sort of thing, I guess."

Martha pulled at a weed without looking up. "Ma, you're still young. Don't be silly."

Noticing a weed Martha had overlooked, Susanna bent down and plucked it out of the ground.

"I was gonna get it, Ma,"

Her mother smiled. "Sure, ya were. How about some lemonade?"

Martha looked up, smiling. "Lemonade sounds fine, Ma. I need to check on little David anyways." She stood, and they walked toward the house, talking when the neigh of a horse stopped them. Turning toward the sound, they shielded their eyes from the afternoon sun, looking toward the empty road.

Martha sighed. "I always expect to see the black mare and James when I hear that sound." She turned back to her mother, who was staring at the woods beyond the garden. Martha turned back in that direction, seeing only the woods and heavy brush at first, but then something moved, and she saw a figure in the shade of the trees standing next to a horse. Fearful, Martha stared at the figure who was watching them, took her mother's hand, and stepped back. The figure stepped from the woods into the sunlight, followed by a black horse.

"James!" Martha screamed as she let go of her mother's hand and ran through the vegetables they had just weeded and repaired. Her bonnet flew off, but she never looked back as she ran toward James as fast as her legs would carry her.

He dropped the reins of the mare, and moments later, Martha was in his arms crying. After they kissed, she looked into his tired eyes. "Where've ya been, James?"

He held her tight, kissed her again, and never answered.

She looked into his sunken eyes with their dark shadows, thinking how thin his face was, and he looked much older than she remembered and was afraid he was sick. "Are ya all right, James?"

"I'm just tired, Martha."

She affectionately touched his hair with one hand while wiping her tears with the other. "Where have you been, James? I was so worried."

"I'll explain one day, Martha, but not now."

Accepting that, she managed to smile as she wiped her nose and tears, then raised her small fist and clenched her teeth. “I ought to punch you one, James Riley.”

He laughed and then took her into his arms again while Mr. and Mrs. Heard watched, giving them time to say hello.

James met his son David Allen Chrisman that afternoon, and in the years that followed, he would take his son Davy for rides on the black mare. And as they rode across the fields he had worked as a young boy, he told stories of his brother Davy, his friend Emmett, and another young boy named Allen Downs.

Twenty-Nine

East Texas - May 1866

Joseph & Mary

The war had been over for a year, and Ethan was home and settled in on the Hall farm, looking forward to having his own place where he, Lori, and their children could live a peaceful existence. Joseph had also returned, settling in with his family on the small farm they had purchased during the war next to Del Hall's farm. The house was small, with only two bedrooms, but Mary happily planned another room to go along with another child someday. Joseph, Del, and Ethan had entered into a partnership working both properties as one, raising the same crops and dividing the proceeds three ways.

The ex-slave Jonah was still with Joseph, living in a two-room shack he and Joseph built close to a grove of trees near a small pond at the edge of Joseph's land. For the first time in his life, Jonah earned a wage for his hard work and spent his evenings staring into the small pond, thinking of the Southern Belle and worrying about Captain Goodman.

Mary was happy and content, but she knew that Joseph wasn't. They argued over the smallest of things, and he often stomped away, disappearing for hours on his horse. He was moody and argumentative, even with the children, and at night their bed was quiet and void of affection. Mary felt helpless, afraid, and alone, and finally, unable to cope with the situation, she confronted Joseph as they lay in the darkness of their bedroom.

"Joseph, what's wrong?"

"Nothing," he snapped.

She laughed, but it held no humor. "That's a lie, and you know it."

He turned away from her and faced the wall. "I'm tired, Mary. Let's just get some sleep."

She stared at the back of his head, feeling more afraid than angry. "Joseph, you've changed. You're hateful and sullen, and you fly off the handle at the littlest thing." She paused, touching his shoulder. "Joseph, please look at me!"

He sighed as he sat up, resting against the headboard staring through the darkness out the window. "I don't mean to be that way, Mary. It just comes on."

She thought about that. "Whether you mean to be or not, you have become quite different since the war. I hardly know you anymore."

He stared into the darkness, considered that for a long moment, and then looked at her face in the dim light. "Do you want honesty, Mary? Are you prepared for honesty?"

Filled with fear, her eyes welled with tears. "Is it me?"

"No, Mary," he said softly. "It's me."

She turned and took his arm. "I don't understand."

Though he could barely see her eyes in the dim light, he knew they were full of sadness and worry and remembered the promises he had made but never kept. The times she needed him when he wasn't there rushed through his memory. Most of all, he remembered the happiness on her face when he told her that they would farm this little piece of land. As unhappy as this place had made him, he stayed because of his love for her and the children, but for no other reason. But he was losing the fight against his own devils, and no matter how hard he tried, he couldn't change what he was.

He put his arm around her and kissed the side of her head. "I do love you."

Reality set in for her. "It's this place, isn't it?"

Joseph sucked in a deep breath and let out a soft sigh. "I'm sorry, Mary, I've tried, really I have."

She thought about that for a quick moment. "I know you have, and I love you for that." She sat up, pulled her knees to her chest, wrapped her arms around her legs, and stared out the window into the black night. How ironic, she thought, that they had survived a terrible war, yet they may not survive the peace. Knowing what had to be done for them to survive what the war couldn't destroy, she bravely wiped the tears from her eyes and face. "What do you want to do?"

He thought for a moment. "I'm not sure."

She settled back against the headboard and looked at him. "I believe you do know."

He turned from the window and took her hand. "All right, I guess I do."

Mary was no fool. "You want to return to Jefferson and the water, don't you?"

"Yes."

"That's what I thought." Her voice trembled as she looked down at her hands in the dim light.

He put his hand on her chin and turned her head. "You wanted the truth."

She smiled softly. "I know."

"I really tried to be a farmer, Mary. I really did."

She looked away in silence, remembering the lonely hours she had spent waiting for him and believing those lonely hours were over now that they had this little piece of land. She had never been one to act on impulse, fearing the consequences of those impulsive decisions, but this was different. Their lives together were in danger of ending. Sitting up, she made her decision, took a deep breath, held his hand, kissed it, and smiled. "All right then, we will sell this place and move back to Jefferson, Shreveport, or even Florence if you want."

In the dim light, he looked at her face, remembering their flight from Florence to escape the war, only to have it find her here in Texas. He remembered the happiness on her face when the war ended, and they became farmers. Now, in the darkness, he imagined the sadness on that same face he loved. "Do you know what you just said?"

She chuckled without humor. "Of course I do." She began to cry. "Don't be foolish."

He sighed. "It would be foolish for me to lose the love of my life."

She smiled and wiped at her tears. "That's so very true."

He took her wet face in his hands and kissed her lips. "I do love you so very much."

Still smiling and still crying, she shook her head. "After all this, you'd better."

"We'll have to sell almost everything," he said.

She smiled bravely. "Perhaps, but we can talk in the morning? Right now, I'm so tired. You've worn me out, Joseph." She turned to the window. "The sun will rise in a few hours, and the children will run through that door, wanting breakfast." She fluffed her pillow, slid deep into the covers, closed her eyes, and waited for sleep.

He watched her for a while before returning his gaze to the window and thought about Shreveport.

Mary lay on her side, watching Joseph sleep, the silhouette of his face dark and mysterious in the dim light of dawn. In a few minutes, the sun would edge over the top of the hills, filling the room with its warm, soft light. She thought of last night's decisions, and now, in the morning hours of this new day, she was filled with fear, second-guessing her reckless decision to pull, take up roots, and move. Wondering where to, she turned onto her back and looked up at the ceiling, thinking of how she had come to love this little farm. It wasn't much, but it was their life together. She had always been a city girl, and the only farm she had ever known was the one Alex worked, and he seemed to love it. Why, then, couldn't Joseph, she wondered? Mary turned to look at his face, curious about the devils that lay hidden deep within, causing him to hate the farm so much. She loved him, and that was the sum of it. Now, she had to put everything aside and prepare for another journey, another new day, another new life. She kissed his cheek, then his lips, and slowly moved her hand over his chest to his stomach.

As the early morning sun shone through the open window with a brand new day, Joseph opened his eyes, turned, looked at Mary's sleeping face, and smiled, thinking of how much he loved her. He put his arms around her, kissed her cheek and then her neck as his hand found the strings of her nightgown, pulling it down around her shoulders. She had missed his touch and the tenderness and knew she would do anything to keep him. They made love, and afterward, in the quiet of their world, they lay together, listening to the new day's early morning sounds. Mary sat up, pulled her knees to her chest as she often did, and smiled at him, looking happy.

He sat up, put his arm around her, and together, they sat back against pillows and headboard, eagerly discussing what they needed to do. They decided that Joseph would approach Del and Ethan to see if they were interested in buying the farm. During her sleepless night, Mary decided she did not want to return to Florence. They considered Jefferson, but Joseph said it was too wild, so they settled on Shreveport, giving him access to the Mississippi the Big Red, and a better chance of finding a job on a sternwheeler.

Mary pushed away her fears and disappointments as they talked, looking toward the excitement and mystery of a new life. They would be together, and that was all that mattered.

Joseph finished breakfast, drank the last of his coffee, and rode to the Hall farm, finding Del and Ethan in the corral next to the barn, pitchforks in hand. Climbing down from his horse, he shook Del's hand and then Ethan's. "I've come with a proposition."

Del and Ethan looked at one another curiously, leaned their pitchforks against the barn wall, and waited.

Joseph got right to the point, telling them about his and Mary's decision to give up farming and move to Shreveport. "I know this seems sudden, but it's been coming for a long time." He smiled, looking apologetic. "I'm not cut out to be a farmer any more than either of you a river pilot."

Ethan considered the land on Joseph's farm. "What sort of price do you have in mind?" He looked at Del and then Joseph. "We ain't exactly rich people."

Joseph chuckled and nodded. "I know that Ethan and I ain't one to try and make a profit from my friends, but I would like to get back my original investment."

Knowing what Joseph had paid for the land, Del gestured toward Joseph's place as he looked at Ethan. "Be a right smart buy for you, Son. Joseph's asking a fair price."

Ethan quickly considered that. "S'pose you're right about that, Pa." Then he looked at Joseph. "If you're sure this is what ya want to do, Joseph. I can't find any fault in the deal." He held out a hand to seal the deal.

Joseph shook Ethan's hand, saying he would be by in the morning so they could all go to Jefferson and see about a loan. "One last thing," he said, looking at Ethan. "I need a favor."

"You just name it."

Joseph looked uneasy. "I want to go into Shreveport first to find work and a place before taking Mary and the children there, and I was wondering if you and Lori would look in on Mary and the boys while I'm gone."

Ethan smiled, putting one hand on Joseph's shoulder. "After what you did for my family and me during the war, Lori and I will be happy to look in on Mary and the children."

Joseph smiled, looking grateful. "Well, then, I'll come over early tomorrow, and we'll ride into Jefferson." Then he turned and climbed into his saddle.

Janice Hall called out, "Joseph."

He turned, seeing her running across the yard, holding what looked like a letter in her hand.

Del took off his hat, looking foolish, and scratched his head. "I must be getting old. With all this talk about the farm, I plum forgot to tell you about the letter addressed to you that I picked up in town yesterday."

Looking puzzled, Joseph leaned down and took the letter, seeing it was from his sister, and the postmark was almost two months old. "It's from my little sis in Tennessee,"

"Hope it's good news," said Janice.

Having a bad feeling about the letter, he thanked her, turned the horse, rode a short distance, and pulled up next to a shady spot under one of several tall oak trees alongside the dirt road. He dismounted, tied the horse to a branch, sat on a flat rock, took off his hat, and set it next to him. He carefully tore off the end of the envelope, took out the letter, unfolded the paper, and began reading.

Dear Joseph Greene,

My name is Laura Stevens. I am a schoolteacher in Hardin County, and your sister, Sissy, has asked that I put her words on paper for you to read.
My dear brother, I have not heard from you since winter last, and I pray this finds you in good health. That said, I have sad news. Pa, Lester, and Billy are dead. They were killed two months back by some terrible men that took what little money Pa had, some horses and cows, then set fire to the house and barn. I was away visiting the Miller's at the time. You remember the Miller's?

The sheriff and his men caught the four men, and they were hanged over in Lawrence County a week past. The sheriff said they were Union deserters too mean and full of killing to go home. The Miller's took me to watch the hanging. Though it was a terrible thing to watch, those men killed Pa and our brothers, and I'm glad they are all dead.

We buried Pa, Lester, and Billy next to Ma. Stevie Miller and I are getting married next month, something that has been planned for a while now. I don't see any reason not to go ahead with the wedding. I think Pa would want that. I guess the place is yours now if you want to come back. I know how you feel about farming, so if you want to sell it, I guess that's your decision.

You can write to me in care of Mrs. Laura Stevens, at the Hardin County School in care of the Gasten Post Office.

Your loving sister,
Sissy

Joseph looked up from the letter and stared at the distant hills for a few moments, remembering the last time he had been home. Crumbling the letter in one hand, and with tears in his eyes, he looked across the road to the hill, the group of trees, and the white picket fence where the three Confederate soldiers lay buried. "The damn war just keeps on killing," whispered Joseph. Then he wiped his eyes with his shirtsleeve and thought about the last time he had seen his pa and Sissy. Several minutes passed while he mourned his pa and brothers, and then he folded the letter, placed it back into the envelope, and shoved the envelope into his shirt pocket. Deciding he would give the farm to Sissy and Steve as a wedding present, he picked up his hat, untied the reins to his horse, and swung up in the saddle.

In the early morning hours of February 27th, 1866, Joseph said goodbye to Mary and climbed up onto the wagon's seat. Ethan slapped the reins against the horse's backs, the wagon lurched forward, then moved across the yard toward the county road. Mary followed for a short distance, stopped, and waved goodbye before returning to the house and the children.

Joseph and Ethan arrived in Jefferson in the early afternoon. Joseph shook Ethan's hand, said goodbye, gathered his carpetbag from behind the seat, and headed toward the pier to purchase a ticket for Shreveport, Louisiana. Discovering the next boat for Shreveport was not until the next morning, he decided to stop in and see if Mrs. Hansen had a spare room for the night.

Minutes later, he walked up the familiar steps to the boarding house and went inside, expecting a warm welcome from Hrs. Hansen. Instead, Joseph was greeted by a man standing behind the counter where Mrs. Hansen was supposed to be.

"May I help you?" the man asked.

"I'm looking for Mrs. Hansen."

The man was tall and thin, and looked to be in his mid to late fifties. He smiled at Joseph with a friendly smile and then told him that Mrs. Hansen no longer owned the establishment and had moved to Shreveport.

"When did she sell?"

He thought a moment. "Seven months ago."

"I wonder why she moved to Shreveport?" Joseph asked himself aloud.

"I believe she wanted to buy a small hotel there."

Joseph asked if he knew the name of the hotel, but the man shook his head no and asked if Joseph was interested in a room. Joseph said he was and signed the register.

Shreveport, Louisiana

Arriving in Shreveport on February 28, 1866, Joseph gathered his baggage, walked out of the cabin on the boat, and made his way along the busy streets. After a short distance, he happened upon a sign reading 'The Hansen' above a rooming house door. With a smile on his face and looking forward to seeing Trudy Hansen, he walked up the steps, across the boardwalk, and stepped into the lobby.

Trudy Hansen stood behind the counter, her back to him and busy at something, so he quietly walked up to the counter and cleared his throat with a loud grumble.

Mrs. Hansen turned, and at seeing him, her mouth fell open with surprise, and then she smiled. "Mr. Joseph Greene." She came from behind the counter. "Why, you're a sight for sore eyes." They hugged, and then she asked, "What on earth are you doing in Shreveport?"

He smiled. "Well, it appears I need a room once again."

Still smiling, she turned and pushed the register and pen toward him. "I think we can accommodate an old friend." Then with a stern look, she added, "I'd appreciate you not bleeding all over my new bedding."

"I promise," chuckled Joseph as he picked up the pen and signed the register.

Trudy motioned toward the parlor. "Come into the parlor." Then she gently tugged at his arm, and after sitting down, she asked about his family and what he was doing in Shreveport. He told her they had bought a small farm, but he just wasn't cut out to be a farmer.

She nodded and smiled while her eyes held understanding in them. "The farm's no place for you, Joseph, no more than it was for my Lyle."

Joseph asked why she had sold out and left Jefferson.

She considered the question for a moment and told him that the place just hadn't been the same after the war. She needed a change, and when a man from the East made her an offer, she grabbed at it, hoping life would be a little better here in Shreveport.

"Is it?"

"It is," she said. "Shreveport is a nice city, not wild like Jefferson." She frowned. "Oh, down by the river in them gambling establishments and brothels, it gets a little wild." She paused. "Not that I've been down there, mind you." She smiled. "But all and all, Shreveport is a nice place to live."

They talked for several minutes, then she grabbed a key. And after they walked up the stairs, she unlocked the door to a room, opened it, and walked in, saying the room was stuffy.

He stepped in, noticing the table and single chair, and smiled as he watched her open the window.

Handing him his key, she said, "It's good to see you, Joseph." She started to leave when she suddenly turned. "Why I almost forgot, a man by the name of Goodman, I believe it was, stopped by not long ago asking after you."

"Captain Goodman?"

She shrugged, "I guess. He said he heard I once owned a place in Jefferson and asked if I knew a Joseph Greene."

He smiled. "He's here in Shreveport?"

"Maybe so. Leastways I saw your Captain Goodman day before yesterday, I think it was."

"Did he say what he was doing in Shreveport?"

Mrs. Hansen considered that. "No, I don't believe he ever did. Seemed a mite disappointed that you weren't around, though." She said goodnight and closed the door leaving Joseph to consider the mystery of Captain Goodman.

The next day, Joseph asked around Shreveport and found out that Captain Goodman was now the captain of a sternwheeler named The Helen. Finding the boat moored to a pier, he went on board and asked where he might find the captain. Shown to Goodman's cabin, he hesitated and then knocked.

"Come in."

He opened the door, stepped inside, and grinned at the figure sitting behind a big desk.

Captain Goodman looked up as a big grin filled his face. "I'll be a son-of-a-bitch," he said. Then he stood and hurried around his desk, pushed Joseph's open hand aside, and gave him a big hug. Goodman pointed to a chair. "This deserves a drink, Laddie."

Joseph realized how much he'd missed that greeting as he settled into the chair and watched Goodman.

While the captain poured two drinks then set the bottle down, he asked Joseph what he was doing in Shreveport.

Joseph explained about selling the farm (again leaving out the details), that Mary and the children would soon be joining him along with Jonah, as soon as he could find a job and a house, in that exact order.

Goodman thought fondly of Jonah. "How is Jonah?"

Joseph chuckled. "Jonah is a mite heavier and a little grumpier these days."

Glad to hear his old friend was doing well, the captain laughed as he handed Joseph a glass of whiskey. "Miss that old Negro." He took a quick sip of his drink. "Well, Laddie, I can't help with the house, but I can offer you a job as First Officer."

"You don't have one?"

Goodman shook his head. "Been saving it for you, Laddie." He paused. "Been looking all over the river for you. The job's yours if you're interested."

Joseph grinned. "Damn right."

The captain took a quick drink. "The Helen's a mite bigger than the Southern Belle, but not quite as maneuverable. She carries more passengers and cargo, and you'll not find a better gaming casino on the river." Goodman looked at him thoughtfully. "Think Jonah will join us?"

Joseph grinned. “I wouldn’t want to be the one to try and stop him.”

Goodman chuckled, looking pleased. “I can hardly wait to see that old Negro.”

The two men talked and drank well into the night, and Joseph listened quietly as the captain told him of the Southern Belle’s fate after the war. He imagined her sitting alongside the river, tilted to one side, frayed, faded, and weathered, leaving her once majestic beauty to the imaginations of those that were now taking her skin. Sometime during the evening, Joseph fell asleep in his chair, so Captain Goodman covered him with a blanket, smiled down at him, and then went to bed.

The early morning noises woke Goodman, and as he slowly got out of bed, he looked at Joseph, still asleep in the chair. “C’mon, Laddie,” he said, shaking him. “We need to find something to eat, and then we have a house to find.”

May 24, 1866 Jefferson Texas

Joseph and his family stood on the dock in Jefferson, waiting to board a steamboat for Shreveport. Still apprehensive about the unknown, Mary bravely smiled and pushed away her fears as she talked with Lori and Janice. The whistle blew, Joseph told Mary that now they had to board and find their rooms, and then he shook hands with Del and Ethan, gave Lori and Janice each a hug, picked up little Edward, and looked at Mary. “We have to go.” Then he turned to Jonah and asked if he had everything.

Jonah nodded, showed Joseph his ticket and his bag with his belongings.

With tears in her eyes, Mary hugged Lori, and then Janice, and Del. Ethan took the hands of Zach and Joseph Jr. while the family followed Joseph up the gangplank. As the boat slipped away from the pier, they waved goodbye to their old friends and looked forward to a new era in their lives in Shreveport.

Thirty

May 1866

Shreveport, Louisiana

Mary sat back, enjoying the buggy ride through the noisy streets of lower Shreveport, curious about this place that held Joseph so tightly in its grasp, and thinking it a strange place with strange people. She tried to imagine what it was like after dark with lighted windows, music, laughter, and all sorts of goings-on. Several women she guessed to be ladies of the evening were on the boardwalks talking or laughing in little groups. Some turned to watch in curiosity as they passed; others were too busy with a man or each other's conversation to look.

This was the world of her husband. A strange and dangerous place that filled some emptiness he carried deep inside, some need she couldn't fulfill, and a place quite different from the places and people Edward and Alex would choose to frequent. Shreveport and the people on the streets began to change as the lower city's sounds faded away, leaving a quiet section of Shreveport for their passage. As Joseph drove the buggy along the busy but quiet cobblestone street, Mary glanced around, thinking this was quite different from the streets that had filled her with uneasiness and fear. This street showed refinement, with men dressed in expensive suits and ladies in long flowing, colorful and expensive dresses as they walked casually along the boardwalk going into or coming out of doorways of stores or restaurants. Suddenly she felt at ease, even welcome.

The buggy was rolling along a quiet, residential street of large, two-story houses, with broad lawns guarded by iron fences and closed gates boasting of refinement and upper class. She looked at Joseph curiously. "Where are you taking us, Joseph? What are you up to?"

He grinned and glanced past her at the scenery. "To the prettiest place in all of Shreveport." He guided the buggy along the street, chasing the clip-clop of the horse's hooves. Mary sat back, accepting his secrecy, listening to the hypnotic sound of the horses while staring at the homes and manicured lawns, imagining the scenes beyond the cold brick and wooden walls.

"You and the children close your eyes," said Joseph.

Mary looked at him, filled with curiosity, and then told the children to put their hands over their eyes and not to peek.

"Same goes for you," smiled Joseph.

Curious at what her husband was up to, she covered her eyes.

Joseph turned onto a stone driveway, passed under an iron archway, then drove along a circular driveway to the front door of a house and stopped. "Don't peek now," he said as he jumped down and ran around the horses to her side of the buggy. "Okay, you can look now."

The children asked where they were. Mary looked at the house and yard and then curiously back at him. "What is this place?"

"Home," he said proudly with a broad grin.

Her face filled with disbelief while staring at the two-story, wooden house freshly painted a pale yellow with white trim. A small porch with two columns protected a large, dark, wooden front door. Rows of multi-colored flowers lined both sides of the front of the house, and a manicured lawn filled the expanse between the circling cobblestone driveway before disappearing back through the gates into the street. A black, iron fence between brick columns bordered the property of grass and shrubs.

He helped her down, and as she stood staring at the house, her eyes welled, and she began to cry. Joseph smiled, knowing they were happy tears, so he let her have the tears she deserved without saying anything. Then putting his arm around her, he pointed to a small wooded area adjacent to the property. "That belongs to us also. It will be a perfect place for the children to play and explore."

"Oh, Joseph," she said softly as she wiped her cheeks with the hanky he gave her. She blushed and laughed with true happiness. "It's beautiful. How many rooms?"

He looked at the house proudly. "Let's see. There's a living room," he held up one finger, "dining room," second finger, "kitchen, study, and parlor downstairs, totaling five rooms," he held up all five fingers of one hand. "Upstairs, we have a master bedroom, another small study we could turn into a nursery…"

"A nursery?" she interrupted, looking surprised.

He smiled. "Yes, a nursery. Don't you want a sister for these rascals?"

She smiled. "You're impossible. Can we go inside?"

"Of course." Then he continued with the room count holding up a finger for each room. "And there are three additional bedrooms upstairs, making about ten rooms in all if my math is correct." He took her elbow and helped her up the brick walk to the front door.

Little Edward followed until he saw his older brothers heading toward the woods, and not wanting to miss the fun, he hurried to catch them. Jonah drove the wagon filled with their belongings to the rear of the house for unloading while Joseph opened the door, picked her up, and carried her across the threshold.

She let out a small scream as she laughed. "Put me down."

He gently put her down in the hall and kissed her. "Welcome home, darling."

She looked into his blue eyes. "I love you so much." Then she began to cry, and as she wiped her face with the hankie, she asked where the children had gone.

He glanced out the door. "They're exploring the woods."

"Tell them to be careful," she said, looking worried.

"The boys are fine, Mary. Let me show you the rest of the house." Joseph gave her the grand tour pointing out the furnishings, explaining the previous owner was so anxious to return to Boston that he sold everything in it. She walked into the living room, sat down on a deep green sofa, and looked up at him, her eyes red and tearing as she smiled.

Joseph sat next to her taking her hand in his. "Now, what's wrong?"

She began to laugh. "Nothing is wrong." She gestured at the house as she softly cried. "This is, well, this is just a bit overwhelming. And while you're so sweet darling, you know nothing about women." She placed a hand on his cheek. "I love it; it's like a dream come true."

"I have another surprise," he said, looking proud.

She shook her head and smiled. "I don't believe I can take many more surprises."

He looked into her eyes for a long moment. "Mary, I know how hard it's been for you with all of the moving and me being gone most of the time."

She started to speak, but he held up his hand to quiet her.

"Over the years," he said, "I've often recalled the day we left your brother's house and the way you looked at it as we drove away." He paused, looking regretful. "I could see the sorrow in your eyes, the same sorrow I saw when we left that little place in Texas to come here."

She smiled, in memory and nodded. "I was happy on our little farm."

"I know you were, and I made a promise to myself that one day, you would have a beautiful home, one that you would be proud of."

She smiled affectionately. "And I am."

He frowned. "I hope so, and what I am about to say may seem a little strange, but I made myself another promise the day I bought this place." He took a piece of paper from the inside pocket of his coat, looked at it for a moment, then at her. "Mary, we'll never move again." He handed her the paper. "This paper holds all my promises."

"The deed to the house?" she asked as she took it.

He smiled and waited for her to look at the paper.

She unfolded the paper and began to read. Finished, she looked up. "I don't understand."

Joseph put his hands on hers, closing them around the paper. "This plot of earth in the cemetery is where you and I will spend eternity." He smiled softly. "We'll both die in this city, Mary, that's my promise. We'll never move from Shreveport. Not ever. We're home at last. After all those years, Mary, we're home."

She put her arms around him and began to cry as she kissed his cheek and whispered, "I love you."

The next day while Mary was unpacking upstairs, Joseph asked the Negro maid to get Jonah from his room above the garage and show him into the library. When Jonah stepped into the library, he was surprised at seeing Captain Goodman standing next to Joseph. His eyes lit up as a big grin filled his face. "Lord be praised Cap'n, I's nevah thought dese old eyes wud evah sees ya again."

Captain Goodman grinned as he extended an open hand. "I wasn't all that sure myself Jonah, how've ya been?"

Jonah smiled, showing a mouth full of white teeth. "I been goods, thank ya."

Goodman nodded toward Joseph. "This lad been good to ya?"

"Ah, yes, suh," Jonah said, still smiling. "He bin jus' fine, he an Miss Mary both bin real goods ta me."

Joseph pointed to a nearby chair. "Have a seat, Jonah. The captain has a proposition for you."

The smile left Jonah's face, replaced by curiosity as he sat down. "Yes, suh?"

The captain sat down on the sofa wearing a big grin. "I hope you're not mad at me over sending you with Joseph."

"Ah, no, suh, I know'd why, Cap'n.

"Good," said the Captain. "I have a new boat, she's called 'The Helen', and Joseph here's gonna be my First Mate. And I was," he looked at Joseph." Or that is, we were wondering if you'd like to come back to work for us. Just like the old days."

Jonah's eyes lit up; his smile grew even bigger as he looked at the captain, and then at Joseph, and then at the captain. "I's surely wud Cap'n, Mistah Joseph. I's surely wud."

"All right then," said the captain, extending his hand. "Let's shake on it."

Jonah took the captain's hand and shook it and then Joseph's as the captain told him to gather his belongings, and he would take him back to the boat so he could get settled in. Jonah stood and hurried out of the room.

Joseph looked at Goodman. "I don't think Jonah was ever very happy with me, Captain."

"Maybe not," replied the captain thoughtfully, then he laughed. "But it looks like he ate pretty well." As the laugh faded, he looked at the empty doorway. "That old Negro was more family than he ever was a slave, and I ain't afraid to admit that I missed him." He smiled at Joseph. "Almost as much as I have you, Laddie."

Joseph grinned, poured two drinks, handed one to Goodman, and then raised his glass. "To us, Captain, to a new adventure."

The years following that May afternoon in 1866 brought good fortune to Joseph and Mary. Among them was another child arriving in early March 1869 they named Allen Greene. But sometimes fate can be fickle and cruel to those she once blessed, and changes began to occur that would affect all their lives, threatening all that Joseph had promised.

June 1873

An early afternoon rain softly tapped at the windows of the parlor while Mary lay curled up on the flower-patterned sofa staring at the open letter lying on the coffee table. Her eyes were red and puffy from crying as she slowly sat up, wiped her eyes and nose with her hanky, and then reached for the letter. Mary re-read the words of Mr. Bernard Larkin, the bank president who had visited her an hour earlier. The thought of Joseph squandering their savings and overdrawn at the bank was more than she could comprehend or deal with. She sat in the dim light, trying to understand how this could happen, hoping it was just an error, which Joseph could fix.

Mattie, their Negro maid, having heard Mary's quiet sobs, stood at the parlor door. "Is ya all rights, Miss Mary?"

Mary looked away in embarrassment. "I'm fine, Mattie, thank you."

"Can I makes ya a cup of tea ta take away the chill?"

"No, no, thank you, Mattie, but would you please check on the children?"

"Yessum, Miss Mary," Mattie turned and left as quietly as she had come.

Realizing the room was getting dark, Mary stood, walked to a nearby lamp, and lit it. Returning to the sofa, she sat down and stared at the letter again, remembering her embarrassment at facing the bank president. He had sat in the big stuffed chair across from her, looking down at the floor while she read the words neatly printed on the paper. He was polite and understanding as they discussed the document and its consequences. With an almost apologetic goodbye, he had climbed into a waiting buggy, and as the buggy drove away, she felt sorry for the man, knowing it must have been an unpleasant task.

She stood from the sofa, walked to the window, and looked up into the gray clouds as the rain beat against the window and small lines of water made their way down the glass to the sill. Thinking he couldn't have picked a drearier day to visit, she turned away from the window, picked up the letter, walked into the library, and set it in the center of Joseph's desk. Hearing the children's laughter upstairs, she looked up at the ceiling, thinking of their future without money, and anger replaced her fears and sorrow.

The children tucked into their beds, Mary lay in bed thinking again about the letter. Unable to sleep, she got up to check on the children and paused at the clock in the hall, counting the hours before Joseph would get home. Returning to her bedroom, Mary sat in a chair next to the window as the concept of an uncertain future filled her with despair. Money had never been an issue for Mary; it was something she had always had. Even while married to Joseph, she never worried about money, and being poor, and without it had never occurred to her, not even during the war. But this was beyond the realm of understanding. She could not believe that Joseph had gambled away their money. Tired and unable to cry anymore, she wanted to sleep, to stop thinking about what had happened. She got up from the chair feeling exhausted, lay down on the bed, closed her eyes, and waited for sleep.

Mary sat alone in the gazebo, watching Zachary and Joseph Jr. innocently playing in the trees on the other side of the yard, happy in their make-believe world. Her thoughts turned to the visit the day before by Mr. Larkin and how embarrassed she was at learning that all of their savings was gone, wasted on Joseph's gambling. The boys laughter from the wooded area filled the gazebo, and Mary thought of her own childhood with Alex and Edward. She missed them and felt especially sad remembering the news of Edward's unexpected death three years ago and the trip back to Florence for the funeral. Wishing he were still alive to provide his wise counsel, she heard Joseph's voice calling to her from inside the house.

Taking a deep breath to prepare herself for what was coming, she wiped the tears from her eyes, straightened her dress, and called, "I'm out here."

He emerged from the back door wearing a smile, took a quick look at the boys across the yard, and sat down next to her.

Not wanting to look at him, she stood, walked to the edge of the gazebo, placing one hand on the post watching the children playing. "The bank president, Mr. Larkin, stopped by yesterday advising me that our account is overdrawn."

Joseph stood and walked to her while he put his hand on the back of her shoulders.

She turned away, trying not to cry, and sat down.

He gripped the railing of the gazebo and stared across the yard at his son's playing. "I had a little run of bad luck and thought I could win it back before you found out."

"A little run of bad luck?" Her voice filled with anger. "Is that what you call it?" Then she turned away and laughed without humor. "A little run of bad luck!"

He turned to her. "It'll be all right, Mary."

Her anger flared, and her face darkened. "How can you say that? It won't be all right, and how dare you even suggest such a ridiculous thing." Then she raised her voice. "We are broke, Joseph. Broke and in debt, thanks to you." She turned away to watch the children while fighting the tears that welled in her eyes. "What the hell have you done? My God, Joseph, you've gambled away over five thousand dollars!"

"I'll make it right."

Without speaking or looking at him, she stood and walked across the yard to reassure their children, who had heard them yelling at one another and had stopped playing. Then without looking back at him, she took them into the house.

He sat back and looked at the empty yard, wondering how he let things get out of hand, and after several minutes, he got up and went inside to the library. He poured a drink and sat at his desk, sipping it while looking down at the neatly folded letter. Setting his glass down, he picked the letter up and began reading. When finished, he placed it back into the envelope, laid it on top of the desk, and drank the last of his brandy. He poured another, walked into the living room, sat on the sofa, and stared out the window, watching the day disappear.

Mary appeared at the doorway. "Dinner's ready."

Neither having much appetite, they picked at their food in silence. It was Mattie's night off, so Mary cleaned up the dinner dishes while Joseph returned to the living room, where he built a fire to take the chill off. Then he sat in the dark with his head resting on the back of the big, stuffed chair, listening to the sounds of the children getting ready for bed mix with the crackling of the logs in the fireplace.

The clock in the hall striking midnight woke Joseph, and realizing he had drifted off to sleep, he stood, walked up the stairs to the bedroom, undressed in the dark, got into bed, and stared up at the dark ceiling, trying to devise a plan to fix what he had done.

Mary turned onto her back and took his hand, holding it tightly against her stomach. “What’re we going to do?”

“I can’t tell you how sorry I am, Mary.”

Her anger spent, she stared up at the dark ceiling and softly said, “I know, but right now, we need a way out.”

Letting go of her hand, he sat up with his back against the headboard.

She sat up next to him and waited for his plans to get out of this mess.

He looked out the window across the dark bedroom and then turned to her. “We can sell half the property.”

She looked at the side of his face in the dim light. “Break up the land?”

He considered his plan. “We can get a good price; it’s prime property.”

She thought for a moment. “I guess we could. The children would miss it, but the rest of the yard is large enough.” She felt hopeful. “What do you think it’s worth?”

He thought for a moment. “Thirty-five hundred.”

Mary was no fool. She leaned forward, looking at him. “You’ve already discussed that with someone, haven’t you?”

He shrugged, feeling guilty. “A few weeks ago, a man approached me about the lot and said he wanted to build a house on the property for his daughter as a wedding present.”

Angry with him, she asked, “Were you just going to sell it one day and then tell me?

Joseph shook his head. “You know I wouldn’t do that.”

“I know no such thing. You gambled away our money without telling me.”

“That was different.”

Mary looked at the closed door, thinking of the children, and then turned toward the window. “I can’t believe you just said that. But please, Joseph, tell me why that’s so different.?”

Realizing that it was a foolish thing to say, he took in a deep breath and sighed heavily. “I guess it isn’t. I’m so embarrassed and upset with myself I’m grabbing at things and saying things that don’t make much sense." He looked at her. "Mary, I truly didn't realize how far I'd gone until I stopped by the bank a few days ago. The bank manager told me I was overdrawn, and at that point, I panicked. You may as well know the rest of it."

She sat forward, looking curious. "There's more?"

"I borrowed some money to win enough to carry us through for a while or until my luck changed."

Mary quickly digested that. "Who did you borrow from?"

"Captain Goodman."

She pulled her knees up under her chin, wrapping her arms around them. "How much?"

"Not much."

"For God's sake," she said angrily but keeping her voice down. "Don't play with me. How much do you owe, Captain Goodman?"

"Around eight hundred dollars."

Without saying another word, Mary grabbed her pillow, got out of bed, and pulled the top blanket off. "I'm going to sleep with Alan." She looked down at him. "I need to be away from you for a while, Joseph, and I need to get some sleep."

"Why can't you sleep here?"

She gave him one of her looks. "Are you really asking me that?"

The next afternoon, Mary sat in the gazebo, remembering her and Joseph's life during the war and the long separations they endured. She fondly thought of his effort at farming, knowing it was something he had always hated, and she smiled, knowing he had done it for her. Mary had never minded his gambling or drinking because that's who he was, but this was different. This was a side of him she never knew, and it filled her with a sense of fear for their future.

Hearing Joseph call out from inside the house, she quickly wiped her eyes and cheeks and sat up as he approached the gazebo. "You're late."

"Not very." He sat next to her with a plain yellow envelope in his hand.

She looked at it fearfully. "What's that?"

Joseph saw she had been crying, and that saddened him. "Open it and find out."

Mary glanced at the envelope, reading the bank's name in one corner, and felt uneasy, even fearful.

"Open it, please," he said softly while handing it to her.

She took the envelope, pulled out the folded piece of paper, unfolded it, and began to read. It explained the sale of the adjacent property for the sum of three thousand five hundred dollars to a Mr.

Morgan Fairchild. "What does one thousand dollars for the first option on remaining property mean?" she asked, looking puzzled.

Joseph cleared his throat and gestured with one hand. "Mr. Fairchild gets the first option on this property, if and when it comes up for sale. To guarantee that option, he is giving us a down payment of one thousand dollars."

She looked at the document. "What if we chose not to sell?"

He shrugged. "The option is for a period of five years, after which we have to return the money with a small amount of interest."

Mary stared at him thoughtfully. "What happens if we don't have the money?"

"Simple," replied Joseph. "We borrow on the house and property from the bank or sell to Mr. Fairchild."

She lowered the document to her lap and looked up, taking his hand in hers. Her eyes were pleading. "Joseph," she said. "You must promise me you won't gamble this money away."

He looked into her tired, worried eyes. "I promise not to gamble, not even a little."

She closed her eyes, shook her head, and looked at him affectionately. "I'm not asking that of you. I never would." She smiled. "You gamble and drink some, and I accept that. Gamble with what you have on you, what we can afford, not with what we have in the bank." She paused. "I married you because I loved who you were, and I don't want to change you." She looked down at their hands and then at him. "But I didn't want you to change from that man either, and somehow you did. All I want now and what I need most is to have faith in you, and that's something I've lost."

He frowned, feeling ashamed. "I know I've hurt you, Mary. I never meant to, and I know I'm a disappointment. But I will never hurt you again."

Thirty-One

July 1873

Out of the Past - Shreveport, Louisiana

It was late evening when the sternwheeler Helen returned from New Orleans, which took longer than Joseph had anticipated. When the last of the lines securing her were in place and the gangplank lowered, he hurried along the pier, anxious to get home. The sounds of laughter and music of the casino spilled from the Helen's second-story windows and followed him to the end of the pier, where he hurried up a dark alley toward the streets of Shreveport and home. The Saturday night sidewalks of lower Shreveport were crowded with the usual drunks, whores, gamblers, and even a few respectable men and women looking for a bit of excitement. Joseph walked along the boardwalk, passing in and out of the lighted doorways and windows, paying little attention to the faces around him because he was in a hurry to get home.

"Joseph," a voice called to him.

He stopped, glanced up and down the sidewalk, then into the street looking for a familiar face to go with the voice, and finding none, he thought he must have imagined it and started walking again. Then hearing his name again, he turned.

"Joseph, you son-of-a-gun."

Joseph grinned as he stepped onto the boardwalk. "Bob Colbert, you bastard, you're the last person I'd expect to see on the streets of Shreveport."

As they shook hands, Colbert grinned. "There are a few worse places." He looked around. "Not many, mind you, but there are a few."

"You still hiding from that stepfather of yours?"

Colbert chuckled. "Nothing quite that exciting, I'm afraid." He placed an arm around Joseph's shoulder, giving him a small playful hug. "Honor this tired southern gentleman by joining me in a drink."

"If you're buying."

Colbert grinned. "I see you haven't changed." He gestured to the door of the nearest saloon. "This way, my friend, and I'll tell you what brings a fine gentleman such as myself to the streets of lower Shreveport."

Joseph grinned as he gestured to the doorway. "After you." Then he followed Colbert through the door, noticing his cane, and recalled Mrs. Trudey Hansen mentioning a man with a cane who had come to visit him.

They found an empty table away from the noisy piano where Colbert ordered a bottle of brandy and two glasses from a thin, balding waiter with a dirty apron. As the waiter left, Colbert glanced around at the men playing cards, picking out a few that looked like easy marks, and then he turned to Joseph. "Tell me, my old friend, what are you doing in Shreveport?"

The waiter returned with a bottle and two glasses, placed them on the table, took Colbert's money, and walked away.

Joseph filled the two glasses. "I live here now."

"You don't say." Bob picked up his glass, smiled, and held it up. "To the South."

Joseph grinned, raised his glass, took a quick sip, and asked, "What brings you to Shreveport?"

"I live here also."

Surprise filled Joseph's face. "I thought you would have settled in New Orleans or even Florence. Why, Shreveport?"

"Yes, one would think New Orleans," Colbert raised his glass. "But here I am." He took a small drink and then looked at Joseph. "Tell me about the knifing back in '64."

Remembering Mrs. Hansen telling him she had run off a drummer with a cane, he asked. "How'd you know about that?"

Colbert shifted in his chair for comfort. "I ran into Captain Goodman someplace, can't recall where, but he told me you were either in Jefferson, Texas or Shreveport. When I arrived here, I asked around, and no one seemed to know you, and being the stubborn ass that I am, I decided to take a few days and ride on a sternwheeler over to Jefferson. When I arrived, I figured the best place to ask about someone was the Sheriff's Office." Colbert grinned. "Not a very trusting man, that one. I had to do some fast-talking, but I finally convinced him we were friends, and he told me about the robbery and where you were staying."

Joseph took a drink, picturing Sheriff Parker sitting behind his big desk, staring up at Colbert, who actually resembled someone he needed to run out of town.

"Well, anyway," continued Colbert. "After my pleasant visit with the sheriff, I stopped by that boarding house of yours and met your lovely landlady." He raised his brow and shook his head in memory. "Not a very agreeable sort."

Joseph grinned. "Mrs. Hansen."

Colbert nodded, looking uneasy. "Yes," he said thoughtfully. "Mrs. Hansen. She's not one to give out a lot of information."

Joseph chuckled. "No, that she isn't."

"Shit, I thought I was going to have to thump her one just to find out if you were going to live."

Joseph laughed. "I wouldn't suggest you thumping Mrs. Hansen, Bob. You just might get thumped yourself."

He laughed, looking convinced. "I can believe that. She looked like a woman to be reckoned with."

Joseph chuckled. "I recall her telling me about a well-dressed man that looked like a drummer asking about me."

Colbert looked up, frowning. "Drummer." Then he laughed. "I guess I've been called worse."

Joseph grinned. "I'm sure you have."

"Damn, that's too bad. Your landlady wouldn't let me upstairs. I wanted to see how you were getting on."

"Well, the truth is, I wasn't much in the mood for company."

Colbert leaned forward, resting his curious face on one hand. "So, tell me, what happened in Jefferson?"

He stared at Colbert a moment, shrugged, and settled back, telling him about winning a large amount of money, the fight in the street, the stabbing, and everything except who did it.

Bob tasted his drink and shook his head, his expression thoughtful. "Too bad you didn't get a look at the bastard."

Joseph picked up his glass and took a drink as the name raced through his mind." It was Charles Whittaker."

Colbert looked surprised. "Charles Whittaker?"

Joseph nodded as he played that night over in his mind. "That's right."

Bob sat back in his chair, looking troubled. "Hell, I've known Charles for years. I've had the occasion to win or lose a few hands from the man from time to time before the war." He paused in disbelief. "I never thought of Whittaker as that sort."

Joseph leaned forward, picked up the bottle, and poured another drink. "Well, neither did I, Bob."

"Are you sure it was Whittaker?" Colbert asked, looking skeptical.

Joseph sipped at the brandy as his mind returned to the dark, lonely street. "Charles and I had been playing cards for several hours, and I was the heavy winner, Charles, the big loser. I had been drinking all night and wasn't as careful as usual."

Colbert sipped his drink as he listened to Joseph tell the story.

Joseph took another drink. "It was late, rather early morning, and the streets were dark and empty. I never saw it coming." He paused in memory. "But I did catch a glimpse of his face. Lucky for me, a deputy happened by and yelled, scaring him off."

Bob shook his head in disbelief. "A guardian angel was with you that night, my friend. I've seen Whittaker use his knife, and he's good."

Joseph's hand went to his shoulder, where the knife had entered.

"It's hard to believe that of Charles," said Colbert. "But I suppose anyone can go sour. The war brought out the darkness in a lot of men's souls, but still, there was something about Whittaker…," he let his sentence trail off in thought, tasted his drink, and then changed the subject. "You do any fighting during the war?"

"No." Joseph settled back, pushing Whittaker out of his mind while recalling the early years of the war. "I put my time in on the Southern Belle." He grinned. "The Union soldiers used us for target practice a few times, but that's about all the war we saw." He told of moving his family out of Florence to east Texas, working on the Big Cypress, Caddo Lake, Red River, and the Mississippi, and finally of trying his hand at farming after the war.

Colbert grinned. "Didn't care for the scenery behind the plow?"

"No, Bob, I didn't, nor did I like the dirt and mud, the long days, and the short nights."

"It takes a certain kind of man to be a farmer, and you and I are not among them."

Agreeing with that, Joseph looked at him. "Where were you during the war?"

Colbert sighed and looked across the room. "I served with the 12th Mississippi Cavalry." He paused to take a drink of brandy and then grinned childishly. "Most of the men with money were off fighting in that hypocrisy of a war, and if I wanted to gamble, I had to go where the soldiers were." He shook his head, looking disappointed. "Not a very intelligent decision on my part."

Joseph chuckled, imagining Bob trying to win money off of broke soldiers.

Bob scowled, shook his head, and settled back in his chair. "Of course, that put me right in the middle of the whole damn mess." He paused. "Something I hadn't thought about until the shooting started."

"Ever get back home?"

He frowned and shook his head. "No, I nevah did, Joseph." He looked troubled. "Thought about it several times, but nevah made the trip." Then he smiled. "But I did get a letter from one of my dear sisters informing me that our beloved stepfather got himself and a good horse killed at Bull Run, as if I gave a damn." He picked up his drink. "Here's to the Yankee that found his mark."

Joseph considered all that while watching Colbert pour himself another drink while thinking he hadn't changed much over the years. A little older, perhaps, but he still cut a handsome figure in his tailored clothes. "What were you doing in Jefferson in '64?" he asked. "I don't recall any southern armies bivouacking around Jefferson."

Bob grinned shyly. "There wasn't, but I was." He sipped his drink. "I had been wounded in the left leg at Harrisburg."

"I was curious about the cane when Mrs. Hansen described you." He gestured to the cane resting against another chair. "I see you still have it."

Colbert picked up his cane, examining it. "I don't need it now. It's just become part of me, like a hat or glove." He set the cane down. "Anyway, having no desire to go home for reasons you're quite familiar with, I stayed with a cousin here in Shreveport until I could return to the 12th Mississippi." He stared into the empty glass for a moment, looking sad. "After Lee's surrender, I ended up in New Orleans for a time, then on several gambling boats along the Mississippi." He looked up, smiled, and shrugged. "I eventually ended up here in Shreveport."

Joseph picked up the bottle and filled Colbert's glass.

Colbert smiled. "I own a little house a few blocks from here."

Joseph looked surprised. "Never figured you for a man that would want to own a piece of property."

Bob looked embarrassed. "Neither did I, but love has a way of changing all that."

"Love?" chuckled Joseph.

Colbert grinned. "Yes, you big asshole, even a man such as I found a woman whose heart is filled with so much love, she is incapable of seeing his sins and vices as evil things."

"You're still full of shit Bob," laughed Joseph, then he smiled. "Any children?"

"Oh heavens, no," he replied, looking serious.

Joseph leaned forward in his chair. "And just who is this unlucky lady?"

Colbert gave him a look. "Why, thank you. If I recall correctly, she is my uncle's niece by marriage." He paused, considering that, then said, "Anyway, they're whom I convalesced with back in '64."

Joseph grinned, "Must have been one hell of convalescence."

Bob looked embarrassed. "Very funny."

"What's her name, and when do I meet her?"

"Her name is Grace."

"Well," Joseph said. "When do I get to meet this, Grace?"

"How about right now?" Colbert said, looking excited.

"Now?" Joseph asked, reaching for his pocket watch. "I'm sure Grace is a nice lady, Bob, but I doubt that she would appreciate you bringing home a drunken old friend at this hour. Besides, I'm a little late in getting home myself."

"I suppose you're right," Colbert said, looking disappointed. "Another time, perhaps?"

They finished their drinks and walked into the night air, stopping at the edge of the boardwalk where the steps led down to the street. Joseph put his hand on Bob's shoulder. "I have an idea. Why don't y'all come to the house next Sunday for dinner? I'm sure Mary would love to meet your Grace and have another lady to visit with. Hell, all she has is the children and me."

"I see your point, Joseph," smiled Colbert. "And I'm sure Grace would love to meet your Mary, as would I."

Joseph gave him directions to his house, and then they shook hands and said good-night. Of all the men Joseph had come to know along the Tennessee and Mississippi Rivers, Bob Colbert was one he had always liked.

A slight breeze played in the leaves above the gazebo, providing a little relief to the warm summer evening while Joseph sat in silence, reading the newspaper and thinking of Charles Whittaker.

"Mistah Joseph," said Mattie.

Startled, he turned and smiled. "Yes, Mattie."

She grinned, apologized, and then told him Miss Mary was with their guests in the library.

He thanked her, pulled his pocket watch from his vest, looked at the time, then followed her into the house, hearing Mary's laughter and the familiar voice of Bob Colbert. Entering the library, Joseph kissed Mary on the cheek, shook Bob's hand, and turned to a pretty, young woman he presumed to be Grace Colbert. "You must be Grace," He grinned. "If not, I'm in an awful lot of trouble."

"No," Grace Colbert said, glancing at her husband. "But my husband would be."

The room filled with soft laughter as Mary took Joseph's arm. "I was just telling our guests how nice it is to finally meet the man you've mentioned so often."

Bob smiled, looking a little skeptical. "Now that worries me." He put an arm around his wife and smiled at her. "You may need to come to my defense."

Grace smiled at Mary. "He does have his good qualities."

Mattie appeared in the doorway, announcing that dinner was ready. Joseph offered his arm to Grace, while Mary took Bob's arm and walked down the hall to the dining room for an evening of social pleasantries and a nice, quiet dinner.

Mary and Grace sat in the parlor, getting to know one another after dinner discussing children, fashion, and pre-civil war life. Joseph and Bob walked the property talking of the days before the war, their first meeting, the war itself, and their concerns over the South without slavery.

"A lot of families have lost everything," Joseph said sadly.

Colbert nodded. "My dear mother and sisters are among them."

Joseph looked regretful. "Sorry, I didn't know."

Bob asked about his family in Tennessee.

Joseph told him of the letter and its news of his father and brother's deaths at the hands of some outlaw Union soldiers. After a brief uncomfortable silence, Bob changed the subject to Shreveport and gambling as they walked back inside to join Mary and Grace for tea before saying goodnight.

Mary and Joseph watched the Colbert's carriage disappear into the late summer night, and then Mary smiled. "I like Grace. I think we'll be good friends."

"I hope so." Joseph closed the door, considering the invitation extended by Bob for a game of cards Wednesday night. As they walked past the library, he asked Mary if she wanted a sherry before bed.

"You go ahead, and I'll join you in the library after I check on the children." Then she started up the stairs.

He went into the library, poured a small glass of bourbon, and then a glass of sherry. He sat down and took a small drink of bourbon and lit a cigar.

Mary joined him on the sofa, picked up the glass of sherry, took a small sip, and rested her head on her husband's shoulder. "I was just thinking of Florence, before the war and Sunday dinners at Edward's."

He nodded. "I'm a bit more relaxed tonight than I ever was with your brothers."

Mary laughed. "Both Edward and Alex adored you."

"Not at first, they didn't." He took a drink and smiled. "I had to wear them down."

She chuckled. "That might be true, but Edward told me many times that he liked you."

"He did?"

She sipped her sherry and nodded. "Many times."

"Maybe," he said thoughtfully. "But I always felt as though I was about to be interrogated by Alex. Edward, on the other hand, watched like a vulture ready to feed once Alex finished me off."

"That's terrible," laughed Mary. "But true, I'm afraid." She sipped her sherry. "Edward always used to say that he liked the way you handled yourself around stuffy Alex."

"I bet he did."

She sat up, looking serious. "That's true, Joseph." She giggled. "He loved to watch you squirm, and after we married, he complained that the enjoyment of those days were gone forever."

Joseph smiled as he thought of Edward. "I miss him at times."

Mary's smile faded. "So do I." She looked sad. "I think he was terribly alone after Sarah's death giving birth to little Alexander." She sipped her sherry, looking sad. "I'm sure his death has been hard on Alex. It was nice of him to take in little Mary and Alexander." She smiled, wanting to forget the sadness. "Pour me another sherry."

Joseph got up, walked to a small cabinet where he poured a half glass of sherry, returned to the sofa, and handed it to Mary. "Are the children tucked in?"

She took a sip, smiled, and raised her glass. "Why do you think I asked for another?"

As Joseph considered that, he set his glass on the table and leaned over to kiss her.

She smiled, putting one hand on his chest. "I'm not relaxed enough. I want to enjoy my sherry and the quiet evening." She glanced at the empty fireplace. "Why don't you build a small fire?"

Joseph looked at the fireplace, then at her. "It's too warm; we don't need a fire."

She looked at him with a flustered look. "I suggested a small fire, not a bonfire for heaven's sake."

With a small fire burning, he returned to the sofa and put one arm around her. She sipped her sherry, and he, his brandy as they quietly watched the flames consume the logs. As she snuggled against him, he could smell her perfume and feel the rise and fall of her body against his with each breath she took. He gently kissed her cheek and neck while she closed her eyes, only to open them and gently push him away with a small smile. "Now, isn't this nice?"

He looked at her face carrying the soft, orange glow of the fire as she sipped her drink, looking at him over the edge of the glass in a teasing way, something she always enjoyed doing. He reached for the glass.

She pulled it away. "Not yet."

He was either quicker than she or she no longer cared, but he took her glass and placed it on the table while she untied the small, silk string at the top of her blouse. He looked at her white skin and the small valley separating her breasts, kissed her gently at first, and then passionately.

The fire was out, and the room chilly when Joseph opened his eyes. Looking at the cold ashes he considering another fire but instead, he pulled Mary closer. Feeling her warm, soft body against his, he gently turned her over, looked into her sleeping face, and kissed her awake from her restful sleep.

They lay in one another's arms, covered by her dress and petticoats for warmth, and at some point, Mary drifted back to the sleep that had held her earlier. Joseph thought about his father and brothers' deaths and decided that he and Mary should take a holiday and visit Sissy and her family one day soon. It was quiet and peaceful, with the drapes still closed, shutting out the early morning sun while keeping the room chilly and in darkness. Hearing the front door open, then close, followed by footsteps in the hall, Joseph said *'Mattie,'* under his breath, listening to her footsteps going past the library door, then fading down the hall toward the kitchen. It got quiet for a few moments, and then the sound of pots and pans made their way from the kitchen to the library. He gently shook Mary and whispered, "Mary, wake up."

She opened her sleepy eyes and glanced around, still half asleep. "What time is it?"

"Not so loud, Mattie's here," he whispered.

The consequences of that caused her to sit up and cover her breasts with her petty coat. "What?"

Joseph raised his head, looked over the sofa toward the door, and whispered, "She's in the kitchen."

Finding humor in their situation, Mary started giggling as she stood while gathering her clothes around her. As she stepped back, she tripped, falling backward onto the sofa letting out a small, shrill cry. Sitting on the sofa covered with her dress and one hand over her mouth, Mary stared at the library door. Then looking at Joseph's expression, she began to giggle.

"Shhh," he said, and then whispered, "She'll hear us." In a hurry to get upstairs, he gathered Mary's clothes, gave them to her, and then picked up his own clothes, put on his pants, and held the rest of his things against his naked upper body. Helping Mary get up from the sofa, they walked to the library door where Joseph listened for any sound from Mattie. Listening to the quiet, he slowly opened the door, poked his head out, and looked up and down the hall.

Mary started laughing, and as she covered her mouth with one hand, she dropped some of her clothing. “Darn,” she whispered.

“Shhh,” he warned again, looking worried.

She put one hand on his shoulder, grinned at him, and whispered, “I’m okay now.” She took his hand and followed him out of the library to the stairs. Thinking of Mattie, Mary softly giggled and whispered, “Boy, wouldn’t she be surprised.”

“Be quiet.” Joseph took her hand and started up the stairs while watching the kitchen door.

Mattie walked out of the kitchen and, seeing them frozen at the bottom of the stairs holding their clothes, stopped in her tracks with wide eyes.

Mary smiled and raised one hand in a faint wave. “Good morning Mattie.”

Mattie glanced from one to the other in silence, trying to decide if she should turn and run or speak.

Seeing the expression on Mattie’s face, Mary began to laugh uncontrollably, grabbed the railing with one hand, and sat down on the stairs pulling her clothes around her. She looked up at Joseph standing on the stairs holding his shirt in one hand, his shoes in the other, staring at Mattie. The scene was too much for Mary as she continued to laugh.

Mattie’s face held shocked surprise, she turned and ran back into the kitchen, and before the doors quit swinging back and forth, Mattie’s laughter echoed from the kitchen, mixing with Mary’s.

Embarrassed and unable to find the humor in the moment, Joseph ran up the stairs, disappearing into their bedroom.

Weak from laughing, Mary slowly stood, braced herself against the banister for a moment, pulled her clothes more tightly around her, and rushed up the stairs to their bedroom, where she fell across the bed in laughter. Turning over, she looked at Joseph standing in the center of the room, holding his clothes, rolled back onto her stomach, buried her face in the pillow, and kicked her feet in laughter.

Mary and Joseph managed to get dressed and go downstairs to a nicely set table for their breakfast. While Joseph glanced through the paper in silence, trying to forget the morning, Mary poured two cups of coffee, glancing now and again at Joseph. Mattie walked out of the kitchen carrying a platter of eggs, sausage, and bread and set everything on the table, trying not to make eye contact with either Mary or Joseph. But as things like this usually happen, Mattie was not able to accomplish that, and she looked at Joseph just as he took a drink of hot coffee. As their eyes met, he laughed, spewing coffee all the way across the table.

Embarrassed yet laughing, Mattie turned and disappeared through the swinging doors while Mary burst into laughter.

Realizing it was going to be impossible for him to eat his breakfast or drink his morning coffee, he got up, kissed his giggling wife on the cheek, and left the house, chased down the stairs by the faint laughter of Mary and Mattie.

Thirty-Two

August 10, 1873

Another Figure from the Past

On the evening of August 10, 1873, a well-dressed, slender man carrying two carpetbags stepped from the gangplank of a sternwheeler onto the Shreveport dock. Taking a quick glance around, he hurried toward the streets of Shreveport, looking for an inconspicuous place to stay, one that was away from the riverfront, gambling halls, and whorehouses, in addition to being inexpensive.

A few minutes later, he stepped into the dimly lit lobby of a small hotel. A middle-aged woman looked up from behind the desk, stopped what she was doing, and smiled as the man set his bags on the floor, asking for a room. She turned the register toward the guest, picked up the pen, and handed it to him while attempting to make idle conversation, which the man rudely ignored.

Placing the pen back in the ink well, the stranger looked at her with cold eyes, his acne-scarred face sullen and without expression. "Key, please."

Giving him a strange look, she turned to the rows of small boxes on the wall behind her, picked out a key, handed it to him, and pointed toward the narrow staircase. "It is the second door on your left at the top of the stairs."

The stranger took the key, picked up his two bags, and quietly disappeared up the narrow, dim staircase while Mrs. Hansen turned the register back around so she could read the scribbled name, **'Charles Whittaker.'**

Charles found his room, unlocked the door, and stepped into the dark room, locking the door behind him. The springs of the bed moaned, complaining from the weight of the two bags he tossed on it as he walked to the window. Standing against the wall as if afraid to be seen, Charles moved the curtain slightly, peered into the street for several minutes, and turned to a small table and lantern. Taking a match from his pocket, he lit the lamp and looked around the small but clean room and the single bed that now owned his two bags.

He glanced at the chest, tall wardrobe closet, a small table, and single chair near a potbellied stove, thinking it would have to do. The room was not unlike the others he had stayed in over the years, some better and some worse. As Whittaker sat on the bed, causing the springs to moan, he thought about the letter in his coat pocket. The bank wouldn't be open until Monday morning, and with luck, he would take care of the business that had brought him to Shreveport and catch a boat back to New Orleans.

He stood, methodically emptied his pockets on the nightstand, and counted the last of his money that totaled thirty dollars and twenty-five cents. Thinking it would have to do, he retrieved the envelope from the inside pocket of his coat, sat back down on the bed, laid back against the headboard with his boots on, and opened the letter. After taking out the neatly folded piece of paper, he leaned toward the lantern and read the printed lettering at the top of the page: 'Gilbert Styles, Attorney at Law, Shreveport, Louisiana.' The letter told of his uncle's recent passing and that he was the sole beneficiary of his late uncle's estate.

Whittaker sat back against the headboard, kicked the two bags onto the floor, and glanced at the letter once again, wishing Attorney Styles had mentioned the amount of his inheritance. Deep in thought about the amount of money he might receive, and hoping there would be enough to begin a new life, he carefully folded the paper and placed it back into the envelope. He got up, undressed, turned off the lamp, and climbed into bed, thinking about the money he would soon have.

A faint breeze made its way through the bedroom window and quietly played with the lace curtains, causing their shadows to dance across Joseph's sleeping face. Opening his eyes, he lay laid still for several moments watching the curtain play in the breeze, then turned to the empty pillow that had held Mary's head. Placing his forearm over his eyes, he thought about going back to sleep, but the clock in the hall chiming eleven in the morning told him it was time to get up.

Sitting on the edge of the bed, with his feet on the small area rug, he held his pounding head in his hands, hoping Bob Colbert felt just as bad as he did.

"Ya's awake, Mistah Joseph?" asked Mattie from the hallway.

He lifted his head and looked at the bedroom door. "Yes, Mattie, I'm awake,"

"Yah bath's ready, Mistah Joseph."

"Thank you, Mattie." He stood with some effort with a throbbing head, reached behind him, gathering a blanket around his naked body, opened the door, and walked across the hall to a waiting tub of hot water, soap, razor, and the suit Mary had laid out for him.

The clock at the top of the stairs chimed noon as he passed it on his way downstairs to the dining room and a waiting plate of food, silverware, and crystal water glasses. He pulled a chair from the table to sit just as Mary walked in from the kitchen.

"Out rather late, weren't you?" she asked rather coldly.

Without looking up, he placed a napkin across his lap. "I got home early."

"Don't be funny, Joseph," Mary said, finding no humor in what he said.

He was in no mood for a quarrel. "I apologize." Then he looked at her. "Yes, it was late. Lady Luck was riding with both Bob and me, and you can't stop when she's sitting on your shoulder." Anticipating her next question, he looked down at the food on his plate.

Looking at him as he ate, she poured him a cup of coffee. "Do you remember what tonight is?"

Joseph contemplated the hot coffee, his headache, and the question. "Aren't we having company for dinner?"

Her voice was chilly and unfriendly. "I wasn't sure you'd remember."

Still trying to avoid a quarrel, he tried to think of something that would make her happy, and in doing so, smiled with a small fib. "Bob and I talked about tonight as we played cards, and he's looking forward to it."

Her expression softened. "Did you invite Captain Goodman, as we discussed?"

Joseph swallowed his food and nodded. "Of course."

She smiled without humor. "You're such a bastard at times."

Stabbing a piece of meat with his fork, he chuckled. "I know, but I love you anyway." He shoved the piece of meat into his mouth and then grinned.

Mary figured she was on a useless course and knew he was just being ornery. "What do you have planned for today?"

"I thought I would spend some time with the boys," he said proudly, knowing that would make her happy. "Unless you've other plans."

If asked, she would have admitted to wanting to slap his smart mouth, but she smiled. "No, I have no other plans. The boys will enjoy that. They've missed you."

He grinned at her. "Why don't you miss me a little more when I'm gone?"

Her face flushed, she glanced toward the kitchen door, smiled, and whispered, "I would have, had you come home at a decent hour."

As she stood next to his chair to pour him another cup of coffee, he put one arm around her and pulled her closer. "I like it when you miss me."

She giggled, glanced at the door, and pulled away. "Honestly, Joseph, you're…well… you're impossible at times."

He glanced at the kitchen door. "Let's go upstairs so you can miss me some now."

Mary's face flushed as she glanced toward the kitchen door and lowered her voice. "Finish eating and go tend to your sons." She turned to leave, getting swatted playfully on the butt.

She turned and gave him one of her looks. "Go play with your children."

Joseph and Captain Goodman enjoyed a glass of bourbon while discussing the old days on the Southern Belle when the doorbell sounded. Minutes later, Mattie showed Bob and Grace Colbert into the library, and after brief hello's poured Bob a brandy and Grace a sherry.

Mary entered the room, greeted everyone, then asked Joseph to pour her a small sherry when she looked at Grace and smiled. "Are you expecting?" She turned to Joseph accusingly. "Why didn't you tell me Bob and Grace were expecting a child?"

Joseph looked surprised, glanced at Bob, and shrugged his shoulders. "Hell, I didn't know." Then he looked at his wife. "And how did you?"

"I just did." Mary smiled at Grace. "A woman carrying a child has a different look about her. When is it due?"

Grace blushed. "Sometime in January."

Mary took Grace by the hand. "That's wonderful. Now our little Allen will have another playmate."

Joseph stepped closer to Bob. "You horse's ass," he whispered. "Why didn't you say something?"

Bob looked apologetic. "Grace made me promise. She wanted to break the news over dinner tonight."

Joseph smiled. "Grace never considered Mary's hidden attributes."

Hearing that, Mary looked at him. "Women can sense such things. I don't know how; we just can."

Joseph smiled, handed a glass of sherry to Mary, and then offered a toast. "To the Colbert's and their child. May it be healthy and a girl." He looked at Bob. "The world is not ready for another you."

Bob laughed. "That may be true, but it is best if the firstborn is a boy."

"I agree," replied Goodman.

"That's not true," argued Mary.

"Of course it is," Joseph argued in the captain and Bob's defense.

Mary looked at her husband. "Why?"

He grinned. "Because that's the way it should be."

"That's ridiculous," replied Mary.

Joseph grinned. "I know, but let's hope little Samuel arrives safely."

Grace and Mary looked at one another and then at Joseph. "Little Samuel?" they said at the same time.

"Of course," he said, grinning. "He'll have my middle name as his proper name and Bob, or Robert, as his middle name."

Captain Goodman's chuckling broke the silence.

Joseph looked past everyone to the far wall. "I can almost hear it now. Samuel Robert Colbert." He smiled. "Has a nice ring to it." Then he turned to Captain Goodman. "Don't you agree, Captain?"

Goodman nodded as he raised his glass. "Amen, Laddie."

Mary scolded Joseph. "Are you trying to frighten poor Grace out of childbirth with such a notion?"

Grace looked at Bob, smiled, and looked at Mary. "That isn't a bad sounding name for a boy."

Joseph was surprised that she took his teasing seriously but very pleased that she would even consider the name and smiled. "I'm sure you will have many names to consider over the months, and whichever name you choose, it will be perfect."

Mattie appeared at the doorway, announcing dinner.

Joseph thanked her, motioned toward the door, and followed his guests to an evening of warm conversation and laughter, which passed much too quickly for Mary.

After saying goodnight to their guests, Joseph closed the door, and when he turned, Mary stood with her hand on the railing. Smiling at him, Mary turned and hurried up the stairs, giggling.

Joseph hesitated, then took the stairs two at a time in pursuit, wishing he didn't have to leave in the morning on a three-day trip to New Orleans.

August 13, 1873

Charles Whittaker

Charles Whittaker was up early and wasted little time shaving and getting dressed before finding a restaurant for breakfast. A few minutes after 10 a.m., AM, he opened the door, ringing a tiny bell above it to the Law Office of Gilbert Styles. Closing the door to the sound of the bell, he glanced around the room.

A balding, heavyset man of sixty looked up from what he was doing and smiled as he placed his pen in the ink well. "Good morning, sir. How may I be of assistance?"

Whittaker took off his hat and reached into his coat pocket, retrieving the letter with one hand and extending the other. "Mr. Styles?"

The man stood and shook Whittaker's hand, finding it clammy. "Oh, gracious, no, sir. I'm Thornton Darbishire, Mr. Style's assistant." He gestured to one of two chairs. "Please have a seat, Mr....?"

"I see," replied Whittaker, preferring to stand for the moment. "I need to see Mr. Styles on a matter of some importance. Is he in?"

"May I ask what the matter concerns, Mister---?" Darbishire let the question trail off, waiting for the man to introduce himself.

Whittaker didn't like being asked by an assistant about his personal affairs, and his expression showed it. "I'd prefer discussing my affairs with Mr. Styles."

Darbishire sat down in his chair while quickly considering the man before him and taking an immediate dislike to him. Darbishire was an educated man from a respectable family with little tolerance for rudeness, especially from someone with clammy hands. He took a deep breath and let out a long sigh while glancing over some papers on his desk, trying his best to be irritating. Finally, settling back in his chair, he looked up. "You are?"

"Whittaker, Charles Whittaker," he replied as if in a hurry.

"Ah, yes. I remember now, Mr. Bromewell's estate."

"That's correct," Whittaker said coldly.

"Nice gentleman," Darbishire said, looking thoughtful. "Too bad he's gone. I always believed him to be a little eccentric perhaps, but he was always quite the gentleman and polite to those he met, unlike some other men." He smiled at Whittaker, enjoying his little implication.

Charles was fidgety, looking impatient. "I'm not interested, Mr....?"

"Darbishire. I'm sorry, but I can't say I see any family resemblance."

Whittaker considered the man a buffoon. "Is Mr. Styles in?"

Darbishire smiled smugly. "Not at the moment, Mr. Whittaker."

Charles held up the letter. "I received this letter a few weeks ago with instructions to see Mr. Styles."

Darbishire was filled with contempt for this rude, condescending, arrogant ass standing in front of him. "Not instructions, sir," he corrected. "We never instruct. You see, Mr. Whittaker, it was I who wrote the letter. That is part of my duties, and I'm sure I never instructed you." He raised his brow. "I believe I suggested. Now, please have a seat." He held out one hand. "May I see the letter?"

Reluctantly, Whittaker sat down and stared into the round, fat face, smiling back at him from behind the desk, which he thought resembled a cat about to pounce on its prey. He hated the fat, little man but had no choice, so he forced a small smile. "When do you expect Mr. Styles to return? I want to get this matter resolved as quickly as possible."

"Of course you do, and I apologize for the inconvenience. If Mr. Styles had known you were coming in today, he would have made other arrangements. But unfortunately, something urgent came up, and he had to leave for a few days."

Whittaker felt trapped, and he was almost out of money. "When did you say Mr. Styles would return?"

Darbishire smiled. "I don't believe I did, but if all goes well, he should return tomorrow on the late train, and that being the case, I expect him in the office Wednesday about mid-morning." He paused and opened the appointment book. "I could place your name in the book if you like."

"As early as possible."

Darbishire nodded, remembering the clammy hands and the absence of the word please, something a gentleman would never forget. This Mr. Whittaker, he thought, had all the qualities of a desperate man, desperate perhaps for money, and in Darbishire's mind, that made him a man very untrustworthy. He donned a pair of spectacles, looked down at the open book, and glanced at Whittaker over the rim of his glasses, then back at the book, enjoying his moment of authority. Taking his pen from the ink well, Darbishire moved it slowly and calculatingly across the page to aggravate Whittaker, which gave him great satisfaction. After a few moments, he looked over the rim of his glasses. "How does 11 a.m. AM fit into your schedule?"

Finally, thought Whittaker while shifting in his chair to retrieve the letter from the top of Darbishire's desk. "Eleven a.m. would be just fine."

"You're welcome, Mr. Whittaker."

Charles stood, walked to the door, paused, and turned to the fat, little man behind the desk, gave him an unfriendly look, then turned, opened the door, and walked out into the morning sun, stopping at the edge of the boardwalk. Putting on his hat, he contemplated his next move, looked at his pocket watch, and seeing it was 11:40 a.m., he decided he could use a drink. Whittaker started across the busy street, careful of riders, buggies, and wagons. But then, hurrying up the boardwalk steps, Whittaker remembered he hadn't had lunch. Noticing a restaurant up the street, he decided lunch would serve his needs better than a drink.

Bob Colbert helped his wife with the dinner dishes and then made sure she was comfortably settled in a chair in front of the fireplace. He placed a blanket over her lap, handed her the book she had been reading, and then kissed her cheek. He smiled, telling her not to wait up, adjusted the blanket, and told her he loved her.

She smiled, wished him good luck, and watched him walk toward the door. It was evenings like this that Grace wished he were a storekeeper instead of a gambler, but that's who he was, and she loved him. Bob Colbert was a gambler by trade and good a one. He loved Grace, treated her with kindness and respect, and often surprised her with trinkets of little value besides the value she placed on them. As the door closed, she looked down at the slight bulge in her stomach, imagining the day she would have a child to keep her company, and secretly hoped her husband would be inspired to go out a little less often then. The day was almost gone, and dusk waited for its friend, darkness, as she looked out the window, watching her husband until he disappeared down the block before she turned away from the window and opened her faithful book.

Bob Colbert entered the Lucky Deuce Saloon taking a place at the bar, said hello to Jim, the bartender, ordered a brandy, and turned to watch the noisy crowd. Across the room, a piano player gently swayed from side to side as his hands glided across the keys to a soft melody wasted on an unappreciative crowd. The only person listening was a working girl long past her prime standing next to the piano, probably thinking of days past, with sweeter, gentler men. A big man dressed in black filled a chair on a podium a few feet away with a rifle lying across his lap. He slowly stood, walked the few feet to the girl, and said something that brought a frown to her face. She touched the piano player's shoulder, then turned and walked among the tables forcing a smile to this man and that one before choosing a lap.

Bob sipped his drink, glancing around the room, recognizing several familiar faces at a table with an empty seat. Walking to the table, he sat down, exchanging pleasantries as he took his wallet from the inside pocket of his coat. Filling his hand with money, he placed it on the table in front of him and waited for the next hand. At first, luck was good to him, but as it sometimes happens, she gets bored and moves on, taking residence on another's shoulder. Habit and knowledge had taught him that when luck leaves, you should follow. Unlike some men, Bob Colbert knew he could not change something that was beyond his control, and he wisely let luck have her way. His pocket watch told him it was ten-thirty. He thought of Grace and their warm bed, picked up his money, said goodnight, and started toward the bar for one last brandy before he left.

At the bar, he blocked out the noise and laughter as he sipped his drink, letting his mind drift back to the war, his wounds, and then of the Tennessee River before the war. He thought of Joseph, their first meeting, and how they had both ended up in the same place after so many years. As his mind thought of Grace alone at home, he gulped the last of his drink, set the glass down, and turned to walk toward the swinging doors. Glancing around the room, he was surprised at seeing Charles Whittaker sitting at a table just a few feet away. He stopped and thought about the story Joseph had told him about being knifed and robbed by the man. Wondering what Whittaker was doing in Shreveport, Colbert made his way across the crowded room to the swinging doors, making sure Whittaker wouldn't see him, and stepped outside. Standing on the boardwalk next to the window, he peered back in at Whittaker, knowing he had to warn Joseph. Seeing the hour on the wall clock inside the saloon window, he decided the hour was too late to visit him without alarming Mary and decided he would tell Joseph first thing in the morning. His mind filled with worry about what would happen if Joseph and Whittaker were to meet, and he decided to visit the sheriff first thing in the morning in hopes that Charles Whittaker was a wanted man. That way, the law would take care of Whittaker, keeping his friend Joseph safe from doing something that could land him in prison or get him hung.

August 14, 1873

Bob Colbert's Dilemma

Bob Colbert lay awake in bed watching the sky prepare for the new day as images of Joseph and Whittaker flashed across his mind, and he knew he had to warn Joseph before the two men ran into one another. He carefully pushed back the covers so he wouldn't wake Grace, sat on the edge of the bed, and started to get up.

Grace turned and opened her eyes. "You were restless last night. Are you all right?"

He turned his head and smiled at her. "I'm sorry. I didn't mean to wake you."

She looked worried. "I've been awake for a while, thinking of the baby."

Concern filled his face. "Are you all right?"

"I'm fine," she said, shrugging. "Just bad dreams."

"About the baby?"

She nodded.

Bob leaned closer, brushed her hair away from her face with his hand, and smiled. "They're just dreams, Grace."

She smiled, feeling foolish. "What bothers you?"

He considered the question and decided to tell her the story that Joseph had told him about being robbed by Charles Whittaker in Jefferson during the war. Finished, he said, "Charles is here in Shreveport."

Worry gripped and held her. "What are you going to do?"

He shook his head, looking concerned. "I have to warn Joseph. I'm sure Charles believes he is dead, and I'm afraid of what Joseph will do if their paths cross unexpectedly." He paused, looking worried. "Joseph could go crazy at seeing Whittaker."

"Is that like him?"

Bob considered that for a moment. "No," he said. "Joseph is one of the most level headed men I know. But you have to understand that Charles Whittaker robbed Joseph and almost killed him with a knife. He still has the scars."

"Then, you need to warn him and hope he doesn't go after this Charles Whittaker." Grace thought about Mary. "I feel bad for Mary if anything were to happen to Joseph."

He explained his idea about visiting the sheriff's office after breakfast to see if there were any old warrants against Whittaker. She told him to be careful. He smiled to reassure her. "Don't worry, my dear. Charles Whittaker is not my problem."

It was ten in the morning when Colbert opened the door to the sheriff's office and stepped inside, surprised at recognizing Sheriff Bill Parker, formerly of Jefferson, Texas.

Bill Parker had been in Shreveport for the better part of two years, enjoying the slower pace compared to that of Jefferson, Texas. Shreveport was a growing community, and the rough, heydays had ended with the South's surrender. These days, the worst thing that happened to Sheriff Parker was dealing with some drunk throwing up on the boardwalk. He looked up from his newspaper as his large index finger poked through the handle of a tin cup that looked small in his large hands. Taking a drink, he swallowed and smiled. "Bob Colbert, if I remember correctly."

Surprised the sheriff remembered their brief encounter in Jefferson, Bob said hello as he walked across the room to the music of creaking floorboards that ended when he reached the edge of the desk Parker sat behind.

"Take a load off, Bob. What brings you around here so early?"

He sat down in one of the three wooden chairs that moaned under his weight and wondered how to begin. His mind made up, he began the story. "I heard the name Charles Whittaker the other night, and while it sounded familiar, I couldn't put a face to it. It's been bothering me, so I was wondering if the name might ring a bell with you."

The sheriff stood considering the name, turned toward the potbellied stove behind his desk, and poured coffee into his tin cup, repeating the name. "Charles Whittaker?"

Bob nodded. "That's right, Charles Whittaker."

Bill Parker turned to the window, watched an old dog walk slowly down the street, sipped his hot coffee, then turned to his desk and sat down. "Name's not at all familiar." Setting his cup down, he gestured to a pile of posters on a table in the corner. "But that doesn't mean there might not be some old warrants with his name on them." He looked at Bob. "You're welcome to take a peek if you've a mind to, but I don't feel like wasting my time on someone that hasn't caused Shreveport or me any grief."

Bob shook his head. "No thanks, Sheriff. It's not that important."

The sheriff settled back in his chair, showing a little more interest. "Where'd you say you saw this feller?"

"Oh, I never saw him, Sheriff, just heard the name, and it seemed familiar, that's all. Could be someone I knew during the war."

Parker looked skeptical. "Hmmm." He took a drink of coffee and looked at Bob over the rim of his cup, and then he set the cup down. "Well, if you find out he's wanted for something, come see me. Don't try and handle this yourself."

Bob shook his head. "Don't worry about that, Sheriff; I'll come straight here." He stood, thanked Sheriff Parker, said goodbye, and walked out of the sheriff's office, considering what to do next. As he glanced up and down the street, he spotted Whittaker on the opposite side, hurrying along the boardwalk. Bob stepped between two buildings and watched as Charles stopped momentarily at a window, adjusted his hat and coat sleeves, and then continued on his journey.

Colbert stepped from between the two buildings and followed until Whittaker disappeared into an office door beneath a sign: Gilbert B. Styles, Attorney at Law. Wondering what Whittaker needed an attorney for, he waited in the shade by the corner of a building, trying to look inconspicuous. Several minutes passed when Whittaker and another man who Colbert presumed to be Gilbert Styles, emerged from the building and walked to the Shreveport Bank just down the street. Curious about what Whittaker was up to, Bob considered his next move and looked toward Gilbert Styles' office. Making a decision, he glanced back at the bank doors, stepped from the shade, and hurried back to the office of Gilbert Styles. His plan was simple. He would walk into the office under some pretext, having no idea what that would be at the moment, and see if he could learn anything about Whittaker's business. Reaching the door, he took a deep breath, opened it, and stepped inside to the tune of a small bell above his head.

A heavyset, middle-aged man dressed in a suit looked up from what he was reading. He smiled, stood, and introduced himself. "Good morning, I'm Thornton Darbishire; may I be of some assistance?"

Bob glanced past Mr. Darbishire into an empty office that he presumed belonged to Mr. Styles. "Is Mr. Styles in?"

"No, sir, he's not." Darbishire smiled as he glanced down at the appointment book. "Do you have an appointment?"

"I'm afraid not. An acquaintance of mine suggested I see Mr. Styles."

Darbishire smiled again with a curious face. "If you don't mind me asking, who might this acquaintance be?"

"Charles Whittaker."

The smile immediately left Darbishire's face as he closed the appointment book. "Charles Whittaker is a friend of yours?"

The man's expression and demeanor told Colbert that Charles Whittaker might not be very popular with Mr. Darbishire. "Well," Colbert said. "The truth is, I hardly know the man."

"I see," replied Darbishire as he studied Colbert with intense eyes. "I find that very strange. You see, Mr. Whittaker just recently arrived in Shreveport." Darbishire leaned forward, resting his elbows on the desk, and folded his hands. "Sorry to say this, but Mr. Whittaker impresses me as a man who doesn't make friends very easily."

Colbert felt awkward, was sure he looked it, and knew the man wasn't buying his story, so he decided on another approach. "May I sit down?"

Darbishire politely pointed to a chair. "Of course."

"Thank you, sir."

A gentleman, unlike Charles Whittaker, thought Darbishire.

"I'm a gambler by trade, Mr. Darbishire, and Charles Whittaker owes me a little money." He shrugged softly. "A gambling debt if you will."

"I see," Darbishire nodded, recalling Whittaker's mannerisms and the clamminess of his hands, a sure sign of desperation.

Colbert glanced at the door, fearful that Whittaker and Styles may return at any moment.

"What did you say your name was?"

Bob thought the fat little man would make a good card player. "My apologies, sir, the name's Bob Roberts, and as I said, I'm a gambler by trade."

Darbishire stared at him, considering the name. "You look more like a man of quality from good stock, Mr. Roberts, not like a gambler."

Colbert smiled. "Thank you, sir. As it happens, I was raised by good God-fearing parents on a plantation in Georgia." He paused, looking sad. "The plantation is gone, as are my parents. God rest their souls."

Darbishire liked the man sitting across the desk from him. He had style and eloquence, both old South qualities from breeding, and obviously a man of intelligence and education. "I had an uncle who was a gambler," he said, looking sentimental. "As a small boy, I would listen to his stories of the riverboats along the Mississippi, of New Orleans, and other such places." The smile of pleasant memory faded to sadness. "Someone shot him in New Orleans during a duel when I was still a young boy. I missed him for a long time."

Bob was getting nervous, fearing that Whittaker and Mr. Styles would soon walk in. "Sounds like an interesting gentleman," commented Darbishire. "Now, you were about to say something before I interrupted?"

Thank God, thought Colbert. "Yes, I was, but I don't feel comfortable giving details, so let's just say Mr. Whittaker lost a few hands while lacking the funds, something that doesn't sit very well with me." He hesitated, hoping he was successful in pulling him into his little scheme. "I'm the sort of man that will go to great lengths to avoid trouble, so I accepted his note. However, I really don't trust a man who gambles without cash, so I have kept an eye on him, and while I'm not proud of it, I followed him here. After he and the other gentleman left, I thought I would see what I could find out." He paused and waited for a reaction, and when none came, he continued. "But I didn't count on dealing with such a man as yourself, and I can see you're not one to be fooled, Mr. Darbishire. My apologies for trying."

Darbishire's chest puffed with pride as his face took on the boastful grin of a politician as he smiled at Colbert. "Well, I do my best trying to read men as they talk. And if I do say so myself, sir, most of the time, I'm pretty much on target."

Colbert smiled politely, knowing time was running out and the game was about over. He stood and extended his hand. "Sorry if I put you to any trouble, sir. I was only trying to see if Charles Whittaker would be able to honor his gambling debt."

Darbishire stood, took Colbert's hand, and gently shook it while looking past him to the door and lowered his voice. "I shouldn't say anything, but it appears that our secretive and rude acquaintance has come into a tidy sum of cash. Shall we say close to $3,200.00?"

Surprised that Darbishire had confided such information in him, he glanced back at the door. "I find that most helpful."

"His uncle passed some weeks back. It was I who wrote to Mr. Whittaker advising him of his uncle's death, and thus the reason for his being in Shreveport." He frowned, looking displeased. "And to be honest with you, Mr. Roberts, the sooner this man leaves Shreveport, the better off the city will be." Then he scowled, shaking his head, gesturing with one hand. "He's a man that is just a little too rude if you ask me, he and has clammy hands."

Colbert grinned. "And not a very good gambler."

Darbishire laughed.

Colbert extended his hand once again saying, "I can't thank you enough, Mr. Darbishire. Ya have put my mind at rest."

Darbishire took Bob's hand and leaned closer. "I believe Mr. Whittaker is staying at The Hansen just down across the street, if that interests you."

"I'm truly indebted to you, sir." Then glancing at the door behind him, he lowered his voice. "I'd appreciate it if you were to forget I was ever here."

Mr. Darbishire smiled. "Not to worry, Mr. Roberts, if that's your real name." His eyes narrowed. "It'll be our little secret. The truth is, I don't like Mr. Whittaker very much."

Bob nodded, thinking Mr. Darbishire was a crafty individual, said thank you, walked out of the office, and glanced back up the street, seeing Whittaker and Mr. Styles on the boardwalk walking toward him. He lowered his head, pulled his hat down, and crossed the street. Reaching the boardwalk on the other side of the street, Colbert stopped and watched as the two entered Mr. Styles' office. Not quite sure what to do with his new information, he checked his pocket watch, seeing it was almost 1:00 p.m. It was early, but he needed a drink to sort things out, so he headed toward a saloon a few blocks away.

The Red River Casino was relatively quiet as Bob stepped through the swinging doors. Three men were at the bar talking to a whore, and two men were at a table in the back, talking to two other whores. He sat at a small table by the window, ordered a beer, and as he drank, he considered the events of the day and the information he had.

He thought about telling Grace all this, but he knew she would probably tell him to leave it alone and stay out of it. But he just couldn't. There was still the chance that Joseph and Charles Whittaker would meet unexpectedly, and that could be disastrous for both men. He was fearful for his friend Joseph and he felt the need to protect him. Taking a drink of beer, he came to the decision that he had to tell Joseph everything.

Bob Colbert stepped down from his buggy, told the driver to wait, walked to Joseph's front door, tapped the brass knocker against the door, and waited. Mattie opened the door dressed in her usual black dress and white apron. They smiled at one another. "Good days to ya, Mistah Bob."

"Good day Mattie, is Joseph at home?"

Before she could answer, Mary responded from the hall, "I'll take care of Mr. Colbert, Mattie. Thank you."

"Yessum," said Mattie as she turned and quietly walked down the hall.

Mary smiled pleasantly. "Joseph's out someplace on the river, but we're expecting him sometime late tonight or tomorrow morning." Bob's demeanor told her that he was troubled, and she worried over Grace. "Is everything all right? Grace isn't ill, is she?"

"Grace is fine, Mary, thanks for asking. I just needed to see Joseph for a few moments, but it'll keep."

Mary became more than just curious about his visit that appeared to carry the resemblance of urgency. "May I be of some assistance, Bob?"

He smiled and shook his head, trying to act casual. "I'll just come back tomorrow."

"As you wish; I'll tell Joseph you stopped by."

"Thank you, and if you would, please tell him I'll stop by tomorrow, perhaps around midday, if that'd be all right."

"Of course." Mary smiled warmly. "You're welcome anytime, Bob, you know that. I'll be sure he gets the message."

He thanked her, turned, walked away, and climbed into the buggy.

Mary watched as the buggy rolled down the driveway to the cobblestone street, sensing something was wrong. Then the children's voices upstairs took her from the mystery, so she closed the door and went upstairs to settle their argument.

A horse's hooves played their lonesome medley on the cobblestone street as it pulled a carriage through the chilly night fog. Inside, Joseph pulled his coat collar up and looked out the open window at the ghostly images of homes and trees passing by the carriage window. He was anxious to get home to a warm fire and a glass of brandy to take the chill off. The carriage slowed, swayed to one side as it turned through the gates of his home, and up the long driveway, stopping at the front door.

Climbing down from the buggy, he reached in and picked up his carpetbag, paid the driver, said goodnight, and walked to the door. After unlocking it, he stepped inside, setting the bag down. Picking up the lantern Mary had left for him on a table next to the door, he walked into the library. Thinking briefly of a fire, he quickly changed his mind, thinking it was too late, so he poured a small glass of brandy and downed it in one gulp. Setting the glass down, Joseph picked up his bag and made his way up the stairs. After looking in on the children, he entered his bedroom, set the lantern and bag down, looked at the lump of blankets covering a sleeping Mary and undressed.

Mary turned over. "How was the trip?"

Surprised she was awake, he smiled. "Uneventful." He climbed into bed. "I didn't mean to wake you."

She moved closer as he settled in. "I wasn't asleep."

Feeling the warmth of her body next to his, he asked, "Have any trouble with the boys?"

"Somewhat." She quietly laughed. "I had to scold Zach a couple of times. I think he has growing pains." Then she looked at him. "Bob Colbert was by earlier today."

Joseph found that curious. "What did he want?"

"I don't know," said Mary. "Bob didn't say. But he acted a little strange, even nervous. He was very disappointed when I told him you weren't expected back until sometime tomorrow morning."

He pondered Bob's visit. "I wonder what that was all about. He's not the nervous type."

"I'm not sure," she said thoughtfully. "But he did seem distant and preoccupied with something. It unnerved me a little."

Joseph considered that. "Do you think something's wrong with Grace?"

"I don't think so. I asked if she was ill, and he assured me she was fine."

"Well," said Joseph. "I guess we'll find out tomorrow. It's probably nothing."

"I hope you're right." She turned and touched his face with her hand. "I've missed you."

Thirty-Three

August 15, 1873

A Strange Sickness

Joseph sat down at the breakfast table, placed the white cloth napkin in his lap, and while Mattie poured his coffee, he picked up the newspaper and looked at the headlines. "Mystery Fever Stalks Shreveport." He took a sip of coffee, opened the newspaper, and started reading about several people sick and some dying from flu-like fever. He read about a mercantile owner collapsing in the street, a Negro mother of three dying at home, and a young girl dying after being sick with a fever for several days, plus several others admitted to the hospital. According to the article, doctors could not agree on the causes, blaming congestive fever, a flu strain, malaria, or a number of other causes, including food poisoning. Joseph finished the article, folded the newspaper, and set it on the corner of the table. As he ate his breakfast, he worried for Mary and the children and considered sending them away for a few days.

Mary walked into the dining room, kissed him on the cheek, said good morning, and sat down. As she poured herself a cup of coffee, she noticed the headlines. "What is making all of those people sick?"

He shook his head thoughtfully. "I don't know, but I hope it's only a few isolated cases of malaria or this bilious fever they're talking about."

Mary considered that. "I read the article while you were getting ready." She looked worried. "It's a little scary."

Concealing his concerns, he shrugged and smiled. "I'm sure it's nothing more than a few isolated cases." He took a drink of coffee and looked at her. "But it might be a good idea if you and the children visited the Hall's until this passes."

"I'll not leave you here and run off to hide."

"It'll only be for a few days," he argued. "Just until this, whatever it is goes away."

Mary shook her head, looking defiant. "I'm not going to run away until we know what this is."

"That's my point, Mary. We don't know what it is, and until we do, you and the children would be better off staying with the Hall's."

"I'll not leave you. We've spent the better part of our lives apart, and I'll not leave you here alone, not even for a week. If you're so worried, come with us."

“All right, Mary,” he said, recognizing a lost argument. “But if this sickness gets worse, you and the children will visit the Hall’s.”

She smiled smugly, having won. “Agreed.”

“I’m going to hold you to that.”

“I know.” Then she looked worried. “Do you suppose all of this has something to do with Bob’s visit yesterday?”

He considered that, looking worried. “I don’t know. Didn’t he tell you that Grace was okay?”

“Yes, but still, all this sickness and his wanting to see you seem a bit more than coincidence. Perhaps they are leaving Shreveport because Grace is pregnant.”

“Maybe.” He finished his coffee. “I think I’ll go see Bob first thing.”

Mary reached across the table and put her hand on his. “I’ll keep the children inside. They can play in the house for a couple of days. Would that ease your worries?”

He smiled, looking relieved. “Yes, it would. Thank you.” Then he stood. “I better go see what brought Bob, by yesterday.”

Grace Colbert answered the door with a friendly smile and told Joseph that Bob was not at home, but he was welcome to come in and wait. Joseph declined politely, telling her that he had some errands to run, and headed toward the gaming halls along the river searching for Bob. As Joseph turned up one of the lower streets of Shreveport, someone called out. When he turned, he saw Colbert hurrying across the street.

“I was looking for you,” Joseph told him. “Mary said you stopped by yesterday.”

Colbert looked worried. “I’ve some news you’re not going to like.”

“Does it have anything to do with this sickness?”

Colbert shook his head. “No.” Then he gestured toward a nearby saloon. “I’ll buy you a drink, and then we’ll talk.”

They found an empty table, and Bob ordered two beers and glanced around the room as if looking for someone. When the beers arrived, Bob took a sip, wiped the foam from his mouth, and looked at Joseph, who was waiting to see what was so urgent. “I saw an old friend of yours the other night.”

Joseph looked curious. “Who?”

Bob glanced around, leaned toward Joseph, and lowered his voice. “Charles Whittaker.”

Surprise held Joseph’s face. “Are you sure it was Whittaker?”

Not getting the reaction from Joseph he expected, Colbert nodded. “Oh, it was Charles, all right.” Then he took a sip of beer.

Joseph leaned on the table with his forearms. "What the hell would bring that bastard to Shreveport?"

"I was a bit curious about that myself." Colbert took another drink of beer and then told him about following Whittaker to the attorney's office, the bank, and of his conversation with Darbishire. "Mr. Darbishire doesn't think too highly of your friend."

"A man of good judgment," smiled Joseph.

Bob sat back in his chair. "I'm betting that he thinks you're dead."

Joseph stared at Bob for a long moment. "I'm sure the bastard does."

"Darbishire told me that Whittaker's deceased uncle who lived in Shreveport left him around $3,200.00."

Joseph stared at the window in thought while touching the scar on his neck. "About twice what he took from me."

Seeing the hate in Joseph's face, Bob wished Whittaker had never come to Shreveport and that Joseph was still out on the river. "He'll be gone in a couple of days, Joseph. Let it go."

Joseph looked at Bob. "Would you?"

"No, I suppose not." Bob looked worried. "You've too much to lose, Joseph. If you kill him, they'll hang you sure as hell."

Joseph looked at him and started laughing. "Do you seriously think I would kill that son-of-a-bitch?" He took another drink of beer and chuckled. "Shit, Bob, I wouldn't waste my time and effort on killing the bastard."

Relieved, Bob settled back in his chair.

Joseph laughed again. "No, Bob, I'll not kill Charles Whittaker. The worst thing that anyone can do to him is to take his money."

Bob leaned forward with his elbows on the table. "You're not thinking of robbing him."

Joseph laughed again. "Hell no, Bob, I'll take it from him in a game of cards."

Colbert considered that for a moment. "He's good, Joseph. It may not be all that easy. What makes you believe that you can beat him?"

He smiled. "Because I can. I beat him before in Jefferson, but the bastard knifed me and took all of my money."

Colbert considered that. "Whittaker's no fool at the card table. He can deal a second card with the best of them, and I know he's damn capable of dealing from the bottom, but neither's ever been proven that I've heard of."

"I know all of that," grinned Joseph. "I've heard all the stories about Whittaker. Don't you get it, Bob?" He took a sip of warm beer. "That's the beauty of it all. The bastard surely believes he killed me and got away with it, and he knows that I looked up at him just as he put that damn knife in me." He took another drink of beer. "You're the only person I've ever told that it was him." His face and blue eyes filled with the sweet thought of revenge. "Can't you just see the expression on the bastard's face if I were to sit down across from him at a card table?" Then he laughed. "And that my friend will be my advantage."

Bob wasn't as confident as Joseph. "And just how are we going to manage that?"

"We?" asked Joseph with a surprised look. "You'll have no part in this, Bob. I don't want Charles after you."

Colbert shrugged. "Unless you know someone else that can arrange a game so you can surprise him, it has to be 'we': you and me."

Joseph frowned as he considered that. "Are you sure you want to get mixed up in this?"

Bob grinned. "At your service, Suh."

Joseph grinned. "As long as you know what you're getting into, but it has to be an honest game. We don't cheat the man." He paused as he sat back in his chair. "I won't do that."

Bob frowned and spoke in a heavy drawl. "Why, Ah surely do resent the implication, Suh."

Joseph smiled. "You're full of shit Bob, now drink up." He waved for two more beers. "We've some planning to do." Then he grinned. "I plan on scaring the shit right out of old Charles, and that will cause him to make mistakes."

The two schemed for the next hour, hatching a plan that would set the scene for a chance meeting between Charles Whittaker and Joseph.

August 23, 1873

The Game

Mary watched her husband play with the mashed potatoes by moving his fork through them and knew something important held him in its grasp. After repeated attempts by her to have a conversation with him, she sent the children off to their rooms. "Joseph," she said in a loud voice.

He looked up.

"Where are you?"

He placed his fork on the plate. "I'm right here."

"No, you're not Joseph. You're someplace else. What's going on inside that head of yours?"

"Nothing's going on inside my head."

She knew differently and pursued the question. "I know you all too well. Does this have anything to do with Bob Colbert's visit?"

The clock in the hall struck eight, and he took out his pocket watch, looked at it, and forced a smile. "I have to get ready."

Filled with worry, she looked at him. "Get ready? What is going on?"

He stood, politely excused himself, and kissed her on the cheek. "No time to explain right now." Then he walked out of the dining room and up the stairs to the bedroom.

Mary was not far behind and sat on the bed as he walked to the wardrobe closet. "Joseph, for the last time, what's going on?"

He glanced at her image in the mirror while putting on his coat. "Nothing. I'm just going into town for a while. Maybe play a little poker with Bob."

"Joseph," she said in a hostile voice. "I'm not one of your dumb, cute, little bar girls, damn it, I'm your wife." She stood and walked across the room. "I know when something's not right."

"We'll talk later, Mary."

She walked to the door and stood with her back against it, looking angry and determined. "You're not leaving this room until we talk." Suddenly fear filled her face. "Have you gambled away our money?"

At first, he was angry that she would think such a thing, but then he remembered that his track record wasn't all that good. He saw the fear in her eyes and knew that he had to tell her everything. If not, he wouldn't leave the house without a fight, and he didn't want that. He walked over to her, took her hand, and led her to the bed. "Come sit with me. I have a little story to tell you."

Curious and afraid, she sat with him on the bed.

"Do you remember when I was robbed a few years back in Jefferson?"

She rolled her eyes. "How could I ever forget that?"

"I've lied to you a little about that night."

"Lied?" She was confused. "Lied about what?"

"I know who stabbed and robbed me that night."

"Why did you lie about that? You could have had him arrested."

"I had my reasons."

She blinked, looking baffled. "What reasons?"

He shrugged. "You wouldn't understand. I doubt that anyone would."

"You're right about that; I don't understand." She looked at the side of his face as he stared out the window in memory of the blood seeping from the bandages she had changed and the scars they had left on his chest and face. Her voice choked. "Who is this man?

"Charles Whittaker."

She ran the name through her memory of names, trying to remember if he had spoken the name somewhere in the distant past. "I don't believe I've ever heard the name,"

Joseph sucked in a deep breath, sighed, and looked toward the window. "He was someone I met in Decatur before the war. We played cards that night, talked, and had a few drinks. Over the years, I'd run into him along the river." He shrugged. "We'd play cards and have a drink, exchange stories, and a few laughs."

"Then you were friends," she said, more of a statement than a question.

He thought about that. "Not exactly."

"What does that mean?"

He grinned and gestured with his hands. "It means what it says, not exactly. We knew one another, and when the war started, he disappeared just like Bob Colbert and a hundred others I'd met over the years. I never saw him again until that night in Jefferson."

"And now he's here in Shreveport?"

He nodded. "That's why Bob stopped by. To warn me."

Her mind and body were filled with fear for her husband. "Is he dangerous?"

Joseph looked at her. "Of course. He almost killed me."

Suddenly she understood. "It's him you're meeting tonight, isn't it?" She paused. "And you want your revenge?"

"Yes," he said in a soft voice. "I want my revenge."

She quickly digested all that he had told her, put her hand on his arm, and pleaded, "Don't go, Joseph, please."

His face filled with concern, and his blue eyes looked sad. "I have to go."

She began to cry as she pleaded. "No, you don't. That makes no sense, Joseph. You don't have to go." She wiped at her tears with the back of her hands, and then grabbed his forearm. "Joseph, please, I've never asked a lot from you, but I'm asking you to please stay home tonight."

He smiled and touched her wet cheeks with his fingertips. His face was gentle, his eyes soft and tender. "It'll be all right, Mary. I'm not looking for a fight. That sort of revenge died inside me long ago."

Her eyes were red with tears. "But you just now admitted you wanted revenge."

He smiled tenderly at her. "I do, Mary, but not his death."

She wiped her cheeks with the back of her hands. "I don't understand."

"It's simple," he said in a calm voice. "Charles Whittaker doesn't know I'm alive, and I intend to show up and scare the hell out of him."

Mary threw up her hands and rolled her eyes. "Now that makes a lot of sense. You're going to scare the hell out of the man that almost killed you. Have you any idea how ridiculous this all sounds?"

Joseph chuckled. "Maybe it does, but that's what I intend on doing."

"You're going to kill him, aren't you?" She looked fearful, her eyes red and puffy.

He stood, took her hand, helped her to her feet, and looked into her teary eyes. "No, Mary," he said softly. "I'm not going to kill him." Then he explained the plan that he and Bob had put together, promising her that all he wanted was a chance to take Whittaker's money. "Money is important to Charles Whittaker, more important than life." He smiled wryly. "I'm a testament to that."

"And if you don't win? Have you thought about that?"

"Yes, I've thought about that." He smiled as he shrugged. "I walk away. All I want is the pleasure of letting him see that he couldn't kill me. That I beat him then, and that I can beat him now."

"I'll ask again, Joseph," she said, looking fearful. "And if you lose?"

"As I said, Mary, I walk away and leave Charles Whittaker with the knowledge that he didn't kill me. That I knew it was him, and that fact will have him looking over his shoulder for the rest of his life. He deserves at least that much."

"Promise me you'll walk away, win, or lose, you will walk away from that man."

He smiled as he touched the side of her face. "I promise." Then he kissed her. "I can't lose Mary. I have an advantage few men have in gambling."

"I don't understand," she said, looking afraid.

He sat down on the bed, gently pulling her down beside him. "Whittaker thinks I'm dead, believing that no one else knows what happened in Jefferson. He has lived the past nine years confident in that lie." He paused and smiled sinisterly. "I can't wait to see his face when he looks up and sees me standing there, big as life."

Mary's expression was doubtful. "How is all that going to help you?"

"Fear causes mistakes," he explained. "And I hope to instill enough fear into Charles Whittaker that he'll make those mistakes and lose at poker."

Mary digested all that and began to feel somewhat certain that he was not out to kill Charles Whittaker. "I think I understand. Will Bob be there with you?"

"He's my Judas."

"He's your what?"

"My Judas goat Mary," he said, grinning. "He's leading Charles Whittaker to me." He turned to the window with a cold and calculating expression. "I will have my revenge or my justice, whatever you want to call it. And I'll get it without putting one single hand on him." He stood, pulled her up from the bed, and kissed her.

She held her arms around him tightly and whispered, "Please be careful."

He smiled tenderly. "I promise. It's only a card game, Mary. It's only a card game." He turned, walked out of the bedroom, down the stairs, and into the night.

She hurried to the window seat, sat down, and watched his dark figure walk down the driveway, disappearing through the iron gates. Fear gripped her as it never had before, and suddenly, she felt the need to be with their children.

The walk from the house to the 'Lone Dutchman Saloon' was a blur to Joseph because his mind and memory were on Jefferson, Whittaker, and tonight. He was oblivious to everyone and everything around him by the time he reached the swinging doors of the saloon. Excitement rushed through him, mixing with other emotions he had little control over, as he stood at the swinging doors. Looking inside while music, laughter, and voices without words spilled out of the doorway, he thought of that night long ago in Jefferson. A man bumped into him, apologized, and went inside, bringing his thoughts back to reality, and then he stepped through the doorway, greeted by heavy smoke, music, loud laughter, and voices. He made his way to the crowded bar, ordered a glass of bourbon, and while waiting, he turned and looked across the room at the piano player pounding at the keys of the piano, ignoring the short, plump women wailing out the words of the song in another key.

The bartender set a glass on the bar, filled it from a bottle of brandy without speaking, and took Joseph's money. He picked up his drink and sipped it while searching the tables until he found the familiar face of Bob Colbert sitting at a table near the far corner. Seeing that

Whittaker's back was to him, he knew he could approach without being seen. The setup was perfect, and he studied the other two men he didn't know at the table. His head filled with excitement; his heart raced, and adrenaline flowed through his body. Without taking his eyes off the table, he gulped down the last of his drink, set the glass on the bar, and made his way across the room, standing in back of Whittaker. "Mind if I sit in?"

Colbert looked up. "Not at all."

The two other men nodded with gestures to sit as Whittaker puffed his cigar and flirted with a pretty young girl sitting at another table smiling at him.

Joseph walked around the table while Whittaker stared at the cards in his hand, pulled out a chair, sat down, and glanced at the other men. One looked about thirty, thin but not sickly and in need of a shave, who he guessed to be a farmer. The other, a little older and heavier, his face bearded but neatly trimmed, Joseph thought was most likely a man of business.

Whittaker glanced at the new player over the top of his cards, and, seeing it was Joseph, his mouth fell open, letting his thin cigar fall onto his lap. Having the presence of mind to stand, he brushed the cigar off his pants before it had a chance to burn his clothing, all the while staring at Joseph.

"Hello, Charles," smiled Joseph as he reached across the table with an open hand. "How've you been?"

Whittaker stared at Joseph as he sat back in his chair and limply shook Joseph's hand, wondering if Joseph knew it had been him that night in Jefferson.

Joseph turned to Bob Colbert. "Hello, Bob. It's been a while." Then Joseph introduced himself to the other two men, shook their hands, and turned back to Whittaker, gesturing to the money in front of him. "Looks like luck is with you tonight, Charles."

Whittaker forced a smile, hoping that Joseph hadn't seen his face in the dark street, or if he had, he would surely be anxious to take revenge. "Good to see you, Joseph."

"Thanks, Charles. I'm probably the last person you expected to see."

Not sure what he meant by that, Charles took out another thin cigar and lit it.

Colbert almost choked on his drink, but managed to swallow it, and then looked at Joseph, hoping he kept a calm head.

Joseph signaled to a waiter, ordered a drink, and then turned to Whittaker. "Let's see," he said, looking thoughtful. "I believe the last time we saw one another was in Jefferson, Texas, back in '64."

Whittaker shifted nervously in his chair, wondering if Joseph was toying with him or didn't really recognize him, and nodded nervously. "I believe that's right," he said, trying to look casual. "I was on my way back to New Orleans at the time."

"Whose deal, is it?" Colbert asked, trying to move the game along.

"Mine," replied the bearded man on his left.

Colbert pushed the deck to him, looked at Joseph, and then at Whittaker. "If you gentleman are through with your reminiscing, can we get on with the game?"

Joseph grinned at Bob and took his wallet from the inside pocket of his coat.

Whittaker noticed the small scar above Joseph's ear and the other running out of his shirt collar. Images of the struggle years ago ran through his mind, and he could still feel the way the knife had cut through Joseph's clothing when he shoved it into his chest. He had been certain that Joseph had died on that street, and then he remembered someone yelling at them and him running away.

The bearded man placed the cards in front of Whittaker, interrupting his thoughts of that night. "Cut?"

While looking at Joseph, Whittaker reached for the deck, knocking over his glass, spilling brandy onto the cards.

The bearded man cursed at Whittaker, telling him to be careful, and turned to a nearby waiter to ask for a towel and a new deck of cards.

Looking embarrassed, Charles apologized while placing his glass upright, and then he picked up his money. As the waiter cleaned the table, he kept glancing at Joseph.

The table cleaned, and a new deck of cards shuffled by the bearded man and cut by Whittaker without incident, the cards were dealt.

The evening went as if scripted by a playwright. Charles and Joseph exchanged silent glances, and after three hours, Whittaker was down only a few dollars. It appeared that Joseph's dreams of breaking the man were slipping away when Charles suddenly announced he was calling it a night.

Joseph began to panic, knowing he may never get another chance. He and Bob glanced at one another, and then he looked at Whittaker. "Stick around, Charles, the evening's early."

Charles picked up his money and shoved it into the inside pocket of his coat.

Colbert spoke up. "Sit awhile, Charles."

Joseph leaned forward. "Shit Charles, it's been what, eight, nine years since we've had the chance to talk and play cards."

Whittaker studied Joseph, still unsure of the man, but settled back into his chair. "Something like that, I guess. I'd say close to nine years."

Joseph gestured at the table. "In the old days, you would never leave a game this early with all this money on the table." He grinned. "The last time we played, I believe I took most of yours."

Whittaker looked at him with a slight grin, remembering how he had gotten his money back, plus a little extra. "You damn near cleaned me out that night, all right."

"Well," Joseph said. "I thought you'd want a chance to win it back." He smiled as he leaned forward with his elbows on the table. "Sort of getting even, as they say."

Colbert glanced from one to the other, fearful this could quickly get out of hand.

Whittaker stared at Joseph, remembering how Joseph had beaten him at almost every hand that night and left the game before he could win it back. He glanced at the clock on the wall above the piano. "It's a little late, and I'm tired."

Bob looked at Whittaker. "Stick around, Charles. The three of us may not have this opportunity again for a while."

Glad Colbert had spoken up, Joseph smiled as he looked at Bob. "Maybe Charles is bored. Perhaps we need to make the game a little more interesting."

Charles wished he'd killed him that night in Jefferson. He looked at the money in front of Joseph, thinking it would be satisfying to teach him a lesson by taking all his money. "What did you have in mind?"

Colbert looked at Whittaker and decided to tease him a bit. "I thought you were leaving."

Charles gave Bob a mean look. "I'll leave when I'm damn good and ready."

Colbert sat back, smiling. "Never meant anything, Charles."

The bearded man looked at the thin man and then at Joseph. "I'd like to know what's on your mind."

Fearing his chance for revenge was slipping away, Joseph knew he would only have this night, and this time to get it.

"I'm waiting," said Whittaker as he took out another thin cigar and put it between his lips.

Joseph took out a match, lit Whittaker's cigar, blew out the match, and tossed it into the ashtray. "Let's up the ante and raise the limit to fifty dollars."

Charles puffed the cigar as he stared at Joseph, thinking he needed a lesson in real card playing. It would be fun to take the fools money as well as Colbert's, proving beyond a doubt that he was the better card player.

The thin man sat back, looking worried. "Little rich for my blood."

The bearded man looked at the thin man and then at Joseph. "I play for fun, so I'm out."

Whittaker glanced at the two, glad they had dropped out since they meant nothing to him. He wanted to take Joseph's money. "It's getting late, gentleman."

Fear gripped Joseph seeing his chance for revenge was slipping away.

Then Whittaker leaned on the table with his elbows. "I've time enough for one, maybe two more hands, so let's really make them interesting." He gestured to the money in front of Joseph and Bob. I see a nice pile in front of each of y'all worth perhaps a couple of thousand each, give or take."

Whittaker was doing just what Joseph had hoped he would, and he cautiously played with the edges of his money, giving the appearance of being unsure or afraid, something disastrous for gamblers.

Charles recognized Joseph's fear in playing for larger stakes, and his ego swelled while his face beamed with confidence. "Come now, gentlemen," he said, looking sure of himself. "It's only money, as they say."

Joseph looked at the other two men as they started to get up from the table. "No need to hurry off, gentlemen." He needed the satisfaction of witnesses to his breaking the arrogant son-of-a-bitch that sat across from him. He wanted that final embarrassment. "I dislike empty seats at a table."

The bearded man shrugged. "I've nothing better to do. I'd like to watch if it's all right with y'all."

The thin man grinned. "I'll stick around."

Joseph smiled. "The drinks are on me." Then he settled back in his chair and ordered drinks all around.

Whittaker looked unhappy about the arrangements. "I'm not too sure I like the idea of an audience."

Joseph grinned. "You suddenly become shy, Charles?" The smile left his face. "There's always someone watching."

Charles looked at Joseph, wondering what he meant. "All right, they can watch. Two hands of $1000.00 each?" Then he reached for the cards, but Joseph quickly put his hands on top of the deck, gesturing to Colbert with a nod. "It's Bob's deal."

Whittaker glared at Joseph then looked at Bob. "So it is. My apologies."

Bob picked up the cards. "Let's make the pot right, gentleman." Then he tossed $1,000.00 into the pot and began shuffling the cards.

Joseph watched as Charles Whittaker set a stack of bills amounting to $1,000.00 in the center of the table. Smiling at Charles, Joseph pushed a stack of bills in the same amount to the center of the table. By now, word of the game had spread across the floor, and the curious gathered around the corner of the room. This was unexpected, but it fit into Joseph's plan very nicely and irritated Whittaker, to his increasing pleasure.

Colbert placed the cards in front of Charles. He cut the deck, and then Bob dealt the cards.

Joseph settled back in his chair, watching as Whittaker methodically picked up each card, studying them as an artist would a canvas. He looked up, meeting Joseph's stare. Joseph smiled at him and then picked up his cards.

Charles discarded three cards onto the pile of money in the center of the table.

Joseph tossed two cards and then leaned forward, staring at Whitaker. "This reminds me of the last time we played Charles. Remember that night in Jefferson back in '64?"

Bob Colbert discarded two cards, and while he dealt new cards, he watched the two, fearing something was about to happen.

Charles looked at Joseph while mistakenly picking up Joseph's cards.

Joseph sat back, looking surprised at the mistake. "Easy, Charles, those were my cards you just picked up."

Whittaker glanced around, looking embarrassed as he turned them over. "My apologies."

The thin man sitting next to Joseph chuckled.

Charles gave him a nasty look, thinking he'd like to cut his throat.

Joseph looked down at his cards, seeing a Queen of Diamonds and an Ace of Hearts, both useless to him.

"Next time, wait your turn Charles," Bob said with a teasing grin, and then he dealt Joseph two replacement cards and Charles three cards.

Charles looked irritated, and his face flushed as he glanced around.

Joseph picked up the two new cards dealt to him, a King of Diamonds and a King of Hearts, and both fitting neatly with his three tens, giving him a full house. Unknown to Joseph, those two Kings would have given Whittaker four kings, the winning hand. But after his error, he was dealt the Four of Spades and two 6's to go along with his two kings, giving him two pairs.

Bob was first to lay down his hand, a pair of Jacks, two deuces, and a Five of no consequence. He grinned, looking at Joseph. "Beat that!"

Joseph placed his cards on the table, showing that he had a full house.

Whittaker stared at the hand, cursing himself for his own debacle, and wondering if Joseph had drawn the two kings that should be his.

Joseph smiled, thinking the odds were in his favor. "Charles?"

Whittaker scowled, tossed his cards onto the table, and sat back in his chair, glancing up at the faces standing around the table and feeling like a complete fool, which infuriated him. He wanted to protest the hand, but he knew it was useless as he watched Joseph pull the money toward himself. His damaged ego pushed aside common sense and good judgment, and he placed one hand on Joseph's forearm. "Let it ride. I'll match it."

Looking surprised, Joseph said, "The pot holds three thousand dollars, Charles." He looked at the money in front of Whittaker. "You don't have that much on the table."

"The bet was two hands for a thousand each, Charles," said Bob. "You want to change that?"

Whittaker sat back in his chair, figuring he could beat both men.

Joseph sat back, looking at the money in front of Whittaker. "That would be a hell of a hand, Charles."

Whittaker's face turned dark as he counted the money in front of him. "I have a thousand on the table and more in my pocket."

"What were the table stakes?" asked a man standing behind Colbert.

Whittaker shot the man a dirty look. "Keep out of this asshole; you're not in the game."

Silence descended for a moment but was quickly replaced by soft-spoken words uttered by the curious gathered around the table.

Bob Colbert sat in silence, waiting to see what Joseph was going to do.

Joseph casually placed the money he had won on top of the small pile in front of him, considering Whittaker's proposal. "All right, Charles," he said, "how much do you have in your pocket?"

"I've about twenty-two hundred on me."

Joseph looked at Colbert. "You all right with changing the bet?"

Bob settled back in his chair, counting his money while sensing Whittaker's impatience, and decided to let him stew a moment. "Too rich for my blood."

Joseph knew what Bob was doing, so he turned to Whittaker. "Alright, Charles, add $2,000.00 to the pot. You can keep the $200.00. He smiled. "I wouldn't want to break you."

That angered Whittaker even more as he reached into his coat pocket, pulled out a stack of bills, counted out the $2000.00 and threw it on the pile of money, and then tossed the other thousand on top of the pile.

"Pot's right with six thousand," said Bob Colbert. The night's drinking was catching up to Charles. He gave Bob a dirty look.

"We'll cut for the deal," said Charles as he reached for the cards, but Joseph put his hand on top of Whittaker's, knowing that he could deal a second card that was hard to catch even if you were expecting it.

Joseph looked from Charles to Bob Colbert. "I think we'd both feet better if Bob dealt," he suggested. Then he looked at Whittaker. "That all right with you, Charles?"

"Fine," replied Whittaker thinking that if Joseph won the deal, he might cheat. Then he looked at Bob. "Deal the damn cards and no funny stuff."

Joseph grinned. "You don't think Colbert would cheat, do you, Charles?"

Whittaker had never figured Bob for a cheat. "Just deal."

Colbert took his time shuffling, which played more on Whittaker's irritability.

"That's enough," Charles said. "Deal the damn cards."

Bob grinned. "Seems you're in a big hurry to lose your money."

The crowd laughed.

Whittaker smiled without humor, giving Colbert another dirty look.

It appeared to Joseph that the night's drinking was catching up to Charles

Bob grinned at him while he shuffled the cards again to agitate Whittaker further. He then placed the cards on the table for Joseph to cut.

Joseph looked at Whittaker. "Go ahead, Charles, you cut the deck."

Whittaker turned to a woman standing behind him. "Back off, bitch, I can feel your hot breath on my neck."

"Charles," said Bob. "You shouldn't talk to a woman like that."

She smiled at Bob as she stepped back.

Whittaker looked around at the crowd's faces complaining they were all too close, and the man he called an asshole earlier told everyone to step back and give them room.

Charles cut the cards, and then Bob dealt them. After they had time to look at their hands, Bob asked, "Cards?'

Joseph noticed Whittaker was hesitant and quickly took advantage by turning to Bob. "Did you ever hear the story of my getting robbed and stabbed in Jefferson back in '64?"

Bob leaned forward, looking interested. "No, I haven't."

Whittaker glanced at the faces standing around the table and then glared at Joseph. "No one's interested in your stories, Joseph."

Looking sincere, Colbert looked at Joseph. "I am. What happened?"

Joseph smiled as he tossed one card into the middle of the table, then neatly placed the four cards on the table in front of him. "Well, it was a good night for me at a place called The Crimson Lady." He nodded at Whittaker. "Charles here, three other gentlemen, and I played until after one in the morning." He looked at Whittaker. "Charles lost a lot of money that night, didn't you, Charles."

"We gonna play cards or bullshit all night?" asked Whittaker.

"Hold on, Charles," Bob said. "I want to hear this. Besides, you haven't discarded yet."

Joseph studied Charles a moment, then looked at Bob. "It was a good night for me. I was ahead by at least two thousand." He gestured with one hand. "But I was tired, and I'd had a few too many drinks." He glanced at Charles. "I said goodnight to Charles and the others and then headed back to the hotel I was staying at." He paused to sip his beer, looking at Whittaker over the rim of his mug. As he put the mug on the table, he wiped his mouth and said, "Guess I was feeling pretty good about the money, knowing my wife and children could use it."

Whittaker looked up from his cards.

Joseph grinned. "Make up your mind yet, Charles?"

"I'll let you know when I do."

Joseph turned to Colbert. "Never saw it coming, Bob, never heard anything either. No footsteps or a sudden shadow to warn me." Joseph paused, moving his head, imitating being struck. "Someone hit me over the head, knocking me to the ground. I was a little dazed when I saw the knife in the moonlight. I tried to block it but got cut right here."

He gestured to the scar next to his ear. "Then a second cut here," he said, touching the scar on his neck. "Then, I felt the blade go deep into my chest." He shook his head. "Thought I was a goner for sure when I was stabbed a second time." Joseph looked at Whittaker. "Old Doc Bradley told me both wounds narrowly missed my heart and a lung."

Bob frowned, shaking his head slowly. "Sounds like you were pretty lucky."

Voices in the crowd mumbled agreement.

Joseph nodded. "The man was probably in too much of a hurry to finish me off."

Still unsure, Whittaker was slowly pulling two cards from his hand while listening to Joseph talk.

Joseph leaned forward and looked him in the eyes. "I'll never forget his face as he plunged that knife into my chest, not once, but twice."

Charles stared at Joseph, knowing he knew it was he who had robbed him that night. His stomach became taut, his heart raced, tiny beads of sweat appeared on his forehead, and his hands began to tremble. He pulled two cards from his hand, accidentally dropping a third card which landed face up, a card he hadn't meant to discard, and reached for it.

Bob quickly placed his hand on the card. "The card's dead, Charles."

Whittaker's expression filled with anger, his eyes cold and mean. "Bullshit!"

Bob sat back in his chair, looked around at the people watching, and then gestured with open hands. "Am I right?"

"You're right, Mister," said a rather large man standing behind Whittaker. "Once the card lands on the table, it's dead, and that's that. House rules."

Whittaker turned, seeing the same man that he had called an asshole earlier. "I thought I told you to shut up."

The big man stepped a little closer, his eyes narrowed. "I shut up before because I thought I might have spoken out of turn, but this is different. And since this is my place, I say we play by the house rules. The card's dead." Then he gave Charles a mean look. "It's that simple."

Sounds of agreement flowed from the crowd as Whittaker settled back in his chair, glancing up at the other faces and then at the card resting on the table.

"Guess ya want three cards now, Charles," smiled Joseph as Bob dealt him three new cards, and one to himself.

Whittaker knew his own clumsiness had caused him to drop two aces, leaving him a ten and one ace. He picked up the replacement cards, finding a ten and another ace, two pair instead of a full house, and cursed his bad luck, but knew this hand could also be the winner. He smiled as he glanced at Joseph, wishing he'd had time to cut his throat that night in Jefferson.

Bob looked across the table. "It's up to you, Charles."

Whittaker looked down at the Ace lying on top of the pile of money he had so clumsily dropped, then laid down his cards. "Two pair," he said. "Aces and tens."

The crowd softly mumbled a string of inaudible words as Joseph placed his cards on the table showing three threes. Bob couldn't believe Joseph had won. He sat back, listening to the laughter and sighs of the crowd and feeling proud of his friend.

The owner of the bar patted Joseph on the back. "One hell of a card game, Mister." Then he turned to the crowd and yelled, "One drink on the house, and I mean one!"

Whittaker stared at the cards knowing he had lost most of his inheritance instead of tripling it as planned. He glared at Joseph for several moments, picked up his hat, the few dollars left in front of him, and then stood and disappeared into the crowd. Joseph settled back in his chair, looking relieved as he smiled across the table at Bob, who was grinning in disbelief. The owner of the bar set a bottle and two glasses on the table. "This is on me, gentleman." He patted Joseph on the back and then disappeared into the crowd.

Joseph poured two drinks, handed one to Bob, and pulled the pile of money toward him. "Strange," he said as people walked away from the table. "Revenge isn't near as sweet as I thought it would be."

Colbert nodded. "Most times, it isn't."

Joseph looked into the brandy in his glass. "Funny the way things turn out. No matter what the reasons, there's something unpleasant about breaking a man."

Bob leaned forward, resting his arms on the table. "He got what he deserved."

Joseph sipped his drink, looking skeptical. "I wonder."

Bob nodded as he smiled. "That's called conscience, Joseph; something our friend never had."

"Maybe." Joseph smiled softly and counted the money into two stacks, putting one in each of his inside pockets, gulped the last of his drink, and stood. "Let's get out of here."

They walked through the swinging doors and paused on the boardwalk, looking into the dim streets and dark recesses of doorways and alleyways, wondering where Charles Whittaker had gone. Joseph suggested they go separate ways and meet at Bob's place to make sure no one followed them. Joseph hailed a carriage and rode around for several minutes before arriving at Colbert's house, finding him waiting on the front porch. "Want to come inside?"

Joseph declined while handing him half the pot. "Here's what you lost and half of what we took from Whittaker."

Bob objected. "I don't want half of what we took from Whittaker. That money belongs to you. I'll take what I bet."

"Don't be ridiculous," said Joseph. "We went into this thing together, and you're taking half." Joseph smiled, then patted him on the shoulder. "Buy Grace a pretty dress and that baby a horse or something."

Colbert smiled and reluctantly took the money, then looked around into the darkness. "I wonder where Charles is."

Joseph glanced around. "Don't know, but I wouldn't be surprised if we saw him again real soon." He extended his hand. "Goodnight, Bob, and thanks."

Bob thought about their evening, recalling stories of Whittaker as he shook Joseph's hand and went inside.

Joseph climbed into the carriage and sat back, knowing Mary would be worried. After the carriage turned the corner, Charles Whittaker stepped from the shadows, knowing that Bob Colbert and Joseph had played him like an amateur.

Thirty-Four

August 24, 1873

Joseph spent most of the afternoon alone in the library with the memory of Charles Whittaker and the previous night's card game. The pleasure he wanted or expected to feel at breaking the man he hated wasn't what he thought it would be. Mixed with the revenge Joseph so badly wanted was the unexpected feeling of pity for the man, which angered him. Then trying to turn the subject away from Charles Whittaker, he picked up the newspaper and read the headlines: Phantom Sickness. The newspaper reported that few officials and doctors could not agree on what the sickness was. The victims falling prey to the mysterious sickness continued to increase, while the authorities and medical profession were unable to suggest a means of protection against it. Joseph folded the paper, placed it on the table, and stared at it, thinking of Mary and the children. He had to convince Mary to take the children and leave the city for a few days, or maybe even weeks.

Mary walked into the library, stood beside his chair, and kissed the top of his head as she looked at the folded newspaper on the table. "All this sickness is a little unnerving."

He looked up at her as he gestured to the sofa. "We have to talk."

Knowing what was coming, she sat down and folded her hands on her lap.

He looked worried. "This sickness with the fever keeps getting worse. More people are dying, and no one seems to know what to do about it. It would be a good idea if you and the children were to leave Shreveport for a while."

"We've already had this discussion, and you know I'll not leave you." She glanced at the newspaper. "I'll not run away and leave you here with that Whittaker fellow lurking around."

"How do you know he's lurking?" asked Joseph, thinking she was being foolish. "He's probably on his way to New Orleans by now."

She looked at him with skepticism. "You and I both know that's not true." Then she sat up with a firm look. "I'll not leave you here alone."

Joseph chuckled. "And what if he finds me? What will you do?"

She shrugged, looking embarrassed. "I don't know, but I'd be here for you."

"And what good would that be if he walked through that door and shot me?"

She stood, looking angry. "Don't belittle my fears, Joseph."

He stood, took her by the arm, sat her on the sofa, and sat beside her. "I wasn't trying to belittle you, Mary, but my point is that staying here changes nothing about your safety. I'm asking you to take the children and leave." He gestured with one hand at the house. "Get them away from this sickness before it's too late."

Mary considered his wish again and remembered the days and nights of loneliness without him during the war. "We have spent too much of our lives apart, so please don't ask me to return to that loneliness."

Silence filled the room as he decided to appeal to her motherhood. "What about the children?"

She looked at the library door leading to the stairway and the children's rooms upstairs. "Maybe you're right," she said softly.

He sighed. "Thank you."

"I'll take them into Texas on tomorrow's boat. I can have a short visit with Janice and Lori Hall, and then I'll return here until this thing passes."

Joseph frowned while considering her proposal and gave in. "All right, Mary, I'll compromise that much with you, but I wish you'd stay with them."

She smiled tenderly and put her hand on the side of his face. "I'll not leave you, Joseph. If you want us to stay in Texas, you'll have to come with us."

He considered that. "You know I can't."

"That's your decision." Then she kissed his cheek and stood. "I'll go pack."

As she left the room, he settled back on the sofa, closed his eyes, and thought of Charles Whittaker.

Joseph opened his eyes to Mary shaking him and sat up, looking confused. "I must have dozed off. What time is it?"

"After nine. The children are waiting for you to tell them goodnight. You've slept quite a while."

"I must have been tired," he said as he stood. "Too late for a story, I suppose."

"It will have to be a quick one. We have to get up early if we plan to catch the early boat for Jefferson."

He smiled. "Once you've made up your mind, ya don't waste much time, do you?"

She laughed softly. "Now, you're complaining because I'm doing what you asked?"

"Actually, I'm quite relieved. But we don't know what time the boat sails in the morning."

"As a matter of fact, I do. I picked up a schedule when I was in town the other day."

He smiled at her. "You were planning this all along?"

"I had hoped by my refusing to leave, you would take us, but I realized that would never happen."

"You'll stay with them?" he asked, looking hopeful.

She shook her head. "Nothing has changed. If you want me to stay with the Halls, you will have to come with us."

"You're right, Mary. Nothing has changed. I can't leave."

"Then I won't stay in Texas," she said matter-of-factly. "Go up and read a quick story to your children. I have to finish packing."

Mary had changed into her nightgown and robe and was sitting on the window seat, an open book on her lap, staring out the window when Joseph entered the bedroom. She turned from the window and the darkness outside as he closed the door and crossed the room. "I dread going without you."

"I know. I hate being here by myself." He looked around the room, knowing the house would be empty without her. "The house creaks and moans without the sounds of you and the children. It's as if it were calling for you."

That pleased her, and she smiled.

"I hate sending you away like this." He looked worried. "But it's for the best. I don't know what I'd do if anything were to happen to you and the children."

"I know. And I have worried about you for countless nights over countless years, and that's why I won't stay in Texas without you."

He thought about that. "Are the boys excited about going?"

Mary laughed softly. "Heavens, yes, they're already fighting about the trip."

Joseph grinned, imagining them fighting, and then his smile faded. "I wish you would stay in Texas."

She smiled at him. "I'll return in a few days."

Giving up, he looked at the book on her lap. "Are you going to read that book all night?"

She smiled shyly. "It's not a very good book."

"Then why read it?"

"Something to occupy my time while I waited." She looked at the book. "I thought it would keep my mind off why I'm leaving tomorrow."

He helped her up from the window seat, took her in his arms, and as he kissed her, his hand separated her silk robe, finding the soft material of her nightgown.

August 25, 1873

The afternoon of August 25, 1873, was a gray, cloudy day with the threat of rain and wind. Joseph, Mary, and the children stood on the pier next to a sternwheeler's gangplank, waiting to say goodbye. He glanced at the other families leaving Shreveport for the safety of east Texas, thinking there was always something for people to run from. Thinking of those who remained, Joseph knew some would die from whatever it was that was hunting them. Pushing that from his thoughts, he turned to Mary and watched as she adjusted little Joseph's jacket.

She looked up, their eyes met in silence, and each knew what the other was thinking as they smiled in a failed attempt to hide their fear. Feeling the tears welling in her eyes, she busied herself with the other children. The boat whistle blew. Filled with words she could not speak, she looked into Joseph's eyes and touched his cheek. Fighting her tears, she moved her fingers along his face to the edge of his mouth and touched his mustache. "We'll be all right," she said in a choked voice. "No need to worry."

But worry did hold him, and she saw it in his face. Fear crowded his emotions, and he wanted her to go but yet to stay. "I know," he said, forcing a smile. "But, I wouldn't worry as much if you'd stay with the Halls."

"But I would worry about you." She shook her head stubbornly. "I'll not leave you alone." She touched his cheek and smiled softly. "Don't forget, I'll return on the evening of the 29th."

Joseph grinned and whispered, "Never."

She smiled.

The boat whistle blew again; a woman screamed, bringing laughter from the crowd. Steam spewed from the tall stacks, and people began mulling toward the gangplank. Joseph picked up their bags and walked up the gangplank with Mary and the children close behind. He handed the bags to a porter and turned to her. "This man will help you to your room." He looked into her red, welling eyes. "Be careful."

She couldn't fight the tears any longer and began to cry. "We will."

Joseph knelt to one knee, looking into the faces of his four children, and then gathering them in his arms, gave them a group hug, and kissed each cheek. "I want all of you to mind your mother and be good while you're at the Halls."

"Yes, sir," said each child. Joseph fussed with Zach's coat. "Son, you're the oldest, and I expect you to help keep your brothers in line."

"I will, Pa."

He looked into Mary's red eyes. "I love you."

She forced a smile but couldn't keep from crying and wiping the tears, looking embarrassed. "I'll be back in four days."

Joseph looked back at the pier, seeing that the big heavy ropes that held the boat secure to the pier untied, falling into the water. "I better go." He kissed Mary, turned, and hurried down the gangplank to the pier. Fighting the urge to run across the pier, jump back onto the boat, and go with them, he turned and walked along the pier for several feet, following the boat as it drifted away from the pier, looking at Mary. She blew him a kiss that he pretended to catch as he had done so many times before, holding it tightly as he watched the boat until it disappeared around the river's bend. Staring at the emptiness of the river for several minutes, he almost wished he had gone with them. Then he turned and walked along the pier to the waiting buggy.

Mary watched the pier fade into the distance, and then, gripped by a sudden chill, she wrapped her arms around herself and followed the porter and their luggage to their quarters. The children fought over sleeping arrangements while she walked to the round portal and looked out at the river bank, worried for her husband.

Joseph pulled at his collar as he climbed into the buggy, and then as he paused, he looked toward town and the plumes of smoke rising in the distance. He knew they were fires of desperate men fighting to kill the invisible death that stalked Shreveport. The fires gave the dark, gray sky an eerie, pink glow as he pulled the whip from its holder, gently tapped the horse on its back, and guided her through the crowded streets of men with their faces filled with fear. Minutes later, he guided the buggy through the iron gates and up the driveway toward the house that looked cold, empty, and menacing in the dark gray afternoon. He drove into the dimly lit stable, stepped down from the buggy, and lit a lantern, filling the stable with a dim yellow-orange glow. The other horses snorted nervously and then settled down at recognizing his calming voice and familiar smell. He unhitched the horse from the buggy, led her into a stall, took off the bit and bridle, and patted her gently on the neck. He made sure each animal had oats, hay, and water before walking into the dim, gray day toward the house.

Opening the back door, he stepped into a small room of coats and shoes, locked the door, and walked through the kitchen. Shadows of images created by the lantern he carried jumped around the room, and followed him across the kitchen to the dining room and into the library. The sound of far-off thunder promised an August rain, perhaps even a hail storm. He paused at a window, moved the curtain with one hand, half expecting to see rain, but found none. The world seemed darker as if night had come early as the storm slowly approached, and he hoped the storm would miss the boat with Mary and the children. Turning from the window, he found a second lamp, and touched a match to the wick, whose light chased away the shadows of the single lamp. He collapsed in the chair, glanced around the room at nothing in particular, feeling the chill of emptiness and solitude. Mattie had the day off, and he wished she were there banging pots and pans in the kitchen, giving some sign of life, or standing in the doorway asking if he was hungry. He was, but he didn't feel like cooking, so he built a fire in the fireplace, poured a drink, and settled on the sofa watching the flames consume the wood, thinking of Mary and the children. The hypnotic flames of the fire made his eyes grow heavy, so he set his glass down, laid his head back, and closed his eyes.

The sound of the clock tolling eight p.m. woke Joseph from a sound sleep, finding that the fire had died, leaving a chill in the room, and one of the lamps had gone out, its glass belly empty of fuel. The other flickered a warning that its life was also ending, so he stood, picked up the dying lamp, and walked up the stairs. Pausing a moment at the top of the stairs to glance at the closed doors of the children's empty rooms, and imagining their laughter, he entered his bedroom with the dying lamp, leaving the hall and the rest of the house to its quiet, emptiness, and darkness. Setting the lamp down, he undressed, climbed between the cold chill of the sheets, turned and looked at Mary's pillow, and thought of her warm body and their last night together. After turning down the lamp, he laid his head on her pillow and stared out the window at the fires along the river, leaving their red, orange glow on the low, gray clouds. As sleep filled his eyes, he closed them as his mind raced toward east Texas, to Mary and the children.

August 26, 1873

Joseph opened his eyes from a restless night and looked out the bedroom window at the red glow of burning homes and shacks mixing with the sunrise's pink and purple glow. As he watched the black smoke drifting skyward, he wondered about the people whose houses were burning south of town. Joseph looked at the empty pillow where Mary's head should be and cursed himself for not going with her. Tossing the covers back, he stood from the bed, feeling the cold floor against his feet, and walked across the hall to the bathroom. Pouring a little water into the soap dish, he made a cold lather with a small bristled brush and looked into the older yet familiar face in the mirror as he applied the lather to his face.

Shaved, he dressed and walked downstairs, surprised and happy at finding Mattie fixing his breakfast. "Why aren't you at home with your family?"

"My oldest gal can manage jes' fine, Mistah Joseph. I thinks ya needs me here whilst Miss Mary's gone." She gestured toward the table. "Now sits down an eats yer breakfast, and after I cleans up, I'll be on my way, if dat be alright wit you."

He smiled. "That'd be fine, Mattie. I appreciate you coming over." He sat down at the table and picked up the morning paper to read while eating a delicious breakfast. The news in the paper gave little hope for the end of the fever and death. The public figures were trying desperately to control its spread before it became an epidemic, which Joseph feared was close at hand. The mayor and other city officials feared it spreading from the outskirts of Shreveport to the inner city.

His breakfast finished, Joseph thanked Mattie, put on his coat, and walked out the front door, picturing the captain standing on the bridge, anxious to leave while scouring the docks for him.

From deep inside The Helen's bowels, the boiler fire roared, spewing her black smoke up the tall, black stacks into the sky. Watching as the black smoke drifted lazily toward the blue sky, Joseph knew she was getting ready to leave, and the captain wasn't going to wait for him. Seeing the gangplank was already up, he ran across the dock, jumping onto The Helen's deck as the lines that held her to the pier set her free to drift into the current. The big, red, wooden paddlewheel at her stern slowly turned, straining to push the boat into the Red River's deeper waters and guide her to her journey south to Alexandria, Louisiana.

Joseph scrambled up the steps to the bridge, expecting choice words from Captain Goodman, but instead found a friendly grin.

"Thought we might have to leave without ya, Laddie."

"Sorry, Captain. Got a late start."

Goodman puffed his pipe. "Well, I'm glad ya made it."

Joseph walked to one of the windows and stared into the distance, thinking of Mary and the children and wishing again that he had gone with them.

Seeing the troubled look on Joseph's face, the captain took the pipe from his mouth and asked, "Everything all right, Laddie?"

Joseph turned to the captain. "Mary and the children left for Texas yesterday until this thing that is making people sick goes away."

Goodman got up from his chair, puffing on his pipe as he crossed the bridge, and patted him on the back. "It's best they left, Laddie. The word is we may be dealing with the likes of the yellow fever."

Joseph looked surprised. "Yellow fever? Are you sure?"

"Well," replied Goodman looking secretive. "I can't swear to it, but I ran into Doc Williams this morning, and that's what he thinks we're dealing with." He shook his head, looking worried. "If it is, we could be looking at an epidemic." He patted Joseph on the back again. "Mary and the boys going off to Texas for a while was the smart thing to do, Laddie."

Joseph looked worried. "Mary's coming back on the 29th."

Goodman looked surprised. "Why in God's good name would you let her do a damn fool thing like that?"

"She said she wouldn't stay in Texas without me."

"Damn it, boy," said Goodman with a worried look. "Maybe you should've gone with them."

Joseph frowned. "I've had that argument with myself all morning."

"When did ya say she's returning?"

Joseph watched several men walk along the far bank, having just emerged with torches from a shack that now burned. "The evening of the twenty-ninth, aboard a boat named The Cypress."

Captain Goodman turned to watch the shack burning. "I'll get you back in time Laddie. The trip to Alexandria and back won't take but a couple of days."

"If you're right about this sickness," Joseph said thoughtfully. "Maybe I should take Mary and get the hell out of Shreveport for a while."

The captain nodded. "Not a bad idea Son. I'm afraid this is gonna get a hell of a lot worse before it gets any better." Tired of talking about the invisible death, Goodman changed the subject. "I heard about that card game between you and that Charles Whittaker fella."

Joseph looked at him with a curious face.

"One of the crew was there."

Joseph turned to the window, looking sullen. "Well, that business is over and done with now."

Captain Goodman turned to the man at the helm cautioning, "Sand bar up ahead."

The man nodded. "Aye, Captain." Then he turned the wheel ever so slightly, maneuvering The Helen around it.

Goodman nodded his approval at the maneuver and then gestured outside, telling Joseph he wanted to talk. After the two walked out of the bridge into the bright sunshine, Goodman leaned on the railing to watch Jonah as he walked across the deck below, busy at some task. "I don't want to sound like I'm preaching," Goodman said. "I ain't your pa, but I'd like to give you a piece of advice."

"Always welcome advice, Captain, as long as it doesn't end up an ass chewing."

Goodman smiled at that as he gathered his thoughts while stuffing tobacco into his pipe. "There were stories about Whittaker up and down the Tennessee River during the war. None of `em good." Goodman put a match to the bowl of his pipe and puffed, creating billows of smoke around his head while watching Jonah on the deck below. "Whittaker's a dangerous man."

In the brief silence of the moment, while the big, red paddlewheel thrashing through the water pushed The Helen downstream, Joseph remembered that night in Jefferson.

Goodman glanced at the side of Joseph's face knowing he needed no further warnings about Whittaker, and then he gestured toward the river. "There's talk about isolating Shreveport, so this may be our last trip for a while. You won't miss much if you return to east Texas with your Mary for a spell."

Joseph looked worried. "I only hope to hell we can get out before they shut us off from the rest of the country."

August 28, 1873

The Red River reflected the fires of burning shacks and other Shreveport buildings as The Helen silently slipped through the dark waters, heading for the pier to tie up for the night. The glow of pinks, reds, and oranges colored the low, gray clouds as the crew stood on the deck. They could hear loud shouting and screams of women filled with fear from the city, mixed with the sounds of buildings collapsing into explosions of sparks and smoke.

Captain Goodman ordered the engines to stop and stuck his head out one of the bridge's windows as the boat drifted toward the piers of Shreveport. A gentle bump announced her arrival against the pier while men quickly jumped from the boat onto the dock to secure the boat. Joseph was on the bridge, looking at the red glow hanging above the city.

Goodman was beside him as they stared at the glow. "Looks to me like we're close to a panicking situation, and when that happens, things get ugly real quick." Looking down the pier, he saw a dozen or so men walking along the pier toward the boat. He put his hand on the handle of the pistol he had tucked away in his belt and shouted. "Who goes there?"

Joseph reached above his head to a small cabinet. Taking out another pistol, he followed the captain to the railing.

It was too dark to see who they were, so Goodman yelled, "If I were y'all, I'd stay on the pier, boys!"

One of the men stopped, and then he gestured for the others to stop, as he then stepped forward, cupping both hands around his mouth. "Is that you, Captain Goodman?"

"It is. Who's asking?"

"Sheriff Parker," replied the man standing on the edge of the pier. "Sorry if we alarmed you, Captain. We were hoping y'all were bringing some medical help from downstream, and if'n ya are, we're here to escort them to the hospital."

Goodman glanced at Joseph, then yelled, "Sorry, Sheriff, but no one would get near us to take off our cargo downstream. But there's a boat coming with doctors and nurses, even some priests. They're a couple of hours behind us."

"Thanks," yelled Sheriff Parker. "It might be best if you and your crew stayed aboard for the night."

Goodman waved. "We plan on doing just that, Sheriff."

The sheriff waved back then led the men back along the pier toward town. Then Captain Goodman hollered at Jonah to get everyone back on board and haul up the gangplank as soon as the lines were secure. He turned to Joseph, looking worried. "Got a bad feeling about all this," Goodman turned to another of his men. "Grab three rifles out of the locker and post three guards with orders not to let anyone on board."

"Aye, Captain," replied the man. Then he turned and walked out of the bridge to get the rifles from below deck.

Goodman turned to the fires of Shreveport. "This reminds me of the towns along the Tennessee River during the war."

Joseph nodded. "If we ain't killing one another, something else is. You ever think that maybe God's a little pissed off?"

Goodman puffed his pipe thoughtfully. "I wouldn't blame Him any, but I'm sure that if He were pissed off, things would be a hell of a lot worse than this."

Joseph chuckled at that, and then he noticed several of the crew jumping onto the pier. "Some of the men are leaving, Captain."

Goodman turned to watch the men. "Those that have families here, I expect. Those that don't will stay on board for the night." He shrugged. "We ain't going anywhere anyway." He looked at Joseph, fearing he was thinking about leaving. "It might be better if you stayed on board tonight."

Joseph considered that a moment. "I think I'll head for home, Captain."

Goodman put his hand on Joseph's shoulder saying, "I can't force ya to stay, Laddie, but it's gonna be a little lonely without Mary and the kids." He smiled affectionately. "An old man like me could use the company."

"Appreciate that, Captain," said Joseph with a regretful look. "But I need to get home and pack a few things if I plan on getting out of town when Mary gets back."

Goodman nodded. "Well, I'm glad you've come to your senses. Want Jonah to go along?"

Joseph considered that. "Won't be necessary, Captain. I'll pack and make sure the place is locked up. I need to leave a note for Mattie and stop by Bob's place to check on him and Grace, and then ask if he would check on the place and the horses until we get back."

"Be careful, Laddie," said Goodman looking concerned. "Things like this bring out the worst in people." He pointed to the pistol Joseph still held in his right hand. "Take that with ya."

Joseph looked down at the gun and grinned. "Thanks, but I won't need this. Things haven't gotten that bad yet."

"That may be," said Goodman. "But I'd feel better if ya took it with ya anyway."

"I'll be all right." He handed the pistol to the captain.

"Suit yerself," said Goodman looking disappointed as he took back the pistol. "You usually do."

Joseph grinned as he patted him on the shoulder. "I best get going."

Goodman watched him walk down the steps to the main deck, past Jonah, who was sitting on a bale of cotton, talking with two other Negroes and watching the fires in the distance. Joseph said goodnight to them and then jokingly told Jonah to keep the old man out of trouble.

Jonah grinned. "Yes, suh Mistah Joseph, I'll take's good care o' da cap'n."

Joseph jumped onto some crates on the pier, climbed down, and walked along the pier toward town. Goodman sat back in his chair, put his feet up, and watched the fires, thinking of the war.

As Jonah and the men watched the fires in the distance, he turned to watch Joseph walking toward the streets of Shreveport in the dim light of the pier. Seeing a figure step from the shadows, Jonah got a bad feeling, sat up, and watched as Joseph stopped and turned. Suddenly the figure lunged at Joseph, and the two struggled. Jonah stood. "Someone's aftah Mistah Joseph, Cap'n." Then he jumped from the boat onto the crates, climbed down, and began running toward Joseph and the other figure, calling out, "Gits aways from Mistah Joseph!"

Hearing Jonah, Goodman hurried out of the bridge, down the stairs to the first deck, and toward the pier, yelling to the other Negroes to get the gangplank down.

Charles Whittaker's blade cut deep into Joseph's chest below the breastbone, piercing his heart.

Joseph gasped for breath as he fell back against a crate, trying to block the second thrust of the knife. As it penetrated between his ribs, puncturing his lung, he managed to grasp Whittaker's forearms. As they struggled, Joseph collapsed to his knees.

Jonah ran along the pier as fast as he could, yelling, "Leaves Mistah Joseph alone!"

Whittaker looked at the big figure running toward them, stepped back, and looked down at Joseph sitting on his knees, leaning back against a crate, his hands trying to stop the blood.

Jonah yelled again, "Gits away from Mistah Joseph!"

Whittaker glanced at the big figure and then stepped forward, grasping Joseph by the hair to cut his throat.

Joseph punched Whittaker in the groin with the last of his strength, causing him to drop the knife, grab his groin, and limp away, disappearing into the darkness.

Jonah yelled as he ran toward Joseph. "Mistah Joseph, Mistah Joseph!" Kneeling next to Joseph, Jonah saw the blood on his shirt and jacket and knew he was badly hurt.

Joseph reached for Jonah with bloody hands and whispered, "Jonah."

The big man took him in his arms, turned, and yelled for the captain. "Cap'n, Cap'n, comes quick!"

Too old to jump from the ship, Goodman had to wait for the gangplank while cursing his old age.

Jonah sat down with his arms around Joseph. "I's sorry, Mistah Joseph, I's sorry, I's sorry I jus ain't fast nuff no mo, Mistah Joseph."

Tears ran down the old Negro's cheeks, falling onto Joseph's face. He started to lift Joseph in his arms to take him back to the boat. "I'll gets ya backs to da boat Mistah Joseph."

Joseph moaned in pain. "It hurts too much, Jonah. Put me down. Please, Jonah, just put me down."

Jonah gently put him down, leaned against a bale of cotton, and held him in his arms while he looked at Joseph's blood-soaked clothes, and then at the blood coming from the corners of his mouth. He knew his friend was hurt very badly.

Joseph smiled as he looked into the old Negro's welling eyes and whispered, "Don't cry, Jonah." Sounding weak, he smiled. "Don't be sorry." He coughed up blood and looked up at him. "It wasn't your fault."

Jonah wiped at his tears. "Da cap'n, he's com'n Mistah Joseph."

Joseph grabbed Jonah's arm tightly as he stiffened with pain and coughed up more blood. "Don't leave me, Jonah," he said, looking afraid. "Don't leave me alone." Joseph's eyes were red and welling as he coughed, spitting blood onto Jonah's old, gray shirt. "Ah Jesus, Jonah," he said, gasping for breath. "I'm dying, don't leave me."

Jonah's eyes filled with tears that left little lines on his cheeks. "Yah ain't dying, Mistah Joseph." He held Joseph tighter in his arms. "Don'ts worry none, I won't leaves ya."

Joseph stiffened, gripped Jonah's arm, and let out a painful moan.

Jonah turned back toward the boat as Captain Goodman and two other men ran down the pier toward them. "I'll gets ya back, Mistah Joseph." He started to lift him up.

Joseph pushed at his arms. "I can't make it, Jonah."

"Yah ain't gonna die, Mistah Joseph, ya gonna be okay."

Joseph began to shiver. "It's cold, so cold." Then he closed his eyes.

Jonah looked at Joseph's face in the dim light of the pier and gently shook him. "Mistah, Joseph. Wakes up, Mistah Joseph, please, wakes up."

Joseph opened his eyes, looking sleepy, and whispered something Jonah couldn't quite make out, so he leaned closer. "What's dat? What's ya say'n Mistah Joseph?" Jonah could feel Joseph's warm breath against his ear as he gasped, fighting for enough breath to whisper a few words Jonah could barely hear.

Captain Goodman knelt beside Jonah, looked down at Joseph, put a soft hand on his shoulder, gently shook him, and whispered, "Laddie." Goodman stared into his eyes for several moments while

Jonah cried, and then he put one hand on his shoulder. "He's gone, Jonah."

Jonah sobbed as he held Joseph in his big arms swaying back and forth as a father would hold a child.

Goodman reached out with one hand and closed Joseph's eyes, then sat down on the pier and looked at the man he had treated as his son while tears made their way down his cheeks. Several minutes passed before he had the strength to stand, and then with the help of the other two men, he and Jonah carried Joseph back to The Helen. After placing Joseph's bloody body on the captain's bed, Goodman told the two men they could leave. He covered Joseph with a blanket, and for the next several minutes, he and Jonah sat in silence, each lost in their memories of Joseph Greene.

After a few minutes, the captain broke the silence in a quivering voice. "I couldn't get off the boat. The damn gangplank wasn't down." He looked at Jonah with red, tearing eyes. "I should've been there."

"I knows Cap'n, me too, but I's too old to run fast anymore."

Goodman stared at Joseph's covered body. "Tell me what you saw, Jonah."

Jonah told the captain how he had been watching the fires in the city and when he glanced at Joseph walking along the pier, he saw a man step from the dark, and he and Joseph began to struggle. "I yells at `em, Cap'n. I yells for him to gets away from Mistah Joseph." Jonah paused while wiping the tears from his eyes and cheeks, and then he looked at the captain. "I try real hard Cap'n, I runs as fast as dese old legs can, but I's too late. Dat other man, he jes' up and run away."

Captain Goodman looked at Jonah, seeing his old, gray shirt covered with Joseph's blood. He stood and patted Jonah gently on the shoulder. "Yah did your best Jonah, that's all anyone can do." He let out a big sigh as he walked to his desk to get a bottle of Scotch and looked across the room at Joseph's covered body. The room was quiet except for the drawer opening, followed by the sound of bottle against glass as scotch poured from the bottle. "Care for a drink Jonah?"

Jonah shook his head answering, "No, suh Cap'n." Then he wiped his face with his shirt sleeve. "I can't b'leves' Mistah Joseph is gone, Cap'n."

Goodman took a drink of Scotch. "Did he say anything?"

"Yes, suh." Jonah looked puzzled. "But it make no sense at all, Cap'n."

Goodman took another drink and waited.

"He spoke a bunch o' words, but ah's only make outs a few of `em." Jonah looked up at Goodman with watery eyes. "Ah thinks maybe he's out o' his head."

The captain took a drink and patiently waited, knowing the old Negro was having a difficult time.

Jonah shook his head, recalling, "Fust he say may, ya knows, like da month an den some wurds I couldn't rightly unerstan'."

"What were the words, Jonah?"

Jonah thought as he relived the moment. "Well, dey was sump'n dat make no sense a'tall, he say someth'n' bout a tear. Mistah Joseph were coughing real bad, an had a hard time talk'n."

"A tear?" Goodman asked, looking confused.

Jonah shook his head, "Yes, suh Cap'n, a tear."

Goodman considered that as he took a sip of his drink. "Jonah, what exactly was it he said?"

Jonah frowned, trying to remember. "Well, Cap'n, I b'lieves it was two words sound a bit like water and tear."

"Water and tear?" repeated the captain looking confused.

"Dat's right, Cap'n, I b'lieves, he say water and tear." Jonah thought for a minute. "He wur cough'n up blood and chok'n. He were go'n quick Cap'n, and ah's barely hurds `em, an only made outs dem words. He says someth'n I nevuh unerstan den, 'may' an den 'water and tear."

The captain finished his drink. "He said Mary, Jonah. Not May."

Jonah looked puzzled. "Yes, suh Cap'n, dat cud be what he was say'n alrights."

"He was thinking of Mary. She'll be getting into Shreveport tomorrow night." Then he stood and looked at the covered body of Joseph. "Whittaker is what he was saying, Jonah. He told you who killed him."

"Who?" asked Jonah, looking puzzled.

"He's a gambler. Did ya get a look at the man who ran away?"

Jonah stared at the floor for a moment, then looked up. "Yes, suh, buts not goods, Cap'n, it were dark, and he was a ways away."

Goodman looked at Joseph's covered body. "I know damn well it was Whittaker getting even with Joseph over that damn card game." He walked to the bed and put one hand on Joseph's covered body. "You wouldn't let things go, would ya, Laddie?" He turned to Jonah. "We'll need a plank or something so's we can carry Joseph to Doc Williams."

"Yes, suh." Jonah stood, left the room, and returned a few minutes later with a plank. They lifted Joseph onto it, and then the captain turned to his desk and took out a small pistol from the top drawer. “Just in case.”

There were several men at Doc Williams's office when they carried Joseph through the door. “Who ya got there, Captain?” asked Doc Williams, looking curious.

Goodman looked sad. “Joseph Greene.”

Another man stepped forward. “Who?”

Captain Goodman looked at the man. “A friend of mine, and who might you be?”

The man looked at him. “Sorry, the name’s Bradley, Doctor Bradley.” He gestured to Doc Williams. “Doc here asked me to come over from Jefferson.”

“Sorry, Doc,” replied the captain. “His name is Joseph Greene.”

Doc Bradley considered the name. “Name’s familiar.” Then he lifted the blanket and looked at Joseph. “Why I know this man. He used to live in Jefferson.” He looked at Goodman. “What happened?”

Goodman looked down at Joseph. “Someone put a knife into his heart.”

Doc Williams stepped closer and looked down at Joseph. “This man’s dead.”

“Hell, I know he’s dead, Doc,” replied the captain angrily.

“Then why bring `im here?” scowled the Doc in return. “I ain’t no damn undertaker. I’m a doctor.”

Goodman’s eyes welled as he dropped the blanket over Joseph. “I didn’t know where else to take `im, Doc.”

Jonah stood inside the door watching in silence, wondering what difference it made.

The room fell quiet, and then Doc Williams put a hand on Goodman’s shoulder. “I’m sorry, Captain. I’m a little tired and irritable. I have been out all day and most of the night seeing too many dead people that I couldn’t help. Just never expected a brutal killing, I guess, not yet anyway.”

Goodman nodded. “That’s all right, Doc. I guess none of us are doing very good tonight.”

Doc Bradley lifted the blanket and looked at Joseph. “I remember the time I patched this man’s shoulder and neck from knife wounds a few years back.” Lowering the blanket, he shook his head, looking sad. “If I remember correctly, he had a family back in Texas.”

“That’s right, Doc,” replied Goodman. “Has a wife and four boys. He sent `em back to Texas a couple of days ago until this fever thing is over. Miss Mary, that be Joseph’s wife, is coming back tomorrow evening.”

Doc Williams put on hand on the captain's shoulder. "Leave him with me. I'll see to it that he's taken to the undertaker."

"Thank ya, Doc. I appreciate it." Goodman looked at Jonah. "Guess we better be on our way to the Sheriff's."

Sheriff Parker looked up from his desk as Captain Goodman and Jonah walked through the door. "I thought I told you and your men to stay on board that boat of yours for the night."

Goodman glanced at the two deputies. "Mind if we sit down, Sheriff?"

The Sheriff glanced at Jonah, seeing the blood on his shirt, got curious, and nodded. "Go ahead."

They sat down, and then Goodman looked at the Sheriff. "Jonah, here and I, well, we need to talk to you, Sheriff."

The sheriff told his two deputies to make their rounds and then go home for the night and return early in the morning. As they left, he stood and walked to the potbellied stove, lifted the lid of the coffee pot, and looked inside, seeing it was empty. "What's on yer mind, Captain?"

Goodman told him that Charles Whittaker had killed Joseph on the pier, and that he and Jonah had carried Joseph back to the boat and then to Doc Williams's place.

The sheriff looked sad and shook his head, understanding where the blood on Jonah's shirt had come from. "I liked that boy. I recall him being knifed and almost killed back in '64 over in Jefferson." He paused. "He always said he didn't know who did the stabbing and robbing, but something always told me he did know."

Goodman frowned. "I don't know very much about that, Sheriff, but I think he did know."

Parker looked surprised, then curious. "Then why the hell didn't he tell me so's I could've arrested the man?"

Goodman shrugged, gesturing with both hands. "Can't say Sheriff, but I guess he had his reasons. I believe it was Charles Whittaker."

The sheriff quickly considered that. "Joseph, go after his revenge on this man?"

Goodman frowned as he shook his head dismissively. "That wasn't Joseph's style, Sheriff, leastways not the killing type of revenge. No, Joseph's revenge was breaking the man in front of a crowd, and then taking his money."

Sheriff Parker nodded thoughtfully. "I was there the night Whittaker lost most of his money in that card game. That man had hate written all over his face." He shook his head, looking sad. "Wish Joseph had told me who it was in Jefferson. Maybe then I could have seen this one coming."

"We all should've," said Goodman.

Sheriff Parker rubbed his chin with one hand while staring at them for several seconds before he gestured to some wanted posters on the table across the room. "A few days before the card game, a fella named Bob Colbert was in here asking about this Whittaker."

Goodman looked surprised.

The sheriff leaned forward, placed his elbows on the desk, and folded his hands. "I thought it a might peculiar of him just coming in here like that asking me if'n I'd ever heard of the man."

Goodman glanced at Jonah and then back at Parker. "When was this, again?"

Parker thought for a moment. "Oh, several days ago. Not really sure. I never gave it another thought until I saw them playing cards together that night, and I asked who the men at the table were."

"What'd ya tell Colbert?" asked Goodman.

Parker sat back, shrugged, and gestured with his hands. "Nothing," he said, looking indifferent. "Never heard the name until Colbert asked." He nodded toward the stack of posters on the table. "I told him he could look through them posters if he'd a mind, but he only smiled and said he heard the name and it sounded familiar. Said it was probably someone he knew in the army during the war and then left."

Goodman digested that story, wondering what Colbert had been up to. "Story sounds a little strange," he said, looking puzzled, and then he stood and gestured toward the door. "C'mon, Jonah. We've taken enough of the Sheriff's time."

Outside he took Jonah's arm and lowered his voice. "This whole thing sounds fishy to me, Jonah. There's more to this, and I aim to find out what it is."

Jonah looked puzzled. "Yes, suh."

Goodman told Jonah to return to the boat. Then he went to Bob Colbert's house, arriving there a little past ten. Seeing one light still on, he knocked, and when the door opened, Colbert looked surprised as he smiled. "Captain Goodman, come in. Can I offer you a drink?"

Goodman stepped inside. "No, thanks, Bob."

"What can I do for you, Captain?"

Goodman lowered his voice. "Joseph's dead, Bob."

Colbert's jaw dropped as he stared at the captain.

Goodman then asked him why he had visited the sheriff a few days before the big card game, when he was asking about Charles Whittaker.

Bob turned and sat on a nearby chair, looking shocked. "Joseph's dead?" He looked at Goodman. "How? What happened?"

"Charles Whittaker killed him." The captain asked again why he had visited the sheriff asking about Charles Whittaker.

Bob Colbert turned and stared into the fire in the fireplace for several seconds, regretting his helping Joseph, and thinking that his friend would be alive today if he hadn't. He told the captain to sit down. Then Colbert retold the story Joseph had told him about the knifing back in '64. Then he told him of Joseph's plan to lure Charles into the card game so that Joseph could have his revenge by taking his money.

The captain stared into Colbert's eyes, considering everything. "Was it an honest game?"

Bob looked surprised, then baffled, and then angry at the question. "Hell, yes, it was an honest game! Joseph had him pegged and knew exactly when to mention the robbery and the stabbing." Colbert smiled with admiration. "Charles believed he had killed Joseph that night in Jefferson, and I'll never forget Whittaker's face when Joseph said he knew who it was that stabbed and robbed him." Colbert chuckled. "Whittaker just about shit his pants. He was so upset he fumbled a card face up on the table. The card was called dead, Whittaker argued, but the owner of the place agreed, and it remained a dead card." Colbert's smile faded as he looked into the fireplace. "Turned out, it was the winning card for Whittaker."

Bob looked at Goodman with a proud face. "Never saw anything like it before, Captain. Joseph was cold and steady. He had this look about him like nothing was gonna beat him." He paused with a grin. "Whittaker was wet and clammy." He paused in memory. "Joseph played the game of a lifetime."

Goodman stared at the fire, imagining the scene, and then he sucked in a deep breath as he stood, sighed, and thanked Colbert.

Bob stood. "How is Mary?"

The captain looked sad, thinking about tomorrow night. "She's coming in tomorrow afternoon. Me and Jonah are going to meet her boat."

"I didn't know she was gone."

"She took the children to some friends in Jefferson. I'm not looking forward to that; it's a hell of a thing I have to do."

Colbert's expression was sad. "I don't envy you that task, Captain." Then he glanced at the bedroom door. "Guess I'll wait until morning to tell Grace, no sense getting her upset."

Goodman looked toward the door, nodded his agreement, and then suggested that if Grace was up to it, maybe they could drop in on Mary. "I have a feeling she'll need someone like Grace."

Bob agreed, shook the captain's hand, said goodnight, and then Captain Goodman made his way back to The Helen, filled with the grief that Joseph was gone.

Thirty-Five

August 29, 1873 – October 1873

Mary Greene

Goodbye My Love

Sorrow and anxiety filled Captain Goodman as he watched the steamboat, Cypress, as she nestled against the pilings, not looking forward to having to tell Mary the terrible news about her Joseph. As the men worked the lines to secure the Cypress against the pier before lowering the gangplank, he looked for Mary among the passengers as his mind tried to gather the words that would soon break her heart. He would sell his own soul to the devil to avoid doing this to this kind lady, but this was where destiny had delivered him, and he had no choice. He found himself hoping she had missed the boat, but there she was, standing at the railing looking for Joseph, her face filled with excitement and anticipation.

Seeing the Captain, she smiled and waved, then hurried along the deck toward the gangplank while he struggled to find the strength and the words to tell her that the man she loved was dead. Joseph was gone, tomorrow and the day after that and the day after that. How can I tell her such things, Goodman asked himself. Watching her as she hurried along the deck of the Cypress, he saw her face filled with the excitement at seeing Joseph, wanting to be with him, to love him.

Goodman wanted to turn away as she hurried down the gangplank to meet the end of her happiness. Goodman's tired, aged eyes welled with tears at the thought of breaking this gentle lady's heart. A whistle in the distance made him look out across the river at another approaching boat, whose tall towers bellowed black smoke into a cloudless evening sky. Taking a deep breath, he glanced back at Jonah, waiting at the end of the pier with the buggy, and then he walked to meet Mary.

She smiled and waved as she hurried along the pier looking for Joseph, but then sensing something was wrong, she stopped a few feet from the captain. A man bumped into her, apologized, and walked on, but she never took her eyes from Goodman's red, welling eyes. "Where's Joseph?"

The captain opened his mouth to speak, but the words hung on his tongue.

Mary looked past him, seeing Jonah standing at the buggy and looking down at his hat. Wondering where her Joseph was, she looked into the crowd only to have a second man bump into her as he hurried through the crowd. She looked at the captain, knowing something terrible had happened. "Where's Joseph?"

Goodman looked into her pleading eyes as he fumbled for the right words, since there were none, and reached for her hand. "Let me help you to the carriage, Mary."

She pulled back, standing stiff and defiant. "What happened to Joseph? Where is he?"

He glanced at the people walking past and then at her, searching for the words to tell her Joseph was dead. "Let's go to the carriage."

She stepped backward, staring at him, looking fearful yet angry, eyes wide, red, and welling. "I want to know where Joseph is."

Finally, he had to tell her. "Joseph's gone, Mary. Our Joseph is dead."

As Mary's knees buckled, Captain Goodman reached out and caught her in his arms, then turned his head and yelled over his shoulder for Jonah. They helped her into the buggy while she sobbed Joseph's name over and over. After Mary and Goodman were in the buggy, Jonah climbed up into the top seat, picked up the reins, tapped the horse, and drove away from the pier. Captain Goodman put his arm around her, and she buried her face against his coat, sobbing while he tried to comfort her from a tragedy that knew no comfort. All he could do was gently pat her back while uttering useless words. "I know Mary," he said in a choked voice. "I know. I loved him too."

Jonah turned onto the main street among the other buggies, carriages, and men on horseback and drove toward her house. Inside the buggy, she sat up, took the captain's hand, held it firmly on her lap, between hers, and looked out the carriage window into the now dark streets of Shreveport. "What happened?"

He took in a breath, letting out a sigh while turning the words over in his mind. "We returned late last night from Alexandria." He gestured with one hand. "Joseph had decided that he was going to return with you to Texas until this was over. After we docked, he wanted to go home and pack a few things. I tried to get him to stay on board, but he wanted to check the house and horses then stop by Bob Colbert's place about something." He paused. "He was killed soon after leaving The Helen."

She turned from the window, looking bewildered. "Killed?" She stared at him, suspecting the truth. "It was Charles Whittaker, wasn't it?"

He looked into her eyes and nodded. “Yes, I believe Charles Whittaker killed Joseph.”

She leaned forward, buried her face in her hands, and sobbed for several moments. Then she looked out the window. “I was afraid this wouldn’t end with that damn game. It went much too deep for that. I could see it in Joseph’s eyes and on his face.”

The carriage filled with sounds from the street of laughter, music, and other city noises as she turned and looked at Goodman. “You said that you believe this Charles Whittaker killed my Joseph, but you don’t sound sure. Why not?”

He proceeded to tell her what had happened. Of Joseph leaving the boat, of how Jonah saw the figure and Joseph struggling on the pier, and Jonah jumping onto the pier running to help Joseph, but arriving too late. Then he told her the words Joseph uttered before he died, of how they carried him back to the Helen and then to Doc William’s place. As he talked, Mary looked out the window, wiping her tears, imagining the scene in her mind. Captain Goodman finished and sat in silence, watching her. “His last thoughts were of you. He spoke your name just before he died.”

She closed her eyes, lowered her head thinking of the last time she saw her beloved husband. “Where is Joseph’s body?”

“At the undertakers.”

“Take me there.”

The captain leaned his head out the window to tell Jonah, and minutes later, he helped her down and knocked on the door of the undertaker. When the door opened, Mary asked to see her husband, turned, and told Goodman she would be out in a little while. Knowing she wanted to be alone with him, he returned to the carriage and waited.

Thirty minutes passed before the door of the undertaker’s office opened and Mary stepped out and walked to the carriage. Goodman got out, helped her into the carriage, and then Jonah slapped the horses and drove away.

Mary sat in silence while Goodman looked out the other window filled with memories and sorrow as the carriage drove up the driveway to the house. The captain helped Mary down from the buggy and into the house while Jonah carried in her bag, placing it by the staircase. She thanked Jonah and invited them into the library, asking the captain if he would build a fire while she fixed a pot of tea. Knowing it was something Mary needed, Captain Goodman motioned for Jonah to have a seat while he knelt by the fireplace and built a fire to take the edge off of the cool room. Finished, Goodman sat in a chair opposite Jonah, listening to the sounds from the kitchen of wood being stoked into the stove, the pot being filled with water from the pump, and the tinkling of fine china. As the house became silent, the faint moan of sorrow made its way from the kitchen. The two men sat in silent stillness, leaving her to her moment of sorrow.

The sobbing stopped, and minutes later, Mary walked into the library, carrying a tray with a teapot, fine china cups with saucers, and sugar. The room filled with the sound of china as she placed the tray on the small table in front of the captain. She turned to Jonah and smiled. "Jonah, why don't you move your chair closer to the table?"

"Yessum, Miss Mary." He nodded, stood, and awkwardly moved his chair while she picked up the teapot.

She poured tea into a cup, handed it on its saucer to the captain, and then filled another, handing it to Jonah while managing a small smile.

The silence was almost deafening, broken only by the clinking of china cups on saucers or the occasional tinkling of a spoon stirring the sugar from the bottom of a cup.

She quietly sipped her tea and then turned to Jonah. "Captain Goodman tells me that you were the first to get to Joseph. Did he suffer?"

Jonah glanced at the captain, unsure how to answer.

The captain nodded.

Jonah's face was filled with sorrow as he looked into Mary's eyes. "Ah's don't thinks so, Miss Mary, he wur hurt bad, but as ah held `em in mah arms, he say 'Mary', then he smiles at me." Jonah looked down at the floor with a sad expression, his eyes red. "Mistah Joseph wents quick, Miss Mary."

"He didn't say anything else, Jonah?" she asked.

His eyes were red and watery when he looked up from the floor and wiped his eyes and cheek with his big hand. "Yessum, he say someth'n dat sound like 'water and tear." He glanced at Goodman. "Dah cap'n b'lieves Mistah Joseph done say dah name, Whittaker." She looked down at her cup, staring into the tea for a long moment, and then she looked up with a smile on her sad face. "Joseph was very fond of you, Jonah. He often spoke of the first day the two of you met on the Southern Belle." She looked down into her cup. "I believe the days aboard that boat were sometimes his happiest."

"Yessum," Jonah said. "I likes Mistah Joseph too, Miss Mary." Jonah wiped a tear from his cheek then shook his head. "Dem were happy days fuh me, too."

The room filled with silence and memory, and then moments later, she placed her cup and saucer on the table and smiled. "I'm sorry, Captain, Jonah, but I suddenly feel tired."

"We understand," replied the captain. Then they both stood and followed her to the door.

She thanked them for their kindness, saying she understood the difficulty the two had faced by meeting her at the boat. She smiled at Goodman and Jonah, saying she would never forget their kindness. She took Jonah's hand in hers and smiled. "I'm glad Joseph was not alone in the end Jonah, and I'm glad you were there with him."

Jonah nodded, looking sad, then turned and walked out the door to the buggy. Then as she took Captain Goodman's hand and held it firmly in hers, she looked into his wrinkled face and red eyes. "They will catch Charles Whittaker, won't they, Captain?"

He looked into her soft grieving eyes. "Damn right, they will, Miss Mary. I'll see to it if I have to hunt the bastard down myself."

She stared at him for a long moment as her expression changed from grief to something else. "I accept that as a promise, Captain." Then she said goodnight and closed the door.

As he turned to leave, a small buggy drove up, stopped, and Mattie climbed out, looking worried. "How's Miss Mary?"

The captain tipped his hat. "I see you got my message. She's about as well as can be expected, Mattie. I think she needs you tonight."

Mattie hurried into the house and closed the door as Captain Goodman climbed up onto the carriage next to Jonah. "Let's go home, Jonah."

September 3, 1873

Dressed in a black dress, Mary Greene stood next to Captain Goodman, holding onto his arm, partly for comfort, but mostly because she needed to feel something alive next to her. A slight breeze played with the black veil she wore that hid her grieving face and red, swollen eyes. Mary was only half-listening to the preacher's words that he read from his old Bible. She was thinking of the things she would miss about her Joseph, such as his grin when he teased her, the way he laughed when she did something foolish, his gentleness with the children, and the way his touch had excited her. She looked away from the pine casket to a large oak tree several yards away, taking notice of the dying gold, yellow, and red leaves mixing with the living green ones against the blue sky.

Such a beautiful day, she thought. Then she noticed the columns of dark, black smoke rising in the distance, a reminder of what had sent her away from her Joseph. Turning from the scene of death and destruction taking place in the city, she glanced at the other faces gathered around the grave. She thought the tall, elderly, white-haired preacher looked distinguished. He was dressed in his best black suit, white shirt, and black tie as he read the verses necessary for the ceremony. His voice carried the words softly yet powerfully as he held the Bible in one hand while gesturing with the other.

Her eyes turned to the captain, standing next to her, and watched the tears that slowly made their way over the deep lines of his weathered face, becoming lost in his thick, gray beard. She felt empathy for him, for she knew that he, too, had loved Joseph, and she found comfort in his grieving. Jonah, the Negro ex-slave Joseph had liked from their first meeting, stood holding his tattered hat with both hands, staring down at his own feet, instead of the pine coffin. He wiped at the lines of tears that made their way down the dark skin of his face. His lips moved slightly as he said a silent prayer of his own for Joseph. She heard Mattie and her family behind her softly praying, recognizing Mattie's tears of sorrow. Bob Colbert stared down at the coffin looking angry, yet sad as Grace Colbert held onto her husband's arm with one hand, the other wiping her face with a white hankie. Sheriff Parker stood next to Doc Bradley, and the solitary figure of Mrs. Trudy Hansen stood a few feet behind them, wiping her swollen red eyes with an already wet, white hanky.

The preacher stopped reading from the Bible, said a prayer, closed the Bible, and stepped back. Captain Goodman, Bob Colbert, Sheriff Parker, and Jonah lowered the coffin into the grave, letting the ropes drop back into the dark hole, and as they landed on the casket, they sent back a final sound. Mary bent down, picked up a hand full of dirt, and tossed it into the grave, watching as it scattered over the pine coffin. She stepped back, allowing Captain Goodman to do the same, followed by Trudy Hansen, the Colbert's, Sheriff Parker, Doc Bradley, Mattie, and her family, and lastly, Jonah.

The mourners paid their respects to Mary, each saying how sorry they were, and the last person to do so was Sheriff Parker. Looking uneasy and glum, he took her hand and gently held it. "We're doing all we can to catch the man responsible for Joseph's death."

Mary looked up at him through her veil that hid her tears and pain and nodded in silence.

Captain Goodman greeted the Sheriff, told Jonah to return to The Helen, then took Mary's hand, wrapped it around his arm, and escorted her to the waiting buggy. Helping her into the buggy, he climbed in and sat next to her. The driver tapped the reins against the backs of the two horses. The carriage began to move along the dirt road toward the iron gates of the Oakland Cemetery.

Goodman turned from the window of the buggy and took her hand. "If I may ask, what are your plans, Mary?"

She looked out the window at the mass of markers as the buggy drove through the archway into the street, leaving her beloved Joseph behind. She drew in a deep breath, sighed, and gestured with one hand. "Go back to Texas as soon as possible, I suppose, and tell the children about their father."

Goodman imagined the scene feeling sorry for her. "That won't be easy."

She reached up under the veil and wiped at her tears. "This will kill Zachariah." Her voice quivered as the tears flowed down her cheeks. "And the others too, but Zachariah is the oldest, and he will take it the hardest, I think, because he understands the finality of death more than the others."

Goodman considered that. "I'm sure he'll be all right, Mary." He wanted to say more but couldn't find the words of comfort for her, so he sat in silence, letting the grief of the moment take the day.

September 7, 1873

It had been four days since Joseph's funeral, and now Mary was anxious to return to east Texas, yet she was dreading the task of telling the children about their father. She had decided to gather up her children and return to Florence and her brother Alex, hoping his presence and influence on the children would ease their loss. Packing and making arrangements to sell the house and furniture kept her busy and her mind off of the pain she felt over her loss.

Mary was in her room, busily going through some things, when Mattie knocked at her bedroom door. "Miss Mary, Captain Goodman, and Sheriff Parker is downstairs."

Mary stopped what she was doing and rushed downstairs to the library, anticipating news about Charles Whittaker.

Captain Goodman was looking at a photo of Joseph, and seeing her, he turned from the photo, looking troubled. "We've bad news, Mary. All roads in and out of Shreveport have been blocked. Nothing's moving in or out."

Disappointed, she turned toward the window, thinking of her children. "Does that mean I can't go to my children?"

The sheriff looked apologetic. "Afraid it does, Mrs. Greene, at least until this yellow fever goes away. The surrounding towns just ain't letting anyone leave Shreveport. Guards have been posted all along the roads, with orders to detain or shoot, if necessary, anyone that tries to get past them. The only people we're letting in are doctors and people that can help with the fever, and no one's getting out."

She turned from the window, looking overwhelmed, and sat down. "I'll have to send a telegraph to the Hall's, letting them know." She looked at Sheriff Parker. "Are the telegraph lines still up?"

Parker nodded. "Yes, ma'am. That is, until the man at the telegraph office gets sick. S'pose you could send a letter, but the truth is, people are afraid to touch anything for fear of getting the fever." He shrugged, shaking his head. "Guess I can't blame `em none."

Mary considered that. "No," she said softly. "I suppose not." The room was quiet for a few moments, and then she looked at the sheriff. "I don't suppose y'all have apprehended this Charles Whittaker?"

The sheriff glanced at Goodman and then shook his head, looking embarrassed. "No, ma'am, but we're still looking."

Mary's expression showed her disappointment as she stood. "Thank you both for your concerns and for stopping by." She walked them to the door where Captain Goodman paused, looking at her with concern. "Anything we can do for you, Mary?"

"Not at the moment, Captain." She smiled warmly. "You've been most gracious." She looked at Sheriff Parker and smiled. "You both have."

They put on their hats, and as they walked toward the waiting buggy, she closed the door and leaned back against it, feeling tired and lonely as she thought of Joseph. Instead of returning upstairs to her room, she went into the library, where she lay down on the sofa and cried herself to sleep.

Mary was dreaming of a thunderstorm when she opened her eyes. Realizing someone was pounding at the front door, she got up and hurried out of the library just as Mattie walked into the hall. Telling Mattie that she would get the door, she found Bob Colbert standing on the porch looking worried.

"Why, Mr. Colbert, you startled me." She stepped aside. "Please, come in."

He stepped inside. "It's Grace," he said, looking worried. "She's pretty sick. Could you come over Mary, I don't know where else to go."

"Have you sent for the doctor?" she asked, looking concerned.

He nodded. "The Doc was by earlier and said there was nothing more he could do. Said she needs to rest and build up her strength." His face and eyes were pleading. "She's awfully sick, Mary."

She turned, talking over her shoulder. "I'll get my coat."

Mary entered the Colbert bedroom, finding Grace coughing, wet with perspiration, and burning with fever. She told Bob to get some cold water and towels, then took off her coat, felt Grace's forehead, and sat down in a chair next to the bed. When Bob returned with the water and towels, Mary dipped the towels into the cold water, placed them on Grace's forehead and neck, and began patting down her arms with another cold, damp cloth. "She's burning up. We have to break this fever."

Mary and Bob Colbert worked through the night taking care of Grace, only to lose her and the unborn child in the early morning hours. Exhausted by the ordeal, Mary walked out of the bedroom, leaving Bob to mourn his Grace and their child. She sat down in an overstuffed chair in the living room and looked at the picture of Grace and Bob, remembering the times they had spent together and of Grace's happiness at being pregnant. Unable to hold back any longer, Mary put her face in her hands and cried, letting her sorrow mix with Bob's muffled sobs from the other room. Sitting up, she listened to Bob in the other room crying for his beloved Grace and wondered how people such as she and Bob ever got past such a terrible loss.

Outside the window, the sun was peeking above the buildings across the street. Its bright, dusty rays came in through the window and flowed across the room, filling it with warm sunlight. She looked toward the bedroom door, gathered her coat, stepped outside, and walked home, leaving Bob to grieve for his wife and child.

Sitting in the parlor, lost in memory of happier times, wishing this was but a bad dream, she knew that she would never see her Joseph again. She would never hear him laugh again or cuddle up against his warm body as he slept next to her.

Mattie entered the room, looking worried. "How's Miss Grace?"

Mary asked Mattie to sit with her, and as she did, Mary told her about Grace and the unborn child.

Mattie shook her head, looking sad and fearful. "What's we gonna do, Miss Mary? Dis thing's gonna kill us all."

"I don't know, Mattie," she said softly. "I can't even leave for Texas to be with my children."

Mattie looked puzzled. "Why nots Miss Mary?"

"The roads are blocked. Nothing's coming into Shreveport, and nothing's going out." Mary looked worried. "I better send the Hall's a telegraph right away."

Mattie looked at her. "I'll go along wit ya. A lady ought not be out walk'n round by herself dese days."

Mary smiled appreciatively. "Thank you, Mattie, but I'll be all right."

Mattie shook her head. "No, ma'am Miss Mary, Mattie's go'n wit ya. Ain't nuth'n stopping me."

"All right, Mattie." Mary smiled at her. "We'll go together. Thank you."

Mattie smiled reassuringly. "I know dem boys, Miss Mary, an dey gonna be all right." Then she stood. "I'll fix ya some tea b'fore we leave. Ya jus sit rights here."

Mary smiled. "Thank you, Mattie, but you must be worried about your own family." She took her hand and gently pulled her back down onto the sofa. "I can manage Mattie, really I can. Keeping busy will help me, and right now, I think you need to be home with your own family."

"I cant's get home till my man picks me up, Miss Mary," Mattie said matter-of-factly. "So's if ya don't mind, I jus' stay witch ya, and fix us some tea, den when my man git's here we all go send dat telegraph." Mattie patted Mary's hands, stood, and disappeared toward the kitchen.

September 9, 1873

In the evening hours of September 9, 1873, two men armed with torches walked along the river south of Shreveport, burning all the shacks that were empty. After torching one shack, they walked to the next and called out to see if anyone was inside. One of the men opened the door, held the torch inside as he poked his head in, and saw a man lying on his side, facing the wall on an old, dirty bed. "Hey, Mister, you okay in there?"

The man lying on the bed slowly turned and looked at them. His face was wet from perspiration, looking sickly. "Get me a doctor."

The man with the torch slowly backed out of the shack, closed the door, and looked at his friend. "He's got the fever. We best go find the Doc."

Wanting to see for himself, the other man stepped inside with his torch, took a quick look, backed out, and closed the door. "Best get the Sheriff. That there's that Whittaker fella everyone's looking for."

They hurried back to town and the sheriff's office, finding Sheriff Parker and Doc Bradley talking with Captain Goodman. They quickly told the sheriff about Whittaker holed up in the shack.

Arriving at the shack, Doc Bradley told the others to wait outside, opened the door, and stepped inside carrying a torch. After several minutes, he emerged, shaking his head. "I don't know if that is Charles Whittaker, but the man's dead."

Goodman took the torch and stepped inside the shack, and looked into the face of the man that killed Joseph. Goodman spit as if to get a bad taste out of his mouth and backed out of the shack. He turned to the sheriff. "It's Charles Whittaker, all right, and he's dead."

Doc Bradley and Sheriff Parker entered into a discussion on what to do about the body.

Captain Goodman listened to them for a moment and then stepped toward them. "Burn the damn place down."

"You can't be serious?" argued Doc Bradley, looking horrified.

Angrily, Goodman turned, walked to the open door of the shack, and looked in at the body of Charles Whittaker for a long moment. Then he turned back and looked at Bradley and Parker with hate on his face. "I say we send the son-of-a-bitch to hell."

"The man needs to be buried," argued Doc Bradley.

The captain's face flushed in anger, thinking of Joseph dying on the pier in Jonah's arms before he could tell him goodbye. "He doesn't deserve to be buried. I'll not let that bastard be buried in the same cemetery that holds Joseph."

Sheriff Parker looked at Goodman, then at Doc Bradley, walked to the door, looked inside, and then turned to Doc Bradley. "I ain't carrying the son-of-a-bitch out of here."

Captain Goodman took a torch from one of the men, stepped inside the shack, looked at Whittaker, and tossed the torch next to the bed. He watched as the flame of the torch set the bedding on fire, and as the fire began to consume the clothing of Charles Whittaker, he backed out of the shack, closed the door, and softly said, "Burn you bastard."

It was almost noon when Captain Goodman climbed down from his buggy, walked up the steps to the Greene residence, raised his hand to use the brass knocker, and paused to take a deep breath, then knocked, and waited.

The door slowly opened, and Mary looked at him, her face tired and weary. "Good morning Captain Goodman. Please come in." She showed him into the parlor, sat down across from him, and waited, hoping he had news of Charles Whittaker.

Concerned for her, he asked, "Are you all right?"

"I'm just tired, Captain. I don't know if you've heard, but Grace Colbert passed away from the fever two days ago."

Goodman looked sad as he looked down at his hat he held in both hands, saying softly, "No, I hadn't heard. I'll stop by and see Bob when I leave here."

"I'm sure he'll appreciate that. I haven't slept a great deal since Joseph's death, and I'm worried about the children." She gestured around the room. "The house is cold and empty. All life is gone from it."

He felt sorry for her and would sell his own soul if he could undo all that had happened. He told her of Whittaker's death, of how they had burned the shack down around his dead body, hoping the news would somehow ease her pain.

Mary sighed and shook her head. "I'm sorry to hear that, Captain."

Surprised at her reaction, he looked at her.

"You see, Captain," Mary said coldly. "I wanted to look into the bastard's eyes as they hung him."

Shocked but understanding her feelings, he said, "Maybe so, but he's dead all the same, Mary, and rotting in hell. Are you sure you feel all right, Miss Mary?"

She nodded and forced a smile. "I'm fine, captain. A little tired is all."

He stood. "I can show myself out. I just wanted to tell you about Charles Whittaker. Try and get some rest, Mary."

"I will," she answered as she stood, touched his arm, and smiled. "And I thank you for your concern, Captain Goodman. You always were a kind and thoughtful man underneath that gruff exterior of yours."

He smiled with embarrassment.

"I'll show you to the door."

He helped her up, walked her to the front door, and waited while she opened it.

As he walked past to leave, she gently grabbed his arm. "Joseph loved you like a father, Captain. I hope you know that."

He smiled as his heart ached, and his eyes welled as he fought not to cry. "And I loved the lad like a son." Then he turned and walked to his waiting buggy.

September 14, 1873

Mattie unlocked the back door, entered the Greene residence just as she had done for the past few years, took off her coat, and hung it next to the back door. The house was quiet as Mattie went about breakfast and coffee. She hummed while she worked to the kitchen noises of firewood stoked into the cold stove, pots, pans, and water. Hearing Mary call her name, she turned with a smile at Mary's pale and sweating face.

Mary's eyes closed as she slowly lowered herself to the floor and sat against the doorjamb, looking faint.

Mattie dropped the pan she held, rushed over to her, and knelt. "Miss Mary, you sick wit' dah fever?"

Mary's face and hair were wet with sweat as she looked up at Mattie and whispered, "Doctor."

Fearing yellow fever, Mattie stood and ran out of the house to get the doctor.

Mattie waited in the library while Doc Williams and Doc Bradley examined Mary, and after several minutes, Doc Bradley walked into the library looking sad. Mattie stood, looking worried and nervously wringing her hands. He looked at Mattie's worried face. "Miss Mary's gone, Mattie; you best go on home. Doc Williams and I will lock up and take care of things here." Then, concerned for Mattie, he looked at her. "Are you feeling all right, Mattie?"

She stared at him as her eyes welled with tears. "I's all right," she said, sobbing, and then she rushed out the front door and ran down the driveway to the cobblestone street and home.

Doc Bradley and Williams covered Mary with a blanket, closed and locked the house, and left. Returning that evening with a wagon, they loaded her body into it and then took it to a building containing several rows of bodies that had succumbed to the fever. The death toll was so staggering that individual graves were inconceivable, so mass graves were dug. It was Mary W. McAlexander Greene's cruel fate to be buried in such a grave just yards from her Joseph. Her final resting place would become known as the Yellow Fever Mound at Oakland Cemetery, Shreveport, Louisiana.

October 18, 1873

Captain Goodman stood alone, staring out across the city of Shreveport, deep in his memories of the happy and innocent years before the war along the Tennessee River.

"Cap'n?" said Jonah in his soft, deep voice.

Goodman turned from the smoke above the city, holding his memories of Joseph and the past, put on his hat, and looked at Jonah. "Ready, Jonah?"

"Yes, Suh, Cap'n," replied Jonah with a sad look.

Goodman looked at Bob Colbert thoughtfully. "What are your plans now, Bob? You staying here in Shreveport or heading back to the river?"

Bob considered that for several seconds while looking at the smoke rising above Shreveport, thinking of his Grace and their unborn child. Finally, he shook his head. "No, I think I'll head out to California. There's nothing for me here any longer."

Captain Goodman nodded, looking sad while his mind filled with images of Joseph. "No, I suppose not." He extended his hand. "Can we give you a lift someplace?"

Bob briefly considered that then smiled and shook Goodman's hand. "I think I'll walk home." Then he shook Jonah's hand and wished them both well.

Captain Goodman turned, and with a heavy heart, he looked toward Joseph's grave and the Yellow Fever Mound where Mary lay buried. He turned away, and then he and Jonah climbed into the buggy. Goodman picked up the reins, slapped them on the horse's back, and drove out of the Oakland Cemetery.

Bob Colbert paused to take a final look at his friend Joseph's grave, the Yellow Fever Mound, and then at the grave that held his Grace and unborn child. Filled with sorrow, he turned and walked through the iron gates. On his way to California, Bob Colbert stopped at the Hall farm, leaving Joseph and Mary's children an unfinished letter from their mother. And like Captain Benjamin Goodman and Jonah, Bob Colbert disappeared into the future.

Epilogue

After the deaths of Joseph and Mary, their children remained with the Halls in east Texas. Joseph's grave at the Oakland Cemetery in Shreveport, Louisiana, had deteriorated over the years, and the headstone, which was probably wood, had vanished, leaving an unmarked grave. With the help of a lady genealogist I hired in Shreveport in 2003, I was able to locate my great-grandfather's grave. The cemetery office had suffered a fire in 1945, destroying most of the records. An old hand-drawn map of the cemetery did survive, with the names of those buried in some of the plots. One of those names written in ink is Joseph Greene. However, there is no record of the people buried in the many mass graves of Shreveport or the Yellow Fever Mound victims just yards from Mary's Joseph. In the spring of 2007, I had a stone placed in the Oakland Cemetery at Joseph's grave reading: **"In Loving Memory of Joseph S. Greene b: 1833 d: 1873 and Mary W. Greene b: 1835 d: 1873 Placed by Richard J. Greene."**

Their Children

In 1877, a young Zachary (Zachariah) Greene ran away from the Halls, taking up residence in San Antonio and working at odd jobs. Edward Joseph (who preferred to be called Joe) followed in 1878. They remained in San Antonio until Zachariah died of a burst appendix in May 1879. Allen Greene left the farm and moved to Chicago, Illinois, where he met and married Louisa Gardner in 1898. They had two daughters and opened a restaurant on the east side of Chicago.

No one knows for sure when, but Edward Joseph (Joe) showed up in Chicago and worked as a restaurant waiter. At some point, Allen and his family left Joe and Chicago, moving to Hot Springs, Arkansas, where Allen died in October 1919. It is said that Joe took to the rails, riding boxcars and sending postcards to his brother Joseph Jr., who remained at the Hall farm. While attempting to hop on a train in Chicago, he fell under the train, losing both legs. The story goes that he was carried to a nearby home for elderly ladies, and a doctor was summoned. The severity of the injuries was too great, however, and he passed away in the early morning hours of a cold February day in 1920.

Joseph Samuel Greene Jr. fell in love with Louisa (Lula) Clementine Chrisman, daughter of James Riley Chrisman and Martha Heard Chrisman, neighbors to the Halls. Joseph Greene Jr. and Louisa Chrisman married in 1888. They had thirteen children, seven of whom passed away before their second birthday. On March 18, 1910, Louisa, while pregnant with her 13th child, slipped and fell waist-high into an irrigation ditch of dirty water. Although she was pulled from the water within minutes, their daughter, they named Mary, was stillborn next to that muddy ditch.

Two days later, on March 20, 1910, Louisa died from complications resulting from infection. Joseph Greene Jr. mourned his wife's loss and lived out his life in Texas, raising his six children as best he could. He never remarried and passed away peacefully on January 5th, 1947. One of their sons, Edward Lee Greene, born January 17, 1907, joined the army and was stationed in Colorado, where he met Bertha Patterson, great-granddaughter of Andrew Jackson Patterson.

Edward McAlexander

Edward McAlexander remained in Florence with his wife Sarah and daughter Mary and followed his brother Alex into politics, serving two terms as Alabama State Representative from 1865 to 1867. He and Sarah had two children, Edward Lee McAlexander, born 1866, and Alex McAlexander, named in honor of his father and dear brother. Sarah died giving birth to Alexander in September 1867, leaving Edward alone again. He lived in Florence with his children until his death on October 13, 1870. What became of his children is unknown, though I have tried to locate some relatives on Ancestry.com. Edward's gravestone reads: **Edward McAlexander MD b: Mar 2 AD 1833 d: Oct 13, AD 1870. He raised himself to eminence in the state, Was Colonel of the 27th Alabama Regiment. After the war, a member of the General Assembly of Alabama. A Soldier and a Patriot, he lived and died in the exercise of every Christian virtue.**

Edward's good friend Ethan Hall returned to Florence only once to attend his dear friend's funeral. Ethan spent his years working his farm in Harrison County, Texas, once a good neighbor to Mary and Joseph Greene, and who gladly took on their children's responsibility.

Alex McAlexander, Edward's brother, passed away in Florence in June 1881, followed by his wife Ella the following year in October 1882. Both are buried near Edward.

James Riley Chrisman

James and Martha Heard Chrisman lived on the Chrisman farm, raising seven children, and moved to east Texas in 1874, becoming neighbors to Ethan and Lori Hall. Their daughter, Louisa Clementine Chrisman, fell in love with Joseph Samuel Greene Jr., and he with her. They married on August 15, 1888. James returned to Tallapoosa County for the funeral of his father, William Chrisman, in October 1882. And for the last time in his life, he visited the graves of his younger brother Davy and friend Allen. James Riley and Martha Chrisman prospered in east Texas until they fell on hard times late in their lives. James passed away a poor and broken man in east Texas in late October 1917.

Martha, now alone and indigent but still proud, received a meager subsistence from the Confederate Soldiers' Pension. When no longer able to live on that meager amount, she moved in with a daughter and son-in-law on their east Texas farm. In the early morning hours of November 12th, 1923, she happily and peacefully passed away thinking of her beloved James and believing he was waiting for her. As long as James lived, he never explained where he had been after the war and why it took him so long to return home. Eventually Martha stopped asking, and they never spoke of it or the war again.

William Riley Chrisman

People in the county of Tallapoosa had their suspicions about who killed Bishop Martin and Ben Rogers, and most people felt the county was better off without them. The Home Guard talked of revenge and vowed that they would find the responsible party and hang him, but no arrests were ever made, and the days soon turned into weeks and the weeks into months. When the war ended, it took with it the mystery of Ben Rogers and Bishop Martin. After William died in October 1882, the Chrisman farm was sold, and the proceeds split between James, his three sisters, and their husbands. Because of her Indian heritage preventing her from owning land, Elizabeth Chrisman was not named in the will. She remained with her daughter, Beth, in Marshall County, Alabama, until her death in 1900.

Andrew Jackson Patterson

Andrew Jackson Patterson and Rebecca Davis were married in October 1862 and endured the war's hardships together. Sometimes late at night, when the sounds of cannons imitated thunder in the distance, they would sit on the roof, watching the flashes in the darkness. But that was as close as the war ever came to the farm, and as the years passed, they plowed their fields, raised their crops, and raised four children of their own. The Negro slave John, never returned to the Patterson farm, and no one ever knew what became of him. His desire for freedom was so strong that it took him from his wife and children, and only fate knows what he found. After the war, Andrew took good care of the Negro families, giving them a place to live and work for wages, meager as they were. One day Matthew's sons left the farm and South Carolina for the life of the northern factories.

In the late afternoon on a hot August day in 1874, Rebecca found Andrew Jackson Patterson lying dead from a stroke behind his plow and horse at age 57. His death broke her heart, and she would never marry again, having lost the only man she ever truly loved. She would live the rest of her life raising their children, each of whom would marry and work their farms in and around Anderson, South Carolina.

Rebecca passed away in early 1907 and was buried next to Andrew and his first wife. Young Daniel, the boy who chased his father's wagon across the fields as he went off to war, married and raised several children of his own. One of them, Sumpter Edward Patterson, a boy much like his father in many ways, spent his spare time reading dime store novels of the old west. The day came when he could no longer resist the call of adventure in the far West. He boarded a train for the Colorado plains with what few belongings he could stuff into an old carpetbag. But unknown to this young adventurer as he rode the train across the Great Plains, the west he had read about was already disappearing. Sadly, he spent his life hungry for the adventure that fate denied him.

YOU DECIDE

The Death of Innocence was the death of a way of life that possibly should never have flourished, to begin with. For some, like the Negro slave, it was a terrible life, their only real freedom coming with death, while for the whites, it was a grander time. I'm not condoning what happened by the name of my story but merely using it to acknowledge that during this period, no matter what the injustices, people lived in a period of innocence never again witnessed in this country, and maybe rightly so.

Some people believe that fate is the hunter, while others believe an immortal being or greater power sets our paths long before we are born. I can't answer which is correct, but like you, I can only ponder what power so long ago set forth a path for the Greene, McAlexander, Chrisman, and Patterson families. However, it was arranged, this path could not be avoided as it raced toward Bertha Viola Patterson, the daughter of Sumpter Edward Patterson and great-granddaughter of Andrew Jackson Patterson.

Unknowingly, she was on the same path that Edward Lee Greene had been set upon by the lives of his parents, Joseph Samuel Greene Jr. and Louisa Clementine Chrisman, and their parents Joseph and Mary

Greene, and James and Martha Heard Chrisman. This path would lead to the meeting and eventual marriage of Edward Lee Greene and Bertha Viola Patterson in a small white church on Colorado's plains, not far from Parker, a small town in June 1927. They had four children; Edward Lee Greene, Jr., Jerold Allen Greene, Malcolm Eugene Greene, and myself, Richard Joseph Greene.

There is a need to mention another family not included in this story who lived with their own struggles; The Bruning family. They arrived from Germany in the 1800's settling first in St Louis, Missouri, then on the eastern plains of Colorado. While they had no instrumental part in the great Civil War, they had their battles with life and Colorado's harsh wintry conditions while living on the Great Plains. I must mention them because it was William and Helen Bruning's daughter, Elsie Katherine Bruning, that one day would marry Sumpter Edward Patterson, who was several years her senior. They would have six children, one being the second oldest, Bertha Viola Patterson, my mother. Unknowingly, and for whatever reason, William and Helen settled at the junction of the paths of the other families; but that's another story.

Acknowledgments

For her support, patience, and inspiration, I dedicate this book to my wife, Cathy. Thanks to the following individuals: My brother Malcolm and his wife Bonnie, Yvonne Patterson, Donna Greene Claybrook, Virginia Robertson, Doris Edmonds, Laurie Thomas, Linda Laminack of the Longview, Texas Library, and Angela Hanson for taking time out of her life to take photos of the headstone of our great grandfather, Joseph Samuel Greene in the Oakland Cemetery located in Shreveport, Louisiana.

Other books by Richard Greene on Amazon Kindle

Wade Garrison's Promise

Wade Garrison is a simple man who, as a young man, came west chasing the stories he had read about in cheap western novels while growing up on a farm in South Carolina. He is not a violent man, and like most men of humble beginnings, he holds his name and promises in high regard.

Watching the pine coffin containing his friend, Emmett Spears's lifeless body lowered into the dark grave, Wade makes a silent promise of revenge. It is a promise that will take him far from the girl he loves and the Circle T Ranch in eastern Colorado.

As young Wade Garrison trails the four men responsible for his friend's death, he will soon find himself unprepared for the death and violence he will find. He is unaware that he will lose himself in the process of fulfilling his promise to avenge Emmett Spears.

God's Coffin

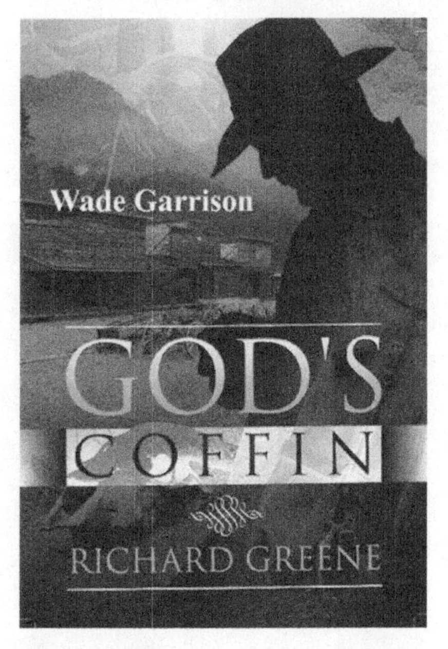

Sequel to Wade Garrison's Promise

Wade Garrison rides out of Harper, Colorado, into the New Mexico Territory in 1872, believing he is riding away from a troubled past.

Now, six years later, his old friend, Sheriff Seth Bowlen, in Sisters, Colorado, is in trouble and needs help. Sheriff Bowlen sends a wire to United States Marshal Billy French in Santa Fe, who, in turn, sends Deputy Marshal Wade Garrison to help their old friend.

Innocently, Wade decides to take his wife Sarah, and son Emmett, with him so they can visit her family in Harper, a small town northeast of Sisters. As he and his family board the train in Santa Fe, he could not have known that a terrible storm of violence was already brewing, and this fateful decision could destroy his wife and child.

Atonement

Sequel to God's Coffin

In August 1878, Wade Garrison took his vengeance against the men who took his unborn daughter's life and tried to kill his wife and son to settle a score. When the last man was dead from Wade's Sharps Rifle, he rode out of Harper, Colorado, a wanted man, and disappeared into the Montana Territory.

Morgan Hunter was a forty-eight-year-old gunman from west Texas wanted for killing a sheriff and his deputy. Fleeing from those killings and riding away from the sorrow that caused them, he rode into the Montana Territory. Unaware of the other, both men rode toward the same destiny.

Sarah looked toward the top of the hill every day, waiting for Wade and his red sorrel mare to come home. The days turned into weeks, and then into months, and still no word of him or from him. The only person she could turn to was the man who was inadvertently responsible for all that had taken place; Sheriff Seth Bowlen.

The Last Ride

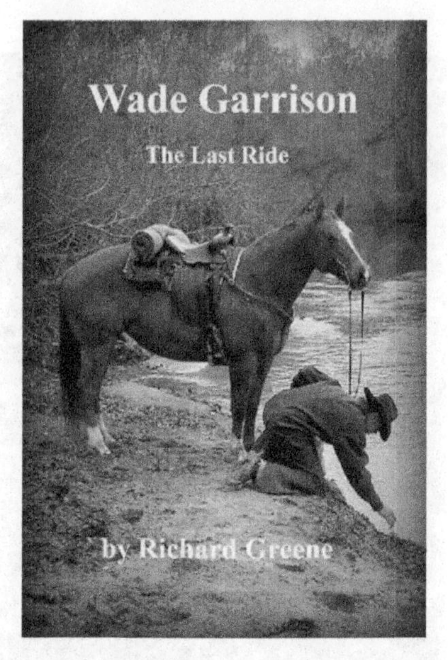

Sequel to Atonement

It has been a year since Wade was shot and nearly died after being found innocent of murder at his trial in Harper, Colorado. Keeping his promise to God and Sarah, his Colt pistol lies tucked away in the bottom drawer of a chest in his bedroom, and the Sharps rifle covered in the rawhide sheath stands in a corner behind the chest. While he misses a United States Deputy Marshal's life, he is content being with his wife Sarah, son Emmett, and daughter Mary Louise on their ranch.

Unknown to Wade and Sarah, he is about to be thrust into a life of violence once again by events in the small town of Harper, Colorado. When the people of Harper seek his help for justice, the old life pulls at him. Resisting those old ways, he fears the town, and his son will think he is a coward. How can he break his promise to not only Sarah but to God?

Feeding the Beast

1951

The Second World War has been over for six years, and the United States is now involved militarily in Korea, termed a Police Action rather than a war. On April 10, President Harry S. Truman fires General Douglas MacArthur, commander of the United States forces in Korea. This action resulted in the president's lowest approval rating of 23%, which remains the lowest of any serving president.

The Denver Police Department protecting a population of fewer than 415,000 residents was small compared to cities such as Chicago, New York, and Los Angeles.

The use of DNA by the judicial system is far in the future. Electric-powered streetcars were the main source of transportation and soon to be replaced by electric buses. Computers were in their infancy, and while most old newspapers and other public records are on microfilm, thousands of documents are not. Not every home could afford a television, so the radio remained the household's nightly entertainment. The closest thing to a cellular telephone was Dick Tracy's two-way wristwatch found in the comics, so the police had to rely on rotary telephones and shortwave radios. Being Mirandized was not an option criminals were given in 1951 and would not be until 1966.

The term 'Serial Killer' would not be coined until 1970 by FBI Special Agent Robert Reesler.

The Last Time I Saw My Dad

This short story is of my last trip to Houston, Texas, to visit my Dad, and the memories that visit brought back of the summers I spent in Houston as a young boy.

Made in United States
North Haven, CT
15 May 2024